P9-EJT-838

Cape Cod

Cape

Cod

WILLIAM MARTIN

WARNER BOOKS

A Time Warner Company

Publisher's Note: This is a work of fiction. Names, characters, places, and incidents either are the product of the author's imagination or are used fictitiously, and any resemblance to actual persons, living or dead, events, or locales is entirely coincidental.

Copyright © 1991 by William Martin
All rights reserved.

Warner Books, Inc., 666 Fifth Avenue, New York, NY 10103

Ⓦ A Time Warner Company

Printed in the United States of America
First printing: March 1991
10 9 8 7 6 5 4 3 2 1

Library of Congress Cataloging-in-Publication Data

Martin, William, 1950–
Cape Cod / William Martin.
p.   cm.
ISBN 0-446-51510-8
1. Cape Cod (Mass.)—History—Fiction.   I. Title.
PS3563.A7297C36   1991
813'.54—dc20
90-50534
CIP

Book design and map illustrations by Giorgetta Bell McRee

For all the family
and all the friends,
across all the years,
who have enjoyed Cape Cod with me

Acknowledgments

My family for many years kept a summer home on the bluffs of Manomet—just south of Plymouth, where the historical Cape begins, and just north of the canal, where the geographical Cape flexes eastward. I could sit on the lawn and, in one sweep of the eye, take in all of Cape Cod Bay, from the beach that protects the Great Salt Marsh to the place where the summer fog hangs above Chatham to the dunes of Provincetown, some twenty-two miles to the east yet near enough to touch.

It was a good place for daydreaming. I loved to study the sailboats skimming along in the summer breezes, the lobstermen tending their pots, the freighters steaming toward Boston, and if I closed my eyes, I could even imagine the *Mayflower* crossing the bay.

Our ancestry was Irish and Lithuanian, but like many generations of Americans before us, we had embraced the story of the First Comers as our own, perhaps because all of us, in one way or another, come from Pilgrims. In fact, an uncle of mine, who was something of an artist, once painted the First Thanksgiving as a family portrait. It did not matter that he was a Catholic priest and so would have been, at the very least, distrusted by the strict Separatists who settled

Plymouth and Cape Cod. The truth of what they did was more powerful to him than the details of what they believed.

In 1957, the year that the *Mayflower II* reached Plymouth, he made us all Pilgrims in oil and canvas. To my Black Irish father he gave armor, helmet, and blunderbuss. To my mother he gave the apron and bowl of the Pilgrim goodwife. To me he gave a hatchet and painted me cutting up the squash for the most famous meal ever eaten in America. I appreciated that. I still do. And though he has passed on, he deserves my thanks.

Of course, many others have helped more concretely with my tale of the First Comers and their descendants. They have helped me in the details and the broad contours and I thank them all, from the shoulder to the hand of Cape Cod.

At Plimoth Plantation: James Baker, Theodore Curtin, who so vividly portrays Master Christopher Jones on the *Mayflower II*; Nanepashemet; Richard Pickering; and all of the interpreters and guides in the village, at the Indian settlement, and aboard the *Mayflower II*, who bring history to life with accuracy, imagination, and passion.

In Plymouth: the staff of the Pilgrim Hall Museum.

In Sandwich: Brian Cullity of the Heritage Plantation.

In Woods Hole: William Sargent.

In Mashpee: Joan Tavares and Richard Scoville, of the Mashpee Indian Education Program; Rosemary Burns and Ann Tannyhill of the Mashpee Archives.

In Hyannis: Marion Vuilleumier.

In Barnstable: Susan Klein and the staff of the Sturgis Library; the staff of the Nickerson Library.

In Dennis: Richard Zisson; Captain George Mabee.

In Brewster: Frederick Dunford, staff archaeologist of the Cape Cod Museum of Natural History, and the rest of the museum staff; Robert Finch; Marion Hobbes; Doris Mullen; David Palmer; Janine and Richard Perry; Robert Wilkinson; and the members of the Brewster Historical Society, who maintain museum and mills.

In Harwich: Joshua Atkins Nickerson II; the staff of the Brooks Free Library.

In Chatham: Tom Marshall.

In Orleans: Susan Nickerson of the Association for the Preservation of Cape Cod; Eldredge Sparrow.

In Eastham: Nathaniel Nickerson.

In Wellfleet: Helen Olsen of the Wellfleet Historical Society; Stephen Kakes; Franny Choate, who can read the water on Billingsgate Shoals the way most people read their mail.

In Truro: Rosemary Broton Boyle.

In Provincetown: Napi Van Dereck; Patti and Ciro Cozzi.

Also, thanks to the rangers and staff of the Cape Cod National Seashore; and to all of the volunteers at all of the Cape's historical societies and in all of the Cape's historical sites, from Aptucxet to Wood's End, whose enthusiasm helps to keep the past alive.

And to a few off-Capers: George F. Amadon; the Reverend Mr. Peter Gomes; Gary Goshgarian; Stephen Martell; the Reverend Mr. George Werner; Conrad Wright and the staff of the Massachusetts Historical Society.

And to my editor, Jamie Raab; my agent, Robert Gottlieb; and, of course, to my wife and children, who never complain.

William Martin
November 1990

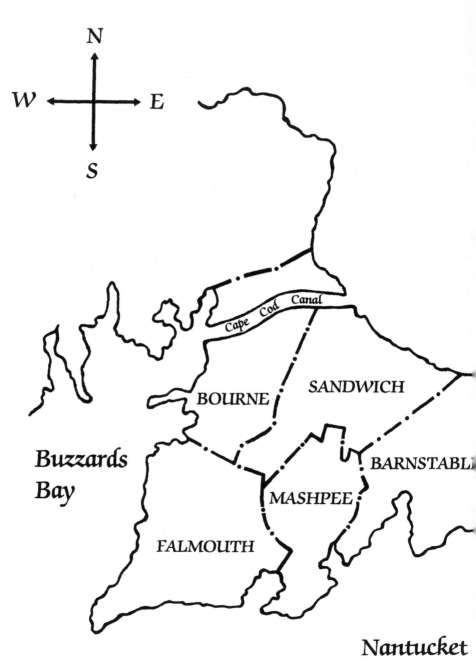

CAPE COD

N
W ← → E
S

Cape Cod Canal

BOURNE

SANDWICH

Buzzards
Bay

BARNSTABL

MASHPEE

FALMOUTH

Nantucket

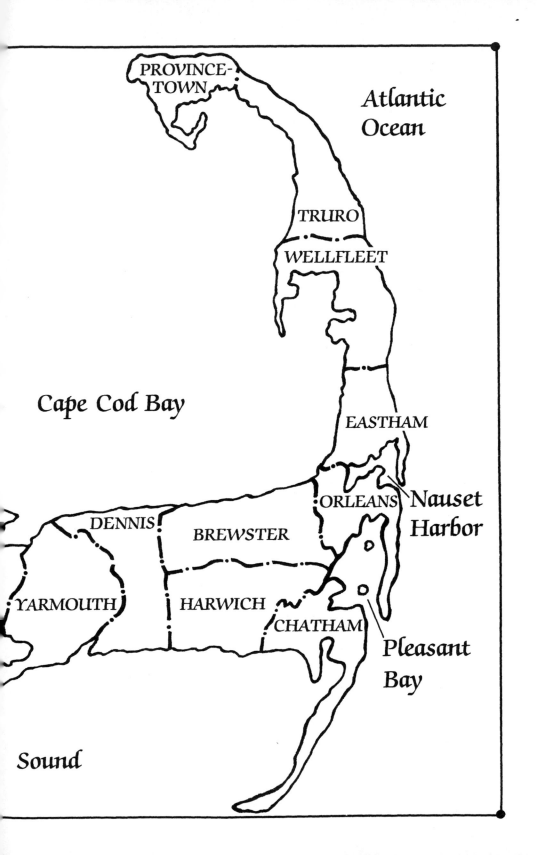

Ezra Bigelow (1590–1660)
m., 1630, Jane Cooper (1610–1698)

Charity Bigelow (1630–1712)
m., 1655, Gideon Horrocks (1620–1761)

Robinson Bigelow
(1632–1654)

Shearjashub Bigelow (1676–1750)
m., 1700, Jane Good (1675–1760)

Ezekiel Bigelow II
(1701–1719)

Mary Bigelow
(1708–1758)

Jacob Bigelow
(1715–1800)
m., 1740, Sarah Doe
(1718–1801)

m., 1738

Leyden Doone
(1738–1807)

Scrooby Doone
(1739–1808)

Elkanah Bigelow (1757–1835)
m., 1787, Delilah Linnel (1760–1841)

Benjamin Bigelow II
(1788–1848)
m., 1810, Achseh Snow
(1789–1865)

Solomon Bigelow II
(1789–1844)
m., 1812, Helen Freeman
(1789–1859)

Abraham Bigelow
(1812–1880)

three children
moved off
Cape

Heman Bigelow (1818–1911)
m., 1846, Jessica Freeman
(1820–1901)

two daughters
moved off Cape

Charles Bigelow (1850–1928)
m., 1887, Edna Fix (1864–1910)

Ethan Bigelow (1890–1973)
m., 1919, Agnes Dickerson (1901–)

Clarence Bigelow (1891–1967)
m., 1920, Jane Perry (1900–1970)

Dickerson Bigelow (1920–)
m., 1947, Elizabeth Deane (1920–1988)

Hiram Bigelow (1923–)

Douglas Bigelow (1950–)
m., 1975, Cynthia Lee   m., 1988, Kelly Jenner
(1950–1986)   (1966–)   .

Douglas Bigelow, Jr.
(1977–)

Anna Bigelow
(1982–)

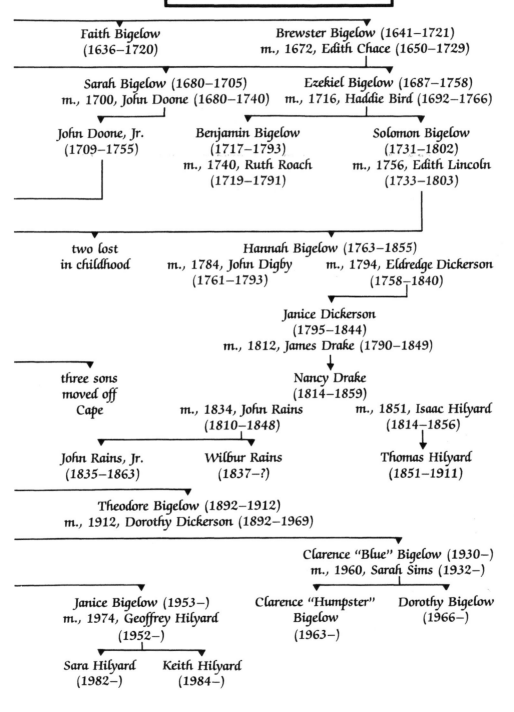

Simeon Bigelow (1594–1680)
m., 1615, Anne Bush (1579–1621)

Faith Bigelow
(1636–1720)

Brewster Bigelow (1641–1721)
m., 1672, Edith Chace (1650–1729)

Sarah Bigelow (1680–1705)
m., 1700, John Doone (1680–1740)

Ezekiel Bigelow (1687–1758)
m., 1716, Haddie Bird (1692–1766)

John Doone, Jr.
(1709–1755)

Benjamin Bigelow
(1717–1793)
m., 1740, Ruth Roach
(1719–1791)

Solomon Bigelow
(1731–1802)
m., 1756, Edith Lincoln
(1733–1803)

two lost
in childhood

Hannah Bigelow (1763–1855)
m., 1784, John Digby   m., 1794, Eldredge Dickerson
(1761–1793)   (1758–1840)

Janice Dickerson
(1795–1844)
m., 1812, James Drake (1790–1849)

three sons
moved off
Cape

Nancy Drake
(1814–1859)
m., 1834, John Rains   m., 1851, Isaac Hilyard
(1810–1848)   (1814–1856)

John Rains, Jr.
(1835–1863)

Wilbur Rains
(1837–?)

Thomas Hilyard
(1851–1911)

Theodore Bigelow (1892–1912)
m., 1912, Dorothy Dickerson (1892–1969)

Clarence "Blue" Bigelow (1930–)
m., 1960, Sarah Sims (1932–)

Janice Bigelow (1953–)
m., 1974, Geoffrey Hilyard
(1952–)

Clarence "Humpster"
Bigelow
(1963–)

Dorothy Bigelow
(1966–)

Sara Hilyard
(1982–)

Keith Hilyard
(1984–)

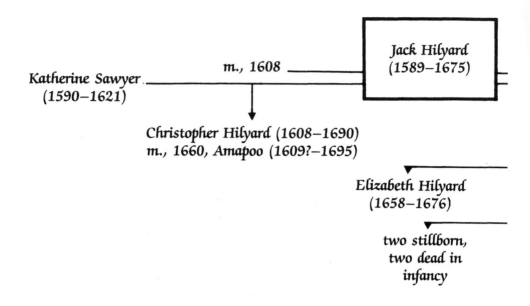

Katherine Sawyer
(1590–1621)

m., 1608

Jack Hilyard
(1589–1675)

Christopher Hilyard (1608–1690)
m., 1660, Amapoo (1609?–1695)

Elizabeth Hilyard
(1658–1676)

two stillborn,
two dead in
infancy

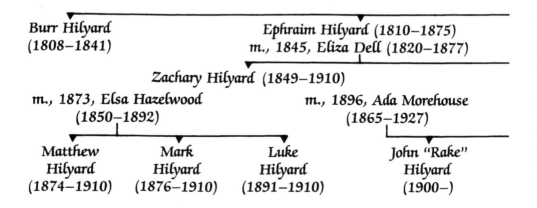

Burr Hilyard
(1808–1841)

Ephraim Hilyard (1810–1875)
m., 1845, Eliza Dell (1820–1877)

Zachary Hilyard (1849–1910)

m., 1873, Elsa Hazelwood
(1850–1892)

m., 1896, Ada Morehouse
(1865–1927)

Matthew
Hilyard
(1874–1910)

Mark
Hilyard
(1876–1910)

Luke
Hilyard
(1891–1910)

John "Rake"
Hilyard
(1900–)

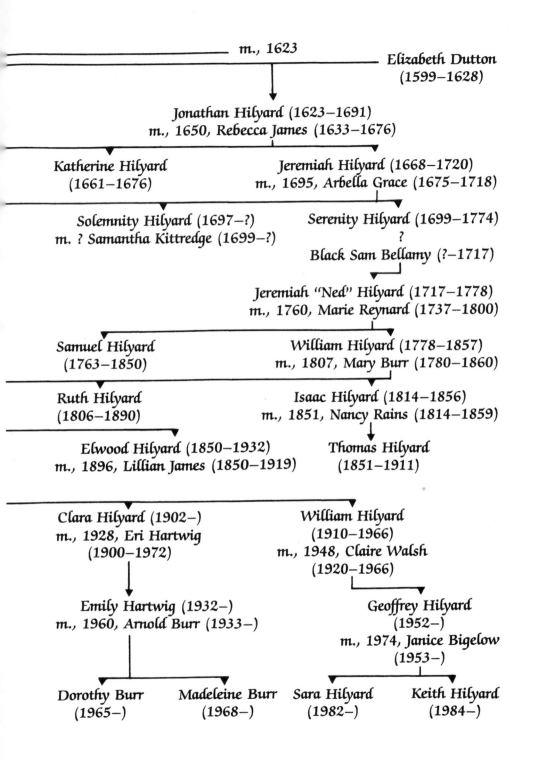

———————————— m., 1623 ———————————— Elizabeth Dutton
(1599–1628)

Jonathan Hilyard (1623–1691)
m., 1650, Rebecca James (1633–1676)

Katherine Hilyard
(1661–1676)

Jeremiah Hilyard (1668–1720)
m., 1695, Arbella Grace (1675–1718)

Solemnity Hilyard (1697–?)
m. ? Samantha Kittredge (1699–?)

Serenity Hilyard (1699–1774)
?
Black Sam Bellamy (?–1717)

Jeremiah "Ned" Hilyard (1717–1778)
m., 1760, Marie Reynard (1737–1800)

Samuel Hilyard
(1763–1850)

William Hilyard (1778–1857)
m., 1807, Mary Burr (1780–1860)

Ruth Hilyard
(1806–1890)

Isaac Hilyard (1814–1856)
m., 1851, Nancy Rains (1814–1859)

Elwood Hilyard (1850–1932)
m., 1896, Lillian James (1850–1919)

Thomas Hilyard
(1851–1911)

Clara Hilyard (1902–)
m., 1928, Eri Hartwig
(1900–1972)

William Hilyard
(1910–1966)
m., 1948, Claire Walsh
(1920–1966)

Emily Hartwig (1932–)
m., 1960, Arnold Burr (1933–)

Geoffrey Hilyard
(1952–)
m., 1974, Janice Bigelow
(1953–)

Dorothy Burr
(1965–)

Madeleine Burr
(1968–)

Sara Hilyard
(1982–)

Keith Hilyard
(1984–)

Cape Cod

PROLOGUE

A.D. 1000

Strandings

Each year the whales went to the great bay. They followed the cold current south from seas where the ice never melted, south along coastlines of rock, past rivers and inlets, to the great bay that forever brimmed with life. Sometimes they stayed through a single tide, sometimes from one full moon to the next, and sometimes, for reasons that only the sea understood, the whales never left the great bay.

The season was changing on the day that the old bull led his herd round the sand hook that formed the eastern edge of the bay.

It had come time for them to fill their bellies and begin the journey to the breeding ground. The old bull did not need the weakening of the sunlight or the cooling of the waters to know this. He knew it because his ancestors had known it, because it was bred into him, in his backbone and his blood. And he knew that in the great bay, his herd had always fed well.

So he sent out sounds that spread through the water and came echoing back, allowing him to see without sight, to know the depth of the water and the slope of the beach, to sense the movement of a single fish at the bottom of the sea or the massing of a giant school a mile away.

And that was what the old bull sensed now.

He turned toward the school, and his herd turned with him. A hundred whales swam in his wake, linked by color and motion in a graceful seaborne dance, by the simple rule of survival to the fish before them, and by the deeper call of loyalty to the herd, their kin, and the old bull himself.

Then the sea was lit by a great flash. The fish felt the coming of the whales, and like a single frightened creature, they darted away. First east, then west, then south toward the shallows they went, and the sunlight flashed again and again on their silver sides.

The dance of the whales rose into a great black-backed wave and rolled, steady and certain, toward the shoal of fish. Soon the stronger fish were swimming over the weaker and splattering across the surface to escape. It did them no good. The wave struck, churned through them, and pounded on, leaving a bloody wake in which the gulls came to feast, while on the shore, other creatures watched and waited.

The old bull filled his belly, and as always in the great bay, the herd fed well. But their hunger was as endless as the sea, and their wave rolled on to the shallows where the last of the fish had fled. Black bodies lunged and whirled in the reddening water. Flashes of panic grew smaller and dimmer. Then came a flash that seemed no more than a moment of moonlight. The old bull turned to chase it, and on the waves above his flukes brought the sand swirling from the bottom.

He had led the herd too close to shore and the tide was running out. In the rising turbulence, he could see almost nothing, so he made his sounds, listened for the echoes, and sought to lead the herd toward safety.

But something in the sea or the stars or his own head had betrayed the old bull. He followed his sounds, because that was what he had always done, and swam straight out of the water. The herd followed him, because that was what they had always done, and the black-backed wave broke on a beach between two creeks.

Still something told the old bull that he was going in the right direction. He pounded his flukes to drive himself into one of the creeks. But he did no more than send up great splashes and dig himself deeper into the eelgrass that rimmed the creek.

All around him, black bodies flopped uselessly in the shallows. The sun quickly began to dry their skin. And their own great weight began to crush them.

The old bull heard feeble warning cries, louder pain cries. He felt the feet of a gull prancing on his back. Then new cries, patterned and high-pitched, frightened the gull into the air.

From the line of trees above the beach came strange creatures, moving fast on long legs. They wore skins and furs. They grew hair on their faces. They carried axes that flashed like sunlight.

They were men. And they swarmed among the herd without fear, and drove their axes into the heads of the whales, and brought blood and death cries. And the biggest of them all raised his axe and came toward the old bull.

But before the axe struck, an arrow pierced the man's neck and came out the other side. Blood and gurgling sounds flowed from his mouth. His eyes opened wide and the axe dropped from his hand.

Now men with painted faces came screaming from the woods. The old bull felt the clashing of the fight and heard sounds of fury unlike any he had known in the sea. Rage swirled around him, stone against iron, arrow against axe, bearded man against painted man. And with his last strength, he tried to escape.

He pounded his flukes but could do no more than roll onto his side, his great bulk burying the axe in the marsh mud beneath him.

Then a bearded man beheaded the painted chieftain and his painted followers fled. The victor lifted the head by the hair and flung it into the sea, but the other bearded men did not celebrate their victory. Instead, they ran off in fear.

For some time, the old bull lay dying on the beach between the creeks. Then the bearded men appeared once more, this time with a woman of their kind. Their axes flashed like the sides of panicked fish, and like the fish, they were fleeing. But the woman stopped and looked at the old bull. She made angry sounds. She picked up a boulder and raised it over his head. . . .

CHAPTER 1

June 30, 1990

Old Men

One of them had seen every year of the century, the other a full three score and ten. One had trouble sleeping. The other wondered where the years had gone. Neither ever awoke without a new pain somewhere or an old pain somewhere else. And neither could drink much anymore, or he'd spend the night at the toilet, pissing out ineffectual little dribbles that wouldn't even make a satisfying sound.

But in these things, they were like old men everywhere. Other things bound them like brothers.

Both were descended from the *Mayflower* Pilgrims. One was grandfather, the other great-uncle, to the same two children. They walked on the beach between the creeks because each owned half of it. And they had detested each other since the administration of John F. Kennedy.

Rake Hilyard walked at dawn. The world was changing quickly, but he found perspective on the beach. Seasons passed, birds migrated, and tides flowed according to laws laid down long before the foolishness began. In the dunes, Indian shell heaps gave evidence of the first men. In the marsh mud, the bones of ancient pilot whales told of the first strandings. Even the sea-smoothed boulders on the tideflats recalled the glacier that left them. And all of it made a ninety-year-old man feel a little younger.

Dickerson Bigelow did not come out as regularly. But after the heart attack, his doctor had told him to walk more, and on the beach, he could work even as he walked. If the tide was low, Dickerson walked on the flats, studied the island from a distance, and imagined what the last development of his life would look like. When the tide was high, he simply walked, his eyes fixed on the sand between his toes, his soul coveting the land on the Hilyard side, his brain scheming to get it.

At high tide on this summer morning, the beach was no more than a twenty-foot strand from wrack line to dune grass, which meant the old men could not avoid each other. But neither would turn back. They had been trespassing on each other's beaches for decades, like warships showing their flags in foreign straits. So they ran out their guns and steamed on.

Dickerson fired first. "Mornin', you old bastard."

"What's good about it, you son of a bitch?"

"We're alive and can walk the beach. How's that?"

"If it was up to you, only *one* of us'd be alive. Then *you*'d fill the creeks and hot-top the beach."

Dickerson Bigelow laughed and ran a hand through the beard that fringed his face. He shaved his upper lip, in the style of an old shipmaster, so that whenever he bought property or petitioned for a permit, he would seem to have sprung from the Cape Cod sand itself, a modern man with the shrewd yet upright soul of a Yankee seafarer.

Next to him, Rake looked like the original go-to-hell dory fisherman—leathery face, dirty cap, dirtier deck shoes, and flannel shirt stuffed into trousers so dirty you could chop them up and use them for chum.

Rake glanced at Dickerson's bony bare feet, the same color as the sand, at the gray trousers rolled up to the calves, the windbreaker draped over the barrel chest, and the knot of the striped tie. "Men don't wear ties to the beach 'less they come on business."

"Our families have quite a resource here, Rake."

"Answer's no."

"Magnificent spot." Dickerson stepped to the top of the dune and looked around.

"Mind the dune grass. That's Hilyard property. Don't want it blowin' away."

"It *is* blowin' away. The whole *Cape's* blowin' away, washin' away, every day. Time to sell, 'fore any more of it goes."

When the Pilgrims came, the land between the creeks had been surrounded by a wide marsh. Then someone dumped some sand in the marsh to make a cart path, then more sand to make a causeway, and later, macadam for a modern road, but the seventy acres of upland, dune, and beach was still called Jack's *Island.* It nestled in the crook of the Cape's elbow, safe from the rage of the Atlantic, sheltered from the northeast wind, but fully exposed to the two families who'd lived on it and fought over it for three and a half centuries.

"Won't sell. Sister won't sell." Rake Hilyard started walking again. "And with any luck, town'll take it *all.* My side and yours."

"Don't be so sure of that." Bigelow went after Rake. He was taller and heavier, but from a distance, he looked like a balloon that the kid in the dirty pants tugged along behind him. "For all the centuries our families have suffered here, Rake, the Lord's givin' us the chance to get somethin' back. Think of the future."

"The *future,*" Rake stopped. "Most men think the land's somethin' they inherit from their fathers. The smart ones know they're just borrowin' it from their kids."

"The future's now, and there's some in your family who agree."

"Who?"

Dickerson scratched at his beard.

"You're bluffin'," said Rake.

"The town meeting won't take this land. Too many strings. And if I have to buy you out a parcel at a time, it could take years. Then it might be too late for all of us."

"Too late already, 'cause if the town won't do it, I'm buyin' *you* out."

"With what? Old lobster pots? The only Hilyard with more than two grand cash money's married to my own daughter."

"Nobody's perfect."

"So what do you have to buy *me* out?"

"The *truth.*" Rake poked a finger at Dickerson. "Straight from history."

"Now *you're* bluffin'."

"History don't lie. 'Specially in a book written by a man who was there."

"What man? What book?"

Rake pulled his cap down and turned toward Eastham.

"You're gettin' senile, Rake." Dickerson watched until Rake disappeared into the glare of the rising sun. He had come to upset his old adversary, to leave him wondering about the loyalty of his family. Instead, he was left wondering himself. As he walked back to his son's house, his eyes fixed on the sand between his toes, his soul frustrated once more in its coveting, his mind traveled back through the story of the Hilyards and Bigelows in search of "a book written by a man who was there."

CHAPTER 2

November 1620

The Book

November 9. Sixty-fourth day. Cold unto freezing yet another day. Position not fixed as clouds cover sky, but soundings show forty fathoms, shallowest since England. The Saints pray hard and regular after sight of land, and God may soon give them heed. In the beginning, I bore them no sympathy. They were like as any cargo, and no better, for all their prayer, than those they call Strangers. But the Saints have gained my respect, the Strangers as well.

Christopher Jones did not bestow respect blithely, especially in his sea journal. He had been a mariner too long, had known too many men to wither in their first heavy gale. He had expected his passengers to wither before the wind ever blew, but they had faced the sea with more bravery than his sailors.

And now they were praying. Perhaps that was the reason for their bravery. The prayer, this bleak November dawn, was the Twenty-third Psalm. Jones considered it a good prayer, though he was not a godly man. He professed belief in the holy Church of England, the prudent course in a world where a man's faith determined his future on earth as well as in heaven. But first and foremost,

Jones was a seaman. He put his faith in the compass and the chart, in the stars and the sun, in his own strong hand on the whipstaff and England's strong oak in the keel.

The Saints put theirs in God and their own understanding of his word. They believed that the corruption of the Roman Catholic Church still festered in its English bastard and would not be cut away until the bastard purified itself of ceremony, of statues, of priests, of all save the Scripture. The English church showed no interest in taking such cure, so the Saints became Separatists, and Separatists quickly became outcasts.

They were simple people, these Saints, simple in their lives and simple in their faith, and their simplicity, thought Jones, had kept them strong.

They did not wither during years of persecution by English bishops and sheriffs, nor after years of exile in Holland, where they found freedom while their children lost their English identity, nor after months of struggling to organize a voyage to the New World. And when their financial backers forced them to accept outsiders because there were not enough of them to build a colony, they did not wither then, either. They dubbed the outsiders Strangers, declared their sovereignty over the venture, and looked west at last.

It should not have surprised Jones, then, that the Saints had not withered during ten weeks at sea.

The *Mayflower* had left Southampton in August, in the time of good sailing. From her years in the wine trade, she had come to be known as a sweet ship in that the ullage from the casks made her bilge smell like a French fermentation cave. But no amount of sweetness could soothe the misery of seaborne motion in Separatist bellies, nor stop a stream of half-stomached salt meat, pickled beets, hardtack, and beer from frothing into the wake, nor overcome the stink of full slop buckets and the stench of seasick vomit that raised more vomit in even the strongest of stomachs.

It was in the nature of men to endure such things for commerce, adventure, or faith, thought Jones, but what pain to modesty it must have been for the women to use the slop buckets without privacy, or to see the sailors hang their arses and balls in the bow ropes and let fly with whatever was in them. After all, these were not tavern wenches or London whores, but goodwives. And what worry the future must have held for any woman who came with children. Indeed, what worry for any woman who had left the safety of a warm hearth, whether for prayer or profit. But they seldom complained and they would not wither.

When the autumn westerlies began to blow, the *Mayflower* went on the tack. For weeks she pounded like a mill hammer against the wind. Those who had recovered from seasickness grew sick again, then sicker still as the westerlies gave way to storms that swirled from the southwest, driving the *Mayflower* off course and leaving her to hull through days and nights of miserable waterlogged beating.

Half-seas over, they were struck by a storm that dwarfed all the rest. Mountains of green water rose with the wind, over the decks, over the spars, over the masts themselves, then rolled over the ship again and again until her seams opened and her main beam buckled with a terrifying crack. Good English oak split amidships and splintered to starboard and port. With every wave, water poured through the boards above the beam, and the sailors feared for the ship. But the Saints brought from their luggage a great iron screw jack and shored the beam. Then they implored Master Jones to press on, for God was with them.

And perhaps he was, but all the same, it grew more miserable each day. Every league closer to the New World was another hour closer to winter. The feeble cookstoves in the fo'c'sle and on deck did nothing to keep them warm, nor did the damp woolens they had been wearing for over a month, nor the bedding that never dried out. But now the closeness of their bodies between decks begat a fetid warmth that kept them from withering awhile longer.

It was good that they had not withered yet, thought Jones, for the worst still lay ahead.

He wiped the quill and blotted the page. He had written enough. His attention was turning, as it did each dawn, to the dark western horizon. He pulled on his sea cape, took his glass, and went out onto the half deck.

"Anovver cold mornin' in the valley of the shadow of death, sir," said Mr. Coppin.

On the main deck, a dozen passengers clustered around one of the elders and read from their Bibles. Their faces were pallid and drawn, their clothes worn and many times mended. Their matted, salt-caked hair and beards crawled from under their hats and across their faces like seaweed. But when they prayed, their voices never faltered.

"Don't begrudge 'em prayer, Mr. Coppin. 'Tis a great comfort, to them what have the gift."

Jones raised his newfangled and most expensive spying glass to his eye and studied the horizon. Smoke gray sky sat atop slate gray sea, and beyond the line that divided them lay America. Only three aboard the *Mayflower* had been there. For Jones and the rest, it remained a collection of words in a few books or a handful of stories from the sailors who had seen it, a new and shining land where men could live in God's bounty or a frightening immensity filled with savages and wild beasts.

ii.

In the shadows of the tween-decks, a man named Jack Hilyard thought about America while he waited for the prayer to end above him. In his right hand he held the slop bucket used by the four families at the bow of the ship, and in his left hand he held his nose.

The ship hit a swell, and a few drops spilled from the lip of the bucket.

" 'My cup runneth over,' " came the voices from above.

With his boot, Jack Hilyard smoothed the liquid into the boards. None would see it, and in the stench of the tween-decks, neither would they smell it.

" 'Surely goodness and mercy shall follow me all the days of my life.' "

Hilyard heard the voice of Ezra Bigelow, one of the holiest of the holies, rising above the others. He laughed to himself, and his eyes searched the tween-decks for some trace of goodness or mercy.

Curtains and canvas rags hung everywhere, forming tiny rooms with walls that waved as the ship rode the swells. Feeble shafts of light illuminated scenes behind the curtains, like *tableaux vivants* at a country fair. A mother tried to suckle her three-year-old, who had stopped eating the salted food. A man crouched by a porthole, held an inflamed wrist to the light, and with his knife, pricked at a pustulant saltwater sore. An old woman wrapped her arms round her waist and coughed. When she stopped, the sound seemed to echo down the length of the ship, but it was other people coughing behind other curtains.

Then Hilyard glanced at his own space, where his wife folded the bedding. She had withstood the voyage better than most, he thought, perhaps because she had more bulk than most. She was strong, and he was rugged, and their son Christopher had the constitution of a sailor. They came from stock that endured, and before long, she would thank him for bringing them to the New World.

The prayer above was nearly completed. " 'And I shall dwell in the house of the Lord forever . . .' "

"Or die of the stink therein," muttered Hilyard to himself, and he stumbled up the ladder to the fresh air. He tripped on the hatch coaming and more of the slop splattered on the deck.

"Amen and apology," said Jack Hilyard to the group.

Elder Ezra Bigelow watched the brownish liquid roll toward his boots with the roll of the ship. Then he slapped his Bible shut. "A better course would be to join in the prayer."

"I prays every Sunday." Hilyard went to the side and dumped the bucket. Then he tied a rope to the handle and dropped the bucket into the sea to rinse it. "If God hears me prayer on Sunday, I needn't bother him the rest of the week. If he don't listen then, he'll for certain ignore me on days he don't claim as his own."

"Every day is his own," responded Bigelow. "And respect should keep thee and thy stinking bucket below until the morning prayer have finished."

"Every day is his own"—Hilyard raised a bucket of clean seawater—"and every day he makes the sun to rise and the tides to turn and the bowels to move." Hilyard dumped the water onto the brownish stain. " 'Tis our duty to answer his call in the great things and in the small. That be a form of prayer, too."

"That, sir, is blasphemy," said Ezra Bigelow with a small note of triumph, as though he now knew the fate of this man's soul.

"Be not so quick to judge," said Bigelow's brother Simeon. " 'Master Hilyard believe he serve the Lord when he empty the nig waste, mayhap he does."

"He'll serve more better," said Christopher Jones, "if he h stones that shit stain."

Hilyard turned to Jones, and in the manner of a good E seaman, tugged at his forelock.

While the Saints considered Hilyard one of the most c erous of the Strangers, Jones held a higher opinion of him. I Hilyard from the North Sea whaling trade. Hilyard's shipn called him the Rat because he was as slender as a ratline ?

strong. And whaling masters had allowed him his independent spirit because few men could better place the lance. Few men on this ship, thought Jones, were better equipped for America.

"The buckets are not to be emptied until after we say amen to the morning prayer," said Ezra Bigelow to Jones.

"Master, you'll forgive me," said Jack Hilyard, "but one of the ladies got the flux. It raise a stench tween-decks and start the others to retchin'. God won't mind if we breaks a rule to stop a bit o' retchin'."

Ezra Bigelow stepped up to Hilyard. He was taller than anyone else on the ship, and whenever he argued, which seemed quite often, he used his own height and the holy height of Scripture to make his points. "What can such as thee know of God's mind?"

"As much as thee, sir, wif all thy learnin'."

"Thou wilt show respect and use the proper form of address. When thou speakst to thy superiors, address them as *you*."

"When *thou* shows respect to me, I'll show it to *thee*."

The savages might destroy this colony, thought Christopher Jones, or the colonists might starve before bringing in a harvest. But it was as likely that they would come apart because Saints and Strangers disagreed over something as petty as the disposal of the morning slop . . . or which word to use for the second person pronoun.

The Saints had recruited some of the Strangers. Others, like Jack Hilyard, had been brought on by the London Adventurers, the financial backers. Most were decent, some devout, and all had accepted the same terms—seven years of contracted labor—forced upon the Saints themselves. But some Strangers had come seeking their fortune first, not their God, and that might be the undoing of them all.

Saint and Stranger faced each other across the mouth of the slop bucket, and for a time, the only sound was the rush of the wind through the sails. On a small ship and a long journey, hostility was unwelcome but inevitable. All waited to see who would strike first, Ezra Bigelow with his lofty rhetoric or Jack Hilyard with his slop bucket.

Then a gull cried. Master Jones did not notice, for the cry of a gull was a common sound to men who plied the European coastal trade. But when the bird cried a second time, Jones felt it at the base of his spine before he heard it. He saw the bird at the same moment that a wild cry echoed from the foretop: *"Land! Land ho!"*

Jack Hilyard and Ezra Bigelow looked up, and Hilyard leaped for joy, because the voice crying out the sight of land belonged to his own son, Christopher.

Bigelow seemed to smile, although his face barely moved. "God gives thy son a great gift, the first sight of our promised land."

Through his glass, Master Jones saw the horizon waver for the first time in sixty-four days. The sight filled him with joy and relief. Though modern man had known for over a century that the world was not flat, no one had seen it from far enough away to know for certain, and even a good seaman like Jones had moments of doubt.

There were few aboard the *Mayflower*—Saints, Strangers, or sailors—who did not rejoice at the cry of Christopher Hilyard. They poured from the tween-decks and the forecastle as though thinking to see the face of God himself. They lined the rail and hung in the rigging and for a few moments forgot the bitter journey just ended.

But their joy was soon tempered. Instead of God's face, they saw only the wilderness. First, black patches of evergreen stood out against the horizon; then gray masses of beech and oak lifted their bare November arms in threat, like soldiers upon a great parapet of sand that rose from behind the curve of the earth, until it stood full before them, a hundred feet high, defying their ship as surely as it did the ocean wearing at its base.

"A continent protected by sand," said Jack's wife, Kate. "The foolish man build his house on the sand—"

"Show more faith," chided Simeon Bigelow. "You see a goodly land, wooded to the brink of the sea. God could have given us no better."

"I sees sand," said Jack Hilyard.

"'Tis what God has offered." Ezra Bigelow raised his voice, as if to raise his own spirits and those around him with the Scripture. "Did not the Israelites face burning sands before they reached the Promised Land?"

"Aye," said Simeon. "Let us give thanks for what the Lord has brought us to."

The chart showed that the Lord had brought them to a peninsula resembling, in all its parts, a man's arm raised to strike a blow at the sea. The chart called the place Cape James, a name John Smith had given to curry the favor of King James. But sailors used the name that Bartholomew Gosnold had given it after fishing here in 1602: *Cape Cod.*

iii.

More had come.

Men in a great canoe, as big as a hillside, driven by white wings on the wind. Men whose faces grew hair like the pelt of the beaver. Men who dressed in layers of colored skins, yet whose own skin was as white as birchbark. Men who brought some good things . . . and many bad.

The canoe, called a ship, was the largest that Autumnsquam had ever seen, and he felt fear, like the taste of blood, rise in his throat.

He had been a boy when *les françaises* appeared in the Bay of the Nausets, fifteen summers before. He still remembered the one called Champlain, who sat on the bow of his canoe and made pictures of the land.

The next year *les françaises* had visited the Nausets again, then sailed south to the land of the Monomoyicks. They stayed too long and would not leave, and there was a fight in which many whites and Monomoyicks died.

More came after that. Some flew the red-crossed flag of the English, others the flowered flag of *les françaises*. A few showed a black flag with a white skull and bones. Some simply fished. Some traded knives and metal for pelts. A few pretended trade only to steal Nausets for slaves, and their evil stained every white.

But in the life of the Nausets and the Wampanoag nation, in the sachemdoms from the tip of the Narrow Land to the edge of the Narragansett Bay, the Great Sickness that followed the white men would be remembered before anything else, good or bad.

It began, they said, to the north, in the Penobscot Land, where the whites fished and traded. It reached Autumnsquam's village shortly after a runner brought news of it. An old man began to shiver and felt great pains in his head. His skin grew hot as a baking stone. His woman bathed him in cold water, and the *pauwau* sang his song. It did no good. The old man died four days later.

But few noticed, because by then, people everywhere were shivering and growing hot at the same time. Little children went so mad with the heat inside their heads that they did not know their own parents. Brave men who had hunted wolves whimpered like old women with pain. Some jumped into the sea to cool their misery, and some of them drowned.

But few noticed, because the Wampanoags were dying everywhere. Autumnsquam did not notice, because he was burying his baby daughter and his own woman.

The dying began in fall and did not end until spring. In some parts of the Wampanoag nation, there were more dead than alive, more dead than the living could bury, and the bones lay bleaching on the sand. For reasons that no man knew, there was less dying on the Narrow Land than in other places, but still there was too much.

Before the white man, there had never been such sickness, the Nausets had never before been dragged into slavery, and the eastern horizon had been the home of the dawn, not the lair of great canoes called ships. Now, the Nausets were no longer friendly to the whites. They enslaved those who were shipwrecked and drove off those who came to trade. But this was the biggest ship that ever had come.

And it was turning south.

Autumnsquam feared that they were searching for the Bay of the Nausets, to steal more of his people and punish them for what they had done to other whites. He would bring the warning, and his people would be ready.

He had learned from his father to measure his gait by the movement of the copper pendants that hung from his ears. If they bounced against his cheeks, it meant that he was running too fast. If they made no motion, he went like the turtle. But if he kept a strong, steady pace, he would feel them swing in rhythm with his gait, and he would go fast yet with dignity.

Because there were fewer now to use the path, much thicket had grown over it, but Autumnsquam was young and strong and wore his winter breeches, and what he could not step over, he went through. For much of the morning, the path took him along the bluff, so that he could watch the white men's ship and keep himself ahead of it.

Then the bluff gave way to long spits of sand that protected the Bay of the Nausets. The path turned inland along the shore, and

Autumnsquam could no longer see the ship. This worried him some, but he kept his copper pendants swinging steadily, stopped only for a handful of pemmican, and soon smelled the cookfires of his village.

At word of the ship, the men took their bows and went to the shore. The women took the children and hid in the forest. And the Nausets waited the day through. But the white men did not come.

Then the setting sun burned through the clouds, sending long rays, like arrows, across the world. The sandspit that formed the eastern shore of their bay glimmered in the golden light. Then the arrows of sun struck something else. At first, Autumnsquam could not tell what it was, this thing that seemed to glide along the rim of the dunes. He was taken by the beauty of it and wondered if it was some new god, come to save them from the white men. Then he knew. It *was* the white men. Their ship was beyond the spit, with only its wings showing above the sand. It had gone south and was now turning north. The white men were looking for a place to land.

iv.

November 10. Yesterday, near dawn, we raised the sand heights of Cape Cod, dead on the forty-second parallel. Master Coppin, who has sailed these waters, said they were a fine landmark—as they proved to be—and no more than a degree north of Hudson's River. There was prayer, some rejoicing, and then dispute.

Some wished to land here, but the elders determined to make straight for the Hudson, where they have charter. So we tacked south and were seeking to turn the elbow of the Cape when we fell amongst shoals and currents so swift that the sand billowed off the bottom as we passed. Coppin had warned of this place, and I had read of it in a Dutch rutter, yet were we near lost when the tide took the ebb and the breakers roared to life around us. The only sound louder was the praying, which I did not discourage.

With night coming and the wind fading, I told them we had no choice but to come about. Else the tide would carry us onto a shoal, where the waves would make short work of us.

At this, Ezra Bigelow grumbled that I was in the pay of

the Dutch, who wish also to settle at Hudson's River. I am rankled. This Bigelow impugns me and henceforth walks a thin line.

We beat north'ard now. Afore dawn, we enter Cape Cod Harbor, safest anchorage in the Americas. There is no more talk of Hudson's River. We are low on beer, and the passengers need solid ground 'neath their feet. Methinks many are pleased to settle here, outside the circle of the Virginia government.

But they must needs create government of their own, for voices of discontent have rose to mutinous pitch since we turned north. Strangers like Jack Hilyard say that without charter for this place, the Saints have no control over them, and they will go where they wish once ashore.

So the elders gather in the steerage cabin where, with strident voice and much debate, they compose charter to bind them till their London men gain legal one. They will ask all freemen and male servants to sign in the morning.

Jack Hilyard, for one, says he will refuse. Ezra Bigelow threatens to clap him in the stocks they have brought for public discipline.

V.

The fire threw shadows on the walls of the longhouse. The men listened with grim faces as Autumnsquam spoke. In the *wetus*, the children cried, and their mothers soothed them. Outside, the dogs barked at the wind.

The old sachem Aspinet threw another log on the fire and watched the sparks rise with the smoke. "The white men may never stop coming."

The others nodded and said yes, except for Autumnsquam. He cast his eyes toward the roof hole, where smoke and sparks escaped. "We are like the embers going up in the night sky. We must send these whites away before our fire is used up."

"We are no longer strong."

"We will only grow weaker if we allow the whites their way." Autumnsquam looked at the others. Their eyes were on him, but their brows furrowed so the sockets were like dark shadows hiding their thoughts. "We drove off whites not four moons ago. Let us do the same with this ship."

Aspinet shook his head. The lines in his face had deepened since the Great Sickness. He had been laid low but had defeated death. This made him stronger in the eyes of his people, though the people themselves had grown weak. "This ship is bigger than any other. It could be filled with warriors. If they have gone north, let them go."

Autumnsquam said no. Though young, he was a *pinse*, a trusted brave and close counselor of the sachem. He could speak his thoughts openly. "These whites think we are weak, so they come to avenge those we have driven off. We must fight them."

He sat back and looked around again. The bodies of the young men glistened with grease. It was all they needed to keep them warm in winter or keep off the bugs in summer. The old men needed dogs sleeping beside them on cold nights and deerskins around their shoulders even in spring.

But the sickness had not burned all the fire from Aspinet's belly. He thought for a time, he sucked a long breath of smoke from his pipe, and he told the others that Autumnsquam was right. They should fight for their land or they were women. Now the others nodded and said yes.

Aspinet handed his pipe to Autumnsquam. "We will wait and watch. If they come south from the rivers of the Pamets, we will stop them."

Autumnsquam sucked on the pipe and passed it to another. "If they come south, they will know that we are not women."

vi.

"In the name of God, amen," intoned William Brewster from the half deck. His had been one of the first and strongest of the Saints' voices, and he had become eldest of the elders.

" 'We whose names are underwritten, the loyal subjects of our dread sovereign Lord King James, by the Grace of God of Great Britain, France, and Ireland King, Defender of the Faith, et cetera, Having undertaken for the Glory of God and advancement of the Christian Faith and Honour of our King and Country, a Voyage to plant the First Colony in the Northern Parts of Virginia, do by these presents . . .' "

Saints and Strangers had assembled on deck, in a cold mist, in the bay of a cold wilderness, to hear the reading of the agreement. One hundred and two souls would be asked to obey, though only the men had been asked to sign. The wife, after all, was the man's chattel and would do as she was told.

Kate Hilyard jammed an elbow into her husband's ribs. "Thou'd better sign if thou knows what's good for thee."

"I don't care how handsome it's writ, I ain't signin'," whispered Jack Hilyard.

". . . solemnly and mutually in the presence of God and one another, Covenant and Combine ourselves together in a Civil Body Politic, for our better ordering and preservation and furtherance of the ends aforesaid. . . ."

"I'll bind meself to nuffin'," added Jack. "I wants a free hand."

"Give a man like thee a free hand, Jack Hilyard, and afore long it'll be down every dress in sight."

Kate was near twice as wide as her husband, and more than once had she laid him out when he grew too ardent or too drunk. She might once have been beautiful, but life in the London streets did naught to preserve beauty. Her skin was reddened by beer and wind, except in the dirt-caked creases around her neck. Her nose bent strangely where her father had broken it with a shovel. And she was missing several teeth. But whenever Jack returned from the sea, she laughed with him and drank with him and surrounded him with her love. And she had given him the strong son now perched in the ratlines above them.

"'Tis a fool's bargain," Jack said louder.

"Then thou be the one to make a mark on it," said Kate.

" 'And by virtue hereof to enact, constitute and frame such just and equal Laws, Ordinances, Acts, Constitutions and Offices, from time to time, as shall be though most meet and convenient for the general good of the Colony, unto which we promise all due submission and obedience.' "

"*Them's* the words I don't like." Jack now spoke out for all to hear.

Elder Brewster stopped reading and looked up. Heads turned all around.

"What words?" demanded William Bradford.

" 'Submission and obedience.' Those ain't in me"—Hilyard wiped the film of mist from his beard and thought after the right word—"lexicon."

"They are in the lexicon of any man who wishes to see the face of God," said Ezra Bigelow, who stood near Bradford.

Jack Hilyard pointed into the gray sky. "There's the face of God"—he pointed to the hook of sand that surrounded them—"and there"—his hand shot toward the bay, where two humpback whales were spouting—"and there most of all."

Ezra Bigelow came off the half deck and pushed his way through Saints and Strangers. "'Tis because of thy voice that this has been writ."

"I won't sign," said Jack Hilyard.

"Thou wilt," ordered Ezra Bigelow, in tone as cold as the mist, "in the name of God."

"We compel no one." William Bradford threw off his heavy wool cape and hat and came down the deck.

He was one of the youngest of the leaders, raised and trained by Brewster, nurtured by Scripture, a scholar of Hebrew and Greek, yet as tall and rawboned and hardheaded as one of Jones's own seamen.

If this plantation had a future, thought Jones, it rested with Bradford.

"Let it be Goodman Hilyard's choice," he said. "A community is well served that has an outsider to look upon and pity."

Kate Hilyard jumped in front of Bradford. "We'll take no pity from no one, Will Bradford, whether Jack signs or not."

"'Tis his own decision." Bradford turned his back on Hilyard and looked at the others. "His fate is in the hands of the Lord, within our community or without."

"You'd like it if I didn't sign, wouldn't you?" shouted Jack Hilyard.

But Bradford did not respond. Nor did Bigelow, who followed Bradford back to the half deck.

Christopher Jones knew the Saints to be courageous men of simple faith and true innocence. Only men of faith and innocence would hope to plant a colony in the wilderness with so few skills. But here was the skill that would hold them together. When it came to defending their power, they could be as shrewd and hardheaded

as English bishops. William Bradford knew instinctively the way to
bring Jack Hilyard into the fold. Ezra Bigelow, for all his declaiming,
knew precisely when to be quiet.

And Jack Hilyard was left shouting like a fool. They hoped he
would not sign so they could exclude him and his family, was that
it? Well, he was as good as they. And what right did they have to
compel any man to sign? He would sign only if he felt like it.

"Jack!" cried Jones, to save him further embarrassment. "Act as
thou wish amongst the elders, but on me ship, act the seaman."

"What be you tellin' me, sir?"

His wife whacked Hilyard on the shoulder. "He's tellin' thee to
sign the agreement."

"A pledge of submission and obedience?"

"'Tis done by every seaman on this ship," said Jones.

"'Tis done by every woman on this ship on the day she marries,"
said Kate. "A woman knows what's needed to build a life."

That drew murmuring approval from several of the women, and
Bradford's wife Dorothy said, "Well spoken."

"If thou don't know that, Jack," Kate added, "thou be a bigger
fool than I thought for bringin' us here."

Jack was no fool. He had pulled after enough whales to know
the need for a firm covenant among men in dangerous places. But
he had come to America to make his fortune, and he had served on
enough whalers to know that the firm covenant at sea most often
enriched those who stayed on land and wrote it.

He tenderly brushed the droplets of mist from the hair around
his wife's face. "I'll sign if the master and me wife thinks it's wise,"
he said. But I'll obey, he thought, only if I think the same.

And Elder Brewster lost no time completing the reading. " 'In
witness whereof we have hereunder subscribed our names at Cape
Cod, the eleventh of November, in the Year of the Reign of our
Sovereign Lord King James, of England, France, and Ireland the
eighteenth, and of Scotland the fifty-fourth. Anno Domini 1620.' "

CHAPTER 3

July 4

The Glorious Fourth

Whatever the Pilgrims faced, they never had to go through this: driving to Cape Cod on the Fourth of July.

And not in a million nightmares could they have seen themselves as wellspring of faith for this cataract of tourists, vacationers, week-enders, day-trippers, campers, swimmers, boaters, fishermen, artists in oil, in water, in Day-Glo on velvet, and lovers . . . of seafood, sun, surf, sex in the sand, art in oil and Day-Glo on velvet, antiques and old houses, condos with clay courts and pools by the beach, tide flats and salt ponds and sunsets at sea.

The first Pilgrims crossed an ocean in misery. Their successors came from every corner of the continent in every kind of conveyance and convenience. And Geoff Hilyard often wondered if they hadn't all been seeking the same thing. But on summer holidays, sitting in traffic a mile north of the Cape Cod Canal, watching through the heat waves as the cars crossed the Sagamore Bridge like ants on a distant log, he couldn't quite remember what the "same thing" was, because these latter-day pilgrims created a steaming, smoking, vapor-locked misery all their own.

"We could have come yesterday and missed this." Janice did not look up from her book.

"I had blueprints to finish."

The Winnebago ahead of them rolled forward. Geoff inched up to close the space so that none of the smart guys sneaking along the breakdown lane could cut in front of him.

"You could've finished down here. Boston's only a two-hour drive . . . unless you go on the weekend."

"From now on I want to be like the old Cape shipmasters. They knew the sea route to Hong Kong better than the land route to Boston." He shut off the air conditioner to keep the engine from overheating. He rolled down the window and was hit by a blast of rock and roll and exhaust from the Ford pickup idling beside him.

"The shipmasters had to *go* to Boston to get their ships." Janice turned a page.

"They went by boat. Open your window."

A car zoomed by in the breakdown lane.

"Look at that bastard," said Geoff.

"In a hurry to get to the promised land," said Janice, so calmly that the sarcasm seemed to float on the surface of her voice like duckweed.

He glanced at her book. "Joan Didion or P. D. James?"

"*Improving Your Sales Approach.* To keep us eating."

In the backseat, eight-year-old Sarah told six-year-old Keith to cut it out. Keith told Sarah to cut it out herownself. Geoff told them both to cut it out, whatever it was.

"They'll be happier on the Cape," said Janice.

In the bed of the pickup beside them, a kid in a B.C. baseball cap was sitting on a lounge chair. A girl in a Body Glove bathing suit was sitting on his lap. They were, as the college students said, swapping spit. Later they'd be swapping a lot more, which made Geoff a little envious. Of what? he wondered. Their freedom? Their youth? After riding out a traffic jam in a flatbed, they'd be too sunburned to swap much of anything. The way they were going at it, even their *tongues* would be sunburned. And Geoff was about to remake his life, or so he told himself.

"Our kids *will* be happier," he said, "and if things get bad, I can always sell my piece of Jack's Island to your father."

"Which would kill your uncle Rake."

"Nothing could kill him." Geoff tuned the radio to the same station playing in the pickup. The group was U-2, and they still hadn't found what they were looking for.

"Neither have you," muttered Janice.

Sarah told Keith that eight-year-olds knew everything and six-year-olds were dumb.

"Last summer," said Janice, "it was seven-year-olds who knew everything and five-year-olds who were dumb."

"I thought we were finished with this," said Geoff.

"You mean dumbness?"

He tightened his grip on the wheel. Her calm voice and serene expression reminded him of a martyr. And her short blond hair made a good halo. It always had. The first time she smiled at him, he thought she looked like an angel. But she hadn't been smiling much lately.

In the rear window of the Winnebago, an old woman tied a ribbon on the head of her miniature poodle.

"Now, *that's* dumb," said Janice.

"What, Mummy?" said Sarah. "What's dumb?"

"That lady is kissing her dog on the mouth."

"Yech!" shouted Keith. "That's worse than kissin' Sarah." And he began to laugh.

"I wouldn't let you"—Sarah laughed right back—"'cause your breath smells like farts."

"Ma-*ah!*" cried Keith, but Ma was laughing, too.

Dad said a dog's mouth was cleaner than a human's, which made everyone laugh harder, and the laughter rolled from kissing dogs to bad breath to Dad's dumb theories while their Voyager rolled on to the Sagamore rotary, where three strands of traffic met and snarled under the sunglasses of the Massachusetts State Police. The silver framework of the Sagamore Bridge seemed close enough to touch, but it was still ten minutes away, and the laughter faded again.

Geoff and Janice had been crossing the bridge when he asked her to marry him. It was 1973, the first warm day of spring, which meant late May on Cape Cod. They had cut classes to sip wine and make love and read Victorian novels in the shelter of some sand dune, and he could still remember the conspiratorial glint in her eye when he asked.

"If I say no, will you drive through the guardrail?"

"I'll have no choice."

"Then I'd better say yes."

He had reached out his hand to hers, and she had placed it on her thigh, at the cuff of her tennis shorts. His fingers had done the rest.

She was wearing tennis shorts this morning, and he still found her thighs irresistible. Halfway across the canal that separated the Cape, like a moat, from the rest of the world, he placed his hand on the smooth skin. "This isn't dumb."

She covered his hand with hers. "Not dumb. Daring."

"And haven't we always been daring?"

"Just ask our families."

ii.

At one-fifty-nine, they parked in front of the house in Dennis where Janice had grown up. She glanced at her watch and put her fingers in her ears.

At two o'clock on the nose, a thunderous explosion rattled the windows of the house, then Dickerson Bigelow bellowed, "The bar is open. Let the glorious Fourth begin!"

When he saw Janice, Dickerson fired the brass starter's cannon again. The blast nearly blew Grandma Agnes off her chair. Drinks spilled, Bigelows jumped, and inside the house, a picture fell from the living room wall. "Ladies and gentlemen," he cried, "it gives me great pleasure to announce that my favorite Hilyards are here!"

Uncle Hiram, family attorney, thrust his hand at Geoff and said, for what seemed like the thousandth time, "Welcome, young Montague, to the house of the Capulets."

Geoff answered, as always, " 'What's in a name? A rose by any other name would smell as sweet.' "

"A rose by any other name would be my Janice." Dickerson threw his arms around his daughter.

She kissed him and tugged at his beard, bringing the usual laughing yelp. A shopworn old greeting, something from Janice's girlhood, had become a comforting tradition for both of them since her mother's death.

Geoff tolerated it. He always tolerated tradition, even if the yelp was just another way that Dickerson attracted attention. And he tolerated Dickerson's knuckle-squasher handshake, which didn't squash quite so much since the heart attack. But he could never stand the stage whisper when Dickerson wanted the family to know how good he was to his son-in-law. "Come to my study in ten minutes, Geoff. I have a little proposal."

"Hey, Grampa," said Keith, "see my muscle?"

Dickerson squeezed the boy's arm and let out a long, low whistle.

Geoff looked at Janice, "Proposal?"

She shrugged and shook her head.

And the Hilyards greeted the other Bigelows—Grandma Agnes, eighty-nine-year-old matriarch, Cousin Blue and his son, aunts and uncles, Bigelows by birth and Bigelows by marriage . . . all members of Cape Cod aristocracy.

Of course, on Cape Cod, aristocracy had little to do with money, achievement, or even education. Millionaires with Harvard degrees and waterfront houses might look down their noses at the natives. But the natives looked at them as little more than tourists. The natives might mow the tourists' lawns or paint their shutters or pump their cesspools. But it was the natives who were the aristocrats, because they had been there since the beginning.

Names like Nickerson, Doane, Crosby, Snow, Sears, Eldredge, Cahoon, Bigelow, and Hilyard appeared on businesses all along Routes 6A and 28. For three centuries they had been appearing on fishing boats, masters' logs, cranberry boxes, saltworks, salvage vessels, the rosters of the U.S. Lifesaving Service, and before anything else, on primitive purchase and sale agreements signed with the Indians.

In most Cape families, there had been Tories and Whigs, solid citizens and scoundrels, empire builders and clam diggers, geniuses and inbreds, and they had formed an aristocracy of strong backs and stiff spines, because nothing came easy on a peninsula surrounded by the sea. It was still said among the Bigelows who ran a Hyannis service station that while the Kennedys had the compound, the Bigelows had the history.

They were not close-knit clans. There were simply too many of them, and after three and a half centuries, some branches were so far apart they had nothing in common beyond their intertwined names. The Bigelows of Bourne barely knew the Dickersons who fished out of Provincetown, or the Bigelow who kept law offices in Boston and Barnstable. But they all knew Dickerson Bigelow, because he made it his business to know all of them. And he invited all of them for the glorious Fourth.

His house had been built in the 1840s, when American architects were looking to classical forms for inspiration and American shipbuilders were creating classical forms of their own. A forebear had invested a sea-made fortune in Shiverick & Sons Shipwrights, then built a Greek Revival house overlooking the harbor where the Shivericks built their clippers. The shipyard was gone, but the house still stood, monument to the same Greek ideal of beauty through efficiency embodied in the clippers.

Geoff thought that way about things. It was the way architects thought.

He liked the library best of all the rooms. The ancient Oriental gave it a sense of history. The books mellowed it, though Dickerson seldom read anything beyond the real estate section. And the artwork reminded Geoff that he was not the first of his family to mix with the Bigelows.

While he waited to hear Dickerson's proposal, he sipped a beer and studied the painting above the fireplace. *Reading the Compact* had been painted by Geoff's great-great-uncle Thomas Hilyard in 1895 and purchased by State Senator Charles Bigelow, Dickerson's grandfather.

Americans had been taught that the creation of the Mayflower Compact was one of the pivotal events in the history of democracy, and artists usually poured the golden paint all over the ship. Tom Hilyard had painted a day so shrouded in mist you could almost smell the damp wool on the dark and brooding figures. The only splash of color was the red quill that Ezra Bigelow offered to Jack Hilyard, and for ninety-five years, people had been arguing over that: was Jack raising his hand to take the quill or to ward Bigelow away?

"That painting proves that our families have been cooperating since the *Mayflower*." Douglas Bigelow ambled in wearing his white trousers and green golf shirt.

"If you believe *that*," answered Geoff, "you've never looked at the painting."

Douglas slipped the bottle of beer from Geoff's hand, took a sip, then handed it back to him. "It shows a Bigelow and a Hilyard making history."

Geoff wiped the mouth of the bottle and drained the beer. He liked Douglas, who was as tall as his father, not nearly as broadbeamed, and far more subtle, except in the choice of his second wife, she of the short skirts, long legs, and gold jewelry heavy enough to bench press.

"How's your golf game?" asked Geoff.

"Long drives, accurate irons, putts like pool shots. How's my sister?"

"Glad to be here for the glorious Fourth—"

"And ready to go back to Boston next week." Janice came in and dropped onto the sofa.

"That's not going to happen." Dickerson lumbered after her, a beer bottle working in his right hand, the necks of two more twined into the fingers of his left. "Now that you've moved back, we're going to keep you here."

Like a bishop offering his ring, he held out his left hand and the younger men each took a beer. Dickerson touched his bottle to theirs. "To the future"—he pointed his bottle at the painting—"and the past."

"And the proposal?" Geoff leaned on the mantel.

"Jan, I know why you love this guy. He comes right to the point." Dickerson sat behind his desk and looked Geoff and Janice up and down. "Nice white tennis shorts on both of you, a powdery pink jersey for the girl, navy blue for the boy." He glanced at his son. "You, too, in all your golfie stuff."

"*Leisure* wear," said Douglas.

Dickerson looked at his khaki trousers and shirt. "In my *leisure* I like to dress like an old fisherman."

"You never fished for money in your life," said Janice.

Dickerson ignored her. "I remind me of where we came from. You remind me of where we're going."

"Grow up, grow old, and die to make room." Bad joke. Geoff knew the moment he said it. Bad hearts and gallows jokes didn't mix.

But Dickerson didn't acknowledge the joke. Only the row of pill bottles on his desk—isosorbide, 10 mg., propranolol, 20 mg., dipyridamole, 50 mg.—acknowledged the heart attack. He leaned on his elbows and looked at Janice. "Honey, you know how happy I am that you've decided to move back so Geoff can make a go of his own firm."

"Geoff decided. I'm going along with it."

"Whatever . . . We're happy. We want you to be happy, too."

Geoff felt the backs of Dickerson Bigelow's unread books closing in around him. "The suspense is killing us. What is it that will make us happy forever, and what do I have to give up to get it?"

Dickerson looked at his son. "In the family for seventeen years and still he doesn't trust us."

"He knows that if we let him in on this deal, we're not doing it because he's the brother-in-law." Douglas slipped a golf ball from his pocket and began to roll it between his fingers.

"It's because he's the best architect in New England, right?" cracked Janice.

"It's because I'm Rake Hilyard's nephew."

"Cynic!" Dickerson Bigelow pushed himself away from his desk and went to the window. Outside, his ancient mother was carrying a tray of hors d'oeuvres toward the back lawn. "I raised a generation of cynics, Ma!"

"Because they grew up around men like you, Dick."

"Never misses a beat," said Janice.

"Neither does her granddaughter," added Geoff.

"And we both love them both," said Dickerson, "just like we both love Jack's Island."

"There's a difference between love and lust."

Dickerson looked at Janice. "Why did you have to go and marry such a smartass?"

"Because I knew that some day, you'd want to do business with him. So stop insulting each other and talk like grown men."

Love and lust had been known to serve each other well, Geoff knew, and if this offer meant a good commission, which would mean a little freedom, Geoff could stand a little of Dickerson's lust.

While the party went on outside, Dickerson talked. Douglas rolled the golf ball between his fingers and clarified. Geoff sipped his beer and acted impassive, as he would in any negotiation. Janice listened, and when she thought her husband too impassive, she asked questions.

The Bigelows wanted to develop Jack's Island. The Hilyards resisted. That much had been known for years. During the mid-eighties boom, the Bigelows didn't even bother to try to develop their side of their island. It wasn't worth the fight with the town and the abutters when there was so much money to be made on the rest of the Cape.

But the boom was over. Real estate prices had turned in a big way. No one was buying middle-priced homes in subdivisions hacked from the scrub pine. Planning boards and conservation commissions were getting tough. And the people of Cape Cod, who shared watershed and coastline but who had always acted as fifteen towns going in fifteen directions, had voted a County Commission to contend with development.

The only land certain to sell—or worth the fight—was waterfront. In a bad market, scarce things kept their value. Douglas said they could squeeze thirty to thirty-five premium-priced one-acre lots out of the island, each one worth three to five hundred thousand once it was perked and permitted. And once they put houses on the land, the profits would double.

"Geoff, sell us your land, convince Rake to sell," said Dickerson, "and you'll design the development we want to call Pilgrims' Rest."

"Modern luxury inside, Pilgrim ambience outside," added Douglas. "Like . . . *Star Wars* meets the seventeenth century."

"What about the permits?" asked Geoff. "The town and county will put you through hell to develop that island."

"We're grandfathered."

"Grandfathered?" said Janice. "How?"

Douglas unrolled a map of Jack's Island, subdivided into scores of 5000-square-foot lots. In the corner was a legend, in the fountain-pen script of someone who had learned handwriting in the old school: "Plan of Land for Pilgrim's Rest at Jack's Island, Brewster, Mass., owned by Elwood Hilyard, Zachary Hilyard, and Heman Bigelow, January 9, 1904, Scale 1" to 100', Charles Berry, C.E., Orleans, Mass."

"I dug this up at the Barnstable County Courthouse," explained Douglas. "They did plans like this for land all over the Cape. Most of them came later than this one, and they were seldom followed up on. This one was forgotten after the Hilyard House burned, but these things retain their weight."

"What good does it do us?" asked Janice.

Dickerson tried to say something, but Douglas was doing the talking now, and he talked right over his father. Since Dickerson's heart attack, Douglas had done so much talking, and done it so fast and so well, that Dickerson didn't even try to top him.

Douglas took his putter from the corner and used it like a pointer above the map. "The genius who laid this out divided the island like a pie, with everybody getting a quarter-acre. If we don't alter the roads or lot-lines, just combine lots to build bigger houses, we have a strong case. I've already gone after several building permits on my side of the island, just to test the waters."

"What did Uncle Rake say about that?" asked Geoff.

"That's when he started his eminent domain drive," answered Doug. "He wants the town to take the whole island."

"He's getting senile," grunted Dickerson.

Douglas dropped a golf ball onto the floor. "If the town rejects Rake, then it's up to you, Geoff. Convince him to sell, and you're in for a fee of a million five—six percent of projected construction costs—plus payment for your piece of land, which may be worth two mil more."

Geoff looked at Janice. Through the telepathy of marriage, they heard the arguments without speaking them: Imagine the prestige. Imagine the income. And it wasn't like he'd never thought of it himself. He had moved to the Cape to create buildings that respected the Cape's history and ecology, whatever that meant. Here was his chance. Besides, if the island was going to be developed, who better to design it?

But Janice knew what else he was thinking, and she said it for him. "This would kill Uncle Rake."

Dickerson grunted, as though his daughter's remark might kill him. "Nothing could kill *Uncle* Rake."

"I need to think about this," said Geoff.

"Take a week," said Douglas.

Janice looked at her brother. "Does he get this offer in writing?"

"In writing!" Dickerson half-rose from his chair, then dropped back as if reminding himself not to get angry. "This is *family*, kids."

But Geoff did not notice Dickerson's effort at self-control. He pointed at the painting. "*They* got it in writing."

Douglas tapped the ball across the rug. "You don't know of anything else they got in writing, do you? Like a book?"

Geoff didn't, and he didn't puzzle over it, either. There was too much else to think about.

iii.

In real estate, three things mattered—location, location, and . . . *Cornhill Road in Truro, views of Cape Cod Bay and Little Pamet marsh, walk to beach, older home, needs TLC.* Geoff and Janice had read the ad when they were first married. They liked the idea of having a place thirty miles from Jack's Island, forty from her father's house. Now the house was an even older home—a living, breathing money pit—but it had appreciated so much that they called it an antique.

They unloaded the car, then gave the kids flashlights, and off they all went toward the crest of Cornhill.

"Nothing makes a kid happier than a flashlight," said Geoff, "except being up past bedtime."

"Nice to be a kid again."

"Nice to have nothing to think about."

Janice took his arm. "Too bad it's not the case."

"Too many things to think about. That's one of the nasty things about pushing forty. That and less sex."

She stopped and put her hands on her hips.

"Just a joke," he said.

She was one of the better things about pushing forty. There was a new hardness at the cheekbones, and the lines were leathering in around her eyes and mouth. But she still had great legs and one of those forthright Yankee faces—a little long in the jaw, a little pinched around the nostrils, never ravishing, but handsome when simple beauty faded. Too bad she was so damn stubborn.

He took her arm, and they walked in silence for a time, following the flashlight beams that danced ahead like fireflies. Then Janice said, "I think you should do it."

In the distance, someone set off a machine-gun string of fire-crackers.

"Sell out my uncle?"

"Talk to him. Tell him the world won't stop because an old man wants to keep things the way they were in 1928."

"You're sounding heartless."

"You're *thinking* the same way."

He slipped his arm from hers and hurried to the crest of the hill, where dozens of happy, half-lit people were singing the ooh-and-ah chorus to the bass thump of distant fireworks.

Around the rim of the bay, the oldest towns in America were celebrating its birth. To the west, above Plymouth, fireworks blossomed and faded like flowers on a distant mountain. To the south, where the land dipped below the horizon, nothing could be seen but white flashes. To the north, over Provincetown, you could almost touch the colors dancing against the blackness.

Janice whispered, "Even the Pilgrims knew you had to move one idea aside to make room for the next."

CHAPTER 4

December 1620

The First Encounter, The First Mysteries

December 1, 1620. Clear, calm, cold beyond freezing. It is said that in the planning of this migration, some argued for the Guianas, but fearing the tropics unhealthful and the Spaniards too close by, they chose America. Of the Spaniards I have heard no good, but no place could be less healthful than this.

Three days past, we sailed to the place called Cornhill, so named because the first explorers from the ship found there buried, amongst Indian graves and abandoned dwellings, a store of corn, some of which they did bring back. Wishing to find the Indians and barter for the rest, but mindful of the wrath they may have incurred in first taking of it, the elders wanted many arms on a second exploration, so I offered the crew.

We shipped in longboat and shallop on November 28, but were much hindered by crosswinds and rough seas and put in after only four miles. All waded ashore, some to their knees, some to their waist in the cold water. And the salt wind that stung our ears turned wet seams and stitches to ice on our legs.

We slept that night in soggy clothes on the beach, and by suncoming, our blankets were covered over with snow. Though all suffered the cold and gripin' bellies, we explored a shallow harbor and two tide-cut rivers, then went up Cornhill, tallest bluff on the bay, covered over with stunted pines, brambles, sassafras, and hardwoods in the protected places. Ezra Bigelow charged his brother Simeon and others to dig into a certain sand hill where the corn was hid, but Simeon hesitated, as it might be a grave that they defiled.

Jack Hilyard said digging was the only way to know if it was Indian corn or Indian bodies in the mound. Simeon, who seems a gentle and honest man, answered that they had come firstly to make amends with the savages. Ezra answered that they had come firstly to guarantee a store of corn and could not make amends with them who would hide from them and do them harm if they could.

Bradford told Simeon to quiet himself, as they would do business with the Indians at the first moment.

Then a rush basket of corn appeared, and Bradford led a prayer of thanksgiving.

In whatever they do, they believe God watches over them. 'Tis a fine confidence, especially when they take what is not theirs.

I returned to the *Mayflower* with the corn, ten bushels in all, and those men too sickly and tired to keep on. The rest of the party—Bradford, Carver, Hopkins, Hilyard, the Bigelows, et al.—returned this forenoon, bringing with them wooden bowls, spoons, rush mats, and other trinkets taken out of empty Indian dwellings.

And Ezra Bigelow spoke of something that struck me as mysterious. North of Cornhill, in a mound near two abandoned dwellings, they found a bow, arrows, cups, bowls, a strange sort of crown, and two bundles.

They ope'd the larger of those and found bones and skull, how long buried could not be told. Some unconsumed flesh remained, and hanks of hair, which was yellow. In the smaller bundle were the bones of a boy, buried also with a bow and beads around his wrists and ankles. Indian king and son? But Indians have black hair. French fishermen? The canvas shirt and breeches on the larger skeleton are sailor's garb. But why buried with such honor? None could say.

After telling his tale, Ezra Bigelow was strangely disconsolate and sought out another disconsolate one, Dorothy Bradford, who has remained at the rail, gazing fearfully at the wilderness, all the weeks we have been here.

In truth, they should all be disconsolate that went out. 'Tis no season to explore, but they must continue. 'Tis no season to build shelters, but it must be done. 'Tis time for me to be sailing, but I must stay.

ii.

Some Nausets tipped their arrows with eagle claws or the tails of horseshoe crabs. Others used pieces of brass traded from white men. But Autumnsquam had learned to shoot a stone-head arrow. With a stone-head arrow, he knew just the force and flight needed to bring down deer or black duck. Bringing down white men would be no different.

He sat before his *wetu*, and with a large stone he chipped at a smaller one. On the ground sat a bowl of finished arrowheads and a pile of unworked stones.

"You make many." Aspinet stood over him.

Autumnsquam looked up. "We need many."

The old sachem sat on his haunches, which pleased Autumnsquam because it was a sign that Aspinet accepted him as an equal. Autumnsquam called to his new woman to bring them food.

"The white men have been here now for one moon, and they have not come south of the rivers of the Pamets." Aspinet picked up a piece of snow crust and sucked on it.

"But they do much north of there. They take Pamet seed corn. They dig into Pamet graves. They steal from Pamet dwellings. White men steal everything." Small chips of stone flew as Autumnsquam worked. "Even us."

"Their women wash clothes on the shore. They would not bring their women on a stealing voyage."

"So they wish to settle. Stealing or settling, they bring no good."

Autumnsquam's new woman came with a bowl of salt herring and put it before the men. He waited until the sachem had taken the first bite of fish; then he took a piece and tore it with his teeth. When she saw that the men were pleased, the woman went back into the *wetu*.

"Her belly grows big," said Aspinet.

"I will not let her be stolen, or lose another child to another sickness. If I do, I will wait for a storm, then point my canoe into the sea."

Aspinet looked for a long time at the young man, then picked up an arrowhead. "Make many more."

iii.

Jack Hilyard awoke like a man. That was what he said whenever morning brought a firmness of the loins, whether from a dream or a need to piss.

The feeble light slipping through the cracks of their little canvas room told him it was before sunrise. He glanced at his son, sleeping at the foot of the pallet. Then he listened. Except for the sounds of snoring and coughing, the tween-decks was quiet. Sleep was a true gift.

The Saints might have their thoughts of God, the Strangers their dreams of a new beginning, but every waking hour was invested by the presence of a wilderness that seemed, even to Jack, to be indomitable. For all of them, sleep had become a small surcease from this vision, a time to restore the spirit as well as the body. And when the spirit was restored, the body might awaken like a man.

Jack pulled his shirt up around his waist, then rolled toward Kate, who slept with her back to him. He bunched up a handful of her shift and pressed against her. She made a sound in her sleep and moved slightly, just enough that he could slip himself between the soft globes of her flesh.

Then he closed his eyes and felt her warmth. He had been cold for days. He had been miserable for weeks. Only Kate had kept him from losing hope. In a life of hopelessness, any woman might make a companion, but a woman who loved you promised the future. In a life of few pleasures, any woman was a gift, but a big woman was an extravagance, and nowhere was Kate Hilyard more commodious than behind. Her warmth coursed through his loins, along his spine, and filled him with a feeling that he could conquer the world.

He wet his fingers and gently tried to waken her. She made a sound of contentment and stretched herself toward his hand. He kept his fingers moving gently in the place she liked most until he knew she was awake, though with eyes still closed.

"Good mornin', my darlin'."

"Thou got hairy balls, mister."

"And a cock that asks if the hen be layin'."

Kate giggled, which made Jack even firmer. Most women were as solemn as priests when they did this. A woman who could laugh with you in the midst of love, she was something rare. And he told her as much.

"Thou art a rare bird thyself, to be wantin' it with thy twelve-year-old son sleepin' at thy feet."

"He won't be wakin' any time soon."

"Do it quiet, then. But not too quick."

And it was as fine a tumble as a man could want. She loved the feel of their flesh as much as he. When he rolled onto her, she welcomed him with her legs and her lips and the breasts that she slipped from her shift. When he began to move, she rolled her heavy hips as lasciviously as a whore. When he growled his pleasure, she whispered, "'Tis true what they say."

"What?"

"The fuller the cushion, the finer the pushin'."

And from the other side of the canvas, they heard Simeon Bigelow whisper groggily to his wife, "What didst thou say dear?"

Kate grabbed Jack's buttocks to keep him from moving. Jack put a hand over Kate's mouth to keep her from laughing.

"What, Simeon?" came another voice from sleep.

"Thou asked me for a cushion."

"I asked a question? What question?"

"Not question. Cushion."

Jack buried his face on Kate's breasts to stifle a snicker. Husband and wife were like two mischievous children. They should have been used to life in the tween-decks. Day and night, the air echoed with the sounds of farting and vomiting and snoring and pissing and coughing, all things that kept a man in this world, no different from the animals. But seldom did the sounds of love break through. To Jack

Hilyard, a man was never closer to God than when his hips were joined to his wife's. The sounds of love should have been as the sounds of morning prayer. But even the Hilyards kept their passion quiet.

"I did not ask thee for a cushion," said Anne. "I got a pallet."

"You distinctly said, 'Push me a cushion.'"

"Pray pardon but I did not. And why didst thou wake me?"

"Thou woke *me* and asked for a cushion."

Kate's body was shaking with laughter, which felt so good to Jack that he had to move once more.

"Where on this godforsaken ship at the edge of this godforsaken wilderness would I expect thee to find a cushion?"

"Right here," whispered Kate. She rolled her hips. And Jack responded, and Simeon and Anne Bigelow continued to argue. And Jack and Kate moved with each other. And Jack tried to hold his consummation but could not. And Kate tried to hold her cry but could not. And Kate turned her head to her pillow to muffle the noise. And the Bigelows fell silent at the sound. But Jack did not notice, and neither did Kate, because for a few seconds, they took each other to another place, away from the cold and smells, the salt food and sad prayers, the fading hopes and winter-killed spirits.

Then the cry that Kate stifled became a cough. She sucked it in and tried to hold it, but it shook her body and reddened her face and finally burst out of her. Jack felt it rack in his own chest. He rolled off of her and held her until the spasm ended.

She wiped her watering eyes with the back of her hand. "'Tis no worse than what anyone else has. But what we just done . . . there's none who has better."

He tenderly pulled her shift over her breasts and stroked her stringy hair. "I'm goin' to build thee and the lad a proper house, darlin'."

"A shelter'll do, Jack. Then build thyself a whaleboat and build us a future on the backs of them big black monsters out in the bay."

"These Saints ain't whalemen. If they decides to settle where there be no whales, I'll break away and expect thee to stand by me."

"I'll brook nuffin' foolhardy, Jack. I told thee that the day of the signin'. But a man of courage, who does what he has to, I'll take him to me bed whenever he asks."

"Thou gives me a strong spine, me darlin'. And a strong son."

Jack looked at the boy, who was sitting up, staring straight at them, eyes wide and curious. When Jack found his voice, he said, "Run along, lad. See what the weather bring for the exploration."

The boy looked once more at his mother's dishevelment, pulled on his breeches, and went out.

"How much did he see?" asked Kate.

"Don't matter. Learnin' 'bout the world, he is. And he knows why we come here. There'll be no fo'c'sles or fishmongerin' for him. Not here. Not in America."

"Excuse me." Simeon Bigelow poked his head over the canvas, and with a small smile he said, "Wouldst thou have a cushion we could borrow?"

Kate laughed and began to cough. "More cushions and less cold would do us all some good."

iv.

But for the explorers, the day brought only more cold. The shallop, under sail, pounded south through the icy spray. Jack Hilyard's cloak froze like a board on his back. Myles Standish's helmet and chest plate had an ice glaze that made him look like a sugar man in the window of a London bakeshop. Bradford, John Carver, Stephen Hopkins, Simeon Bigelow, and the others hunkered down while the waves broke over the bow of the shallop and sent up a mist that rimed their hats, hair, and sword hilts.

Mates John Clarke and Robert Coppin were in command, as Jones had chosen to remain on the ship and care for his cough. Ezra Bigelow had stayed behind as well, having dug into enough graves that he claimed to need a respite from the face of death.

Jack was glad to leave Bigelow at the rail beside Dorothy Bradford. Jack and Bigelow had become natural adversaries, like the sperm whale and the giant squid, and he could not understand the trust that others put in Bigelow. Even William Bradford treated him like a brother.

Jack thought that, in most things, Bradford molded brains to his courage and good sense to his faith. But Jack would never have sailed off and left *his* wife at Ezra Bigelow's side. Had Kate been as frail as Dorothy Bradford, Jack would never have left England at all. That was the difference 'twixt a man of the world and a man of faith. The one never forgot his good sense. The other believed that the same

God who warmed his English hearth would care for him in the wilderness.

Jack did not think that with all the things God had to do, he was watching this miserable corner of the earth, so Jack would do it for him. While the others kept their heads out of the wind, Jack watched for creeks and inlets and, most of all, for whales, which they found, along with a handful of Indians, on a small bay some ten miles south of Cornhill.

The Indians were cutting up a dead drifter and ran at sight of the explorers. This seemed a bad portent. Still, Jack said they were fools if they did not settle on a bay that drew drift whales and was a full five fathoms deep. But they were most of them farmers before seamen, and deep anchorage meant less than a spit's-depth of black earth. So they named the bay Grampus for the abandoned whale, rejected it for the thin topsoil, and continued south.

They stopped for the night just north of where the armlike Cape bent its elbow. There, they built a barricado of logs and boughs and gathered at the fire to give a prayer of thanks. For what, Jack did not know, as they lacked the good sense to settle on Grampus Bay, and how many more chances would God give them? While they prayed, he borrowed the mate's spying glass and went down to the beach to continue God's work.

The tide had ebbed from this corner of the bay as though flowing from a shallow bowl. Flats now stretched for miles, a bleak muddy plain dotted with freezing pools and flocks of gulls gabbling busily about, gossiping and laughing like old women on market day. Jack wondered if they laughed at the fire glimmering feebly in the dusk . . . or at the praying around it.

Through the glass, Jack scanned the southern coast. There was an inlet near the elbow, and west of that, two creeks. Between them stretched a beach, beds of eelgrass, and a collection of shadows that looked, in the fading light, like boulders, all of the same size and shape. He steadied the glass on the gunwale of the shallop to better see.

"'Tisn't appreciated when one of our number will not pray with us." Simeon Bigelow's voice, even in rebuke, was gentler than his brother's, as if the voices and features reflected the men. Simeon was near as tall as Ezra, but fleshy and rumpled where his brother was hard and precise. Even his beard, a rough black tangle, contrasted with Ezra Bigelow's pointed chin whiskers.

"More whales." Jack handed the glass to Bigelow and pointed toward the land between the creeks. "Enough oil to pay off all the debts of this group in one motion."

"They look like boulders." Simeon lowered the glass. "Come mornin', thou may seest more clearly."

"Come mornin', we must go there."

"I be not the man to ask." Simeon began to dig for something in the shallop.

Jack grabbed him by the elbow. "Thou be the man to ask *for* me."

"Why shouldst I ask for thee?"

"Thou be a man of good sense and broader mind than most."

Bigelow straightened himself and removed Jack's fingers, one by one, from his elbow. "I hold the same beliefs as my brethren."

"But thou got charity in thee. Thou knows that, for all me rough words, I wish to see us survive as much as any." A cold wind snapped over the flats and blew the brim of Jack's hat against the side of his head. He pulled it lower on his ears. "These flats be bounteous full, Simeon—whales, fish, shellfish. 'Tis a good place to settle."

"Come mornin', make the case thyself." Simeon smiled. "'Twill benefit thee if they settle there."

v.

Morning came as no more than a graying of the gloom. The woods above the campsite were still deep in darkness. The flats were gray, the sea grayer. Even the sand seemed gray. The gulls stood like gray sentinels on the flats. And the shadows of other shorebirds darted through the gray sky, their nervous swarming a sure sign of change in the weather.

From the woods, Autumnsquam watched. His face was painted black, his body covered with animal grease. He had come for war. During the night, he and the others had tested the white men by howling like wolves in the woods. The whites had roused themselves and fired off their guns, and many of the Nausets had lost their courage. But Autumnsquam would not let them run. Now he counted only one white man for every three Nausets, and by some arrogance or stupidity, the whites had carried most of their weapons to their canoe, then had gone back, unarmed, to their little square of logs and boughs on the beach. Autumnsquam crawled to Aspinet and said the time had come.

Jack Hilyard was watching Simeon Bigelow melt goose grease over the fire. "Through the mist, nuffin' can be seen of the beaches to the south."

"Then thou hast little to say."

"I'll say no matter, when the mood 'round the fire warms."

Myles Standish stood at the opening of the barricado. Not the cheeriest of men, his demeanor had worsened as several had elected to carry their guns and gear to the shallop, to be ready to go when the tide rose. Hunger made him even angrier. "What breaks our fast, Master Simeon?"

"Hard tack in goose grease and a gill of beer."

"For *this* we leave our guns unguarded."

"Repast fit for a king," said Bradford cheerily.

Jack Hilyard cleared his throat. "I knows a way we'll all eat like kings, with sterling brung by whale oil—"

Nothing more of what he said could be heard above the wild cries that came from the woods.

"Wolves?" said Bradford.

Stephen Hopkins rushed into the barricado, "They are men! Indians! Indians!"

And a shower of arrows whistled through the air. Three shafts thumped into the ground around Jack. One struck the kettle and splashed grease onto his breeches. Another landed by his boot. A third pinned Simeon Bigelow's cloak to the ground.

Jack felt a familiar chill at the nape of his neck, which was good, because a little fear sharpened the senses and steadied the hand. But too much fear froze men to their boot soles, and for a moment, none of the others could move.

Then Standish proved the worth of a soldier among farmers and shopkeeps. Though he had no target, he raised and fired his snaphance at the woods. The thunderous roar frightened the Indians into silence and roused the explorers from their shock.

"Arm yourselves! Now!" Standish shouted.

"Fear not the arrows," cried Bradford, finding his courage. "God is with us."

"And dressed most of you in armor!" added Jack.

"But the guns be by the shallop!" said Hopkins.

"And you bloody *fools* for leavin' 'em there!" shouted Standish.

"*I* be no fool," cried Jack. "Mine be right here."

"And there are two more," said Bradford.

"Be quick with 'em, then," ordered Standish, "and the rest of you ready yourselves to run for the shallop."

Jack looked at Simeon, who was still crouched in fright, and held out his gun. "Fire the match."

Another flight of arrows came in, some digging into the sand, some fluttering to the ground, a few tearing into the cloaks drying above the fire, and every one rooting Simeon Bigelow more firmly to his fright.

"Fire the match, Simeon," said Jack evenly, "or we'll none of us get out of here alive."

With shaking hand, Simeon pulled a burning stick from the fire and touched it to the slow match on Jack's musket.

Standish was now standing in full view of the Indians, letting arrows bounce off his corselet while he reloaded. When a stone-tipped arrow struck the armor near his neck, he snapped it in half and spat on it.

This infuriated the Indians, who screamed out a strange cry— "*Woach, Woach, ha ha hach woach*"—and sent down another rain of arrows.

"Do all the spittin' you wants, Captain." Jack raised his matchlock and pulled the trigger. The hammer snapped, touching the smoldering cord to the powder in the pan. There was a small flash, then an explosion that once more shocked the Indians into silence, but this time, their fear neither grew as great nor lasted as long.

Standish ordered the unarmed men after their guns. "Run, you bloody fools. Run now!"

And as the white men fled down the beach, the Indians burst from the woods to give chase.

"Run!" cried Jack.

"Be men of faith," added Bradford.

"And you be men of the musket!" cried Standish. In the firelight, his face now shone as red as his beard.

Bradford and John Carver rushed out with their matchlocks, dug their rests into the sand, fitted the barrels, and took aim.

Standish pointed at the shadows churning down the beach as though driven by the wind. "Aim together," he ordered calmly. "Together, now. Fire!"

The noise of the guns frightened the Indians back into the woods.

Their kick knocked Bradford into Jack, who fell against Carver, who fell onto the seat of his breeches.

"On your feet," ordered Standish. "The savages muster courage to come at us next. Load and pray we have help from the shallop presently."

Then they heard the men at the shallop calling for a firebrand.

"Bloody fools!" roared Standish. "What soldier lets his match go out?"

"What soldier leaves his gun three hundred feet from his side?" answered Hilyard. "Simeon, another firebrand."

Simeon poked his cutlass through the logs. "There be no more small pieces."

"Then a log! Take a log!"

"Take it where?"

"The shallop!" roared Standish. "Without a firebrand, matchlocks be no better than clubs."

Bradford drove the ramrod into his gun. "Be of good courage, Simeon, and be quick. God be with you."

But Simeon stood staring at the flames, in the grip of terror.

So Jack took sterner measures. He kicked Simeon square in his breeches. "A firebrand, man! Fail in this and the colony dies!"

And Simeon Bigelow found his courage. He poked at the fire until a burning log came free. He wrapped it in his cloak, then threw it onto his shoulder and ran.

At the sight of his shadow bursting from the barricado, the Indians sped forth once more. But fear and the flames on his shoulder made Simeon run faster than any demon.

He fired the matches of the men at the shallop and a three-gun volley exploded so loud that a flock of gulls lifted from the flats. Amidst a splattering shower of white gull shit, three more stepped forward, fixed rests, fired, and put the Indians to flight.

These white men were demons, thought Autumnsquam. They made targets of themselves, but arrows did not pierce their clothing. Nor did war cries frighten them nor fire burn them. And their weapons made noise that could shake the ground. But even if the other Nausets were afraid, he would show bravery.

He stepped boldly from behind a tree and bellowed a war cry. The white men raised their weapons at him, but he did not flinch. Two shots exploded around him, but he did not run. He answered them with two arrows of his own.

These savages were demons, thought Jack Hilyard. Even in bitter winter, they wore nothing but breeches. They painted their faces, they screamed like animals, and after they attacked, they disappeared into the blackness of the forest like night creatures at dawn. And now this bold one was standing their musket shots and shouting defiance.

So Jack aimed his matchlock. Autumnsquam aimed his bow. One stood at the edge of the trees, barely visible for the blackness around him. The other stood before his campfire, a black shadow in the light. Autumnsquam's arrow whizzed by Jack Hilyard's ear. Jack's shot struck a tree and sent splinters of wood flying at Autumnsquam.

The Indian felt a pain that was more humiliating than excruciating. He gave a last defiant cry and ran off with the others.

The explorers ran into the woods and fired off their pieces, then gave two shouts to show they had no fear of the Indians. The shouts echoed feebly through the trees and, in men of less faith, should have inspired fear. No sound could have been lonelier. But men who knew God as intimately as the Saints could never be lonely, no matter how vast the wilderness.

So they offered a prayer, then congratulated one another on their bravery. None spoke of marksmanship.

Simeon Bigelow, praised for saving the day, said he hoped they could make peace with the Indians.

"Peace comes when you prove you be ready for war," said Standish, who paid Jack Hilyard the high praise of calling him "a good man in a fight."

"Pray that he is as good in peace," added Simeon.

After they were away, William Bradford proclaimed that henceforth, they would know the beach by the name First Encounter.

Jack Hilyard had no interest in naming names. He was looking toward the south coast, but the mist remained so thick he could not see the beach between the creeks, nor could he persuade them to put in so near to where the savages had attacked. They were not so foolish as to think a second fight would end as well. So Jack restrained his instinct to call them women and quietly promised Simeon that soon, he would return to the land between the creeks and claim it as his own.

From the woods, Autumnsquam watched them go. He would send word along the Narrow Land, and by the time runners reached the small villages of the Scusset, the story would tell of the Nauset victory that drove the white men into the sea. Autumnsquam would not object. Truth took many forms, and his bravery would be the heart of the tale. But there would be no need to send runners beyond the Scusset, for north of that was the land of the Patuxets.

And the Patuxets were no more. They had lived on the best harbor in the bay, with fish and shellfish in abundance. They had taken their water from a fine spring, climbed hillsides that gave long views of sea and countryside, and cleared wide fields for corn. But the sickness had killed them all. In the land of the Patuxets, there would be no one to care at the coming of the white men.

Autumnsquam could not have known that an Englishman called John Smith had charted this bay and given the name *Plymouth* to the Patuxet land. Or that the men in the shallop would arrive there that day and decide that the fresh water, the defensible hills, the cleared fields, and the lack of Indians were all part of God's plan . . . for them.

vi.

December 13, 1620. Cold, clear, wind NW. The return of the explorers after eight days brings as much rejoicing as the news that they have found a site for settlement.

All listened with excitement to the stories of the voyage, and the place that will be their new home. But joy and excitement were not long-lived for the terrible news awaiting William Bradford. It was left to Brewster to take him inside and tell him.

Those who pressed their ear to the cabin door heard no sobbing, nor the piteous howl that some would give on learning that their wife had fallen from the ship and drowned. When Bradford emerged, he carried himself erect and answered to every kind word, "'Tis God's will."

Perhaps. But a master can shut his eyes to nothing aboard his ship, so I called the elders together in my cabin. Brewster said that Dorothy must have fell overboard in one of her night moods. The others agreed, as her driftings about the deck were well known.

I then asked Ezra Bigelow, who has been most nervous and jittery-seeming since she died, what he did that night. He summoned an indignified air and asked why such question was put to him.

I answered that he had been seen beside her many times since we anchored, and that when her husband went on his latest voyage, he stayed behind and was seen in the night to take her hand.

Elder Brewster, a just and wise-seeming man, asked if there were truth in my words. Ezra answered that he loved Dorothy Bradford like a sister, which seemed enough for Brewster, though not for me.

I said that the night of her death, I did study the coast in the chartkeeper's cabin. The deck being deserted, the sound of voices drew my attention. Sharp voices they were, 'twixt Ezra and Dorothy, as though they had come to some terrible pass.

This brought torment to Bigelow's face, but angrily he told me I eavesdropped, and for that he had no respect. I answered that I gave no care for his respect and what happened on my ship was my business, broad daylight or no.

William Brewster demanded that, were I charging one of their firmest members with the death of Dorothy Bradford, I give evidence.

Then came William Bradford himself, saying he would brook no suspicion of Ezra, a godly man and good friend. With shaking voice, he said the wilderness so terrified his wife that he believed she had taken her own life.

All gasped at this. Ezra told Bradford that grief colored his talk. He called Dorothy a woman of good faith and admitted that he had spent many hours with her that night, that they had talked of the frightening wilderness and God's love, but never did she mention the taking of her own life.

And Brewster ended the meeting. He thanked me for my scrupulosity and assured me that the elders were more scrupulous than I. He chided Bradford for suspecting something so sinful of his wife. And he said that Ezra Bigelow was exonerated by his honesty.

If the elders want him, let them have him. After a month in the New World, they know full well that the dangers they face be far more pressing than a single accident, if accident it were. Every man, innocent or not, will be needed.

As for me, I've done my honor in this.

CHAPTER 5

July 5

Murder on the Mayflower

The next morning, Geoff rose early. He started the coffee, then went onto the deck that faced the rising sun. He loved the early morning on Tom's Hill, the light that slanted in over the hillside, the gentle warmth before the heat of the day, the nearby quiet that let him hear the faroff sounds.

Down on the Little Pamet Marsh, a blue heron was poking its bill into the grass. Geoff watched its slow and careful movement and marveled that such a delicate creature could be related to the gulls squawking above Pamet Harbor. But then, he had often marveled that Janice could be related to Dickerson Bigelow.

Then the phone rang, frightening the bird into the air.

Geoff grabbed the phone, brought it outside, and picked up the receiver before the second ring.

"Geoff, did you know there was a Tom Hilyard painting called *Murder on the Mayflower?*"

"George?"

"The one and only."

"The only one who calls before seven o'clock in the morning."

"I'm so lagged I can't sleep. From Tinseltown to Provincetown, seven hours on commercial airlines, a hundred years on the time machine."

Janice came stumbling to the screen door. People did not normally call at this hour. Geoff put his hand over the receiver and whispered, "George." That explained it. George was not normal people.

She went into the kitchen and poured a cup of coffee. It had begun. The gathering of the boys. There were three of them. Harvard had thrown them together as freshmen in 1969, and they had been friends ever since. Times changed, along with careers, addresses, wives and lovers, worldviews, values, and dreams, but the boys still gathered on the Cape each summer to renew their friendship. And quite often, "boys" was the operative word.

"Do you know about this painting?" George was saying.

"No, but he did so many—"

"You're supposed to be the Tom Hilyard scholar."

"I like the later stuff. He did Pilgrim paintings to pay his bills, like me designing tract houses or you writing sitcoms."

"Then you're not interested in an art auction?"

"I have to see Rake today. Real estate talk."

"The Bigelows trying to screw the Hilyards again?"

Geoff watched the heron settle back onto the marsh, but he did not answer. George had a way of getting to the truth.

"Among the items up for bid," George went on, "is *Murder on the Mayflower.*"

"I guess I could go up Cape to see that." And he would take any excuse to avoid Uncle Rake.

It was one of the quirks of local geography that driving *up* Cape meant traveling south or west. Cape Cod, which Thoreau called "the bared and bended arm of Massachusetts," ran forty miles from the shoulder to the elbow, forty more from the elbow to the fingertips. Chatham was at the elbow. From there to the canal was called the Upper Cape because it corresponded to the upper arm, although it was at the bottom of the map. From there to Provincetown was called the Lower Cape, although it was *north* of the Upper Cape.

This could confuse tourists, who called the Upper Cape the lower Cape and the Lower Cape the outer Cape. But the term "outer Cape" sounded so logical that even the natives would not pretend to misunderstand. Of course, they might confuse things a bit more by mentioning the mid-Cape, the bicep between Yarmouth and Brewster, or the outer Cape's back shore. And if tourists asked where the front shore was, they found there wasn't any, but there was a bay side.

Geoff and Janice were driving up Cape in Geoff's '84 Chevy Cavalier, which he kept in the garage at Truro. Geoff considered it the perfect New England car: too beat-up to be worth stealing, but nicely broken in at 64,000 miles.

George Flynn, who sat in the backseat, said he preferred their van, which he had nicknamed the *Now Voyager*, after the Bette Davis movie. "And we could call this shit box the *Pocketful of Miracles*. It's a miracle the damn thing runs."

"So walk."

"Not until I know the dirt." He leaned over the front seat. "The Cole sisters who owned the painting, weren't they connected to the Bigelows somewhere along the line?"

"We're all connected somewhere along the line," said Janice, who rode shotgun. "My great-grandfather, Charles—"

"The congressman?"

"State senator was the best he ever did. His son married my grandmother's sister, but he died and she married into the Coles and—"

"Somehow, somebody ended up with an undiscovered Tom Hilyard in their attic," laughed Geoff. "Let's leave it at that or we'll need a diagram to figure it all out."

"So why are they selling?" asked George.

"Have you lost weight?" asked Janice.

George slapped his belly proudly. "Ten pounds."

Since college, he had always carried a little extra flab, and no one had ever noticed. The weight was part of the personality, along with a willingness to say whatever was on his mind and a boyish laugh that took the edge off whatever he said.

"Don't lose any weight in the wallet today," said Janice. "Either of you."

Tom Hilyard paintings were not too pricey. Tom Hilyard had not been that good. But bidding could drive them up, and Geoff had been tempted more than once. Janice liked the paintings they had inherited—one of the stark House on Billingsgate series and one of the Pilgrim paintings—but until Geoff took her father's deal, they could afford no extravagances.

"A painting no one's heard of since it was painted," mused George. "Seems a little mysterious."

"Stop thinking like a writer," said Janice.

"How can I think like anything else when Cape Cod vibrates with history, drama, the spectacle of brave men and women carving a new world from the wilderness?"

"You should be on the chamber of commerce."

George laughed and pointed to a road sign rolling past. " 'First Encounter Beach.' How many hot little adolescent asses will squirm this very day in the sand where the battle for North America was joined between the forces of Christian enlightenment and the Manichean aborigines?"

"You're still thinking like a writer," said Janice.

"And you're thinking like a curbstone. I'll bet you don't even care that Dorothy Bradford's death is the first murder mystery in the recorded history of America."

Geoff glanced at the rearview mirror. "Mystery?"

"Why would her husband write a book that chronicled *everything* the Pilgrims did until 1647 and say absolutely *nothing* about her death? Some say she fell overboard. Some say she jumped because she knew she didn't have the guts to face the wilderness. Some—"

"Some say she was pushed?" offered Geoff.

"Well, *I* wonder about it."

"This isn't exactly a big deal," said Janice.

"Maybe not. But if we can learn how other people face their worst times, maybe it can help us."

"Isn't that why you write sitcoms?" she asked.

" 'Legal Eagles' has great social significance." George pretended to get uppity. "And Dorothy must have been awful unhappy . . . a husband who couldn't figure out where to settle and the wilderness staring her in the face."

"*That* I can identify with," said Janice.

ii.

"Five thousand dollars, ladies and gentlemen. We won't entertain anything less for this beautiful and historically important work by Thomas Hilyard."

"He's right about the historically important part," whispered George. "Make a bid."

"Make one yourself," said Janice. "We can't afford it."

"We can," said Geoff.

Janice shook her head. A breeze came up from Pleasant Bay, and the awning puffed like a sail. A hundred people had come to buy armoires, settees, Oriental rugs, laquered tables brought by sea captains from China, and paintings.

There were auctions on Cape Cod almost every week. Some were little more than garage sales with carnival barkers, but some purveyed the treasures of the past. And an estate auction like this, where the provenance of each item was well established simply because it came straight from the house, was prized by the public and dealers alike.

A young woman in the third row took the bid for five thousand. The auctioneer called for five thousand five hundred.

The painting, displayed on an easel at the front of the tent, was twenty-four by thirty-seven inches. It was not a great work. It did not vibrate with life or light. In fact, it was so dark that the gilt frame nearly overwhelmed the image. But the subject gave it mystery.

The rail of the *Mayflower* ran diagonally across the image, from bow to stern. A lantern in the cabin at the stern provided the only source of light. In the foreground, a woman shrouded in a cape looked out at the blackness. And from the shadows a shadowed man moved toward her.

"Tom Hilyard thinks old Dotty was pushed," said George excitedly. "Let's make a run at this."

Five thousand five hundred was taken by a balding man at the back of the tent. The woman in the third row countered with six.

Janice sensed they were right about the historical importance, especially because the plate identifying the characters had been removed. Tom Hilyard had actually named the man who killed Dorothy Bradford, and somebody, sometime, had not been too happy about it. A solution to America's first murder mystery. But when the auctioneer called for six thousand five and Geoff's hand started up, Janice grabbed his forearm, historical importance be damned.

She knew he could have lifted her off the floor. He had taken to working out regularly and was stronger now than at twenty-five. That was fine with Janice. And she liked the way his features gained character with line. Once he had looked gentle and introspective. Now "experienced" was the word for the way he looked, if not the way he acted. And when she saw the I-want-it stare that made him look like nothing more than a thirty-nine-year-old kid trying to embrace another fantasy before he was forty, she wanted to strangle him, or at least break the arm she was squeezing.

But that might have caused a scene. So she held his arm until the man at the back of the tent took the bid.

"Six thousand five hundred. Do I hear seven?"

George leaned around Geoff and looked at Janice.

"You're on your own," she whispered. Up went his hand.

"Seven thousand to the gentleman in row eight. Do I hear seven five?"

George whispered to Geoff, "Put up half and I'll take the other half. Let's start the summer off right."

"We don't have the money," Janice whispered in Geoff's other ear. "Don't do it."

"Eight!" called the woman in the third row, and a little williwaw of excitement spun through the crowd.

"Eight five," came the voice from the back of the tent.

"Nine!" cried George.

"The gentleman says nine. Do I hear nine five?"

There was a slight pause before the man at the back raised his hand.

"And ten?"

For a moment the words hung in the air. The bidding had slowed. Perhaps ten would take it. Geoff looked at George, then at Janice. She squeezed harder.

"I'll make the decision," he whispered and began to peel her hand away.

Then the woman in the front called, "Ten." And before Geoff could get his hand up, the bid bounced to ten-five, then eleven.

Geoff's hand relaxed, as though it had gone beyond him.

Janice said, "Thank God for her."

"Are we out of it?" George whispered.

Janice squeezed Geoff's arm again.

"Lighten up," Geoff said to his wife. "I think so," he whispered to his friend.

Quickly the bidding ran to fifteen thousand, and the murmur grew as steady as the breeze off Pleasant Bay.

"Fifteen five."

"Sixteen."

Those in the back watched the man. The rest stretched their

necks for a look at the young woman, who seemed to most of them no more than a pile of strawberry blond hair and the padded shoulders of a tan business suit. George shook his head in amazement. Geoff squinted at the painting. Janice folded her arms and gazed over Barleyneck to Pleasant Bay.

Finally, at eighteen thousand dollars, the woman became the owner of a Thomas Hilyard. When the gavel fell, the applause burst, as if everyone knew they had seen the best duel of the season. The woman stood now and gave a small, gracious bow to the gentleman in the back.

"Good taste in paintings. Pretty, too," said George.

iii.

Geoff agreed. He agreed so completely that he followed the young woman, her two male companions, and the painting out to the road. George followed Geoff, while Janice stopped to chat with a friend.

The young woman was nearly six feet tall and as brusque as bleach. When she saw Geoff, she gave him the mildly annoyed and momentary glance that every woman perfects to ward off unwelcome males. But when he introduced himself, his name got her undivided attention.

"You're related to Rake Hilyard, then?"

"You know him?"

"Everyone who knows Cape history knows him."

"A student of Cape history?" George squinted in the sun. "Is that why you bought the painting?"

She gave George the kind of neutral smile that said she gave away nothing she didn't have to. "One buys a work of art for many reasons. This has been purchased for the Old Comers Plantation. I'm the director of collections."

George looked her up and down. "You must have a pretty good . . . er . . . endowment. To spend eighteen grand on a painting, I mean."

"We have an excellent genealogy collection as well, although *your* family may not be represented."

George smiled. He admired a good insult, even at his own expense. "Hilyard thinks somebody pushed Dorothy Bradford?"

"A lot of people have thought that for the last three centuries or so. Tom Hilyard is just one more. My real interest is as much in his technique as his narrative."

"Why the interest in my uncle?" asked Geoff.

The larger of her two companions, who were apparently bodyguards, reminded her of their schedule.

She kept her eyes on Geoff, tuning out everything else. "Not only has your uncle seen the whole century here, but he also knew Tom Hilyard. That makes him doubly interesting. I did an oral history with him."

"Rake can talk a cat off a fish wagon," said Geoff. "As owner of three Hilyard paintings, he'll be glad to know someone's just paid the highest price ever for one."

"Do you own any?"

"Two. I was hoping for three."

"I'd love to see them sometime." She took a business card from her jacket pocket and handed it to Geoff: Carolyn Hallissey, Old Comers Plantation, Orleans, Massachusetts. "You should do an oral history with us, too. The Cape's changed more in your lifetime than in the previous three centuries."

George was still laughing when her car went down Barleyneck.

"What's so funny?"

"When a woman asks you to do something oral, you're supposed to say, 'When and where?' "

"I was going to show her mine if she'd showed me hers."

"Her what?"

"Her Hilyard Pilgrim painting."

"Which one do you have?"

"*The Gravediggers.*"

CHAPTER 6

February 1621

The Gravediggers

Christopher Jones wrapped a blanket around his shoulders and opened his log. He looked forward to his writing. It had become a way to drive off the winter phlegm and make springtime come sooner.

> *February 7, 1621.* Bitter cold, steady NW wind, sky as clear and thoughtless as a dead man's eye . . . and of those have I seen too many. There is death on the ship and death on the land. Of the ship's company, I have lost eight, and more are laid low. Were I of a mind to challenge the winter sea, I would have but ten able bodies to man the rigging. And whilst the passengers do labor to build their houses, their chief activity is burying their dead.
>
> To the six dead of December and the eight of January have been added five more this month. Some lie sick in the tween-decks, on the same foul pallets they have used since we sailed. More lie in the common house, which has in truth become a charnel house. Most have congestion of the lungs. Some show also the bleeding gums and swole joints of the scurvy.
>
> Samuel Fuller, their chirurgeon, has bled many to drain

the ill humours, so that the sweet smell of congealing clots sickens the air. Giles Heale, ship's doctor, has physicked them in hope of cleansing the illness through the bowels, but many are so weakened that they cannot move and must lie in their own filth till tended by the few who are healthy.

William Brewster and Myles Standish have not faltered, though Standish has lost his wife. Kate Hilyard washes vile linens in the brook. Simeon Bigelow aids her in the dressing and feeding of the sick. Ezra Bigelow tends to sick spirits, going from pallet to pallet, asking for favorite Bible passages, which then he does read. In this does he show a constancy that makes me question my earlier suspicions.

And at dusk, when they have finished work on their own house, Jack Hilyard and his son go to the common house to learn how many have died that day. Then they climb the hill to a place by the ordnance platform, hack through the crust, and dig what graves are needed. Then the bodies are brought up. The procession is small, for there are few who can walk, and quiet, for the Indians must not know how many have died. The dead are put into the ground without ceremony, as is their custom, the graves then being covered with pine boughs and brush to hide them.

Only one was buried last night. Simeon Bigelow turned the first shovelful of sand onto the body of his own wife Anne. "She is with God now," he said. "She has finished her work. We yet have much to do." In the Indian fight, it is said that Simeon showed great fear afore saving the day. No man who has looked so bravely into the mouth of the grave could ever be called coward.

Surely God guides these people, else they could not endure. As my sailors die, their friends desert them, steal their victuals, take their blankets. As the passengers die, their friends show love and faith that surpass anything in my knowledge. They show it even to the dying sailors who mocked them for their piety and prayers. This is charity. This is Christianity.

Jack Hilyard was not a prayerful man, but each night he bowed his head and said his amens, because prayer was all they had, prayer and the slow lengthening of the days. No man could warm the winter. No man could stop the snow. And no man could avoid the sickness, unless protected by God or in a place far away.

When he lay by Kate's side in the night, he begged her to leave the dying and go with him to the land between the creeks. But she said no. They had signed the agreement. They could not survive without the community, nor the community without them.

And so the Hilyards did what they could, until a miserable sleeting afternoon in late February when Jack came to the common house. He stood at the door until his eyes made friends with the gloom. He held his breath, for the smell of death was as bad as the sight of it. Then he stepped over bodies and beds and looked about for his wife. She should have been at the chimney, bent over the stockpot.

"She'll be on the pallet in the corner." Simeon Bigelow put a hand on Jack's shoulder, and Jack felt the chill travel from the hand down the length of his spine.

She had been coughing more of late, her clothes hung looser around her frame, and at night, the heat from her body was enough to warm him without blankets.

"Coughin' blood, she is, Jack," said Simeon, "but she's hardy, like thee and the lad."

Jack knelt beside her and took her hand. Her skin was flushed from fever and the heat of the fire, so that she looked to be filling with life rather than losing it.

"See what thou's done to thyself," he whispered.

She gripped his hand, and her breasts shook with the coughing that raised a foam of red spittle to her lips.

What a bitter place he had brought them to, thought Jack. What hell he had put them through. What foolish dreams he had dreamed.

William Mullins, who lay in the next bed, was suddenly seized by a spasm that sat him up and doubled him over and left him weak and wheezing when it was finished. Jack knew that before long, he would be dumping sand onto the waxen face of Master Mullins, and he resolved that his wife would see no more death.

"Simeon, I'm takin' her to her own house," he said.

"Jack, thine own house . . . thou hast not finished the roof. Think of the night wind blowin' through the thatch."

"We'll keep a fire, day and night."

"I'll stay here," said Kate. "Be about the business of buildin' houses, or there'll none of us survive."

But Jack would hear no argument. With the help of the Bigelows, he carried her across the path they had hacked in the sand, and named Leyden Street, to one of the half-dozen dirt-floored houses that formed the settlement.

He knew she would live. She was as solid as others who had survived. And what's more, he was praying for her, on his knees, with his head bowed and his hands folded. God would not desert them.

It did not bother Jack that people who had prayed harder than he every day of their lives were dropping like geese in flight above a starving village. That simply affirmed his belief that God favored most those who bothered him least.

Day and night, Jack mopped Kate's brow, held her, prayed for her. Christopher piled wood to keep the fire high. Simeon Bigelow brought goose broth from the common house. And on the third day, Jack went out to hunt.

Though this would later be called the Starving Time, there was game in the woods and marshlands, but seldom enough healthy men to hunt. There were fish in the waters, but they had not brought hooks of the proper size to catch them. Wild blueberry and blackberry formed the underbrush, but birds and winter winds stripped them bare before the settlers. And the red fruit that the Indians called crane berry, which grew wild in the sandy lowlands and might have saved those who died of scurvy, went unpicked for its bitterness.

That night Jack brought back three ducks. Two he gave to the common house and one he roasted for his family. As he turned the duck on the spit and the fat sizzled in the fire, he spoke of spring.

"Never mind spring. Just care for the boy," said Kate.

Jack went to her pallet. "We'll both care for the boy. God'll see to that."

She gripped his hand and pulled herself up to a sitting position. Her face and neck reddened with the effort, and her eyes opened wide, as though she were seeing beyond them, into a future she would never know. "God have his own plans—"

"I'm prayin', darlin'."

"Do right by the boy."

Jack tried to make a joke. "It's him what has to do right by us. Don't thee, lad?"

On a stool in the corner, Christopher eyed the duck. He was scrawny like his father, tall like his mother, and a greasy shock of black hair scraggled down his neck. "'Tis what you say, Pa."

"There," said Jack. "He knows."

"He *trusts*, but I *know*. I know what thou's plannin' . . . to go off alone and look for drift whales. But thou signed . . ." The cough was starting again. She clutched at Jack's forearm. "'Tain't time. . . . Thou needs help."

"I've thee to help."

She struggled to keep the cough down. "There's good men here, good teachers for the boy. Help 'em start their future, and they'll help you build—" The cough exploded like a shot from a minion.

Jack drew her to him and told her she would be fine. And he told her again, and again and again, while the little room filled with smoke and the smell of sizzling fat.

Finally Christopher said, "The duck, Pa. 'Tis burnin'."

But Jack held his wife until the coughing stopped. He could feel her bones now, poking through in places he had never felt them before. He shut his eyes tight, but tears began to trickle down his cheeks, into his beard.

And Kate whispered, "The duck, Jack. 'Tis burnin'."

iii.

" 'Yea, though I walk through the Valley of the Shadow of Death, I fear no evil. Thy rod and thy staff, they comfort me. . . .' "

They had buried so many here that they no longer missed lanterns, especially on nights when the full moon spilled its freezing light onto the snow. Three bodies went into the graves that Jack Hilyard insisted he dig, although Myles Standish and William Brewster had offered to do it for him. Degory Priest and Alice Mullins were placed in their holes. Then the body of Kate Hilyard, wrapped in her best cloak, was lowered into the ground.

Ezra Bigelow recited the psalm. Though the Saints did not believe in elaborate remonstrations over the dead, Ezra knew the comfort the Twenty-third Psalm could bring, and in these terrible days, all needed comfort. He had tried to quote the psalm to Dorothy

Bradford on that awful night, but she would not listen. He had offered it to her husband, and it had soothed him. Even a Stranger like Jack Hilyard could feel its power and promise.

Ezra knew the psalm by rote, as he knew most of the Bible. But he held the book when he prayed, because the book told their reason for being, and their reason for being *there*, and it would be their salvation. With the book to guide them, they could climb from the valley of the shadow of death to this hilltop of death itself and know that God would not desert them. He had a purpose for both the living and the dead.

A young woman named Priscilla Mullins, who had already buried her brother and would soon bury her father, stared at the body of her mother. Simeon Bigelow stood with his arm around Christopher. Master Jones folded his hands and bowed his head. And Jack Hilyard, stock-still and wordless, leaned on his shovel at the foot of his wife's grave.

" 'Surely goodness and mercy shall follow me all the days of my life, and I shall dwell in the house of the Lord forever.' "

Ezra glanced across the open grave mouth and told Jack to turn the first shovel. But Jack neither looked up nor moved.

Ezra whispered, "Jack, the first shovel."

Jack still stood motionless.

"The Indians may spy, and the dead must be buried," Ezra said more urgently.

Jack simply looked at Ezra, and his breathing grew harder, so that steam came in long freezing plumes from his nose.

Ezra then asked Master Jones if he would do the burying. Without a word, Jones took the shovel that young Christopher held and dug it into the sand.

None by that frigid grave mouth would ever forget the sound Jack Hilyard then made.

"It was as if," wrote Jones in his log, "the shovel struck Jack's belly rather than the earth."

Christopher, hearing the sound again decades later, would remember the hopelessness he felt on that dark and grieving hill. Priscilla Mullins cried out in sympathy with Jack. Simeon Bigelow heard the cry of Job, so utterly human that it made him wonder that he had not cried out himself at his own wife's death. And Ezra Bigelow heard the sound of Satan bursting forth, not simply a cry of grief but an utter denial of the psalm's power and God's plan.

Jack jumped at Jones and grabbed the shovel. "I be the grave-digger! I know death better than any of you." And he sent the sand splattering onto his wife's legs.

"Jack," said Simeon, "let me do it for thee." He reached for the shovel, and Jack pulled it back with such force that Simeon nearly fell into the hole.

"I be the gravedigger. Me and me boy." Jack thrust the shovel upon his son, then picked up his own. "Come on, lad, help me bury thy mother and them other poor dumb souls what come here thinkin' God was watchin' over 'em."

At that, Priscilla Mullins began to sob.

"Shovel, boy." Jack Hilyard whacked his shovel against his son's.

Christopher looked down at the shovel, then into the hole. "I can't, Pa. I can't bury her."

"Shovel the sand, damn thee!"

"Jack!" cried Simeon.

"Have respect for the dead," said Ezra Bigelow.

"I respect 'em. I respect 'em more 'n thee. I *do* somethin' for 'em. I *bury* 'em." Then sand and ice crystals flew in the moonlight. Faster and faster Jack's arms went, as if he had been seized by mad-ness. Had this colony the time to worry over witchcraft, he might have been burned on the spot as the warlock priest of some black coven, doing his evil ceremony in the moonlight.

Jones tried to grab him, but Jack pushed away and held up the shovel like a club.

"I be the gravedigger," he cried. "I bury the dead, so's them what prayed the dead would live don't waste their energy as well as their breath."

"'Twas God's will," said Ezra. "All is God's will."

"Why do you talk like this over my mother and your own good wife?" Priscilla Mullins wiped her tears from her eyes. "I've lost two dear ones, but my prayers were not wasted."

"Mayhap not. But mine were," answered Jack.

"Damn you, Jack." Simeon Bigelow ripped the shovel from Jack's hands. "Take your boy home and grieve this venom out of you."

But before Simeon's words could calm him, Ezra Bigelow put himself between Jack and the grave mouth. "Aye. Go home. Stay longer, you coast too close to blasphemy."

"Blasphemy?" cried Jack. The word was a quick match striking powder in his brainpan. "Blasphemy? God treats me prayers like dung and I fear blasphemy?"

Ezra Bigelow looked at his brother and the others. "If you care for this man's soul, quiet him." Then he took Priscilla by the elbow and started down the hill.

"Go!" screamed Jack. "Go back and watch more of 'em die, and pray in their ears while they do. Then pray over their meat when they're dead."

"Pray for yourself."

"God damn you Ezra Bigelow, and God damn your prayers."

"Quiet yourself," urged Simeon. "Think of the boy."

"I do think of him, all the time." Jack strode to the top of the hill and shook his fist at the moonlight. "I do think of him, 'cause God won't, God damn him."

"Blasphemy." The word rushed out of Ezra Bigelow as though Satan were crushing his chest. "Blasphemy!"

"I blaspheme the blackness!" shouted Hilyard.

"Quiet afore the whole colony suffers!" Ezra cried.

"How much more can the colony suffer?" Hilyard looked again at the sky. "God damn thee, thou cold, heartless, hidden bastard of a God."

"No more of this!" cried Ezra Bigelow in a voice as terrifying as Hilyard's own.

"God damn thee for lettin' us think thou hear our prayin' whilst the best of us"—Jack's voice cracked—"the best of us"—he dropped to his knees—"whilst the best of us goes into the ground."

Jack's blasphemy was finished, and the terrible pain of faithlessness now poured forth in great gulping sobs. The others were running up the hill to comfort him, but Ezra went no farther than the grave mouth. He knew that God would not hold the grieving words of a Stranger against the colony, though Ezra would hold them against the Stranger himself.

iv.

By the time the sun was up full, its light dancing like quicksilver on the sea, Jack Hilyard and his son were four miles south of the settlement, on an Indian trail that curved along a high bluff. They carried what they could of blankets, clothes, a hammer and saw, some dried beans, and a greasy duck. The boy wore Jack's cutlass, and Jack kept a match smoldering in the metal box on his belt.

He had decided he could pay no heed to love or sentiment. He had good friends in the colony, for certain. They had comforted him in the night, given him what beer they had, and stayed with him until he slept. But they could not protect him or the boy from the sickness. And while Kate's last request had been for them to stay with the colony, Jack believed the sickness had clouded her mind. In health, she would have told him to heed the voice inside him, especially when God left him to his own devices. After last night, Jack expected little help from God, and even less from those who held regular conversations with him.

He wondered if God had bothered to tell Ezra Bigelow where sickness came from or where it went. God had offered no answers to Jack on the matter. He could think only to get himself and his son away. Better to chance savages and starvation than scurvy and the coughing death.

He looked over his shoulder. Christopher was striding steadily along the path, his hand on the sword hilt, his head tilted slightly to keep the boil on his neck from rubbing against his collar. The boy was acting the brave soldier and Jack's chest filled pride.

Christopher had not spoken since they slipped away. That was not unusual. He was a quiet lad, and any twelve-year-old with any sense listened more than he spoke. Indeed, anyone of any age who had seen what Christopher had might have been struck dumb as a stone. But there was strength in youth, and even in the worst of times, Christopher watched and listened and sought to understand what passed before him.

He now had no mother, no confidence in God, and no community beyond his father and the stunted pines along the path. His sense of the uncertainty of things was great. But he found meaning where he could, and like all boys, he seized on physical things, on the pain of the boil, on the weight of his pack, but most of all on the cutlass hilt in his hand. His father had shown confidence enough to give him a man's weapon, and pride overcame his fear.

Just before nightfall, they reached the north bank of a tidal river that snaked from the bay into the pine-covered hills. They were at the shoulder of the Cape, in the sachemdom of the Scussets. And here the boy saw his first Indians.

They came on the flood tide, driving their canoe upstream

through the last red glow of dusk. The canoe was laden with pelts, but the Indians did not labor at the paddles. They steered with short, powerful strokes and let the current sweep them toward the campfires glimmering in the valley.

This world belonged to them, thought the boy. They rode like spirits on the water. One wore a loose deerskin shirt, the other nothing more than a coating of grease, as though neither felt the cold that made Christopher's knuckles ache. And the colors of the canoe and the deerskin and their copper adornments, indeed the color of their very flesh, seemed to be drawn from the reds and deepening browns of the dusk around them.

This world belonged to them, he thought again. And they belonged to it.

At the bend of the river the Indians were met by others, who helped them lift the canoe out of the water and carry it up the valley.

"What are they doin', Pa?"

"Makin' a portage, it looks like."

"Where are they goin'?"

"With all them pelts, they must be traders. May be an easy way to get that canoe into the water on the other side."

Not far beyond the hills were the headwaters of another tidal river that flowed southwest. But Jack's thoughts were on another place.

He pointed beyond the mouth of the river, to the beach that ran east into the gathering night. "Once it's dark, we'll take to the strand. And keep to it we will, so's not to miss the place or stumble into any villages. In a day and a half, we'll be there."

"Will the Indians let us stay where the whales beach?"

Jack gave out with a short laugh. "I seen what a piss-poor job they done flensin' a blackfish. When I show 'em how to do it proper, they'll make me lord bloody mayor."

V.

February 15, 1621. Seas calm, air cold, damp mist freezes on rigging and decks. This may prove the worst month yet. Three more have died, another half dozen have taken to beds. Even William Bradford is laid low, feverish and unmindful of anything but his own misery.

And Simeon Bigelow now brings distressing news. The day after his wife's burial, Jack Hilyard and his lad went hunting, promising return when they had a full sack of ducks. After four days, Simeon grew worried and went to Jack's house, where he found missing Jack's hand tools and other truck which would not have been taken hunting. Simeon reckons that Jack and his son are run off and asks me to fetch them back.

Had Hilyard jumped ship, I would have punished him myself. But Simeon is made of kinder stuff. He says only a man who has lost a wife can know the pain of a man who loses one, and this colony cannot lose strong males like the Hilyards.

These words do not move me, but Simeon believes Jack has gone to a place where whales strand. If I am to whale here next year, I must needs know where the beasts are to be found, 'specially stranders, which are good as gold sovereigns on the beach. So I send word ashore that I go on another seal hunt. In truth, 'twill be a manhunt.

vi.

It had been several days since Autumnsquam went into the woods, to a place of tall trees near a creek. He had chosen a pine with a wide girth and chopped it off as close to the ground as he could. He had stripped it of bark, which he could use as covering for his *wetu*, pushed the log into the creek, and floated it to the beach where he had fought the white men. There he had spread dry pine boughs and wood chips across the top of it and started his fire. Ever since, the fire had been smoldering into the log, slowly hollowing out the center, while he shaped the outside with a stone ax.

He was sharpening one of the ends, so that it would go smoothly through the water, when Aspinet came out of the woods. Two others were with him, and Autumnsquam's first thought was for his woman. Her time had nearly come. If they brought news of her, their faces said that it was not good.

Instead, they told him that the Namskakets had seen a white man and boy building a *wetu* on Nauseiput, the place between two streams. A few days earlier, runners from the sachem Iyannough had brought word of a white man and boy walking east along the Great Salt Marsh. Iyannough knew they were not the whites who stole people from his village, and so he let them pass. The next day, the Nobscussets had seen them near Sesuit, and the Setuckets as well.

"Iyannough could have killed them," Autumnsquam grunted. "Or the others. But they wait for the Nausets."

"Iyannough saw no reason. He is young like you, but he may be wise."

"If Iyannough had been our sachem, white men would live here now, on our land. But we"—Autumnsquam thumped his hand on his chest—"taught them fear."

"Fear drove them no farther than the Patuxet land. And now they are back."

"So we kill them. We kill any who try to settle."

The old sachem shook his head. The sinews in his neck stood out like pieces of twine. The copper pendants glittered in his ears. "They may come to trade knives or metal or because other whites do not like them."

Autumnsquam poked at the smoldering coals in his canoe. "There are more of us, so we should kill them, or soon there will be more of them, and they will kill us."

"They have powerful weapons," said one of the others.

"Clumsy weapons," said Autumnsquam. "A Nauset can shoot five arrows for every shot from the white man's gun."

"But in the Patuxet land they have put up guns as long as canoes, guns like those *les françaises* shot from their boat. They say that with these guns, the white man can sit in the Patuxet land and shoot all the way across the bay."

Autumnsquam did not like the sound of this, so he chopped at the canoe. "You hear the counsel of cowards."

"The whites have powerful guns and powerful gods."

"A god more powerful than Kautantowit?"

"Powerful enough to kill the Patuxets and give their land to the whites."

Autumnsquam spat on the sand. Since the fight, his fame had spread and his arrogance had grown. "Do not insult Kautantowit."

"Kautantowit will not be insulted if we show patience."

Then one of the others pointed to the bay. A sail had appeared. The white men's canoe was coming.

Autumnsquam looked at Aspinet. "If you do not kill them when there are few, many will follow . . . and quickly."

vii.

February 16, 1621. Calm, clear, wind NW and steady. At dawn we left the harbor and did ride a booming wind south southeast 'cross the bay. Less than five hours passed, and we were approaching the coast.

Knowing of the flats here, I arrived as the tide took flood, following blue channels through the green shoal water to within a few rods of the beach, where we struck sand. My sailors wished to wade ashore, but I forbade it, knowing that many who did the likewise in November caught their death. And we were safer in the shallops, as the savages were watching. We could see some on a beach to the east, which Simeon recognized as the site of the First Encounter. Those we did not worry about, being far away. But others, we knew, watched from woods all around.

So we kept our eyes sharp and rode in on the tide. The sand was scattered with bones, tail flukes, blackfish heads from a recent stranding, and cakes of ice what wash in as these flats freeze over.

Leaving half the company at the shallop, we followed boot prints over the dune grass and into the woods, and soon our noses followed the smell of roast duck. In a small opening amongst the trees, we found an Indian house of bent saplings covered with bark. A duck was spitted on the fire in front of it. We raised our guns to the ready and called Jack's name.

A voice greeted us from behind and gave start enough that the speaker was near shot. 'Twas Jack. His gun was primed, and his boy held a cutlass.

Simeon said we had come to take him back. But Jack bade us come into the dwelling he had fashioned and join in victuals. He would show us the richness of this place, offering us clams, the duck, which we ate of, and the bitter red berry that grows in the lowlands.

Twas a most fine spot. Jack said he chose it because he had found here a square of stones, several paces on each side, over which he would build a true house. The stones were all of the same size, like ballast stones, and went down deep, which I found most puzzling, as it looked like the work of a civilized man.

But Simeon's only interest was in bringing Jack back. He said that otherwise, his brother Ezra would fetch the agreement with Jack's name upon it. "He will force thee by law and keep this island from thee forever."

Jack said the island belonged to the Indians, and the Saints could have no authority over it. Simeon answered that the Indians might not let him live past that night, but if he would leave, Simeon would speak for him when settlement were allowed here.

Then I spake. "Though God took thy wife, he left the lad in thy care. Do not betray God's trust." I had not known I would say these words. I have never used God's name, save in vain, when bending men to my will. But this winter has shown me God in men like Simeon, and such words as these do come more easier.

And coming from me, they touch a man like Jack. He now saw the true danger he had brung to his boy by venturing into Indian country and said that for the good of the lad, he would come back.

Simeon cried thanks to God and took Jack in manly embrace. But there was another thing that bothered him —the axe Jack now carried.

It was iron, covered in much rust, except where Jack had sanded and sharpened it. The blade was flared wide, more than the span of a man's hand, and on the shaft was engraved a strange kind of writing, here shown:

Simeon said it should be put back in the Indian grave from which it came, but Jack said he found it in the mud when digging for clams. Simeon disbelieved this, for what metal can survive seawater? But there was no time for disputation, as the tide was turning. I am a practical man and know the value of such things, so I told Jack to keep the axe, though it, too, puzzles me.

When we were away, I saw smoke curling up above the trees. I asked what burned. Jack said he had fired his hut so Kate would not be confused.

"Kate is with God," said Simeon gently.

Jack's eyes turned from Simeon to me to the smoke rising above the trees. "Aye. She'll not be needin' our little house."

Then he did put his arm 'round his son, who seemed much perplexed in his father's changes, and watched the beach 'twixt the creeks. Then he watched the smoke mixing with the clouds.

I know not what the Indians call that place. But on my chart, 'twill be called Jack's Island.

CHAPTER 7

July 6

Jack's Island

Geoff could make the run from Pamet Harbor to Jack's Island in forty minutes. Why put up with Route 6 traffic when you could lean on the throttle, get your Grady White up on the water, and shoot south with the wind burning your face and the hull like a giant jet ski under your feet? Why watch the unspooling of Route 6 strip malls, motels, and gas stations when you could follow the route of the Pilgrim shallop from Truro, along Billingsgate Shoals, past First Encounter Beach, and into the Restricted Zone?

Restricted because of the *James Longstreet,* a Liberty ship grounded on the Eastham flats in 1944 and known ever since as the Target Ship. For thirty years, military fliers had bombed, rocketed, and sandbagged the old hulk, but she never sank, because in twelve feet of water, she had no place to sink *to.*

Geoff liked the *Longstreet.* Any shipwreck could inspire images of romance and high tragedy. But the *Longstreet* also showed just how hard it could be to get rid of your trash. After all those bombs and all those winters, the damn thing still sat there, in two rusted pieces, dominating the bay from Brewster to Wellfleet.

And like a lot of trash, she was still dangerous. Small-charge target ordnance and misfired rockets lay unexploded on the bottom.

And there was always the possibility that something, from the vibration of an outboard to a direct hit by an eight-ounce sinker, might set off an old bomb and send some family and their Chris-Craft to meet the Pilgrim Fathers.

People generally ignored the warnings. Fishermen claimed the hulk attracted baitfish, which in turn attracted big fish, which of course attracted fishermen. Day sailers were always cruising close, just to gawk. And Geoff had once watched a board sailer go *through* the break in the middle of the ship, which was maybe the stupidest thing he'd ever seen.

After speeding through the Restricted Zone, Geoff watched for the dead trees that marked the channel into Rock Harbor. To the right of that was Skaket Creek, then the mouth of Nauseiput Creek, eastern boundary of Jack's Island. A small flotilla of Sunfish was pouring out of Nauseiput, white sails and yellow sails and a few bright red ones, booming and jibing across one another's paths like butterflies. A bit farther west were the main house and the sailing camp barracks. Geoff aimed west of those, east of Jack's Creek, toward the trees in the center of the island.

The boat stopped with a whoosh of sand about twenty feet from the beach, accepted practice on the tideflats. Two hours before, the flats had been a mile-wide strip of seaside desert. Two hours later, they would be covered in ten feet of water. A small wonder of nature, which could also be a big pain in the ass if you got stranded a mile from shore.

Geoff left his anchor in the mud, then followed a path over the dune and into the pines that thickened to form a typical Cape Cod woodland—carpeted with brambles, draped with wild grapevines, more intimate than majestic.

Up ahead, Rake's barn appeared. Three lobster buoys hung in the back window like props from a tourist's photograph. Beyond the barn stood the house, a classic story-and-a-half Cape: shingles weathered silver in the salt air, blue trim peeling from windows and gutters, central chimney, symmetrical windows, foursquare, solid—

"Coffee, son?"

The words came from behind and startled him. Rake was standing in the barn, filling two mugs from his new coffeemaker. "Emily and Arnie give it to me. Figured should use it."

That was how Rake greeted people—in mid-conversation—even if he hadn't seen them for months. He said a man his age didn't have time for howdy-do's . . . or too many pronouns.

Geoff stepped into the barn that felt more like a time capsule. A Haig & Haig pinch bottle, the spoils of rumrunning, rested on a brace between two studs. A clam rake hung from a rafter. One of Tom Hilyard's old easels was leaning in the corner, next to a sign: Right Fork for Hilyard House Hotel. A 1960 Kennedy bumper sticker was pasted above a window.

The trapdoor was open and a work light was shining in the cellar below. "Come to help clean out the root cellar, or did Dickerson Bigelow send you?"

"You know what he wants?"

"Same thing he's always wanted."

"What if I told you I thought it was a good idea?"

"Give this island over to a bunch of condoms?"

"It's condos. But Bigelow wants to build houses. Emily and Arnie think it's a good idea." Geoff knew that sounded lame.

"Don't listen to *them*," said Rake. "They got my sister Clara sittin' in a room, starin' out the window like she was in some . . . nursin' home. Owns the whole sailing camp and—"

"Times are changin', Rake."

"Times are always changin'. Date changes every midnight. Week changes every seven days. Seasons, too. Got to make the change for the good."

"I agree."

"So why do Dicker's biddin'?"

Like a kid trying to escape a grilling, Geoff looked for a distraction. He peered into the hole. There was a dustpan and brush down there. It seemed that Rake had been cleaning off the old stones that formed the foundation.

"Heard of something'll make whatever Dickerson's offerin' look like an old shell heap," said Rake.

"An art auction to sell Tom Hilyards?"

"Talkin' *millions*. Not a few grand put up by some museum gal."

"The oral historian?"

"Plannin' to talk to her?"

"She's just some snoop with a tape recorder."

"That's what *I* thought, till she started askin' things that told me more than I could tell her. Things to keep this island from Dicker Bigelow forever."

"What things?"

The old man glanced beyond the house, toward the road. "What's goin' on out there?"

"What was she telling you about?"

"That." Rake kicked an old doorstop and went out.

The doorstop was a piece of fireplace wood, stripped of bark, heavily varnished, and screwed to a little mahogany pedestal. The plaque said, *"Mayflower* log, July 31, 1958."

What the hell was this? Why couldn't he say anything straight? What did this have to do with anything?

"Rake!" he shouted, but the old man was striding down his driveway, and something had caused him to drop into what he called his fuck-'em-let's-fight-about-it stride.

On Jack's Island, the only road crossed the causeway, made a loop, and left. Normally, Bigelows used the west side of the road, Hilyards the east. When a car passed Rake's house from the west, it got his attention. When it stopped across from his house, it got his inspection. When it was a van like this one, from which two men unloaded plumb lines, plot plans, and transits, it got him mad.

"Hey! What the hell are you doin'?" Rake stomped across the road.

"None of your damn business," said Humpback Bigelow, whose name had nothing to do with his posture. His father was called Blue because at six feet six, two hundred sixty pounds, he was the biggest thing that grew native on the Cape. Humpback was an inch shorter, fifteen pounds lighter, and so was nicknamed after a smaller whale. He didn't mind. He much preferred the name Humpback—or better yet, the Humpster—to Clarence.

"What the hell are you doin'?" repeated Rake.

"None of your damn business." In twenty-seven years, the Humpster had learned almost no manners and didn't know that a civil engineer wore something more civil than khaki trousers and a T-shirt with a pack of smokes rolled in the sleeve.

"Take it easy, Rake," said Arnie Burr. "We're here to shoot the boundaries of Geoff's property."

Geoff loped down the driveway after Rake. "Wearing the surveying hat today, Arnie?"

Arnie's family had been on the Cape since the Revolution,

breeding a long line of receding chins, prominent noses, and skinny chests. To these Arnie added the personality of a sculpin and a hairline that looked like the prime meridian going over the pole.

Arnie knew how to do a little of everything, a Cape Cod trait. He was a licensed civil engineer. He could pound nails, dig post holes, and in the warm months, he ran a sportfishing charter, though repeat business wasn't his strong point. The business of running the sailing camp he left to his wife, Emily, because Arnie didn't like kids.

Geoff had learned that firsthand after his parents died in a 1966 auto accident. Rake and his sister Clara wanted Geoff to attend school in Brewster, but Clara's daughter Emily was named guardian, and she said the kid was smart enough to go to private school. Arnie added that his parents' double indemnity made the kid rich enough, too.

So Geoff spent his adolescence at Phillips Exeter and always thought he had been cheated out of life at Jack's Island. He never wondered if Arnie might have been right. He just knew Arnie didn't want another kid around. Of course, Arnie sent his own daughters off to school when the time came. Now they lived in California, as far from him as they could get.

"What are we surveyin' today, Arnie?" asked Geoff.

"Nothin'!" The back of Rake's neck burned mad red. "They're gettin' out of here."

The Humpster laughed the way someone does when he feeds a chicken bone to a dog. Then he spread the legs of the transit and stood it in the middle of the road. "Nobody keeps me from my work. Not even some screwy old man."

"Screwy, am I?" Rake took a poke at the Humpster, who wound up his right hand as if he might send the old man into the bay.

Geoff knew the Humpster was nasty enough that he wouldn't pull any punches, so he jumped between them. "Let's talk about this, boys."

But Rake sent a roundhouse over Geoff's shoulder, straight at the Humpster's nose. His aim wasn't what it used to be, and he hit Geoff in the side of the head. Then the Humpster grabbed for Rake, and Geoff grabbed for the Humpster, and they were all scuffling and yelling at once.

Let go . . . Back off . . . Quit it . . . He called me screwy . . . You ARE . . . Quit it . . . Back off . . . Fuck off . . . QUIT IT . . .

YOU fuck off . . . Back OFF . . . Get off my land . . . We ain't on it, you screwy old bastard . . . He said it again. Let me at him . . . C'mon, you old . . . BACK OFF . . . *Oomph* . . .

Geoff sent the Humpster into the side of the van, and his big ass put a dent in the door. He bounced back with a wild right, which Geoff ducked. This exhausted most of Geoff's street-fighting skills and reminded him that no matter how often he pumped the Nautilus, he was in over his head with the Humpster, who did this kind of thing for recreation.

So Geoff grabbed the transit and pointed it like a pike. "Back off, you big tub."

This brought Arnie Burr into the fray because Arnie was, above all else, cheap. "That transit cost money! You want to break it? Put it down."

"Call off your whale," said Geoff.

"Back off, Hump."

Geoff put himself in front of Rake, who was twitching around, trying to get another shot in at the Humpster.

"I don't know what we're fightin' about," said Arnie. "We got permission to be here."

"From who?" demanded Rake.

The Humpster aimed his finger at Geoff. "Him."

Rake looked Geoff in the eye. "You?"

And Arnie turned on Geoff, too. "Your *wife* gave permission. We're checking your land against the 1904 lines."

Geoff saw betrayal in Rake's gaze and a fury so pure that it drained all the color from the old man's face.

"Your *wife*," Rake said. "Bigelows do stick together."

Arnie chuckled at this. He had married into the Hilyards, but he had sided with the Bigelows, too.

Geoff couldn't stand Arnie. He knew Rake couldn't either, so he let Arnie have it. This always made him feel good and might get him back into Rake's good graces. "I didn't give permission for any survey, Arnie, so pack up and get out of here."

"The land's community property, ain't it?" Arnie set the transit back in the van. "What's yours is your wife's. And if you can't control what she's sayin', it's no reason for us to lose a fee. Somebody pays for our time."

The Humpster pointed at the dent in the door. "And you'll pay for that, smartass."

"That's *your* ass," answered Geoff.

The Humpster gave him the finger.

Geoff turned to Rake, "Bright guy, the Humpster."

"At least you know what side he's on," said Rake, and that was all he said.

ii.

MLS. Multiple Listing Service. The bible of the real estate trade.

MLS. More Lousy Summer houses. The book for Barnstable County contained photos and statistics on over two thousand houses, from multimillion-dollar waterfront beauties to the little shacks back in the hills.

MLS. More Little Surprises. "Old Cape Cod charm and village convenience" could be a falling-down place on Route 6A that smelled of fish caught in 1892. "Some saltwater views, walk to beach" meant that if you climbed onto the roof, sometime in January, when there were no leaves on the trees, you might see some blue in the distance, and you might be able to walk there in an hour, if you had no beach umbrella, cooler, chair, bag, books, or two-year-old grabbing at your heels.

MLS. More Lost Saturdays. Much Luckier Somewhere else. My Life is Slow. Cape Cod real estate was slow. That was why Janice would have been luckier to be somewhere else, doing something else, instead of wasting her Saturdays waiting for the phone to ring so she could take some vacationer to see "Old Cape Cod Charm, convenience, saltwater views, and a walk to the beach."

Janice had missed the mid-eighties boom, when a two-holed outhouse on an eroding bluff appreciated at thirty percent a year. Now the only property sure to sell was the expensive stuff on the waterfront. That was why the Jack's Island development made sense.

Outside, a car door slammed and Geoff got out of a station wagon. He'd come by boat from Jack's Island to Sesuit Harbor, then by thumb to the restored Victorian house on Route 6A, home of Bigelow Development.

She put up her hands. "I've heard all about it, Geoff."

"You had no right to send them down there."

"Douglas asked me. I didn't think they'd go this morning. But *you* shouldn't have picked a fight with them."

"You're *pushing* me, Jan." Geoff slammed his hand against the side of a file cabinet. It echoed off the refinished floors and white walls and framed prints of Bigelow projects.

"Ahoy, there." Dickerson came downstairs from his office. "We're in a place of business." He poked his nose into Douglas's office. "But no one else here, so slam away. Bottle it up, you might get a heart attack, like me."

"I thought Rake would drop dead when he saw the surveying equipment," said Geoff.

Dickerson's eyes widened in their little bags of flesh. "Surveys. Good idea. Get those topos and old plot plans into the hands of the architect. Stimulate his brain."

"We haven't gotten that far, Dad," she said gently.

She had been here less than a day, and already it was clear: Dickerson had lost it. He used to spend the morning on the telephone or in the field, chatting, cajoling, raising holy hell. Now he was up there at his desk, behind his row of pill bottles, reading *Field and Stream*.

"Dad," she explained, "Douglas says that if we win at the town meeting, we have to be ready for the Conservation Commission a week from Tuesday. We have to talk to them before we do anything else. We have to shoot boundaries around Rake's property, in case he won't give in, flag trees, get the botanist in to mark off wetlands. These things can't wait."

"Yeah, yeah. Can't forget the Conservation Commission."

Now she looked at Geoff. "That's why I told them they could work on our property."

"*Our* property?" said Geoff. "You mean *my* property? Or do you think it belongs to Bigelow Development already?"

She looked down at her notepad and drew a rough map of Jack's Island. She wrote "Bigelow" on one half. Then she drew the road through it . . .

Geoff put his hands on the desk and looked into her eyes. His sunglasses had left large white circles on his face, which made him look slightly depraved. "I was just starting to feel my way with Rake when those two ruined everything. Now he won't even talk to me."

. . . And then she divided the Hilyard half into segments. One belonged to Geoff. A larger one to Rake. The sailing camp on Nauseiput Creek belonged to Rake's sister, Clara.

"Feeling your way with Rake," said Dickerson, getting himself back into it. "Does this mean you've committed to us?"

"I don't know." He aimed a finger at Janice. "Just don't push."

She looked at the finger. She thought about biting it. "The property's yours *and* mine, by marriage."

"That's why Rake's so mad."

Janice looked at her father. "If you had come to Cape Cod to be 'the architect who cares,' wouldn't you want a commission like this, to show what you could do?"

Geoff slipped on his sunglasses. "That would depend on how much I cared . . . about Cape Cod, that is."

"We been here as long as you, Geoff," said Dickerson. "We care as much. Don't forget that."

Geoff looked at his wife. "See you tonight."

Tonight. The gathering would continue. She couldn't count on George. Maybe Jimmy Little would help her. He was the most cynical of all of them. And he was an Indian. Tonight. In the dunes.

iii.

The dunes that formed the hand of Cape Cod and the long curling fingers of Provincetown had themselves been formed from Cape Cod's forearm. Some people saw something biblical in this. Like Eve being fashioned from Adam's rib. Others, who took their metaphors from science, thought of skin grafts or tissue transplants.

But to understand the forces that had shaped Cape Cod, you needed a biblical sense of God's power . . . or a modern faith in the science of geology. A good imagination helped, too.

First you had to imagine ice, a shimmering glacial sheet nearly a mile thick, grinding south across the continent. Then you imagined mild breezes blowing up from the south. Then you got in the car and drove Route 6 from Sandwich to Orleans, along the line of hills formed twelve thousand years ago, when the glacier met the mild air, dropped a load of rock, and dissolved into rivers that carried debris south, creating the flatlands from Falmouth to Chatham. The terminal moraine and the outwash plain.

When you turned north at the Orleans Rotary, you could now imagine the glacier on the Atlantic side, flowing west to create the tablelands of the Lower Cape.

By the time you reached the place where Truro sloped toward Provincetown, the glacier was gone, but like the phoenix, was reborn in the seas that rose as it melted. Ten thousand years ago, Cape Cod ended at Truro. The glacier had left the arm without a hand, so the sea chewed into the tablelands and swept sand northwest. Soon a barrier beach curved into the bay. Marshlands formed within its protective arc. The forearm grew thinner. The hand took shape.

And the wind always blew.

It started in Labrador and came on as relentless as the ice had been before it. Grain by grain, it raised the sand into waves and wave by wave the sand rose into great cresting combers that would have flooded the land, but for the long-bladed grasses that held it until vines could bind it and trees could take root.

After the glaciers, the wind, and the leaves of grass had done their work, the settlers came. They cut the trees for firewood, they foraged cattle on the ground cover, and in not much more than a generation, the sand was set free to roll once more.

Now there were thirty cottages among the mountains of sand in the Provincelands. They were small and old. None had electricity or protection from the winter. Their only luxury was solitude. But on a summer night, they looked like small garnets of light in a great black matrix of sand.

George Flynn stayed in a cottage at the base of a dune that each year crept closer to his back door. He had a single large room with a table, desk, sofa bed, kerosene lamps, wood stove, and water pump. It wasn't the Hollywood Hills, and if he hadn't been able to walk to Provincetown, he wouldn't have been there at all. But he said that if he summered in the dunes that inspired Eugene O'Neill, he might eventually figure out how to write like him.

The talk at George's table began with old friends playing catch-up, gossip, and tell-the-latest-joke. After dinner and wine, it began to follow wild arcs that swooped from the crests of the dunes, where the summer wind still moved the sand, to the floor of the cottage, where a woman's bare foot slid toward a man's.

"The Indians called Jack's Island Nauseiput, which meant the place between two streams . . . unh . . ."

"No footsie!" cried George. "Jimmy never says 'unh' unless someone's playing footsie with him."

Jimmy's wife, Samantha, elbowed George in the ribs. "C'mon, we're among friends here."

"Play footsie all you want," said Janice, "but only with your husband."

Samantha got an evil little glint in her eye and made a show of massaging her foot against Geoff's.

Geoff laughed and sipped his wine.

"Don't you envy Jimmy?" Samantha asked.

"I never envy my friends."

"Oh, Geoffrey, you're no fun anymore."

What Geoff envied was the intimacy of one bare foot touching another beneath a table, a hidden promise of passion while everyone else talked about Indian legends. *Feel the sandy smoothness of my toes and just wait till later.*

The first time Geoff sat at the Bigelow dinner table, Janice slid the sole of her bare foot halfway to his thigh while her father talked about the impact of Nixon's trip to China on Cape real estate. Now, Geoff would have been thrilled beyond envy of—or even passing interest in—Samantha, if his wife would play a little footsie with him. But they were not on the best of terms, and neither of them was barefoot.

What the hell. He'd make the gesture, maybe break the ice. He moved his foot across the floor and touched hers. She was wearing sandals, and he had on Converse basketball shoes with soles like steel-belted radials. It just wasn't the same.

Her eyes flitted toward him, as though he had brushed her arm. Then she looked back at Jimmy.

"These Indians didn't know about glaciers and erosion and so forth, so they invented the legend of Maushop the Giant to explain things. Maushop pricked his finger once, and his blood fell on the Great Salt Marsh, and that's where the cranberry came from. And he knew a magic song to lure the whales into the bay and . . . unh . . ."

"Oh, Christ," cried George. "They're at it again."

Samantha giggled. She was slightly drunk and very giddy. "If we can't do this here, where *can* we do it?"

"Certainly not at Pride's Crossing," said Jimmy.

Samantha pulled a long face and sat up primly. "But of course

not, Mr. Little." She was fair and blond and very delicate, and there
had been hell to pay when she announced to her social-register family
that she was marrying a Mashpee Indian.

Jimmy had the copper skin, the high cheekbones, the almost
Oriental eyes, the straight black hair of the Wampanoag. He had
grown up never trusting the treaties, as he said, and his cynicism had
been an invaluable tool on his journey from the ponds of Mashpee
to a corner office in a New York law firm.

"Would Maushop object if we built a development on Nauseiput
Island?" asked Geoff.

Jimmy grabbed his beer can. "Don't ask me a serious question
when I'm playing footsie with my wife."

"So ask him a *stupid* question," said Janice. "Did you know
that the only wood remaining from the *Mayflower* is a piece of timber
that Rake Hilyard is using for a doorstop?"

"What?" cried George.

"Baloney," said Geoff.

"Really." Janice laughed. "The old man thinks it's going to save
the island. I'm afraid he's getting senile. Geoff hates to hear me say
it, and I hate to say it myself, but . . . *senile*."

Geoff waved his fingers, as if to tell her to shut up. But he had
brought the whole thing up in the first place.

"We can't leave important decisions in the hands of someone
who may not be competent," she said. "Can we, Jimmy?"

Jimmy squared himself to the table, a good lawyer listening to
a client. But Samantha sabotaged him with her foot. Jimmy's face
cracked; then he began to laugh.

"There she goes again," said George.

"We can't carry on a serious discussion when everyone's horny,"
said Janice.

"So, we either talk about sex, in which case you four go off to
the dunes and leave me to choke the chicken, or we discuss something
stupid, like a doorstop."

"Stupid is right," said Geoff. "A piece of varnished firewood is
all it is. The plaque calls it a *Mayflower* log."

"A log," said George, "or *the* log?"

"It's just an old joke. What does it matter?" Geoff held out his
glass.

"Does this mean I'm driving?" asked Janice.

"If you're not careful, you'll be walking."

"Before you two whisper any more sweet nothings," said George, "are we talking log as in piece of timber from a ship the fate of which no one knows? Or log as in captain's diary?"

"If no one knows where the ship ended up," said Geoff, "how in the hell would they know where the log went?"

"Bradford's diary disappeared before the Revolution. Seventy-five years later someone found it in England and bang!" He clapped his hands. "Big sensation."

"Where is it now?" asked Janice.

"In the state archives."

"What's it worth?" asked Geoff.

"Millions."

George gestured to the bookshelf where he kept his research material for a play on the Quakers and a signed studio photo of Bette Davis. "I have the Morison edition. Good footnotes, good job of modernizing the spelling without spoiling the antiquity of the syntax."

Geoff locked his fingers behind his head and rocked back in his chair. "Did you ever read the part where they find the kid screwing the turkey?"

"In a famous document of history," said Janice, "you remember *that*."

"Spare us the details," added Samantha.

"The details are amazing." George went to the bookcase.

"I've heard the details of what they did to the Indians a hundred times," she answered.

"That's so I can make you feel guilty whenever we have a fight." Jimmy slid his foot across the floor to her.

"The Indians got off easy compared to the adulterers and the turkey-fuckers and—God forbid—the committers of other unnatural practices," said George.

"I don't suppose you mean the gays," said Janice.

" 'Sodomists' is the word they used." George reached for the Bradford diary, but another book caught his attention. He pulled it down and began to riffle through it. "Samuel Eliot Morison is the only one who mentions the log, as far as I know. Ah." George found the place and held up the book. *"The Story of the 'Old Colony' of New Plymouth,* published 1956 by Knopf." And he read, " 'It is too bad that we have no log or sea journal of the *Mayflower*; it would be priceless now. Master Jones doubtless kept one, but as he died shortly after returning to England, his widow probably used it for wrapping paper.' "

"Typical male remark," groused Samantha.

"Priceless?" said Geoff.

"Lost and gone forever." Janice held out her glass. "Pour me some more wine."

Outside, the breeze blew and sand grains rolled down the dune.

CHAPTER 8

April 1621

Witawawmut's Head

April 5, 1621. Wind steady, WNW, sky clear. The Cape slips below the horizon. The seas rise. The ship takes life. The men go to their tasks with fresh spirit, well pleased to be shed at last of Plymouth and the Saints.

Springtime comes and with it gentle winds to push us home. Gentle may they remain, for we are undermanned and topheavy, with half the crew dead and naught but ballast stones in the hold. I crowd no sail. I've not the sailors for it, nor confidence that even so sturdy a ship as this won't pitchpole with an empty hull.

I be more confident that them I leave will survive empty bellies and half-empty plantation. Fifty souls, sturdy in constitution and faith, have lived through the winter.

And in these last weeks have they made a treaty with Massasoit. Though his stronghold is well SW of Plymouth, he is chief of all the tribes to the tip of Cape Cod. He sees in the white settlers, or more truthfully in their ordnance, an ally against the Narragansetts, his enemies to the west.

This is to the good. But the grace of God must continue to pour down on them, so that they may grow their corn and fill their larders and unburden themselves of the debt they owe the London Adventurers. Their work in the wilderness is barely begun. But God will help them. Of that I doubt not. . . .

"God *damn* them," boomed Thomas Weston.

"I know now I be in London," said Jones, "as if noise and stench weren't reminder enough."

"God *damn* them, I say. And if you like it not, sir, God damn you, too." Thomas Weston circled his desk like a bear in a pit, looking to lash out at one of the dogs.

Christopher Jones sat calmly in a chair by the window.

Neither Weston's bulk nor his anger moved Jones, who understood as well as Weston the theatrical use of the temper. He studied Weston's cheap finery—red hose, port-stained red waistcoat, plumed red cap hanging on the peg—and concluded that the Saints' agreement with Massasoit was surely more honorable than the dealings they must have had with this man.

"They sent nothin'? Nothin' at all?" cried Weston. "Not a single bloody pelt? Nor yard of cedar? Nor even a few roots of sassafras? Nothin'?"

"They be near half of 'em dead. And the rest of 'em be half dead. Thanks be to God you got plantation at all, weak as 'tis."

Weston dropped into his chair, hooked a leg over the arm, and swung it in annoyance.

"'Tis their weakness," continued Jones, "has kept 'em from answerin' their agreement."

"More weakness of judgment than of hands, I'd aver." Several pieces of pork were tangled in Weston's beard, and the real food was garnished with a carbuncle that looked like a red cherry at the corner of his nose.

As an apprentice blacksmith, Weston had learned that in the modern world, iron could do more than gold to better the lot of the common man. Now he did his ironmongering at a hall in Aldergate Ward while, in the barn behind, a dozen bellows fired furnaces in which smiths fashioned the ingots and the implements he sold.

He had made good from humble beginnings and looked to do better. Into his circle he had drawn others of like mind, men of commerce who sought to become men of speculation and, perhaps, of wealth. They called themselves the London Adventurers, and they looked across the sea, to a land where the woods were endless and the beaver roamed by the millions. There would always be men like the Saints, who wished to cultivate such a place, and they would always need men like the Adventurers, who let their money do their cultivating for them.

Weston pulled a quill from his inkwell and wrote out a letter of credit. "You'll give over your sea journal and anything else you got in writin' 'bout this voyage."

Jones laughed as he would at a sailor questioning an order. "Not only does the ale make your nose red, it clouds your brain, sirrah."

"Sirrah?" Weston stalked across the room and stood over Jones. "I be a man of business. You call me 'sirrah' once more, I'll bake your head in one of me furnaces. Teach you some manners and a bit of sense."

Christopher Jones stood slowly. His clothes now hung upon his body, and circles had darkened under his eyes. Though he now felt the full weight of his fifty years, he was not yet one to threaten. "Me journal be me own business, me own and any barrister what calls for it in law court. That's why I keep it. If you want to see it, that's where you'll see it . . . *sirrah.*"

"Very well, *Master* Jones." Weston went back to his desk and picked up the letter. "Let's us not forget our business be undone till I pay you the last part for your ship."

Then, outside the window, there was a great commotion of flutes and tambourines. A clown carried high a placard: At Two of the Clock this Day, *The Taming of the Shrew*, by the late Will. Shakespeare, Royal Globe. And behind came actors costumed as Italian nobles and harlequins, dancing and singing to the delight of the crowd that was as perpetual in these narrow streets as the waves at Cape Cod. It was May, and the spirits of London were near as high as its smell. Jones realized how seldom he had heard laughter the last ten hard months.

Waiting for him at Rotherhithe was a woman who was anything but shrew. He longed to laugh with her and lie with her and feel her soothing hand upon his brow. And after a few days at her side, his cough would fade and his strength, which now he showed in sham, would come back to him in earnest. So he sat again, to conclude this business quickly.

"I be but one man." Weston's voice lost all threat. He simply waved the letter in the air as if to dry it. "I must answer to others, who worry for their money."

"As do we all."

"Then you see me predicament. A glimpse of the journal can hurt no one, but only bring them sympathy."

"What beyond sympathy do you seek?"

Weston stroked his beard, and a piece of the pork came away in his hand. He studied it for a moment, then popped it into his mouth. "A narrative of the winter. Aye, just that. So's I know what they face and know better the way to help 'em."

Jones did not believe this scheming ironmonger for a moment. Weston would seek in the log some piece of knowledge to use against the settlers, something to make them redouble their efforts. But there was nothing he could bring to bear upon them that they would not bring upon themselves. It had been his good fortune to have made a covenant with honorable men. Even Ezra Bigelow had proven his constancy in the miserable first winter.

Outside, the parade had gone past. Laughter and music had been swallowed by the din of the streets. Jones wished simply to go home, and he had some small sympathy for Weston. Just as Weston would face difficulty convincing his partners that the Plymouth settlers still deserved their support, Jones would face it from his should he fail to deliver final payment for the voyage.

So he left for Rotherhithe that afternoon. He coughed much of the way home, but in his pouch he carried Weston's letter. Weston, for his part, now had the log.

ii.

It was during the warmest days that Autumnsquam finally met one of the whites. It was his bad fortune that he met a boy, for he had sworn that he would kill any white who came within shot of his arrow, no matter the agreements that the far-off Massasoit had made.

He was digging quahaugs near the place of the winter fight when he saw four runners far out on the flats. It seemed that they were floating above the sand, on a layer of water. But that was just some magic of Geesukquand, the sun spirit, who played this trick on everyone's eyes in the warm months.

When the runners came close, their feet touched the ground,

and they looked like ordinary men—two Manomets, one of Iyan-nough's Cummaquids, and a white boy who had been found wandering between the Scusset and Manomet rivers. The Manomets had brought him to Iyannough, who now sent him to Aspinet.

Sweat poured from the boy's face. The sun had reddened him so that he looked like a cooked fish belly beside the healthy-skinned Wampanoags. He had tied his heavy moccasins around his neck so that he could run barefoot across the flats, and he wore also a string of shells.

"We gave him a necklace because he ran well," said one of the Manomets, "all day, without complaint."

Autumnsquam asked the boy his name. The boy did not understand. The Nauset thumped his chest and said, "Autumnsquam." Then he pointed at the boy, who jumped back like a dog ducking the hand of a stranger.

That was good, thought Autumnsquam. He pointed again, and the boy said, "Christopher . . . Hilyard."

"Chris-to-pher Hil-yud." Autumnsquam tried the words.

Then the boy pointed to himself, to the south, and pressed his hands to the side of his head in the sign of sleep.

"He has done that three times," offered one of the others.

"Sleeps to the south?" Autumnsquam looked toward the land between the creeks. "Nauseiput?"

The boy made the gestures again.

"You sleep tonight with the Nausets."

At the village, there was great commotion. The women and children scurried from their *wetus* to see the white boy, and one ran off to fetch the men, who were fishing. Autumnsquam sat the boy on a log outside his own *wetu*, and the women and children gathered around in a great circle of curiosity.

But Autumnsquam wanted no welcome. Let this boy be frightened. Let all whites be frightened, for all time. To keep them frightened, Autumnsquam glowered. And as he was a *pinse*, a trusted brave and counselor, the rest of the Nausets did as he did . . . but for one.

This one had been born in winter and was now old enough to crawl. Like a crab he scuttled from his *wetu*. He stopped at his father's feet and looked up, then he saw the new face. He had not yet learned to fear strangers, so he smiled.

The white boy smiled back. The baby sat on his fat behind and smiled even wider. The children at the edge of the group smiled, too. And Autumnsquam chewed on the inside of his cheek to keep his own face from warming.

Then the white boy took off his beads and gently placed them around the baby's neck. And the laughter of the Nausets could be heard on both shores of the Narrow Land.

Christopher stayed three days with the Nausets, exploring, fishing, and playing with Autumnsquam's little boy. Then his people came for him. They grounded their boat on the flats but would not go up to the village, fearing another fight. Autumnsquam thought that was good, though the Nausets wore no paint and had no plans for war. He sent word to the village, but he and the others stayed on the beach and kept their bows in their hands.

The wind that day was a warm wind, from the southwest, and it carried the stink of the sweated white bodies straight into Autumnsquam's face. The boy Hil-yud did not smell bad, but the smell from the whites' canoe was like a great heap of dried seaweed and dog dung drying in the sun.

He could not go closer than the length of three canoes, but there was one amongst them that he sent forward—he whose corn had been taken in the Pamet land seven moons before. And the whites, for all their bad smell, did better than Autumnsquam could have dreamed. They gave a knife as gift and by sign and word, promised to make good for the corn. And they did not smell so bad.

Then, toward sunset, the whole tribe brought the boy through the woods. This was good, thought Autumnsquam, because it showed how many there were of the Nausets, and even if the whites had made a treaty with Massasoit, the Nausets were still to be feared. Sachem Aspinet stopped on the shore and made a sign of peace, then brought forth the boy, bedecked in beads and shells.

Autumnsquam was glad he had met Chris-to-pher Hil-yud. If the whites were to live there, it was better to know that some whites were good. Then Autumnsquam recognized the man running toward the boy. It was the one he had tried to kill in the winter fight, the one who had tried to kill *him*.

The father embraced his son. He said soft words, then angry words. The boy pointed again toward Nauseiput, and the father embraced him once more. This was good, thought Autumnsquam. Men who could be mad at their sons and glad for them at the same time could not be all bad.

With one arm around the boy, the father went to Aspinet and

took out his knife. This made Autumnsquam reach for his tomahawk. But the white man had planned no deceit. He made a gift of the knife to Aspinet, and the Nausets cheered.

Then the boy drew his father toward Autumnsquam. If the white man recognized him, he did not show it. Instead, he offered his hand. Autumnsquam would not embarrass the sachem and so touched his hand to the white's and gave a smile to the boy. Then the white man, who grew much hair on his face and looked like a scrawny dog, gave Autumnsquam a knife.

In the flashing of the blade, even Autumnsquam forgot the flash of this man's gun. But to the white man's smile, he simply nodded. They now owed each other nothing.

The boy, however, owed something to a little Nauset girl, or she to him. She pushed through the crowd and called his name, "Chris-to-pher," as if he had taught it to her.

Her name was Amapoo, Autumnsquam's niece. She still carried much in the way of little girl plumpness, but her womanly parts had begun to bud and would soon blossom. She ran forward and put a necklace of moon snails around Christopher's neck, causing his face to turn a bright berry red.

Autumnsquam had never seen such a thing in one of his own, but he knew what it meant. And it would not be good, if it came to pass.

iii.

"The prodigal son returns!" cried Simeon Bigelow as the shallop took the breeze.

Jack threw his arms around his son. "Thanks be to God."

"Prayin' again, are we?" grunted Ezra Bigelow.

Jack scowled at the figure hunkered in the bow. "This time, God answered."

"Aye," said Simeon Bigelow, securing the halyard to a cleat. "'Tis God's gift."

"'Tis God's gift we were not massacred lookin' for the young wastrel." Ezra Bigelow's face was shadowed, his eyes barely visible beneath the broad-brimmed felt hat.

"'Tis the gift of good Indians," said the boy defiantly. "They treated me like a cousin."

Ezra raised his head. "Another blasphemer we have, come aboard in savage ornaments."

"A boy," said Simeon gently.

"Tell me lad," growled Myles Standish from the stern. "What made thee run off?"

"I wanted to meet Indians and see if they used our island in summer."

"What island?" said Standish.

The boy glanced at his father, who gave a slight shake of the head.

"An island thou may have seen in winter?" said Ezra, "whilst 'twas said thou wert . . . hunting duck?"

"Dammit lad!" Jack Hilyard leaped to his feet so suddenly that the shallop listed. He pulled off his hat and struck his son across the face. "Never run off again. Never!"

The boy's cheeks reddened again, but he cowered only a bit. Had his father been truly angry, he would have struck with a bare hand.

"Thou worries us into our graves," Jack Hilyard swung the hat again.

"Sit, Jack," cried Simeon, "before we turn over."

"Aye," said Ezra, "add no lies to thy blasphemy."

"Lies?"

"The boy run off, for he sees the world through the father's eyes and sees this . . . island as a place to 'scape the law and the Word." Ezra stood and propped himself in the bow, like a preacher in a pulpit. "For breaking our laws, for running away and causing able-bodied men to venture into Indian country, I pledge to the son, and to the father who raised him, that *never* will they have what they seek here."

Now the boy saw true anger in his father's eyes, anger shot first at Bigelow, then at the boy himself. His father called him a bloody moron, then tore the necklaces from off his neck and flung them into the sea.

iv.

In the life of the bay, nothing was wasted. The men of Plymouth learned that lesson well the first summer. Massasoit's Indians taught them to use herring from the bay to richen the soil: plant one herring in every hill of seed, and plant corn, beans, and squash together. The cornstalks grew tall from the herring, the beans twined around the corn, and the prickles on the squash vines grew out to protect them all from the rabbits.

Come autumn, when the oak leaves turned red and the salt marshes gold, they got in a harvest worthy of a great feast. For three days, they partook of the abundance God had given them, whilst offering hospitality to Massasoit and his men. They ate turkey and venison and looked to the second winter with a confidence as great as their faith.

Yet in a few days more, another ship arrived, the *Fortune*, carrying thirty-five more souls, thirty-five more mouths to feed. The ship also carried a new patent, making this settlement legal in the eyes of the Crown. And it carried a letter, more like a cannon shot fired from London four months before.

In it Thomas Weston berated them for keeping the *Mayflower* so long and sending her back empty. He warned that unless they delivered *something*, they could not count on the support of the Adventurers. William Bradford, now governor of the plantation, shot back his own angry letter and, to prove their constancy, had the *Fortune* loaded with cedar planks and pelts.

They survived the second winter. Warm shelters and full bellies went far toward fighting off disease. And in June of 1622 hopes rose with the arrival of the *Charity* and the *Swan*. But those ships brought both bad news and bad seeds.

The French had stopped the *Fortune* on her voyage to England and stripped both her passengers and her cargo. Their good friend Christopher Jones had died of consumption in March. And Thomas Weston had quit the Adventurers.

This meant also that Weston had quit his support of the Plymouth Plantation. But he wrote that he looked to friendly dealings with Plymouth: witness the sixty men he had sent on the *Swan*, charged with building a plantation that he intended himself to join. Weston had given no thought to feeding these sixty, or to their character. Those problems he left for Plymouth.

By fall Weston's men had moved north about twenty miles to a place called Wessagusset to make a settlement, but they were lazy and improvident and soon needed food. They asked Plymouth for help, so Bradford traveled to the Nausets, who traded corn for English hoes. But by February, Weston's men had once more sailed themselves into hard straits.

They drank too much, molested Indian women, and were forced at last to hang one of their own for stealing Indian corn. When they made themselves servants to the Massachusetts in exchange for food, they earned the Indians' contempt.

About this time, the sachem Massasoit took to his deathbed. The Saints dispatched Edward Winslow to his side. Winslow found death to be no more than a massive case of constipation, which he cured with a physic. In thanks, Massasoit gave him warning: not only were the Massachusetts planning to rub out the Wessagusset colony, but Plymouth as well, and their sachem Witawawmut had visited both the Cummaquids and the Nausets to bring them into his alliance.

Though Plymouth had no use for Weston's men, they could ill afford war. True, they had enclosed their settlement in a great diamond-shaped stockade and at the highest point had built a blockhouse, which served also as meetinghouse, a place strong enough, in Ezra Bigelow's words, to keep out both Satan and the savage. But there were no more than a hundred fifty in Plymouth, and the Indians still numbered in the thousands.

So Myles Standish led an expedition north to cut off this Indian conspiracy at the root. He took only eight men, all the plantation could spare, but he made certain to take those who were reliable in a fight, Jack Hilyard among them.

For several days, they lived at Wessagusset, in the same miserable conditions as the other whites, and endured the insults of the Massachusetts, who walked freely through the settlement, brandishing knives and taking what they would. The Indians found it most comical that the Plymouth men spent time fixing one of the sorry houses, as though planning to stay. Like goodwives, the Plymouth men swept and cleaned, put shutters on the windows, and even built a strong new door.

On the third evening, Myles Standish and Jack Hilyard were sitting together on a stump when the one named Witawawmut came into the village. He was tall and muscular and wore his hair in long plaits that fell to his shoulders. He wanted a man to gut fish, and there was one here who did this in exchange for corn.

There was bad blood between Standish and Witawawmut from their first meeting in a Cummaquid village. Witawawmut had contemptuously called Standish a midget, and Standish had nearly killed him. Now the Indian went past as though Captain Shrimp—a name used only behind Standish's back—were no more dangerous than the stump he sat upon.

Witawawmut called several times and finally spied his man asleep under a tree. He cast a look at Standish, then pulled aside his breechclout and pissed into the man's face.

For all the bad temper in his red beard, Standish knew the way to bide his time. He whispered the word "tomorrow" to Jack Hilyard and smiled at Witawawmut.

The next day, Standish invited Witawawmut, his partner Pecksuout, and their two retainers into the house for a parley. He stationed four men outside, while Stephen Hopkins, John Billington, and Jack Hilyard waited inside.

The Indians seemed to fear nothing. These whites were unarmed, and how much more dangerous could they be—even Standish—than the craven beggars and scratchers who had been there for six months?

Jack Hilyard sat at the table in the middle of the room, in a shaft of light that fell through one of the little windows. Beneath the table, he held Standish's own snaphance. He did not like a bit of this. After the First Encounter, he had found the Indians to be honest and worthy in all their dealings. But only the strong survived. That much he was certain of. And he now had a new wife in Plymouth. To protect her and the babe in her belly, he would kill all the Indians to Narragansett Bay if he had to.

As Witawawmut entered, Jack pulled back the hammer and felt the flint scrape against his thumbnail.

Standish spoke a few words to the Indians. At the last of them —"We wish only to know how we may be friends"—the door was barred from the outside. Men at each window slammed and barred the new shutters, and the room fell into riot.

Standish snatched Pecksuout's own knife from around his neck and stabbed him in the heart. Jack Hilyard pulled the snaphance from under the table and killed Witawawmut with a deafening shot. One retainer threw himself at the door. Billington pulled him back and broke his neck with a single blow. The fourth surrendered, but it did him no good.

They would make of him an example, if it would stop a war. They dragged him outside and hanged him.

Then Standish asked Jack Hilyard, "The axe I did see in your belt, be it sharp?"

"Like a razor."

"Then give the great Witawawmut a shave."

They broke up the Wessagusset colony. Any who were willing to meet Plymouth standards were allowed to return with them. The rest put aboard their small ship, the *Swan*, and went to join the English fleet fishing at Penobscot.

The returning warriors went straight to the governor's house, where Standish placed a bundle of bloody rags before William Bradford.

"Is this what I think?" asked Bradford.

Standish urged him to open it. Bradford hesitated, so Ezra Bigelow peeled away the rags to reveal, first, the greased black hair and feathers, then the painted forehead, the eyelids half closed, the mouth half open, the tongue lolling grotesquely at the corner, and the raw neck meat that looked like chicken guts and bone.

"This be the one they called Witawawmut. A most arrogant *pinse*," said Standish.

"Very good," said Bradford. "Now take it away."

"Mount it, Captain," said Bigelow.

Bradford shook his head. "A savage custom."

"The better to frighten the savages," said Standish.

"Aye," added Bigelow.

"We do not want fear." Bradford folded the rags loosely around the head again. "We want peace."

"Fear ensures peace," said Ezra Bigelow. "Fear and punishment for the Nausets."

"We are not strong enough to punish them," said Bradford, "nor have we evidence 'gainst them."

"We have the word of Massasoit," said Bigelow.

Jack Hilyard did not wish to stay an extra moment. He wished to tell his new wife of his bravery, his new and most pregnant wife, most pregnant and most envied by those who still waited for women from England. But he had to speak. "I be the one what took this *pinse*'s head."

"Bravely done," muttered Ezra, "after he was dead."

"I *killed* him first," said Hilyard, "when you was nowheres to be found."

"Speak your piece, Goodman Jack," Bradford interceded.

"The Nausets be allies. They saved me boy and dealt corn for Weston's men, too."

"They saved your boy to put us in their debt. They traded corn to get good English hoes," grunted Ezra Bigelow.

"They be savages," added Standish. "Had we not give Massasoit a good shit, even *he* might have been down on us."

"We've not strength to fight them all," said Bradford.

Bigelow picked up the head and held it by the hair so that the jaw dropped open and long strands of fluid dripped from the neck. "Let this be our weapon. Mount it. Let 'em see what we do to our enemies. Let 'em see our anger and spread word. Let 'em think we come in all wrath, with musket and cannon, to punish the plotters. Let fear be our ally."

And Bradford agreed, for Bigelow spoke good sense. The head of Witawawmut was put upon a pike at the meetinghouse, so that the people of Plymouth could study it each Sunday on the way to service.

Christopher Hilyard studied it each day. He watched a crow perch on the top of it and peck until he pulled the tongue completely out of the mouth. He watched swarming flies blow the flesh full of eggs. And when his father took guard duty atop the blockhouse, Christopher went with him and watched the maggots hatching in the eye sockets.

Such contemplation was not good for a young boy, his father said, but in Christopher's confusing world, Witawawmut's head seemed the heart of confusion. Why had it been put up to frighten the Nausets, who had shown only friendship since the first fight? Why was this Indian not simply buried, and the memory of his enmity buried with him? This world belonged to them, he thought, and they to it.

To Christopher, this head bespoke his father's hatred of those who had befriended him. His father's new wife bespoke his own eclipse in his father's eyes. Now Christopher longed to leave his father's house and see once more the smiles of Amapoo and the Nausets.

But among the Nausets, there were few smiles.

Even in that enlightened time, trial by ordeal was used to determine guilt. A man accused was put to a test. If he survived, God was showing favor. If he did not, he was guilty.

The Nauset sachem Aspinet had conspired with no one, but

upon hearing of Witawawmut's head and the white men's wrath, he and many of his people were struck with fear and fled into the marshes. Within months, the misery of life there made them easy prey for the diseases that now came each winter. When word reached Plymouth that Aspinet was dead of pestilence, it was taken as a clear sign, not of misunderstanding between white and red, but of red guilt.

Some Nausets, however, refused to flee. If the white men attacked, Autumnsquam would die rather than leave his home. Others believed that even if they fled, the white God would chase them into the marshes and strike them with sickness. But if this God was so powerful, Autumnsquam wondered, why had he not struck *him* first? After all, Autumnsquam deserved punishment. It had been he who promised that the Nausets would join Witawawmut's war.

It would have been bad work, killing the boy Chris-to-pher Hil-yud. But Autumnsquam would have done it. He would have done it for his own boy and for his people. Many Wampanoags, rising against the whites, falling on them at night, killing the forty or fifty men-at-arms, killing the women and children . . . He would have done it . . . for the future.

Now he feared that the people of the Narrow Land would never rise up. Some villages were even sending gifts to Plymouth. They would accept the white man's terms and the white man's gods. First, they would accept the whites who were smart and dangerous, like those of Plymouth. Then they would accept the ones who were lazy and crude, like those of Wessagusset. And it sickened him. Had it not been for his boy, he would rather have left his head on a pike beside Witawawmut's.

V.

"Be you certain we can handle this tub?"

"A shallop's the finest tool what was ever made for the sea, master. She'll handle this blow like a three-poler."

"And only the Indians knows this coast better'n—"

A mountainous wave rolled over the boat, filling her ankle-deep with water.

A crude one, who was also smart and dangerous, was shaping a course for Plymouth. He had crossed the Atlantic on a fishing vessel, telling his mates he was a blacksmith. That was partly true, but he had not told them that his name was Thomas Weston.

The Council for New England had grown more vexed with Weston than ever the Plymouth men had. He had sent ships to New England without permission. He had charged them to fish where they would, for the ocean was free. He had funded the renegade Wessagusset colony, for New England was too big to be controlled by a few men. And none of it was lawful in the eyes of Crown or council. So had he been prohibited from setting foot anywhere in New England.

Weston had read the decree, taken a false name, and sailed for New England, council be damned. No man or royal authority could keep him from his investment. But when he reached the fishing fleet at Penobscot Bay, he learned that no man in his colony had done anything to *protect* his investments, and the *Swan* could not be found. His speculation had fallen to pieces.

But he never dismissed an idea that might prove profitable, and he had brought with him a sealed iron box. In it was something to use when there was time for the wildest of speculations. It was the sea journal of the *Mayflower*, and the time had come.

As blacksmiths were not well suited to the sea, he had found a pair of fishermen who would take him to Plymouth. However, but for the Saints, he had never judged men well. They were north of the Merrimac River when the seas rose and the shallop began to ride like a leaf in a rushing stream.

"By'r Lady!" cried the one who said he knew what he was doing. "We be headin' for the breakers."

"Hold her steady!" cried the one who had said he knew where they were going. "Or we'll be in pieces."

"The wind's got her!"

"Then bring her about!" cried Weston.

"Shut up," cried one.

"He's right!" shouted the other.

Through the sheets of rain Weston saw the breakers wearing on the bar a hundred yards from the beach. "Throw out an anchor!" he screamed.

"Shut up!" cried one.

"He's right!" cried the other as a wave broke over them and carried his mate into the black boil of water.

Now the shallop began to turn with the force of the waves. Weston grabbed his box and clutched it to his chest, "Bring 'er about!"

"But the tiller's gone!"

"It's the tiller*man* what's gone."

"We be adrift! And bloody sinkin'! Bail!"

"You brung no buckets, you damn fool."

"Use that." The fisherman lunged for Weston's box.

"No!" Weston pushed the fisherman away.

The sea rose and the fisherman followed his mate into the abyss. A moment later, it swallowed Weston as well. . . .

vi.

They were Penobscots. They had come with pelts to trade at Strawberry Bank. Now they had new knives, beads of glass for their women, a copper kettle, and buckets of white men's beer for the long walk north.

Thomas Weston had his old knife, a purse containing ten pounds in gold, a rucksack of clothing rescued from the surf, and the iron box which, somehow, he had clung to when the sea sucked him in. If there was anything of luck in this, it was the season. Had it not been summer, he would have frozen to death. But after the storm and the miracle of his deliverance, he had dried himself in the sun, and now had many hours of daylight in which to travel.

He had taken a path that snaked through marsh grass as tall as a man and as dense as thatch on a roof. He had not gone far when he heard laughter and men speaking in a strange tongue. His first thought was to hunker down in the rushes and let them go by.

But there was no time. They were rounding the bend now. And their chatter was ceasing as, one by one, they saw the big, bedraggled white man blocking their way.

Weston puffed himself up to his full five feet nine and squared himself on the path. If he understood one thing, it was the power of bluster. He clutched his iron box to his chest and resolved that he would not even step aside.

The Penobscots were not warlike people. But like the Nausets, they were of two minds about white men, who brought some good things and many bad. The Penobscots who met Weston may have decided that in his box and rucksack he carried some of the good things. And for all the bad they had endured, perhaps he owed them.

An Indian said hello.

Weston set his jaw and nodded. He guessed the Indian had learned English while working with the fishing fleet.

"Got pretty red feather in hat."

"Aye." The feather had stayed in Weston's hat, which had stayed on his head during his ride in the surf. It was not nearly as pretty as once it had been.

The Indian took a gourd from his bucket of beer. He was as tall as the Englishman, but his chest and shoulders were scrawny. And none of his mates looked much better. Weston thought he might handle them all.

The Penobscot smiled. His face was pitted from the pox, and his body was covered with foul-smelling grease. The Penobscot, however, was in no way bothered by the mosquitoes, which feasted on Weston's neck and had been biting through his hose since he entered the marsh.

The Penobscot offered the gourd. "Drink for feather?"

Weston was tempted. A draft of beer for a feather. A true bargain. But in mongering, he never accepted the first offer. It showed weakness. So he shook his head.

The Penobscot did not seem disappointed, as though he understood the game of barter. He ran his hand over the ridge of hair on his shaved head. "What bird?"

Weston did not understand.

The Penobscot drank down the beer, then said. "Me want feather from red bird. What bird? Cardinal bird?"

"No bird. Dye. Red dye." He realized immediately that he had blundered.

The Penobscot looked at his friends and said something that caused them all to grumble. Then he pulled his knife and swung it toward Weston's neck, screaming, "Red no die. White die. Then take feather."

One of the Indians grabbed Weston's left arm. He tried to swing loose, but another grabbed his right, causing the iron box to fall to the ground. One of the others grabbed it, while the leader slid the knife from Weston's belt and pressed it against his chest.

"Give me my box."

"No talk or thee die."

The Indian took Weston's knife and sliced through the wax seal on the box. He pulled it open, his face filled with anticipation, until he saw . . . a book. He turned the box upside down and let the book drop to the ground. Then he looked inside for secret compartments; then he threw the box into the rushes with a curse.

He took Weston's rucksack and rifled through that. Then he grabbed Weston's change purse from his belt.

That Weston could not countenance. With all his might, he swung his body so that the Indian on his left slammed into the one before him. Then he bit the nose of the one who held him by the right arm. Then . . .

He woke in the bright, broiling sunshine . . . or something woke him. Was it the vicious pain at the back of his head or the curious feeling in his crotch? He rolled over, and the rushes scraped against his back, which was burned like meat. Then something bit him, bit him right at the tip of his manhood. He screamed and leaped to his feet. Sharp claws sank into his foreskin and he screamed again. But there was no one to hear. He did not know where he was or what had happened. He knew only the pain.

And there were crabs—crawling, scuttling, shuffling—everywhere.

He reached down and snapped off the claw so that the crab fell away, but the claw remained, fixed to his foreskin like a pincer. He was naked, barefoot, bitten all over by mosquitoes, and like a scalded dog, he began to run. He did not even think to look for his rucksack or his clothes or his book. It would not have mattered, for they were all gone.

CHAPTER 9

July 7

Husband and Wife

Something felt nice, somewhere below the snap of his pajamas. At first it had no focus, because he didn't. His mind was still wandering through some dreamscape of fish wrappings and ship's logs and fancy houses overlooking the bay. Then the feeling came to settle between his legs.

Every couple had their special time. For Geoff and Janice, it was morning. Especially at the Truro house.

When they bought it, the second floor had been a rabbit warren of badly lit rooms and sloping ceilings, where anyone over four feet tall banged his head getting up to pee. Their friends, of course, had been happy for *any* Cape Cod roof over their heads on weekends, but why did it have to be so damn low?

So Geoff had decided to put in a skylight, one of those double-insulated Velux numbers he was always calling for when he designed attic makeovers. If he could call for one, he ought to be able to install one. It took him two days, but he cut the rough opening, framed it, fit the window, secured the flashing, and with inordinate pride, found a place for every screw, bolt, and nut that had gone splattering across the floor when he first opened the box.

The next morning, sunshine streamed through the skylight to wake them, and they made love, first with Geoff on top, then with

Janice, so each could enjoy the view. Both pronounced the skylight a success.

Children got in the way of mornings, and like most couples, Geoff and Janice had become creatures of the night. But sometimes, in high summer, the sun might wake one of them before the kids did, and that one might wake the other. And that might lead to something more.

"This is unexpected," he whispered.

"I felt your sneaker last night. I wasn't in the mood to feel anything else. Let's say I'm reopening negotiations."

He slipped an arm around her and drew her to his face.

She offered him her neck, where the aroma of Chanel still lingered. She liked sunrise passion, but passionate sunrise kisses were another matter, especially after an evening with George Flynn's garlic-town bouillabaisse. She would rather kiss a furry old sock.

He slipped a hand under her nightgown. "You must have been dreaming."

She hiked up her nightgown and threw one of those long, smooth thighs across his waist. "The kids'll be waking up any minute."

"Do you need something?"

"Day twenty-seven."

He raised his hips. She lowered hers. And they met. At first they moved slowly, without the frantic speed of youth, the fear that it might end before it began. It was one body greeting another, old friends getting comfortable.

Then they stopped. They did this to prolong the pleasure. Sometimes they would try to see how long they could last before one of them moved. Sometimes they would try to take themselves to another plane by talking about flowers or baseball or maybe the weather, and all the while, the urge to move would be growing, the excitement tightening their voices . . . but the longer they lasted, the better they finished.

She pushed down. "You made me mad yesterday, Geoffrey. I didn't deserve it."

"You sent Arnie Burr and the Humpster to Rake's house with a transit and a set of plot plans." He slipped her nightgown off her shoulders and pressed his lips to a breast.

"That feels nice." She sat back on his thighs, to enjoy the touch of his tongue, then pushed him away. "I want an apology."

"All right. I'm sorry. Whatever I said, I'm sorry."

"Accepted." She plucked a gray hair out of his chest. "You aren't getting any younger, Geoff. You shouldn't pass up a big opportunity."

"This is sounding more like a real talk."

"It's a good time to say what we think."

"Say much more, and your visitor may think he's not wanted. Either that or his owner will roll you over and finish what you started while you talk right through it."

"All right. Besides, I'm getting sweaty."

"So let's do something worth the sweat."

He pushed gently. She met his motion. The headboard began to creak. A sound rose from his chest. She sighed and closed her eyes. But even in the midst of love they always kept one of their senses sharpened to the outside world, and Geoff heard . . . *something*. He stopped and gripped her waist.

It was the scuffling shuffle of feet pajamas on a sandy floor. Janice dropped to her pillow like a tern hitting the water.

"I heard a noise," said Keith sleepily.

"Noise?" muttered Janice.

"Something banging." He rubbed his eyes. *"Ka-thumpeta, ka-thumpeta, ka-thumpeta."*

"That was Daddy."

"What was he doin'?"

Janice yawned. "His exercises."

"Oh . . . I'm hungry, Mom."

"Go downstairs and get a Pop-Tart."

"Dad says Pop-Tarts are shit."

"So eat an apple," growled Geoff.

The boy started to leave, but first he said, "Mom?"

"Mmm-hm?"

"Why are you sleeping with your leg on Dad's stomach?"

"Because she *likes* me," growled Geoff.

"Oh . . . I like you, too." Then Keith went off.

Janice listened for the perplexed whine of Kermit the Frog on the television set. Then she slid her body back across Geoff's. "Where were we?"

"Wherever we were, we're not there now."

"I hope that stuff George read—about that *Mayflower* log, I mean—I hope you're not still thinking about that."

"C'mon, Janice—"

"I want an answer. Don't forget what's at stake."

"Don't forget *my* stake." He rolled her over, and the talk ended.

They began to move together. She closed her eyes. Another sound vibrated from his chest into hers. This time they would get there. This time . . .

And from somewhere in the house came a cry of terror.

"Sarah!" Janice pushed Geoff off and ran for the door.

"Where is she?" Geoff pulled up his pajamas and ran after her.

They scrambled through the upstairs, from their bedroom in the front, through Keith's room, which backed onto Sarah's, then a step down, around the chimney, into the skylit dorm with five beds.

Snapping and buttoning themselves as they went, they stumbled down the back stairs toward their daughter, who stood at the bottom, looking into the bathroom, screaming, "Nooo!"

Janice pulled her away from the door. Geoff sprang from the third step, landed, and squared himself in the doorway, ready for whatever he would face . . . but not for what he stepped in.

"I'm sorry, Daddy, I just flushed and . . . and the water came right back up, and I tried to stop it but I couldn't—"

The water was still coming up, overflowing the rim, running across the floor in a fine yellow film to bathe Geoff's splintered feet. He pushed the cover off the tank and raised the float. After a moment, the overflow stopped.

"I'm sorry, Daddy," said Sarah. "I only did . . . you know, number one, and I didn't use too much toilet paper, like you always yell about."

"It's all right. Go and have a Pop-Tart."

As she scurried off, Janice appeared in the doorway with a mop and bucket. "I thought you said Pop-Tarts tasted like shit."

"I said they *are* shit. They taste pretty good." Geoff sat on the edge of the ball-and-claw tub and began to rinse his feet.

"It's only kid pee, Geoff." She slapped the mop on the floor and began to soak up the flood. Her breasts swayed gently beneath her nightgown, but the mood was lost.

"It's the biggest problem we have."

"C'mon, Geoff." She squeezed the mop into the bucket. "You and I have bigger problems than an overflowing toilet."

"Not us. The whole Cape. The whole damn world. But especially the Cape." He grabbed a towel and dried between his toes. "A reason to question this development."

"You say you had this pumped in April, and it's backin' up already?" Blue Bigelow smiled. His teeth were stained brown halfway down and yellow the rest of the way, and he seemed not at all bothered by the stink rising from the cesspool. "You got a problem."

Geoff stood at the lip of the tank. If Blue could stand the smell, so could he. "Why are you so happy, Blue?"

"I'm workin', which is more than I can say for most construction men on Cape Cod." He turned to the Humpster, who was standing by the truck. "Almost down, turn 'er off."

"Let 'er run a little more." The Humpster leaned against the truck, one of those big red tankers with a shit-covered hose squirming like a tail out the back and a smell that seemed to be rusting the paint from the inside. On Cape Cod they called them honey wagons.

"Kill 'er *now*, you stupid son of a bitch," shouted Blue, "before she starts suckin' air!"

Maybe everyone should treat the Humpster like a stupid little boy, thought Geoff. "Glad I got the A-Team. I thought you guys didn't get dirty anymore."

"I never let my boys forget what's important." Blue jammed his hands into his back pockets, which caused his flabby pectorals to stretch against his T-shirt like two water balloons. "It's great to be— what is it?—*vertically integrated*. Development, money, materials, construction—all in one little company. Your father-in-law handles the first two, gives me the orders, I do the second two, and we get on fine. But when you're vertical, it means you go from the ground up."

"Starting with the hole for the shit?" said Geoff.

Blue nodded. His first chin moved against his second, which moved the third. Most native Cape Codders were like their trees— closer to the ground, a little scrawnier than the mainland variety, and stubborn. The Bigelows got the stubborn part right, but someplace along the line, a *big* gene had been bred into them, and it always seemed to pop up in Bigelows that Geoff didn't like.

And Blue looked even bigger, because the crew cut made his head look so small. "Like I tell my boys," he went on, "never get out of septic tanks, no matter what."

The Humpster might have heard this joke a hundred times, but he gave a laugh that was as false as his father's friendliness. Geoff knew that when Blue joked, even the dumbest of his employees was smart enough to laugh.

"There's always money in septic tanks," said Geoff.

"Damn right. Sooner or later, people always stop doin' what they like to do. When they're kids, they like to watch cartoons, but that changes. When they get older, they like to screw a lot, but that goes, too. Some people even lose interest in eatin'."

"Not you."

"Not yet." Blue slapped his belly. "But one thing's for sure. We all want a good shit every day till we die." Then he called into the house and asked Janice to flush a toilet.

The water rushed down the pipe from the house. They looked into the hole and watched it splatter into the tank. "I'd say you got problems."

"Yeah, and a plugged line ain't one of them." The Humpster dragged a hose to the edge of the tank.

"Failed system, more likely," said Blue. "That and an uncle who don't know what's good for him."

"Now I know why the A-Team came."

The Humpster sprayed the sewage off the grass around the lip of the tank, and some of it splattered onto his father's trousers. For this he got another "Stupid son of a bitch!"

"You work in shit, expect to get some on your pants," said Geoff.

"You could have it all over this place before you're finished." Blue looked around the yard.

The old house with the Greek Revival trim stood on an acre of land halfway up Tom's Hill. There were ancient apple trees growing in the front yard, taller locusts all around the boundary. A hedge shielded them from the paved road below and from the dirt road that led up the hill.

Across the marsh on Cornhill, modern houses turned glass faces toward the sea, but the backside of Tom's Hill had remained rural, a quiet little swatch of a Cape Cod long past. Its exquisite privacy had been a mistake of time rather than design. The nineteenth-century fisherman who built this simple house had had room for fruit trees because the land had cost less than the nails to build the house. And while you could see the ocean, there were no sweeping vistas of blue, because, for a fisherman, the sea was nothing more than a place of work and death.

In keeping with the house, the cesspool was about the oldest design you could find, nothing more than a stone cistern porous enough for liquids to leach into the surrounding sand, while bacteria consumed the solids. It was efficient enough, as long as there weren't too many cesspools putting pressure on the sandy soil, and as long as the sand remained permeable.

Cape Cod's water came from a single giant aquifer, a reservoir of fresh water floating precariously between the sand above and the salt water below, like curaçao floating between the cream and the crème de menthe in one of those fancy drinks. And if they kept building, someday all the cesspools might overwhelm the sand's filtering ability, and some wells might start to pump gray water. Clam flats had already been polluted by tainted runoff. And if the aquifer was depleted, salt water might mix with fresh and destroy the whole system.

But all of this caused Blue Bigelow to smile, because whenever a septic system failed, the state required upgrading to what it called Title V standards, and Blue made big money. He pumped out the shit, he designed the system, and he put it in.

"If you need another pump real quick, you can start thinkin' about Title Five. But you're an environmentally sensitive kind of guy, so you won't mind much."

"How much?"

"Could be five or six grand, could be twenty-five or thirty. It all depends on how the glacier went through." Blue lit a cigarette.

Geoff closed his eyes and waited for the explosion of sewer gas.

"That's where your second problem comes in."

"Rake?"

"You and him are sittin' on a lot of money at Jack's Island, and you may need it to solve your first problem."

"What do I owe you for the pump?"

Blue waved a hand. Even his friendliest gesture carried some threat. "Just lean on that uncle of yours to let go of the land. I got a lot of people who want work."

"If I don't?"

"You ever seen a honey wagon let go on your lawn? Ugliest thing you ever saw. Shit everywhere, toilet paper, Tampax, used rubbers. Christ knows what's in *them* these days."

The Humpster started the truck. A puff of blue exhaust billowed out.

Blue stepped onto the running board and, for the first time, stopped smiling. "Straighten the old man out before that town meetin'."

Janice came running out to say good-bye.

Geoff told her, "Your father's cousin is charming me."

As Blue climbed into the cab, she shook his hand. "All his charm is in his bulldozers."

"Without bulldozers, the world's got no use for architects, honey."

Geoff slammed the door after him.

"A used rubber layin' in a pile of shit." Blue shook his head. "Make you give up sex for a year."

Geoff and Janice watched the truck rumble out to the road. The Humpster couldn't make the turn on the first try, or on the second. So the words "stupid son of a bitch" got louder, and his face got redder. Finally Blue jumped out and directed the truck, with gestures and more "stupid son of a bitches," out the driveway and down the access road.

"If I thought you had any of his genes, I'd give up sex for *life*." Geoff climbed into the Chevy. "He and his son make me hope there *is* a *Mayflower* log."

She reached through the car window and put her hand on the wheel. "Go chasing it, and you *will* give up sex—with me, anyway."

"An idle threat, after this morning."

"Low blow."

"Sorry." He threw the car in gear and grinned like a kid. "Let's run away like we used to. Find some sand dune and just . . . do it all day long."

She folded her arms and looked over her shoulder at the house. The sound of a Warner Brothers cartoon could be heard through the screen door.

"No good, huh?"

"That's the past. The future's staring you in the face. And where are you going?"

"To lay this *Mayflower* log stuff to rest."

"Dammit, Geoff!" She slammed her hand so hard on the car roof that he felt the sound in the bridge of his nose. "This is *just* what I asked you not to do."

"I can't always do what you ask, honey." That was a mistake. He knew the minute he said it. He put on the sunglasses that he used to shield himself from those serious brown eyes of hers.

So she banged her hand on the roof again. "My father and brother are trying to do something for all of us, and you waste time with myths from senile old men?"

He backed down the driveway. A quick retreat. But she walked along beside the car. "You say you can't always do what I ask, but you *never* do what I ask. When I said 'No, Geoff, don't leave Withers and Johnson, there's not a better architecture firm in Boston—' "

"I wasn't a partner, Jan." He shifted into drive. They had fought this fight too often already. "I was passed over. Up or out. I was going to do small detailing on big jobs for the rest of my life."

"The pay was good."

"The job sucked."

She turned toward the house.

He called her, but she wouldn't stop. "After what George read last night, this log has me interested."

Now she stopped. "Be interested in your family. Helping my father and brother to develop that island should interest you. Whether your kids can flush the toilet should interest you."

"A book that Samuel Eliot Morison said was worth millions interests me, too. That would buy a lot of septic systems."

"We only need one."

"And one day to track the story down. That's all I'll take."

"I said you were a dreamer when you wanted to move us all to Cape Cod. I said I was a damn fool when I went along. But I was wrong. *You're* the damn fool." She went inside and slammed the door.

Yes, he thought, all the Bigelows had a stubborn gene. Rake had warned him at Thanksgiving dinner during his junior year at Harvard. Geoff had casually mentioned that he and Dickerson Bigelow's daughter were taking the same Colonial History class, and he thought she was pretty nice.

Rake had poured gravy onto his stuffing and said, "Be careful. A Bigelow is a person who got all the answers but don't know any of the questions."

CHAPTER 10

August 1623

For Unlawful Carnal Knowledge

Ezra Bigelow read the sentence: " 'For having a child born six weeks before the ordinary time of woman after marriage, fined for uncleanness—' "

"Unfair!" cried the mother, and the baby in her arms began to scream.

"Quiet the woman," Governor Bradford stood on the platform at the center of the settlement, flanked by William Brewster and Ezra Bigelow.

"And the *child*," added Bigelow.

The sun beat down on Plymouth like God's all-seeing eye, good reason why half the population chose not to witness the punishment. After all, some had actually *committed* the sin for which Jack Hilyard and his new wife were being sentenced.

"You'll not quiet a woman of good character," shouted Elizabeth Hilyard, and the baby began to shriek.

"Easy, Bess," said Jack from the whipping post, "thou frighten the child."

"Tell 'em we never knew each other till marriage," she cried. "Deny the sin!"

"No denial carries weight when the evidence is in your arms," said Ezra Bigelow.

Jack's neck was as brown as an Indian's, the rest of his skin cream white. "Afore the sun broils off me flesh, finish your readin' and take it with leather. Then pray nature never make a liar of thee."

"Nature is God's handmaiden," answered Bigelow. "She does his biddin'." And he finished the sentence: "Fined for uncleanness and whipped publicly at the post, then man and wife both to stand in stocks till sunset."

The whipman assured Jack Hilyard he meant no ill will.

"None taken," answered Jack. Then he looked at Christopher, now fifteen and naught but hands and feet and sullenness. "Take thy mother inside till this be done."

Christopher scowled. Jack knew he resented it when anyone called *her* his mother. Secretly he approved of the punishment for *her*.

"I'll go nowhere." Elizabeth handed the baby to Christopher. "Take him out of the sun."

It was clear that Christopher felt less resentment toward his half brother, and no boy wished to see his father's back stripped, so for once he did as she told him.

And Jack took the punishment bravely. None in the plantation expected otherwise. Though he was loud and rebellious, he had a harping iron for a backbone, even as it was laid bare. With every crack of the whip, he ground his teeth and tried to think on the strange humor of his predicament.

He had fallen in love with Elizabeth as soon as she stepped from the *Fortune*. He was not alone. Widowed on the voyage, this strong-backed young Saint of twenty, with flaxen hair, fair features, and all her teeth, had drawn single men like the marsh drew webfoot foul. And the Brewsters, who took her in, ate quite well of the duck and fish brought to their door by her suitors.

That she chose Jack Hilyard was a source of surprise to all, from the Brewsters to Jack himself. He was eleven years her senior, with a sullen son, but he had built a solid house and had ambitions for this life as well as the next, and both mattered to Elizabeth.

Churchgoing was law in Plymouth, but for Elizabeth, Jack went smiling, read loudly, sang in full voice, and made his son do the same. He no longer spoke of breaking the agreement to go off on his own. And once they were betrothed, he made no attempt to lie with her, though he thought, on some nights, to feel the ghost of Onan take his hand.

It seemed a sad joke, then, that his back was stripped because his wife had been delivered early. It could only be punishment for past sins. Or perhaps the elders, who should have been praying for the life of his weakling infant, were jealous that he had gotten the girl.

Time in the stocks chastened most, but by day's end, Elizabeth was spewing bitterness. Her wrists were rubbed raw, her back was cramped into a fishhook, and she was ready to renounce all association with the Saints. "I hate 'em. With all me heart."

"Thou's a good girl. God knows." Jack moved his shoulders and told her to do the same. He had stood often in the London stocks, and he knew that the cramps they suffered now were as nothing to what would come when they were released.

"If I saw a priest," she said, "I'd have him turn me papist, this very minute."

"None of that, now." It was the voice of Simeon Bigelow, bringing the key to release them.

The settlement was quiet. Most families were taking the evening meal, and few had interest in the stocks.

"Hasn't been too bad, then?" said Simeon.

"Mortifyin'," said Elizabeth.

Jack twisted his neck, like a chicken peeking out of its coop. "Can't compare to London. There, a man in the stocks suffers scorn and rotten fruit the whole time. In Plymouth, him who's without sin casts the first stone." He thought that sounded most Saintly. "Now let us out."

Simeon shook his head. A sliver of sunlight still sat on the hilltop. "The letter of the law, Jack."

"Damn your laws, along with your brother," said Elizabeth. "Me babe cries for the breast."

Simeon grasped her hands, which protruded from the wood. "Forgive him, Bess. This is a fragile outpost on the edge of blackness. God protects us for he knows we push the blackness back. But if he sees the blackness block out our own light—"

"I done nuffin' black."

"God knows, but we have laws. Betimes the laws do hurt, but they show the way."

"No more sermon, good master. Let me out."

Just then a man came lumbering down Leyden Street from the blockhouse.

Though he wore motley clothes two sizes too small, he had a familiar face, and Jack thought he recognized the gait, or what he saw in the glance. It was the look of a Londoner, and Jack expected rotten fruit to follow.

"Excuse me, good master," the man said to Simeon, "but where be the house of Governor Bradford?"

"Weston?" said Jack.

The man stepped closer. His face, covered with bites and bruises and a few more carbuncles, warmed in recognition. "Jack Hilyard. If ever a man ends up in the stocks of Plymouth, 'twould be thee." He shook the yoked hand.

"Thou be far from London and well worn."

"Thomas Weston." William Bradford had come out to see the Hilyards and saw instead his former patron, reduced now to beggary. He looked him up and down, as though in no way surprised. "Uncertain and mutable are the things of this unstable world."

ii.

The Hilyards ate well that night for all their pains and cramps. Sympathy brought food from many a house. All knew the need for the blindness of the law, but more than one child had been born before a full nine months, and food always eased pain in a hungry place—a baked bass, a bread of corn flour, long beans snapped succulent from the garden, a bucket of clams, a summer-fat duck roasted and still hot, a pudding made from all the kinds of berries growing wild.

"I should stand the stocks more often." Jack cut up the fish. "Belly cheer and good beer make the pains fly."

"But not the humiliation." Elizabeth held the baby to her breast while she served out the squash.

Christopher Hilyard tore silently at the duck.

"For a meal like this, I'd face another *year* like this," said Weston, downing a draft of beer.

Word was about that the original London Adventurer, for whom few had good to say, had journeyed on foot from the Strawberry Bank trading post at Piscataqua. They might have begrudged him this meal. But he was entitled to some small hospitality . . . as long as he did not stay.

Weston had made Jack Hilyard's first harping iron and many more after. When Jack had tired of whaling and moved in with Kate's fishmongering family, Weston had given Jack a job selling supplies to cooperages. When Weston began to recruit Strangers for the *Mayflower*, he had encouraged Jack.

"Would that I'd picked more like thee for Wessagusset, Jack, and more like these Saints."

Elizabeth spat out a disgusted laugh.

"Bess . . ." chided Jack.

"Me face burns from the sun, and me pride burns from the embarrassin'." She sat. "I would leave here the first chance."

At that, Christopher looked up.

"After a certain lad led us on a dangerous hunt two years ago," said Jack, "Ezra Bigelow promised he'd *never* let us go where we wants."

With his sleeve, Christopher wiped duck grease from his mouth. "I went to meet Indians. Human people like us. Not heads to be mounted on pikes."

Jack snatched a duck wing from his son's plate and pushed the succotash toward him. "Mix some beans and corn with that duck, boy, or thou'll be quackin' afore dawn."

"Ezra Bigelow . . ." Weston chewed on the name along with his fish.

"Bloody hard man," said Jack.

"Bloody bastard," said Elizabeth.

"Bess," said Jack, "that's no language for—"

"She be right, Jack. Bloody bastard. He sat with Bradford when I spake to the governor." Weston belched and held out his mug for more beer.

Jack filled it. Elizabeth shifted the baby from one breast to the other so skillfully that the men did not notice. Christopher settled back into silent combat with the duck.

And Weston went on. "I told 'em I needed pelts to sell, to provision meself and the *Swan*, should ever I find her."

"If the elders give *thee* beaver charity, this colony might mutiny." Jack pulled a fish bone from his mouth. "The pelts be saved for the next ship. We be in want of clothes and implements."

"Thou talk like the governor."

"Him and me has little truck."

"'Cept when he punish us," said Elizabeth bitterly.

"The governor be polite enough to me," said Weston, "but Bigelow, he damned me."

Jack was not one to spare words, even with an old friend who had fallen on hard times. "Thou deserted us, then damned us with sixty worthless beggars who damn near brought the Indians down on us. Thou *deserve* a little damnin'."

Weston slammed his beer mug down. He had been a master of high dudgeon, but after all his reverses, there was little of it left, and he was saving it for someone else. So he shrugged. "Business be business. Should the elders stake me, I'll find them sixty beggars and the *Swan* and turn 'em all 'round smartly."

"With what in return?"

"I've hope of another ship and good supply. If the elders help me, they'll have anythin' they stand in need of."

"But thou lost their trust. Once 'tis lost, 'tis bloody hard to get it back, 'specially Ezra Bigelow's."

"This Bigelow, was he a friend of Dorothy Bradford?"

"The Saints be all friends."

"How did Dorothy Bradford die?" asked Weston.

"Fell from the ship, she did."

"Accident, then?" For the first time since he stepped inside the house, Weston had stopped eating.

"Aye."

"Did Bradford hold anyone to blame?"

Jack shook his head. He had stopped eating, too. Only Christopher continued to gnaw duck bones.

"Bradford never spake 'gainst Bigelow?"

Jack shook his head again. "They be fast friends."

"Show me Bigelow's house after the meal," said Weston, "that I may talk with him in private . . . about business."

iii.

Ezra Bigelow lived a simple life. In the eyes of the Saints, it was one of exemplary virtue. Most of his time he spent as a governor's assistant, helping to fashion the foundation of a church-state that one day would reach from Cape Cod to Narragansett Bay. He also did a share in the cornfields, and he hunted, though he was not the best man with a musket. Words were his weapon, and he believed his words were inspired by God.

Inspiration came to him each day from his Bible, and he spread it to the colony whenever Elder Brewster did not wish to preach the Sabbath. There were no official ministers in Plymouth, none who could baptize or give the Lord's Supper, but Ezra always reminded the people, when he stood before them of a Sunday, that they were the body, head, and heart of the church, and God's Word was its soul.

He and his brother Simeon had raised a two-room house near the foot of Leyden Street. They had agreed that when one married, the other would move out. But few women had come to the colony, and none for the Bigelows.

Ezra prayed that God would send him a helpmate, but he had not dwelt upon his loneliness since the terrible night when Dorothy Bradford died. Instead, he dwelt upon the Bible. And he had little sympathy for those who could not do likewise when the flesh tempted them.

For the church-state to survive, order had to be preserved in the public things and the private as well. People could not go wandering off at their own whim, nor could the natural members between their legs.

Ezra knew that Jack Hilyard had violated both of these tenets. He had no qualms about the punishments he urged, either when they fetched Christopher back from Nauseiput or after the birth of Jack's new babe. Ezra knew the infant to be undersized, an eight-month infant at best, but he was certain that Jack Hilyard had committed the act of uncleanness with Elizabeth before marriage, just as he had sneaked off to Nauseiput himself, six months before his son went alone, and so deserved what punishment he got.

With his brother gone visiting, Ezra he would relax with Leviticus, which encouraged the lawgivers.

The dark came earlier in August, but Ezra considered it a high calling to make his own candles, because the candle illuminated the Word and the Word illuminated the world. Whenever he cooked goose or swine, he went into the marsh and cut rushes. These he trimmed to twelve-inch lengths and soaked in animal fat, which congealed around the rush, and there was his candle. The holder was a simple clip attached to a dish of pewter or brass. The flame burned small but intensely bright.

"Good evenin'."

Ezra looked up from Chapter Twelve, The Purification of Women after Childbirth. "Yes?"

"Your door be open. May I come in?"

"I spake my mind at the governor's house," Ezra said impatiently. "Lest you wish to discuss Leviticus—"

"Ain't that the one what gives all the punishments for when we bung hole horses and goats and such?"

"Death."

Weston had not toyed with a man in some time. He was not certain of his ability or of his size, which, before his time in the wilderness, had been so dominating that he had seldom needed to toy. "Aye, death. And death to the man that have another man's wife?"

"The punishment for adultery is so stated. From Leviticus comes also 'eye for eye, tooth for tooth.' And as you deserted us, so have we deserted you. Good night." Ezra looked down at the book.

Weston came closer. "I know of another book, more recent. It tell of the first months here, and—if I be wrong, strike me dead—it tell of adultery . . . and murder."

Ezra Bigelow put down his Bible and studied the face dancing in the shadow of the rush candle. "What murder?"

"Dorothy Bradford."

Ezra Bigelow wore only black and white, yet even in the dimness, what color there was seemed to drain from his face. "An accident, as stated in our records."

"That's not what Master Jones wrote in his sea book."

"What did he write? Where is the book?"

Weston shrugged. His purpose was better suited without the book, as only *he* could interpret what Jones had written of that night. And he could ignore the good things written later of Bigelow. "I cannot tell thee where the book be, but it damn thee, Master Bigelow. It damn thee for certain."

Bigelow jumped to his feet and slammed his hands on the table. "I am a godly man, sir. No adulterer . . . and no murderer!"

"As a godly man the world sees thee"—Weston stroked his beard—"but the words of that book could bring terrible scandal on a godly man, and a godly plantation."

"Bring forth the book, that I may read it."

Weston pulled out a chair and sat at Bigelow's table. "In good time, master. In good time."

iv.

At suncoming, Ezra Bigelow stepped over the ruts in Leyden Street and hurried to Governor Bradford's house. The cocks crowed in their pens, the dogs barked at the black-cloaked figure, and Ezra stopped to study the stream of smoke rising from Bradford's chimney.

The young governor had taken himself a new wife, Alice Carpenter Southworth by name, and Ezra wished not to disturb them. If the smoke rose in healthy billows, they were up and about. If it was only a wisp, it meant the fire was still banked and the house quiet.

Ezra saw no smoke. As he considered whether he would wait or return later, when others might interrupt private conversation, he heard Alice's voice come sleepily through the open window.

"Ooh, la, good master, such greetin' to wake me."

"My rod and my staff, they comfort thee."

There came a sound of laughter, more intimate and personal than anything Ezra Bigelow had ever heard, at least from his friend Bradford. There then came the sounds of man and woman taking their pleasure. The ropes beneath the mattress creaked and the headboard thumped against the wall of the house. And out of respect, Ezra moved off.

After all, it was sin to dwell on thoughts of the flesh, and listening to such sounds could only torment a man who had no woman. Ezra looked out at the blue sea and tried to drive from his mind the vision the sounds conjured. Between husband and wife, it was an act of holiness. Between others, or played out in the mind, it was merely lust.

And now—especially now, after the untoward appearance of Thomas Weston—Ezra Bigelow had to avoid giving any appearance of lust. For he was a godly man.

"Good morrow, Master Bigelow!" A few minutes later, Bradford came to his window and looked into the clear sky. "'Tis a fine day the Lord hath made."

"Good morrow, Master Bradford. May I enter?"

"Aye. And break thy fast."

"Good day to thee, master. How fare thee?" Alice gave Ezra a small curtsy, like a well-bred goodwife. She had already drawn the coverlet over the bed in the corner and was now at the hearth, stirring porridge. How he longed for such a sight in his own house, for a bed tight-slept and well used.

"Care thee for porridge?" Bradford seemed in bright spirits.

Ezra shook his head. "My thoughts did wake me . . . on Thomas Weston."

Bradford sat at his table. "I've thought on him myself. Given his necessity and past favors, it may be our Christian duty to help him."

Ezra slipped his hands beneath his cloak to still them. "He deserves eye for eye, but Christ taught charity."

"Fifty beaver skins, then, and begone with him." Bradford tested his grainy gray meal and found it too hot.

"He did ask for a hundred."

"Come, Ezra, he's a monger. He barters. Ask for the heavens but settle for the earth, ask for the earth but settle for a colony, ask for the colony but settle for a plot." Bradford blew on the porridge, tested it again, and slipped the spoonful into his mouth.

"Fifty pelts will not provision the *Swan.*"

"Aye, should ever he find it."

Ezra came close and spoke the words he had memorized. "I oppose unwarranted gifts, but I have prayed hard on this and do change my thinkin'. Weston favored us formerly, and fair treatment of him now will bring favor from him in future. Treat him ill, and count on his enmity forever."

And William Bradford agreed. They were simple men, given to prayer and honest work and sound sleep each night. In complicated matters, they listened to the counsel of their friends. In the responsibility he had carried for near three years, Bradford listened to his assistants. "A hundred skins, then, done with discretion. We'll tell the other assistants, but the general population must not know, for we'll be hard put to explain such charity."

"'Tis wisdom before charity, done in anticipation of what Weston may do for us."

V.

At midnight, Ezra Bigelow met Weston, Jack Hilyard, and Christopher near the mouth of Town Brook. He had brought a tipcart covered in straw beneath which were a hundred beaver pelts. He pointed a bony finger at Hilyard. "Reveal any of this, and I'll find reason to stock you for a month."

"I give Tom me word."

While Jack and his son loaded the pelts onto a canoe, Ezra drew Weston up the path. It was a moonless night. But for the torches flickering at the corners of the stockade, Plymouth was in blackness. Jack could see nothing of Bigelow and no more than Weston's outline. But his mates used to say that he could hear a whale breach before anyone else saw it. So he listened hard, for, considering the men, there had to be dirty dealing somewhere in this.

". . . the book."

"This is the truth . . ."

". . . what you promised."

Weston spoke of leaving before the tide turned.

"Thou hast not brought the book? But our bargain?"

A book and a bargain. Jack was right. Dirty dealing.

"The Indians did strip me. 'Tis gone, in truth."

Bigelow's voice rose. "This is *not* what was promised."

There came the sound of hawking. ". . . my spat-on palm means truth. I'll speak none of this . . ."

And Jack could hear no more. Soon after, he and his son and Thomas Weston pushed off, leaving the black figure of Ezra Bigelow standing like death on the shore.

All that night, they held close to the coast, so that they could wade ashore if the sea overturned their canoe. But the night was calm, and by dawn, they reached the mouth of the Scusset, the place where they had first seen Indians.

Christopher gazed east, along the upper arm of the Cape. "We could follow the beach, Pa, be at our island by nightfall."

"*Our* island." Jack laughed at that, more in anger than amusement. "Our island be no more than a dream to wake thyself from, lad, thanks to thy wanderin' ways."

And there was no further talk of their island. They rested until the tide turned, then pointed their canoe upstream and, like the Indians, let the current take them through the valley. When the water grew too shallow, they carried the canoe over the mile-long path and down to the headwaters of the Manomet. That night, they camped near the mouth of the Manomet, a place the Indians called Aptucxet, "at the little trap river."

Word had come that a Dutch trading pinnace was on the south coast, and might stop here, as here was the only place on Cape Cod where canoes could pass from one side to the other without facing open ocean or dangerous shoals. Thus it was the best place for traders to deal with Indians or with a white man who owned a hundred pelts of beaver.

Thomas Weston slipped off his boots and put his feet by the fire. A big toe poked from his hose like a shrew poking its nose from a burrow. "It might be that a canal could be dug over that portage we took today."

"Canal? We're lucky we has shelters." Jack put another log on the fire.

"You could sail straight on to Plymouth without ever seein' the shoals that did trouble you so in the *Mayflower*."

"Sail right up to Ezra Bigelow"—Jack leaned back and threw his words after the sparks rising into the night—"ask for a hundred pelt, beaver or otter, no matter."

Weston gave a growling laugh. "It be a grand world."

Jack smoothed a pelt and placed it on the feet of his sleeping son. "I hear thou gets all the pelts thou wants, if thou knows 'bout a certain . . . book."

The grease in Weston's beard glistened in the firelight. "I did forget tales of thy sharp ears. Well, there be no book, nor anythin' else to use 'gainst Master Bigelow, 'cept this." He tapped his temple.

"Bigelow's not one for bluff or bluster."

"I be the best bluffin' blusterer what ever there was."

"Thou asked last night about Dorothy Bradford. . . . This book of thine, does it talk of her?"

Though there was not an Englishman for twenty miles, Weston slid closer to Hilyard and lowered his voice. "Jack, hear the counsel of one who was born poor, got rich, got poor, and who'll get rich again. Forget books that be lost forever. Think of trade."

"Don't be changin' the talk, Tom."

"I be tellin' thee why I come here. To get started again, in trade. Trade's the thing. Trade whale oil, trade pelts, trade the land if you can." Weston strode to the edge of the river. "Start here."

"Start what?"

"A tradin' post. The Indians trades pelts to thee for trinkets. Thou trades pelts to the Dutch for profit."

Jack looked out at the river mouth. The new moon had risen, a rapier of light glimmering above black water and blacker land. "And the book?"

"*Trade*, Jack. To man or nation, trade matters more than faith. After that, there be no more to tell."

And no Dutch came that season. So Weston went north and found the *Swan* floundering from one Penobscot fishing settlement to another. He provisioned her with beaver charity and repaid Plymouth, as Bradford wrote, with "reproaches and evil words." But he never again spoke of book or scandal. This might have been because he considered it a secret to use again. Or perhaps a perverted sense of honor kept him from destroying the reputation of Ezra Bigelow and besmirching the colony he had helped to start.

When he sailed for Virginia, to test his skills as planter, trader, and member of the House of Burgesses, Weston did not even go with thanks. He called them good beggars on his behalf and bade them good-bye.

Ezra Bigelow prayed in thanksgiving at his leaving. Jack Hilyard prayed for knowledge of a book that would give him sway over Bigelow and the island called Nauseiput. Elizabeth prayed that the elders would heed her husband, who now urged them to build a trading post on the Manomet.

She had determined that she would pray like a proper Saint and keep house like any goodwife. But until she could move her family away from those who had punished her so unjustly, she would bring no more children into the world. Upon news of this, Jack seethed.

vi.

In the land of Autumnsquam, the Nausets seethed as well, but with fever. As the cranberry vines reddened and the geese took flight in the year that the white men called 1623, another plague came. It swept through the marshes where some still hid from Plymouth's wrath. It struck in villages where there were good shelter and plentiful food.

Autumnsquam had once killed a wolf with his bare hands. He

had fought the white men in the dawn light. He had refused to be frightened by Witawawmut's head. But all the courage he could muster meant nothing in the face of this sickness.

His woman died before him and left Autumnsquam alone to watch their son die. He held the boy to his chest and covered him with kisses. He did not care that the sores on the boy's forehead broke against his lips. He would be glad to join his family as soon as Kautantowit would take him.

He buried his boy beside his wife and buried the others who had been his friends. Then he sat back and waited for the fever and the sores to come to him. But they did not.

After many days, the wind rose, the rain slashed down, and he heard the roar of the sea beyond the bar. It called to him like the voice of Kautantowit. So he paddled his canoe into the east wind, and as he drew close to the inlet, he saw the breakers raging.

Three times he tried to run the inlet, and three times the sea threw him back. The breakers that he prayed would swamp him did not let him beyond the bay. It was not his time to die. Perhaps it was a sign. Perhaps one day, Kautantowit would call him to wipe this land clean of the English and their god. He went back to his dying village and prayed that it would be so.

vii.

Elizabeth Hilyard prayed as well, for four years.

In that time, she did not conceive again. But she could not deny her husband his due. He was, after all, her master.

Though a Saint, she had grown up in a most unsaintly section of London and there had heard of a way to prevent the man's seed from entering her body though the man did. She took boiled sheep guts—meat casings—and fashioned sheaths that her husband could wear when he came to her. He objected, but she promised that if he wore them, she would never turn him away. She kept her promise and they remained, at least outwardly, good citizens.

Each spring, Jack pressed the elders to permit whaling. But the whales seldom coasted close to Plymouth and the elders would yet permit no settlements in distant parts of Cape Cod. Then he would press them on the need for a trading post at Aptucxet. Press them for anything, his wife said, that might get the Hilyards away from Plymouth.

In 1627, the London Adventurers echoed Jack's words on trade. After farming and husbandry had ensured survival of the plantation, the Adventurers suggested that Plymouth's best hope to work off its debts would be in trade. And the London market craved pelts.

So Plymouth bought land from the Manomets, made treaties with the Wampanoag nation and the Dutch at New Amsterdam, and built at Aptucxet a trading post more capacious than any Plymouth house, with two large rooms, an upper chamber, loft, and root cellar. The Indians would bring pelts of beaver, otter, muskrat, even mink. The Dutch would come with glass, pottery, cloth, and the metal goods the Indians coveted. Plymouth would trade in the fruits of its husbandry. And all would benefit.

For Jack Hilyard's foresight, for his bravery against Witawawmut, and perhaps as recompense for punishment that many considered unjust, Bradford named him proprietor. Ezra Bigelow was glad to be shed of Hilyard, his bitter wife, and his nettlesome elder son. And the Hilyards were glad to move some twenty miles to the shoulder of Cape Cod. Jack would see little direct profit, but much in the way of goodwill—from Plymouth and his family.

On the first night, he found it in the upper chamber. Beside the rushlight, Elizabeth removed her skirt and petticoats. Then she slid her black stockings down her legs. Then she took off the bodice that encased her upper body and the bum roll that fullened her hips. Then, though the night humors were known to be a danger to the naked body, she pulled her shift over her head and stood, for the first time, completely bare before him.

"I've no fear of the night air," she whispered. "And I brung no sheep's guts to Aptucxet."

He leaned on one elbow and his eyes caressed the whiteness of her body. "It surpass my knowin'."

"What?"

"Why thou choosed me, when all them fine Saints lined up for thy hand."

"Two reasons." She knelt on the edge of the bed, bringing her sex so close to his face that the smell of her intoxicated him. "Thou art thine own man. And thou hast that—" She threw back the coverlet.

His shirt formed a little tent above his loins. "Thou knows the words to make a man feel manly."

She pushed the undershirt up toward his waist. She made motion to sit upon him, then hesitated, as if she had forgotten something.

His heart nearly quit when she lowered her mouth toward his root. He had heard of this done, for a price, by London whores. Now, in the exquisite privacy of Aptucxet, far from the prying eyes of the colony, his wife would do it for him. Then she stopped. He understood. They were rebellious, not depraved, and sodomy was sin no matter where done. She wet her fingertips with her tongue and anointed him. "Now, let us make another child, a free child."

Jack put his head back and thought how blessed he was.

In the loft, Christopher heard the creaking of the bed ropes and wished the same blessing for himself. He was nineteen, tall and brawny, with a thickening beard that made him seem all of a man, in no way connected to his wiry father. And there was a sullenness about him that masked a questioning nature.

The sullenness derived from questions that could not be asked in Plymouth, as they challenged the faith of Plymouth. There was but one church, said the Saints, one path to God, and the fate of all was predestined. But Christopher had befriended Indians who visited Plymouth, had learned their language, had heard of Kautantowit, of Geesukquand and Habbamock and all the spirits of sky and earth, and he had found meaning in them. They explained the world in a way that men could understand.

And that, he believed, was what faith should do. If one set of beliefs could not teach men the way to live in harmony with their world and themselves, what should men do but seek God in another way? It was for certain that eight hours each Sunday upon a hard meetinghouse bench had never explained to him why the head of one who sought to save his land should rot at the meetinghouse door.

Thus it was a happy day when his father charged him to go among the Cape tribes and speak of Aptucxet. He yearned to meet the Nausets once more, to seek Kautantowit in the marshes and beaches, and perhaps see the smile of the girl named Amapoo again.

After three days' journey, in which he visited many villages, he came to Nauseiput Island, shining like a ruby in the October light. Several Saquatucket families lived in the clearing where Christopher and his father had once tried to settle. The Saquatuckets had built their *wetus* around the old foundation hole, in which a heap of discarded shells rose higher each day.

Sepet was the sachem. He was white-haired, with skin hung in pouches where his chest muscles had been, and he dwelt without women or children. "Our world changes. We are fewer each year. And Kautantowit . . ."

"He must be sad."

The old man rubbed the saggy flesh of his breast. "Who can say? Sad, or mad that we do not praise him?"

"Tomorrow I visit the Nausets."

Sepet poked at the fire and laughed bitterly. "Do you know the name of their new sachem?"

"Autumnsquam?"

"So we wish, but his name is George. He takes an English name to be a friend of the English."

"What of Autumnsquam?"

"Sad and lonely, like me. The sickness of pox took his woman and his son, like mine."

Christopher bowed his head. "I must see him."

"He lives near the round pond on the bay, with his niece, the girl Amapoo . . . and her man."

That night Christopher slept on Nauseiput, in Sepet's *wetu*, on a bed of deerskin. But he did not have blissful sleep. He dreamed of Autumnsquam's baby, adorned with shells, and woke in a sweat. He listened to the wind in the trees and the rattled breathing of the old Indian beside him, and after a time, he slept again. Then he dreamed of Amapoo, and it was a dream so intense that he woke in the middle of a night-come.

The next day, with anticipation and trepidation, he moved on to Nauset. He remembered from six years before that Aspinet's village had spread a great distance both north and south along the shore. Now there were few columns of smoke rising anywhere in the Nauset land. The fields looked to be planted more with weeds than corn. The children were scrawny. The dogs bared their teeth. And many *wetus* were stripped of covering, nothing more than bent saplings, like skeletons in the sun.

In respect, Christopher first visited Sachem George, half brother of Aspinet. George wore an English cloak, grinned a great deal, and promised that all the Nausets would bring their pelts to Aptucxet.

Christopher gave him a new knife, then went north to the round pond.

There he found two dwellings built on the shore. Autumnsquam sat before one and chipped flint with a stone. Beside him were three large rush baskets, each overflowing with arrowheads.

Christopher held up his hand. *"Poo-ne-am."* Greetings.

Autumnsquam was startled. His hand went to his tomahawk, but after a moment, he recognized the white man. "Hil-yud? Christo-pher?"

"Autumnsquam, *netomp.*" My friend.

"Appish, Chris-to-pher." Sit.

"I bring my father's greetings . . . and his sorrow."

Autumnsquam looked up at the leaves of maple and beech. "My boy rides the southwest wind with Kautantowit."

"I will remember his smile always."

Autumnsquam turned his eyes back to his chipping, as though the memory filled him with too much sorrow to contemplate.

"You make many arrowheads."

"We will need . . . We will not speak of arrowheads. You made my boy laugh. You are welcome here."

And they talked the afternoon through, of the growth of Plymouth and the shrinking of Nauset and the turning of the earth.

Toward sunset, she came. He saw her from a distance, crossing the sandbar that separated the pond from the sea. She balanced a basket of clams upon her head and walked a respectful distance behind her husband.

"They are together two years but have no children."

"They have time."

"I would give her a child myself, but she is my blood."

The husband, named Spoospotswa, was young but scrawny and sunken-chested. His cough echoed ahead of him like the call of a sick bird.

Amapoo, however, had grown well into womanhood, not tall, but with good flesh on her shoulders and arms, a healthy round face, and the firm breasts of youth. Christopher could not see her legs, as she wore a skirt of marsh grass, but he thanked God that Wampanoags did not consider uncovered breasts a cause for lust.

Before Autumnsquam said his name, she recognized him. She put down her basket and came to him, filling her face with a smile. He wished to take her hand, but feared that her husband might take offense. And if he accidentally touched her breasts, his breeches would betray his manhood.

So he bestowed his gifts. Autumnsquam received a hatchet, Spoospotswa a knife that made him Christopher's friend for life, and Amapoo a looking glass.

That night Amapoo put on her best deerskins and hung copper pendants in her ears. Her husband did not notice. He sat by the fire and watched its reflection dance on the blade of his new knife. Nor did he notice that Christopher could not take his eyes off his woman.

Christopher stayed three days. He slept in Autumnsquam's *wetu*, though each night he was kept awake by Spoospotswa's coughing. He fished, helped with the harvest of corn, and quietly yearned for Amapoo.

When it came time for him to leave, Amapoo offered to go with him along the sandy paths as far as Nauseiput. Spoospotswa had little interest in a journey, but Autumnsquam said he would accompany them and visit his old friend Sepet. Christopher was happy for the companionship, though he would have been happier had Autumnsquam stayed behind.

Old Sepet welcomed them all. And that night, the shell heap in the foundation grew higher. The women served, the men ate, and each time that Christopher glanced toward Amapoo, her eyes shone into his.

It was past midnight when he rose from his pallet and went down to the beach. He looked out at the eelgrass where his father had once found an axe and wondered at his predicament. Why, when there were a dozen girls his own age in Plymouth, had this one never left his mind? How could he ever love her, when she had taken a man of her own?

"It is a good moon." She came out of the darkness and sat by his side.

"A bright moon." He felt his heart begin to race.

"The last warm moon. The southwest wind still blows, like Kautantowit's breath. But soon, the wind will be Chepi's wind, from the northwest, the demon wind. Then the dying will start once more."

"I will pray that it does not."

"To your god or to Kautantowit?"

"Both."

She smiled. Her teeth were strong and white. "You speak like a *pauwau*, a medicine man. You have great wisdom."

He put his arm around her and drew her body close to his. She smelled of wood smoke and deerskin. "Tomorrow I must go back to my people, and you to your man."

"But we will come to trade."

"I will be glad to see you."

She raised her hands to the sides of his face, and it was as if she had touched his manhood. When he kissed her, he tasted the sea.

"Stop this." Autumnsquam appeared on the dune grass above them. "She is not your woman."

Christopher jumped up, despite the stiffness between his legs. He tried to speak, but his knowledge of the language did not enable him to lie.

"Her man may be sickly, but it is her duty to make Nauset children."

"I am sorry, but—"

"She cannot go with another man or she will be banished. We need our healthy women. Leave now." Autumnsquam threw Christopher his rucksack and hat.

"I came to him," said Amapoo.

"Tell no one. You cannot be with this man. Go up to the women."

She took Christopher in her arms and pressed her lips to his. "Wunniish," she said fiercely. Farewell.

"Wunniish." Christopher looked once more at Autumnsquam. "I am a Hilyard. You can trust us."

"I trust you in trade. Not with my niece."

viii.

In the following months, many Indians put their trust in the Hilyards and were not disappointed. They would trade what they had from the Dutch or Plymouth, and if they had no barter, they would pay in wampum, one shilling for white shells, two shillings for black. Soon enough wampum could be exchanged for goods anywhere along the coast.

Autumnsquam went with pelts and wolfskins. He was much impressed by the size of the white man's house and great stone fireplace, and he was flattered that Jack Hilyard invited him to eat at their table and sleep by their fire. But when he returned to Nauset, he would tell Amapoo that such a house was a bother, big and clumsy, like the white man's weapons.

When Autumnsquam went to Aptucxet in the time of the herring moon, he found many Indians already there, filling the big room. In the center of them was Massasoit, sachem of all the Wampanoags, holding a baby boy.

"What is his name?" asked Christopher.

"Metacomet," said Massasoit.

Autumnsquam was drawn to the baby. "He has the eyes of a warrior."

Massasoit turned his broad face to the young *pinse*. "You are a Nauset?"

"Aye."

"Send my greetings to George."

"George sends his greetings to you." Autumnsquam traded a muskrat pelt for some of the sweet powder that the whites valued so highly. He touched his little finger and tasted, then offered some to Massasoit. In his heart, he blamed Massasoit for making peace when war would have been better. But to show disrespect to the sachem would show disrespect to all Wampanoags.

He gave sugar to Massasoit's baby, who cried for more.

Massasoit laughed at this like a proud father, which filled Autumnsquam with sadness and envy. "My son likes English things. They even give him an English name."

"What?" asked Christopher.

"Philip."

Autumnsquam felt the baby's grip and remembered his own strong son. Let them call you Philip, he thought, but when Kautantowit calls to me, I will call to you by your Wampanoag name. Then he saw the wide blue eyes of Jack's son Jonathan, gazing at the sugar. Had the pox not come, his son would be the age of this one, so pretty and innocent. He smiled and gave little Jonathan the rest of the sugar, which caused Metacomet to scream all the more. And the laughter of Wampanoag and English came near lifting off the roof.

That night, Autumnsquam ate with the Hilyards, what they called a chowder, made of quahaugs cooked in the juice from a cow. He liked their food and liked to look at Jack Hilyard's yellow-haired woman. But he had come with news. He did not want to tell it, but Amapoo had insisted. Spoospotswa was dead of the coughing disease.

ix.

Soon Christopher was making monthly journeys to remind the Cape Indians of the good things that could be had at Aptucxet. And for him, there was a good thing at Nauseiput. At each new moon, he would smell wood smoke before he crossed the western creek, and Amapoo would be waiting in the clearing. Old Setep was dead, and his little band had moved off to join a larger village, so Nauseiput belonged to Christopher and Amapoo.

And Christopher gave himself completely to Amapoo's ways. By day, he wore a breechclout and dug clams on the flats. By night, he took off the breechclout and she her deerskin and they locked their loins together. They loved each other in the woods, on the beach, sometimes in the warm bay water itself. Then, as if they knew that neither God nor Kautantowit would let it go on, they went back to their people.

Autumnsquam told his niece she needed a man who could hunt and fish and build her a *wetu*. She could not make a half-white child by a white trader. Jack told his son that if the colony learned of his fornication with an Indian woman, they would punish him and his family both. But neither Jack nor Autumnsquam could deny nature. And the young people were drawn to each other on every moon.

Then Elizabeth Hilyard came to deliver the child that she and Jack had worked so long to make.

Her pains began on an afternoon in early July. As Christopher was at Nauseiput, five-year-old Jonathan was sent to fetch the Manomet medicine woman.

Jack held his wife's hand, feeling as frightened as she and more helpless by far. They prayed together, as she was still a godly woman, and she endured six hours, her eyes moving constantly from Jack to the Indian woman who, by signs and sounds, tried to put her at ease.

Jack would never forget Elizabeth's bravery, nor how hard she pushed when the old woman made the sign, nor the fear that came into her eyes when the old woman patted the top of her head and shook it, then patted her behind: the baby was not coming head first but breeched.

Then the old woman pointed to her own chest as if to say that she would save the child. Elizabeth smiled through her pain, and Jack felt better, though he did not speak of the blood now soaking the bed beneath his wife.

The old woman slicked her hands with animal fat and tried to slip them into the womb. After great effort and great pain, which Elizabeth endured with great strength, the baby was delivered. It was a little girl.

And it was dead.

Whatever heartache Elizabeth felt was short-lived, for she bled to death that night. There was nothing the midwife nor the Manomet *pauwau* nor the prayers of Jack Hilyard could do to save her. The life just ebbed out of her, like a river of red.

Two days later, the Plymouth men arrived. Ezra and Simeon found Christopher digging a grave, while off at the edge of the woods, a squat, fat Indian girl was picking berries with Jonathan.

Ezra glared at the girl but spoke to Christopher. "Thou showest great arrogance to bring her here."

Christopher threw a shovelful of sand at Ezra's feet.

Simeon said, "Where is thy father?"

"Follow the smell."

They found Jack in the great room. Elizabeth lay on the table, uncovered. The baby was wrapped in a sheet beside her. And the stench was like thick phlegm in the air.

Jack turned a blunderbuss onto the Bigelows. "Come no closer."

"They must be buried, Jack," said Simeon gently, as though he noticed no smell.

"Send them on their"—Ezra held his sleeve across his mouth —"send them on their way to God."

"Get out."

Simeon pulled out a chair and sat.

Ezra, for once, did as Jack asked. He went stumbling out the door and gulped down a breath of fresh air. Then he turned his eye to the gravedigger, whose transgression had been the true reason for his journey. "The Manomets say thou were not here when thy stepmother's time drew nigh."

"'Twas nothin' I could've done to save her."

"And thou brought the Nauset girl back with thee?"

"She would not let me return alone."

"Then thou dost not deny that thou wert with her?"

"Would it serve purpose?"

Ezra looked toward the berry patch. The laughter of Amapoo and the boy mingled with the birdsong.

"He grows without faith."

"His mother taught him well."

"Who shall teach him now?"

Then the trading post door swung open and Simeon stumbled out. He breathed in fresh air, then called for sailcloth, a heavy needle, and thread. Soon after, he emerged with Jack.

"Thou hearest good sense, Jack," said Ezra softly.

"The Lord work in strange ways . . . or so Simeon say." Jack looked down at the open grave.

"Thy friends work for thee."

"Be thou my friend?"

"I shall give thee a chance to start over . . . away from the sad memory of this place."

Simeon shook his head, as if to tell his brother that this was neither the time nor the place, but Ezra had never been known for subtle dealings. He waited long enough for the sailcloth containing Elizabeth and the baby to be placed in the ground. Then he took Jack inside and presented his plan.

"We need thee at our trading house on the Kennebec, Jack," he began. "We need experienced hands there, and thou may count on a good Plymouth family to keep little Jonathan growing strong in the faith whilst thou do our biddin'."

Jack looked out at the berry patch, where Jonathan was again picking berries with the Indian girl. "I cannot go without me boy . . . Elizabeth's boy."

"'Twould only be for a little while," said Simeon. "Elizabeth would want this."

"God will profit the boy in Plymouth and thee at Kennebec," added Ezra.

Christopher's face appeared in the window. "Do not do this, Father."

"*Thou* may go to the Kennebec, too," said Ezra. "Indeed, thou *shouldst*. 'Tis wide country for a profane young man."

"If I refuse?"

"Go where thou wilt, but know that some in the colony would make carnal knowledge between white and Indian a capital crime."

And Jack understood. Ezra was forcing him to choose between sons. He could take Christopher two days' sail away, while leaving Jonathan to be raised a good Saint and taught a good trade. Or he could go to Plymouth with the boy and leave his firstborn to wander the wilderness alone.

He studied the dead coals in the fireplace, then looked at Simeon. "Be this the verdict of all the governor's council?"

"Some fear that to mingle the white and the Indian bring danger. Nauset men cannot take kindly to this . . . use of their women."

"'Tis more than mere use!" shouted Christopher.

Ezra's body uncoiled like a whip from the chair and snapped his voice toward the window. "Some fear that *thou* endanger thy *soul* by lying with a heathen, and the soul of the colony by thine example."

"I will find my way."

"See that thou dost not block the way of the colony." Ezra softened his voice, as though attempting to speak with reason. "This is yet a small Christian outpost, boy. But others will follow us, and they will put up a great house upon our foundation. We must build it hard and pure."

Were his son not the object of these words and Ezra Bigelow not the speaker, Jack might have cheered. He did not look much beyond what he could see in each day's light. But he could see no future for a son with an Indian wife.

Now Simeon Bigelow went over to the window and took Christopher's hand. "Thy compliance will set well for the day when thou hope to purchase land."

Where Ezra built great houses for the future, thought Jack, Simeon made small huts for the modest hopes of his brethren.

"Nauseiput?" Christopher asked.

"Never there," answered Ezra. "But land on the bay, from which thou may chase whales."

"Let us go to the bay now," said Christopher.

"Prove thy constancy, first," said Ezra. "Make atonement for your . . . dalliance. Go to the Kennebec."

"If I take him there," asked Jack, "can I buy the place named Billin'sgate, when the time come?"

To this, Ezra Bigelow offered his hand.

Free of grief, Jack would never have taken it. As it was, he thought to threaten Ezra Bigelow with the book and see what came of it, but he had neither stomach nor strength for such scheming.

He looked out at little Jonathan, who sat cross-legged beside Amapoo and picked through the bucket of blueberries. The boy's cheeks were stained with juice, hers also. These Indians were like children, thought Jack. He could not leave either son among them longer, for the world was changing quickly. Only those with hard heads, or hard hearts, would survive. So he would harden his heart and go to the Kennebec, and he would make Christopher go with him. And someday, they would hunt whales in the bay. . . .

Then he heard the voice of an Indian. He looked out and saw Autumnsquam raise . . .

CHAPTER 11

July 7

Indian at Aptucxet

. . . his hand and wave. He wore his best finery—leather and deerskin, beaded headband and wampumpeag, but in place of moccasins were a new pair of Converse 100s.

"Why aren't you out chasin' ambulances?" Massasoit called to Jimmy.

"He chases ambulance *companies*," said the Indian woman stepping out of the Aptucxet trading post.

"That's why they call him a *corporate* lawyer," said Geoff Hilyard.

Ma Little cackled at the expense of her big-deal son and threw her arms around Geoff's neck. Everyone had called her Ma since she took in her first foster child at age nineteen, and she'd borne two of her own, Jimmy and Massasoit.

Massy Ritter did not resemble his half brother. He would not have looked out of place in a lithograph of slave life. This was not unusual among the Mashpee Wampanoags. Nor was his German surname, because the town of Mashpee, where Massy and Jimmy grew up, had begun as Cape Cod's Indian reservation and over its history had welcomed a lot of people the wider world rejected.

Mashpee took Yankee surnames from white overseers, Hispanic names from Cape Verde Islanders, German names from Hessian prisoners who liked Mashpee enough that they stayed on after the Revolution, and African blood from the Cape Verdeans and runaway slaves.

Of course, the Indian population of Cape Cod had needed new blood, or it might have disappeared entirely.

There were perhaps two thousand Indians living on Cape Cod when the Pilgrims arrived. No one knew for certain. But white diseases had already begun their work on the naive immune systems of the Native American. Within a century and a half, there were only five hundred adult Indians on Cape Cod. Their ancestors had sold most of their lands for kettles and English hoes, then moved to reservations, known as plantations, or to Praying Towns where well-meaning ministers taught of the white god who sent diseases in his wrath and took them away in his mercy.

Mashpee was the first and largest of the plantations. By 1763, it was the only one left. And considering how poorly white overseers had done by the Indians of Cape Cod, the Mashpee Wampanoags petitioned the king of England for self-government. The king granted the request, a rare demonstration of good judgment. But when the thirteen colonies could not convince the king to grant them the same thing a few years later, dozens of Mashpee men joined the rebellion, perhaps on the principle that more freedom was always better than less. Most of them died. Many of their widows married Hessians.

But their sacrifice did Mashpee no good, because after the Revolution, the state of Massachusetts put overseers in charge of the town once more. Some served well. Others enriched themselves at the expense of the Indians. When they left Mashpee in 1834, they left it in poverty.

For over a century, the world left Mashpee alone, and Mashpee got along just fine. It was the Indian town, a bad address, in spite of the trout ponds, salt marshes, and fine south-facing beaches. Then, in the 1960s, developers discovered the town and its undervalued land and began to buy. They built condos in the pine woods and golf courses near the beaches. They closed off ancient fishing grounds. They gained political power. The Wampanoags, seeing their town wrested from them, brought suit to have open lands entrusted to the tribe. And an idealistic young lawyer named Jimmy Little joined the fight to retain something of his people's past.

When the case was heard in 1977, every real estate developer who could draw breath held it and waited.

"They're just after somethin' for nothin'," Blue Bigelow had announced. "They're not *real* Indians, anyway. Just Mo-nigs."

"What's a Mo-nig?" Geoff had asked.

"Mo' nigger than Indian."

In subtler language, this theme was developed by attorneys who fought the suit. And they won. Mashpee boomed. Control of the Board of Selectmen passed to white newcomers, and the three hundred Wampanoags of Mashpee couldn't do much about it.

Some, like Massy Ritter, didn't care. They fished a little, drank a little, and played sullen with outsiders, just as they always had. Others, like Jimmy, moved on to make their way in the world. And then there was leathery old Ma, who could still tell you about Kautantowit, Geesukquand the Sun Spirit, Maushop the Giant, all the spirits of sky and earth.

Six days a week, she ran a deep-sea fishing charter out of Falmouth. On the seventh, this member of the Mashpee Tribal Council took off her baseball cap, put on her deerskins and beaded headband, and educated the tourists about the people who had greeted the Pilgrims. And what better place to do it than in the town of Bourne, at the birthplace of American business?

The Aptucxet site had been discovered in a pasture around 1850. There was nothing left of the building, nor much interest in it then, because knowing the history of the land was less important than wresting a living from it. But in 1920, tercentenary of the Pilgrims' landing, the Bourne Historical Society raised money to construct a replica on the ancient foundation. By then, the tourists had found Cape Cod, and Cape Codders had begun to sense that after the beaches and boat harbors, history might be their best drawing card.

The Aptucxet replica perched on the banks of what had once been a tidal river and was now the widest canal in the world. While twentieth-century ships flowed by, you could feel the pull of the past at Aptucxet.

That was why Geoff liked it. That was why he liked the whole Cape. History had survived in the gentle curves of Route 6A, in the magisterial sweep of the Great Beach, even in the junk that burned-out business executives sold when they bought captains' houses and put up *Antique* signs. Of course, for every 6A curve there was a neon-and-macadam mile of Route 28. And for every old house, there was a strip mall.

But on the Cape, you could still find the connections, forge the links with a past that made you feel rooted to the land and the people who had lived on it, then integrate your vision with the surroundings. That was how Geoff tried to work at the drafting table, and it was a good way to live: find the connections, put it all together, die happy.

And what better link with Cape Cod's past could there be than Indians at Aptucxet?

"Take some literature, Geoff." Ma Little pointed to a table covered with pamphlets. "Wampanoag youth programs, unemployment, success stories like Jimmy Little, Wall Street Lawyer."

Ma was smiling, but Geoff heard a little resentment, a little disappointment. Her son came back every summer and did *pro bono* work for the tribe, but that didn't change the fact that one of the best and brightest had moved away.

"Geoff needs your expertise on an old Cape myth," said Jimmy.

"I'm your gal. You want to know about Maushop the Giant, or—say, how's that feisty old Rake Hilyard?"

"Yammerin' away about the log of the *Mayflower*," said Jimmy. "Ever heard of it?"

"No, but that don't mean it don't exist."

"We're trying to figure out how the log could stop the development at Jack's Island," said Geoff.

"I thought there was a commission for that now," said Massy.

"There's a commission for everything," said Jimmy. "But you can't stop development. We learned that in 1977. If you don't want the bad guys to do it, you help the good guys. The world's changing."

Ma folded her arms, and raised her chin. "Changin' too damn fast."

"You've never heard a legend about a log?" asked Geoff.

"Ma says there's a legend for everything." Massy took a surf caster from under the pamphlet table. "Then she starts tellin' one. That's when I go fishing."

"A legend for everything." Ma watched Massy amble off toward the canal, then turned an eye onto Geoff. "Are you using a legend as an excuse to avoid something?"

Geoff could never tell if she was really mad or just theatrical. It was one of the reasons he liked her. "I'm not sure what I'm doing, Ma."

She grunted at that, then grabbed Geoff's arm in one hand and Jimmy's in the other and dragged them into the trading post.

There were two large rooms on the first floor, with low ceilings and pine walls. In the smaller room, the curator, dressed like a seventeenth-century Englishwoman, was giving a tour of the artifact collection. But the main room looked as it might have on a day in the 1620s, and it gave Geoff a strange chill to stand there.

Barrels of corn, flour, and salt were piled in one corner. A musket stood in another corner. A stew pot hung in the fireplace. Deerskins lay beside the scale. And the board was set with wooden bowls and spoons, as though the proprietor would soon be coming in for dinner.

"Take a look at this," said Ma.

A large square-cut piece of granite, unadorned and unlabeled, sat on the floor by the staircase. It was marked with four large letters and perhaps a dozen smaller letters beneath them.

"The Bourne Stone." Geoff had heard about it.

"Stepping-stone of the First Indian Church in Bournedale, built in 1682."

Jimmy said, "What does this have to do—"

Ma raised a finger to her lips. *Shut up and listen.* "It's made of granite, rare on Cape Cod."

"There are glacial erratics all over," said Geoff.

"This stone was *found* like this. Cut, squared, inscribed. The Indians dragged it to the meeting house, but set it writing-side down. They thought the letters were devil markings."

"Then why use it at all?" asked Jimmy.

Ma pretended not to hear that. "There's not an Indian today who can tell you what these letters mean."

"No Egyptian can tell you what the hieroglyphics mean," laughed Jimmy. "So what?"

"A Harvard professor says the writin' is Iberian—like Spanish —for 'A proclamation. Do not deface. By this, Hanno takes possession.' An Iberian named Hanno may have been here five centuries before Christ's birth."

"Who believes that?" asked Jimmy.

"Well . . . some do, Mr. Wall Street Lawyer," she answered with a defensive little catch in her voice. "And others believe it's Scandinavian."

"The Vikings?" asked Geoff.

"A Swedish tourist said they used stones like this for boundaries all over Scandinavia."

"*There's* evidence for you," said Jimmy.

"If this stone proves that someone was here before Columbus,"

Geoff asked, "why isn't it one of the most important finds of the century?"

"Because these are just Wampanoag ideograms, and there's no one left to read them." Jimmy went to the fireplace and dipped his finger in the stew pot.

Geoff studied the strange angular lettering on the stone. There was something vaguely familiar in the graffiti. But that was the point. Legends had many ancestors. Nothing could be categorical. Maybe there was a log, maybe not. A wise damn Indian to answer a legend with legend.

Ma gave him a little wink, as if she knew that he knew what she was telling him. "The Wampanoags have legends about how Maushop made the Cape, but the whites say it was God or a glacier. And the whites have legends about who discovered America"—she nodded toward the rock—"but the Indians know it was discovered before the whites got here. Legends answer the hard questions."

"With the wrong answers." Jimmy looked at Geoff. "Don't give up professional fees and land sales for a legend."

"I raised a cynic," said Ma.

"I grew into one."

"A cynic who counsels his friends to chew up Mother Earth because it don't matter no more."

Jimmy put on his sunglasses. "The world's changing."

Mother and son were at each other again. That hadn't changed in years. But over the door was something new—a harpoon, and maybe a joke to cut the tension.

"Hey, Ma," said Geoff. "Why don't you stick him with this?"

"I'd like to." Ma came over. "They say the first man to work here went whale hunting later on. We don't know who he was, but I'll bet you he had more gumption than men today."

"Is this his harpoon?"

"It's a symbol of gumption. That's what you have when you don't accept what is." Ma touched the metal. "Some say it takes gumption to stop the world from changin'. Some say it's the ones with gumption who *do* the changin'. My boy's made up his mind on it. Where do you stand?"

"On my own two feet" was the answer he gave. And the commission from the Bigelows would keep him there. Independent, well off, able to work and support his family.

"Right in the middle" was the answer that went through his

head. He loved Jack's Island just as it was. And what if Rake was doing more than spinning some legend to give himself confidence in the future? What if there really was a log?

More questions. This hadn't gone as he had expected. All right. Janice would understand if he dug a bit deeper, for peace of mind. She would have to.

ii.

When Geoff Hilyard called, Carolyn Hallissey told her secretary she could see him on Wednesday.

Then she ordered the file the detective agency had prepared on the major players in the *Mayflower* log business.

She scanned the vitals—height, weight, years married, ages of children—and read the interview with Geoff's former boss: "As smart as anybody here. But thought he was getting mundane projects— housing developments and rehabs—while his contemporaries did glamour stuff, skyscrapers and all. We gave him houses because he was good at them. So one day he just left. A lot of it had to do with his independence. I don't think he had ever been happy in a big firm." A loner with ambition. A helpful insight.

Then she read his financial information: fifty thousand in savings, just enough to live on for a year, a small IRA, mortgages on two houses, loans on a new Plymouth Voyager and a twenty-three-foot Grady White with an oil-injected Yamaha engine.

Someone—either Carolyn's boss or the detective—had written, "Like in-laws, mortgaged up the ying-yang. Unlike them, some liquid assets. Will probably go for the deal."

She closed the folder. She didn't care about the deal. Her job was to find out what he knew about the log . . . if it existed.

iii.

Janice was in no mood to understand what Geoff was after, nor was she in a mood to finish what they had started that morning. Geoff knew the night was lost when he told her he still had questions about Jack's Island and the log.

"Did you talk to Rake again?"

"He wouldn't talk to me."

"Then forget it." She turned her back in bed and curled herself into a ball.

But Geoff kept talking. About harpoons and whales. Not exactly pillow talk, and not very topical. He was looking for connections. "They say Jack Hilyard was a whaler."

Janice twitched herself into the mattress like a dog tamping down the grass.

"He chased them in open boats and flensed stranders on the beach."

"Hilyards . . . always chasing something," she muttered.

That was a connection he would not dispute. "We used to kill them; now we try to save them." He listened to the wind chimes playing in one of the apple trees by the door. He felt the sea breeze pushing in through the windows. "The Center for Coastal Studies in Provincetown has a call list of volunteer whale savers. They help push pilot whales off the beach, cut humpbacks out of nets. I may join up."

"You do that, Geoff." She mixed annoyance and sleepiness in her voice, like a child nodding off to avoid something troubling. "Save the whales."

"Save them . . . hunt them . . . either way, you're just trying to be part of something greater."

She lifted her head off the pillow and looked at him. "You save the whales. Let Rake save the log. I'll save the family. Then we'll see who ends up as part of something greater." Then she went to sleep.

And Geoff dreamed of whales.

CHAPTER 12

October 1650

Papists Come to Plymouth

"We got us a big one, lads. Humpback for certain." There was no knowing the mind of a hungry whale, but Jack Hilyard had been watching a cloud of gulls, and from their motion had plotted the beast's progress halfway across the bay. "He spouts black blood afore sundown."

It was autumn, and for Jack, the high time had come, when the southwesterlies lingered like a maiden's kiss on the land, when the blue water rolled in long, gentle swells, when the spouts blew up like little silver clouds above the bay.

His son Jonathan pulled at the first oar. Beyond him was a woman dressed as a man, a strong woman with big hands and a face marked by the scars of the pox . . . Amapoo. Burly, black-bearded Christopher sat forward of her. And in the harpooner's seat, wearing a necklace of whales' teeth and a blue frock over his breechclout, sat the Indian called Autie.

"Humpback sink when dead," he said. "Better chase onto flats."

"Thou just worry 'bout the dart."

"Last time, me dart good, humpback sink." Autie, who still preferred to be called Autumnsquam, had learned many English words. A smart Indian had to, because the English used words like weapons.

It had been six years since the whites came to Nauset and asked to live on the land. They had given some good things—knives and copper, warm blankets, iron kettles, colored beads—and the Nausets had said yes, the white men could live there.

But when the Nausets tried to hunt in the places they had always hunted, the whites told them they could hunt no more. The Nausets answered that they could not be kept from their land. They were part of it and it was part of them. But the whites pointed to papers that the Nausets had marked and said the Nausets had sold them the land, and "sold" meant they could never use it again.

This "sold," thought Autumnsquam, was a word more killing than a gun.

"Thou struck deep, but not deep enough," said Jack. "Now, thou bloody heathen, now's a chance to redeem thyself."

"Redeem." The worst weapon-word. They talked of a redeemer, the Son of God, sent to earth to die for men's sins, before men had even committed them. What kind of god was this, who killed his own son because he was mad at sinful men? Some Nausets had accepted this strange story because the English sent good men like Simeon Bigelow to teach it. They promised that if the Nausets accepted the Jesus God Ghost, the Nausets would be accepted by the whites now flooding the land.

Autumnsquam accepted nothing. He believed in Kautantowit and the spirits of the sky and the earth. But he could throw a harpoon through the eye of a needle, so the Hilyards accepted him, no matter what he believed.

The Hilyards were the best whites to buy Nauset land. They traded fair and paid him a fair share of every whale they slaughtered. And in this New World a Nauset could buy much for his people with a fair share. So when Autumnsquam prayed to Kautantowit for the uprising that would drive the whites into the sea, he prayed also that the Hilyards would be spared.

The world had turned many times since he had seen the Hilyards on that sad day at Aptucxet.

Jack and Christopher served at the Kennebec trading post for seventeen years while Jonathan reached manhood in the home of a devout Plymouth Saint and boatwright. Jonathan visited his father each summer, but as his apprenticeship came to demand more of him, his visits grew shorter. As his training in the faith revealed his father's failings and his brother's profane ways, his visits grew shorter still.

By 1644, Jonathan had grown into a fine boatwright and an upright member of the church. In that year, young Plymouth men formed a parish in Nauset, which they renamed Eastham, and Jonathan bought forty acres of white cedar marsh from Autumnsquam. Not long after, in hope of bringing his father back to the breast of the church, Jonathan invited him to Eastham. And Jack dreamed once more of the whales.

"'Tis time for thee to go," Christopher told Jack, "afore thou grows too old for the hunt." But Christopher would not go back to Plymouth with his father. He left the trading post and disappeared into the Maine wilderness.

Little was known of Christopher's doings after that. From time to time, he appeared at trading posts with pelts, but soon disappeared again. It was said that he pursued Indian beliefs and lay with Indian women, though none had conceived by him. It was even whispered that he had taken an Abenaki wife. This was the truth, and it was good that it could not be proved, or he might have been hanged.

On Cape Cod, Jack Hilyard began as a drift whaler, flensing humpbacks that floated ashore or blackfish that beached in herds like cows. But as more men wandered the wrack line, carving their initials into stranded blubber, there were fewer whales to go around. Then Cape towns put a tax on drifters, because ministers, with the inspired logic of holy men, declared such whales to be gifts of God, thus the property of God's church. And Nauseiput Island, where pilot whales most often stranded, now belonged to Ezra Bigelow.

But each fall, a man could stand anywhere on the bay and count spouts the day through. All he needed was a boat and the courage to use it.

Jack had the courage, and Jonathan built him the boat. It had to be light because it would be launched from the beach, so Jonathan made it of white cedar, light yet tough. It had to be maneuverable, because a wounded whale was a dangerous creature, so Jonathan gave it double ends to change direction in an instant. And it had to be big enough to stand up to the waves that roiled the bay in whaling season, so Jonathan made it a full twenty-four feet long, with five thwarts for five oarsmen and a fore-and-aft sail for swift running.

Then Jack raised a tower on the tip of Billingsgate Island, the place promised him that sad day at Aptucxet, and from there he watched the horizon for whales. One morning in 1650, as he shielded his eyes from the sun, he saw a familiar brawny figure striding over the sand.

It was Christopher, wearing two feathers in his hat and a necklace of wampum around his neck. He said his Abenaki wife had died and it was time for the Hilyards to hunt the whale together. The first day that Christopher and Jonathan hunted with their father, tears nearly ran down Jack's cheeks, but he looked at the sea and blinked them away.

Autumnsquam envied Jack his sons, even if one was too holy and the other not holy enough. He had only his niece, who dressed now in a man's clothes so that the elders would not know of her doings with Christopher.

"Me bloody good heathen, Jack Bloody Christian Hilyard. Me no need no bloody redeemin'."

"That's foul talk, Autie," said Jonathan.

"Aye." Jack laughed. "Foul talk from a foul old *pinse—*"

"Who needs no redeemin'," said Christopher, "so long's he can dart the iron and bring his niece whalin'."

Amapoo glanced over her shoulder and gave him a smile. They were both in their forties, had both lost spouses, and had come once more to care for each other, though they were now old enough to be circumspect in their affections.

Jack held the steering oar and watched the whale. "A big 'n, lads, awesome big. I swear, if God come back tomorrow, he'd come as a whale, not some holy man."

"God's come already," said Jonathan, "as a simple carpenter."

Autumnsquam grunted.

At the oars they kept the cadence. The gentle swell rolled, the gulls circled, the smooth black body surfaced and spouted and sank again. Then the water ahead of them went rough, the dark blue beneath it turning to green, then to a milky white.

"Stoppin' for a little lunch, he is," said Jack.

Autumnsquam shipped his oar and looked over the side. "Silversides come!"

"Amapoo, fill your bucket," said Jack, his voice now tightening. "The rest mind your tasks."

"Mind the line!" added Christopher calmly.

"Big mouth come," Autumnsquam hefted his harpoon.

Jack peered into water. "Aye, a big 'n for certain!"

The whale was rising through a green cloud of sand. The great maw was open. The surface was boiling with thousands of fish driven upward. And then—

"He breaches!"

A hole opened in the sea, curtained with living baleen fabric, alive with sand eels. The water splattered and danced with silver panic, and the hole in the sea made a sound, a great snort that resounded in the chests of every person aboard. Then the curtain closed over the fish and the whale showed himself full to the boat.

There was a smell about the beast, rank and fresh at once, a smell of land and of sea, of past and future. And there was a majesty about him, for certain. Like a king reclining after a meal, he settled back and set his eye upon his tiny subjects.

This was the moment to fill Jack Hilyard with awe. What madmen they were to challenge His Majesty the Whale. What fools . . . Then he shouted, "Strike 'er, Autie!"

And the Indian darted his iron deep into the rich black blubber.

For a moment, the whale stopped, as though shocked by the arrogance of such an attack. He swung his long armlike flipper to pluck out the harpoon. Then he raised his flukes and slammed the water in insult, sending up a wave to capsize the boat and chastise the boatmen.

Then he sounded in a forty-ton dive.

The harpoon line screamed around the loggerhead at the stern, slapped over the thwarts, and tore through the chock like a saw hacking the boat in half. It played out with such speed that the loggerhead began to smoke. Jack shouted for Amapoo to wet it and she splashed water everywhere.

In an instant, two hundred feet of line went as taut as a bowstring. Then it began to play a strange groaning tune as the boat was pulled from a northeast heading due north. Then they were off. The flying spume soaked them all. The air rushed past like a gale. And as the little boat pounded against the waves, every backbone pounded against the base of every skull.

The whale hauled them north eight miles, all the way to the tip of the Cape. Then he stopped. The long, low rays of the October sun burnished the sandhills and glistened on the back of the beast. When he spouted, a little rainbow danced in the mist above him.

"Out with the oars," said Jack. "Now, he be ourn."

Then the whale gave another great snort and sounded with such force that Jack nearly tumbled overboard. The loggerhead was torn from the cuddy board and flew down the length of the boat, smashing this way and that, knocking Amapoo senseless and cutting a deep gash beneath Jonathan's eye. Then the whale was gone, line, loggerhead, and all.

"Bloody Christ," said Jack Hilyard.

"Bloody Christ no redeem us, Jack Bloody Christian Hilyard. Me throw good, me stick good. But thee make damn bad boat." Autumnsquam put his hand under the cuddy board and waved his fingers through the loggerhead hole.

"'Twas God, not the boat. God wished the whale to live." Jonathan wet a cloth and held it to his cheek while his brother splashed water onto Amapoo's face to bring her around.

"I suppose God wished us to live on Billins'gate 'stead of Nauseiput," muttered Jack.

"I know not God's mind on that matter," said Jonathan, "though he saw fit to give the island to Ezra Bigelow."

Autumnsquam's eyes shifted from father to elder son. Talk of Nauseiput often came after they failed to catch a whale, or missed a stranding, or spent a day hauling wood to barren Billingsgate. And such talk brought out an old anger. But today, Christopher was not listening. He was studying a curl of smoke at the tip of the Cape.

It was a wild and a desolate place where men cut wood and ran cattle, but where none chose to live. Still, the harbor it encircled was the safest refuge between French Acadia and Dutch New Amsterdam, and many flags had been seen there, among them the fleur-de-lis of the French privateer . . . and the skull and crossbones.

Jack called for his glass.

"No pirate would want us," said Christopher. "We got nothin'."

"We got a damn good boat."

"We got damn no-loggerhead boat," said Autumnsquam.

Jack swept the glass over the harbor but saw not a single mast. Then he settled on the smoke. "Bloody Christ."

"Pirates?"

"Men pilin' green brush to make smoke."

"How many?"

"Four. Two in breeches and two . . . in dresses!"

"Men in dresses?" said Jonathan. "Sodomists?"

"Frenchmen, methinks."

French papists is what they were, two sailors and two shipwrecked Jesuits in black robes. Jack had never seen papist priests before and was greatly surprised that they smiled and shook hands like ordinary men. Their leader, Father Gabriel Druillettes, said they were on diplomatic mission when blown off course, and he begged passage to the place he called Pleymout.

"It be twenty mile to Plymouth," whispered Jack to his sons, who stood by the boat, "and I don't much trust papists, or men in dresses."

"Master Bigelow says the robe covers a forked tail," muttered Jonathan.

"And some Eastham Protestants spend more time manurin' their brains than their corn rows," said Christopher.

Jonathan gave his brother a hard look. They were no more alike in appearance than in beliefs. The younger shaved his face smooth and wore his clothes for no more than a week at a time. The older hid his face behind his black beard and had not removed his greasy leather jerkin since spring.

"I simply ask if they can be trusted," said Jonathan.

"They be men," said Christopher. "And shipwrecked. I say we show 'em charity. Right, Autie?"

Autumnsquam stood on a dune and studied the staff that the priests had planted in the sand. It was topped by a crucifix on which Christ writhed in agony. Though he had heard plenty about God's son, he had never before seen him, as the Saints did not permit the worship of godlike images. "They know good torture. Give 'em ride."

"We save our baggage," said Father Druillettes, "but only the box that Père Daladier 'olds do we want."

Jack glanced at the younger priest, who clutched a metal box like the first Gospel. Daladier was tall and ghostly, with reddened stumps for thumbs and forefingers, ugly scars where his fingernails should have been. As Jack stared at the hands and wondered what strange rite of self-flagellation this had been, he noticed a foundry stamp on the corner of the box.

His eyes were no longer sharp, nor could he read, but the symbol seemed strangely familiar. Jack touched the damaged fingers, pretending sympathy while moving them to better see the stamp.

"Torture," explained Father Druillettes. "Iroquois devils."

With great pride, Father Daladier said, "Jésus-Christ give me strength. Jésus-Christ do not desert me."

The hands now had Autumnsquam's attention. "Why Iroquois do this?"

"I try to bring·them the true faith."

"More holy men. More true faiths."

"T.W." Jack remembered. This symbol stood for a name. His first harpoon showed the same mark. And his memory had been marked for many years by the man who made it. T.W. Thomas Weston.

"I guess Plymouth ain't so far after all."

ii.

The Community of Saints that the Old Comers had envisioned had existed for only a brief time at Plymouth. True, William Bradford and his favored assistants were regularly elected. They made laws and meted out punishments as good scholars of the Bible, and they still oversaw all land purchases. But Plymouth had grown so quickly that it had long ago burst its boundaries, both physical and spiritual.

Where once the people worked on communal farms and small plots, they now owned acreages stretching north to Scituate and south to Cape Cod. Where once the settlements had hugged the coast, they now reached far into the New England forest.

Most roads still led to Plymouth, but new ones went to a town forty miles north, near the mouth of the river Charles. There, a far richer group of religious rebels had arrived in 1630. Within a year, they had brought thirty shiploads of followers to the place they named Boston, and their population had created a fine market for the fruits of Plymouth farming and husbandry. This meant more substantial homes and a better life for most everyone in Plymouth. But by 1640, Puritan Boston had surpassed Plymouth in all save longevity.

Moreover, Bradford and his assistants had determined that they could no longer restrain settlement of Cape Cod. The Indians were docile, the patents secure, and the people already moving there of their own will. The towns of Sandwich, Barnstable, and Yarmouth were founded around the first parishes. Then a ten-mile stretch was reserved for those like Ezra Bigelow, who had assumed the colony's debts to the London Adventurers. This was known as the Old Comers'

Tract, and within its boundaries was the island that Jack Hilyard had coveted but Ezra Bigelow had claimed.

By 1644, the fortunes of Plymouth had sunk so low and the population had dwindled so far that there was talk of moving the First Church itself to the fertile plains of Nauset. Though the idea was deemed too radical to carry out, enough of the newer generation left that Bradford was moved to call Plymouth "an ancient mother, grown old and forsaken of her children."

Nevertheless, to do business with the colony, men still paid their respects to the ancient mother, and two priests paid theirs at the home of the governor.

Extra logs made the fire blaze on Bradford's hearth on the night that the priests arrived. Whale oil lanterns were lit instead of rush candles. An Araby rug was laid upon the table. The governor's pewter and Venetian glassware were brought out. And he wore his finest red cloak and waistcoat.

As it was a Friday, Mrs. Bradford served striped bass, the nut-sweet staple of late fall. Ordinarily the good Protestants of Plymouth made special effort to eat meat on Fridays, having no use for the superstitions of Romanism, but they always showed respect to men of faith.

And when the meal was finished, Bradford brought out one of his small treasures, a bottle of brandy given him by Governor John Winthrop of the Massachusetts Bay Colony. Jack Hilyard had not tasted brandy in many a year. Had Father Druillettes not insisted that his rescuer join the feast, Jack would not have tasted it on this night, either.

Seated with Bradford were the proprietors of the Kennebec Trading Post, William Paddy, Thomas Prence, Thomas Willett, and John Winslow. Myles Standish was there to lend his opinion on military matters. And the long, pinched face of Governor's Assistant Ezra Bigelow glowered across the table at Jack.

Bradford and Standish were now graybeards, worn down by time and the cares of the colony. Merely to look at them made Jack feel like a stubborn old fool for shore whaling at the age of sixty.

But Ezra had aged little, perhaps because he did not take a wife until he was forty, perhaps because his life had been, in most things, a success. He had fathered two daughters and two sons, prospered in farming and trade, kept to his faith and kept others to it as well. And if he carried some dark secret from the days of the *Mayflower*, it did not show. His hair was chimney-black, and the more colorful clothes he now wore considerably softened his aspect. But his talk with Jack began sharply. "Hast thou trespassed upon my island of late?"

"I'd not touch it with me longest harpoon."

"I know thou covet it, but my Indian tenants keep good eye there."

"Good prayin' Indians they are," said Jack.

"Aye, who hear the preachments of my brother Simeon. Others on Cape Cod still resist. I disdain congress with such heathens till they be converted."

Jack knew the intent of this remark. He wondered what Bigelow might say, should he learn that one of the "men" in his whaleboat was a woman.

Their pleasantries were interrupted when John Winslow rose to introduce the guests. "Gentlemen of Plymouth, I have come to know Father Gabriel Druillettes as a good man and true. He well deserves the name by which he is known through all Acadia—the Patriarch."

Father Druillettes gave a little bow. Though it was said that he worked as hard as any man in the French missions, neither his round belly, his somnolent eyes, nor the new black cloak he wore over his cassock suggested privation. And he conducted himself with diplomatic grace, even among men whom tradition had made enemies of his nation and his faith.

"The Jesuits," continued Winslow, "have undertaken to bring Christ to the Abenakis on the Kennebec. We must approve."

"Indeed," said William Bradford.

"Aye," added Ezra Bigelow. "Knowledge of Christ from the papist is better than no knowledge at all."

Whatever the priests had come for, thought Jack, they would not get it from Bigelow, unless it was the *book* they had brought in that metal box on the sideboard. All through the meal he had tried to keep his mind off the things the book might contain. But for twenty-seven years, he had wondered.

After introductory compliments, the priest begged permission for the Jesuits to continue missionary work near the Kennebec trading house.

"And if we say nay?" asked Myles Standish.

Ezra Bigelow tugged thoughtfully at one of his eyebrows. "Perhaps you will send ships from Acadia and seize our Kennebec house, as you did the house at Penobscot."

"*Excusez-moi, mais* . . . but that is fifteen years ago," answered Father Druillettes, "and the *jésuites*, we 'ad no part of it."

"Yet we did never regain our post at Penobscot," said Standish.

"Good gentlemen!" John Winslow jumped up once more. "Father Druillettes is interested in the Christ we worship, not the commerce we pursue."

"He is a papist." Bigelow waved his bony hand, as if that was enough explanation.

"We have not come together to argue theology," snapped Bradford. "We have grievance 'gainst the French over the Penobscot, but if French priests would teach the Word to the Abenakis, and we have not the ministers to Protestantize them, it is meet for us to give our assent."

"*Merci*, M'sieur le Gouverneur." The priest bowed. "We interest also in *une entente* . . . an alliance. We bring, as you say, the Word to the Abenakis, but west of them are the Iroquois, who 'ave the devil for a god."

To Father Daladier, these words were like the ringing of the bells in the papist mass. He raised his hands, spread the six fingers and four stumps, and showed them around as though showing the holy host. Then he placed his hands on the table and folded what fingers were left.

"The Iroquois pull out all his nail, then cut off the finger which are consecrated to 'old the sacred bread."

"Blasphemy," whispered William Bradford.

"Amen." Jack Hilyard finished his brandy with a slurp, but the governor did not refill his glass.

"Others the Iroquois crucify. They make fire 'round the cross, and as the priest watch the flames burn them, the savage cut off their cooked flesh and eat of it. This they call Iroquois communion."

"God have mercy," whispered Bradford.

"Bloody heathens," said Standish.

Father Druillettes let the story hang a moment in the air. "In Baston, and now 'ere in Pleymout, I ask for 'elp of good Christians to put down these 'eathens."

"Mon-seur Droo-lay," said Bigelow. "Our colony is not threatened by the Iroquois. Neither is the only trading post we have left in Maine. What vantage is there to help the French in anything?"

"Much good will come, m'sieur." Druillettes waved a hand at Father Daladier, who stood and went toward the sideboard.

Jack Hilyard took the brandy bottle and poured himself more in spite of Bradford's scowl. He drank it down quickly and waited for the revelation. But it did not come.

Instead, Ezra Bigelow stood and smacked his hands on the table. "I see *no* good from an alliance with the French. War is usually more imminent with them than with anyone else. Better to make our alliance with the Iroquois against the French papists."

Father Druillettes' face flushed as red as Bradford's waistcoat. He raised his hand, and Father Daladier stopped in his tracks. "M'sieur le Gouverneur, is this your belief?"

"You must forgive Master Bigelow. He speaks harshly."

"*Et l'entente?*"

"What did Boston say?" demanded Bigelow.

"That the Kennebec is yours, so the decision is yours."

"Let us think upon it," said Bradford.

"*Très bien,*" said the priest. "*Et merci. Maintenant, excusez-nous.*" He folded his hands before him and left with Father Daladier and the box close behind.

Jack grinned at Ezra. "Still makin' friends wherever you goes."

iii.

Father Jacques Daladier had withstood Iroquois torture, but he could not withstand Jack Hilyard's curiosity.

Jack and the priest spent the night on cornhusk mattresses in the great room of William Paddy's home. Father Druillettes retired to a feather bed on the second floor, while Jack's crew slept in the barn, well cheered by the beer he had brought them. It was a crime to give beer to Indians, but a small offense, thought Jack, when one of the Indians was a woman who slept at the side of a white man. Jack also brought a bucket of beer into the house. He mixed it with whaling stories and a bit of sympathy for a lonely Jesuit's fingers, and led the talk toward the metal box.

Father Daladier had to grip the mug between his palms because he had no thumbs. "The beer, it is good. Most time I drink water."

"Terrible stuff." Jack spoke in a low voice, so as not to awaken anyone else. "We run low on beer and had to drink water the first winter. When it come spring, half of us was dead, me dear first wife amongst 'em. There's plenty that think 'twas the water what done it."

The priest licked the foam from his mustache. "The water, it is not good for any man."

Jack stared into the fire. "Them was hard days."

"That is what the Capuchins tell us."

"The who?"

"The missionaries of Port Royal *en Acadie. Quand ils . . . Ex-cusez-moi, mais mon anglais, n'est pas bien, et . . .*"

Jack couldn't speak French, but he sensed that the priest was starting to feel the beer. He poured a little more. "These Ca-poo-chins, how'd they know 'bout us?"

"*Ils l'ont lu . . .* er, they read in a book."

Somewhere in the house, someone was snoring. Jack could feel the vibration in his chair. He took a deep breath and said softly, "What book?"

"The book we bring in the iron box. *Les capucins,* when they 'ear that the Patriarch comes to Pleymout, they say, give this book if it will make *une entente.*"

Jack Hilyard studied the firelight in the priest's glassy eyes. "What is this book?"

"The journal by the master of the ship that brought them."

"Christopher Jones?"

"*Je ne sais pas.* I do not seen the book. I know only that it tell the story of great dying and great faith. We think to give it to the men of Pleymout this night, but M'sieur Bigelow—" Daladier shrugged and slid his mug across the table for more beer.

Jack gave up the last of his own. "Bigelow spoilt the gift-givin'?"

"We are friends with Winslow, but this Bigelow is no friend with us. Père Druillettes say 'e wait for *une entente,* armed men in the field 'gainst the Iroquois, before 'e give the gift. Until then, *pas de mot.*" He pressed his fingers to his lips, in the universal gesture for silence, and seemed startled that the index fingers were not there.

"The book goes back to Port Royal, then?"

The priest nodded.

"Would the Patriarch let a ignorant whaler read it?"

"No. It is a secret."

"Well, how'd the Ca-poo-chins get it, then?"

"I tell too much already, but that is the part *plus intéressant.*"

That night, Jack Hilyard slept by the fire, and as he drifted to sleep, the story of the book's journey entered his dreams. The orange glow of the fire still danced before his eyes. Out of it came five Indians. They called him Weston Bloody Christian and ordered him to give over the box. He tried to protect it, but they tore it from him and pulled it open, and out dropped the book.

The fire burned brighter and he felt greater heat. In his sleep, he kicked off his blanket. The Indians were holding him over the flames with the book in his arms. One of the Indians was speaking in his own tongue, but Jack understood.

"Do not burn the book. The black robes say that God is in books. They read from books, then kiss them and hold them up to the sky. When they make their God from bread, they see how to do it from the book. We will give this to the black-robe priests to please them."

The Indians took the book from Jack's arms, then threw him into the fire. He awoke with a shout, covered in sweat. The fire was burning down, the flames glimmering weakly on the great room walls. He reached for Elizabeth . . . or Kate, as he did each night, but a priest with mangled hands was snoring beside him, so he pulled up his blanket and slipped back to his dream.

A candle glimmered on the chapel walls. With a hand pierced by nail holes, a priest turned the pages of the master's journal. "The Indians bring it to one of our outposts to gain favor. The missionaries send it here to Port Royal. But it is useless." He slid the book across a table, and Jack picked it up.

"Useless to the French," whispered Kate, and her face became that of Elizabeth, "useless to the French, but for us, it do buy Nauseiput."

iv.

Four years later, Port Royal lay quiet in the cool August sun. Cattle grazed in the fields. Smoke from cookfires curled into the sky. And the river ran like a ribbon of blue down from the green hills.

"Somewhere in that town," whispered Jack, "be the metal box that hold the key to our future."

"I came for no metal box," said Jonathan. "What we do we do for the colony. 'Twill never be forgot."

"What we do we do for ourselves," grumbled Christopher.

"Find the Capuchins and there be the box," whispered Jack to Christopher.

"All you Massachusetts men," cried the English sergeant, "into the boats!"

"Forget not the Plymouth men!" added Robinson Bigelow, eldest son of Ezra.

"Right well call yourselves *king's* men. Into the boat!"

On the poop deck of the *Augustine,* the drumbeat began. A moment later, it was taken up on the *Hope* and the *Church.* On the distant hills, the cattle began to run. On the fortress walls, men began to scurry. And down the valley rang the frightened sound of church bells on a Wednesday morning.

Christopher Hilyard felt in his own gut the pounding terror that the drums were meant to drive into the people of Port Royal. He had no fear of whales, angry elders, or Cape Cod Indians, but he had not been made for war.

Three sudden clouds of smoke shot up and out from the fortress walls. The thundering crump of three cannon pounded against the drumbeat in Christopher's belly. Three columns of water rose around the *Hope.*

"Pay no mind," called Major General Sedgwick from the poop deck. "God will let no cannonball strike us."

"Lest we be fool enough to get in range," whispered Jack.

"Sedgwick speaks true," chided Jonathan. "God protects the righteous."

"Then for certain he'll show *us* no quarter," said Christopher.

Ezra Bigelow had been a prophet, after all. Whenever the struggle for faith and empire flared in the New World, England and France were no allies. The men of Plymouth had supported Father Druillettes, had even convened the United Colonies in New Haven to hear him present his case. But no English army had taken the field against the Iroquois. And now an English army was moving against the French.

It had begun in disagreement between England and the Protestants of Holland. They had gone to war over trade, which, as Thomas Weston once said, mattered more to nations than faith. Lord Protector Cromwell, seeking to carry the conflict to the New World, had commissioned Boston Puritan Robert Sedgwick to raise an expedition against the Dutch at New Amsterdam and had sent seventy

Roundhead troops, veterans of Naseby and the Irish Wars, to stand with the Colonial volunteers.

Robinson Bigelow, a student at Harvard College, brought the call to Plymouth. Like his father, he believed that the future of Plymouth rested in the hands of the more powerful Massachusetts Bay Colony, and thus was it in Plymouth's interest to join the expedition. But the men of the Plymouth Colony had known only good dealings with the Dutch, and only a few volunteered, among them Cape Cod militia captain Jonathan Hilyard.

Then, just before the English flotilla left Boston, word arrived that the Dutch had sued for peace. And there sat Sedgwick, with three ships and a hundred and thirty men, yearning to fight for lord protector and country. In such circumstances, what would any good Englishman do but turn on the French?

To entice more Plymouth men, young Bigelow sent word that they were now attacking Saint John, Port Royal, and the Penobscot trading post that the French had stolen from Plymouth twenty years before. When the name of Port Royal was heard at Billingsgate, the Hilyards became Cromwellians and Jack the oldest volunteer in the army.

Now Christopher feared that he might vomit. With each thundering shot from the fortress walls, the knot in his throat nearly unraveled onto the men clambering ahead of him into the longboat. But he held on. Foul the helmet of one of Cromwell's Roundheads and find yourself on the end of his pike.

They landed beyond range of the guns and fanned out on the coastal plain below the fortress. By noon, the siege was neatly laid. And for the rest of the day, people from the village and the surrounding countryside streamed toward the gates, their children and livestock in tow. And for the rest of the day, the Hilyards studied the spired building that rose to the right of the fort.

The Capuchins had erected a church and seminary at Port Royal, and it would seem that they were not about to leave it to the English.

"They think God'll pertect 'em," Jack said to Christopher as they ate an afternoon meal of salt meat, hardtack, and beer, "so they're staying close to their house."

"'Tis them bloody guns'll do the pertectin'."

All day, the French had kept up the artillery fire, as much to show the abundance of their munition as their displeasure.

"We needs to get into that church, fortress be damned."

"It be scarifyin' work, Pa."

"Don't be losin' thy spine after all these years. Nauseiput be *our* island. *Ourn* from the time of the First Comin'. And this be the way to get it."

"It do us no good if we be dead."

"Before *I* die, I'll bring me sons to Nauseiput. 'Tis me dream. I be old, but thou and Jon—"

"I be forty-six."

"Younger 'n me, and in need of that master's journal."

"I never needed it yet." Christopher tore a piece of salt meat with his teeth and tried to swallow it.

"Had I that log twenty-odd years ago, no Bigelow would've broke up our family and set us to wanderin'. Wif your taste for Injun women, you need a weapon 'gainst that man. So screw up the courage in that big gut of yours and think on the future."

"The future." Christopher managed to swallow the meat. "Aye."

They told Jonathan nothing of the plan they made, for he would not have understood. He had no love of Nauseiput, nor any hatred of Ezra Bigelow. He was merely a brave Protestant answering the call of Cromwell, bravest Protestant of them all.

Around four hours after noon the doors of the fortress swung open and out marched a hundred and twenty men. Though the French had supplies to last five months, they did not choose besiegement. Better to end the engagement quickly than suffer Englishmen or hunger for too long.

In the camp, the drums began to beat and the men formed their ranks.

Christopher Hilyard moved into position behind his father. He was no child to be taken by dreams of battlefield glory, no veteran of the Civil War carrying the banner of Protestantism. His goal was simpler. From the day that he first saw the Scusset Indians riding their canoe toward dusk, he had dreamed only of being like them. From the day that he saw Witawawmut's head, he had dreamed only of peace.

To gain the island where he had known his happiest moments, he had joined this little war. He longed, as much as his father, to live on Nauseiput. And for Nauseiput he would conquer his fear. He swallowed the knot in his throat and shambled off, eyes fixed on his father's skinny back, hand around the stock of his gun.

A mixed company of Massachusetts and Plymouth men had been given the right flank. Massachusetts men held the left. And in the van, separated from the flanking Colonials by twenty yards, were the red and blue tunics, the fierce helmets, and the pikes of Cromwell's soldiers.

To a European general on a hilltop, this engagement might have seemed like poor men's war indeed. A few pennants fluttered in the sun. A handful of English advanced toward a line of fewer French. A tiny fortress, surrounded by rude dwellings, sputtering smoke and shot like an angry old man, stood the prize. And the vast Acadian wilderness paid no mind to any of it.

But for the men in the lines, who heard the thundering cannon, felt the ground shake with each shot, saw the enemy through a curtain of dirt and smoke, a few minutes of bravery and chance would determine their fates.

As he advanced across the grass, Christopher felt his wampum necklace tighten around his throat. He watched the sack at his father's belt swing in rhythm with his gait. He listened to his holy brother Jonathan sing the Twenty-third Psalm like a song, while Robinson Bigelow kept up a brave line of talk for them all. And none of it made him feel any the braver.

Then the French stopped. They dug their rests into the ground and mounted their muskets, which caused some of the green Colonials to hesitate, a few to fall back. But the Roundheads kept up their thudding step, and the sergeant who commanded them shouted to the flanks, "Run now and let their cannon shred you. Close with 'em and watch 'em fly."

"Aye!" cried Robinson Bigelow. "Show your courage or leave the field to men!"

"Give 'em good Protestant fire," added Jonathan Hilyard. "And remember what these bloody French say. The English may best the Dutch at sea, but one Frenchman's match for ten English on land."

"We'll not brook *that*!" shouted Jack Hilyard from the column, as though he truly believed it.

"Run that lie down their gullets!" cried Jonathan.

Jack dropped back and whispered to Christopher. "I sometimes marvel that he be me son."

"Or my brother."

"Remember, no matter what be said, when the volleyin' start, we see fire comin' down from that church."

"Aye," grunted Christopher.

"Halt!" The sergeant had not taken off his helmet all day, and in the heat, his face looked to have been cooked to the metal like beef to a grate.

His disciplined Roundheads ceased their advance, and the Colonials did likewise.

Now the artillery quit. A gentle wind drifted across the plain and blew the smoke off toward the ships. The field grew quiet. The soldiers had drawn close enough to settle the issue themselves. Though their muskets were not accurate weapons, when many were fired at once, a great gust of lead was blown toward the enemy. Thus were men grouped tightly to kill and be killed.

The English sergeant ordered the flanks to fix rests.

And the French sergeant ordered his men to fire. But of the fifty French weapons fired, at least forty were poorly sighted, aimed by shaking hands, or improperly powdered, so that only four shots reached the English.

God, fate, or a French marksman chose Robinson Bigelow as one of the four. His beaklike nose, which had earned him the name Honker, was blown apart. He dropped his cutlass, spun about, and came stumbling toward Christopher.

Now the English sergeant gave the word. A thunderous volley echoed from the flanks. But Christopher did not hear it. His eyes were fixed on Robinson, who held his hands to his face, as if to hold back the blood welling like springwater through his fingers. "Robby, lad—"

Now the English sergeant ordered the charge, and his regulars lowered their pikes. But Christopher put his arms around Robinson Bigelow and tried to lower him to the ground while all about him he felt the nervous scuttling of leaderless militiamen, men seeing the effect of French gun on English flesh for the first time.

Robinson Bigelow's eyes were the eyes of a cow the moment after the butcher had slit its throat. Where the ball had embedded itself, the blood bubbled up unstanched. He opened his mouth to call the charge, but first poured out blood from the shattered bone behind the nose, then strange, squashed sounds from a voice that no longer had an upper cavity to give echo. He spun away from Christopher, staggered against someone else, and fell face-forward into the grass.

Jonathan Hilyard drew his cutlass and tried to take command

of the right flank. "C'mon, lads. Let's show 'em what good Protestants can do."

Most did nothing but mill about.

Only the Roundheads were closing, with their pikes pointed and their voices bellowing a fierce animal roar.

The French were no more disciplined than the New England volunteers. While their first rank attempted to clear and reload, the second rank stumbled forward in undrilled haste. They presented their weapons. They took aim. And the pikes of the English professionals struck.

Now Jack Hilyard shouted, "What's that just come from that house over there? Smoke?"

Christopher was supposed to answer, but he was cradling Robinson Bigelow in his arms and trying not to vomit.

"Act like men!" Jonathan came back among them. "Others gain all the glory."

"Let others die," said Christopher.

Jonathan whacked his brother with the side of his cutlass. "Bloody coward! Avenge Robby Bigelow 'stead of losin' thy stomach."

"But, Jonathan," screamed Jack Hilyard, "up there, they be shootin' at us!"

The smoke was thick enough that none could dispute what Jack said. The French might have been firing from every house on the flanks of the fort. In truth, there was no fire. The Roundheads had driven into the center of the French, breaking their line and their spirit like rotten staves.

Jack knelt beside Christopher and shouted, "They're *firin'* on us from that house, son. I say teach 'em a lesson."

Christopher looked at Robinson Bigelow. "He needs help."

"He's beyond help," shouted Jonathan. "Now get up and help yourself . . . and your company."

"If your own brother won't join the fight," said a Massachusetts man, "don't expect us to do for you."

Jack grabbed Jonathan by the arm. "I just seen more smoke from that house." He pointed to the church. "Let's take a handful of men and bring a bit of glory to Cape Cod!"

"I attack the center. Attack what you will." Jonathan stepped over the writhing blood spring of Robinson Bigelow and led a dozen of the bravest at the French line.

Jack led a dozen of the most cautious toward the spire.

"*Arrêtez-vous!*" The wizened little friar stood blinking in the bright sunlight when the door came smashing into his hallway.

"Where be your guns?"

"*C'est une église, un sanctuaire. Allez-vous-en.*"

"Your guns? *Vo-tra fu-sils?*"

"*Fusils? Nous sommes prêtres. Nous n'avons pas de fusils.*"

"These be priests!" said one of the Massachusetts men.

"I seen *guns*," insisted Jack. He also saw a great refectory to the left and a library to the right.

He ordered three men upstairs, two more into the refectory, and he shoved his son into the library. All through the house could be heard the pounding of heavy New England boots and the angry chattering of the French priests. The angriest of all was the one who stood at the door and now followed Jack and his son.

"*Vo-tra fu-sils?*" demanded Jack again, and he swept a pile of books off a shelf.

The priest screamed and jumped at Jack, who slammed him against the doorjamb.

"Father!" cried Christopher. "We be Christians."

"We be fightin' for our future, lad, so take that frighted look from your face and help out."

Jack swept through another shelf of books, of saints' lives, of Thomas Aquinas, of Franciscan philosophy. All crashed to the floor, and the priest jumped at Jack again.

Jack pushed him at his son. "Hold the little pest, or thou won't ever dig clams on Nauseiput."

Christopher Hilyard threw his arms around the priest and drew him to his breast, as if to protect him. Blood trickled from the priest's shaved pate down into the little white fringe of the tonsure.

Christopher thought, Enough blood. I have seen enough blood for a lifetime.

Then came the crash of another shelf, a muffled cry of excitement, and Jack said, "Now!"

Christopher spun the priest toward the window and the view of the battle, which had turned to a rout. The priest tried to pull away, but Christopher was near twice his size, and for all they had gone through, he would not let his part in the plan fail.

"Look, little priest. Look at what fools we be, we French and English."

"*Mère de Dieu,*" muttered the priest at the sight.

Then Christopher held up the hand still covered with Robinson Bigelow's blood. "Look at what Christians can do to each other."

"*Mère de Dieu.*"

Jack slipped an iron box from the sack on his belt. It was sealed with wax and contained a captain's journal that Jack had bought in Boston. Its pages were blank. This he dropped into the mess of papist books on the floor. Then he knelt and touched his dream, while Christopher tried to wipe the blood from his hand.

CHAPTER 13

July 9

Old Comers and New Buyers

Never mind the name. How in the hell did Jack Hilyard ever get his *hands* on this place? That's what Janice wanted to know.

At Radcliffe, she had written her undergraduate History thesis on Cape Cod land grants, and she knew that Jack's Island had been part of the Old Comers' land, a tract that included present-day Brewster, Harwich, and Orleans.

Old Comers. Even in the seventeenth century, they distinguished between the ones who got their fence posts in first and all the rest. Before anyone called them Pilgrims, all of the first settlers were called Old Comers and sometimes First Comers. But the Old Comers who paid off the colony's debts were a special group whose service had earned them control over a vast stretch of Cape Cod. They were revered men. Little was known of Jack Hilyard, except that he wasn't one of them.

"It may be," she had written, "that he earned this island because of service in the trading posts, though he had already been given a tract on Billingsgate Island. It may be that he was allowed to purchase the island after his family fought at Port Royal in August 1654. Jonathan Hilyard is singled out for bravery in the only eyewitness account of the battle. According to Plymouth records, the sale from

Ezra Bigelow to Jack Hilyard occurred soon after. The two events may be related."

Maybe, maybe not. What was important now was how in the hell to get the whole island *back* so that they could put it to work.

To reach the sailing camp, she took the east road through pitch pine woods, past the campers' army-surplus barracks, and she wondered how a few dozen well-sited, well-designed houses could do anything but improve this.

Rake Hilyard said they couldn't, and Geoff no longer seemed to be sure. But Hilyard men were dreamers. Hilyard women were different. Cousin Emily ran the sailing camp and liked the Bigelow deal. Her mother Clara was one of the oldest of the Old Comers, and even if she had sided with Rake, she was someone you could reason with.

The main house was a classic turn-of-the-century ark, with high peaks and gables and great rambling porches. Perfect for a sales office.

A dozen students were draped on the veranda. Some looked like homesicks waiting for parents. A few were brandishing fiberglass bows and arrows. And one little kid was sitting on a step, scratching at the runniest case of poison ivy Janice had ever seen. But what self-respecting kid would care about poison ivy when he had sailboats, the tennis court, the archery range around him?

In the big rooms downstairs, voices echoed and phones rang and hundreds of sandy bare feet wore the wax off the floor. Even in its last season, the business of the sailing camp went on. But upstairs, where the family lived, the rooms were quiet and the floors were still shiny.

The wheelchair pivoted at the sound of Janice's knock. "What? Who is it?" Clara's eyes were failing. Most of the time, she kept them turned to the sea.

"It's me, Janice."

"Who?" The old lady wet her lower lip with her tongue.

"Janice. Geoff's wife." She came closer.

The rheumy old eyes examined her, the hanging lip tightened into a bit of a smile.

"How are you?"

"Rotten." That was what she always said. "Arthritis so bad it's like havin' baseballs for joints. Hemorrhoids so bad it's like havin' fireballs in my—"

Janice gave her a little box of chocolates.

"Soft centers?"

"Of course."

"Can't chew 'em otherwise. Can't chew. Can't walk. Sometimes can't even breathe." She pointed to the oxygen tank in the corner.

Janice noticed the smell of urine, something new in Clara's decline, and sadly pervasive.

Janice tried to remember the Clara who kept two dozen lobster pots in the bay, just for fun, and could knock back highballs like a fisherman. It hurt to look for her in this old shell, but Janice tried, because Geoff's aunt had been the first Hilyard to treat her like family.

"Has Rake talked to you lately?" asked Janice.

"The only one who does . . . *talk* I mean. Everyone else sounds like they think I'm their dog. 'Do you want your supper? Do you want to go for a walk?' Rake *says* things."

"Has he talked about what you might do if you lose at town meeting?"

Clara narrowed her eyes, and the lower lip worked back and forth several times. "You got a pen and some paper?"

Janice looked around the room.

"You won't find 'em here. That bastard of a son-in-law of mine took 'em all away."

Janice dug into her bag and pulled out a little notebook and a plastic Bic with the cap chewed off.

The old lady snatched them and opened the notebook on her wheelchair tray. Then she fitted the pen between her fingers and wetted her lower lip with her tongue.

"What are you going to write?"

"A new will." She lifted her hand onto the paper and tried to move the pen. Her fingers were so arthritic that she looked as if she were trying to push a giant piece of thread into the eye of an invisible needle. A few wavering words took shape: "I, Clara Hilyard Hartwig . . ."

"Can I help?" Janice gently slipped the pen from the ancient fingers.

"Put down that I am cutting Arnie and Emily out. If the town won't take our land at the town meeting, I'll *give* it to them for conservation."

Janice's hand froze. "Clara . . . have you talked this over with anybody?"

"No. And if you won't write it, give it back."

Janice held on to the pen and paper.

"Come to think of it, Emily and Arnie want to sell to your old *man.*" Clara snatched the notebook back. "Why did you come here, anyway?"

"To see how you were."

"You came to sweet-talk me, just like Emily and Arnie. I always thought you came 'cause you liked me." Clara handed back her chocolates. "I thought you were a better person."

That hurt, but here was Janice, scuffling around with chocolate boxes, hoping to persuade Clara to do something she had resisted all her life, simply because they couldn't wait for her to die.

The truth, beyond what was said on the glorious Fourth, was that the Bigelows were in a cash crunch and had to start development soon to get out of it. Janice's brother had told her in the office that morning. She suspected there was more, that her brother was the cause of the crunch, and when she pressed him, he wasn't too clear about how he planned to get them out of it. She didn't trust Douglas much. Nobody had trusted him much since he'd divorced his first wife and started slicking back his hair.

But when it came to talk, Douglas was still a pro, and he knew exactly what to tell his sister. He begged her to trust him and swore her to secrecy . . . for Dad. Dad knew they were in trouble, but he had been in the hospital when the worst of it came in, and Douglas had done what was necessary to rescue them. "If we go down, the old man will die," he had said. For Janice, there was no more convincing argument. So however badly she felt, she had come to do more than just visit old Clara.

Maybe she would start by humoring the old lady. So she took back the notebook, tore off the top sheet, and dropped it on the wheelchair tray. Then she wrote out the will and read it back, just to show Clara how impractical it sounded.

"If the townspeople are too cheap to buy the place," she asked, "why just *give* it to them?"

Clara just held out her hands until Janice gave her the notebook. She signed it. Then she sat back and smiled. "Why? Because my daughter married a son of a bitch and turned into a bitch herself."

Right on cue, Arnie Burr appeared in the doorway, wearing a sheaf of arrows and holding a fiberglass bow. "A visitor, Clara?"

"Yeah, you plannin' to shoot her?"

"I should, for tellin' us we could survey land when we couldn't."

Arnie shot a little arrow of a look at Janice. "But I'm teachin' the camp archery lesson today."

Clara talked to Janice, as though Arnie weren't there. "He can't get business on his charter boats, and there's nothin' to survey until Rake and me die, so he gets himself up like a half-assed Cupid and teaches camp kids how to shoot arrows into each other."

"What's on that paper, Clara?" asked Arnie.

The old lady grabbed the sheet from the tray and tried to stuff it into her dress.

But Arnie snatched it away. " 'I, Clara Hilyard Hartwig . . .' We told you, Clara, if you want a lawyer, just ask us."

"Lie." She looked at Janice, "I wrote a will and they found it under my mattress and took it away from me."

Arnie shoved the paper into his pocket. "Clara, we don't want you doing something you might regret."

"I regret that my daughter married *you*."

"We love her, Janice, but she's stubborn." He snapped the bowstring, as if he was itchy to use it.

"We all love her, and we want her to be happy." Janice gave Clara a kiss on the forehead, and Clara looked at her like a dog that knew it was being put to sleep. Janice scurried out like the dog's owner. What Clara, with her terrible eyesight, did not know was that she had grabbed the first sheet of paper, which showed only her own scrawl.

Her signed bequest was in the notebook that was now in Janice's purse. But it couldn't be legal, could it? Janice almost didn't want to know.

ii.

Rake Hilyard sat at his dining room table. He had his telephone, his typewriter, his scratch pad, and all the papers and articles he had collected over the years . . . on just about everything that had interested him.

He called it his office. His niece Emily called it a firetrap. Rake guessed she said that so that some night her husband could burn the place down.

It was ten-thirty in the morning, and he had already made forty phone calls to remind people about the town meeting. His ear felt like a piece of pounded veal. But if the taxpayers would take the island, the Bigelows could be stopped from ripping it to pieces.

He took his breakfast plate out to the kitchen and threw it into the sink. Egg yolk had dried on his fork and his chin. He had lived to be ninety and ate an egg every day, damn the doctors. He smoked, too, damn them all.

Helluva thing that a man had to petition a town meeting because he couldn't trust his own family. But there it was. Even Geoff and his Bigelow wife wanted to develop the island.

And a helluva thing how it all seemed to start at once, noises about Bigelow trouble with the banks, then the talk that it was time to develop the gem of Bigelow properties, Jack's Island, then the appearance of the 1904 subdivision that might allow the development to proceed whether the town objected or not, then the visit from that Carolyn Hallissey. More than funny.

He slipped the list from his pocket. After Carolyn Hallissey's visit, he had written down everything he had ever heard or wondered about the log. He thought that if he looked at the black and white for long enough, like a scientist studying results, he'd be sure to see connections.

While he reheated a cup of coffee in a saucepan, he thought of a good hiding place for the list. He should protect it, because it might be the treasure map for millions of dollars. And there was something in that log that had scared Dickerson Bigelow's grandfather to death in 1911. Rake remembered. It had to do with the painting Carolyn Hallissey had bought a few days before.

He wrote "*Murder on the Mayflower* by Tom Hilyard" at the bottom of the list. Then he heard a sound.

Out front? Now on the side. Now in the back.

He had been waiting for this. He had suspected for some time that somebody was watching him.

Hide the list. He went up the stairs to the picture on the landing. That would be a good place. Right there, inside the backing. Then he went up the rest of the way to the bedroom and grabbed what he called his security blanket, a pump-action shotgun.

He wasn't surprised that they—whoever *they* were—had finally decided to break in this morning. Rake had driven off at seven o'clock to have his car serviced. Then he had walked the two miles back with the Cape Cod *Times* and a quart of milk under his arm. Which meant there was no car in his driveway and the place looked deserted.

And the damn jogger, the one who'd been running by every day for the last two weeks, was snooping in the backyard. Cute disguise, that jogging suit. Let someone put on a pair of silk shorts and some astronaut shoes, and he looked as innocent as a kid hunting for a lost dog. Rake had been around long enough to know that nothing was innocent.

"Hello?" The jogger was at the back door now, calling into the house. He was about twenty-eight, blond, and bland enough to be some graduate student waiting on tables at night so that he could go to the beach during the day. A bead of sweat dripped off the tip of his nose.

And a shotgun pressed against the back of his neck.

Rake couldn't tell if that was sweat or something else he saw running down the guy's leg a moment later.

The jogger said he'd sprained his ankle and wanted to use the phone. Rake said he wasn't born yesterday and told him to go use a Bigelow phone. The jogger limped off, muttering about a crazy old man. The limp sure looked real, but you couldn't be too careful.

iii.

Geoff Hilyard sat beneath the skylight in his studio. He had resolved to work, but his mind kept wandering to the Brewster town meeting that night.

Rake and Clara were offering their land, provided that the town would acquire the rest of the island for conservation. Probable cost, six million. Nobody thought the article would pass. The Board of Selectmen opposed it. So did the Finance Committee. But Rake had gotten the signatures to put it on the warrant, so the meeting was called.

If the article passed, Geoff would be off the hook, and well paid for any land the town took. But he would lose the commission, the chance to do something big. But he loved the island. But the money and prestige from a big commission . . . It had been like that all morning, a leapfrogging game of contradictions playing inside his head.

He had an old topographical map of the island pinned to the wall above his drafting table, along with photographs he had taken of the high-peaked Aptucxet replica, the 1793 house where Rake lived, and the barn behind it.

He often found that sketching something old gave him new ideas. He used a 2b pencil on yellow trace. It felt familiar in his hand. And it felt good to be in his office, in the loft of the barn behind his Truro house, right beneath the skylight where he worked best. Janice was right. This was was what he should be doing instead of treasure hunting.

He drew Rake's house from several angles. Nothing came. He studied the deep slope of the Aptucxet roof. Did the first Jack's Island house look like that, or was it the more conventional saltbox? And what of the barn? It was said that Quakers met there in the days of the persecutions. He drew it.

By the mere act of drawing, he was taking another step toward taking the job, toward wanting it.

"Traitor," a voice whispered up behind him, and Geoff spun about with his 2b pencil like a knife in his hand.

George's fleshy face was grinning at him.

"For a big guy, you move quiet."

George slapped his belly. "I'm losin' weight, remember. You start pushin' forty, you have to toughen up. Otherwise, the young ones won't look at you."

"You ought to find someone to settle down with. It's dangerous out there."

"Tell me about it." George looked over Geoff's shoulder. "I brought my metal detector."

"Metal detector? You're kidding."

"No. You'd be amazed at the conversations you can start. We could walk the beach, pretend we're looking for the metal clasp of the *Mayflower* logbook. Maybe we could both make a friend. We'll find you a girl."

"I don't need any more friends right now. And Jimmy's right. The log's just an old legend." Geoff began to sketch the barn.

"Jimmy's a tight-ass, in the figurative sense, of course. Ever since his tribe lost the Mashpee land suit, he's gotten whiter and whiter and tighter and tighter, just buried his anger. He's no fun anymore. Take it from one who knows. You can't hide things."

Geoff sketched in the roofline and drew the door. "So why am I a traitor?"

"You're sketching elevations for that island. And you don't want to do it."

"But I'm an architect." Geoff felt George boring in. He concentrated on the point of the pencil and sketched a door. "Did you know that Quakers used Jack's Island for their worship at the beginning?"

"Now *there* was a group that let it all hang out." George flopped onto the cracked old leather sofa that smelled like the barn. "They said what they thought, did what was right. I read a lot about them when I was younger . . . before I did what was right for me."

"Before you came out?"

George shrugged. "History has metaphors for all of us. The Quakers were treated almost as badly as . . . well, as guys like me."

Geoff drew a bay window on the side of the barn. He thought about the courage of the Quakers, the first faith to challenge the orthodoxy of the Pilgrims. Courage . . . gumption.

These words went together, like Ma Little's conundrum: Who was more courageous? The changers, like Dickerson, or those who resisted change, like Rake?

"Like I said when you were wondering about moving down here"—George locked his hands behind his head and looked up at the ceiling, more like the patient than the doctor—"sometimes you just have to flip the bird to the whole world."

"It's not that simple when you have a family."

"It will be if you find that log."

"Or if I take the Bigelow deal."

Inside the bay window, Geoff drew the heads of four Quakers. A family, doing what they thought was right . . .

CHAPTER 14

October 1660

More True Faiths

"What they do?"

"Sit."

"What else?"

"Nothin'. Just sit, like loggerheads."

Jack Hilyard and Autumnsquam peered through the oiled-paper windows at the people inside the barn.

They sat on benches arranged to form a square. Mostly they were silent, but from time to time, the spirit came upon one who declaimed from Scripture or gave personal witness or spewed criticism of the colony's leaders.

Then Christopher Hilyard would ask, "Who doth not quake at the word of the Lord?"

And the Indian woman at his side would answer, "Only those who love him not."

Those in the barn called this worship, but in the eyes of Plymouth and Massachusetts Bay, it was subversion.

"Bloody Quakers," muttered Jack.

"More true faiths."

"Bad enough they get me own son to join 'em. But now comin' here to hold their foul meetin'. I've a mind to turn 'em out, I do. Chris and his squaw, the bloody lot of 'em."

"He your son, she my niece, even if they both bloody Christians. No turn out."

Jack kicked at the soil and stared out to sea. In the beginning, he had never looked out from this place without feeling the urge to pinch the back of his hand and assure himself he was not dreaming. But after five years, the island was his for certain, and he dreamed only of keeping it.

He had even given it the name in Jones's journal. Jack's Island it was called, and it showed Jack's shaping hand.

A two-story post-and-beam house had risen in the middle of a clearing. Not far from the back door was the well sweep, though Jack rarely drank water. Beyond that lay a huge pile of firewood, for in this land of plenty, he would never be cold again. About twenty feet back of the house, he had built a barn over the root cellar he discovered that first winter. And where once a path had led through oak and beech to the water, an open field now rolled to the tryworks, where oil was rendered from whale blubber and smoke stained the sky like sin upon a clean soul.

As it was the Sabbath, the smoke was sin in truth as well as metaphor.

The trees behind the barn had fed the first trying fires, and tall hardwoods across the island had fallen to keep the fires burning, to keep the oil flowing, to give the people of Plymouth and Boston and London itself the essence of Cape Cod whale, distilled from godlike majesty to a clean, pure beam of light. In Jack's eyes, such work was worthy of any Sabbath.

The colony disagreed. And it seemed that a delegation was coming to make their point. Or perhaps it was the presence of the Quakers that brought them, for nothing had so challenged the colony as this new form of devotion, not even the French.

In either event, a shallop was plowing down from the northwest, riding the incoming tide, and Jack cursed at the sight of it.

"Want put out try fires?" asked Autumnsquam.

"They seen the smoke. No sense actin' afeared of 'em now." He pounded on the door of the barn.

"Our service be not finished," said Christopher from within.

Jack kicked at the door. "'Twill be when that Plymouth boat gets here."

Those words were enough to swing open the barn door and summon forth the soldiers of a new religious rebellion. They neither hurried nor seemed troubled that Colonial officials were coming, perhaps to arrest them. They made their good-byes with cheer and trooped off toward the inland path.

Jack watched them for a time—old Goody Privet, the Smiths and their five children from Eastham, the Stubbses and the Burkitts from Yarmouth—simple people whose lives had a simple center. If they failed to grow their crops, catch their fish, cut their firewood, they died. But when they sought to simplify their faith, they complicated their own lives and confused everyone else's.

"Get thyself home and put on clothes of color," he said to his son.

"Black be good enough."

"It be a badge of defiance," said Jack.

"And who hath been more defiant than thee?"

"I done it quiet. That's why we got this island."

"Quiet defiance, in some places, be called cowardice."

"Stop." Autumnsquam put himself between father and son. "Bad word for son to say to father." He stamped his foot on the ground for emphasis. He was smaller than either of them, scrawnier even than Jack, but he had always commanded their respect, had insisted on it. He could not, however, stop the bad words now.

Jack looked at his son. "I done no grovelin' when the French fired on *me* that day. Nor did thy brother."

"'Twas that day I became a follower of the Gospel of Inward Light, when I saw Robby Bigelow's face shattered because men chose to make war and call it holy. I make war on no man, nor do I grovel for any."

"Instead thou goes to Boston and defies the Puritans like a damn fool." Jack looked at Autumnsquam. "Gets himself banished from the Massachusetts Colony, he does. Gets his ears cut off for good measure."

"White men know good torture. Now know good talk, father, son, both." Autumnsquam whacked a forearm against Jack's chest, then Christopher's. His whales'-tooth bracelet jangled like a shaman's bag of bones. His whales'-tooth necklace, which he wore like a collar, pressed angrily into his flesh. "Good talk. Talk good."

But Jack kept his eyes on his son. "After Boston, he comes back to the Plymouth Colony and invites his Quaker friends to my island for a little Sabbath blasphemy."

"'Tis no blasphemy to follow thy conscience and the Bible, 'stead of ministers and magistrates," said Christopher. "And this island be mine as well as thine. We did terrorize defenseless priests and blackmail a grievin' man to gain it. We each paid a piece of our soul for a bit of freedom. I use mine as I see fit."

Jack glanced again toward the beach. "We'll chew on all this later. Get Amapoo out of sight."

"She be my wife. She stand by my side."

Amapoo cast her eyes toward the ground. She wore a black dress with a white collar and now called herself Patience, but shiny copper pendants still hung from her ears and beaded strings held her long hair in place.

"Then the both of you get out of sight."

Christopher led Patience into the house, though it was Jack's suspicion that they would not be there for long.

"Very sad," said Autumnsquam.

"What?"

"Amapoo and Chris. They learn 'bout Kautantowit. But thee boy turn back to Bloody Christ, and she go with him. Very sad. Bad talk. Bad talk."

"Aye." Jack peered down at the beach, where the shallop had just grounded. "Methinks I see the gray beard of Ezra Bigelow."

The world believed it was grief that turned Ezra Bigelow gray. Jack knew there was another reason.

On the night that the messenger brought the news from Port Royal, Ezra Bigelow cursed God. He went out into the darkness, like Jack Hilyard so many years before, and shook his fist at the heavens. Of all the Englishmen to fight, why had God chosen *his* son, his brilliant boy, flower of his faith, future of his colony, foe of its French enemies, why had God chosen *his* son to be martyred in the grass of Acadia? Robinson had died a true Christian soldier, they said, but still he was dead, and the only one to die.

As the days passed and his hair, strand by strand, began to go gray, Ezra found himself turning to the Bible after all, and he found comfort—in Lamentations, in Job, in the joyous conclusion of Luke. He saw that God, in his own good time, had come around to visiting upon Ezra the pain that few men escaped, and in his own good time, God would bring Ezra and his son together again.

Jack Hilyard came around to visiting Ezra a week later, in his own good time.

Ezra knew of Christopher's kindness to Robinson on the field and thanked Jack. "I understand why Jonathan joined that expedition. But thou and Christopher art neither of thee orthodox men."

"We went for booty. That make us as orthodox as any."

After the French had capitulated, those who wished were allowed to take to their ship. The rest, including the Capuchins, were given "freedom of conscience," though the missionaries lasted little more than a year under English masters. In return, the French were made to yield up more than ten thousand pounds' worth of weapons, skins, and supplies, and every English soldier earned a share.

"Thy portion could not have been great," Ezra said. "Thou lost more than a month of whaling season."

"Me portion was nothin' as compared to this." Jack pulled from his pocket a transcription from Master Jones's journal.

The next morning, Ezra's hair and beard were the color of a gull's back, and Jack was preparing to go to Nauseiput. . . .

Now the Plymouth visitors found Jack in his new barn, sharpening a flenser. Autumnsquam stood at the door, harpoon in hand, like a picket.

"A fine day to sail down from Plymouth," said Jack.

"Hello, Pa." Jonathan Hilyard had taken a Plymouth wife and moved back to the seat of the colony, where now he captained the militia. "We come as representatives of the General Court."

"We come also as friends," said Ezra Bigelow.

Jack touched iron to the grindstone and tiny sparks flew in the shadows. "Me *son* proclaims himself from the Gen'ral Court, and *Ezra Bigelow* calls himself friend. The world does change too much."

" 'Thou shalt keep holy the Sabbath' has not changed since Moses," Brewster Bigelow clamped a hand on his hip. He was nineteen, the youngest of Ezra's children. He wore a green waistcoat with yellow satin piping and had just enough hair on his face to cover his boyish blemishes.

Jack pretended to ignore him. "We found us a fine big drifter up Billin'sgate way."

"Fine big stinker," said Autumnsquam.

"Aye. Must've been there a week. 'Tis a true marvel you didn't smell him in Plymouth. Flensed him on the beach, we did, then hauled the blubber down here, stink and all. If we didn't try him out today, he'd've been too far rotted for anythin' but manure." Jack tested the edge of his iron with his thumb and now looked at the younger Bigelow. "The Lord wanted us to use that whale, son. So he put him on that beach."

"A broken Sabbath ain't why we come, Pa." Jonathan went over to the grindstone and knelt beside his father.

"How be me granddaughter?"

"Healthy as a horse."

Jack's smile folded his face into a thousand creases. "A little beauty, she is, and me pride for certain."

"Come spring, there'll be another."

Jack gave out a hearty laugh. "Thou old cock."

Jonathan blushed. "I've a lovin' wife, Father."

"And a lovin' old dad."

"But a Quaker for a brother," said Brewster Bigelow.

Jack looked at Ezra, who remained in the sunshine, beneath the shadow of his wide black hat. "Easy to see where the lad come from, Ezra."

"The colony knows Christopher's a Quaker," said Ezra.

"I never seen a Quaker in me life."

"What be Quaker?" asked Autumnsquam.

Ezra glanced at the old Nauset. "Better a praying Indian at Portanimicut Plantation, my friend, than a lying Indian at Jack's Island."

"Me no need plantation to learn 'bout white God. Plantation for lapdogs. Me free. Me pray to Kautantowit. And"—Autumnsquam raised the harpoon—"me no lie."

The harpoon whizzed at Ezra, past his ear, and buried itself in the oak on the far side of the clearing.

"Arrest this bloody savage," Brewster ordered Jonathan Hilyard.

"Me no bloody. Tree bloody."

Sure enough, a red stain was trickling down the gray bark. Autumnsquam walked past Bigelow and pulled the harpoon out of the tree. On the tip of the blade, a squirrel still twitched. "Kautantowit send us dinner. Squirrel stew. Nuff for two. Me go fix now."

Ezra watched the Indian amble off. Then he went into the barn. "Thou hast always had a fondness for renegades, from Thomas Weston to that Indian—"

"To the Quakers," said Brewster.

"Thou knowest of Marshal Barlow?" Ezra took off his hat and wiped the perspiration from his forehead.

"The one what ferret out Quakers up Sandwich way?" Jack began to sharpen a lance, feigning indifference.

"He's been given jurisdiction over the whole of Cape Cod," said Jonathan.

Jack noticed Brewster Bigelow poking through the line tubs and hay bales at the back of the barn. "What be you lookin' for?"

"These," he said triumphantly and lifted a long bench from out of the hay. He placed it in the middle of the floor, then pulled out a second and placed it at a right angle to the first. "There are two more, enough to form a meeting square. The fine for allowing a Quaker meeting, sir, is five pounds or twenty lashes, and a freeman can be disenfranchised as well."

"And the fine for *bein'* a Quaker?" demanded the man who now appeared in the sunlight outside the barn.

"Well, Chris," said Jack with a false grin. "Thy brother Jonathan come to see thee."

Brewster Bigelow looked at Jack. "Never seen a Quaker? Lying to a governor's assistant is yet another fining offense."

Jack pressed his blade to the grindstone. "What about dartin' a lance into a assistant's son?"

Christopher strode up to Jonathan. "Thou comest as a representative of the colony. Well, here I be, brother."

"We come to warn thee, Chris. Do not break up services and curse preachers, like some of your breed. And take the oath of fidelity to the colony."

"'Tain't my way to break up another man's worship, but Quakers takes no oaths."

"Then you'll be flogged and fined forty shillings in every town you enter," said Brewster Bigelow.

"I've had worse." Christopher pushed back his hair to reveal the little curls of reddened flesh on either side of his head.

"Boston does not dally with heretics," Ezra said approvingly. "If 'twere my choice, we'd follow their lead . . . cut off some ears, hang the leaders instead of warnin' them out. Plymouth tolerates too much."

"Why can thee not tolerate men of conscience? 'Twas conscience drove thee and thy kind to come here forty year ago."

"*We* damned bishops and pomp. *You* damn magistrates and ministers, too."

"We seek only to strengthen our personal bond with God, to make it as simple as the meeting of sea and sky at the horizon."

"And in the doing, you would destroy all that we have builded here, the whole house of God." Then Ezra saw the woman standing in the sunshine outside the barn. "Even unto fornicating with heathens."

Jack Hilyard stopped the grindstone. He could not feign indifference at this. If Chris attacked the governor's assistant, he would pay with all the flesh on his back.

The anger stiffened his shoulders, but Christopher remained motionless. His new faith had changed him. "She be a Christian now. And she be me wife."

"She is not thy wife lest thou appear afore a magistrate," said Bigelow. "A gatherin' of Quakers cannot legalize marriage 'twixt *whites*, much less savages."

"Were thy son Robinson a Quaker, Master Bigelow, he'd be with us this day."

These words seemed to strike Ezra Bigelow with more force than a blow. His head dropped to his chest, and his shoulders shook with a sob.

Brewster Bigelow snatched the lance from the grindstone, nearly slicing off Jack's fingers. He spun, and pressed the point against Christopher's chest. "Out of respect for thy brother, we come here to warn thee, and thou dost foul *my* brother's memory."

"Thy brother died in me arms."

"He did not die so that Quakers might challenge his faith and his government."

"He died for foolish men and foolish principles."

Jonathan jumped between them and pushed the lance away. Though Brewster seemed close to killing him, Christopher did not move an inch. He was as stubborn as Jonathan was earnest, and they were both of them braver than bull whales. Jack had long ago given up trying to understand what drove them. But his pride in them was great. Were he to lose one, he would be as likely to crumble as Ezra Bigelow seemed now.

"Get out, the lot of you," Jack cried. "Get out and let two fathers talk."

"What may you say to my father that—"

Jonathan grabbed Brewster by the collar and Christopher by the sleeve and dragged them out. Then he kicked shut the door, leaving the two old men in the shadows.

The light now came through the cracks and windows in dusty yellow shafts, causing the lines in Jack's face to deepen, the tears to glisten in Ezra's eyes. There were few of them left, these Old Comers, and for all their enmity, they felt an ancient bond, like half brothers born of the same womb.

"We loves our sons," said Jack, "whether they be good Reformists or—"

"Deluded Quakers."

"Thou understand me, then."

"Fathers do understand each other where sons are concerned."

"One of me boys embraced your way and the other turned elsewhere. I tell thee honest I don't much care, so long's they honor their old dad."

"A high hope," said Ezra softly.

Jack pointed a finger at Ezra Bigelow. "But if Chris be banished or get his back stripped for what he believe—"

"I cannot stop the colony from keeping to its laws."

Jack tried to set his jaw, though he no longer had back teeth enough to shape an aggressive face. "I did keep me word to thee. In exchange for this island, I did keep the master's journal secret. But I still has it, Ezra, and it say things 'bout thee and Dorothy Bradford—"

"Her death was an accident."

"Yet did thou bargain with me."

"To protect the names of those who stood by my side." Ezra pulled himself out of his slouch as if he could pull himself out of his grief. "No man chooses scandal."

"The very reason I'll break me word if ever I see Fat Barlow comin' after me boy." Jack's front teeth were no more than a few yellowed snags, but still he could smile, especially if he meant to show malice. "When a bunch of rantin' Quakers challenge what the Old Comers built, a tale of funny doin's on the first ship might give 'em somethin' juicy to rant over, whether it be true or not."

"Thou art an unprincipled man, Jack Hilyard."

"A simple man wif simple needs. I wants to keep this piece of land, and I wants to protect me sons."

Ezra folded his hands behind his back and raised his chin, so that his beard pointed straight at Hilyard's nose. "All right. Give over the journal, and I'll do what I can to turn the colony away from thy boy, no matter what he believes or who he lays with."

"Thou still strike a fine pose, but I ain't so stupid as that." Jack tugged at Bigelow's white whiskers.

Ezra slapped the hand away. "Then save him thyself."

The friendship of fathers and the half brother bond were never so strong as enmity between a man who made rules for others and one who lived only by his own, between a man who had buried the past and one who would dig it up.

Ezra turned and stalked to the door, but stopped there as if struck by a sudden pain. He brought his hand to his breast and pressed like a man trying to keep from bursting open.

"Ezra? What ails thee?"

Ezra raised his hand as if to say this would pass. Presently, he stood more upright, wiped away the beads of sweat from his forehead, and seemed to regain himself. "'Tis all for the best, Jack, that we make no bargain on the book. My conscience on the matter is clear."

"Mine, also."

"I would leave this life with my head high, knowing that I took no hand in permitting a Quaker pestilence to thrive in the colony."

Jack stepped close to Ezra and looked for the shroud of death that it was said could sometimes be seen upon living faces. "Thy time grows short, then?"

"So my heart would tell me."

Jack thought a bit on this, then brought his face even closer, as if to kiss his old nemesis farewell, and he whispered, "I'll not miss thee."

Ezra pulled open the barn door and cast his eyes on Jack for what would be a final time. "Watch for the sheriff on the next Sabbath, and if thou holds more Quaker meetin's in this barn, watch that thou don't lose this island."

ii.

Four times the following week, Jack went through the woods to the house on Skaket Creek to beg Christopher and Patience to move their meeting to some patch of off-island woods. But they refused.

It had been the marshes, more than whales or white cedar, that drew settlers to Cape Cod. Most colonists were farmers before anything else, and the marshes that spread for miles behind the beaches and around the creek mouths yielded fodder for all the cattle from Sandwich to Eastham. It was true that cattle fed on salt hay needed more fresh water, but on Cape Cod, there was an abundance of that as well.

On Saturday Christopher and Patience went onto the marsh to cut hay. Jack knew they were doing it not to feed their forty head of cattle, but for a better view of Marshal Barlow, should he come riding over the marsh. At the end of the day, they brought a cart of hay up to the barn and loaded it into the loft. Then they took out the benches and arranged them in a square. In a Quaker way, they were preparing for war.

From a perch atop his woodpile, Jack watched them go arm in arm down the path. It was good that they had each other and their faith, he thought, because they seemed intent upon losing everything else.

He was not one for musing, but the strangeness of these Quaker ways lay heavy on his mind. Though his hair had long since whitened and his skin had been boiled red by sun and incessant wind, he had reached threescore and ten without feeling old. Wisdom, a grandchild, and the gaining of Nauseiput had kept him vibrant. Now age was descending as quickly as night.

With the russet oaks fading into shadow, Autumnsquam brought Jack a bucket of beer, the great leveler of men.

"I do need a draft," Jack said. "Sometimes methinks I've nothin' else left."

"Thee got good land," said Autumnsquam. "Thee got two son."

"I may have to fight for the land 'cause of the sons."

"Once this land belong to Indian. Once I have son. Now Nausets is children who pray at white man's feet, and land . . ." Autumnsquam dipped the tankard into his bucket and drank. "Thee got what me dream of."

Jack looked out onto the darkening ocean. Not a light shone anywhere on the water or along the north-running coast. It was the time of day when Jack felt most alone, yet most surely in the presence of God. For who, other than God, could turn the great blue bay to blackness so easily? What more devotion did men need make than to do their work each day and watch God darken the world each night, to see in the coming of the night what came at last to all men? There was simplicity beyond anything his sons now sought.

"Autie," he said, "thou hast *friends*. Friends be better'n sons sometimes. Thou fights all thy life to get thy sons together in a good place, and one decides to raise his childrens in Plymouth, while the other goes about challengin' the law . . ."

High above them, a gull squawked and dropped a long white stream that splattered onto the roof of the barn and trickled down the shingles. Jack sipped his beer and studied the stain. "Autie, that barn be good for nothin' but catchin' gull shit and Quakers. What say we burn it down?"

"I say you stupid Jack Bloody Christian Hilyard." Autumnsquam drained his beer and got up. "Go to bed."

"Where you goin'?"

"Sick of stupid bloody Christians. Go to Portanimicut. See some Indian."

"They're all Christian Indians there. Simeon Bigelow's done a fine job in his prayin' town."

Autumnsquam grinned. "Some still make fuck with free Nauset."

"Thou old cock. I'd like a bit o' that meself."

"Thee too old." Autumnsquam shouldered his harpoon. He always carried it in the woods because there were wolves in the woods and wolf heads brought bounty from the colony. "Thee no burn barn, I find ugly squaw make fuck with thee."

By the time Autumnsquam reached the King's Road, the moon was up full, a big yellow hunter's moon that blotted up the stars and warmed the black ground. But even in the moonlight Autumnsquam saw the orange glow in the sky above the island.

"Jack Stupid Bloody Christian Hilyard," he muttered. Then he made for Portanimicut and the best bloody Christian he knew.

iii.

Marshal George Barlow of Sandwich relished his work. No man doubted that. He gave out punishment with a smile and sought out Quakers as though charged by God himself. But there were some in the colony, and not all of them Quakers, who gave the devil more credit for George Barlow.

He was a glutton and carried a glutton's bulk about on the back of his horse. He was a drunkard and wore a monstrous red nose as a badge of dishonor. But worst of all, he was an abuser of the office given him by the magistrates.

While collecting fines for the colony, he collected tribute for himself—a bolt of good cloth from this Quaker, a bolster tick from another, a copper kettle from a Quaker woman who had nothing else in which to cook. And around the pommel of his saddle he carried a whip of three knotted leather strands that he was more than happy to use on the backs of Quaker men or women.

They were the perfect fugitives. When chased, they did not run, and when captured, they did not resist. He could not be certain that the other inhabitants of Jack's Island would be as docile. That cantankerous old rodent Jack Hilyard was better with a lance than most men were with a musket. And living with him was the Indian harpooneer in the whales'-teeth ornaments. Barlow unfurled his whip, then urged his horse ahead.

But before he went far, he heard . . . *singing*.

Quakers did not sing. At some of their meetings, they barely spoke. And these voices were behind him, sounding loud and off-key, in no way pleasing to a Christian ear. No more than half the singers seemed to know the words to the hymn they sang, because the singers were Indians. A procession of perhaps fifty was marching down the path from the King's Road, and leading them, like Moses, was Simeon Bigelow.

"Good mornin', Marshal Barlow." Simeon cradled the holy book in his right arm, while in his left hand he swung a walking staff. His wild beard and mighty girth were known to praying Indians from Portanimicut to Sandwich. For his work among them, he was near as revered in this colony as Moses had been in his.

"Reverend Bigelow—"

"Not Reverend. Never been ordained. Just a Christian spreadin' the good news."

Simeon Bigelow stopped beside Barlow's horse, while the Indians paraded onto the marsh, led by one in a blue coat who wordlessly bellowed out the tune to the Fifteenth Psalm. As he went by, this Indian gave Barlow a smile and a broad wave, and the bracelet of whales' teeth jangled at his wrist.

"Who is that?" Barlow demanded.

"One from my Portanimicut Plantation. A fine prayin' Reform-ist."

The Indian took to the planks that led across the marsh, spun back to the others, and swung his arms as though directing a chorus. He sang and shouted and jumped from one foot to the other, like some long-legged bird.

"A lively old Christian," said Simeon.

"Aye," answered Barlow suspiciously. "Does he know there's a Quaker meetin' goin' on over there this very minute?"

"Quakers?" Simeon threw back his head and gave a laugh. "We been invited for an orthodox service."

Barlow leaned down, bringing his veined red nose close to Bige-low's beard. "I got this knowledge from your own nephew Brewster."

"A lad of strong imagination. But look you at my Indians. For every one in leather breeches or deerskin dress, there be another in a cloak or woolen skirt. I spent twenty years teachin' 'em to be good Christians. Wouldst I be so dumb as to expose them now to"—he nearly spat—"Quakers?"

In the middle of the island, Jack Hilyard was watching the smoke rise from the foundation hole into which his barn had collapsed. His head throbbed, less from beer than from shame, and he struggled to compose words that would explain what he had done.

"Thee son love thee much." Amapoo came up behind him.

Jack turned. "And I love him. That's why I done this, Ama-poo . . . Patience."

"I think he know, but he still mad."

"I don't want to lose this island."

"Him neither. But he no want lose his soul."

"Do you Quakers . . . do you forgive folks?"

"Christ forgive his killers."

Then Jack heard a strange sound . . . singing. He took Patience by the arm and went toward the marsh.

First he saw his son and the Quakers, clustered at the top of the path. Then he saw a long line of Indians winding across the marsh. He could not believe that it was Autumnsquam who was leading them, cutting antic capers in the mud and acting as though he were plainly out of his head. Nor could he believe that Marshal Barlow, after a last look across the marsh, was going back the way he had come.

"Friend Bigelow!" Christopher shouted, his voice echoing joyously through the woods. "Thou art friend indeed."

"The Lord's house has many mansions." Simeon came up the path behind his Praying Indians. "I see no reason for the Quakers not to live in one. Any more than I would deny my flock their holy songs."

"Nor do I," shouted Jack Hilyard, pushing his way through the Indians and Quakers now gathered at the top of the path. "The Portanimicut Prayin' Injuns be invited to feast with us this afternoon, and the Quaker families be invited to meet in me *house* if they can find nowheres else."

"The marshal may come back," warned Simeon.

"Let him come."

"You'll not burn your house if he approaches?"

"'Twas not me what burned the barn, Simeon. 'Twas fear." Jack looked at Christopher. "This island be a free place, free for any faith me son wants to follow. Free for as long as I can keep it so."

From the marsh, Autumnsquam watched Jack Hilyard and his son shake hands. It made him glad. He had saved his friends and their land another week. But it was their land now, not his or his children's.

He had let the procession go by, let them continue to sing the white men's song even after Barlow was gone, and as he watched them going up from the marsh, he knew that they were all lost to him now, Amapoo and all the praying Nausets. They were all bloody Christians. They had forgotten Kautantowit. But none of them knew that it was Kautantowit who had saved the island, Kautantowit who had sent the shitting gull to warn him.

The old Nausets had believed a man could know the way of life by watching the passage of the seasons. In October, while the sun still warmed the earth, mellow reds came into the oaks and crept through the bear grass and bogs. Old age came to the year, and serenity descended on the land.

Autumnsquam had seen sixty cycles pass. The landscape had turned red around him. But the sky had turned to smoke above him, because in October the white farmers burned off the tall trees to widen their fields. Autumnsquam felt no serenity, nor was he a part of anything, not even of Jack Hilyard's little island. And the gull was circling above him once more, crying its lonely cry.

Jack wondered why Autumnsquam was still standing like a scarecrow out on the marsh. He waved, but Autumnsquam did not move.

"Chris," said Jack, "go tell him we be butcherin' one of the swine. That'll get him up here."

Christopher loped down onto the marsh. "Autie—"

Suddenly the Indian's hand shot into the air, and the whalebone bracelet rattled at his wrist. "So long, stupid bloody Quaker!"

"Autie!" Christopher started after him.

But Autumnsquam turned and ran toward the mainland. When he reached the edge of the marsh, he waved again. "Go back. Plenty good bloody Christian squaw back there now. They no care what color their god. They no care what color their babies!"

"Autie, wait!"

"Me follow gull." Autumnsquam glanced again at the bird, which had wheeled west, and then he was gone.

CHAPTER 15

July 9

Town Meeting

Conceived by the Pilgrims, idealized by Jefferson, admired the world over . . . Geoff Hilyard sometimes thought the town meeting had as much in common with Franz Kafka as it did with the Founding Fathers.

In the old days, it had been held in the Victorian town hall, an intricate filigree of rooflines and turrets, delicately shingled and painted in warm tones of cream and yellow, a perfect symbol for the mingling of Gothic complexity and American optimism in small-town politics.

But small towns got bigger, and now the meeting was held in the gymnasium of the new school up in the scrub pine. There was nothing wrong with it, as school buildings went—a lot of interconnected brick boxes with big casement windows and plenty of parking—but it could have been anywhere in America. After it got dark and the quartz lamps threw that vibrating orange light onto the grounds, it could have been anywhere in the solar system. And the gym smelled of jockstraps.

The only town official expected to support Rake was Bill Rains, a member of the Conservation Commission.

"Hello, Geoff." Rains was standing at a table on which were

piled pamphlets: Don't Let This One Get Away! "Where do you stand?"

"On the floor."

"This development is going to meet some stiff opposition, Geoff. I'm going to lead it."

Rains was a sixties radical from Chicago, with a potbelly and a little Cape ancestry. He had come in the mid-seventies to paint driftwood and mellow out and had seen, even then, that development was turning parts of the Cape into a giant suburb. Now he made his living as a naturalist on a Provincetown whale watch vessel and spent the rest of his time, so Dickerson Bigelow said, stopping other people from making *their* living. Geoff knew that was a bit strong. He liked Bill Rains, but he thought the nature-boy beard and flannel shirt were as much of an affectation as the new look on Doug Bigelow, who was just coming in the door.

Doug wore a dark shirt, a dark sport coat, and a silver-buckled western belt, and whatever he put on his hair made it shine like the hood of the black BMW he had bought after his divorce. There was no question that he looked better in his mid-forties than he had ten years before. Was it the golf-course casual by day and the Mel Gibson–cool by night? Or his second wife, the blonde with the attention span that did not distinguish between a town meeting and *Moby Dick*. Doug had come alone.

He picked up one of the pamphlets. "You can throw these out, because we're going to win, Bill."

Rains kept his eyes on Geoff. "If *you* refuse to sell, it will put a very big crimp in this project."

"I'll keep that in mind." Geoff left environmentalist and developer to bicker and caught up to Rake in the registration line. "We have to talk."

"Got nothin' to say." The old man rolled his sister ahead of him in her wheelchair.

The poor old bastard. He'd gone and dragged her out of her sickroom, as though one more vote might turn the tide.

"Name and address," said the woman at the desk. "Address first."

"Jack's Island Road. John 'Rake' Hilyard and Clara."

"Evenin', Rake." The woman crossed the names off the voting list. "I haven't seen you in a dog's age, Clara."

"That's because she lives a dog's life," said Rake.

"How are you, Clara?" Geoff knelt in front of her.

She didn't seem to know him. "Huh?"

"How are you?"

"What do you care?" Rake rolled the wheelchair over Geoff's toes.

Janice was sitting in the front row of the non-voting section, beneath the west backboard.

A few rows behind her sat Jimmy Little and Ma. What the hell were *they* doing there? Jimmy shrugged, as if to say that *he* didn't know, either.

Geoff also noticed Hiram Bigelow, senior partner of Bigelow, Holden, and Hoar, the law firm that would fight every obstacle put before the development. Uncle Hiram nodded.

Behind him was one of those people who could spoil a night, a face so nondescript it would leave you wondering for hours *if* you knew him, and then where the hell you knew him *from*. He shoved a stick of gum into his mouth and threw the wrapper on the floor.

Geoff settled in beside Janice. "I can't believe Rake brought Clara."

"Neither can her daughter."

Emily Burr had just finished giving Rake hell in a stage whisper that could be heard all the way to the ladies' room, where she was now headed with a cigarette.

"Mad enough to need a smoke," said Geoff.

"If I smoked, I'd join her," said Janice.

"Sell any houses today?"

"No. Make any decisions?"

"Did you know Quakers held meetings in Rake's barn?"

"Does that mean no?"

The gavel fell, which was good, because they didn't have anything else to say.

A town meeting was supposed to be a democratic thing. But why was it that the ones who owned the waterfront property always went for the chairs on the floor, while the ones in the sweat-stained caps, who lived back in the hills, as hand-to-mouth proud as their ancestors, always took to the stands at the sides? What counted, Geoff knew, was that out of forty-seven hundred registered voters, these two hundred or so gave enough of a damn to come out and debate an issue in the July heat.

There was a process for this as time-honored as the Mayflower

Compact. The moderator read a proposal. The sponsor spoke. The Board of Selectmen, the Finance Committee, and the Planning Board had a say, then anyone else who had an opinion, pro or con.

Sometimes it worked with enough simplicity to warm the rockiest Yankee rib. Propose, debate, amend, vote in the open so everyone knew where you stood, then get on to the next issue because there were fields to clear and fish to catch in the morning and everyone had to get home to bed.

And sometimes it was like life in the world that most of the Off-Capers had come to escape. A pro said his piece and was answered by a con, who was then rebutted by the pro. The con might have consorts con the pro, who would then call for proponents to the pro to pro the con, who would then get sick of the whole thing and shout "Move the question." Then they'd vote to see if they would vote or keep up with the pros and cons, and then . . . It was easy to understand why people elected legislators to go through this torture.

The first article was an appropriation of $180,000 for a class-A pumper to replace the one the fire department had been using since 1957. Passed without opposition.

The second: "To see if the Town will vote to approve the first week of October as Brewster Black Locust Week." This was the kind of issue that got more attention than it deserved, but the debate gave you an idea of how people were thinking.

For the pro, a bookstore owner transplanted from New Jersey, in rumpled seersucker sport coat and old-fashioned boat sneakers, altogether reminiscent of Fred Rogers: "We who live on Cape Cod know autumn as the most beautiful season. We lack the foliage of Vermont or New Hampshire, but that's no reason why the discerning tourist shouldn't be encouraged to see the mellow reds of our marshes and the golden yellow of our black locust groves. This tree isn't native to Cape Cod, but like so many of us who aren't, it thrives here. It was brought from the South in the 1800s, to grow in the nitrogen-poor soil, and Cape Cod would be a bleak place without it. The black locust deserves honor, especially at a season when the guest houses are putting up their Vacancy signs and could use the business."

Geoff squirmed. Janice twitched. Over on the middle aisle, Rake and Clara sat and listened.

For the con, an old matron whose family had held a pew in the First Church since the War of 1812: "I don't care if the locust *is* a tree. The first thing it is is a *bug*. You can look it up . . . in the

Bible. A *bug*, always bringin' the plague and whatnot. If tourists aren't smart enough to come down here in the fall, I don't think we should honor a *bug* just to get their attention. How many tourists would come if it was Brewster *Bug* Week? Or Cape Cod Cock-a-roach Week? Who wants tourists in the fall, anyway?"

Article 2 failed. Geoff was a little disappointed. He thought it might have been good for a laugh.

The warm-up was over. On to the main event, Article 3: "To see if the Town will vote to authorize the Board of Selectmen to acquire by purchase or by gift or to take by eminent domain under Massachusetts General Laws, Chapter Seventy-nine, and to commit to the control of the Town of Brewster Conservation Commission for conservation, recreation, and watershed protection purposes," et cetera, et cetera . . .

The warrant listed Jack's Island as it appeared in the assessor's map, twenty-five acres of which would be purchased in a friendly taking at a cost of two million dollars. Thirty-five acres taken by eminent domain for four million more. The Finance Committee report: eight to nothing against. There were better ways to spend the town's money.

The first speaker was Bill Rains. As he came to the microphone, Geoff heard a little undertow of noise, as though a lot of people had heard too much from him already. He ignored them and made his pitch, concluding: "The protection of Jack's Island is as important as protecting Nauset Marsh. If we keep losing threads of our past, if we keep letting more woodlots be plowed up and turned into condominiums, if we always surrender to the almighty dollar, we lose a sense of who we are."

"I know who I am," shouted Humpback Bigelow. "I drive a bulldozer."

The moderator banged his gavel and said speakers were to be recognized before they spoke.

Rains looked up at the Humpster. "It's people like you who give inbreeding a bad name."

The moderator banged his gavel again. The Humpster got a confused look on his face. He turned to his father, and his lips formed the words "What's inbreeding?"

And the debate wore on. We don't have the right, just because *we're* here, to close the bridge and say no one else can come. But this is a fragile place. But we've spent enough money. But if we don't spend more, it lowers the value of all our property. But . . . But . . . But . . .

Across the gym, warrant pamphlets flapped back and forth in the heat. Geoff couldn't see his aunt's face, but even she was fanning herself, sore joints and all.

The taxpayers had acquired hundreds of acres in recent years to protect the open space, watershed, and character of the town. Some considered it too little too late. Others wanted all land to remain in private hands. But this was certain: with each purchase, tax rates went up, and at some point, people said *enough*. Some argued that development demanded more services, which caused taxes to rise even more, but that was a hard one to put over.

A selectman, speaking for himself as a builder, warned that if there was no more construction, there would be no more jobs, then no more retail sales, no more cash flow. "Then we sink back into the magnificent rural poverty from which we came."

Good point, thought Geoff, and maybe a good idea.

"People before plants," said someone from the other side.

The two gray heads on the center aisle shook in disagreement. The makeshift fan flapped away in front of Clara's face.

Someone asked about the Cape Cod Commission.

"They'll have their say if the developers get past us, the Conservation Commission, the Planning Board, and the Zoning Board of Appeals," shouted Bill Rains. "I say cut it off right now. Send a message. We've given up enough of this place. Cape Cod is no longer for sale."

"He's getting strident," whispered Geoff.

That brought Doug Bigelow to the microphone, and Geoff sensed Hiram Bigelow, Doug's uncle, twitching nervously nearby. Dickerson had shown the sense to stay away. It was not good strategy to reveal yourself too soon. But Doug liked to talk.

"My wife and I *live* on Jack's Island," he said.

A voice in the crowd corrected him: "Your *second* wife."

That brought a few snickers, and someone whispered, "The mother of his children lives in Boston now."

Doug smoothed his hair and kept talking. "We won't foul our own nest or feather it at the expense of our town. After all, my family has owned that island since the Pilgrims."

And Rake Hilyard jumped up. "So has mine!"

The moderator banged his gavel. "You have *not* been recognized. Respect the civility of the process, please. If anyone else speaks out of turn, I'll have him removed."

Rake had always been a stubborn old fighter, but he had always believed in the civility of the process. He sank into his chair like an old house collapsing into its foundation hole.

Douglas continued as though Rake had not even spoken. "You can't stop development. You can't stop people from having kids and needing places to live. So trust someone who's been here as long as . . . *almost* as long as the Indians."

That brought a clearing of Ma Little's throat. Heads turned and the moderator raised his gavel. Ma simply looked at the ceiling as though she'd farted and wanted to seem casual.

"Vote *against* this article," Doug said. "Leave private property in the hands of private people, just as our forefathers did."

Geoff wiped the sweat from his forehead. "These July meetings get hot . . . windy, too."

"About to get windier," said Janice.

Rake shuffled to the microphone. Clara's fan stopped moving.

"Lived on Jack's Island for most of *my* life, too." His voice was weaker than usual, as though he could smell defeat. "My sister and me can remember all the way back when the hotel burned down. And we want this done. Buy our land. Keep it for the future, for the kids and the wildlife. Make the sailing camp a community center. I was a big supporter of the National Seashore thirty years ago. And . . ." He lost his place and began to fumble with his papers.

Someone else asked for the floor.

Old Rake pulled himself up and snapped, "Got the floor, and no one takes it till I'm finished."

That made Geoff feel better. He hated to see the old man losing the edge.

"So why don't you just *give* the town the land?" called out Blue Bigelow.

The gavel banged. "Out of order."

"Yes, yes, guess I've thought of that. But we've lived on the land for three centuries. Land's everything. Always has been. Can't just *give* it away. Besides, if we *give* our piece, it don't stop the Bigelows from doin' *this* all around us—"

And with a flair for the dramatic that Geoff would never have expected from Rake, the old man unrolled a copy of the 1904 subdivision. And that raised holy hell.

A lot of people hadn't heard about it, or had heard only rumors, but there it was, a nightmare vision for a well-zoned town, drawn in tiny eighth-of-an-acre lots across the waterfront.

"If you don't pass this article," said Rake, "the Bigelows can cover that island in egg crates, make the whole place look like a cheap motel."

Someone said the town had successfully fought these grand-fathered plans in the past and they would fight this one. Someone else responded that the only way to guarantee the island's survival was to buy it. Someone else said it was *still* too much money. And Douglas promised that his family would construe the plan as liberally as possible. To which someone whispered, "Like you construed your first marriage?"

Finally, someone called, "Move the question!" and the voice vote was taken: A resounding *no* to the article, 1904 plot plan not-withstanding.

"My ear tells me the measure has been defeated," said the moderator. "We'll count only if there is a motion."

"So moved!" cried Rake Hilyard.

"Stubborn old bastard." Geoff had to laugh in admiration.

And the crowd groaned. It was hot. Fans were flapping, and the mosquitoes had picked up the scent of two hundred sweating bodies wafting out the open doors of the gym. But Rake Hilyard never quit.

Those in favor of the article held up their voting cards first. Sixty or so, including Rake Hilyard. Not a bad showing, but not good enough.

"Geoff," whispered Janice, "Rake is holding up your aunt's hand. She isn't doing it herself."

"It's the arthritis," said Geoff.

"Are you sure?"

Geoff glanced over at Emily. Her hands worked steadily at her knitting. Her husband Arnie nodded off in the heat. "*They're* not worried."

The defeat was swift, the gavel final. The town did not want Jack's Island.

Rake grabbed the handles of the wheelchair and rolled his sister toward the door. No one else stood. No talk drowned out the squeak of the wheelchair wheels. It was as if the Hilyards were allowed to leave with their pride intact. Rake stood as straight as a dock piling, and Geoff almost cheered him.

"Didn't expect to win," said Rake when Geoff caught up to him in the lobby after the meeting. "But ain't finished yet."

Now Bill Rains came through the crowd. He was sweating in his flannel shirt. "Well, Rake, you and Clara better think about giving the property to the town, and I'll get ready to give them hell when we inspect the island."

Rake looked around until he spied Doug Bigelow, who was chatting with Blue and the Humpster by the trophy case. "Do that, Bill, and I might do it, too. Just might give away my land after all."

Doug Bigelow looked up as though someone had called him a communist.

Rains crouched down and asked Clara, "What do you think about— Hey, is she supposed to have one eye closed and one open like that?"

"Huh?" Rake looked at his sister.

Geoff touched the old woman's wrist. "Clara!"

Even before she saw her mother's face, Emily was shouting, "Give her air! Give her air!"

So naturally, everybody surged forward to see who it was that needed air. The Humpster was pushed into Doug Bigelow, who was pushed into Emily, who hit Rake, who nearly fell over the wheelchair, which rolled over Bill Rains's toes and right out the door.

"For chrissakes," cried Emily, "get her before she rolls all the way to the beach!"

Geoff and Janice caught her before she made it to handicapped parking. It was clear, even in the eerie orange light, that air was something she no longer needed.

"The poor woman," said Janice. "They never gave her the chance to change . . ."

"Change what?"

"Never mind."

When the ambulance light flashed off into the summer night, no siren was needed.

In a pool of orange a small group talked to reporters for the Brewster *Oracle* and the Cape Cod *Times*, and the mosquitoes took it all as great sport.

"This is now in the hands of the Conservation Commission, and we'll be inspecting the property next Tuesday, the seventeenth," said Bill Rains. "And I know we'll have some strong objections to construction there."

"This is no time to be discussing business," responded Doug Bigelow. "I'll only say that my company will comply with every regulation. The law gives us certain rights."

On a bench in the shadows, Rake sat with Geoff and Janice. He seemed too shocked to leave. "Never knew she was dead. Just held up her hand, thought she was tired."

"She *was*," said Janice gently, "so she went to sleep."

Sometimes Geoff knew exactly why he loved her.

"Got no choice now," said Rake.

"Don't think about selling now," said Geoff.

"Ain't thinkin' about sellin'. Gotta find it."

"What?"

"The log of the *Mayflower*. It's out there."

"Sure it is," said Janice.

Maybe it *is*, thought Geoff.

In the shadows, someone chewed a fresh stick of gum and wrote down what he had just heard.

Now Ma Little came over and sat down beside Rake. "Too damn much talkin', Rake, that's what done her in. Too damn much talkin'. Too damn many talkers."

"Let's go, Ma," said Jimmy. "You saw what I said you'd see. The town was against this. And it killed poor Clara."

In his blazer and business face, Jimmy looked about as sympathetic to Geoff as Doug Bigelow did. "Like I told Geoff, time's are changin'."

Ma took Rake's hand in hers. "You're right, Rake. The town's wrong. That's all there is to it. So stand your ground."

Rake patted her hand.

"And if them bulldozers ever come, you call me, and we'll meet 'em right on the causeway, with shotguns."

"We're too old for bloodlettin', Ma," said Rake.

"Maybe so." Ma pulled her cap over her eyes. "But it wouldn't be a bad way to die."

CHAPTER 16

March 1676

Bloodletting

Though the bright sun promised spring, the wind still stung of winter as Jonathan Hilyard led his family across the cornfield to Clarkes' garrison house. There he embraced them all and promised that he would return straight after meeting.

"Pray hard for the end of this thing," said Jonathan's wife, Rebecca. "I wish to take my family to worship again."

"Plymouth be three miles away. 'Tis a dangerous walk," answered Jonathan. "God will understand why we keep our women to home."

"Pray for the Injun's head." Eight-year-old Jeremiah slipped his words through the space where recently he had lost his milk teeth.

"We never pray for such things," chided Elizabeth, the eldest daughter.

Jonathan tousled his son's hair. "'Tis the head of a devil we pray for. God will hear us."

"Oh, la," said fifteen-year-old Katherine, "sometimes methinks 'tis God visits these things upon us for our sins."

"You listen too much to Goody Clarke," said Rebecca.

"The Lord does not punish us, Katherine. He *tests* us." Jonathan Hilyard strapped on his bandolier and shouldered his musket, like a practiced captain of militia. "He sends this Injun to warn us 'gainst growin' weak or complacent."

"Give me a hatchet and I'll chop off his head myself." Jeremiah hacked the air with his hand.

"Just see that the women bolt the garrison door, son. Worry for thine own head afore the Injun's."

The Injun was Metacomet, or King Philip, and his head had become the most valued trophy in the colonies.

Jonathan's father had beheaded an Indian called Witawawmut, and for fifty-five years, there had been peace. Witawawmut's skull had become the symbol of English strength, while Christ's Cross had become the sign of English decency. But there were many among the Wampanoags who saw English decency as nothing more than a way to conserve English strength. Whether by the dealings of the General Court or the threat of the musket, the English were populating the land with their white children and filling the air with the three white spirits they called one God.

When Metacomet's father, Massasoit, had signed his treaty, he had seen the First Comers as allies against the Narragansett but as no threat to him. There had been only fifty of them, after all. Now there were thirty thousand. The Massachusetts Bay Colony had grown westward toward the Connecticut River. The colony at New Haven had spread north. The religious rebels of Rhode Island had settled round Narragansett Bay. And Plymouth Colony, though hemmed in on three sides by the sea, filled steadily with families, and each family wanted a hundred acres, and each son of each family would one day want a hundred acres more.

To make room, the whites had united to rub the Pequots from the face of the earth. Through land purchase and Praying Towns, Plymouth had rendered the tribes of Cape Cod guests in their own land. And yet, until Massasoit died in 1661, peace was ensured. The old sachem was a man of his word, and perhaps he could not admit that his fair dealings with a few whites had been the undoing of his people.

When his son assumed the throne at Mount Hope on Narragansett Bay, however, he heard the warlike counsel that his father had rejected. He heard it from the young men who feared the loss of their world. He heard it from the old men whose world was already gone.

The war began in the summer of 1675. Historians would chronicle the stream of events that flowed from Massasoit's death to the opening shots. But like water running downhill, war was simply inevitable.

Whites and Indians first skirmished in the town of Swansea, on Narragansett Bay. The Indians won the fight, so the English raised a fine army to chastise them but could not find them. The Indians then struck at Dartmouth, east of Swansea. They burned the town and captured those Quakers too slow or trusting to reach the safety of the garrison house.

Each Quaker was hanged by his wrists and sliced neatly around the waist. Then his skin was peeled up and off like a shirt. To the Indians, skinned Quakers were little different from the beheaded Witawawmut. Torture and terror were fair weapons in war. And this they saw as the final conflict. One side would survive, the other disappear forever.

Not all Indians joined the fight, however. On Cape Cod, there was tense quiet in the Praying Towns and tribal villages. Ministers like Richard Bourne, Samuel Treat, and Simeon Bigelow labored to keep the peace and spread the Word of Christ among the Indians. But as the raids crept closer to Plymouth, the General Court decided that even Praying Indians could not be trusted. In hope that isolation would succeed where word of Christ might fail, they prohibited any Indian from crossing the Scusset River.

Still, in much of the Plymouth Colony, isolation was more common to the white settler than to the Indian. For all his efforts, the white man had far to go before he wore away the wilderness. His settlements and cornfields were like brightening Christian stars in the firmament of heathen forest or, to Indian eyes, like white pockmarks on the face of a virgin.

Jeremiah Hilyard watched his father and the Clarke men cross the cornfield and turn north on the Plymouth Road. Their leaving left him the oldest male at the garrison house. It did not matter, however, for they would not allow him a gun or even a hatchet. If he had a hatchet, he would cut off the head of any Indian who dared . . .

He sat on the stump that the Clarkes used for a chopping block and kicked at the dried bark. The sun was warming quickly and felt good on the side of his face. Off in the woods, the crows were squawking at something, and above him the gulls circled and cried like lost children.

He hated Sundays. Bad enough to listen to the minister at Plymouth. At least the meetinghouse had light and air. Here he would have to lock himself into the garrison house, with its tiny windows and three-foot-thick walls, and listen to that old crone Sarah Clarke read from the Bible.

"Jeremiah!" called his sister Elizabeth. "The reading begins. Come quick so that I may bolt—"

She said not another word, and Jeremiah later prayed that she had not another thought. At the strange sound she made, he turned and saw her stagger against the doorjamb. She touched the side of her head, where her hair had been matted into a deep groove. Then the tomahawk struck a second time, and she collapsed into a pile of bloody green wool.

"Beth!" screamed Jeremiah. "Ma! Injuns! Injuns!"

His sister Katherine's pink dress appeared in the dark doorway, and the tomahawk opened her fair face from hairline to chin.

Jeremiah had heard of Satan and his minions. They were everywhere, said the minister, even in the godly town of Plymouth, but the entrance to Clarkes' blockhouse had suddenly become the entrance to their hell. As Satan gave a war cry and rushed inside, his devils burst from the distant woods, swarmed around the house, and flew toward the door in frenzy. Jeremiah heard the women scream and the devils bellow, and then he heard tomahawks striking skulls like stones striking pumpkins in the field.

The urine ran down his leg. He tried to run himself, to run for his father, but his legs turned to pudding. He tried to cry out, but his throat closed up and his father was surely too far away to hear him.

Then Elizabeth Clarke's suckling infant came hurtling out the door, its head stove in at the soft spot that mothers told children never to touch.

And Jeremiah felt the words in his own mouth: "The Lord is my shepherd. . . ."

Elizabeth Clarke rushed after her babe. Her nursing breast, covered with blood, flopped above her bodice.

"I shall not want. . . ."

An Indian lunged out the door after her. As she fell upon her babe, he fell upon her, driving his knee into her spine and pulling her head back with a jerk.

"He maketh me to lie down in green pastures . . ."

The Indian's knife flashed. A line of red appeared at Elizabeth's forehead; then her yellow hair came off all in a piece, like an animal pelt.

"He leadeth me beside the still waters. . . ."

Elizabeth Clarke picked up her dead child and staggered to her feet. She looked like an old man with a bloody bald pate and fringe of yellow around her ears. She took three steps toward Jeremiah and collapsed.

"He restoreth my soul . . ."

Jeremiah was praying out loud now, and the Indian holding the bloody scalp was coming toward him. He turned to run, but another caught him and lifted him off his feet. Now he screamed and, from within, heard his mother cry his name. He kicked at the Indian and broke free, but a tomahawk glanced off the side of his head and sent him staggering through the garrison door . . . into hell.

He saw his sister Katherine, faceless and hairless on the floor, and the Clarke children, like dolls thrown heedlessly by the fireplace. He heard screams of horror and hatred. And where he had always smelled the warmth of women, musky yet sweet, he smelled man-sweat and bear grease, deerskin and blood.

"He leadeth me in the paths of righteousness for his name's sake. . . ."

Lights burst before him as a tomahawk sent him hurtling toward the fireplace. He struck the mantel and fell to the floor. His senses began to close out the horrors. Then his hair was pulled back and a knife came to his forehead.

"Nooo! Not his hair!" His mother's scream was followed by a thunderous explosion that blew the Indian off Jonathan's back. The room fell to silence, the momentary and deafening sound that came after a gunshot in a small space.

Then his mother's body was on top of him, her fingers twining into his hair. "You've killed all my babies! but you can't take their beautiful hair. Their—"

Her fingers closed so tight around a curl that he thought she might pull the hair out by its roots. Then he felt her blood running down the side of his face, and her fingers were no longer moving.

Yea, though I walk through the valley of the shadow of death . . . He kept the words inside his head now, because if the Indians heard him, he would die for certain.

Old Goody Clarke was screaming, "Get out, you filth! Get out of my house."

I shall fear no evil. . . .

"Granny Clarke! Help! No!" It was Abigail, the oldest granddaughter.

From the bloody safety beneath his mother's body, Jeremiah peered across the floor at Abigail's yellow dress. Moccasins moved toward her. Red splattered the yellow. The girl's body struck the floor, and her lifeless eyes looked along the boards at Jeremiah.

"Lord have mercy!" screamed the old woman.

Thy rod and thy staff they comfort me. . . .

The boy could see the feet of old Goody Clarke, stumbling and scuffling amidst moccasins and leather breeches. There came the *thwanging* of a pan against an Indian skull, a grunt of pain, then men laughing.

Thou hast prepared a table before me, against them that afflict me. . . .

Then a pistol thundered. A table flew into the air, sending bowls of hot soup splattering across the floor. An Indian landed a short distance from the boy and his body curled itself around the hole in his belly.

Thou anointest my head with oil; my cup runneth over . . .

His mother's blood was trickling down his neck.

Surely goodness and mercy shall follow me all the days of my life . . . Surely. Surely this is a dream, a horror, from which my father will awaken me, will save me.

"Oh, you bloody savages," shrieked Goody Clarke. "You have killed me! 'The Lord is my—' " The old woman dropped to her knees, the pistol still smoking in her hand. A line of blood appeared at her throat. Her eyes opened wide and lost their luster. She tried to say more, but the line of blood widened into a grotesque gaping smile, and she fell onto the floor.

And I shall dwell in the house of the Lord forever.

ii.

Wet snow swirled in from the sea and bent the pine branches close to the ground. Jonathan Hilyard nearly froze when he strayed from the planking and sank to his knees in the icy spring tide. He might have let himself settle forever into the ancient peat, except for his mission . . . and the boy walking behind him.

But what the boy was thinking he could not know, for the boy had spoken only in psalms since the attack. On the island, Jonathan took the path that led toward Nauseiput Creek and the tiny house where, he prayed, he would find light and warmth against this bitter darkness.

"Why, Jon!" cried Christopher. "Thou art a long way from home."

"I no longer have home. Nor wife nor girls, neither."

"God have mercy."

"Aye. He had mercy enough to save my son." Jonathan shoved Jeremiah through the doorway before him. "But no more."

Jonathan told them that the Eel River settlement was gone, houses burned, livestock slaughtered, eight muskets with powder and shot stolen, every woman and child save Jeremiah tomahawked to death, and him spared only because they thought him dead. Then Jonathan collapsed into a puddle of melting snow by the fire.

Christopher and Patience had reached their sixties in the serenity of faith. Quakers had endured persecution for nearly a decade, but for the Quakers of the lower Cape, Jack's Island had always been a charmed place. There they had held meetings that proclaimed their freedom of mind and spirit, yet known full well that they were protected from persecution by Simeon Bigelow's singing Praying Indians and the blasphemous Jack Hilyard. In the bad times, Christopher and Patience had shielded many a branded Quaker. Now, it seemed, God was asking them to shield Jonathan and his son.

"God work in strange, awful ways," said Patience.

Jonathan looked at her with hatred in his eyes. "'Tis thy people work in strange ways . . . monstrous ways."

Christopher gripped Jonathan's arm. For his age, he was still burly and powerful, and his fingers tightened like line around a loggerhead. "Hold thy tongue, brother. Tar not the good with the bad brush."

But Patience was not offended. Her name fit well. She put her arms around Jonathan's neck and told him he would feel better if he cried. He was a lost child, staying strong for his own child, and Patience made herself his mother. He had not cried since he was a boy, but he pressed his face against her breast and let the tears sting his eyes.

Christopher looked at Jeremiah. Most little boys were shocked when they first saw their fathers cry. Jeremiah simply picked at his stew.

"How be thee, son?"

"The Lord is my shepherd."

"He is that."

iii.

By morning, the world had been reborn in cold brilliance. Ice crystals in the new-fallen snow glittered like jewels. The green creek and blue bay danced with caps of white. It seemed to Christopher that God had scrubbed the darkness from the world before scrubbing the blood from the minds of Jonathan and Jeremiah Hilyard.

But after breakfast, Jonathan prepared to leave.

"Thou cannot go now."

"I must."

"Stay and visit Father. He speaks of thee often."

"No time. Let him know nothin' of what's happened. 'Twill kill him for certain."

"Where thee go?" asked Patience.

"Captain Pierce raises a company to pursue the raiders. I come to raise Cape volunteers and Praying Indians for scouts. We'll find these savages and kill 'em."

Christopher held up his Bible. "The Lord saith, 'If thine enemy strike thee, turn the other cheek.' "

" 'I will pursue after mine enemies and overtake them.' " Young Jeremiah spoke for the first time that morning. " 'And I will not turn again until they are consumed.' "

Christopher recognized the Eighteenth Psalm and was chilled to hear such words from a boy. In Plymouth, they were taught the Old Testament well, he thought. Pray they were taught the New Testament also.

Jonathan embraced his son. Then he and Christopher went out into the snow-blinding sunlight. "Should I not come back, raise the lad up as a soldier of Christ, a good Reformist. 'Twill give him more better chance than the Quakers of Dartmouth ever had. Or my women."

Christopher saw a misery in his brother's eyes that faith would never relieve. No man could lose his children so horribly and still look kindly upon God's inscrutable ways.

For all the women he had lain with, Christopher had fathered no children. It was the only regret of his life. But if God had given him his brother's fate, he would gladly have taken childlessness in its place. As it was, he felt that his heart had been torn from his chest, but his grief could be nothing as to what his brother now bore.

Then, through a stand of trees, Christopher and Jonathan saw their father slouching along the beach, as he did each day.

"Does he come to visit thee?" asked Jonathan.

"Some mornin's, aye, 'less Autumnsquam be with him."

"Autumnsquam? He disappeared fifteen year ago."

"Sixteen. Yet each mornin', Pa pisses on the tree where Autie harpooned the squirrel. Then he asks the tree if his harpooneer wishes to go a-whalin'. Should Autie come to his mind's eye, he will walk the beach, watchin' for drifters or spouts, chatterin' the whole time to his friend. Then will he home, where my mother or yourn await him."

"He's lived too long. Pity he did not die afore this."

"Aye," said Christopher. "Pity us all."

"Tell him not. God may have the mercy to take him afore he hears." Jonathan strapped his musket to his shoulder and trudged off through the early spring snow.

iv.

The first warm day made Autumnsquam sweat. He limped, though he was not lame. The one beside him held a poultice to his ribs, though he was not wounded. The three with them showed elaborate concern, though they were in truth more worried about the column of white soldiers now rounding the riverbank bend.

"They see us," said the youngest warrior.

Autumnsquam glanced over his shoulder. Five Indian scouts were moving out ahead of the column while the rest quick-marched after. To their left, the last chunks of ice were breaking up in the

Pawtucket River. To their right rose the forest where the whites would die.

"The dogs send their Wampanoags out first," said the youngest warrior.

"Those are Nauset Wampanoags," said Autumnsquam. "Nausets who pray to the white man's God."

"Are you not a Nauset?"

"I believe in Kautantowit and the spirits of the sky and earth. I am a true Nauset."

This true Nauset had come far from his Cape Cod land. His wanderings had taken him through forests, across rivers, and finally to the sachemdom of the one for whom he had bought sugar at Aptucxet. He had never forgotten the strong cry and stronger grip of the baby Metacomet, and he had prayed that Kautantowit would not let Metacomet's generation pass without an uprising. Kautantowit had heard his prayers, and Metacomet had heard his warnings of a white wave sweeping westward, carrying the old customs and the old spirits away.

When the war began, Autumnsquam went to the Narragansetts as Metacomet's envoy, to bring them into an alliance. The Narragansetts said no. They had signed a treaty with the English of Boston. But while Autumnsquam stayed at their stockade town in the Great Swamp of Rhode Island, the English of Boston attacked and slaughtered three hundred, by shot, by cutlass, by sharpened pike. They killed men, women, and children without distinction. Then they burned all the dwellings, so that none would know shelter there again.

So much for English treaties and English treachery, said Autumnsquam, and he brought the survivors, vengeful and vicious, into the fight. Now an alliance of Narragansetts, Wampanoags, and Nipmuks was driving the whites back all along the frontier. They struck from out of the forests like the wind. They burned towns, massacred garrisons, killed livestock, and left the whites to stumble about like fools in the forest. Or they led the whites into their traps.

This one had been set by Autumnsquam himself, and so certain was he of success that he offered himself as bait. After all, he was old, and should the trap fail to close, his death would be of no great loss. Yet so impressed were the Narragansetts that several had volunteered to help him.

Now the small band went along the riverbank with their "wounded ones," moving slowly enough that the whites could keep them in sight, but not so slowly that they would be caught. At the place where the river bent again, they took a path into the woods, and the whites followed.

The Nauset scouts called for the Narragansetts to stop, but Autumnsquam's friends hurried him toward a boulder that sat like a *pauwau's wetu* in the middle of the woods. Beyond the boulder, the land sloped to a gully in which lay three hundred Narragansetts, their faces painted black to distinguish them from the Nausets, their weapons ready in their hands.

The whole of the white column, sixty or seventy in strength, had entered the woods now. Their cartridges dangled like baubles from their bandoliers. Their corselets glimmered like silver in the sunshine that slanted through the bare trees.

At the boulder, Autumnsquam fell to the ground, making a great show of rubbing his leg and motioning for the others to go without him.

The English were so close now that he could hear the jangling of their cutlasses, smell the stink of their white bodies, see their faces. Though he had lived his life, his heart pounded hard in his chest, for every man wanted another day. And though his eyes sometimes played tricks on his mind, he thought he saw a familiar face near the front of the column. But all whites were big and wore hair on their faces. And he was an old man.

He could worry no more about the tricks of his eyes. It was his voice that worried him now. It was an old voice, not used to the war cry, and to spring the trap he would have to be heard all the way to the riverbank. He breathed deep. He prayed to Kautantowit. Then he leaped to his feet and cried "Hi-hi-hi-hi-yeah!"

As a flock of starlings took flight, the Narragansetts rose screaming from the gully.

The whites stopped like men who had seen the earth open before them. The leader called for retreat, and his soldiers pivoted smartly, straight into a wall of arrows and musket fire from the Indians who had sneaked up the riverbank behind them.

That the fight went on for two hours was tribute to the bravery of the enemy. Each time that Autumnsquam fired his musket, he was secretly proud of the Praying Indians and sobered by the ferocity of the whites. Even when surrounded by five hundred they fought like demons, back to back, first with deadly musket fire, then with cutlasses and knives, and finally, as the circle closed around them, with bloody bare hands.

When it was over, Autumnsquam went among the dead, not to scalp them, but to pay them tribute. The smell of gunpowder hung like a bad spirit cloud in the air. Tree trunks all around had been splintered by lead shot. The ground was a bloody red mud. And now the victorious Narragansetts were sharpening their knives for the stripping.

Autumnsquam did not know any of the Nausets who had fallen, but he was drawn to the body of the familiar white. He had not shot at this one, though each time he looked during the fighting, there were more dead Indians around him.

A young *pinse* reached the white man first. He pushed aside the bodies of two Narragansetts to get at the man's bandolier, which he slung over his shoulder. Then he picked up the man's hat and put it on his head. "How do I look?" he asked Autumnsquam.

"No good."

The young *pinse* took off the hat and threw it away. Then he pulled out his knife and grabbed the white's forelock.

"Not this one," said Autumnsquam. "He fought bravely. Show him respect."

"No respect for the enemy. I claim his things and his scalp . . . and his balls if I want. It is the way of war."

Autumnsquam could not deny that. Many of the warriors were now wearing warm woolen coats and felt hats. Sachem Canonchet was trying on a shiny corselet. Two dogs were rooting around in the bloody crotch of a dead white man. And those unlucky enough to be alive were screaming as the stripping knives went to work. It was the way of war. But this was no nameless white, and he was still alive.

"This one is mine," said Autumnsquam.

The young *pinse* jumped up. There was blood on his blackened cheek and across his bare chest. "This one killed my brother. He is mine."

"I set the trap. I baited it. I choose him."

The young *pinse* held his knife under Autumnsquam's nose. "Can you stop me from taking his hair, old man?"

"If I go to Canonchet, he will give me what I ask and you will get nothing. If *you* give me what I ask, you may take this man's musket and go well armed to the next fight." Autumnsquam picked up the gun and put it into the young man's hands as a peace offering. It was enough.

"Respect your white warrior. I will go and find *his* brother and kill *him*." He shook the musket and ran off.

Autumnsquam crouched down and whispered, "Your brother, he still stupid damn Quaker?"

Jonathan Hilyard's eyes flickered. An arrow had passed under his collarbone, close to his heart. He bled from slash wounds in his legs and belly, and the side of his head had been bashed by a tomahawk.

"Thick-headed stupid bloody Christian Hilyard," said Autumnsquam. In all his prayers to Kautantowit, he had asked for the safety of these bloody Christian Hilyards. Now Kautantowit had put the safety of one of them into Autumnsquam's hands. Answer your own prayer, the Great Spirit was saying. You have helped to start the war you prayed for. Now help to save the whites you prayed for. If you ask for opposite things, it is up to you to make them come to pass.

v.

After a few days, the boy Jeremiah began to speak without psalms. It would not be long, Christopher knew, before he spoke of the massacre at Clarke's garrison house. Others were speaking of it already, as a few local Indians—well known to the Clarkes and unknown to King Philip—had been arrested, convicted, and executed.

So early one March afternoon, when the wind was lighter than usual, Christopher went to his father's house with a bucket of beer. Jack was splitting logs, small ones, piling them neatly as he went. He seemed glad for a reason to stop. Father and son, now both old men by the calendar, sat on the woodpile, and the son told the father of the bloody doings at Clarke's garrison house.

As if he had not the strength to grieve, or perhaps to comprehend, Jack sipped his beer and said simply, "Our women, they all be taken afore their time. Why does God do this to us?"

"He works his good in awesome strange ways."

"I been alone forty years. Where be the good in that?"

"Job has the answer, I think."

Then Jack studied the smoke curling from the tryworks, "Think thou we'll see more blackfish afore Easter?"

The next morning, the Hilyards sailed their shallop up to Barnstable, the center of the whale oil trade among the bay towns. Boston oil dealers came regularly because the harbor was deep and the spit that protected it was the site of the best tryworks on Cape Cod. At the dock, the Hilyards got a fair price for the fifteen barrels they brought. Then they went up to the village.

Barnstable was becoming a prosperous place, as colonial towns went. The cattle had good forage in the salt marshes. The tryworks supported the church. The shipmen had the harbor, and the merchants and tradesmen served a growing population. Along the County Road, there were fine two-story homes with real glass windows, a meetinghouse, a blacksmith, a trading post, and Crocker's, the most famous tavern on the Cape.

Jack wished to go straight there, but Christopher waved the supply list. "We need molasses, cloth, nails . . ."

As they rounded the corner from the Millway Road, they were struck by a strange quiet. Ordinarily the dust of business hung thick above the County Road, but today the townspeople were clustered in front of Crocker's, listening to a man read solemnly from a sheet of paper.

Christopher asked the blacksmith what passed.

"The marshal reads the list of the dead."

"Dead?"

"The Pierce Massacre."

"Pierce? Massacre?" The words struck Christopher Hilyard like a lance.

Before he could usher his father and nephew away, Christopher heard his brother's name tolled out over the crowd. Then he heard his father's scream of horror at all they had lost, a cry of fury at God, a sound that echoed across fifty-five years. And once more, Christopher knew the hopelessness he had felt on that dark and grieving hill in that terrible first winter.

vi.

It began to rain that afternoon. Autumnsquam thought the rain might soothe Jonathan's fever, so he kept moving. He had taken a horse from a field in the town of Rehoboth and made a pallet of a blanket and two saplings which he could drag over the sandy roads.

He had not removed the arrow, as that might have caused its wound to bleed more. But he had dressed the other wounds with boiled moss and put a poultice of herbs on Jonathan's head. For the fever, he had made a broth of red cedar leaves and maple twigs, but that had done little good.

Near the headwaters of the Scusset, Autumnsquam stopped and looked for a canoe. In the old days, the Scussets always left their canoes, and a man in need might borrow one to get to the bay. But the old days were gone.

vii.

Jack Hilyard listened to the rain pound upon his roof. Night came fast, and with it, he prayed, sleep. And if the sleep were forever, he would pray for nothing else. These last two days had been enough to make any man look warmly upon his own death, even a man who had come at last to believe that God lived only in the minds of men.

The cold rain that fell upon the sea fell also upon the body of his son somewhere to the west, and it cared nothing for either of them. Of those who had gone before, of his two good women and Ezra Bigelow, all that was left moldered in the sand of Plymouth Colony. No heaven greeted Elizabeth or Kate. No hell burned Bigelow for what he might have done to Dorothy Bradford. There was no heaven or hell but here, and no devils but those that walked the earth.

And Jack would make the earth a better place if he killed one. So he climbed out of the bed where he had tried to numb himself with beer and sleep and with the feeling of his own ancient body reshaping itself for the womb. Then he went downstairs and loaded his pistols. They would be good for killing devils.

viii.

Before nightfall, Autumnsquam passed through Moskeetuckqut, the Great Salt Marsh, where the whites now fed their cattle. He could see them in the fields, big shadows clumped dumbly together in the darkening rain, like land whales, but without the dignity or courage.

Autumnsquam had taken this road when he left Cape Cod. Then it had been a sleeve of sand through the tall trees. Now the trees between the road and the bay were near gone, cornfields rolled away to the south, and there was not a quarter-mile distance between any of the houses.

At the supper hour, he came to the village of Barnstable. It had grown mightily since the day he followed the flight of the gull. For near half a mile, the white man's buildings stood side by side, staring out at him, wondering at him. If someone challenged him, he would tell the truth: he had fought at the Pierce Massacre and was taking a white survivor to his family. He would not say he had fought on the other side.

But cold rain and good-smelling stews kept the people by their fires. Not even the marshal came out as Autumnsquam went by.

East of the village, the land rose, and the horse labored to pull the pallet. His flanks were lathered and his gait uncertain. If he faltered, Autumnsquam would have to seek help in the village. And some Praying Indian might say that this one did not march out with Captain Pierce. And Jonathan might not remember old Autie through the heat of the fever. And then the whites would know.

So Autumnsquam jumped down to lighten the load, and when they reached the top of the rise, he let the animal rest. He could see the harbor and the tip of Cummaquid itself, the wild stretch of sand that protected the salt marsh. In the Indian language, Cummaquid meant "long point," but the whites called it Sandy Neck. Where once the Nauset had met the Cummaquid to trade and feast, an orange trying fire fouled the sky.

Even the land had lost its dignity.

ix.

"I worry for Father Jack." Patience stirred clam chowder over the fire.

"I put him to bed and gave him beer. He will sleep." Christopher warmed his hands, then his backside, over the flames, but he knew that this night, nothing would warm his soul.

"Still I worry for him."

"I worry more for *him*." Christopher looked at the boy, who sat on a stool, rocking back and forth, speaking again and again the first verse of the Twenty-third Psalm. "He has not the strength of experience nor the resignation of age. Me and thou, we know of God's ways. And Father knows enough to sleep."

"No man sleep on the night he learn his son dead." She wiped her hands on her apron. "I go to him."

"He curses Indians, and God, too. He curses them for taking all the Hilyard women." Christopher slipped his arms around her girth. "I did not remind him that one Hilyard woman remains, and she is an Indian."

Amapoo smiled. Though her hair had gone gray, her teeth were still even and straight, and her pockmarks had faded into soft wrinkles on her face. "A Quaker Indian."

X.

Simeon Bigelow shuddered to hear the awful news, and he sorrowed to go among the *wetus* and tell the women that their men had died with Captain Pierce and Captain Hilyard.

That night, he convened a service to remember the dead and pray for a just end to the war. But among the Nausets who gathered in the candlelight of the little meetinghouse, Simeon heard as much anger as grief. Their men had died for those who did not trust them enough to let them leave Cape Cod alone, who thought them better off in Praying Towns and plantations than living free in the land of their fathers.

One young man, named Keweenut, was bold enough to say that King Philip might even have had the right idea.

Simeon Bigelow sensed that a single small incident might make his Portanimicut Plantation explode, and if the Nausets joined the fight, so might all the other Cape Cod Indians, and then there would be disaster for all.

When he had comforted his people as best he could, Simeon resolved to go and comfort his old friend Jack. He asked Keweenut and some of the others to accompany him on the four-mile walk, so that they could see that the suffering of the war touched both races.

xi.

Jack put on his cloak and felt hat, shoved the pistols into his belt, and lit his whale oil lantern.

In the barn he reached under the floorboards and pulled out the axe. He had found it in the mud, though he no longer remembered where. He had used it to chop off an Indian head and bring peace that had lasted fifty years. He would use it now to bring peace again.

He unwrapped the canvas and wiped off the oil that protected the axe head against rust. The metal glittered in the lamplight. He ran his thumb over the blade, then across the strange letters engraved in the iron. He wondered what devil god they paid worship.

A bloody cold night it was, and rainy, too . . . a miserable night to walk to Portanimicut, but the perfect kind of night to kill devils.

Autumnsquam tethered his horse to a tree near the edge of the marsh. He had not forgotten his last sight of this place, red and gold in the warm October sun. He had thought never to see it again. Now it appeared like death, a black mass in the sheeting rain, a sodden bog surrounding it.

He could not cross the marsh on horseback. The tide was high and the animal too exhausted to pull himself through the muck. Nor could Autumnsquam carry Jonathan on his back. He was an old man, after all. He would need help. He covered Jonathan as best he could, then stepped onto the planking.

Meanwhile Patience came through the woods to Jack's house. It was raining so hard that several times the flame in her lantern was splashed and guttered.

But she had been right about Jack. No man could sleep on the night he had learned of his son's death. Lamps glowed in every room, and sad light slanted from every window. She pushed open the door and called, but there was no answer. Up the narrow stairs she went to the bedroom. The bed was turned down and rumpled. Then she glanced out the window and saw the light moving south toward the marsh.

She lowered her own lantern and threw open the window. She called Jack's name, but the rain washed away the sound.

When Autumnsquam was halfway across the marsh, he saw the lantern swinging toward him. It stopped for a moment at the top of the island path; then it descended. At first, the old Indian felt the urge to run. Instead, he waved and called, "Hallooo!"

Above the steady pounding of the rain, Jack thought he could hear voices. It might be the wind, or it might be the devils. If he put out his lantern, he could see into the distance, but then he could not see the way in front of him, and if he stepped off the planking, he would sink into the mud and they would kill him.

Then, more clearly, he heard a man shouting "Halloo!" Then he heard a woman calling his name from behind. A light was appearing at the top of the island path, and two more lights were glimmering to life on the far side of the marsh.

The devils . . . surrounding him. But Jack Hilyard was too old to feel panic. He gripped the handle of one of the pistols and prepared to fight.

The woman on the island path was coming after him. Her lantern was descending . . . but she was an Indian. She would try to stop him from doing what he had to do.

He pulled a pistol and fired. Her lanternlight disappeared. Then he drew the other pistol and turned toward the shadow now stopped no more than twenty feet away.

"Who's there?" shouted Jack. "Speak or I'll shoot you, too."

"It Autumnsquam. Old Autie, Jack Stupid Bloody Christian Hilyard."

Jack remembered. He almost smiled. But no. It was a trick . . . a devil Indian who knew an old name . . . a devil whose friends were now hurrying after him with their lanterns.

"Autumnsquam's dead," he said.

"No." The shadow came toward him.

Jack lowered his lantern so that he could better see in the dark rain.

"I bring your son to—"

Jack fired. In the muzzle flash, he saw white whales' teeth shatter as the ball struck the Indian's throat. White whales' teeth . . . Autumnsquam . . . The devil was the great dissembler. Autie was not coming back. . . .

Now Jack pulled the axe from his belt and rushed toward the lanterns entering the marsh from the mainland.

"Jack! Stop!" someone was shouting at him, a familiar voice, a white man's voice, but the only face he could see in the lanternlight was Indian.

Satan took many forms . . . and spoke in many voices.

"Stop!"

Jack barreled into the Indian, swinging the axe as he went. The Indian shouted and tried to sidestep, but Jack swung hard and felt the blade bite into flesh and bone.

"Jack!" screamed one of the others. "God has given us a miracle."

"Tempt me with no miracles. Satan tempted Christ with miracles in the desert. See what happened to him!" Jack knew that the Indian was not dead, so he raised the axe again.

"No, Jack! Thou'll start a war!"

Jack recognized the voice of Simeon Bigelow. "I finish one."

Simeon grabbed Jack's arm.

Jack pushed him back and swung the axe. If Satan could take the form of Autumnsquam, he could as easily become a white preacher. "Get back."

"But Jack, thy son—"

"You've killed him—" And the grief-mad old man turned his axe at another old friend.

Simeon was bigger than Jack, but near as brittle, and as he tried to wrench the axe away, he slipped, pulling the axe and Jack with him into the soaking marsh.

The black rain poured down. Its black sound roared down. And the blade of the axe split Jack Hilyard's breast.

xii.

It had begun in blood, and that was as it ended. It had begun in horror, but for the Hilyards, some small measure of order was restored, some sense of God's mercy remained. An ancient father died before his son after all. A son returned from the land of the dead to raise up his own son in the name of the Lord. A wife survived the pistol shot that shattered her lantern. And two old friends, one who brought the future, one who had been the past, were laid side by side in a small grove of pines near Nauseiput Creek.

Young Jeremiah read from the Twenty-third Psalm as though he truly understood it. Jonathan leaned on Patience and she upon Christopher. And Praying Indians filled the woods.

Simeon prayed once more for a just end to a terrible war. He thanked God for his goodness, and then, as an afterthought, he thanked Kautantowit. He knew it was a small blasphemy, but it seemed to please the older Indians, and it would have pleased Autumnsquam.

Then the strange funeral procession wound its way back through the woods and cut-over meadows to Jack's house, where Patience had prepared a repast in honor of the dead.

"Thou shalt never know how pained I am at killing thy father," said Simeon to Christopher before they went in.

"'Twas an accident."

Simeon shook his head. "Had he killed an Indian, or an Indian killed him, there would have been terrible days on Cape Cod, days to make Satan happy."

"Thou hast done more than any man to keep Satan at bay. My father said thou wert the most best man he ever knew. And he kept somethin' I think it meet for thee to have."

Christopher led Simeon to the new barn that had been built on the site of the first one. Pulling back a trapdoor, he climbed down into the ancient hole, and after a few moments he found the ballast stone that his father had split in half many years before. Fitted neatly behind it, the color of the earth into which it had been pressed, was a wax-sealed box. Stamped in the corner was the foundry mark of a man long dead. Inside was the narrative of a people who would grow large in the memories of their children.

He pressed the box into Simeon's hands. "Read this, old friend. Then do with it what thou wilt."

"What is it?"

"The sea journal of Christopher Jones."

Simeon hefted the box as if to feel the weight of history. "Jones was a rough man, but a good'n."

"He admired the First Comers, though he spoke as well of their failings."

Simeon looked into Christopher's eyes. "Did he speak of my brother and Dorothy Bradford within the same pages?"

Christopher could not tell what Simeon knew or suspected, and so he merely nodded.

"Is that the reason thou now owns this island?"

"We went through much hell to get this place. If God favor papists, we may burn in hell for our effort. But that book worked its magic upon thy brother . . . rightly or wrongly."

"Why give it to me?"

"'Tis an ode to faith and bravery, written by a man of little faith. Thou art a man of faith and bravery preachin' to those with little faith." Christopher patted the box with his hand. "Thy faith and bravery saved this Cape from the horror that Jonathan's family suffered at Plymouth. This book is an ode to thee."

Simeon looked at the box, then at the axe that lay against the grindstone. "I will take the box if you rebury the axe, as once I asked your father to do."

"Done."

"The axe is not somethin' I care to look on again." He held up the box. "But this will I read."

And he read both the good and the bad of it. And yes, it told of his brother and Dorothy Bradford dallying on the deck of the *Mayflower*. Yet it spoke most delicately of delicate matters. And during the dying time, Jones spoke of Ezra, of all the First Comers, as men of strong faith and Christian kindness.

When King Philip's War ended, however, their descendants proved that for all God's interest in their affairs, they had learned little of God's mercy.

King Philip was run to earth in August, in the same Rhode Island swamplands where he had heard the warlike counsel of Autumnsquam and the others. What hopelessness he felt for his race when the whites at last encircled him would never be known. He was shot, beheaded, drawn, and quartered. His hands were sent to Boston, his head to Plymouth. The four pieces of his torso were hung in the trees.

This did not shock Simeon. He had seen Witawawmut's head rot in the sun. He knew the language of war. But he could not understand the new path to peace. He was in Plymouth, when the captives of the last battles were brought through. Wampanoag men and women, linked by chains and rope, their children clutching at their sides, had less the appearance of beaten enemies than of broken hearts. Most of the men sensed that they were leaving their land forever, and this journey was their last walk with their loved ones.

Plymouth had suffered greatly, though in truth no worse than the Indians. The colony had incurred bills of great magnitude, 27,000 pounds in all. The tax levy had been enormous. But still the debt remained. So it was decided that those who had caused the war— or, more truthfully, those who had lost it—would pay for it.

The proposal, forwarded by many of the most learned men of the colony, and most vociferously by Brewster Bigelow, was to sell the captured Wampanoags into slavery.

Simeon never forgot the sight of families broken up on the hallowed ground of Plymouth, within the shadow of the burial hill where the First Comers lay. This was not what God had wanted, nor what William Bradford would have permitted. But it was done.

Some of the luckier Indians were given to Plymouth men in payment for wartime loans. These might be well treated and see their loved ones again. A few might even gain freedom and move to the Mashpee Plantation on Cape Cod, where many Wampanoag families had fled. But the rest were marched on to Boston. From thence would they be shipped to the West Indies, to be sold and to die in the pestilent climate.

"'Twas not necessary, nephew," Simeon told Brewster as they watched the Wampanoags straggling sadly north under the muskets of the Plymouth militia. "A hand of peace would have done you better."

"'Twas Satan put 'em here, uncle. Every minister believes that. They proved it at Clarkes' garrison house. We do the Lord's work in wipin' 'em from the earth."

"They be humans, no different from us in their hearts."

At the sound of Brewster Bigelow's laughter, Simeon resolved that he would not share with such men the story of their fathers' faith. He saw, in that beaten chain of Indians, the perversion of the beliefs that had driven the First Comers across the Atlantic. Christopher Jones's journal of faith and sacrifice could never restore what was lost when those Indians were sent to the slave ships, nor could it inspire men who would make such a terrible choice.

So he went back to Portanimicut and wondered what he would do with the sea journal.

At Jack's Island, Christopher Hilyard wondered what he would do with the axe. He thought to bury it again in the marsh mud where his father had found it. It was the beheader of Witawawmut, the killer of his father and perhaps of many others unnamed. But he could not deny the strength he felt when he held it. And in the wilderness, even the most peaceable Quaker admired strength.

CHAPTER 17

July 11

Iron Axe

"Shouldn't you do something to protect the axe?" said Douglas Bigelow. "Encase it in Lucite or something?"

"Then I couldn't touch it." John M.—for Manuel—Nance pushed a button pad to disconnect the alarm, then took the axe out of its case. "I like to touch it."

The blade passed under Doug's nose. He was supposed to admire it while sensing the subtle threat.

"You could shave with it"—Nance twisted his wrist, causing the blade to flash and the strange letters to flicker—"or chop off a head."

Doug looked out at the fog on Pleasant Bay and wondered what he was doing in Nance's library. But he already knew. He was surviving.

John M. Nance—from Provincetown to Chatham in one generation, from the home of fishing boats and bohos, where the houses were small and the streets were crowded, to the Cape Cod capital of preppy, where even some of the *locals* wore lime green trousers with their blue blazers. John M. Nance, son of a Portagee and a Pilgrim, great-grandson—so the rumor went—of a runaway slave, looking as respectable as the dining room at the Chatham Bars Inn . . .

And as white. White Lacoste shirt, white tennis shorts, white sweat socks. The only color the little Union Jack on his Reebok sneakers. But for all the whiteness, he tanned as well as anyone Doug had ever seen. He didn't burn and peel like his English ancestors or darken to Portuguese olive. He *browned*, like a good American who'd never heard of skin cancer or the thinning of the ozone layer.

He admitted to being sixty-two, though people took him for forty-five or so. His hair was black, no dye job, his current wife was thirty-two, and his features were as smooth as the bow of his cigarette boat.

He lived on Shore Road in an enormous Colonial Revival with black shutters, twelve-over-twelve windows, wings like studding sails, views of Pleasant Bay, and a secretarial staff so he didn't have to go to Boston but once a week.

"This axe reminds me of how hard I had to fight to get here . . . and who I had to chop up."

Doug uncrossed and recrossed his legs, as if to say he was a busy man.

"Nice pants," said Nance.

Doug was wearing lime green pants with little blue whales spouting red steam. Good golf-course pants.

"So Clara's dead. One down, one to go."

"That's cold-blooded," said Doug.

"I say what *you* only think. The privilege of money."

Doug hated to admit it, but Nance was right.

"Now that we're over the eminent-domain hurdle, you're looking better." Nance twirled the axe in his hands. "But it would be nice to have Rake Hilyard's piece, too."

"We may not have much choice."

Nance spoke very softly and pointed the axe at Doug, "I didn't save you from the banks to hear you say *that*."

Iron Axe Ventures was a major player, known for shopping malls in Maine, ski condos in Vermont, strip malls everywhere, money, limited partnerships, tax shelters, accelerated depreciations, smart lawyers, money, deals, deep pockets, more smart lawyers, more money, smart investors, smart advertisers, smart sales force, and even more money for all the smarts.

Bigelow Development was small-time by comparison. To win the game on Cape Cod, they needed the backing of the big boys, especially now that the business cycle, rather than the tree-huggers, had cooled the development fervor on Cape Cod.

Nance's company had targeted Jack's Island during the early eighties. Nance had proposed a joint development—ninety condo units, conference center, tennis courts. Dickerson Bigelow turned him down. After all, there was a . . . history between them.

And Dickerson had never needed partners. He had developed only his own land, with short lines of credit and no interference, building a company with twenty million dollars in equity and a reputation to match. Then, as the Reagan recovery began, Dickerson had started listening to his son.

Leverage. That was the word Douglas used. Leverage that turned twenty million into fifty or sixty or more. Big developers did it in Boston with every project. Big business did it on Wall Street every day. And they did it in Washington every fiscal year. The whole damn country was leveraged. So why not Bigelow Development?

With Douglas making more decisions and Dickerson deferring to him, the Bigelows had built all over the Cape—big condos near the water, small subdivisions in the scrub pine, strip malls along Route 28. And they were not alone.

For a while, builders couldn't build fast enough, and environmentalists couldn't stop them. The Cape population jumped—retirees, construction workers following the work, commuters who claimed they didn't mind the two-hour drive to Boston, people who needed no more than a terminal and a fax to work anywhere. Somewhere along the line, Douglas had divorced and remarried. His father questioned his personal sense but not his business sense. After all, the banks were leveraged, the builders were leveraged, the buyers were leveraged, everybody was making money. And then it stopped.

Massachusetts stopped booming. Money stopped flowing. Builders had satisfied the demand and then some. In two years, inflated property values dropped by twenty-five percent. The Bigelows were caught with too many houses and too many strip malls and too little cash.

And because of leverage there was debt. And when the Bigelows couldn't service their debt, the banks called the loans. And since the banks were in trouble, they weren't offering new lines of credit to overextended builders. It happened to a lot of people.

But what about twenty million in equity? Most of it was tied up in property, and as property values fell, twenty million was suddenly worth less than ten, with a cash position of less than two.

It wasn't surprising that Dickerson went down with a heart attack.

And when his survival was in doubt, he signed power of attorney over to his son . . . for everything.

Doug knew he needed two things—a loan and collateral. For collateral he had the 1904 subdivision. For the loan he took the 1904 plan to a man who had once tried to make a deal for Jack's Island. After all, to Doug, deals were like weather systems, sometimes bringing big storms of money, sometimes fizzling into nothing. He couldn't turn one away simply because there was a . . . history.

"The clock is running, Doug. Acquisition should go to ten million, including utilities. With forty units of premium housing, we should still see ten million clear." He turned the axe in his hands once more. "But we can't let this old Rake Hilyard get in the way, or your hesitant brother-in-law."

"Don't worry about them."

"And your father? Does he know who saved his ass yet?"

"He's still pretty weak. He hasn't asked many questions. He'll see the intelligence of this alliance."

"It's no alliance. I'm taking back what your father took from me. You get a service fee."

Doug got up. "We've made a deal. That's all."

"Nine months. Perked and permitted in nine months. The whole island." Nance brought the axe down so that it cut through the blotter and into the mahogany desk. It was not the first time he had done it.

ii.

The morning after they buried Clara, Geoff went to see Rake, even though the old man had treated him like the red tide at the funeral.

He called Rake's name and let himself in. There might have been a time when Rake cleaned his house, but not in the last thirty years. The rooms were piled floor to ceiling with newspapers, and the dining room table was covered with magazines, pamphlets, letters, photocopies, coffee cups, Hostess cupcake wrappers, and in a foxhole in the middle of the mess, a typewriter with which Rake fought his battles.

Geoff read the sheet on the platen: "Dear Miss Hallissey, I have considered letting you see some material that may aid in the search for—" There it ended. What was he giving her? And why was he putting his trust into the hands of a stranger?

"Rake!" he called through the house, across the backyard, and into the barn. Then he went down to the water and called again.

It was a close day, humid enough to rot sand, and a gray mist blanketed the bay.

"Gone fishin'." Emily was loping down the beach from the sailing camp. "Took off in his Boston Whaler as soon as he had enough water to get over the flats, fog be damned."

Emily was in her fifties and never much of a beauty. Her nose took care of that. And she had not been very lucky with men, either. Maybe it was the muscles from hauling sailboats or the no-nonsense way she wore her hair, or maybe it was that *attitude* that had intimidated suitors. Here was a woman who wouldn't go to pieces if a man left her. She'd simply have another smoke and get on with things.

Competent. That was Emily. Maybe that was why she had stood Arnie Burr all these years, and weathered her mother's death without a tear.

"Has Rake ever mentioned anything to you about the log of the *Mayflower?*" asked Geoff.

She gave him one of her cigarette-cracked laughs. "Last night, after I told him we were selling. He wanted to go through Ma's room."

"Why?"

She set a cigarette between her lips. "To see if she'd *left* anything. Arnie said there'd be no snoopin', so it got nasty—Rake doesn't like Arnie much, you know—and Rake said his sister wouldn't want us sellin' the camp. He thought she might have put it in a will somewhere. Arnie threw him out." A match hissed in Emily's hand. "Arnie can be a bastard sometimes."

She sucked the flame into the tip of the cigarette. With the butt still between her lips, she blew a stream of smoke out the corner of her mouth and tossed the match in the sand. Nobody could smoke a cigarette better. "So then Rake started in about the log. He said he'd buy up the whole island with it, and if he couldn't, it still had things in it to keep the island safe forever."

"Safe . . ." Geoff stared off into the fog.

"What in hell is he talkin' about? Do you know?"

"I don't even think *he* knows."

"Well, one thing I *do* know: when we clear probate, we're sellin'." She flicked an ash. "We've had enough. Pressin' for deposits in May, hand-holdin' the homesicks in July, watchin' that no one's caught in the August squalls, hopin' none of the female counselors miss their periods in September."

"You and your mother brought a lot of happiness, Em."

"Now it's time to get some back."

Geoff looked at the island. "It's getting harder for me to imagine houses from one end of this beach to the other."

She pointed him toward the Eastham shore, where the fog was beginning to lift. "Do you think that the first Englishmen who stood on this beach could have imagined houses from Rock Harbor all the way to P-town?"

iii.

Emily was right. Change was inevitable. The sailing camp didn't make financial sense anymore, and the barracks along Nauseiput Creek were a worse eyesore than anything he would ever design.

So why did he feel so bad about the chance of a lifetime? As the fog blew in and blew out and blew back in again, he tried to avoid the question a bit longer by keeping his appointment with Carolyn Hallissey.

Old Comers Plantation was part museum, part library, part tourist attraction, a special genus of Cape Cod museum like the Heritage Plantation in Sandwich. It perched on the edge of Portanimicut Pond, which fed into Pleasant Bay, and had once been the estate of a Pilgrim descendant who had made a fortune in munitions during World War I.

The lawns were clipped like putting greens. The daylilies bloomed in a fugue of colors that promised to play all summer. The pines and hardwoods were groomed like bonsai. And if you kept an eye closed, you hardly noticed the "Kiss Me, I'm on Vacation" T-shirts or the kids complaining to their parents that there was nothing here that was *fun*, not the antique windmill or the replica of a Nauset lifesaving station or the reproduction of a Wampanoag longhouse or the library that was the center of the collection.

Carolyn's office was on the second floor of the main house, in what had been the master bedroom.

Alone in a bedroom with Carolyn Hallissey . . . Geoff settled into a wing chair opposite her desk and watched the fog drift up the inlet from Pleasant Bay and tried to act cool.

Carolyn called for coffee. "I'm sorry to hear about your aunt. I never got to talk to her."

"Why?" Be a bit aggressive. Don't go giving her the advantage by letting her know you think she's gorgeous.

"Well, whenever one of her generation passes on, we lose another little fiber of the fabric."

"Is that why you went to my uncle?"

"Am I missing something here? Are you mad that I outbid you for that painting or something?"

Too aggressive, he thought, so he smiled. "It's just that you seem to have an inordinate interest in my family."

"Your family has had an inordinately long presence on Cape Cod. And I have a grant to do oral histories on old Cape Codders. That's simple enough."

"All right, I'll ask you a simple one. When you visited my uncle, did you talk about the *Mayflower* log?"

She put on a pair of glasses and raised her chin, as though studying him through bifocals. He guessed the glasses were a prop. "I may have." She pressed the intercom and told her secretary to bring the Hilyard folder with the coffee. "We'll read the transcript."

Very cool, he thought. And now she was letting the silence sit between them, to see what might flow from it. She hadn't gotten to be the director of this well-endowed little place at—what? thirty-one?—without learning how to look bulletproof.

But Geoff had sat through enough sessions with critical clients and stubborn bosses to know that there came a time when the best thing to do was *shut up*. Make the other guy feel nervous, force *him* (or her) to ask a few questions, get to know *her* (or his) mind before you said anything else.

The staring ended with the coffee, brought by a young man who couldn't have been more than twenty-three. He had one of those haircuts that took everything off the sides and left the curls on top, and he wore fashion's latest attempt to usher the business suit into the twenty-first century—a sort of brown Eisenhower jacket and trousers that made him look more like a bellhop who'd forgotten his hat than the avatar of the sartorial age.

"How's his dictation?" cracked Geoff when he left.

"David's excellent at what he does. At night he goes home . . . to Provincetown." This last came with a significant little nod about certain young men from P-town. Then she started the tape recorder on her desk. "Where were we?"

"Are you now taking my oral history?"

"Are you giving it?"

"I need to be romanced before I do something so . . . intimate."

She slipped off the glasses. They absolutely *were* a prop. "In the present line of conversation what would you consider . . . romantic?"

"More on the *Mayflower* log. Since he talked to you, my uncle has decided that all he has to do is dig into the right dune and he'll find it. I'd like to know what gives, so that I can disillusion him."

"You shouldn't disillusion old men. Illusions are all they have left."

"My wife thinks she knows a younger man with a few illusions of his own." That, he thought, sounded as bad as "My wife doesn't understand me."

But Carolyn acted as though she hadn't noticed the lame pass. "You understand how important illusions are. Your uncle showed me his barn, and I saw a doorstop—"

"The *Mayflower* log. Would you bid on it if you found it?"

She gave him a deep, sexy laugh that suggested a lot more than it said. "So it's the talk of *money* that turns you on. Of course I'd bid on it. We're talking about one of the most significant finds since the invention of the stitched binding." A note of awe crept into her voice. "The Bradford diary has its own perspective, and *Mourt's Relation* was written by apologists, promoters trying to tell their friends in England how great it was here. Christopher Jones was just a shipmaster, probably very practical and uncultured. His log might tell us no more than the way the wind was blowing, or . . . it might show history with all its blemishes."

"Blemishes make it more valuable?"

"People love to know the dirt. Who's screwing whom and so forth. Dirt brings history to life."

"So, how much for . . . blemishes?"

"Recently a letter by Thomas Jefferson sold for three hundred thousand dollars. I'd guess something like the log would go on the block for millions."

"Could you afford it?"

She ran her fingers through her long hair, a very casual gesture. Perhaps it was *meant* to be, which made it less casual but no less attractive. "We have some rich members on the board. Real estate fortunes from the mid-eighties. They support Old Comers Plantation so the world won't think they're Cape rapers. Their motives may be hypocritical, but their money's green."

Now Geoff knew why she had charmed Rake. She could freeze you out with a cold smile or give you a friendly frown that pulled you so close to her prejudices that you thought the whole world was us against them.

She took the folder from the coffee tray. It was about six inches thick, filled with Xerox copies, documents, clippings. "We're trying to tighten the scholarly focus here by organizing files on the historic Cape families. We collect what's been written about a family, photocopy everything from family letters to deeds, cross-reference them, and try to build a picture of how the Cape came to be what it is."

He went to the desk and looked over her shoulder. He tried to ignore the aroma of Shalimar coming off the back of her neck, but if he had really wanted to ignore it, he could have stayed on the other side of the desk. "Do you have anything for Jack's Island?"

"Most of the records were lost in the Barnstable County Courthouse fire in 1834, but we have this." She flipped to a copy of an ancient ledger filled with tiny script. "From the records of Brewster Bigelow, son of one of the Old Comers, found in the attic of the family home in Barnstable. It dates to 1717."

"The year the *Whydah* sank," mused Geoff.

"Considering the myths I've heard about Black Bellamy—"

"That he's one of our ancestors?" Geoff laughed.

"There may be some connection between his ship, the *Whydah*, and this." She pointed to an entry. " 'Purchased of Jeremiah Hilyard, November 9, 1717, the certain property called Jack's Island, bounded by Nauseiput Creek on the east, Jack's Creek on the west, and all the marsh southward to the mainland, for the sum of one hundred pounds.' "

"What makes you think this relates to the *Whydah*?"

"That." She pointed to a painting above the fireplace.

Geoff had been so busy looking at Carolyn that he hadn't noticed the distinctive style of Tom Hilyard's narrative period. Five figures were jammed into the frame, two facing three. On one side, a comical-looking old man in nightshirt and cap held up a lantern while behind him his wife held a blunderbuss. On the other side, faces contorted absurdly in shock, were a young white woman and two Indians. *The Arrest of Serenity.*

CHAPTER 18

May 1716

Serenity and the Pirate

The boy who had survived through prayer the massacre at Clarkes' garrison house grew with a straight spine and a firm faith and married a woman more devout than himself. He took her to the Eastham farm his father had bequeathed to him, and there they brought six children into the world, of whom two survived infancy. The boy they named Solemnity, and he grew so strong in the faith that they sent him to Harvard to study the Word of God. The girl they called Serenity, more in hope than in fulfillment.

In the spring of 1716, there came to Cape Cod a handsome giant of a man whose beard was so black that it gave him his name. Black Bellamy he was called, and he wooed the young woman whose great-grandfather had come on the *Mayflower*, and he promised he would return a spring hence to marry her. Then he sailed for the Caribbean, while the belly of Serenity Hilyard grew large.

There was talk of punishing her for unlawful carnal knowledge. Two days in the stocks was the proper sentence, one for the evidence beneath her apron, a second for refusing to identify the father. But Justice Doane said such punishment was too severe for a woman with child, and Serenity was too stubborn to give up the father's name.

Besides, everyone thought it was Sam Bellamy did the begetting.

If he came back, he would be punished. If not, his absence would be punishment enough for Serenity. No scarlet letter would brand her. No elder would bar her or her child from meeting. There was mercy in Eastham, after all. And her stubbornness was seen by most as a virtue—not so lustrous as purity, perhaps, but enough to gain her the respect of those who damned her sin.

Respect did not ease her father's mortification, however. To let his daughter's bastard be born beneath his roof was almost too much to bear. Yet how much worse would it be to put her out? asked his wife, Arbella. What kind of parents would they be then? What kind of Christians?

Serenity felt the first pains on a raw morning in February 1717. The wind had swung 'round to the northeast, and snow clouds were blowing in. Arbella wrung her hands, then sent her husband to fetch the midwife, Goody Doane. But Goody Doane was off to tend another young woman, and this one had a *husband*.

Jeremiah had learned to brook those insults he could not rebut, and with the first flakes fluttering down, he pulled his cloak around his neck and headed down the King's Road to Goody Snow's. There the news was the same, though more gently offered. Goody Snow had gone to the aid of Mrs. Bangs, near Sunken Meadow Pond, and could offer no help until Mrs. Bangs had been delivered.

So Jeremiah took to the road once more. He was forty-nine, as strong and stubborn as the pin oak that rooted in the sand and dared the wind to blow it down, with a face that might have been cut from the hard oak wood itself. What he had survived in youth had prepared him for God's arbitrary ways, and neither birth nor death disconcerted him. But the sight of Sarah Daggett coming through the snow nearly caused him to cry out in shock.

"I guess thou be needin' a midwife." She was stooped and wrinkled and had only three teeth, and it was said that she always wore her bonnet because she had more hair on her chin than on her head. It was also whispered about that she was a witch.

"How could you know our need?"

She touched a finger aside of her nose. "I smelled it."

Yes, he thought, a witch. Why else would she have left her distant sandspit and traveled by shallop and on foot to meet him here on the road? But what would be more fitting than a witch to birth a bastard?

ii.

Serenity was eighteen, with wild black hair and eyes that could change from green to blue as quickly as the sea on a bright windy day.

She had resolved that she would present Sam Bellamy with a healthy child, no matter that the midwives of Eastham might shun her, no matter the truth of the tales now reaching Cape Cod, tales of plunder and murder and great flaming hulks left for dead upon the sea. Her Sam, they said, had become a pirate. She would not believe it until he told her himself.

When her labor began, she slid a box from under her bed and put it beside her. In it she had packed an hourglass to time the pains, clean swaddling, a sharp knife to cut the cord, thread to tie it, and a leather strap to bite on, so that her parents would not hear her scream. After all, her mother was no match for anyone's pain, and she would give her father no satisfaction for the suffering brought on by her fornication.

She was biting hard on the strap when Goody Daggett shook the snow from her shawl.

"Another biter, eh?"

The pain was rising to its peak. Serenity drove her teeth into the leather.

"Bite down, darlin', bite down." The old woman winked at Arbella, who stood on the other side of the bed, her arms folded tight across her deflated breasts. "Just like all the rest, bitin' and fightin'."

"I bit the strap through six births," said Arbella. "What other way is there?"

Serenity felt the pain receding now. Her body relaxed and settled back onto the bed. She closed her eyes and tried not to think. Then she felt the strap slipped from between her lips. A warm wet cloth was passed over her forehead. Outside, the wind whipped the snow against the house, but Serenity was aware only of the old woman's touch.

"You came far," said Serenity.

"I smelled the air this mornin' and said there'd be babies by nightfall."

"Just by *smellin'*?" Arbella unconsciously took a step back from the bed.

"Smelled a storm, I did. Nobody sees it, but babies is always born when there's storms. And I knew there'd be one lass who might go beggin' for a midwife."

"But all the way from Billingsgate Island?"

The old woman smiled, as if to say that the journey was not so bad if you had a broomstick to ride on. "Serenity's as good a girl as any, I'd say."

"She'd be better if she had a father for that child," said Jeremiah from the doorway.

"The child's got a father," snapped the old woman. "How in holy heaven does thou think it got in there? Just be thankful it's got a strong mother."

"The father will come," Serenity said softly.

Jeremiah looked out at the snow. "Not this night."

Goody Daggett ordered him out, then took the girl's hand. "Now let me show thee why they sometimes calls me a witch."

Serenity fixed her eyes on the old woman's face. Arbella's lips moved in a psalm; then she leaned close to hear the witchcraft.

"To ease your pain, we're going to use . . . the air."

"Spirits?" said Serenity.

Arbella looked around the narrow birthing room.

"Just the air."

"The air? What foolishness is this?" demanded Arbella, perhaps disappointed at such simplicity when she expected spells and newt's-tongue stew.

"God put air on this earth so's birthin' women could ease their pain." And she told Serenity simply to breathe when she felt her womb tightening. Breathe fast and shallow, she said, in-out-in-out-in-out, and faster as the pain reached its peak.

"What about the strap?"

"The strap means thou's fightin', and there's nothin' finer than a woman with some fight in her." Goody Daggett rubbed her smooth old palm over Serenity's belly. "But that little beauty in there don't want thee fightin'. He wants thee acceptin', givin' thanks. So do the most natural thing there is. *Breathe.* God'll take care of the rest."

And he did. Blizzard and birth pains kept up the night through, but Serenity breathed hard and harder, and only at the end, when it came time to push, did she cry out. And the name she cried was Sam, again and again. Sam. I'll birth you a son, and we'll all three live happy. Sam. Come home. Black Sam. Black Sam Bellamy.

And whatever warmth her father had felt for her went cold. Until that moment Jeremiah had prayed that it might have been a Cape Cod lad who had done his daughter, someone dishonorable and cowardly, for certain, but not the one they said was a pirate. When the baby's cry rose above the wind, Jeremiah did not run into the room, as he had done at the births of his own children. Instead he pulled down the Bible and sought out the psalms.

It was left for Serenity to summon him, and however reluctantly, he went. She looked radiant, joyous, and, for one of the few times in her life, serene. "His name will be Jeremiah Edward, Father."

Goody Daggett had said there was no better way to soften a man than to give his name to a child.

"Jeremiah Edward *what?*" he asked coldly.

Serenity's smile faded. "He shall bear the last name that I bear . . . whatever it might be."

"That name'll be Hilyard, for no decent man'll have you now."

"Jeremiah Edward Hilyard, then." She looked down at the black hair nestled against her breast. "But we'll call him Ned."

The snow fell for two days more. When the sun appeared at last, three and a half feet covered the open fields, six-foot drifts rose against houses and hillsides, and Jeremiah was like to go mad with the chattering of the women and the squalling of the babe who now bore his name. So he put on snowshoes and went among his cattle. All but one had survived. He butchered that one and put out marsh hay for the rest, then began the seven-mile walk to his property in the north parish of Harwich.

At Christopher's death, Jeremiah had inherited Jack's Island. He preferred Eastham, but he could never sell such a fine piece of salt marsh and upland. So he let a group of Praying Indians live there in exchange for half the money earned from cattle, hay, corn, and drift whales. This he set aside for the education of his son, Solemnity.

And Solemnity was much on his mind as he came upon a funeral procession digging through the snow. A thousand Praying Indians bore to his rest the body of Samuel Treat, Eastham's minister and righteous voice for the Indians of Cape Cod. Jeremiah had prayed that one day his son would replace Treat on the Eastham pulpit, when he had done with Harvard and prepared himself for the call. But Treat had died too soon. Now Solemnity would have to wait.

Because of Serenity's sin, he might have to wait forever.

iii.

Springtime came slowly to Cape Cod. On even the clearest day, a cold east wind kicked up after noon and kept coming until dark. With clouds to feed it, the wind turned wet as well, bringing fog and mist and rainy gloom that sat for days, as heavy upon the soul as upon the sand itself. And in the spring of 1717, not even the smile of an eight-week infant could brighten the gloom at Jeremiah Hilyard's cottage.

Serenity said she would leave when summer came. If Sam Bellamy returned, she would go with him, because pirate or no, it would mean that he loved her. Otherwise, she would simply leave and never think on him again. She did not know where she would go, but she could not sit by the fire and nurse her child for many nights more, while her mother clicked knitting needles and told her how well she took to motherhood—for a *husbandless* woman—and her father read aloud from the Bible, as if to drive her sin from his house.

She felt the sucking at her breast grow gentler. She knew the babe was close to sleep. She had come to know, from merely his touch, what he wanted and what he liked. When Sam Bellamy's beard first scratched her breast, she had cried out in shock and pleasure at the intimacy. But here was an intimacy that no lover could equal. Here she gave life to life. As she gently removed his mouth from her breast, she thanked God for the child, however he had come.

"This is the night." Jeremiah looked up from the Bible.

"What?" Arbella sat in a Bradford chair beside the fireplace, her hands working steadily at her knitting.

"This is the night that the Lord will send Black Bellamy to Cape Cod."

"'Tis foul weather for sailin'," said Arbella.

The wind had backed out of the northeast earlier in the day, and the rain had begun just after nightfall. The second great storm of Anno Domini 1717 had begun. Now the little house on the Nauset Plain shivered in the gale.

"Does this prophecy appear in your Bible?" asked Serenity.

"A just God sent a great blizzard to take a great man like Reverend Sam Treat. He sends a foul no'theaster to drown a foul fornicatin' pirate like Sam Bellamy."

She looked at her baby. "The God who makes this child fatherless is not just."

"The *father* made him fatherless. And considerin' the father, the child's the better for it."

Serenity stalked up the stairs and put the baby into his cradle. When she came back to the great room, she was wearing her cape.

"Where are you goin'?" demanded her father.

"To show a just God my face. Let him see that some don't cower."

"You defy God?"

She took a lantern from the shelf and filled it with whale oil. "I defy the darkness."

But it was more than mere darkness. It was a wild, howling blackness of a storm that shook the trees and drove the rain like shot against her face, that sent the clouds scudding across the sky and produced, beneath the wail of the wind, a deep and steady roar that seemed the sound of creation itself.

She followed the sound, and it led her to edge of the earth. Even through the blackness, she could see the boiling surge a hundred feet below, hear the awesome thunder of it, and feel the ground quiver each time it tore into the bluff.

But Serenity was not awed. She had come to shout defiance, to show God the face of one who would not fear him, of one who would never cease to ask him why, and who would start by asking why she had been born in this miserable corner of the earth, to a psalm-singing father, a devoutly superstitious mother, and a brother upon whom all the love and hope of the family rained down.

What wonder that she was nothing like her name? These simple Protestants called their children after things they admired, Faith, Hope, Solemnity, even Wrestling and Increase, for the sons they hoped would wrestle the devil and increase the faith. But never would they name one Defiance.

It was defiance had driven her into the arms of Sam Bellamy. Her father had told her to resist him. But how could she resist Sam Bellamy? Cape Cod farm boys talked about the number of herring they needed to manure a good cornfield, Cape Cod fishermen about the number of cornfields a good herring catch could manure. Sam Bellamy spoke of London and the Caribbean and the riches he would seek among the sunken treasure ships of the Spanish Main. He said no woman of his would hoe corn rows or make sewing needles from fish bones.

She would never forget the sense of danger she had felt when he first slipped his arms around her and told her he loved her. She knew he was no more than a wastrel looking for a warm quim. But she stepped back and raised her skirts, and when he entered her, she felt that she had defied the world.

As she drew breath to shout her defiance this night, she saw something that caused her to call God's name instead. Two lights were glimmering through the black rain—the stern lights of a ship, a mile north and not more than a mile offshore. The lights were moving, which meant the vessel was still making headway, but she had entered the graveyard of ships.

That was what they called the back shore from Chatham to the Provincelands, where great underwater waves of sand shifted with the current and rose from the sea as the tide ran out, protection for the bluffs against the full force of the Atlantic but treachery itself for the mariner lost in a gale.

Serenity raised her lantern and began to run. She knew that by dawn, there would be dead men on the beach. She prayed that Sam Bellamy would not be among them.

She had not gone far when the stern lights stopped and began to swing toward shore, as if the captain were turning toward her lantern. In panic she doused the flame. She had heard of mooncussers, plundering scoundrels who waved lanterns to lure lost ships onto the shoals.

The lights stopped. Their motion had no bearing on her lantern. The captain had seen that wind and sea were taking the ship, and he had thrown out the anchors to hold her off the outer bar. The giant flukes had dug into the sand and the cables had snapped taut, turning the bow straight into the northeast wind. It was a last desperate maneuver, for a ship on the run could ride the waves, but a ship rooted to an anchor was no more bending than a fence post.

Serenity was close enough to see in the blackness the black shadow of the ship and the waves exploding skyward as they struck. Then the stern lights began to slide. The anchors could not hold against the force of wind and sea, and the flukes became like great plows, cutting furrows across the sandy bottom.

And Serenity ran, driven by the fear that her father's prophecy had come true. She imagined Sam, screaming orders at terrified seamen, flogging them into the rigging to save what was left of the blown-out sails, driving them forward to cut the cables for a final seaward run, firing his pistol to keep them from the liquor store, where some would seek strength or oblivion, and clinging to the helm that might already have shattered the mate's arms in a mad come-about spin. Her Sam, facing death because he had come back for her after all.

Then the lights stopped moving. The ship had struck. A wave swept over the great shadow and the lights were gone.

iv.

The crying of the gulls woke Serenity, the crying and the strange quiet. The roar had receded, had all but ceased. There was sand in her mouth. Her cloak was soaked through. And her breasts ached with the fullness of her milk. She crawled out from under the holly bush where she had collapsed and looked over the edge of the bluff.

The clouds were lifting off the horizon, like a ragged curtain, revealing a lurid band of red sky and a sea the color of slate. That sea now rolled over a shattered shoal of wood a thousand feet offshore, and with each crump of the surf, it carried more debris to the beach, so that the sand was strewn, for a mile in either direction, with spars and line, casks and crates, bolts of cloth and bottles . . . and bodies.

Serenity pulled herself to her feet, and the bluff collapsed beneath her. Her stomach dropped; then her head seemed to follow it. She fell a hundred feet in an instant, tumbling and spinning down the steep embankment like a little girl in a giddy, dangerous game.

She had forgotten that storms could tear great chunks of sand from the bottom of the bank, leaving the bluff loosened and unsafe. But there was no gentler fall, and no faster way to reach the beach. She landed, sitting upright, a few feet from the body of a man in a fine greatcoat. He lay on his stomach, his head twisted at a strange angle.

"Sir?" she said. "Sir?"

The man did not answer.

She crawled over to him and nudged his shoulder.

He did not move.

She rolled him onto his back, and he sloshed like a half-filled cask. Water bubbled up out of his mouth. His eyes stared blankly at the gulls. And beneath his greatcoat he wore nothing but breeches and a cutlass.

Not the dress of a civilized gentleman. She looked around at the other bodies, broken and bloated, dressed in rough clothes and rags. Pirates . . . honest men . . . She could not tell. Some of their faces were serene, sleeping peacefully in death. Others were twisted grotesquely, mirroring the last sight that had passed before their eyes.

She staggered among the bodies, protected from the horror by a numbness, an icy cold that came, not from her wet clothes or the wind, but from within. She knelt beside this one, turned over that. She did not smell the gassy stink puffing from the mouths or recoil at the clammy flesh and stiffened limbs. She called for her Sam, but the only answer came from the gulls.

Then someone groaned. She stopped and looked around.

The sun had appeared on the horizon. Flecks of light danced on the gray water like bloody coins, and the bluffs were turning red behind her. Down by the water, someone was rolling over, lifting himself to his knees, looking about to make sure he was in this world and not the next.

At first she was frightened. Here was a pirate, a desperate man. Then she saw the whales'-tooth necklace and cried out his name.

John Autumn stood and tried to run, but he tripped over a shattered spar, and gold coins fell glittering from his pocket. He stared at them for a moment, then at Serenity, and like a frightened animal, began to limp up the beach. He did not go far before he collapsed in the sand once more.

She knew him. He had lived on Jack's Island, and they had played as children. He claimed Autumnsquam as uncle and Serenity's great-aunt Patience as aunt. He said it was Patience who had fixed the necklace of Autumnsquam and given it to him. No one was certain of such things. There were many legends. What was certain was his seamanship. He knew the Cape shoals as well as any, and it had been rumored that he had taken his knowledge on the pirates' account with Black Bellamy.

She knelt by his side. "Was this Sam's ship?"

He pressed a finger to his lips, as though he could not tell her. His hair was a tangle of salt and snarls, his dark skin darkened by his time in the southern sun. And whatever had given him the gash on his forehead seemed to have knocked him senseless as well.

"Johnny, my Sam! Tell me about my Sam."

"Can't stay." His left foot and ankle were twice the size of his right, but still he tried to rise.

"You'll be goin' nowhere on that leg."

He grabbed a broken piece of planking and levered himself to his feet.

"I'll help you. Just tell me about my Sam."

"Can't stay. Can't stay or I'll hang."

"I bore his child, Johnny. Tell me."

"Cap'n Sam's dead."

Serenity felt the milk in her breasts let down, whether from fullness or the sudden rush of emotion, she did not know. "Is he among these dead?"

He shook his head again. His mind seemed to be clearing. "The last I seen him, he lashed hisself to the helm. I was goin' to cut him loose when we turned turtle."

"Were you . . . were you really pirates?"

He pulled a piece of eight from his pocket. "You'll find these on most. Weighin' 'em down to their deaths. Look through the wreckage, you'll find plenty more. If I could stay, I'd be rich." He scanned the top of the bluffs. "But they'll be comin'. Soon they'll be all over the beach."

He dug the plank into the sand and tried to move again, but he did not go far before giving up. "I have gold enough in my pockets to let you and your babe live half a year in Boston. I give it all to you if you get me up that bluff."

The sun was full above the horizon. Its light was now hard and white and made the dead on the beach seem of no more value than the broken spars and smashed casks. To the scavengers who soon would come to pick over the wreck, they would be worth less.

Serenity told Johnny to get himself to the base of the bluff. Then she went about the business of collecting two hundred feet of line. She found a length wrapped around one of the broken spars, another around a cask, another lying loose. For all her exhaustion, she worked quickly, stopping only to pick up gold coins spilled from a dead man's pocket. She could not bring herself, however, to put her hand inside.

She tied the line under Johnny's arms. Then she climbed to the top in a switchback pattern, as she had when she was a little girl disobeying her father's order to stay off the bluffs.

At the top, she wrapped the line twice around a tree. With Johnny using his arms and his good leg, she hauled him to the top and hid him in the small clump of bushes where she had collapsed.

"You can't leave me here," he said.

"No one'll see you, and I must go to my baby." She put her hands on top of her rock-hard breasts and massaged them. "I'll come back with my father's cart."

"Where can we go?"

"Jack's Island?"

"They'll be waitin' for me there."

"Do you fear witches, then?"

"I fear nothin' I don't believe in."

"Then we'll go to Billingsgate, to Goody Daggett's."

v.

The news spread quickly that Bellamy's flagship, the *Whydah*, had struck the bar. And a haul from pirates' heaven she was, a three-hundred-ton trader and slave galley taken off Jamaica with twenty thousand pounds of gold in coin and dust, indigo, ivory, Jesuit's bark for quinine, and an armament of eighteen twenty-four pounders.

No one knew how many people plundered the wreck in the days after. It was the law in Massachusetts Colony, which by now had swallowed up Plymouth Colony, that whenever a ship was wrecked, the town clerk took possession until proper disposition of vessel and cargo were made. This meant until the town and colony took their share.

A more time-honored law said that abandoned vessels were the property of those who salvaged them, and in the God-fearing hamlets of Cape Cod, this was the law that mattered. After all, Cape Codders lived isolated and independent at the edge of the earth. They endured nature's worst and counted the best as part of God's Providence.

From the *Whydah* they hauled off spars, line, broken barrels, casks of wine, planking, whatever cargo survived the surf. One man even found an elephant tusk rolling in the waves. Many found pieces of eight and other coins. And a few found more than ever they would admit.

Captain Cyprian Southack, sent by the colony a few days later, found nothing. The seas were too rough to save any of the treasure that the shoaling sands had begun to bury, and few Cape Codders had any intention of surrendering what they had secreted in their barns and mattresses.

When they did not bring forth their spoils, Southack sent men to every farmhouse on the Lower Cape. One he sent was a Cape Cod barrister whose family was well connected to the Colonial government—Ezekiel Bigelow, son of Brewster.

During the second week of May, he and his associate, a fat Boston man named Worthington, reached the settlement at Chequesset Neck. They sailed over to Great Island and stayed the night at the sign of the Spouting Whale—"Samuel Smith, he has good flip, Good Toddy if you Please, The Way is Near and Very Clear, 'Tis just beyond the trees." After they turned in, Smith sent word to his aunt, Sarah Daggett, that the king's men were coming.

The next day, they crossed Jeremy Island to Billingsgate Island, the windswept stretch of dunes where Jack Hilyard had put up his first tower. Other whalemen still kept a tower, trywork, and whaling house on the island. Fishermen had also come, and oystermen as well. Most built shacks to stay for a season, though a few lived there the year through, Josh Daggett's widow among them.

"What do thee want?" Goody Daggett squinted in the harsh sunlight, of which there was no other kind on Billingsgate Island.

Ezekiel Bigelow removed his hat. "We come to ask, marm, if you've anythin' from the pirate ship *Whydah*, or know of any who does."

She laughed and her three teeth stood out like jokes in a sermon. "Oh, most certain I do. I've fifty gold sovereigns in me budge, if thou cares to fish for 'em, and me cat's got a gold bell 'round her neck give to 'er by Black Bellamy hisself."

"We merely do a job, marm. And what about him?"

John Autumn glanced up, then went back to carving a piece of whalebone. He little resembled the Indian people remembered. He had taken off his necklace, shaken his hair out of its English knot, and sat by Goody Daggett's door, bare-chested and breechclouted, with a blanket around his legs to conceal his splinted ankle.

"He ain't been off the island in two weeks, 'cept to go up to Sam Smith's and fetch me a bucket of beer."

Bigelow brought his face close to the Indian's. "Do you sip the beer as you bring it?"

John shook his head.

Worthington grabbed the Indian by the chin and twisted his face. "A question was asked. Answer with your tongue."

Control your temper, thought Serenity, who hid beneath Goody Daggett's bed. She had come to Billingsgate that morning to tell of the rumor now running about Eastham: the only known survivor of the *Whydah*, a carpenter kidnapped by the pirates, had seen Johnny Autumn's body on the beach as he climbed the bluff before dawn. When he came back with the townsmen, the Indian was gone.

"I ask you, Injun, do you sip any of the beer?"

"No. That crime for Injun."

"Indeed." Bigelow smiled, though his cheeks remained hollow. "How came you by the gash on your forehead?"

"I hit him with me fryin' pan when he come late with the firewood," said Goody Daggett.

"Hear, hear," said Worthington.

Serenity felt little Ned stirring in her arms. He was awakening, and he managed to get out a cranky little squawk before she could get her breast into his mouth.

"What was that?" asked Ezekiel Bigelow.

"What?" said Goody Daggett.

"Who else lives here?"

Goody Daggett pointed across the dune to a shack on Grampus Bay. "The Hatch brothers, but they be fishin'."

Then came a louder squawk from the back of the house.

The king's men looked at one another, and Johnny gripped the knife beneath his blanket.

Serenity held the baby tight. If they found Sam Bellamy's woman here, it would mean the end of freedom for Johnny the pirate and for those who had hidden him.

There was another squawk and old Goody Daggett laughed. "That's Lucinda."

"Lucinda?"

"Talkin' to Josh again."

"Josh Daggett? Your husband?" said Bigelow.

She shifted her eyes onto Worthington and gave him a little wink. "Dead he is. Five year now."

Worthington stepped back. "Then who's Lucinda?"

The old woman went inside. There were more squawks and the tinkling of a little bell, and she returned, cradling her cat in her arms. It was, of course, as black as pitch.

"Lucinda, say hello." Surreptitiously, she scratched a fingernail on the cat's asshole and made it squawk.

Worthington took another step back. "They *said* you were a witch."

The old lady offered the cat to Worthington. "Stroke her fur and she'll bring you luck. A cat who can see the afterlife's a rare thing."

Worthington raised his hands. "I've seen enough. Let us leave this old crone and her Indian . . . and her black cat."

Ezekiel Bigelow looked hard at Goody Daggett. "Do not play at witchcraft, marm. 'Tis still a capital crime."

Goody Daggett gave the cat's bell a tinkle. "Who can know what a cat sees?"

When they were gone, she broke out the beer and served Johnny first. "Thou be safe now, son. Haul me firewood and water, and stay as long's thou likes."

Johnny reached into the bucket of oysters he had harvested that dawn. He opened one for Goody Daggett.

"The pirate's whore, the Indian, and the old witch of Billingsgate. That's what they'll call us." Goody Daggett sucked in the oyster. "I say piss on 'em all."

Little Ned began to fuss, and Serenity shifted him from one shoulder to the other. "My father has softened some, now that Sam's dead."

"Thou can't stay there, darlin'. He'll smother thee. Him and all the holy faces of Eastham." The old woman slurped in another oyster and wiped the juice off her chin. "That's why I lives out here, with no company but the wind and Lucinda."

The baby continued to fuss. Serenity shifted again, but he would not quiet.

"Give him." John took the baby and laid it on his knees. Then he reached under his stool and brought out the whales'-tooth necklace. Miraculously the crying stopped, the tiny eyes focused, the hands reached for something new. John teased the fingers a bit, then slipped the toy into them.

"As skillful with him as with the shoals," said Serenity.

John smiled. "He can have it."

"But, John—"

"I'll never wear it again, not with king's men huntin' me."

"And Ezekiel Bigelow leadin' 'em." Goody Daggett spat. "Him and his people are hard ones. Always has been."

"It's said Simeon was a good man," offered Serenity.

John nodded. "He told me I was good's any white man. But he had strange parts, too. Old Keweenut, from Jack's Island, he told me once him and Simeon buried a box at Cornhill by the light of a full moon."

"What was in it?"

"He never said. Just big magic, that's all."

"Big magic." Serenity looked at Goody Daggett. "Sounds like somethin' for a witch."

She cackled. "Ain't no such thing as a witch."

Serenity came regularly to the island after that. She might beg a ride on a fishing boat at the Herring River or make the long walk over the dunes. Naturally her father objected to her wanderings. He feared that she was studying witchcraft and would one day be hanged for it. He would have greeted that fate more warmly than the truth —that she was falling in love with the Indian Johnny Autumn.

No man could have been gentler with Ned, and none had ever been gentler with her. Johnny and Ned would play for hours, and when it came time to leave, the baby would always cry. While the baby slept, Johnny and Serenity would talk. And what he told her sometimes made her cry.

Yes, Sam Bellamy had been coming back for her. He loved her so much that he endangered riches and crew for her. He talked of her so much that hardened pirates yearned to see her eyes change from green to blue like the sea on a bright windy day.

Serenity did not entirely believe him, but she listened for hours to the stories. And soon, it was *his* admiration that she heard, not Sam Bellamy's.

Johnny said that most pirates were like Serenity, rebels against a world that put every person in a place above which he could not aspire. He took his lesson from Bellamy, who had proclaimed he would not "pin his faith upon a pimp of a parson who neither practices nor believes what he puts upon the chuckleheaded fools he preaches to." Bellamy called himself a free prince. And there was a girl on Cape Cod he sought to make his princess.

Some days, Serenity and Johnny would not talk, but simply sit beneath the sailcloth awning beside the house and stare at the blue distance. Or watch in silence as the gulls circled and swooped.

And some days they would be filled with anger at the injustice

of life. What crime, Johnny once asked, was there in stealing the
Whydah? She had been built as a slaver and named for an African
port where the slaves were sold. Every ounce of gold she carried had
been tarnished by the tears of black-skinned men now gone into
chains. "We punished them slavers as sure as the storm punished
us. And for that they'd hang me."

Serenity put her arms around him. "They'll never find you,
John. I promise."

"I can't stay here forever. And if I leave, I can never be seen
with you."

"Do you wish that? To be seen with me?"

"I dream of it, like Sam did."

He wore only a breechclout, and she did not deny that the sight
of his flesh excited her as much as his words. In the bedroom, Goody
Daggett snored beside the baby. On the bay, the fishermen worked
their nets. And Serenity slid her hands down his flanks and untied
the leather around his waist.

Then she lay back on the cool sand beneath the awning and
drew him onto her. Against her clothes, his nakedness felt all the
more sinful. But this was not sin or rebellion. It was need. And no
baby could fulfill it, nor any father's psalm. She undid her bodice
and pressed his face to her breasts. Then she raised her skirt.

There was no other preliminary, because all had been preliminary to this. He entered her and she clung.

She moved to the island soon after and set herself up in an
abandoned shack. Her father objected, but she gave her solemn
promise that she would study no witchcraft. The few who lived year-
round on Billingsgate Island paid her no mind. Most of them had
run away from something as well. But the fishermen and whalers
who came for the warm months were mostly family men and church-
goers, and so Serenity and John remained circumspect in their affections.

And never did they sail together to Billingsgate town, which
now was growing three miles north, within the harbor that Great
Island, Jeremy Island, and Billingsgate Island itself created. Together,
Serenity and Johnny showed their faces only on the lonely dunes.

One late August eve, at Goody Daggett's, they ate the corn that
Johnny had coaxed from the sand with a dressing of bluefish heads,
seaweed, and crushed shells. When they were done, Goody Daggett

said that nights were growing shorter and winter would soon be upon them, so they had best think about leaving. "For there be no place bleaker, and I'll not have bleak faces when the world's too bleak for words. I'd rather have nothin'."

But Serenity and John could not leave together. And if they stayed, the fishermen's wives might finally come to gossip. And what if the gossip brought back the king's men?

"Thou hast a bit of gold, hasn't thee?" asked Goody Daggett. "What thee picked up from the beach?"

"'Twould let us live a few months, somewhere," answered Serenity, "were there a place Black Bellamy's woman and an Indian could live without suspicion, or a place we could spend Spanish pieces of eight without gettin' the attention of the colony."

Johnny poured more beer for the women and took some for himself. "Even at Smith's, they say the king's men keep a sharp eye for such coins."

"'Tis true enough, that." Goody Daggett sipped her beer. "I did forget."

Serenity put her hand on John's. "So, we need a miracle."

Johnny placed his hand on hers. "Or big magic."

vi.

When he saw Johnny Autumn appear at Jack's Island, Keweenut laughed and cried. He was old and his left arm was a useless hook and he said his mind lived in days that would never come back. They talked of Autumnsquam and Amapoo. They talked of Jeremiah Hilyard, who let Indians live on Jack's Island, of Jack himself, whose axe had crippled Keweenut so long ago. And they talked of Simeon Bigelow, who had reminded them of their dignity. Then Johnny asked about the big medicine that Simeon and Keweenut had buried many years before.

The next night, beneath flickering torches, Johnny, Keweenut, and Serenity dug into the sand near the base of Cornhill. After several tries, they found an old rush basket filled with rotted seed corn. Inside it was an iron box.

"Simeon say he bury it in the place where they first take Indian corn," explained Keweenut. "He give back big magic of truth."

"Truth?" asked Serenity.

"In that box."

Serenity peeled away the wax seal and found a book, preserved almost perfectly in dry sand. " 'The Journal of Christopher Jones, Master of the *Mayflower*, July 1620 to May 1621.' We must take this back to Billingsgate."

"No," said Keweenut.

"But—"

"I say I show it. I do not say you take it."

Johnny held a torch over it. "Read. Then we argue."

Serenity pushed back her shawl and sat on the sand. For three hours she read aloud. For the first time in months, she stopped thinking about her little Ned—watched over that night by Goody Daggett—and the hard future that faced them. When she was finished, she was convinced that they should take the book because it could change that future.

"No," said old Keweenut. "I promise Simeon I keep the story and pass it down. Now I old, so I pass it to Johnny. He pass it down to the next Nauset, if any left. Pass the story of big medicine in Cornhill. But the book must stay in Cornhill."

"But can you not see what this is?" Serenity begged.

Keweenut shook his head.

"It tells the story of the First Comers, the ones what took the Cape away from you. It's a big truth that would be worth much money to a learned man."

Keweenut shook his head again and squared his English hat on his head. He had done all that he would.

Serenity looked at Johnny, whose eyes were sunken shadows in the torchlight. "This book could save you, Johnny. A certain king's man might wish to keep its truth hidden. He might even pay."

Then Keweenut spat in the sand. "How this hurt king's man?"

"It says there were villains among the First Comers. And their name was the name of a king's man."

Johnny pulled his blanket around his shoulders and told her to quiet herself. The dancing of the torchlight made his face look even more skeletal, as if he had surrendered, right there on Cornhill, to the extinction of his race.

Well, Serenity would never quiet herself or let him surrender. "You know the name of the villains, Johnny. 'Tis *Bigelow*."

And Keweenut snatched the book from her hands. "You will not say bad of the Bigelows."

"A Bigelow may have pushed a woman off the First Comers' ship," said Serenity. "And his son sold Indians into slavery. And his *grandso*n would hang Johnny. Villains."

But Keweenut would not waver. He said he could not see what good the book would do for the children of enslaved Wampanoags or for Johnny. He said the best man he had ever known was the Bigelow who buried the book. Now a Hilyard wished to take it. So he shook his crippled arm at Serenity. "Your great-grandfather did this. Do not tell me of bad Bigelows. And do not steal the book, or Habbamock will curse you."

So they resealed and buried the box, and Serenity resolved that she would come back before long, damn the threats of the evil spirit Habbamock.

When they returned to the beach, their whaleboat was gone, lifted off by the spring tide. After searching up the beach and down, they huddled together in the cold September night, wondering what had become of the greatness of their people, and how they would get home.

They decided that walking the King's Road would be better than staying there until the tide returned their drifting boat. If they were lucky, they could reach Chequesset Neck by suncoming, Goody Daggett's by breakfast.

However, luck was no more with them than it had been with Black Bellamy. They did not make it through Truro. A farmer tending a sick cow saw them and took his suspicions over the hill to Constable Freeman, who was waiting with a blunderbuss when the remnant of a great people straggled into the village.

He might have let them go, except for the white woman. No decent woman was about in the middle of the night with Indians, unless she was up to "witchly doings," and so they were arrested.

vii.

The silver oar, symbol of the Admiralty Court, glimmered like pirate's treasure in the sunlight. From her cell window, which looked down a narrow alley toward North Street, Serenity could see nothing else but backs and raised fists and children peering through their parents' legs as the procession of pirates went past.

Eight were hanged in all, Johnny and seven from a second ship that sailed north with Black Bellamy.

One of the few mercies of Serenity's imprisonment was that she did not see the hanging, though she was able to hear it in the noise of the crowd that lined the route. When their roar loudened, she knew the prisoners had reached the gallows. When it ceased, she knew that the end was near. She imagined the nooses being fitted and the Reverend Mr. Mather reading a final psalm. Then came the bloodcurdling cry that was part cheer, part shriek at the sight of eight men sent to God.

She buried her face in her hands and cried bitterly. She tried not to imagine the twitching legs, the blackening faces, the grotesque erections that rose as the men died. She tried to think only of that day in the dunes when they had first made love.

There would be no more love for Serenity. She had been given five years' hard labor. When her child was weaned, he would be taken from her, and she would be sent to a workhouse to serve out her sentence. Keweenut was deemed innocent. Despite her reputation as a witch, Goody Daggett was given the mercy of the court.

The women's jail was a rat-infested old house close by the waterfront. There were bars on the windows, but in deference to the softer sex, there was clean straw on the floors and some privacy in the small rooms.

Serenity had been given the room closest to the keeper's fireplace, so that her baby would get a bit of warmth. Prostitutes and those taken in gaming were farthest away. Women who failed to keep holy the Sabbath or who neglected their husbands occupied the middle rooms. And those who had somehow lost grip on sanity, who tore at their hair or tossed horse dung at passersby, were put all in a single room and left to thrash.

But Solemnity Hilyard would not shun his sister, and he visited her on the night that Johnny was hanged.

"Oh, Lem, this life can be misery." Serenity threw her arms around her brother's neck and began to cry.

He did not recoil at the touch of her dirty clothes. He was two years older, decades beyond her in demeanor. His jaw and forehead seemed to have been smoothed by a sculptor to remove any traces of passion. His brown frock, matching waistcoat, and breeches were the image of probity for the putative minister.

He stroked her snarled hair. "Our Lord knew misery in this life, Rennie. He is our example."

"No sermons, Lem. I've the Reverend Mr. Mather for that."

His eyes filled with warmth, as though he remembered that this was his sister, not some parishioner come for counsel. "No sermons, then. You were never one for sermons."

"How's mother?"

He shook his head. "This comes hard to her."

"No harder than to me." With the back of one of her fingerless gloves, she wiped her nose.

"Father is wounded as well. And your brother prays for you."

"No prayers." She pushed away. "Except for little Ned."

The baby, now nine months old, slept on the pallet in the corner. Solemnity sat beside him.

"Watch for bedbugs," his sister warned.

He touched the baby's black hair. "The Lord makes them so beautiful."

"Even a pirate's child?"

"He loves 'em all."

"Father doesn't. He'll not take little Ned in. I must give him to the colony to care for." She drew a tattered shawl tight around her shoulders. "What'll he become then?"

"Might you also ask that if he is raised by Pa."

"Pa, he's blood, no matter how sour." She sat next to him. "Besides, Pa did good enough by you."

He took her hands in his. "Now that you've a child of your own, you may know how unquestioning is a parent's love, no matter what the child may do or the parent may say."

She looked down at her filthy fingernails and tried not to cry. She was sorry for nothing, but she would have given anything to be back on the plains of Nauset.

"I will persuade Father to care for the child, if Mother has not already," said Solemnity.

She looked into his eyes. "Thank you, Lem."

"If I can't persuade him, I'll care for the child myself."

"I love you, Lem, no matter how different we are."

"We may be more similar than you think, sister." He drew her once more to his arms. The lone candle cast a huge dancing shadow on the wall.

"Not in faith," she whispered.

"In our passions . . . in our questions."

She pushed back from him and looked into his eyes. "What questions have you?"

He laughed, as if he had revealed too much of himself to her. "What were you doing in Truro the night you were arrested?"

And in the guttering light, she told the only man she trusted of the journey to Cornhill and of the book she had found buried there. She told him more than she had told the court, far more than he asked.

viii.

The journey down from Barnstable was a long one for an old man, but Brewster Bigelow had dreamed of making it many times, and as Ezekiel had told him, there would be no better opportunity than the present.

"I can serve you tea," said Jeremiah Hilyard, inviting Brewster and his son to sit in his great room, which was merely the largest room in a very small house.

"Tea will do." Brewster Bigelow daubed a handkerchief at his running nose and took the Bradford chair by the fire. He removed his hat, but he left his cloak around his shoulders. His father had many times described the debates among the Saints who wished to sail to Virginia and those who thought the Guianas would be the place for settlement. His father said that those who went to warmer climes lacked the industriousness to build godly colonies. In this Brewster disagreed, but in most things, the child had become the man.

He had inherited the faith, the faith in the faith as an instrument of betterment for those around him, the commitment to colonial service, and the consuming desire to own land. And there was one parcel he had wished to own since the day that his father sold it.

"Where is your wife, Mr. Hilyard?" asked Ezekiel.

"Taken to her bed."

"Fever?" Brewster Bigelow pressed his handkerchief to his nose and began looking for the door. An old man could not be too careful.

"Sadness."

"We saw the boy out by the marsh, clutching the skirts of a goodwife."

"Goody Daggett." Jeremiah's voice sounded softer, older.

"You trust her?" asked Ezekiel.

"She proves her charity, even if she is a witch. She'll go home when my wife can care for him."

Ezekiel, who was thirty years old, showed all the patience of an older man in his dealings. "We are heartfelt sorry for what you have suffered, Mr. Hilyard. Most indeed."

Brewster, who was seventy-six, had the impatience of a man who sensed that his time was short. "The child is a blot upon your family shield."

"He's my grandson, like it or no."

"True enough. True enough." Brewster coughed several times. "If you have honey, I'll take it in my tea."

Jeremiah put three spoons of tea into the pot, then poured steaming water from the kettle.

Ezekiel drew closer, squinting slightly as the steam rose around his face. "Your grandson is God's child before all else. But in a family such as this, with aspirations such as yours for Solemnity, the child may prove an embarrassment."

"Indeed." Brewster hacked several times more. Then he picked up the poker and pushed at the fire to raise more flame. "A man whose sister has fornicated with a pirate and brought his bastard—"

Jeremiah Hilyard slammed the pot on the table. "I've suffered enough on this. And my wife even more. We need no more visitin' *friends* like you two."

"You do, if we bring advice." Brewster raised something to his mouth and spat it into the fireplace.

"You've brought nothin' ever before. I'd not even see you were you not a Harvard overseer."

"A task my father takes most seriously," said Ezekiel. "After all, Harvard was founded to advance the ministry and increase our understandin' of Holy Writ. Its honor must be jealously guarded."

At the mention of Harvard, shining star in the firmament of America's ministry, Jeremiah calmed his anger and poured the tea. "What is your advice?"

"Solemnity has a bright future," said Ezekiel. "Perhaps at Harvard, perhaps in the local ministry. But his family connections will stand against him, now that you've taken Black Bellamy's bastard into your house."

Brewster rose from his chair. "You will need to go far to make amends in the eyes of the world. But if you do, you may guarantee Solemnity's future."

"See that no future comes to the bastard child," said Ezekiel. "Allow Serenity no inheritance to pass on."

Jeremiah Hilyard let a rare smile cross his face. "You want me to sell Jack's Island."

Brewster waved his hand as though the remark were an insult. "Your girl must have no inheritance. Only through hard work and honesty can her child atone for his father's sin and prove that he is worthy of the community."

Jeremiah's smile faded. "You do not speak in jest?"

Ezekiel leaped in to close the breach his father was opening. "Sell the land as assurance to the people of Cape Cod, to the people at Harvard—"

—"whose ear we have"—

—"that you believe firmly in the education of Solemnity Hilyard. Give *him* the money. Let it not fall into hands that were fathered by evil."

"Then you want me to sell it . . . to you?"

"We have not only Harvard's ear, but the church's as well." Brewster Bigelow began to cough, a face-reddening, eye-watering attack of catarrh that almost drowned out the words that mattered most, as though they mattered not at all to Brewster. "A word from us, and Solemnity will be called to the First Parish of Harwich."

"Harwich?" whispered Jeremiah. "A ministerial call to Cape Cod?"

The coughing ceased instantly. "Aye. Harwich."

And Jeremiah agreed, for his piety was great, as was his dream for his son. And his spirit was broken. The seventy acres of upland and fifty of marsh were sold for the princely sum of one hundred pounds. The buyers were the family who first had owned it, the Bigelows of Barnstable. And within a week of assuming the deed, they ordered Keweenut and the other Indians who lived there to leave.

ix.

Serenity spent the next five years living in the barn of a man named Gideon Glint, who oversaw seven women, renting them out to the

rich merchants of Boston as scullery maids. Her brother visited from
time to time. By horseback, the journey from Cambridge to Roxbury
took less than two hours. And he wrote to her regularly, though his
letters often brought bad news.

November 30, 1717

Dear Sister,

Hope you are well. I must tell you that Father has sold
Jack's Island to the Bigelows. It embarrasses me to say that
he intends to donate the money to my education and the
upkeep of the Eastham parish. I begged him to do otherwise, but he was adamant. I am sorry for you and for little
Ned. I will try, in some way, to see that some of this comes
to you.

Serenity burned the letter, scorned her father, and cursed the
Bigelows. Lem she forgave.

February 9, 1718

Dear Sister,

With overwhelming sadness, I report the death of our
mother. Shortly after you left, she took to her bed and never
rose again.

This leaves Goody Daggett as the only woman in little
Ned's life. She stays now in Eastham to be with him. She
is surely no witch but an angel of mercy.

As for mother, Father says she died of a broken heart. I
urge you not to believe this or to blame yourself. I think
she died of consumption. We shall miss her, but the Lord
works in strange ways.

Serenity blamed herself for nothing and thanked God for Goody
Daggett. Her father she blamed for his unbending belief that every
storm was a sign from God and every sin received quick retribution.
Was God punishing Serenity by Arbella's death? Or Jeremiah? Or
was it simply Arbella's time to die?

October 10, 1718

Dear Sister,

Good news. I have been called to the parish of Harwich,
to assist the Reverend Mr. Stone in his pastorate. This is

a fine position for someone only recently ordained. I am told that Ezekiel Bigelow was most vocal in my favor. The townsfolk have deeded me ten acres of woodland and a small house, plus a tax on all drift whales. I admit to you, though to no others, that my ambition reaches somewhat higher than this. Before I finish, I will preach in Boston, perhaps in London. But this is a fine situation for the nonce.

I pray that I may serve them well and that I may now be a stronger influence on little Ned.

She prayed for his happiness, and she prayed for her boy. Lem would realize his ambitions. Of that she had no doubt. But would her boy ever come to know her? How could he when he visited her only on the rare occasions when Solemnity could come to Boston?

April 9, 1720

Dear Sister,

I once told you that we were more alike than you thought, in our questions and our passions. And just as your passion undid you, mine has undone me.

I will be blunt. There was in the parish a young woman named Samantha Kittredge, formerly of Yarmouth. She is the wife of Captain Hezekiah K., who works the coastal trade 'twixt Boston and New York and is away for many weeks at a time.

In her loneliness, she came to me for Bible study. I was smitten, as, it seemed, was she. One night, while endeavoring to study Ecclesiastes, we came to study each other.

I would have been the wiser to have taken her to some bower of bliss in the woods. But—here I speak frank—her hair was the golden color of marsh grass in September, and her lips, as they formed the holy words, were a communion I could not resist.

The Reverend Mr. Stone discovered us in flagrante delicto. Samantha now wears a scarlet letter upon her breast and has moved to Truro. Her husband will not have her, and she is too mortified to return to Yarmouth. I was forced to beg public forgiveness and step down. I am undone and drifting. Father is devastated.

Whatever order there was in Serenity's life was torn away. There was discipline aplenty. Mr. Glint was not averse to using the whip when it pleased him. And there was structure for every day. But Lem's letters had reminded her of her life's center. Her boy had been cared for, and her father, and the flock of Harwich. Now she did not know if she pitied Lem or their father more.

July 12, 1720

Dear Sister,

Father is dead. He was harvesting oysters near Billings-gate when a squall struck. His boat was found overturned, his body washed up on Lieutenant Island. May God have mercy on his soul.

I fear that he welcomed the squall. We wounded him, you and I, and he spoke often of meeting God to discuss his failings. He was a simple man who believed simply, a strong man with strong faith.

I must tell you that Bigelow has made an offer on the Eastham property. It is most generous, and as my indiscretion has left me without prospect, I need income, as will Goody Daggett in bringing up the boy.

I am in no state to raise a child and have sent Ned to Billingsgate with Goody Daggett. By selling the Eastham property, I can guarantee their support.

She cried for her father, though she had never expected that she would. She worried for her little boy. And she raged at her brother. She wrote back, urging him not to sell the land. Goody Daggett was resourceful, after all. And how could he do more business with the Bigelows, "who have a history of treachery dating from the First Comers?"

October 9, 1720

Dear Sister,

It is done. Father made me the sole heir to the property, and I felt it necessary to sell. Half of the money have I given to Goody Daggett for Ned's care. Half have I kept for myself. As for besmirching the Bigelows, I reject it totally. They are the only ones who have helped me.

Through the good offices of Ezekiel, I have been given opportunity to redeem myself in an Indian parish at Cumassakumkanet, Sandwich. I will be assistant pastor to Amos Colt, Indian by heritage but a fine Christian. I intend to put thoughts of Samantha behind me and devote myself to the good of Mr. Colt's flock. Their meetinghouse is a wooden Methuselah. Rebuilding it will be the first task of my new life.

X.

The following week, Solemnity went begging at the Bigelow law office, on the first floor of the Barnstable home that Brewster Bigelow had built in 1700, a monument to the wisdom of owning land and studying the law. It carried two full stories, with three roof dormers, and was painted a hard slate gray, but softened with buff-colored trim and green shutters. Between the Cape and Cambridge, Solemnity had seen no finer edifice, outside or in. There was pine wainscoting in every room, high ceilings, fine flocked English wallpapers, Turkey carpets, and French draperies pulled back to reveal the life of the town passing by.

Barnstable was shire for the whole of Cape Cod, and it was not by chance that Brewster Bigelow had constructed his home directly across the road from the county courthouse. Any who needed assistance could not help but turn to a family who hung their shingle before such ordered beauty, and in Brewster and Ezekiel, they were seldom disappointed.

Solemnity held his hat by the brim. His hands were blistered, his thumbnails blackened from working a hammer, his clothes here and there splattered with whitewash.

Brewster looked him up and down. "Not what I would expect on a minister."

"I would have dressed in something more appropriate, but in a poor parish, the stipend does not allow for new clothes. And I try not to use the money from the Eastham property too quickly."

"Marshal it well." The old man's laugh turned into a cough that became a hack. Then he spat at the spittoon, which he missed, and not for the first time.

"I am scrupulous," said Solemnity.

"See that you're as scrupulous about Indian maidens. You've no more land to sell, should your codpiece come undone again."

Solemnity bit at his cheek to contain his anger at such condescension.

Brewster peered at the document in front of him, saw something he did not like, and excised it with his quill. "Land is a powerful asset, boy. My father understood that. My son as well."

"Land is a treasure," said Ezekiel, coming in from the adjoining office. "And how can we help one who has sold us so much?"

Solemnity described the work on the meetinghouse. They had sawed, nailed, painted. All they lacked was a new stepping-stone, the old step being wood that had rotted away. He said that as a boy, he had discovered a stepping-stone buried at the barn on Jack's Island, and he sought permission to dig it up.

"A damn nest of subversion, that barn," said Brewster. "Doesn't surprise me a bit to see what you've come *to*, you and your sister, considerin' the line of blasphemers and heretics you come *from*. They never deserved to own that island."

"May we have the stepping-stone?" asked Solemnity, as solemnly as he could.

"Take it. But nothing else, not even hay straw for your horse. That island's Bigelow property again, as it always should have been."

Ezekiel spoke more gently. "See Shearjashub. He lives in the main house."

"You have my thanks."

"There may come a day when you can do something for us." Ezekiel pulled a half crown from his waistcoat pocket and flipped it to Lem, who barely caught it before it hit his nose.

"Buy yourself a new suit of clothes to wear when you come to Barnstable."

Solemnity weighed the money in his hand, then put it into his pocket and left.

Through the open window he could hear Brewster Bigelow's cough doing battle with a tired old laugh. Brewster would cough himself to death not many months later. It would be said that he died a happy man, though his happiness would be measured in acres rather than friends.

xi.

The next day, Solemnity rose at suncoming and borrowed Amos Colt's horse cart. He did not say where he was going, because the new stepping-stone was to be a surprise.

It was an exquisite October day, a port wine day, he called it, when cranberry and bearberry, maple and oak, even poison ivy, came a deep, rich red. But as the leaves turned, trees across the Cape were being burned to make more pasture. Their smoke smudged the blue and tinged the air with the scent of passing time. And somewhere high above, a flight of geese honked their way south.

Lem envied them their freedom and wished, in a way, that he could be like them: "Consider the birds of the air . . ." But he could not be like them. He could not leave. His sin condemned him to service, and who better to serve than the Indians? Who else would have him?

But many thoughts crossed a man's mind on a five-hour cart ride, and even a minister might commit a few of the seven deadly sins if he had an active imagination.

Pride came first. The Bigelows had wounded Lem's pride often. And never more grievously than the day before. He cursed himself for asking favors of men who had swindled his family while handing out half crowns of false pity.

And from pride flowed anger. He had been sorely tempted to throw that half crown right back in Ezekiel's face. Or stuff it down Brewster's rasping throat. He hated the Bigelows for their condescension and scheming. He envied their success and money.

Pride, anger, hate, envy . . . the antidote for these was more pleasant contemplation, but even that could lead to sin. Solemnity counseled that when temptation crossed the mind, one should think on the transcendent love of God. He tried, but thoughts of God's love were less appealing than those of Samantha Kittredge.

He considered her ocean-blue eyes and warm smile, her skill with a blueberry pie, and her insights into Scripture. She had seen things in Ecclesiastes that surpassed the knowledge of the greatest scholars. But inevitably his mind settled on the smoothness of her thighs, the rise of her nipples against his lips, the unspeakable bliss of entering her body. Even on the cart board, he could feel himself stiffening in his breeches.

He willed her images from his mind, but they did not stay away for long. And eventually, he surrendered. It was lust, yes, the fifth deadly sin of the journey, but he loved her in other ways as well. And it pained him beyond words, sometimes beyond endurance, to think he would never be able to have her.

At Jack's Island his pain was magnified like a beam of sunlight passing through a glass. This had been his family's refuge from the prying eyes of the colony. Had he owned it now, he would have made it *his* refuge as well, a place to go with Samantha, to satisfy his love and, yes, his lust.

But the Bigelows had traversed the marsh with a sandy road, the better to move off the corn, cattle, fish, and whale oil. They had stripped most of the trees that Jack Hilyard had left, so that even on a port wine day, there was a barrenness about the place that Solemnity had never known as a boy. The cattle chewed wherever greenery grew. The picked-over cornstalks waved sadly in the breeze. Puffs of topsoil blew into the dry October air.

There was no refuge here, he thought. In truth a man could go to the ends of the earth and find no refuge from the eye of God.

He spent little time on the island. He found it too painful, and he liked Shearjashub and his sons no more than any other Bigelows. He went straight to the barn behind Jack Hilyard's saltbox and dug until he had freed the square-cut piece of granite all around.

With long bars, Shearjashub's sons levered the stone out of the sand. With brute strength born of ignorance, they lifted it onto the cart. Then they went back to their work. They were not ordinarily hospitable, and they had all voted to remove the Reverend Mr. Hilyard from their parish after he was taken in adultery. They offered him neither drink, conversation, nor comment upon the strange lettering across the face of the stone:

Beneath this were a dozen more scrawls.

Lem knew something of Wampanoag writing, which was more a series of pictures than sounds, but he recognized nothing of the symbols he had revealed when he brushed the sand away from the rock. Who had drawn them? An Indian tribe long gone? But what tribe built in granite? Indians built nothing to last. They believed that only the earth lasted.

He had preached to them that only God lasted. But as he battled each day with his thoughts, he had begun to believe that only love lasted.

He made for home. Night came on. The stars turned out. He felt their cold gaze and wondered. What could God care of the earth in the majesty of the universe? What did God care for the devotion of the colony in the black enormity of the continent? Would God care if a minister chose love over holy loneliness? Was this strangely marked piece of granite a stepping-stone to God's stars or a penitential weight he would carry through his life, as meaningless as the letters drawn upon it?

He stopped the wagon. He was not far from home. The air still smelled of brush fires and carried the honking of the geese that flew both day and night because the season fled fast.

With his shovel, he levered the stone off the back of the cart, and it thumped into the sand. Someone would find it and perhaps use it well. Then he turned toward Truro and the woman he loved.

xii.

There was no one to greet Serenity when she was released from the workhouse two years later. Goody Daggett had grown too feeble to travel. Solemnity and his woman had long since disappeared. And none of the good people of Eastham would welcome her, let alone bring her back. So Goody Daggett and the little boy sent her a bundle of clothes and enough money for passage home.

The clean skirt, apron, and shawl felt strange and wonderful, a foretaste of the freedom that came when Gideon Glint's door closed behind her for the last time. She walked the two miles to Boston, breathing deep of the smells of wood smoke, horse dung, and low tide that hung like fog over the steeples and hills of the grandest town in America.

At Long Wharf, she arranged passage with a fishing captain. Then she bought a whole cone of sugar. She broke off a little piece and let it melt on her tongue, sweet communion with freedom. The rest she wrapped in paper and put under her arm. Then she went to the Old South Meeting House and asked for a colleague minister, the Reverend Thomas Prince, of whom she had heard in her travels about the kitchens of Boston.

At Harvard, Prince had begun to accumulate books and papers

related to the history of the colonies. Now he had created, in the steeple room of the church, a collection of antiquities he called the New England Library.

Serenity had little trust for churchmen, but she needed knowledge to make her plans and so would risk what information she had. Besides, Prince was a Cape Codder by birth, and that counted for something.

"What kind of book is it that you have knowledge of?" asked the Reverend Mr. Prince.

"In truth, 'tis not knowledge."

"Then what?" He was a young man, not yet out of his thirties, but already balding and bad-tempered.

"I've heard stories about the log of Master Jones."

Prince gave her a blank stare, made all the blanker by the backs of the books that surrounded him. "Is this a name I should take to heart?"

"*Christopher* Jones, sir, of the *Mayflower*."

The demeanor of Mr. Prince seemed instantly to change. He closed the book before him and leaned across his desk. "The *Mayflower*?"

She nodded slightly, as though uncertain of what she was telling him.

"You've heard legends? From whom?"

She gave a nervous little laugh, revealing the brown edges of decay around her teeth. She was only twenty-three, but five years of servitude had aged her quickly. "I worked in so many places, Your Honor, 'tis hard to remember."

Prince furrowed his brow and studied her with a hard minister's eye. "Do you waste my time, woman?"

"Oh, no, sir. No, indeed." She fiddled with fringe on her shawl.

"No . . . I don't think you do." He went to one of the bookcases behind him and pulled down a vellum-bound book. "Here is a journal begun near the same time as the *Mayflower* log, if there be such a thing."

He placed it on the table in front of her. "The memories of William Bradford, governor of Plymouth Colony for most of its existence. Borrowed from the family."

She ran her hand over the smooth leather. It seemed to be in perfect condition. Then she opened it. The pages were filled with a small, tight script, entirely legible.

"Have you ever seen a book of this vintage? Or felt such rough paper? A century old?"

She shook her head.

"Are you certain? Such a volume could be worth hundreds of pounds."

This was what she wanted to know. She would spend the packet ride balancing those hundreds of pounds against the revenge that she had long plotted on the Bigelows. They had taken her family's land for a pittance, for two pittances, and she had been unable to stop them. She had no certainty that the log would discomfit them, but they might pay to protect the memory of their *Mayflower* ancestor. Would they pay hundreds of pounds?

"Where might one sell such a book?" she asked.

"To this library," answered Prince. "Do you have it?"

She shook her head again.

"On your honor?"

"My honor?" She laughed at that.

He leaned close to her. "You will go far toward redeeming it, should you bring the book to a place where history and scholarship are honored."

She smiled. "If I find it."

xiii.

The little boy did not at first recognize her. He was playing in the sand beside the shack when she came over the dune.

"Hello, Ned."

He stood and stepped back.

"I'm your mama."

"My mama's in jail."

"I . . . I brung you a present." She reached into her apron and pulled out the sugar.

The little boy eyed the gift, but still he would not go to her.

Then Goody Daggett came out of the cottage. She had tried to prepare the boy for his mother's return, but for five years, he had connected his mother with long journeys to a barn near Boston. Goody Daggett gestured for Serenity to remove her shawl.

The covering fell away, so that the low November sun struck the side of Serenity's face.

"Mama!" The word burst joyously now, and they ran to each other's arms.

She clung to him as though he were life itself, and from this time forward, he would be. She had refused to cry for five years, but she could contain her tears no longer. She had returned to what was left of her family. And she would never leave.

"Don't cry, Mama," said Little Ned.

She wiped her nose on the back of her sleeve. She wiped her hand down the front of her new skirt. Then she crumbled off a piece of sugar and popped it into the little boy's mouth.

By moonlight she went once more to Cornhill, though this time she went alone. She did not dig far before she found the rush basket. With shaking hands and cold-stung fingers, she pulled it out of its hiding place, then plunged her arm into the ancient corn. She reached to the bottom, then to the sides. She ran her arm all around. Then . . .

Her cry echoed from Cornhill to Tom's Hill and lost itself in the marshes above the Little Pamet. She dropped to her knees and pounded the sand. The log was gone, and with it her future.

Had Solemnity done this? Or had the old Indian Keweenut hidden it someplace else? Keweenut was too frightened of his legacy to move it. It was Solemnity, then, for certain.

She damned him. She damned them all. Solemnity had stolen her future. The Bigelows had stolen her land. One might even have sold the log to the other, neatly closing the circle of treachery.

She damned them all again. Then she felt the tears rising again, but this time she did not permit them. She had to stay strong for her boy. She dug her fingers into the sand and squeezed as though holding on to the earth itself. She had been swindled and betrayed, but she would not be defeated . . . ever.

CHAPTER 19

July 11

The Works of Serenity

"One of the Indians in the painting is supposed to be Johnny Autumn. He was hanged after the wreck of the *Whydah*. When I saw the painting, I did some digging," explained Carolyn Hallissey.

"You didn't find much."

"Records from the trial. Legends from the locals. You know . . . Was Black Bellamy coming back for Serenity or for an Eastham girl named Maria Hallet, or was he just coming north because the heat was on in the Caribbean?"

"Plus juicy tidbits about Serenity's brother." Geoff flipped through the pile of sheets and found the quote from Paine's *History of Harwich*: " 'After his scandal, Solemnity Hilyard spent a brief time ministering in a Praying Town. Later he and the woman disappeared on the same day. Neither was ever heard from again.' "

"A man of mystery," said Carolyn.

"And the mystery of the log?"

"In the whole folder there's not a mention of it."

"Then maybe it *did* wrap Mrs. Jones's fish guts, just as Samuel Eliot Morison says."

"Maybe." Then she leaned close, as if letting him in on a secret. "But . . . what . . . if . . . it . . . didn't?"

He liked her. He was cynical enough to know she might be

giving him an act. But he liked her, because she liked what she was doing. He would have liked her even if she hadn't been the best-looking museum director he'd ever met. Pretty faces were a temptation, but enthusiasm . . .

"I'd love to bid on that log," she said. "I'd love to *find* it even more. It's how careers are made."

That helped. The career-driven ones were easier to resist. Their motives were obvious.

"Why do *you* want to find it?" she asked.

"To settle my mind about it . . . and get the money."

She slipped her arm through his and led him toward the door. "Two honest motives for two treasure hunters."

They flirted right out to his car and said good-bye. Nothing wrong with any of it, as long as he went home to his wife. Of course, he and Janice hadn't finished what they started a few mornings before, and things had been downhill ever since.

He liked what he'd read of Serenity. As the fog burned off, he took a right at the National Seashore Visitors' Center and followed Nauset Road through the area where she had lived.

There would have been few houses in 1717, even fewer trees. All across the Cape, mature stands of hardwood had fallen in that first century to make boats, shingles, firewood, and farmland. Men had changed the face of the Narrow Land in two generations. Now scrub pine and locust were so thick that you couldn't see half the summer houses scattered across the Eastham plain. It was comforting to know that if given a chance, nature could cover her scars.

The land of Serenity sat now in the middle of the National Seashore and so would be safe forever . . . but it was the Bigelows who had sold that land to the government in 1961. And they had swindled it out of the Hilyards. A harsh word, but what else could he think? Jeremiah had died, Solemnity had disappeared, and Serenity had moved to Billingsgate. Why on earth would she have moved to a sand dune, unless she'd lost everything? "Swindled" was the word. He found himself getting angry.

At the Nauset Coast Guard Station, he turned north along the cobalt blue sea.

It was pretty stupid, getting mad over something that had happened so long ago. But sometimes history had a way of surfacing right in front of you, and you had to face it. A half mile offshore, a salvage vessel was anchored over the remains of the *Whydah*. Treasure hunters had found Black Bellamy's dream and now dreamed it themselves, hauling millions in gold and artifacts off the bottom.

Carolyn Hallissey had said she hoped to anchor an old ship in Portanimicut Pond and make it the *Whydah* museum, so that people might see pirate artifacts and find a *connection* with men driven to go "on the account." She had used Geoff's word, and it made him like her even more.

Find the connections. Study the flow of people through time or a place or an old house. Speculate on the things that made their lives unique and yet like yours. You didn't do it because it was your job. You did it because it was a way to understand. Find the connections and die happy.

And if there were connections to be made with pirate artifacts, imagine what might be found in the journal of the sea captain who had brought the first settlers to this place.

ii.

When he came home Janice was browning onions and garlic in a pan of olive oil. "Were you working?" she asked.

"At Old Comers Plantation."

"Doing what? Taking tickets?"

"Are we arguing tonight?" He stood in the kitchen doorway so that she couldn't escape. The original house had had three good-sized rooms back to back—parlor, dining room, and great room with beehive ovens and hand-pump plumbing. But in some misbegotten modernization, the beehives had been torn out, the plumbing redirected, and a galley kitchen squeezed into a pantry at the back, a cramped little piece of New York on the shores of Cape Cod Bay.

She dropped a fistful of linguini into a pot of boiling water.

He took out two Molson's Goldens, wiped the lips of each can clean, popped them, and put one beside the range. "I don't hear 'Sesame Street.' Where are the kids?"

"At my grandmother's." She eyeballed a cup of white wine into the pan.

A collander of mussels was draining in the sink, a can of tomatoes stood open beside the stove.

"No kids, mussels marinara . . . We can't be arguing tonight."

"We're looking for answers."

"How's the toilet flushing?"

"That's a question. Everything's going down fine. For now."

The wine reduced. In went the tomatoes, followed by a dash of oregano, a bit of basil. All done as though he were not standing two feet away. She could ignore him the way Larry Bird could make passes—no eye contact at all.

"I have an answer for you," he said. "I was at Old Comers doing research."

"You've made up your mind?"

"About one thing. This *thing* between our families has had a lot of chapters since the *Mayflower.*"

She dropped the mussels into the sauce and threw in another shot of wine.

They ate on the deck, in the quiet of the July evening. The mussels marinara tasted of sun and sea. The Washington State Chardonnay calmed her temper and cleared his head. They talked rationally. They disagreed like adults. They drank more wine.

"The future's been dropped in your lap, Geoff. You can't throw it away because of the past. Think of me. Think of the kids."

"If Clara had lived, she might have signed the sailing camp over to the town and taken this out of my hands."

Janice looked into her glass. "She didn't. Be thankful the decision is still yours to make."

Twilight faded. Except for the sound of an occasional car gliding by the foot of the hill, the calm of the summer night embraced them.

"You know the difference between you and me?" he said.

"Aside from the obvious ones?"

"You grew up here. You know how depressing it can be in the winter, when the hillsides are brown and half the people from Bourne to Provincetown are collecting unemployment while they wait for the tourists."

"Winter can be nice, but it's damn lonely," she said.

"Even lonelier on a narrow bed in a gloomy New Hampshire prep school, staring at the picture of John Lennon curling off the wall, humming 'Good Day Sunshine' and thinking of those boyhood summers, fishing with your father on salt-fog mornings when you were so into the fish you wouldn't notice the fog burning off. But just before it disappeared, you'd look up and see wisps of it in the air, like spun silver . . . Memories like that get a lot of people through the winter."

"I have memories, too. We have them together." She refilled their glasses. "But spun silver feeds the November rain."

"I know. I've thought a lot about it." Then he took her hand and led her down the hill, through the locust grove, to the barn. In his office, he flipped on the track lights above his drafting table.

"Geoffrey . . . elevations?"

"Just sketches."

"They're beautiful."

There were a dozen views of seventeenth-century reproductions. All had the steep-pitched roof and narrow clapboards of the Aptucxet trading post. Some had the traditional diamond-pane windows; others had Palladian windows at the gable ends. And he had begun to toy with floor plans as well, all roughly rendered in 2b on yellow trace.

She looked at them as though he'd just given her Picasso's sketchbook. "*This* is what you were made to do, Geoff."

"I'm no fool, Jan. That's a lot of damn money your family's offering."

"It's the future. Let me go get some more wine."

But she never made it to the house.

After a few moments, Geoff heard the sound of running water. At first, it puzzled him, so he went down the stairs.

Her sandals were on the threshold, her T-shirt and shorts just beyond. His eyes followed the path that led to the outdoor shower stall at the end of the barn. Bra . . . panties . . . steam. As she turned beneath the spray, the places that the sun never touched glistened in the starlight.

"C'mon in, the water's fine."

Geoff stripped and joined her. They kissed with wine-tasting tongues, then kissed again and tasted the water caressing their faces. He soaped her breasts and behind. She washed the part of him that grew against the curve of her belly. The water flowed over them, making their skin like a single surface. The steam rose into the sky. The dark embraced them.

She whispered, "If you want to feel your fantasy, you have to give as good as you get."

A thought fled through his mind: *always negotiating*. But it was a good deal.

He slid to his knees in the gentle spray. He let his tongue play gently over her nipples and follow the moisture toward the dark blond cleft. She hooked a leg over his shoulder, and . . .

The headlights hit her right in the eyes.

"Who the hell is that?"

"Turn off the water. Maybe they'll go away."

The gentle spray stopped. The headlights went out.

Janice peered over the top of the stall. Geoff, still on his knees, poked his head out the side and looked up toward the driveway.

"Whose car is that?"

"Can't tell."

The cool night air quickly went cold on wet skin.

The car door opened with an ungreased *thwop*.

"I'd know that sound anywhere." She shivered.

"Geoff! You about?" Rake's old voice cracked. "Geoff! Janice Bigelow! Kids!"

"Be right up!" Geoff reached into the locker beside the stall—towels, soap, and two white terry-cloth robes. He offered one to Janice. "To be continued."

"I'll finish by myself . . . the shower, that is."

Rake was smiling like a fisherman who'd filled his boat while his friends were getting skunked. "Didn't take you away from somethin', did I?"

"Just a shower."

Rake looked toward the sound of the spray. "Showered under a palm tree in the Pacific for two years. Never did it with no pretty girls, though. Always fightin' two or three other guys for the soap."

They went inside, and Geoff got out two beers. Before he could ask any of his questions, Rake began to answer them.

"Went cruisin' this mornin', out over Billin'sgate. Needed to think." Rake dropped a large box on the table. Then he took off his hat and scratched through the white hair. The hard old face softened when the hat was removed. "Decided it's you and your Bigelow wife or nobody. . . .Too old to have nobody."

"What's in the box?"

"Don't go gettin' buck fever. 'Tain't the log." He lifted the lid off the box, revealing a pile of yellowed, hand-lettered sheets. "Broadsides, written by Serenity Hilyard herself."

Geoff riffled through them, and a residue of disintegrating paper came off on his fingers. "Writs of Assistance are Rubbage" was lettered across the top sheet.

"Been keepin' 'em since I was a boy. Tom Hilyard found 'em

in the wall of the house on Billin'sgate, in the busted-off barrel of an old blunderbuss. My father kept 'em, give 'em to me. *Was* plannin' to show 'em to that museum gal—"

Janice came in, looking fresh and not the least bit frustrated in her terry-cloth robe.

"But better off trustin' my own relatives." Rake looked at Janice. "Even if she *is* a Bigelow, Clara trusted her."

"Yes. Yes, she did." Janice went to dry her hair.

"She's a little, uh, skeptical about all this." Geoff tried not make any fast verbal moves. Treat Rake like a nervous deer who had finally decided to trust the salt lick by the back door. "*I'm* ready to listen. I just wish you'd come to me earlier."

Rake was squinting toward the bathroom and the whine of the hair dryer. "She wants the development, don't she?"

"Tell me about the log."

"Takin' this a step at a time, Geoff. Not givin' all my trust till you've earned a little. That's my way."

"Where'd you first hear about the log?"

Rake shook his head. "Not where'd I *first* hear of it. Where'd I *last* hear of it? That museum gal. Someplace, sometime, she seen somethin' that led her to me."

"The doorstop?"

He rubbed a hand over the quarter inch of gray stubble on his chin. "Read about Serenity, son. Tell me what you think. Maybe I'll tell you more." He went to the door.

"Wait a minute, Rake. You haven't touched your beer."

"Don't want to drink too much, don't want to say too much, 'specially if there's somebody here"—he glanced at Janice, reappearing from the bathroom—"who's skeptical. Read what's in this box, then say how skeptical you are."

Janice took Rake's arm. "We love you, Rake. Geoff and I and the kids, too. We just want to do what's best for everybody."

"Somethin' in that log scared your Great-Grandpa Charles plain shitless back in 1911. It might scare your pa today." He pulled on his hat and gave the brim a little snap with his finger.

The car door *thwopped*; the valves clattered to life.

"I'll talk to you tomorrow," said Geoff from the deck.

The fog was blowing in from the east on a cooling night breeze. It struck Geoff on the insteps, traveled up his bare legs, under his robe, and made his balls shrivel. He hated when that happened.

iii.

The right thing to do. Had to give 'em that stuff, and if they read it right, give 'em more. But no sense in tellin' too much, and never tell how little you *really* know.

Past the gas stations in Wellfleet . . . fog gettin' thick . . . Hunch forward. Always good to hunch forward, get closer to the windshield, easier on the eyes. Night drivin' got harder and harder. . . .

Had to get home and study the list. Get old, need to make lists. Otherwise, forget your asshole if it wasn't drilled in.

Fog so thick, couldn't even see what Indiana Jones was doin' on the drive-in screen. *There* was a guy you could use. Archaeologist with a bullwhip. Show *him* the list. Let him figure what Tom Hilyard meant by "The book of history will set us free from the evil that bricks us up."

Fog even thicker . . . No matter. Don't give a damn about strip malls and motels in Eastham. . . . Should slow down, but the nitwit on your tail, why don't he pass?

Comin' up on the rotary now. Not many brake lights. Fog too thick, and not many out at this hour, but *still* that jerk behind you, pushin' you along . . . Be an old bastard and put on your brake.

That backed him off. . . . Hated rotaries, especially in the summer, with all the tourists who'd never seen one before . . . Stop, go, start, stop . . . Accident every day. Even worse in the fog.

Off the rotary, into the dark, and . . . *good.* No lights ahead. Nervous damn stretch—two lanes runnin' straight and flat through pine woods for thirteen miles, speed limit fifty, and damn-you-straight-to-hell if you were an old man who didn't go over forty. Somebody always itchin' to pass. Tourists comin' the other way. No wonder they called it Suicide Six.

Damn that bastard . . . Right up on your tail, and flashin' his lights! Put your foot on the brake. Make him pass . . . but they've put up those rubber stanchions. He *can't* pass.

Three flashes, then one, then three . . . Morse code? For what? "Get off the road you old bastard"?

Well, foot to the brake and fuck him . . . forty, thirty-five. High beams in the rearview . . . Three flashes, then one, then three. Fuck him, let's fight about it! Twenty-five—

Bang! Son of a bitch bumped you! Slow down—no, speed up.

Thirty, thirty-five, forty . . . Right on your tail, high beams still flashin'. *Bang!*

Swerve to the right and grind on the shoulder, curve to the left and *thwump-thwump-thwump-thwump*. Rubber stanchions against the rocker panel and . . . *bang!*

Hold on, hold on, the overpass is comin'. Can't swerve if he hits you there. Hold *on!* Think of a followin' sea, a followin' sea and a high wind . . . Now, deep breath, to calm the churnin' gut, deep breath. *Bang!*

Three-one-three, three-one-three. Faster now, faster.

Eyes on the rearview, eyes on the road. Here he comes. *Bang!*

And now a flash to the left—a reflector. A bicycle! At eleven o'clock! Shooting out of the fog like a PT boat at a Jap destroyer. Can't hit a bicycle!

Hard a-starboard . . . Rake's 1968 Oldsmobile Cutlass bounced over the shoulder. The grill struck the bridge abutment, and the engine burst through the dash.

iv.

The glow had faded. The wine was wearing off, there were dirty dishes to wash and mussel shells to bundle before they began to stink, and Rake had reminded them both that this problem wasn't going to go away because Geoff had drawn a few sketches.

It was just as well. Geoff's balls hadn't relaxed yet. A cold wind or a good scare always pulled them tight. He was still cold and now a little scared of this Serenity and what she might pull him into.

There were broadsides on the Stamp Act, the king, the coming of rebellion, and one called "Tar and Feathers and Comeuppance."

Begin at the top of the pile. "Hey, history major," he called to Janice, who was still banging around in the kitchen, "the Writs of Assistance? What and when?"

"They were 1760 or '61. . . ."

CHAPTER 20

April 1760

Comeuppance and Rebellion

The great whales were gone.

It was true that the blackfish still came. Cape Cod farmers rowed after them and slapped the water with their oars and drove them, in great lowing herds, onto the beach. But a blackfish carried no more than a barrel of oil while the humpback and finback were huge living casks—thirty, forty, even fifty barrels in a single beast—and they had been hunted from the bay as surely as the wolf from the woodlands.

To men weaned on thundering flukes and cedar-boat sleigh rides, herding pilot whales was a landlubber's life. But there was another whale—faster, meaner, far more powerful—who took the whole Atlantic for a feeding ground and in whose battering ram of a head was an oil so white it resembled sperm. Sometimes he rode the sea currents close to the back shore, and sometimes he sailed as far as the African coast.

And Cape Codders were the first Americans to lash tryworks to the decks of their ships and go after him. And the first Cape Codders were from Billingsgate town. And among them was a man named Ned Hilyard, who wore a whales'-tooth necklace and could stick a harpoon in a half-guinea coin at a hundred paces, which skill far outweighed the tales told about him and his notorious mother.

In her youth, said the good people of Billingsgate, in her wild youth, they said, eyes ablaze with indignation and jaws slack with excitement, before her hair went gray and her teeth began to fall out, Serenity Hilyard had been a Smith's Tavern whore, and one of the best, a quim that could service a dozen dirty whalers in a night and a smile that could steal a dozen souls.

Few who damned her whoredom knew that she used her body to provide for her child, then to buy law books in which she sought what she had once dug after in a Truro sand hill: comeuppance for the Bigelows of Barnstable. She had read in the law as voraciously as any Harvard prince. She had taught herself complaints and torts, land transfers and deeds, and had found nothing untoward in the sale of Jack's Island or the Eastham farm.

So she gave up her dream of regaining her land, but word spread through the meaner taverns and meeting places of Cape Cod that Serenity was one who would help. Men in need sought her out when they wished to word themselves well before the court or comprehend a complaint brought against them, and she turned none away, neither thieves nor smugglers, Indians nor niggers, nor the forlorn French Acadian girl who appeared that spring. Her name was Marie Reynard, and she asked Serenity to bring suit for the return of the ship that was confiscated when she and her band of exiles were washed up on Cape Cod.

Serenity laughed and reminded her that there was a war between the French and English. The Acadians were unfortunate victims. Then she invited this exile to sup with her and her son Ned in their Billingsgate house.

Goody Daggett's ghost must have put some strange potion in the cod muddle that night, because Ned and Marie fell in love at the table. It was called the Age of Reason, but Serenity could find no answer beyond witchcraft for the attraction of such opposites.

Ned was forty-three, Marie twenty-three. His hair was black, his eyebrows a scowling line across his forehead, his skin tanned brown as seaweed. She was blond and fair, with a complexion the color of clean sand. He had learned from his mother to expect nothing good of the world and went with his fists clenched. She had been an innocent, grown like a flower in the Acadian soil, now staring bewildered at all that had afflicted her people during the latest war between England and France. But a month later they were married.

The people of Billingsgate town were scandalized that *anyone* would fall in love with a French papist. And they were shocked that one of the wildest men on Cape Cod would fall in love with anyone.

After all, Ned Hilyard had darted irons not only into hundreds of whales but also into a few men. And he took his profits in whale oil, they said, so that he could defy the Crown.

British law did not permit importation of molasses—basic ingredient of rum, basic manufacture of New England—from any but British ports. Molasses from the French and Dutch Indies, however, was of higher quality and not subject to the Crown's ninepence tariff. So each winter, Ned loaded whale oil onto his sloop and sailed to the warm Indies. He sampled the whores, traded oil for molasses, and smuggled home a handsome profit. Come spring, he went a-whaling again.

But in the year after his marriage, Ned kept close to Billingsgate. He had a family and a house to build, and in all his life, he had never known the purity of bliss he found in the arms of Marie Reynard, or the satisfaction in labor.

He chose a spot protected by low dunes, dug holes for brick pilings, and built a four-room house that hunkered out of the wind like a battened hatch. He used cedar shingles for the roof and sides, but for sheathing and floorboards he stripped the wood from the abandoned whale house at the tip of the island. After all, without whales, there was no use for a house, and on the lower Cape, wood had grown as scarce as Indians.

A man could stand on the Eastham tablelands and, looking east or west, see salt water with hardly a leaf to block the view. Along the bay, from Eastham to Chequesset Neck, stretched a sad swath of land where the First Comers had found forest, where their descendants had grown grain, and where the topsoil now swirled with the wind. In Provincetown men had been cutting wood and grazing cattle for decades, and like Lilliputians loosing Gulliver's bonds, they had freed the great dunes that now rolled across the landscape.

Mother Nature, it seemed, had turned against Cape Cod just as Mother England had turned against the merchants and shippers of Massachusetts.

That winter, the surveyor general of customs in North America requested renewal of the Writs of Assistance, enabling officers of the Crown to enter any premises and search for contraband without warrant. Given the growing debts from the French and Indian War, the Crown intended to prosecute the writs vigorously, especially against molasses smugglers.

For Ned, this was a minor discouragement. He always had his harpoon. For Serenity, it was something more, because the customs inspector for Barnstable was named Solomon Bigelow, and it was said that he kept spies.

ii.

"The *Serneriny*'s comin' out," said Scrooby Doone.

"The who?" said Leyden Doone.

"The *Serneriny*, what cousin Solomon wants us to watch."

"It's *Seren* . . . *Seren* . . . *Serentity*, you dumb fool."

Scrooby Doone was a gangling youth with a prognathous jaw and an Adam's apple that hopped about like a three-legged dog when he talked. Leyden Doone was stockier than his brother and dumber than most four-legged dogs. They had sprouted from a branch of the Bigelow family tree, just below the limb from which both of their parents had sprung. Cape Cod was still an isolated place, after all, and the grandchildren of Brewster Bigelow were not the *first* first cousins to marry and produce offspring of less than ministerial intelligence.

The Doones were the keepers of Jack's Island. They raised cattle, cut marsh hay, and grew corn, which they fertilized from the herring-black streams of spring. Simple tasks for simple men. And because they were simple, Cousin Solomon had set them a higher task. If they performed it well, none would suspect them.

"We better follow her," said Scrooby.

"To the Indies? Don't know the way." Leyden was leaning over the side of their catboat. He had dropped the sounding lead to gauge the depth, but in the time it took him to haul it in, he had forgotten what it said.

"She just goin' into Rock Harbor, you dumb fool."

"Smarter'n you."

The *Serenity* tied up at Rock Harbor, unloaded nothing but a few pieces of paper, then ran up to Sesuit Harbor in Dennis and did the same. Then she made for Barnstable.

"Should we keep followin' her?" asked Scrooby.

"Nobody smuggles pieces of paper. 'Sides, I'm hungry."

So the Doones let the *Serenity* sail on and didn't report to Solomon Bigelow that she had been delivering Serenity's first broadside to the bay-shore towns.

WRITS OF ASSISTANCE are RUBBAGE

PEOPLE OF CAPE COD! I WRITE because I am a lover of TRUTH, which comes not from acceptance but from dispute. In thought will we formulate our argument. In argument will we learn the TRUTH. Tell me that the WRITS OF ASSISTANCE benefit the commonality and I will tell you that they are the VERIEST RUBBAGE.

With the KING HIMSELF will I argue, for I am determined to oppose with all the powers God gives me all writs of slavery and villainy, as these foul Writs of Assistance. King George says the rights of his people are dearer to him than the most valuable prerogatives of the CROWN. To that I say, DENY THOSE RIGHTS TO THE BRITONS OF AMERICA and we will choose to call ourselves AMERICANS!

While certain Barnstable attorneys and customs inspectors lick their chops to do the Crown's work, the people must WHET their BLADES!

The Anonymous Outcast of Billingsgate

"Who is this bloody liar?" Solomon Bigelow slammed one of the broadsides onto the table in his brother's office.

"Whoever he is, he speaks boldly." Benjamin Bigelow thought he might know the Anonymous Outcast, but he had no intention of revealing his suspicions.

Benjamin was forty-three, a man of great substance in the community, great probity in business, great girth in the belly. Solomon was twenty-nine, tall, scrawny, and already going gray. The elder brother had inherited their father Ezekiel's legal practice, the younger their grandfather Brewster's impetuosity. Benjamin had been appalled to learn why Serenity Hilyard hated them. If Solomon learned that she had written the broadside, he might sail to Billingsgate and burn down her house.

Benjamin looked at Solomon's reflection in the mahogany tabletop. "Whoever it is, he deserves not the least attention till he comes into the open and fights like a man."

Solomon tore the broadside into pieces.

But there would be more, because Serenity had found a new weapon. Cape Cod had neither newspapers nor printing presses. To give an opinion, one stood before the tavern and declaimed it, spoke at town meetings, or lettered as many broadsides as writing cramp would permit and tacked them in places where they might be read. A woman shunned in public could find no better forum than the broadside, and Serenity's pen soon poured forth vitriol against the writs. A mother whose son smuggled molasses could do no less.

iii.

A hearing was held on the writs in February 1761, in the council room of the Boston Town House. Arguing for the Crown was King's Attorney Jeremiah Gridley. Speaking in opposition was James Otis, of an old Barnstable family, who had resigned as advocate general of the Admiralty Court in protest. All wore their finest white wigs, and the Boston *Gazette* told the story.

> King's Counsel Jeremiah Gridley defended the writs as a loyal subject. "I urge the court to uphold them. They are the legally justifiable means by which Customs Inspectors may bring to an end the outrageous and injurious trade that permits smugglers to circumvent payment of duties that should benefit every soul in the colony."
>
> But James Otis carried the day, beginning straight after dinner and concluding at six o'clock by the chime of the Old South bell. From exordium to peroration, his voice never faltered, the stentorian strength of it seeming to carry all the way to Cape Cod.
>
> He began by proclaiming, "I am determined, to my DYING DAY, to oppose, with all the powers and faculties God has given me, all such instruments of slavery on the one hand and villainy on the other as this Writ of Assistance is."
>
> He concluded with the audience wrapt in silence. "Let the consequences be what they will, I am determined to

proceed and to the call of my country am ready to sacrifice estate, health, ease, applause, and even life. The patriot and hero will do ever thus. And if brought to the trial, it will then be known how far I can reduce to practice principles which I know to be founded in truth."

On Billingsgate, Serenity Hilyard read the *Gazette* and heard not only an echo of her own words but the rumbling of a distant storm. If the former king's advocate general turned against His Majesty, what might come next?

A few days later, the former king's advocate general and his slave ran a sailboat onto Billingsgate Island. The man was dressed in a fine cloak and tricorn hat, and his stockings were as white as a gull's belly. Under his arm, he carried a broadside.

Serenity was accommodating a toothache at the time. It was a common affliction, but she suffered more often than most. Some said it was because of her taste for raw sugar. Others blamed her bilious opinions. She still had front teeth, but one canine was gone, the other nothing more than a rotted stump. Mostly she ate cornmeal mush, chowder, beans cooked to pulp, and sugar melted on the tongue. When her jaw began to throb around a tooth, nothing but seawater and rum passed her lips. The cold seawater soothed the throbbing momentarily. The rum dulled the senses more generally.

This one was a molar, and unless Ned pulled it, her face would swell till the infection burst her skin and drained into the cloth tied around her jaw. Life could be misery.

The man knocked on her door. "Good afternoon, marm."

"A damn sight gooder if you carry a vial of laudanum."

He was in his mid-thirties. He had a round, full face that had seen little sun, powerful shoulders, but the delicate hands of a scholar. "I seek the Anonymous Outcast of Billingsgate."

"Wouldn't know him." Serenity offered strangers suspicion and the sight of her blunderbuss before trust.

"Some on this Cape think they know her by name. I would talk with her."

She squinted in the harsh sunlight. "Who are you?"

"My name's Otis." He tapped the broadside. "I would tell her that I borrowed the terms 'slavery' and 'villainy' to describe the writs. Unusual yoking of words, yet most apt."

Serenity forgot her toothache. This formidable Cape Codder,

written about in Boston papers, praised for his eloquence, a visionary, had come to flatter *her*. Ordinarily, those who praised her eloquence could not read or write, and those who flattered her other parts came less often as she aged. But he faced a test before she let him into the house. "What of the last paragraph? The one about Barnstable attorneys and customs inspectors?"

Otis smiled, revealing even, straight, tea-stained teeth. "I grew up in Barnstable. I know the Bigelows well. And I tell you, marm, I'd rather see the writs in the hands of the French."

She flung open the door of Goody Daggett's old shack and offered him tea spiked with rum.

"Whence came the molasses for the rum?" he asked wryly.

"The rum is a gift." Ned stalked in the back door, and with no more greeting, picked up the bottle and splashed rum into Otis's teacup. "'Tis impolite to refuse a gift."

Otis lost neither calm nor wit, but raised his cup. " 'Deny those rights to the Britons of America and we will choose to call ourselves Americans.' Heady sentiment. The time may come when others agree. And *they* will be called patriots."

"I'm a woman who's spent her life lookin' at things from the outside, the bottom, and the back-end-to. I speak for them like me. If that makes me a patriot"—she touched her cup to his—"then, to patriotism."

"A fool's idea in a fool's brain." Ned took a swallow from the bottle.

Otis pointed to Ned's sloop, the *Serenity*, tugging at her cable in Blackfish Bay. "With a writ of assistance, a royal agent can search your vessel, your house, your mother's house, even your w-w-w-wife's budge for molasses."

"I've lived with the writs. I see no need for broadsides about 'em. And you'll speak no more of my wife."

"This here's an important man, Ned," said Serenity. "Treat him like one."

"I treat him like any man."

"But will the Crown treat you like an *English* man?" asked Otis. "With the writs, a customs inspector needs no more than your bad reputation to search your house."

"He may need no more than the broadsides of the Anonymous Outcast." Ned drained the bottle and headed for the door. "I say stretch your neck for no man."

"I'd rather stretch my n-n-n-neck than have it wrung," shouted Otis, with sudden violence.

It was said that he was given to strange fits and strange deeds, stutterings and inappropriate obscenities, sudden sea changes of temperament that passed as quickly as they arose. Who but an impulsive man would sail half the day to speak with an anonymous outcast, thought Serenity, when there was so much more of consequence to be done?

Otis tugged at his waistcoat, then tugged again, as though his anger twitched outward to every finger. Then he was calm and smiling. "Miz Hilyard, you stretch your neck, and I'll stretch mine, or we'll *all* swing in the wind of the king's farts. That's what I've come here to say."

iv.

As the currents of Cape Cod Bay had built Billingsgate Island, the currents of history would build the sandbar that Otis began in the Writs of Assistance speech. As he railed in Boston against the Acts of Trade, the Sugar Act, the Stamp Act and wrote *The Rights of the British Colonies Asserted and Proved*, Serenity stirred the waters of Cape Cod with her broadsides and found that the colonies were full of rebellious outsiders like her. As Boston mobs hanged tax collectors in effigy and destroyed the homes of rich royal officials, Serenity urged them on. "It is HIGH TIME," she wrote, "that the rich families learn that every man can rise as high as they, no matter how lowly his birth."

And none of this pleased Black Bellamy's bastard. He knew that Bigelow kept spies, and one day, Bigelow would come after him. Then there would be trouble, whether he carried contraband or not. So he went back to whaling and left the smuggling to those whose mothers were not so fiery. After all, he was now a man of responsibility.

Samuel Edward Hilyard was born in 1763. He sucked at his mother's breast while she lettered broadsides. He learned his first words as his grandmother dictated them. He took his first steps behind a father who stomped out whenever the women began their troublemaking work.

In June of 1768, word arrived that two regiments of British

troops were on their way to Boston to support the latest round of taxes, called the Townshend Acts. This time Boston mobs would be kept in check, and resisters would be shipped to England for trial.

In the General Court, James Otis cried, "Let Great Britain rescind: if she does not, the colonies are lost to her forever."

And on Billingsgate Island, the little boy once more smelled ink and heard the scritch-scratch-scritch of quills upon parchment.

"Outside on such a cold day as this?"

A shadow loomed over the sand hill where the boy played. When he tried to conjure his father during his absences, he saw the whales'-tooth necklace before anything else. He reached out and touched the white bone. "Did you kill many whales?"

"Fifteen. We'll make Wellfleet the greasiest town in Massachusetts, or we should be tried out ourselves." Wellfleet: Billingsgate town had grown so rich—or "greasy," in whalers' talk—that it had broken away from Eastham and renamed itself. There were some who feared that the colonies might try to do the same thing. But what man would wish to see the dispute with England erupt into war? What hope, Ned often asked his mother, would whalemen have, or coastal towns, if the British warships that seemed so stately and swift when viewed from the foretop were put to the use for which they had been built?

Ned pulled out a small paper sack. "I brought you molasses candy. Horehounds, they're called."

Little Sam put one on his tongue. The only thing sweeter was the company of his father after so long.

"Ned!" called the boy's mother. "Welcome back."

Then Grandma Serenity said, "Just in time to sail 'round the bay with a new broadside."

"I've been six months at sea. I'm not ready to play messenger boy." He stalked into the house and snatched a broadside from his mother's hands. " 'Troops in Boston are a desecration . . . the customs administration of Solomon Bigelow an obscenity.' "

Little Sam sat in his sand hill and listened.

"All truth." That was his grandmother.

"Stay out of this!" shouted his father.

"No one can stay out of it, no one with principles."

The boy scooped sand into his hands and let it run through his fingers.

"Your principle is to taunt the Bigelows. But they can come and take the *Serenity* if you make 'em mad enough."

"They've already taken our past and our future."

What did this mean? the boy wondered. Who were these Bigelows that they could do all that his grandmother said?

"My future's out there playin' in the wet sand when he should be at the warm fire. I'll do nothin' to endanger him."

"You're doing nothin' *for* him."

"I challenge sperm whales for him."

"Give him a *country*, if you're man enough. Teach him principles. If not, we'll put up the broadsides ourselves."

"You'll put up no more slanders on the Bigelows!"

The little boy covered his ears.

"You can't burn those!" shouted his grandmother.

But the sparks swirled out of the chimney. Then the door swung open and his father marched out. "Let's go fishin', son. We'll put food on our table while those damn fool women worry about taxes and . . . principles."

The little boy hurried after his father, stumbling over the dune grass and struggling through the deep sand like a gosling chasing the gander. After they had walked some distance, his father stopped and the boy nearly ran into him.

With a sound that they felt as much as heard, an osprey passed over them and swept out over the bay, solitary and serene, until she saw her fish. Her talons glanced off the surface as delicately as a tailor's needle on fine silk. Then she rose to the top of the rickety tower, where Jack Hilyard had once scanned the bay for whales, and she fed her chicks a fine meal of fish.

"She's a brave old bird, and she knows a good principle. Stretch your neck for those you love. No one else."

v.

But Ned stretched his neck, if only a little, and if only to keep peace in his family.

When he was not whaling, he sailed the *Serenity* around to the bay towns to put up his mother's broadsides. And little Sam went along. His father was already teaching him how to handle the forty-foot sloop, and he relished the company of his father's whaling mates,

Square Henry Stubbs and Charlie Kwennit. Stubbs was, quite simply, square—square head, square body, legs no longer than his upper torso, and a character as sharp-edged and solid as a building block. He said little and spat a lot and hauled line faster than any man alive. Kwennit was the great nephew of an Indian named Keweenut and, at twenty-three, the youngest harpooneer in the Wellfleet trade.

In some towns, the Hilyards were greeted warmly by those who had taken to calling themselves patriots. In other places, they met unfriendliness. But the unfriendliest place they ever visited was the British Coffeehouse in Boston.

For months the customs commissioners who frequented the coffeehouse had been writing to London, questioning James Otis's motives and slandering his character. Otis considered himself a loyal subject of the king, honestly attempting to improve the governance of the empire, and he had responded to the commissioners' letters by placing a notice in the *Gazette* in which he called them liars and all but called them out. When Serenity heard of the dispute, she lettered fifty broadsides in support of Otis, whose behavior, it was said, had grown more volatile as the struggle between Crown and colonies had grown more intense. She told her son that Otis of Barnstable needed all the friends he could get. Then she pressed the broadsides into his hand and begged him to deliver them to the coffeehouse where Otis often went to debate.

The air was thick with tobacco smoke and the sweet smell of burned coffee beans that night. Ned took a table in the corner and ordered two cups of Cuban. Little Sam stared at the bright red coats and powdered wigs. The British officers stared back in amused fascination, as though the Hilyards were a pair of apes.

Soon an officer—who had even powdered his face—minced over and said, "Excuse us, old chaps, but what time do the offal pits open?" This brought a dose of hilarity from those within earshot.

Little Sam thought his father might break the man's back. "Offal" meant "shit," and Ned Hilyard never brooked an insult. But to Sam's surprise, his father sat there and stared, as still as a figurehead.

The officer wrinkled his nose and sniffed the air. "I thought you'd know. It seems you've been there recently."

When this pansy-face went back to his table, Ned whispered, "There's nothin' meaner than a British officer showin' off for his friends."

Just then a man appeared in the doorway.

"Otis," whispered Ned. "A damn fool with a foul mouth, a short temper, and a lot of ideas we could do without."

"Grandma calls them principles." The boy looked toward the doorway as James Otis swooped, like the Billingsgate osprey, toward a table in the center of the room.

A thick-waisted man in a black frock stood and stepped away from the table. His name was John Robinson, chief customs commissioner. "You have a bloody nerve coming in here, after what you put in the *Gazette.*"

"Hear, hear," said the powder-faced officer.

"I answer calumny with truth. You wouldn't recognize truth if it bit you on your p-p-prick, assuming you have one." Then he looked at the others. "I demand an apology from all of you. Hutton, Paxton, Burch, Bigelow—"

Little Sam remembered that name. He looked at his father, who still sat motionless.

Bigelow stood. "I apologize for nothing."

Sam thought Bigelow's voice sounded like the cry of a scavenging gull, and he had the look of one, with his beaklike nose and prematurely gray hair.

"Solomon, I pummeled you when we were boys and I'll pummel you now."

"Physical threats, is it?" bellowed John Robinson. "You impugn our honor, you invade our good fellowship, and now you threaten us."

"I demand satisfaction of you, sir."

"What satisfaction would you prefer?"

"A gentleman's satisfaction."

"If it's a fistfight you wish, it's a fistfight you shall have." Robinson unbuckled his sword, then reached out to tweak Otis's nose, as though he were no more than a naughty boy. Otis raised his walking stick, and Robinson raised his in answer.

There was a sharp, violent motion—that was all little Sam could be certain of—and Otis's hat flew across the room like a spinning kite.

A light went out in a corner. Red coats and broadcloth surged around Otis. Angry shouts struck little Sam like blows at the back of the neck. He turned to his father, but Ned remained in the chair, eyes shifting from the fight to the door to the broadsides on the table before him.

Otis lashed left and right and until a walking stick struck his head like a mallet driving a bung into a keg.

Now Sam felt his father's hand, lifting him through the dark mass of men. Like a glimpse of hell, the boy saw into the middle of the brawl. Fists were flying. Blood and bone showed in the middle of Otis's forehead. And the scavenging gull Bigelow was driving Otis to the floor.

"Papa, he needs help."

"Yes." It was powder-face. "Help the poor chap."

"I'll help *you*"—Ned drove a knee upward—"to be the girl you'd like to be." The officer struck the floor and grabbed his balls while the Hilyards hurried out.

"Papa!" Sam shouted as they reached the cool September night. "You should help your friend."

Ned grabbed the boy by the collar. "I told you, son. Stretch your neck for none but those you love. Now hurry. Stubbs and Kwennit are waitin' at the pub."

The boy pulled away. His eyes were filling with tears. "You're a coward. You left your friend to be hurt."

"He was *not* my friend, and 'tis *not* my fight."

A fishmonger went by, pushing a smelly old cart. "Coffeehouse sounds like a rowdy pub."

"My pa won't help."

"Can't blame him. There's redcoat officers in there."

"His *friend's* there, too." The boy's voice cracked, and he began to cry. He did not want to. His father always told him that brave men did not cry. But bravery no longer seemed in demand.

Then his father smacked him on the back of the head. "Stay here and stop cryin'."

The boy sucked in his breath and watched his father stride back into the coffeehouse. Moments later two redcoats flew out the door like partridge flushed from cover. Then a chair exploded through a window, sending glass fragments glittering like jewels. A customs commissioner followed the chair and landed on the glass shards.

The little boy wanted to cheer, but the grunts and punches and shattering glass frightened him beyond words. Bravery was dangerous. Perhaps they should have left after the ball.

Then his father lumbered out the door with the unconscious Otis slung over his shoulder. "Run, lad! For the boat!"

A half-dozen men came stumbling out after Ned, and they would have caught him, but Square Stubbs and Charlie Kwennit were never far away. When they heard shattering glass, they left their beers in the pub and came running. The square head of Square Stubbs butted three royal officials into oblivion, and Kwennit's harpoon handle carried away the rest. Charlie swept the boy into his arms and Stubbs took Otis and they ran for the boat.

ASSASSINS IN THE COFFEEHOUSE!

It has now been a month, and we can say it in truth: They did not kill him, but they gained their DASTARDLY GOAL! Royal customs commissioners lured James Otis into their British Coffeehouse and picked a fight. One man against many walking sticks. James Otis was SAVAGELY BEATEN, and would have DIED, but a BRAVE Cape Codder pulled him from the maelstrom.

He lives. His GREAT HEART beats. But his GREAT MIND is broken. The words of GENIUS resound no more. He is among us, yet gone.

DOFF your hats when you pass his Barnstable Home. Let him feel your LOVE as he watches the parade of HISTORY that now must leave him behind.

SPIT when you pass the Courthouse at Barnstable, where Customs Commissioner Solomon Bigelow spends his days when he is not lounging with the other assassins in Boston. He claims self-defense. He claims honor and constancy as a descendant of the First Comers. He is a HYPOCRITE.

James Otis opposes TYRANNY even now, by his very existence. Let his BRAVERY be our example. Let his FATE be our inspiration.

COMEUPPANCE awaits those who stand in the way of history. And for those who twist it, who hide behind it to protect their guilt, COMEUPPANCE will come in a book that proves their villainy from the time of the First Comers.

Little Sam Hilyard had recently learned to read, and he read this broadside many times. His grandmother said she had used his description of the coffeehouse fight and so he was one of the authors. Sam was so proud he decided to save the sheet in the broken-off barrel of the old blunderbuss, with which he stalked sea monsters and imaginary Tories on the dune.

One Tory, Solomon Bigelow, read this broadside in the small grocery that his aunt Nabby kept beside the Barnstable County Courthouse.

Widow Nabby was a big, fleshy woman, as opinionated an old Tory as there was. She often said that Solomon took his bad temper from her and it was the best part of him.

" 'A book that proves their villainy.' What does the writer mean?" asked Solomon, whose eye was still bruised from a blow he had not even seen in the coffeehouse.

"Sail down to Billingsgate and find out." Nabby measured three cups of tea leaves from an East India Company chest. She put the leaves into a sack. Then she began to shave sugar from a cylindrical loaf. "Do we even know who the writer is?"

"Benjamin won't say, but Scrooby and Leyden think it's the Hilyard woman."

"So go and flog the old hag."

Solomon pressed his finger to his lips and glanced toward his daughter, who listened to every word.

Nabby pulled a peppermint stick from a glass jar. "There you go, Hannah dearie. Take that out and watch the world go by."

"Thank you, Aunt Nabby." She was five years old, with chestnut brown hair and the look of a child whose knowing far surpassed her years.

Solomon tucked the tea and sugar under his arm. "A visit to Billingsgate may be in order."

"No!" The door opened and Benjamin stalked in. "Tea and sugar, Aunt Nabby, and don't be filling my brother's head with notions of vengeance."

"This Anonymous Outcast has been slandering us for years," said Solomon.

"Addlebrained Otis has forgiven his assailants, except for Robinson. The next person you attack may not be so conciliatory. And conciliation is the order of the day."

"Spoken like a lawyer." Nabby laughed.

For her part, Serenity Hilyard feared she had divulged too much about the book, but she had written in a passion of fury. She knew that Otis might have ended as he did—sometimes incisive, usually scatalogical and incoherent—without a visit to the coffeehouse. But it was the Bigelows she was after. They stood for all that she opposed. The rebellion that she was helping to birth would justify her life, because it would bring them low, even without the *Mayflower* log. And the rebellion came quickly.

vi.

By the spring of 1774, the future did not look promising to Benjamin Bigelow. Liberty poles were rising on the town greens and thunderclaps of rebellion were rolling across the bay, and so he journeyed to Boston. As a man of the law, he wished to discuss with royal authorities the protection of county records and deeds. As a man of property, he wished to discuss with like men the threat to them all.

He called first at the home of Governor Thomas Hutchinson. Though the men dined alone, Benjamin wore his best white wig, a neat burgundy suit with brass buttons, and the newest ruffled shirt in his wardrobe, for it would be his last meeting with an old friend. They had attended Harvard together, broken bread at the table of the Reverend Mr. Thomas Prince, concurred on the Writs of Assistance, and when the mob destroyed Hutchinson's home during the Stamp Act riots, Bigelow had offered him a room on Cape Cod.

Hutchinson picked at the crumbs of cheese around the cheddar wedge on the table. He was tall but frail, with delicate features and shoulders that seemed far too slender to support the weight His Majesty had placed upon them. "I sail for England, and General Gage welcomes two more regiments to Boston. How will Cape Cod take to that?"

"No better than Boston."

"The names on their Committee of Correspondence—"

"Names of traitors." Bigelow was considered a solid man, calm in demeanor, careful in speech, at fifty-seven the very study of the judicious attorney. His fleshy white face, framed by the wig, seemed set in marble, with gray stones for eyes. Seldom did he use a word so strong as "traitor."

"Some respectable names among them. Cape Cod names as old as your own—Nye, Freeman, Otis, Crocker, Sears."

"All men who should know better."

"I'm surprised to see no Hilyard."

"The Anonymous Outcast? Simply a nay-sayer."

Hutchinson sipped his wine. "'Twill be a great joy to escape the nay-sayers. I intend to revive my scholarship. Perhaps even write another volume of Massachusetts history."

"Pity you'll not have the Reverend Mr. Prince's New England Library to draw upon."

"I shall borrow a few of the books"—he poured more wine— "for safekeeping. Only God knows what may happen here 'fore the Crown regains sway. 'Twould be a true sin if manuscripts like Bradford's history were lost to rebel mobs."

"My worry is for the deeds in the county courthouses."

"You protect the deeds. I'll protect the history. After all, my great-grandmother lived in Bradford's time."

"Anne Hutchinson—something of a rebel herself."

"They were all rebels, even *your* ancestors."

Bigelow nodded gravely, though he did not like to be reminded of such truths. "Rebels of the *soul*. That distinguishes them from the mob."

Hutchinson leaned close to Bigelow. "There is a manuscript of the First Comers that even now may be in the hands of the mob. Have you ever heard of the log of the *Mayflower*?"

Bigelow shook his head. A small trickle of powder fell from his wig and settled on his shoulder.

"Mr. Prince believed it to be in the possession of your friend the Anonymous Outcast of Billingsgate. She alluded to it in one of her excrescences against you, just after the Otis incident."

"Prince is long dead, Excellency, and I have never been much for such tales. I'm a man of the here and now."

"Even a man of the here and now may imagine the use the mob would make of a manuscript that portrays the First Comers as rebels. Should you discover the existence of this thing, move quickly, for it may be a dangerous symbol."

Benjamin Bigelow seldom moved quickly in anything. "Act in haste and repent at leisure" was a motto close to his heart. And as he had heard nothing about this mythical *Mayflower* log, he saw no reason to speak of it to his brother, who grew more nervous all the time, like an unsaddled horse hearing the trumpet sound.

Throughout the summer, Benjamin tried calmly to present the Loyalist position. What could be more suicidal, he asked of his Whig friends, than to rebel against the greatest military power on earth?

What could be worse for Cape Cod than the British fleet sinking shipping and raiding towns at will? "Economic ruin will result. And for what? A few pence tax on tea?"

But while he conciliated, others inflamed. Solomon, a customs inspector rendered all but useless by the Whigs' Solemn League and Covenant against importing British goods, railed on in the taverns about fools who would destroy prosperity to call themselves patriots. Aunt Nabby shouted her contempt for every patriot parade and refused to give up her tea when local agitators came to enforce the covenant. She would damn well sell what she wanted where she wanted.

They and those like them were a walking provocation but nothing as compared to the Intolerable Acts, which closed the port of Boston and brought more troops to the city and more ships to the coasts of the Cape. Benjamin Bigelow told his wife that he no longer held hope for the future. But still he was shrewd and careful and tried to gauge the position his family should take when the fighting began.

Before he could decide, a choice was forced upon him by the first openly treasonous event of the Revolution. It was a fine September day, and the county court was about to open the autumn session. But the Crown had revoked the right of the Massachusetts court to select jurors. Trouble was in the wind, and Benjamin was in his office when he heard the beating of a drum.

What frightened him was that they were not a mob but an unarmed army. Dr. Nathaniel Freemen, on a fractious black stallion, rode at their head, the drummers followed, and then, in columns of two, came a thousand men or more.

They called themselves the Body of the People. They marched into the town and packed themselves in front of the courthouse, blocking the high sheriff and Justice James Otis, Sr., father of the patriot, from taking their seats. In the most polite terms, Otis ordered them to retreat. In the most polite terms, they refused. The court did not open.

That accomplished, the Body of the People turned their attention to the officers of the Crown and the Loyalists in Barnstable.

By now Solomon and Benjamin, their wives, and Solomon's son and daughter, were watching from the upstairs windows of Solomon's house. The so-called patriots were taking some people from the crowd and leading others from their houses and forcing them to sign public recantations. There was no violence, but a fine measure of intimidation in the presence of the Body of the People.

Two men went into Aunt Nabby's grocery and came out a moment later, their recantation flying after them. "I'll sign nothin'! I'm a loyal subject and always will be. And if you put that damn liberty pole up in my town, I'll chop it down with a butter knife if there's none man enough to do it."

The crowd roared with laughter at the furious old lady, but Solomon whispered that she was braver than he. Then he suggested they slip out the back and down to the wharf, where they could sail away on one of their schooners.

"Nothing of the sort," said Benjamin.

"We can't refuse. They may tear us apart."

"We shall sign," Benjamin said placidly.

"Sign? Are you daft?"

"Sign. If they win, we win. If they lose, we have been coerced. Refuse to sign and suffer the consequences."

And little Hannah asked, "Does this make us patriots?"

"No dear," answered Benjamin. "We are simply being expedient."

That afternoon, up went the liberty pole, gaily painted and topped with a gilded finial. That night, it was cut down. No one knew by whom, but the next morning, Widow Nabby announced that justice had been served—if not in the court, at least on the town green.

The following night, justice was served to the Widow Nabby in the form of tar and feathers and a ride on the severed pole. Whatever she had said about the cause of liberty, she recanted. Whatever the cause of liberty had gained at the courthouse, it lost.

vii.

TAR AND FEATHERS AND COMEUPPANCE

We have warned them not to stand in the way of history. We have told them that comeuppance awaits, and still they chop down liberty poles and laugh at the future.

Ask the Widow Nabby what happens to old crones who

hold to old ways. Ask her if the turpentine burned when they took off the tar and feathers. Ask her BIGELOW relatives about history. They have tried to hide it and hide from it. They have denied that they are TORIES and liars, but the Book of History proves otherwise, and someday, they will meet their comeuppance.

"It was terrible, what they did to her," Serenity told her grandson a few nights later. "But she's a Bigelow. And nobody gets my blood boilin' faster."

"Speakin' bad about her won't make her nephews give back Jack's Island, will it?" The boy threw several driftwood sticks onto the fire.

"If there's rebellion, the Tories'll sail off to Canada. They can't take their land with 'em."

"But the Bigelows signed the pledge." The boy was now eleven. His hands and feet had begun to outgrow the rest of his body, and his grandmother thought that his mind was outgrowing the hands and feet.

"They're liars. Always has been." She took a mouthful of rum and held it around her remaining tooth. "I sure wish your Pa was to home. I could use a good man with the pliers."

"Why . . . why must we get toothaches, Grandma?" The boy folded his legs and sat before the fire.

"'Tis a fair question, lad." She tightened the cloth around her head, which squeezed her jaw and soothed the pain. "Because we're slaves. Women are slaves of men. Men are slaves of gover'ments. Gover'ments intone the name of God. And God makes us all slaves to pain, then looks down on us like we look down on a nest of ants afore we step on it. So I write my broadsides."

"Because you're mad at God?"

"To break the chain and set us free." She took another mouthful of rum, which puffed out her cheek like a wineskin.

"Is the book of history about God?"

Serenity tried to laugh, but it hurt her face too much. "It's about good men and God and slaves to God. The lost log of the *Mayflower*, the Bigelow book of comeuppance. And what a tale it is, of Indians and First Comers, battles, murders . . ."

The wind came out of the northwest, booming down in gusts that were the first breath of winter. The black cat named Lucinda the Tenth purred by the fire. And Serenity began the story. She had told the boy's parents, but they had been little interested. Just a book about something that happened a hundred and fifty years ago. What importance could it hold?

She hoped the boy would have more imagination. "I first was told of it by a pirate who was also an Indian—"

Then the boy heard a sound.

"What?" asked Serenity.

"A sail lowerin' or the clank of an oarlock."

Serenity took a swallow of rum. Below the wind, she heard the crump of the waves hitting the beach. It sounded as if the tide had turned and was rising. If they were coming, they would take the tide. And she had never deceived herself: some night, they would come. "My ears ain't too good, lad, but if you think you heard somethin', bar the door, and bring me the blunderpiece."

The color drained from the boy's face.

"'Tis prob'ly nothin'," she said. "But go out the back and fetch some help."

"The Hatches?"

"They're off fishin'. You'll have to go to the Tebbets."

"They're almost as far as my ma."

"They're the closest there is tonight. Now bolt the door like a good lad."

As Sam touched the bolt, the door blew into his face, striking so squarely that the world went black before him.

"Comeuppance is here." The first man through the door wore a hood and was dressed in black.

Under the seat of her chair, Serenity had fastened a lethal little pistol called a duck's foot, a spread of five barrels, all fired by a single pull of the trigger, the perfect weapon for the sea captain facing mutineers or the old woman facing intruders.

She pointed it at the four hooded men now crowding through the door. "Get out!"

She would have done better simply to fire, because the back door burst open, and as she turned, the man in black smashed an axe handle into her wrist. The duck's foot fell to the floor, her arms were pinned behind her, and a rag was stuffed into her mouth.

"Comeuppance," repeated the man in black, his voice sounding like the cry of a querulous old gull. "*Comeuppance.* You like the word, don't you?"

Serenity tried to speak.

The black hood came close. "Scream and you're dead." Then he plucked the gag from her mouth.

"My grandson?"

Two of the men had trussed the boy and gagged him. Then they picked him up and threw him like a sack of oysters into the sand.

"He'll be fine," said the one in black, "as long as his grandmother cooperates."

"Get out."

One of the men knocked the kettle off the fireplace hanger and put up a bucket of tar. Then he threw several logs onto the flames to make them jump.

"When my son sees your boat, he'll come in here and harpoon the lot of you."

"Your son's a thousand miles away. And there's none on this island who'll hear you scream over a blowin' wind."

"You won't hear *me* scream. Now get out, afore I sic every Son of Liberty on Cape Cod after you."

The man took a spoon from the table and dipped it into the hot tar. Then he brought it over and held it under her nose. "This is what happens to old crones who think Tory ways are wrong."

"So, you can read, eh?"

"Tar and feathers and comeuppance."

The burned stink of hot tar stung her nostrils.

"We'll make it boil, so it covers good." He let a glob fall onto the table and spread out before her.

One of the others stirred the tar until it fell smoothly back into the bucket. "Ready."

Another one dropped an old feather pillow onto the table. "Let's *do* her."

"Did you tell your wife where you'd be tonight?" said Serenity. "Or do you wear that hood 'cause you're too ugly to find a woman who'll look at you?"

"I ain't ugly," said the one with the pillow.

Another one brought over the tar. "She won't be so feisty after this."

"Shut up," snapped the man in black. Then he turned his hood at Serenity.

She tried to see his eye color and gauge his measurements. She would remember their gaits, their clothes, the shoes they were wearing. But she would never forget the voice of the one in black.

"There is one way you can avoid the tar, woman."

"I'll recant nothin'."

"Tell us where to find the so-called book of history."

And she grinned. "You're a *Bigelow*."

For a moment, the black hood was motionless, soundless. But the nervous, chicken-head twitching of the others told her she was right.

"I'm anyone who's heard about the book," said the black hood.

"You're a Bigelow."

"The book of *comeuppance*, woman. Tell us where it is and escape the tar. Refuse and suffer like Widow Nabby."

"Then *you* don't have it?" She had wondered for decades if her brother had sold the log to the Bigelows. Now she knew. He had taken it with him, wherever he went.

The man in the hood stared at her for a moment. Then he took a spatula covered with tar and brought it toward her. "We'll start with the hair first. Like Nabby."

Serenity looked at the others. "This ain't about Tories and Whigs. This is about Hilyards and Bigelows. Do this for politics, if you want, but don't let this Bigelow bastard do it for what he wants from me."

"Where is the book?" demanded the man in black.

"I don't know." She closed her eyes and clenched her jaw as the boiling tar burned a patch of her scalp.

"Where is it?"

"Get out, Solomon Bigelow. Or are you Benjamin? Which coward are you?"

"I'm a Tory, sunk like the Sons of Liberty to frightenin' old crones." He took more tar and poured it onto her head. It was so hot that it soaked through her hair and burned through her skin and set her brain on fire.

"Where is it?"

"Get out!" she screamed. "Get out."

The man in black ordered one of the others to sprinkle feathers on Serenity's head, and they fell like gentle snowfall on a burning bed of ash.

"Now strip her," he commanded.

"No one stripped the widow Nabby," said Serenity.

"Then the book? Where is it?"

"I don't know. It disappeared. Sixty years ago."

"Who would expect the truth from one who has lied so often on foolscap?" He tore the top of her dress away.

"We're Tories, man, not *monsters*," protested one of the others.

But the man in black tore off her shift. "There. Nothing but a hag."

Serenity's head felt as if it were covered with a burning hat. Her breasts shriveled in the cold air. But she would fight with every last fiber, because it was bred into her, in her backbone and her blood. She aimed a kick to his groin and nearly lifted him off his feet.

He struck her face and screamed, "Bitch!"

She kicked like a trapped deer, at everything in sight. She struck a shin, then another groin.

And the man in black grabbed the tar bucket from the fireplace hook. A tarring might go no further than a few cold daubs on the hair, for a little chiding. Or it could threaten a victim with burning and suffocation. The man in black may have planned on the first but was giving the second, dumping the tar over Serenity's shoulders and breasts like a bath of fire.

Her flesh seared and blistered, and the smell of her own death burned into her head. But still she would not surrender anything, and if she screamed, it would be with the same voice of defiance she had brought to the beach on that night almost six decades before. "Damn you! Damn you all for bloody night-ridin' cowards!"

"This is what happens to old crones who stand against good men of the Crown." And he dumped more tar onto her back.

She screamed and damned them again.

Then the feathers flew around her head and up her nose, and she nearly passed out from pain and fury.

The man in black tore into the chest of drawers by the fireplace and the box of broadsides on the table.

"The book's not here," she said. "You'll never find it."

"Liar!"

Two of the others ran in a long painted pole with a gilded finial, the liberty pole from Barnstable, cut down again and brought to Billingsgate. They raised Serenity, kicking and cursing, though every move caused the cooling tar to pull on her flesh and lift more skin from her burned back.

They were losing their taste for this. They had started willingly enough, but the old woman's pain seemed to be draining them of their hatred. If they rode her on the rail, they would do it simply because it was the final act of a miserable little dumb show that had been played out in every one of the thirteen colonies.

"Enough," said one of them. "She's had enough."

"She's the chief rabble-rouser on the Cape," said another. "She's the cause of all our troubles."

"Rail her and run her," cried the leader, "like they did to my aunt."

"Bigelow!" screamed Serenity, finding the last reservoir of fury. "I damn you. I damn you Solomon Bigelow. I go to my grave with the knowledge of your comeuppance."

"Take your own comeuppance!"

He pulled her whale oil lamps from the table and smashed them, one on the floor, the other against the wall. The flames bit hungrily into the dried old boards. "If comeuppance is here, it'll soon be gone."

Outside, young Sam woke face down in the cold sand. He heard his grandmother's wail. Then he saw her riding out of her own cottage like some figure of myth, half human, half-feathered, borne aloft by a group of hooded retainers.

"I damn you all! I damn Loyalists and Tories and all . . . all . . . all!"

Flames began to jump in the house, and a hooded figure appeared in the doorway, screaming like a scavenging gull, "Comeuppance! Take the comeuppance you have threatened so long!"

Then a living fireball burst from the door—Lucinda the Tenth, her back in flames, streaking across the dune and disappearing into the sea. . . .

The northwest wind that fed the flames drove the Tory boat back across the bay. By the time the other islanders reached the house, it was a tower of fire that lit the sky from Provincetown to Plymouth.

They found Sam first, and he led them to his grandmother. She lay face down in the rising tide that each day carried a little more sand away from Billingsgate Island. Nature changed the face of the world over centuries. Men and women had much less time. Serenity had used hers well.

And young Sam Hilyard resolved that someone would pay.

CHAPTER 21

July 13

Billingsgate Shoals

"She must have died near here," said Geoff.

"Tarred her and feathered her and set fire to her cat." In the bow seat, George applied zinc oxide to his nose. "This is going to be *fun*."

"Fun . . . yeah," said Jimmy.

Geoff ran the boat right into the heat waves rising from the remains of Billingsgate Island. Twice a day, this sandbar rose from the sea, drawing clam diggers, scavengers, gulls that came to pick over the dogfish carcasses, and guys like George, with their metal detectors.

"C'mon," Jimmy was sitting in one of the fighting chairs, stripped to the waist, ready for a fight. "This is our day to fish. Every boat on Wellfleet Harbor is up by the eight-can."

"We're fishing for history." George jumped into ankle-deep sand and then took something that looked like a minesweeper off the bow.

"Playing treasure hunt on a ghost island won't bring back Rake Hilyard," said Jimmy.

"Maybe Serenity's death holds the key to Rake's," answered Geoff.

"The key to Rake's death was the one in his ignition. A ninety-year-old man shouldn't have been on Suicide Six on a foggy night."

"The cops claim he swerved to avoid hitting an animal." Geoff put on his sunglasses and jumped down. "He wouldn't have swerved to avoid hitting *me*."

Jimmy shook his head and snapped a pencil-popper onto his steel leader.

"She's here," said George. He had the look he got whenever he saw great art or a great menu in a restaurant window.

"You won't find her with a metal detector, George."

"Humor me, Geoff. The broadsides say she knew about a book of history. That's why Rake wanted you to read them."

It had been sixty years since Billingsgate had been above water at high tide. The sea had spread the island south and east into an enormous mutton-chop of a shoal, leaving piles of red-brick rubble scattered across the sand like the gravestones of a vanished settlement.

"They call this Cape Cod's Atlantis."

"Except this was no myth." Geoff felt almost reverent, in spite of the ridiculous image that George cut in white ducks, Panama, and metal detector.

"Her spirit's here."

"We aren't going to find it with that thing."

"I once found a piece of eight washed in from the *Whydah*. Serenity might have buried the log in some kind of metal box sealed with wax. If she buried it four or five feet down, you'd find it right at the surface now." George's sweeper made a little beep. He dug with his toe and turned up a pop top.

Geoff stood in the center of the shoal and pivoted slowly to absorb the view that Serenity would have seen—the bluffs of Great Island, Wellfleet Harbor, the Eastham shoreline running south, the blue bay glimmering in the sun. The contours had not changed since she had been here. He could almost feel her.

And just as she had been stalked by Tories, it seemed they were being stalked by a big Chris-Craft anchored down at the point. One guy was fishing, another was looking north through a pair of binoculars. He could have been looking at anything, but since Rake's death, Geoff had begun to suspect everything.

Now the sound of the big Chris-Craft engine came thrumming across the shoal, sending Geoff back to his boat and his binoculars.

"Looking for more connections?" Jimmy was casting into a few feet of water.

"Those guys in the Chris-Craft connected with us about ten minutes after we left Pamet. They've been around us ever since."

"Jeez," said Jimmy, "maybe they're *following* us."

"We know why *we're* here. Why would anybody else be, when all the fish are hitting at the eight-can?" Geoff pushed his sunglasses up on his head and focused on the transom, but the high-sun shadow and the big wake rolling out made it impossible to read. "Did they catch anything?"

"The one with the rod just pulled in three blues on three casts."

Geoff lowered the binoculars. "Only one guy fishes, and as soon as he starts to get some action, they leave?"

Jimmy shook his head, as though losing patience with all this. "So maybe they have to get to work."

"Who worries about work when the blues are hitting?"

"So go after 'em."

Geoff checked the depth of the water. "We won't lift off for another ten minutes."

George came up to the boat with the metal detector slung over his shoulder. "Maybe they thought we made 'em."

"*Made* 'em." Jimmy laughed and cast his plug over a tide rip. "You sound like an amateur. You both do. Amateur troublemakers and intriguers. Stick to your own jobs."

There should have been an argument over that, but the first bluefish of the summer hit Jimmy's plug and tore off a hundred yards of line. And boys would be boys when the bluefish hit. Geoff grabbed the gaff. George grabbed another rod.

The fish burst from the water in a perfect arc of blue muscle. It seemed to hang in midair until it heard the shouts of excitement echoing across the flats. Then it shook itself violently, slammed into the water, and began to run.

There was a feeding frenzy coming. It had begun down near the tip of the shoal, where the mystery boat had been. Now it was working its way north. Thousands of hungry bluefish, churning up the water, chopping up the baitfish, biting at anything from Castmasters to slow swimmers to the foil gum wrappers that the man with the binoculars had left floating on the water.

ⵊⵊ.

"Hi, Janice. Phyllis Baxter here." Janice scribbled the name on the notepad in front of her. Maybe if she saw the words, she could remember the face.

"How're you, Jan?"

Someone should tell her she talked too loud on the phone. Of course, not many people were calling the offices of Bigelow Development these days, so *any* voice was welcome.

"I'm fine." Janice sketched a round face, short hair, a big ear-to-ear smile, and said, "Glad to be back."

"I always say the good ones can smell a turnaround. They get in when everyone else is getting out."

Jewelry. Janice drew a pair of orange earrings the size of honey-dipped doughnuts. "I'm in for better or worse."

"Don't worry, dearie. It can't *get* any worse." After Phyllis complimented someone, she reminded them she had been doing this for thirty years. She was no blue-haired dabbler augmenting her Social Security, no mommy showing houses when the kids were off at school—and by inference most of the other female brokers were. Phyllis knew what was *really* happening in the wild world of Cape Cod real estate.

And what was really happening this week: "A divorced mother of two—who wore sunglasses on a cloudy day, which may mean she's a battered wife—was sent by a friend. She's moving from New York to get away from her ex-husband, which *definitely* means she's battered. She's got a buck and a quarter to spend—"

Janice wrote $125,000 on her notepad and shifted the telephone to the other ear.

"—but a sale's a sale. She saw this house in Eastham. Your listing, rotten location, right on Route Six, rotten location, rotten little rat-hole house. But if *she* likes it, we call it Convenience with Cape Cod Charm. I suppose anything's better than New York."

Janice drew a big apple. Inside it she wrote $7,500, standard commission on $125,000. Then she wrote $3,750, the share her office would receive in a co-brokering arrangement. Then she wrote $1,875, her share of the office share.

"Could you show it?" asked Phyllis Baxter.

Through the window, Janice saw her husband hefting a leaky trash bag out of the back of his Chevy.

She flipped through her book and found the listing. "I'll meet you there in half an hour. Gotta run. . . . Geoffrey, I hope you're planning to clean the fish blood off the floor."

Geoff stuck his head into her office. "Some welcome for the hunter-gatherer."

She heard his footsteps thump down the hallway to the little kitchenette at the end. The bag of fish hit the sink, and the refrigerator door popped open.

From his office, Doug's voice echoed off polished hard wood floors and white-painted walls, "Just what I want—more bluefish."

"Did somebody say bluefish?" Dickerson came down from his upstairs office. "I'll take two. Cook 'em on the grill with a little mayonnaise."

Geoff came back to the front office—three desks, only one occupied on a slow day in a slower market. "We hit a blitz up at Billingsgate."

Doug came through the French doors that separated his office from the agents', the old dining room from the parlor. "How you holdin' up, Geoff?"

"Life goes on."

Dickerson put a fatherly hand on his shoulder. "Two deaths in a week . . . tough."

"I'm trying to keep it in perspective."

Did they mean *any* of this? Geoff always handed out bluefish to everyone after a blitz, but that wasn't why he was here. Janice could see it in his eyes. Now that Rake was dead, he controlled more land. He could rewrite the deal to get better terms, or he could kill it completely. She didn't know what he planned, and she didn't think he knew either . . . until now.

On her notepad, she drew the island once more. Then her father said "Soooo," which usually meant he was going to ask a blunt question. She raised her pen from the page.

"*Soooo*, Janice tells me that before the . . . sad events of the last week or so, you'd done some sketches."

Doug sat on the edge of a desk and began to swing his leg. "We can't tell you how pleased that makes us."

"Keep your lime green pants on," said Geoff.

"We all have to keep our pants on," said Dickerson. "We don't clear probate for six months. But if we get our ducks in a row—"

"I'm not worrying about ducks."

Doug's leg stopped swinging. Dickerson ran his hand through his chin whiskers.

"Rake showed me some things the night he was killed," Geoff said.

"Killed?" said Doug.

"I think he was run off the road."

Janice scratched out her sketch of the island. This was worse than she thought. "Who killed him, Geoff?"

"I don't know. Maybe the people who followed us in a boat this morning."

"And who were *they*, Geoff?"

"Fishermen." Doug laughed. "They saw you in your Grady White and figured you knew where the fish were."

"I don't think so," said Geoff.

And Dickerson Bigelow blew up, lost it entirely. Once, he would have stayed and argued or cajoled or played the bullying businessman until he'd brought Geoff around. But he was getting old. And he was no longer in control. The best he could do was sputter, "Janice, you married a damn fool," and stomp up the stairs.

A door slammed, then popped open again. "And tell him to keep his damn bluefish!" *Slam.* The whole house shook.

"Dad's offended," said Janice.

"If Geoff's accusing us, I'm offended, too," said Doug.

"I'm not accusing, I'm speculating."

Doug picked up the phone. "So speculate with the state police. According to them, everything about the accident was consistent with the maneuver to avoid an animal—speed, skid, direction of travel. No evidence of foul play."

"Have they speculated on the log of the *Mayflower*?" asked Geoff.

"A Rake Hilyard hoax."

"Now Rake's dead and I inherit half of his property—"

"And the hoax," muttered Janice.

"And now," added Douglas, "you think you owe it to him to do what he would have done with his property, even if that is exactly nothing?"

Geoff looked at Janice. "Your brother understands better than you do."

Doug came over to Geoff. "We need to let the Conservation

Commission walk Jack's Island next week. We can't even *think* of the next step until they've marked off the wetlands and we've settled those arguments."

"I won't stop you, Doug. But don't be too broken up if *they* stop you."

Janice couldn't take all this civility any longer. She shoved a few papers into her purse and took her MLS book. "My father's right. I married a damn fool. I have an appointment."

• • •
iii.

"Hi, Jan. It's so good to see you again."

This must be Phyllis Baxter. Janice couldn't quite remember. But there were the earrings, bigger than doughnuts, more like inner tubes. And the teeth—big, square horse teeth set in a mouth that was always open. She remembered now.

Phyllis introduced her client. Janice shook the young woman's hand—very soft, very white. Jet black hair that made her skin look even whiter, and a white raincoat, though it was a sunny afternoon. Her height might have been impressive if not for the tall-girl slouch and the twitchy way about her. Like a battered wife.

It was none of Janice's business. Show her the house. If she liked it, sell her the house, then pity her because she couldn't find anything better.

They exchanged a few pleasantries—very few, because they couldn't be heard above the traffic on Route 6. Then they went inside.

"Isn't this *cozy*," bellowed Phyllis, still competing with the roar of the traffic outside.

About as cozy as the inside of a stove carton, thought Janice.

"Is there a fireplace?" asked the woman.

Janice looked at the listing sheet. "I'm afraid not."

Phyllis peered through the little windows above the kitchen sink. "Your kids'll like the backyard."

Janice looked out the windows by the television, at four lanes of traffic. "Just keep them away from the front."

Phyllis gave her a scowl. It wasn't their job to worry about people's kids, unless the people could afford to give the kids something better. "What are the taxes here?" she asked, trying to keep it going.

"Four hundred."

"Very reasonable."

"For this place, robbery," said Janice.

Phyllis asked for the listing sheet, as though it might hold the key to the sale. "Well, *this* is a little bit of history. It says this house was moved from Billingsgate Island. Imagine that."

"Half the houses on Cape Cod have been moved," said Janice, "from Billingsgate, from Monomoy Island, from one side of a lot to another. . . . We can find her a nicer house."

"We'll do our best." Phyllis gave Janice a smile that could have bitten a board nail in half.

Janice said she could think of a few places in this price range, and she promised to call Phyllis. The young woman thanked Janice for her frankness and made only one stipulation: a fireplace.

"I'd love to be able to sit with my kids beside a roaring fire. Fires are happy things."

Everybody should have a fireplace, thought Janice, and a husband who didn't hit her . . . or play the damn fool when the big moment of his life arrived. The more houses they built, the better the chances that this poor woman would get her fireplace.

iv.

"Now, what's this I hear about a metal detector on Billingsgate?"

"I report what I see."

"You can interpret, too, I hope." John M. Nance tapped a golf ball toward the hole on the putting green in his backyard. It rolled to within an inch of the cup and stopped. "Otherwise, my money is wasted."

"The night Clara dies, Rake says he has to find the log. The night Rake dies, he visits Geoff with something. And the day after Rake's buried, Geoff's on Billingsgate Shoals with a metal detector."

"Do you think the log is buried on Billingsgate?"

"Maybe." The bland-looking young man wore a gray Puma warm-up suit with yellow piping. He chewed Juicy Fruit gum and dropped a yellow wrapper onto the putting green.

Nance was in mid-putt. His putter stopped. He glared at the wrapper.

The young man began to explain why the log might be on

Billingsgate, but Nance's eyes were on the wrapper, which he studied until the young man picked it up.

"The log is *not* on Billingsgate Shoals, Mr. Lambeth. We've known that from the beginning." Nance followed through and missed his putt. "Your initial report said this Geoff Hilyard would go for Bigelow's deal. Now he's going after the log. That could kill the deal, though we don't know how."

"So he's changing his mind."

Nance tapped another ball. "This much is certain: if he goes for the log, it would be better if we found it first. If he goes for the deal, we *have* to find it first."

"Where will he look next?" The young man unfolded another stick of gum and put the wrapper in his pocket.

"That's what I pay your agency for."

"We do industrial spying . . . corporate intelligence. We don't even like divorce work. We're new to this."

"So am I." Nance tapped another shot at the cup. "But if Hilyard's following the history, he'll turn to Sam Hilyard next. Sam holds the key."

CHAPTER 22

June 1776

Sam and the Doctor

Sam Hilyard aimed the glass at the horizon, where a tall tree of sails reflected the dusk. "She's carryin' a full spread, Pa. Royals, t'gallants, mains'ls, tops'ls."

"She's the *Somerset*, all right, lad. How far?"

The motion of the *Serenity* made the glass unsteady, so Sam wrapped an arm around a shroud and rested it on a ratline. "She's hull down."

"And night comin' faster than she is." Ned clapped his son on the back. "We beat 'er again, lad. We sleep in Boston tonight."

Nothing in this rebellious world made a boy feel prouder than to sail with his father under letters of marque. Nothing made him feel more of a man than to elude once more the *Somerset*, sixty-four-gun ship of the line. And nothing better slaked his thirst for revenge than to raid British shipping and Loyalist havens along the Canadian coast. The Hilyards had become privateers.

Sam looked astern, at the prize ship lumbering along in their wake. The Halifax-bound merchantman *Ramshead* had surrendered without a fight, which was all for the best. The *Serenity* carried four six-pounders and a pair of swivels, but the Hilyards much preferred bluff to cannon fire. "Will we get her into Boston, too?"

"Canvas, paint, English-made nails—a cargo to bring a fair price on Long Wharf," said Charlie Kwennit. "With Square Stubbs in command, give no worry to the *Ramshead*."

"Worry instead about the captain of that bloody giant out there." Ned pointed toward the sails of the *Somerset*. "We been slippin' his blockade a year and a half now."

"Do you think he knows who we are?"

"Know who we are?" Ned Hilyard gave out with the kind of laugh to fill a son with confidence. At fifty-nine, he was still a young man in step and strength. He even looked younger, having shaved his mottled beard. But more than a shave, thought Sam, it was his father's refusal to be cowed by anything that gave him the vigor of youth. "I damn well *hope* he knows who we are. I'd be sore disappointed if he didn't "

Sam laughed with his father and felt the gentle roll of the sea, speaking to him through the soles of his bare feet and soothingly along his backbone, as though he were another singing line on the *Serenity*. He watched the night rising from the eastern horizon and crossing the sky like a great canopy to cover them. And he could think of no better place to be, no matter that the *Somerset* stalked them.

ii.

Dr. William Thayer could think of no worse place to be than the sick bay of the *Somerset*, even when the task was as simple as lancing a boil on a sailor's neck. He barely touched his knife to the reddened mound of flesh before the blood splattered and the tallow-colored core came popping out.

The sailor, a hairy Devonshire ape named Tom Dodd, asked to see what had caused him such pain. With a cotton cloth, Thayer removed the festerment from the facing of his coat, where it had come to rest. Dodd studied it, nodded approvingly, and said that a core the size of his little toe should be good for an extra tot of rum.

Thayer agreed. Rum was one of the few things that made life tolerable for any of them, especially for a ship's doctor who practiced on pox-ridden old drunks snatched from waterfront pubs, on homesick farm boys who had sought excitement but found wormy beef, floggings, and forecastle buggery instead, or on career sailors who considered this misery their happiest home. Dodd was among the last, and he knew all the tricks for gaining an advantage or an extra tot.

But Thayer had seen enough of Tom Dodd. The only rum he would be getting was soaked into a cloth and used as a poultice. Thayer said the rum was good for drawing out the poison, of which there was a long measure in the look that Dodd gave him before going off to torment some young seaman.

Thayer took a few swallows of rum himself and went on deck to clean the stench of Tom Dodd from his nostrils.

"A fine evening, sir. Marvelous twilight."

Captain George Ourry studied the western horizon through his glass. "I am no connoisseur of twilights."

"Of privateers, then, even as they elude you?"

Ourry turned his gaze to Thayer. He was a dark man, tall and shroud-slender. "There is blood on your waistcoat, Doctor."

"I've just—"

"Cover it with pipe clay. I'll not have one of my officers looking like a Covent Garden butcher"—he wrinkled his nostrils—"or smelling like a grog bucket. I've warned you about your taste for rum, Doctor."

"Aye, sir." Thayer took a few steps toward the companionway, then stopped. "'Tis a fine twilight just the same, sir. 'Twould do you a bit of good to study it."

Ourry raised the glass to his eye again. "I prefer to study that sloop and her prize, learn her movement and her silhouette, the way the master shapes his course to the wind. Loyalists have been known to pass information about privateers like that, and one day, Ned Hilyard will make his mistake."

"Hilyard . . ." Thayer peered at the sail, nothing more than a black triangle against the red western sky. "'Tis a name I've heard."

"Perhaps because the rebels have nothing to celebrate but their piratical privateers."

iii.

That was true, as HMS *Somerset* and the Royal Navy had closed New England waters to everything else. And Cape Cod had suffered more than most. In Wellfleet, whaling ships rotted at anchor. In Falmouth and Barnstable, merchantmen sat with masts stepped down and deck boards rotting in the sun. And from Plymouth to Provincetown, men of property tallied their losses.

The most loyal of these men had moved to Nova Scotia or the British-controlled islands south of the Cape. But most of them were loyal to their money before anything else, and so they trimmed the sails of their conscience to the prevailing wind, which blew the Bigelows to Boston for the auction of the *Ramshead* and her cargo.

To the surprise of many, not the least of them Ned Hilyard, the Bigelows also wished to discuss other business with Ned Hilyard.

They said they intended to fund a privateer and they knew Ned to be the best commander on the American coast. They offered him partnership in a sixteen-gun topsail sloop, fast enough to outrun a Royal Navy frigate, powerful enough to take on an armed East Indiaman laden with goods.

And the unspoken reason for the visit was that the Bigelows feared Ned's fury, should ever he learn the truth of Serenity's death. What better way to deflect suspicion than to ally themselves with her son?

Benjamin still regretted the night he had told Solomon what he knew of the book of history. Solomon regretted the night after and admitted that, every night since, he had dreamed of a burning cat. It had been merely prudent to burn the house where the book was hidden, he said, but his temper had overcome his prudence.

And because this happened often with Solomon, Benjamin did the talking in the tiny cabin of the *Serenity*. Ned listened, questioned them about their loyalty to England, which they assured him was in eclipse, and he promised to bring an answer to Barnstable in two weeks.

This pleased young Sam, for while the men were meeting in the 9cabin, their children were meeting on the deck.

Hannah Bigelow's father had told her to wait by the gangplank and read the book he had bought for her on this, her first trip to Boston. She preferred to watch the boy splicing rope near the bow. The boy nodded to her. She smiled at him. And the boy nearly put the splicing awl through the palm of his hand.

"So . . . you're a Bigelow?" He summoned the courage to cross the deck while clenching his fist to hide the blood.

"You're the grandson of Serenity Hilyard," she said. "I read all her broadsides."

Sam did not know how to take that. He was not skilled in polite conversation, especially with Bigelows or brown-eyed girls in yellow sunbonnets. "She's dead."

"I know. You're bleeding." She took a handkerchief from her sleeve and pressed it into his hand, and he was smitten.

iv.

July 10, 1776, the night the Hilyards would come to Barnstable to dine and deliver their answer. A night, thought Hannah, to have patriots beneath her roof, not abstainers like her father and uncle.

In Philadelphia, the Continental Congress was confronting the cold logic of independence. On Cape Cod, the Committees of Correspondence had convened to vote their instructions. And in every town save one, the vote had been yea and duly forwarded to Philadelphia.

In Barnstable, one hundred thirty men had debated the question. Sixty-five abstained, thirty voted in favor of independence, and thirty-five voted not to send *any* word to Congress. The patriots of the town were furious. Men of property had predicted that independence would mean poverty, and thus had they controlled the vote.

Benjamin Bigelow had abstained and told his brother that to vote otherwise would be to jeopardize their carefully balanced seat on the fence of rebellion.

Hannah was mortified. After the visit to meet the Hilyards in Boston, she had hoped that her father and uncle would take the van of rebellion. She had even begun to sew a Grand Union flag— thirteen red and white stripes for thirteen colonies and the Union Jack for their English heritage—to fly from their privateer. But the family table talk still smacked of expediency.

Hannah knew another word for it: "hypocrisy." Her mother told her to restrain such opinions until she had grown to womanhood.

And she grew closer to that each day. Her breasts had begun to fill and rise, the tips to grow more sensitive. She kept a supply of menstrual cloths at the back of her drawer. Many of her dresses no longer fit her widening hips. And the revolutionary ideas that had taken life when she visited the *Serenity* now boiled in her mind like the forces changing her body.

Her father said her patriotism was simply a passion of youth. But it was more. In the grandson of the Anonymous Outcast, Hannah had found a hero to fill her daydreams of romance and rebellion—a boy her own age, and already a *privateer.*

Hannah put on her best blue skirt, a white apron, a buff-colored shawl, and gold ribbons for her hair. This, she was certain, would shock her father. She waited until she saw the Hilyards arrive; then she dabbed a bit of vanilla extract behind her ears and hurried to the top of the stairs.

Men's voices boomed from the foyer. The air was filled with the promise of new business. But Hannah saw only Sam. His untied black hair reached his shoulders, his face was burned by sun and blotched by blemishes, yet he was already as tall as any man around him. In the foyer of one of the finest houses on Cape Cod, surrounded by Turkey carpets, English wallpapers, mahogany, brass, he seemed the finest thing that Hannah had ever seen. She straightened her skirt and went down to him.

"Your hat, sir?" She took the tricorne from his hands. She was glad for her full skirt, to hide her shaking kneecaps, gladder still that his sunburn did not hide the flush in his face when he looked at her.

Then Hannah curtsied to the fathers, who inspected her from the hem of her blue skirt to the gold ribbons in her hair. And as she had hoped, her father's brow furrowed down to collect his fury.

But Ned's laughter restrained him. "I may question your patriotism, Bigelow, but what Loyalist would let his daughter dress in the colors of a Continental officer?"

Solomon Bigelow gave Ned Hilyard a thin smile.

The Bigelows served lamb, summer squash, green peas from the Bigelow garden, and a Burgundian wine that was among the last of its vintage in blockaded New England. With it, Ned Hilyard toasted General Washington, and Benjamin toasted the future of Massachusetts privateering. Solomon and his son Elkanah raised a glass to each.

But there good fellowship ended. The ordinary decorum of the dining room, which would have kept the men from talking of business or politics until the ladies had retired, did not pertain in these troubled days. Business was the reason the Hilyards had come and politics the only other talk that mattered.

"By using Cape Cod boatwrights, we can build a new sloop for five thousand five hundred twenty-five Continental dollars," said Solomon.

"Indeed," added Benjamin. "We figure close."

"Something at which you seem skilled," said Ned.

Hannah was not surprised at the hardness in Ned's voice. She thought him a hard-looking man. She much preferred the gentle face of his son, whose gaze met hers whenever she looked across the centerpiece.

"Close figuring is the sign of a prudent man," Benjamin sounded no more than conversational.

"Is that why you chose to figure so closely at the Barnstable meeting on independency?"

For a moment, there was silence. Hannah looked again at Sam, who looked down at his plate, as though embarrassed by what his father had said, or was about to say.

Then Solomon slammed his wineglass on the table. "I resent your inference, sir."

"Then explain your vote as the gesture of a patriot."

" 'Tis our belief," said Benjamin calmly, "that self-determination—an American Congress sending American representatives to Parliament—should be our goal. Independency will destroy most of us in the achieving, and the rest of us *if* we achieve it."

"You talk like a coward," said Ned Hilyard.

"I'm a man of *principles*," answered Benjamin.

"If your principle opposes independency, why fund a privateer?"

"Because we wish to survive," said Solomon angrily, "as we will, with or without your piracy to support us. I for one will be glad to go without, if it means we do not have to endure your son leering across the table at my daughter."

Hannah felt her meal turn to suet in her throat.

Ned Hilyard pushed his plate away and stood. "I have no principle but revenge. I came here because a bond with the likes of you might sooner or later lead me to my mother's murderers. But she'd tell me not to dirty myself, even if you offered me command of the *Somerset*."

Whatever might have followed, there came a sudden explosive clanging of the bell in the First Church steeple. Wineglasses tumbled to the floor and the tablecloth was pulled askew as all leaped to the windows.

July twilight gave the color of flame to the white clapboards of the church. The bell pounded, and above it now came the sound of a single word, bellowed up and down the County Road by a young man on horseback. "Independency! Independency!"

"My God, they've done it," said Solomon to his brother.

"They've *done* it, by God," said Ned to his son.

It was a strange crowd that gathered before the church, as divided in its beliefs and emotions as those who had convened at Bigelow's table. Some cheered the horseman's cry and pounded one another on the back. Some shook their heads and walked away. Most stood numbly in the middle of the road, confronted at last by the enormity of what had been done.

The rider pulled out a long sheet of foolscap, blew the trail dust away, and began to read. " 'When in the Course of human events, it becomes necessary for one people to dissolve the political bands which have connected them with another . . .' "

Hannah stood at the edge of the crowd and craned her neck to see. Her father and the others were somewhere in the throng, and young Sam was standing on top of a picket fence, his arm around a tree trunk.

"Come with me," said Hannah.

"Where?"

"A place where we can see."

" 'We hold these truths to be self-evident, that all men are created equal . . .' "

She led Sam back to her father's house and up the stairs to the end of the hallway. There a window looked through the maple branches at the church.

" 'He has plundered our seas, ravaged our Coasts, burnt our towns, and destroyed the lives of our people.' "

They listened in the gloaming to the transgressions of King George. They looked at each other. They looked at the crowd. Their shoulders touched. The sweetness of her vanilla scent struck his nostrils. The closeness of the young patriot made her heart pound. She drew her teeth across her lower lip. He fidgeted with his waistcoat buttons.

" '. . . these United Colonies are, and of Right ought to be Free and Independent States . . .' "

Her face shone in the fading light. "This is the most thrilling moment of my life."

Sam Hilyard wanted to say something equally impassioned, but he felt only an overwhelming desire to kiss her, which was exactly what she wanted him to do.

The kiss was awkward, more formal than romantic, and both

of them wondered if they were doing it properly. It could not, however, have been more exciting in atmosphere or alchemy. But then what? Would they kiss again? Embrace? Neither knew the decorum for these things, and Solomon Bigelow allowed them no chance to learn.

"Bloody sneak!" Solomon's fist struck Sam in the face and knocked him onto his seat.

"Father!"

"The world comes apart, but I still rule this house!"

Sam felt the urge to stand up and fight, but he was numbed beyond thought by the pain that had so suddenly replaced the pleasure of his first kiss. He tried to rise, and Solomon's boot sent him tumbling down the stairs.

"Get out, or you'll get comeuppance you won't forget."

Sam landed on the Turkish carpet. *Comeuppance*. The word sounded strangely familiar in the raging voice. But Sam could think only of flight.

"Father!" Hannah ran to the top of the stairs.

"Pack your things. You're bound for Cousin Emma's."

"Halifax?"

"The rest of us may have to endure independency, but you'll go where it's safe"—Solomon glared down at Sam—"from these patriots."

Sam stood and staggered to the door.

There would be no arrangement between the Bigelows and Hilyards, no more kissing between their children. The Bigelows would live in fear of what Ned Hilyard might learn, and Ned Hilyard would learn nothing from the Bigelows.

v.

On a September afternoon two years later, HMS *Somerset* rode at anchor in Provincetown Harbor.

The flogging was nearly over—two dozen with the lash would teach a Cape Cod fisherman that he was in the Royal Navy now, not hauling nets on his uncle's sloop. There'd be no back talk when the mate ordered men aloft in a heavy blow.

"Twenty-two." A strip of flesh tore loose, and the blood splattered. "Twenty-three!" The whip whistled again.

"He's gone out, Captain," said the mate.

"Complete the punishment."

"Let me feel his pulse," said Dr. Thayer.

George Ourry kept his eyes on the prisoner. "Complete the punishment."

"I am the medical officer!"

"Proceed, Mr. Speel."

The mate nodded and called for twenty-four.

Ourry said the best discipline for any crew was the punishment of one of their own. That the prisoner himself no longer felt the lash was of little consequence. Every man aboard, three hundred sailors and two hundred marines, could imagine his own back stripped of flesh in the hot sun. Ourry would allow no doctor, fresh from the grog bucket, to intervene in this demonstration of his authority.

"Twenty-five! Punishment completed. Ship's company, on 'ats!" cried the mate.

Scrooby Doone and his brother Leyden did not put on their hats, because they were not members of the ship's company. If they showed disrespect, this captain might flog *them*.

Ourry fixed a cold eye on the Doones until the bos'n explained that they had been sent to the Provincetown anchorage by the Loyalist Solomon Bigelow, whereupon Ourry invited them to his cabin.

While Leyden studied his reflection in the brass lamp above the chart table, Scrooby planted himself before the captain and recited his speech. "Mr. Bigelow said I should tell you Ned Hilyard's plannin' a smugglin' run up to the Scusset, then overland to the sloop he keeps in the Manomet. From there, he plans to run south to New York."

"How do you know all this?"

"Me brother and me, we . . . we hears things."

"What's he smuggling?"

"Salt." Leyden made a face at his reflection in the brass. "Bay-shore lads been makin' it so the army can salt they beef . . . if they got any."

"Aye, and they say they'll carry it on they backs afore lettin' bloody British get it," added Scrooby.

"*Bloody* British?" said Ourry.

Scrooby threw back his shoulders, and his Adam's apple danced in time to his song. " 'God save our noble king. God save our gracious king. God save the king.' "

Ourry inclined his head slightly and allowed a smile to flicker at this pair of inbreds. "Very good."

Leyden brought his face to within a few feet of Captain Ourry and stretched his lips like an ape. Then he pursed them as though about to kiss the captain.

"*What* is he doing?" asked Ourry.

"He likes you brass buttons. They make he face look funny. He ain't too smart."

"Smarter'n you." Leyden elbowed his brother.

"Our gracious king will consider knighthood for both of you, if you have dates and times for Hilyard's journey."

Scrooby reached into his back pocket, then into the pockets of his waistcoat, then his hatband.

And Leyden pulled a slip of paper from his shoe. "Smarter'n him."

"No, you ain't." Scrooby grabbed the paper out of his brother's hands, smoothed it, and gave it to the captain. "Mr. Bigelow says burn that after you read it. And *he's* a smart man."

"Tell him his intelligence is appreciated."

The Doones tugged at their forelocks like good sailors and left. From the stern gallery, Ourry watched them raise sail and point southwest.

"You sent for me, Captain?" Dr. William Thayer knocked and stepped into the cabin.

"Do you think there are many like those two marching with Washington? Or are all the village idiots Loyalists?"

"I wouldn't know, sir."

"Come, Doctor, I've allowed you ashore to tend their sick often enough. Our chaplain has preached in the sorry little churches of Truro and Provincetown. Yet no one can say how large or sturdy is this rebel vessel that sails on a Loyalist sea."

"Those who heal the sick are welcomed wherever they go, sir, so my perspective is limited."

"Aye. In many ways, Doctor." Ourry stepped away from the gallery.

"Many, indeed, sir." Thayer tugged nervously at his waistcoat and realized that one side was higher than the other. Without looking down, he began to fumble for the misplaced button.

"Trouble with the uniform, Doctor?"

Thayer dropped his hands to his sides.

Ourry poured a glass of port. "Drink?"

Thayer was somewhere in his forties, but they were hard years that had grayed his hair and splotched his skin. "No, thank you, sir."

"We're showing a long measure of willpower this afternoon. Especially after the outburst on deck. Or did we partake of Dutch courage?"

"The seaman will live." Thayer's hands returned nervously to his waistcoat. "He's my only concern."

"Your insubordination would be *my* concern, but I've received information on Ned Hilyard, which makes *you* a rather insignificant matter."

"Thank you, sir."

"I can punish *you* any time, simply by cutting off your grog. But Hilyard's been slipping my noose for two and a half years now, raiding merchantmen from the Saint Lawrence to the Indies, running food to the armies in the south, hiding himself in bays and inlets whenever he's at home. . . . All of this reflects rather badly on me, you know."

"Yes, sir." Thayer found the misplaced button. He adjusted it and those below it and smoothed his waistcoat. "A captain cannot afford bad reflections, either from those he blockades or from his medical officer."

"Now that you've straightened your buttons, polish them so that *they* reflect well on *you*." Ourry glanced out at the coastline and the few shacks of Provincetown. "There is little enough honor here, Doctor. Bringing a privateer to justice will satisfy our . . . nobler instincts."

vi.

Rock Harbor nestled in the elbow of Cape Cod, in the south precinct of Eastham, two miles east of the place that was still called Jack's Island in spite of the best Bigelow efforts to rename it. Ned had moved his family here because Billingsgate had proven to be a vulnerable place, and the narrow channel through these flats made Rock Harbor safer haven than most. Shallow-draft vessels might ground on low tide, and no frigate could come within cannon shot.

Torches of tallow-soaked marsh grass sputtered and spat, and a dozen men hurried to load the *Serenity*.

"There's a tide waitin' to turn," said Sam.

"Where's your pa?" asked Square Stubbs.

"Sayin' good-bye to Ma."

Stubbs laughed. "Quite a man, fillin' his wife's belly at his age."

"You're speakin' of my *mother*."

"And a fine woman she is." Stubbs rolled a barrel of salt to the hold. "But it's your pa who's—"

"Load salt, Stubbs." Sam was now fifteen, tall, bony, better proportioned by the month, and more experienced than men twice his age. He had fired six-pounders at merchantmen off Nova Scotia, lost his virginity to a Dutch whore on Saint Eustatius, faced the dirtiest weather on the Atlantic. He missed Charlie Kwennit, who'd gone off to stand with the Mashpee Indians in the Continental Army, but Stubbs was still there, as square as ever, and Sam was thankful for it.

"Sammy," Stubbs was saying, "you have to admire a sixty-one-year-old man who can still—"

"Enough of that!" Ned Hilyard strode out of the shadows, his wife close behind.

"Take care of him, Square Henry," said Marie. "I would not have our new baby born while his father and brother rot on a British prison ship."

"Nothin' more than a little night sail up the Scusset," said Stubbs. "Child's play."

And the *Serenity* slipped away at midnight, beneath a cloud-covered sky, on a calm sea.

Sam stood at the bow and watched for British boats. His eyes had adjusted so that he could distinguish three shades of black—dark for the sky, darker for the sea, and darkest for the land to the south. They were abreast of Jack's Island now, where lived a few farmers of Bigelow blood and a hundred head of Bigelow cattle that seemed suspiciously safe from British shore parties.

He stared into the darkness and allowed his resentment to boil, as it always did when he thought of the Bigelows. One day, when the Hilyards had built a fortune from privateering, he would take the Bigelows' land and marry their daughter and give them the come-uppance they deserved for all that—

The shot exploded at such close range that the *sound* nearly knocked Sam Hilyard to the deck. Two more shots burst, one from either side, and in the orange nightmare flashes, Sam saw six British longboats with bow-mounted four-pounders racing out of Nauseiput and Jack's Creek like a pack of dogs.

"Man your guns, lads!" Ned grabbed one of the swivels he kept shotted at the transom, touched a quick match, and the gun thundered. He was answered by musket fire that tore across the deck and killed two of his sailors.

Sam and Square Stubbs worked furiously to load one of the six-pounders. They had not been ready for this.

"Where did they come from?" cried Stubbs.

"It's my fault," answered Sam. "I missed 'em."

"No mind. Just load."

They rammed the powder cartridge into the gun, then the ball. Stubbs primed the gun from a powder horn, and they ran it just out as the first longboat bumped the hull.

"Tilt 'er!" cried Stubbs.

Sam advanced the quoin to lower the angle of the shot, then Stubbs fired the hole. The gun flashed, covering the attackers in smoke and thunder, but the ball shot over their heads and buried itself in the mud.

"They're too close!" cried Sam.

"Get ready to fight 'em by—" A musket ball caught Stubbs in the eye. He turned, as if he might say something, then collapsed.

The terror made Sam's balls rise into his gut. After their first victories, he had never been frightened in a raid. And with every success, experience had burnished the confidence of youth. Now, in the smoke and noise of a nightmare, he knew that even young men died.

The marines came over the starboard bulwark, driving their bayonets into the Yarmouth men at the second gun. Five muzzles flashed from the stern, and three marines fell to Serenity's old duck's foot pistol. Sam grabbed a worming iron and started aft, to die at his father's side.

But a musket butt smashed into his head and the world went black.

vii.

"'Ere we is in the gut of the whale, like Jonah 'imself, in the gut of the whale. Breathe deep the good stink, lads, breathe deep

and breathe well, for there's no smell quite like it. 'Tis the belly
of 'ell."

"Shut up, you bloody fool."

Chains clanked, as though someone were trying to pull free from
something. "Call me a fool and I'll choke you to death, choke you
to death, to death. Call me a fool and I'll choke you to death. I'll
squeeze your damn throat till you can't take a breath."

The darkness was so complete and smothering that Sam Hilyard
thought he was in the grave.

"I'm Miffle," said another voice. "I broke the back of one of
me mates in a fair fight. John Judge, he's a deserter, and Barmy Burt,
'e's just Barmy. What about you?"

Did they mean him? Sam wondered. And who else?

"We . . . we're privateers."

"Pa?" said Sam. "Is that you?"

"Sammy? Thank Christ."

Sam's senses were coming back to him now. He could not see,
but he could hear, and most certainly could smell the stench of the
place, wherever it was, and feel the throbbing in his head and the
chafing at his wrists and ankles. He was in irons. And there were
giant iron chains all around him.

"So your name's Sammy?" said Miffle.

"Sammy, Sammy, blippy, blammy, a fine-lookin' lad with a
buggerin' bum."

Ned Hilyard growled, "Anybody who touches that lad—"

"Easy, mate," said Miffle. "We all done somethin' to earn this
'ole. We're all criminals in the eyes of the Lord."

"In the eyes of the Lord? Are . . . are we dead?" asked Sam,
with less panic than he would have expected.

"We might as well be," said Miffle.

"Am I blind?" asked Sam.

"No. We're in the cable tier," said Ned, "the cable tier of the
Somerset."

From the corner there came a burst of hysterical laughter.

"Shut up," said John Judge the deserter.

But the laughter went on with another rhyme. "We live in the
tier with shit and with snot. We drinks the bilge water when the
weather gets hot."

"That's why 'e's barmy," explained Miffle.

"Aye, there's piss in it. We can't 'elp it, though. We gotta piss somewheres."

Sam felt the physical presence of his father, to the left of him. He moved in that direction until his chains stopped him. "Pa, we got to get out of here. We got things to be doin'."

Burt's laughter vibrated in the blackness.

There was neither day nor night in the hole where the anchor chain was stored, for there was no light. Sam did not know how long he and his father stayed there with Miffle, John Judge the deserter, and Barmy Burt. They talked. They slept fitfully. Only the meals of salt beef, water, and biscuit gave rhythm to time.

And the darkness took on weight, like black wool pressing against Sam's face. There were times when he thought he could not breathe, times when he was sure he was blind, times when he found himself smiling as Burt began to laugh at nothing. Of their capture he remembered only the sight of Square Stubbs, one eye staring as blood poured from the other. His dreams of privateering riches faded before the simple need to survive.

"Pa, I want to go home."

"So do we all," said Miffle.

"'Ome," said Judge, "or Truro, or anyplace where a man"— his chains clanked in the darkness—"where a man can be free."

Then came the laughter again. "I want to go 'ome, go 'ome, go 'ome, and get me dick stroked by a 'and not me own."

"Shut up," said Miffle.

"Think on your ma." Ned's voice came calmly out of the blackness and embraced his son. "Think about the bright sun . . . the sea . . . a fair wind."

Barmy Burt farted and laughed.

Sam imagined himself at the helm of the *Serenity*, and for a time his mind was free of its hell. It soared through layers of blue. It soothed itself beside the rhythmic surf. It wandered the dunes of Billingsgate and led him to a place where Hannah waited in the sunlight.

But when he saw the sunlight at last, it blinded him.

Chained to the others, the Hilyards were led through the darkness of the orlop deck, past the hammocks on the berthing deck, upward to the gun decks.

The rays of sun pouring through the ports struck Sam's eyes like hot needles and broiled away the sight of the black thirty-two-pounders. At the companionway, the sunlight burned down the hatch and turned the backs of his eyelids to fire. He brought his hands to his face to hold out the light.

Then the drums began to roll. A marine poked Sam with his bayonet and ordered him above.

"They're 'angin' me." Miffle's voice filled with terror.

"Easy, mate," said Ned Hilyard.

"They're 'angin' all of us." Barmy Burt began to laugh. "'Ang us by the neck until death do us part. 'Ang us till we give up the ghost with a fart."

"Shut up," said John Judge.

Sam's head pounded. He grabbed for his ears, and the bright sunlight seared through his eyelids. He covered his eyes, and the drums assaulted his brain.

"I didn't mean to kill 'im," screamed Miffle.

"Easy!" said Ned again.

Sam opened his eyes and peered through his fingers. Two marines were unlocking Miffle and Judge.

"No," cried Miffle.

"No and no, and away we go, to the place up above or the one below!"

Sam covered his ears against the drums and poems and, for the first time, saw the face of Barmy Burt, like a bearded death mask planted with two rolling eyeballs.

"I go to freedom," said Judge calmly.

"And we three follow, like pigs to the wallow."

"Shut up," said Sam.

"Let him be," said Ned. "Worry about yourself."

Sam looked at his father and was shocked. Ned had been bowed and whitened by his time in the cable tier, though his jaw was still stubbornly set.

As his eyes adjusted, Sam widened his gaze. The deck was lined with rows of red-coated marines and sailors in rank, and at the stern, like ministers to the king they served, stood the officers in royal blue. How foolish they had been to confront this power.

"Are we goin' to die, Pa?"

Ned Hilyard looked at his son. "Not if there's a God."

"God?"

"Serenity has his ear, and she's fillin' it with advice right now."

"But she defied God."

Ned winked. "That's why he might listen to her."

The drums ceased then, and the sentences for murderer William Miffle and deserter John Judge were read: death, under the Articles of War.

"We're next, we are, for a noose and a swing, to 'ell we all go to meet beggar and king."

"Shut up," said Ned.

The drums rolled again. Burt began to laugh. Sam was shaking. But Ned remained as motionless as a rock. Miffle and Judge were stood on the bulwarks and nooses put around their necks. They were both offered hoods, which they refused. They were asked if they chose to jump or to be pushed, and neither could answer. Judge turned his face toward the hills of Truro. Miffle cried that it had been a fair fight.

The drums beat the death roll, and the mate droned a psalm. The captain in glittering brass buttons raised his hand to his shoulder, causing the drummers to cease as if they had been shot. When he dropped his hand, Miffle and Judge dropped toward the peaceful sea like birds . . . until the ropes snapped and broke their necks.

Sam Hilyard felt his father's leg press against his, to stop it from shaking.

"Be strong, lad."

The captain turned his gaze onto the three who remained. One of the officers, a disheveled-looking man with splotchy skin and misbuttoned waistcoat, hurried forward to inspect them.

He felt Sam's pulse, tugged at a few of his teeth, and gave him a gentle smile. Sam began to think he might not hang.

"Scurvy?" said the captain.

"Not yet, sir. But I would recommend against any further chaining of these men."

"Of course." The captain stepped closer, though he held a handkerchief to his nose for the stink coming off them. "And I agree. They will not be chained."

"The captain won't chain us. The doctor says no. But now will 'e 'ang us . . . or let us die slow? I don't give a mother's *fuck*." Burt stuck out his tongue and revolved it as though it were a curious snake coming out of its hole.

If any in the crew found this humorous or were taken by Burt's defiance, they were wise enough not to show it.

Captain Ourry watched the tongue for a moment, a faintly amused expression on his face, then ordered Burt back to the cable tier.

"But, Captain?" the doctor ventured.

"I'll not have him contaminating the ship." Ourry raised his gaze and his voice. "I'll not tolerate insubordination from any. Even one who's gone daft." Now he lowered his voice and stepped close to Ned Hilyard. "Is that clear?"

"*Heaven help* us if it ain't." The stink of Ned's breath knocked Ourry back, which may have been his intention.

Ourry held the silk handkerchief to his nose and turned to the first lieutenant. "Read the sentence."

"For privateering against His Majesty and smuggling contraband through blockaded waters, Jeremiah Edward Hilyard and Samuel Hilyard, under the Articles of War, do hereby forfeit their vessel and shall be—"

Here Sam closed his eyes and prayed that Serenity had gotten God's ear.

"—conveyed to New York to be interned aboard the prison ship *Jersey*."

Practically a death sentence, thought Sam, though not immediate. He fixed his eye on the Union Jack and thanked the God who had heard Serenity.

"But," said Ourry, "you have a choice. Your Mother Country enjoys a very active whale fishery off the river Plate in South America, filled almost exclusively by Cape Cod men. A harpooner like yourself—"

"I'll join no traitors givin' comfort to the enemy," said Ned.

"Very well, then." Ourry's expression did not change. "Until the dispatch sloop arrives from New York, you shall serve before the mast, replacements for Miffle and Judge."

"I think not, sir," said Ned softly.

Sam looked at his father and gave his chains a shake, but his father's eyes were locked to the captain's.

"You think *not?*" Ourry's dark brows and long, pointed nose were warmed by the most mirthless smile that Sam Hilyard had ever seen. "He thinks *not!*"

"Pa," whispered Sam, "workin' a mast is better than sittin' in the hole."

"'Tis principle, son."

"Principle?" said Ourry.

Ned laughed. "A fine time to be developin' principles, but there it is. We're prisoners of war. We can't be forced to work for the enemy."

"You vile creatures, you're *pirates!*"

"We're *privateers*, sailin' under letters of marque from the Council of Massachusetts."

"In honorable language, *pirates*. You should thank me for letting you out of your stinking hole."

" 'Twas *you* put us there. Just as King George tried to put all of this"—Ned waved his hands around the sweep of the Cape, from the Provincelands to the highlands of Manomet—"in chains. But no matter how much you flog us or tax us, you can't put chains on our principles."

Sam Hilyard tugged at his chains once more. From the time of James Otis, his father had always considered himself and his family first. Principles be damned.

"A fine speech." Ourry looked at the crew. "This *pirate* refuses an order. This *pirate* does not understand naval discipline. Mr. Speel, teach him with fifty lashes."

"Fifty!" cried Sam. "You can't."

Ourry strode to the taffrail, as though he had not heard that remark, and when the doctor approached him, he raised his hand in warning.

Sam looked at his father. "You said the smart man picked his fights."

"Serenity picked one that was too big, too. But God heard her. That must say somethin' for principles."

Fifty lashes stripped every scrap of flesh from Ned's back and shoulders, like a massive burn. The captain ordered him back to the cable tier, but the doctor insisted that he be brought first to sick bay.

Thayer dosed Ned with laudanum, then washed his back in seawater, as good a medicine as there was for a flogging.

Through the haze of the drug, Ned called for his son, and Sam was brought to him under marine guard.

"Will he live?" Sam asked the doctor.

"I hope so, son. But fifty lashes is a . . . a brutal punishment for a man of any age, and your father—" .

"He's strong."

"Aye. In more ways than one."

Sam knelt by the cot. The scent of his father, which had grown so comforting during their time in the cable tier, had become an unfamiliar sweet stink of blood and raw flesh, something that struck the back of the throat rather than the nose.

"That captain, he won't get away with this, Pa. I'll—"

Ned shook his head. "The smart man picks his fights. And the smart man don't stretch his neck for revenge. He don't for anything, save family or friends. Remember that."

"Then why—"

Ned tried to laugh. "Sometimes an idea just creeps up and bites you in the ass."

"It's a good idea, Pa, freedom."

"We were free on Billingsgate, son, afore all this started. That's one kind of freedom. But—" A wave of pain caused his body to shudder.

"The laudanum wears off," said the doctor.

But Ned managed a few more words. "Real freedom . . . liberty . . . that's hard. It gives you principles. It forces you to make decisions."

"I'll get us free again, Pa. I'll think of somethin'."

Ned touched his son's hand. "I'm free now, lad."

"But you go back to the cable tier." Sam could not understand this kind of freedom. He thought the laudanum clouded his father's mind. How could they gain their freedom in chains, or seek their revenge?

Four longboats put out from the *Somerset* the next day. Three carried detachments of Royal Marines on a foraging party. The fourth carried the body of Ned Hilyard.

viii.

In Halifax, Nova Scotia, a young girl named Hannah Bigelow spent each Thursday afternoon poring over the weekly *Intelligencer*, searching for stories of the war. She was never disappointed, because Halifax was the largest Atlantic seaport in Canada and the point of refuge for most of the Loyalists who had left New England.

The paper made it seem that the rebels were losing. It went on about Washington's floundering campaign and underfed rabble while giving the American victory at Saratoga scant attention. The alliance with France was treated as satire. And the fact that American ships were taking British prizes in the English Channel was of little consequence. But when a privateer that had tormented Halifax was captured, the news was trumpeted.

All of this worked its way on Hannah, and she came to decide that her passion had simply been girlish enthusiasm. A young man named John Digby helped her in this. He was seventeen, intelligent, of a good Falmouth shipping family that refused to remain in Massachusetts when mobs came to rule.

Hannah and John went to the dock to see the *Serenity*. They had to ask which ship it was, because the name had already been painted over. A British officer proudly took them aboard and pointed out the bullet holes and bloodstains on the deck. "The father and most of his crew are dead. The son is bound for the prison ships."

Hannah went home and cried. For all her change of heart, she had never forgotten Sam Hilyard or the excitement of their first kiss. She prayed that he would survive the prison ship, though she could not imagine him in chains.

ix.

Fire? An open seacock? A torch in the magazine? How would he do it? Night after night, Sam lay awake in his hammock, and he plotted. Somehow he would send Captain Ourry and the *Somerset* to the bottom . . . if he survived the berthing deck.

"A fine-lookin' lad with a buggerin' bum," a strong temptation for a seaman away from women too long. It was that hairy ape Dodd, fingering his bottom again.

Sam tried to move, but Dodd's weight pressed down on Sam's back. His breeches were torn down. Something long and hard and, it would seem, covered in grease, entered his body where things usually went out.

Sam let out a muffled cry and tried to roll over.

"Just be quiet now, lad."

"Get off. Get away."

"You gots a friend in old Tom. There's some would use you, then pass you 'round to their mates, but you be good to old Tom, and 'e'll pertect you from all the rest. Just . . ."

The pain was terrible, tearing. Was this what women felt when men did them? It couldn't have been, or there would be no human race.

Dodd's stubbled face scratched the back of Sam's neck; his breathing came harder and faster.

Somehow Sam managed to get his knife out of the little pocket in the bottom of his hammock. Dodd's eyes must have been closed, because he did not see the knife, and he must have been near finishing, because he never felt it in his nostril until it sliced.

Dodd muffled his cry, so as not to wake the rest to his buggery, but with blood spilling everywhere, he grabbed Sam by the throat and began to strangle him. Had their weight not spun the hammock over, Sam's dreams of revenge might have died right there. But when they struck the deck, Sam freed his knife hand and pressed the blade against the thing still poking at him. Dodd's member deflated, and with it his fury.

By now, the scuffle had awakened some of the other sailors. It was unlikely that any were shocked by what Dodd was doing, but it was certain that the young Yank, who held his knife in one hand and pulled up his breeches with the other, made his reputation that night.

Sam could have been berthed with the powder monkeys and drummers. But he was too big for their work, and they fell under the province of the junior officers. He preferred to be among common seamen. If he fought off their advances, he would not be caned for it.

So Dr. Thayer had given him the knife, violating the captain's rule that no seaman could have one except in the rigging. Ourry did not even permit sailors to shave themselves, as a straightedge made a dangerous weapon. Instead, barbers worked through every watch to keep the crew beardless. But Dr. Thayer believed that one young man protected from buggery was a soul saved in a world of corruption. Sam definitely agreed.

And the sailors, though far from noble, were not fools. When they saw that Sam would protect himself, they gave him respect. Even Tom Dodd would offer instruction when they were assigned to the same station, as every man wanted a smart mate in a heavy gale. The sailors taught him how to handle the complex of lines that controlled a great square-rigger, and they taught him a few simple rules for survival aboard a British ship of the line.

He should never awaken a sleeping sailor, as most feared midnight sodomy. Instead, when searching for his hammock in the dark, he was to move quietly and sniff. When he came to a hammock that did not smell—at least to him—it was his.

He should never waste his piss over the side, but go into the open vat on the orlop deck, so that when there was a fire, they would not have to use drinking water to fight it. No one warned him that the smell and the swarm of bugs above the vat would nearly strangle him.

Before eating any ship biscuit, he should rap it on the table to shake out weevils and worms. If he found an especially lively weevil, he should save it for the races, in which crewmen bet their grog rations on the fastest bugs.

And above all, he should never take one of the ship's rats as a pet . . . or cross Captain Ourry.

The rats seemed to pay more attention to Sam than did the captain. It was as if Ourry considered his victory over the Hilyards so complete that he no longer needed to offer them the respect of an enemy. The father had died because he refused to work. The son had seen the error in this and had taken to the rigging like a sick man to the waters at Bath.

And that was what Sam wanted him to believe. But Sam had seen only the error in his father's reasoning. Freedom could not be won if a man chose chains. There was no honor in a principle if it killed you. Once Sam overcame his grief, he came to believe that, for all his calm courage, his father had lost his mind and chosen imprisonment over freedom, death over life.

So Sam went about his tasks with care and obedience. He sought no attention, good or bad, while he planned the revenge that would gain him his freedom. It would come, he was certain, if he bided his time.

When a sail hove in sight one November afternoon, Sam learned how little time he might have to bide. The *Somerset* was riding the swells like a balky horse, and Tom Dodd was teaching him the lines and blocks that supported the mainsail.

"This 'ere's the main yard 'alyard, three lines run through the 'alyard jeer block. You got leech lines and buntlines, too, and parrels 'round the masts, but the main yard 'alyard's the most important— Say, are you listenin'?"

Sam's eyes were turned toward the south.

"You lose this 'ere block in a 'eavy blow, the 'alyard runs out, the parrels don't 'old, the yard comes down, you lose mains'l, main-top, and control of your ship—"

"What ship would that be?" Sam pointed to the horizon.

"Oh, my." Dodd feigned a cry of sadness. A scab had formed at the corner of his nose, and he looked more poxed than ever. "That's the dispatch ship from New York. You'll be gone by nightfall. You're dead, lad. At least, if you'd let me bugger you, there'd be someone to remember you." Dodd patted Sam's behind.

"Remember my knife."

That evening, the captain sat with Dr. Thayer and an enormous man in a dirty brown coat, Master Kindle of the schooner *Julia*. On the table before them were a decanter of port, two glasses, a half-eaten meal of mutton, potatoes, carrots, and a bundle of dispatches.

On the captain's carpet stood Sam Hilyard, as summoned, patiently awaiting the captain's attention while his empty stomach gurgled like a bilge pump.

"Have a look at him, Kindle," said Ourry at last. "Another one for that vermin scow on the Brooklyn flats."

"A 'orrid place, the *Jersey*, and gettin' worse."

"Have you much typhus?" Dr. Thayer sipped his port.

"There's typhus, starvation, and the rats is fatter than the prisoners. But young lads is always welcome."

Ourry patted his mouth with a linen handkerchief and went over to Sam. He was not wearing his cockaded hat and so seemed slightly more human. "Principles. This lad's father died for . . . principles."

Kindle attacked his joint. "Cape Cod mutton's a principle *I'd* die for, Cap'n."

Ourry looked into Sam's eyes. "Kindle doesn't understand principles. He's too hungry."

"Aye-aye, sir." Sam stood at attention and looked straight ahead, resolved to show neither fear nor disrespect.

With thumb and forefinger, Ourry pinched the flesh of Sam's chest. "Such a fine specimen. 'Tis a great pity to lose you to starvation, pestilence, *principles*. But you must go, as your father would have done."

"I'll . . . I'll miss the *Somerset*, sir."

"Will you, now? And what would your father say?"

"He's . . . dead, sir."

For some reason, Ourry found this answer more humorous than

anything that had happened since the Hilyards came aboard. He laughed in the boy's face, threw his head back, and laughed from the back of his throat. "Dead indeed, along with the principles he so conveniently espoused after he'd finished raiding innocent commerce."

"My father, he did what the colony asked, sir," said Sam. "I do what I must."

"Principles are slippery things, Kindle."

The fat man gnawed on the mutton leg. "Aye."

"Some men let their principles kill them. Others let their principles die. And either way, hate follows. This lad hates me because I killed his father. But could he hate one who showed him that his principles were merely illusions?"

"My hatred's real, Captain."

"That's good. Hate keeps a man alive."

"Honest lad," said Dr. Thayer. "Honest lads make good sailors, Captain."

"Perhaps . . . perhaps." Ourry returned to his meal, rubbed his napkin over his brass buttons, and picked at his food.

Sam had come with contrition and yet had demonstrated spirit. He could do no more, and he resolved now that if he was banished to the *Jersey*, he would fall on Ourry and kill him, consequences be damned.

But Ourry, it seemed, was not finished with Sam. There were many lessons to teach these rebels, and the best rebels to learn were the youngest. "Gentlemen, I hate to have a man leave my ship hating me."

"They either leaves lovin' you . . . or dead." Kindle poured a shot of port down his throat and began to laugh.

"You're very crude, Kindle."

Kindle stopped laughing instantly.

Dr. Thayer bit his cheek to keep from smiling.

"'Twas a joke, sir, merely—"

Ourry raised his hand for silence, then turned his gaze onto Sam. "Master Kindle brings word of French shipping. We go in pursuit tomorrow. I will show you that your principles *were* illusions. All men are *not* created equal. There is no man in the fo'c'sle my equal. And no rabble of colonials and French the equal of good English oak. The *Somerset* is England, lad. Stay with her and see the good sense your present course describes. Then"—Ourry smiled—"will you love me."

Back in the forecastle, Tom Dodd grinned across the table at Sam Hilyard. "So we still be shipmates. There's 'ope yet."

"None for you." Sam stuffed a piece of ship biscuit into his mouth without rapping it on the table. He held it until he felt the worms tickling the back of his throat, which caused him to gag and bolt for the piss vat. There he vomited up biscuit, salt meat, and corn stolen from a Cape Cod field. Then he took a deep breath of urine stench, which caused him to vomit up a wad of green bile as well. This earned him a place in sick bay, where he could plan his revenge without fear of Tom Dodd's greased prick.

There was a strong smell of drink from Dr. Thayer but a strong air of sympathy as well. He said Sam need not eat wormy biscuit to earn the safety of sick bay, but simply ask, and the doctor would concoct a reason.

"This can be a miserable, corruptin' life, and a lad like you, Sam, he's not ready for corruptin'."

Sam thanked him for all his kindness and for the knife.

Around four bells, the wind came up.

"Doc?"

Thayer was reading, huddled beside a bucket of hot coals suspended on a ceiling chain. "Aye?"

"The wind. What direction is it?"

Thayer cocked his head, studied the motion of the bucket and his lantern. "No'theast, I'd guess."

"Good." Sam knew that the tide would be running hard on the flood when they left. He pretended to sleep and prayed that the gale kept up. When the doctor blew out the lantern and went to his berth, Sam went to work.

He took the doctor's bone saw from the instrument case and, with all his stealth, sneaked up to the spar deck, past the marine watch, to the mainmast rigging, and up to the main yard halyard. His allies were the dark of a moonless night and a wind that boomed so loud it blew away all the subtle sounds of an anchored ship.

He chose a spot just below the jeer block, where three heavily tarred, fist-thick lines formed the strongest point of the halyard, and he began to cut. It took him most of an hour to finish his work. He severed two completely and left the third hanging half-cut. It would hold, he was certain, until morning, when this would be his station, and either he or the *Somerset* would meet their end.

The wind blew hard and steady the night through, sweeping every cloud from the sky and raising whitecaps even within the anchorage at Provincetown. It was still booming well after dawn when the *Somerset* weighed anchor and left the harbor under topsails and drivers.

From High Pole Hill, the villagers watched her go. From the mainmast, Sam Hilyard watched the villagers. The moment the sails of the *Somerset* dipped below the horizon, they would rush for their fishing boats and make for the cod holes. And if the *Somerset* struck the bar, they would rush to her. His survival might depend upon them, though in truth, he had stopped worrying about survival.

His desire to destroy the ship had become so concentrated and pure that nothing else mattered. A grown man might have looked down from the maintop at the guns, the red-coated marines, the officers bellowing commands, and chosen to fight the French instead. Sam looked up and out, at the Narrow Land washed in long, low rays of gold, at the roiling blue sea and the stretch of blue above, and he summoned his courage.

Once the ship had rounded Wood End and swung north, the captain called for mainsail and foresail, maintop and foretop.

"Get to it, Sammy my lad." Dodd grinned at him. "And don't fall. I'd never forgive meself."

"Get too close, and *you'll* be doin' the fallin'."

They stood on the lines above the main yard and let out sail, as they had done a hundred times before, but this time, Sam reached up with his knife and cut into the last strands of line in the jeer block. And so skillfully did he cut that not even Tom Dodd saw him do it.

"Can't 'ide in sick bay forever, lad," Dodd was saying as he busied himself with his work.

"I always got my knife." Sam flashed it under Dodd's nose.

Dodd gave a laugh and took to the ratline. Sam thought to hack a bit more, but he knew now that the halyard could not hold under the strain of the mainsail. So he dropped to the deck with the other sailors.

As the *Somerset* rounded Race Point and entered the Atlantic, the gusts swept straight across the sea, and every wave struck the bow like a shot, sending spouts of white spume into the air while the deck pitched wildly.

Captain Ourry veered several points north to swing beyond the bar before turning south. Once he passed Head of the Meadow, with the highlands of Truro to starboard, the wind would be his ally, chasing him far and fast down the forearm of the Cape. But he first had to beat against a northeast gale and a running tide that conspired to put anything that floated on the beach.

He ordered the men aloft once more, to ready them for the next sail change.

Dr. Thayer watched Sam climb the mainmast just behind Dodd. He had been watching Sam all morning, for when a sailor feigned sickness, his mates were known to push him harder the next day. And Tom Dodd was the sort who might push literally.

Dodd was the first to step onto the main yard line, and something caught his attention. He was gesturing for his mates to stay on the crosstrees while he grabbed two pieces of line to splice them.

Thayer pushed past a squadron of marines and went down the deck for a better view.

Sam Hilyard had wrapped his arm in a length of line and leaned out, as if to help Dodd repair the broken line. A brave lad, thought Thayer.

"A vengeful lad," whispered Dodd, "who cuts the 'alyard I taught 'im about."

"Never."

"It was you at this station a few minutes ago." Dodd's eyes shifted to the other sailors, none of whom could hear his talk over the wind. "I got the goods on you now, you sweet little buggcr."

"And I got 'em on you." Sam did not hesitate or think an extra second on what he did. He leaned out and put his foot on the main yard. From the deck, it looked as if he was reaching for one of the loose lines.

"No!" cried Dodd. "No more weight—"

Another gust boomed from the northeast, carrying Dodd's cry away from the ship, and the last halyard broke. Leech lines and buntlines snapped like thread. The parrels screeched down the mast. Dodd's eyes and mouth formed three ovals of terror, and he fell, the sail billowing around him like a shroud.

Sam had done it. He swung back to the crosstrees as the main top, torn loose from its stays, slammed against the mast and sent three more sailors screaming toward the deck. Sam held tight to the line and tried not to hear.

Now sailors came rushing from below. Marines who never showed fear in the face of rebel muskets began to mill about in panic on the spar deck. The captain's brass voice trumpet flashed in the bright sun. And the *Somerset* lost headway.

Had the northeast gale abated suddenly, had the tidal current been gentler, had he not been here on the treacherous back shore of Cape Cod, George Ourry might have saved his ship. But he was quickly turned broadside to gale and tide, and then he was doomed.

From his perch, Sam saw the light green water of the Peaked Hill Bar just a hundred yards to starboard. He thought that Ourry might throw out his anchors to hold her off, but enough canvas was set that if the anchors held, the wind might blow the masts to pieces. And so the captain screamed at the officers, the officers at the mates, the mates at the sailors, the sailors at the marines, and the marines at one another.

And now, with the shoal water not twenty yards away, Ourry rushed down the deck and looked up at the mainmast.

"You up there! Restring the block! You must . . . *Hilyard!*"

And good English oak struck the American sandbar with a tremendous crash. The deck tilted to starboard. The sea pounded up and over the port side. George Ourry fell amidst a tumble of red coats and white wigs and was nearly crushed by a loose carronade that rolled across the deck and killed three marines. Dr. Thayer grabbed the rail and nearly went over the side. Men flew from the masts like ants flicked from a stick.

Sam, still clutching a line, swung out over the water and back toward the mast like a pendulum, and in the second before he made fast, he decided his chances were better in the freezing Atlantic than ever they would be with the furious brass-buttoned figure now picking himself up from the tumble of marines on the spar deck.

He pushed off with his foot, swung far out over the Peaked Hill Bar, and let go.

For a moment, he hung suspended in midair, looking back at the ship. She lay against the bar, the waves pounding over her, the Union Jack flapping impotently at her stern, and he decided that if this was his last vision, it would be enough. Then he struck the icy water and nearly passed out.

In the rolling surf, he managed to grab a broken spar, and clutching it with all the stubbornness he had gained in fifteen years on Cape Cod, all the cussedness he had inherited from his grandmother, all the will he had learned from his father, all the life he had drawn from his mother, he rode the rising tide to the beach.

For a few moments, he lay exhausted at the wrack line, and then, above the pounding surf, came the sound of . . . cheering. He looked toward the low bluffs and recognized this as Head of the Meadow. Provincetowners had gotten here quickly from High Pole Hill. The people of Truro had turned out as well. Eyes were always watching for ships to founder, and *Somerset* was the biggest thing ever to hit the back shore.

There were hundreds of them lining the bluff to watch the death of the ship that had so long invested their coast.

The cheering grew louder as the day wore on and Captain Ourry tried to work his way off the bar. He threw over food crates and casks, which were carried to the beach, where the scavengers fought over them. He threw over cannons to lighten his load. He put out a longboat with rowers, but the waves swamped them and drowned the men, and the people bellowed and screamed over the steady roar of the day.

Their hatred, thought Sam, was greater than his own, with so little reason. From them the British had stolen corn and cattle; from him they had taken a father. He wrapped himself in a blanket that a charitable soul had given him and sank to his knees. He could no longer watch the dying ship. This was war, but he was bitterly sorry for those he had killed, even for Tom Dodd.

Then the tide lifted the *Somerset* off the bar and pounded her, bow first, onto the beach, as though she had been sailed there.

The screaming of orders had ceased on her quarterdeck. The cheering had faded on the beach. Only the thunder of surf and wind remained, like a living presence between the rebels and the shipwrecked men. HMS *Somerset* carried two hundred marines and sixty-four cannon. But because of her list, the starboard cannon could be brought to bear on nothing more than the sand, and the port cannon simply pointed down the beach.

"'Tis time to strike, Captain," said Dr. Thayer.

Ourry's hand was frozen on the hilt of his sword. His eyes were fixed on the sand beneath his ship.

"Damage, Mr. Speel?" he asked the mate.

"Starboard stove in. Port side battered. God knows if the keel's in one piece."

Ourry raised his chin as if to allow some invisible noose to be passed over his head. "She cannot be refloated, then, and fighting their militia is pointless."

"The better part of valor, sir," said Thayer.

"Valor, honor, principles . . ." Ourry looked at Thayer. "That Hilyard boy was on the main yard."

"He went over when we hit the bar. He was trying to fix the broken halyards."

"Perhaps." Ourry gazed up at the Union Jack, now blowing out straight and strangely proud in the wind. "Strike."

The flag fluttered down. On the beach, a great cheer exploded.

In the cable tier, Barmy Burt was laughing and crying at the same time. He sat in a pool of urine and stared at the thin shafts of light now cutting through the cracks in the hull.

Dr. Thayer unlocked him and helped him stand. "We're goin' ashore."

"Are we 'ome?"

"Not exactly."

"Yes. We're 'ome. We're in dear old, merry old, jolly old England, where Britannia rules the waves. We been chained and been throttled and damn near been drowned, and the captain, 'e's made us all slaves. But we're proud, yes, we are, of the bravery we've showed, in subduin' them nasty old Yanks, and now all we ask is a soft friendly bed and the captain can kiss both me shanks!"

As Militia Captain John Otis would write, there were "riotous doings at the wreck" that day. The men of Provincetown and Truro divided the spoils, Provincetown taking a third and Truro two-thirds of everything from marlinespikes to bread casks to the brass fittings from Ourry's cabin. A Truro man even tried to take possession of a North Carolina Negro who had joined the Somerset crew.

Sam sat in the sand and listened to their negotiations, democracy in action, while Ourry marched down the beach behind his crew, last of four hundred eighty survivors to leave the Somerset under guard of the local militia. Sam had won, yet was he drained of joy as surely as he had been purged of hatred. In a way, he felt as stranded as the great hulk now swarming with scavengers.

But he would soon enough find his bearings. Word reached Truro village that he had escaped, and word came quickly back that his mother had moved there to be near her husband's grave and her son's anchorage. She was staying at the home of Samson Rich, and she was now in labor.

Thus did she become the patient of the Cape's new doctor, William Thayer, and his assistant, Mr. B. Burt.

Before that day was out, Sam stood in the borning room of a house on the Little Pamet and met his brother, Edward William Hilyard. With one hand, his mother held the infant to her breast, and with the other, she reached out to Sam.

He jammed his hands into his pockets and tried to keep the boy in him from crying. "I'm sorry. 'Twas my fault that we never saw the ambush that night."

She twined her fingers in his hair. "God has a purpose for everything, son."

The familiar sound of her soft French accent filled him with joy and sorrow both. He knelt at her bedside and pressed his face to her cheek.

X.

"This war is far from over." Dr. Thayer stood outside with Sam. The booming gale had finally passed, and a quiet November cold was settling on the land. In the Rich cottage, women were preparing a meal, and the sound of their chatter was tonic to men who had been so long aboard ship.

"I done my part," said Sam.

"A fact I'd not make light with. Should His Majesty be victorious, you may pay for your sabotage."

Sam looked sharply at the doctor.

"That would be Ourry's word for it," Thayer said, "though others would call it an act of war. I considered what you did a great release. I could not have stood the ship another week, or I'd have drunk myself to my grave."

"But now you're a deserter."

Thayer pretended to ignore this. The sun's last rays were reaching up the little valley. The bay was going gray in the fading light. "What are we looking at? I'd best know, that I may become native quickly."

"The Little Pamet River. To the left is Tom's Hill. To the right, that's Cornhill."

A flight of geese came in and settled in the river.

"Cornhill . . ." mused Thayer, "*Cornhill. That's* where your name comes from."

"Where?"

"A book I once read, about this place and the Separatist settlers. It mentions Cornhill and goes on at great length about a man named Jack . . . Jack *Hilyard!* Ever since I heard your name, I've racked my brain over that." Thayer laughed, like a man who had found a lost penny.

"What is this book?"

"I believe it's the log of the ship that brought the Separatists a hundred and fifty years ago. The *Mayflower.*"

Sam tried to calm himself. "Where did you read it?"

"Doctors with a taste for the grape often end up aboard His Majesty's ships. And they often are found, before that, in waterfront taverns."

Comeuppance . . . The word began to echo again in Sam Hilyard's head. Comeuppance . . . revenge. He drove it away.

"I once tended a young man who'd been beaten in a tavern brawl, the wastrel son of a Hertfordshire squire, he was. As I hailed from the same town, he invited me to spend time at his father's estate. The squire took great pride in his library, which contained an ancient Bible, a Shakespeare Folio, and the log of the ship *Mayflower.*"

"Do you remember the name?"

"Of course. Bellamy."

Down by the marsh, Burt was picking cattails. For the first time since Sam had met him, he was neither laughing nor muttering to himself. He was singing, singing his poems in a most pleasing voice. He was free, but Sam felt the past chaining him into another cable tier.

"Did this book speak of a family named Bigelow?"

"It sounds familiar. Though I must admit I was well filled with Madeira most of the time." Thayer fixed his eyes on the horizon. "Terrible vice, the grape. Destroys a man's brain, then his gut. Perhaps here I can start anew, 'fore it destroys me."

Comeuppance . . . Sam heard his grandmother's word again, mingling with the call of the gulls. The book of history was in a town called Wheathampstead, Hertfordshire, in the hands of a family called Bellamy. What would his grandmother want him to do?

Then he heard the cry of his baby brother. He had had enough
of comeuppance. He wanted to feel his mother's love. And the love
of a spirited Cape Cod girl, exiled now in Nova Scotia. How would
comeuppance win her, when comeuppance would bring her family
low?

CHAPTER 23

July 14

The List

"Get out of bed," said the voice on the other end of the line.

"George?"

"The *Somerset* is out."

"It's six-thirty."

"Bring Keith and Sarah over to Head of the Meadow. They'll see something they'll never forget."

It had happened before, most recently in 1973. The sea got to raging, moved out a few truckloads of sand, and exposed the remnants of a mighty warship. Then the tide surged back to bury her again.

Must have been the thunderstorms that did it this time. All night the squalls gusted through. Geoff slept fitfully. Janice tossed beside him in the strobing light. But if either of them thought about a little middle-of-the night tumble to make them both sleep better, they didn't do a thing about it.

Now the sun slanted through the trees, and the mist rose from the wet pavement, making the morning feel as though it came from out of the past, fresh and unsullied. And Geoff took his son adventuring. In Boston he had been one of those seven-to-seven fathers—gone before the kids were up and out past their bedtime. It was one of life's lousy ironies that most people's work demanded the biggest piece of their time just when their kids needed them most. On Cape Cod, Geoff thought he could give his kids what they needed and keep working, too. But lately he hadn't given them a thing.

A promise of doughnuts did more to get Keith into the car than the chance to see the *Somerset*. Sarah chose to sleep in. "Can I buy two chocolates, just for myself?"

"Sarah likes chocolate, too."

"Yeah, but she didn't come."

"She didn't care about an old British warship. That's guy stuff. But we'll get her a chocolate. Just because we love her."

Keith shrugged. He could be convinced. "So what kind of doughnut does Mom like?"

"Butter crunch."

"Then we'll get one of them, too. We love her, too."

"Yeah." But she was making it more difficult.

The road cut across the Little Pamet Marsh, rose out of the valley, and passed the ramshackle Rich house, an old Cape that always got Geoff to wondering what life had been like when the Truro population was a few hundred and ships like the *Somerset* marauded the coast.

At Head of the Meadow Beach a small crowd had gathered, mostly surf fishermen and beachcombers like George.

"Where's the ship?" asked Keith. "You said it was as big as the *Constitution*."

"It was, once." Geoff laughed. "But it was stripped, then burned so people could get the metal out of it, like nails and spikes. Then the waves pounded on it."

It was pretty disappointing, actually—a thirty-foot piece of keel, a few charred ribs sticking out of the sand, and the sparkling blue Atlantic ignoring it altogether.

George was sweeping around the ribs with his metal detector. When he saw them, he shouted, " 'The annals of this voracious beach! who could write them unless it were a shipwrecked sailor?' "

"You've been reading Thoreau again," said Geoff.

The detector beeped. George told Keith to dig. The boy hesitated a moment, as though something in the sand might bite him, then he pulled out . . . a pop top.

"The British knew about boating safety," said an old man photographing the remains. "No glass beer bottles on the boat."

George laughed at that, and the old man introduced himself as Thomas Digges, professor emeritus of history, Dartmouth College. He was very tall, with very white hair and a sun-dried face. "I'm something of an expert on the *Somerset*."

"So where are the cannon?" asked Keith.

"Hauled off to Fort Independence in Boston under the command of Paul Revere, who had rowed past those very guns on his way to his famous ride."

" 'Just as the moon rose over the bay, where swinging wide at her moorings lay the *Somerset*, British Man-o-War; a phantom ship, with each mast and spar across the moon like a prison bar. . . .' " George loved to show off his arcane knowledge—like Longfellow's "Paul Revere's Ride."

"So what put her on the bar?" Geoff was half listening while he watched Keith scamper down to the water's edge.

"Edward Rowe Snow suggests she lost her main yard halyard," said the professor. "But he was more entertainer than maritime historian. The log at the Naval War College in Greenwich makes no such mention. Besides, what captain would have allowed something like that to deteriorate?"

"Or admit it if he had?" said George.

"Ourry blames it on the treachery of the back shore, but he hints at sabotage. We know he had captured some privateers. It could have been one of them . . . young Sam Hilyard, for example."

There was some surprise at that. Geoff was surprised that Sam had been there. The old historian was surprised that Geoff knew so little about his forebears.

Geoff said, "He wrote a batch of letters to Hannah Bigelow that my wife read, and he built the house my uncle lives—lived in. But this *Somerset* story is news to me. You say he sank the ship?"

"If Snow's theory is correct, he could have done something in the rigging. Or it might have been ship's physician William Thayer. He stayed in Truro when his mates were marched off to Boston, became the local doctor, raised a family here. You have to wonder why he would leave the verdure of his native Hertfordshire to live on what by then was nothing more than a desolate arm of sand. And I wonder why you don't know more about your famous ancestors, sir, so you can tell your son."

Geoff looked at the boy playing tag with the waves. "I wonder myself."

ii.

Janice ate a butter crunch doughnut and managed to be civil to George as he rattled on about the ghost ship.

"All's I saw was a lot of burned wood," said Keith around a mouthful of doughnut.

"That's all it was," said Janice. "They can't even be sure if it's the *Somerset*."

"Naval archaeologists are convinced."

"*Archaeologists.*" Janice said the word as though it were a mouthful of shit, because in real estate development, wherever archaeologists tread, delays were sure to follow.

George brought his baggy face close to hers and, perfect mimic that he was, said "Developers" in the same tone of voice.

She looked at Geoff. "You should spend more time with Jimmy and less with this troublemaker."

"That's the nicest thing I've been called in a long time." George laughed and headed for the bathroom.

"New house rules," she shouted. "If it's yellow, let it mellow. If it's brown, flush it down."

Geoff started to laugh, but she cut him off. "Not funny. If we need a new septic system, you're going to have to sell something or get some kind of job other than treasure hunting." She finished her coffee and buttoned the grim taupe-colored linen suit she wore with her mood.

Geoff scratched his stubble. "The doughnut was a peace offering."

"A peace offering would be more architectural drawings, or a promise that you were over the foolishness about Rake's murder, or a commitment to stop looking for that stupid legend."

Now George came out of the bathroom. "Pity, Jan, that you have to sell real estate on such a gorgeous day."

"Somebody's got to make some money around here."

"Nice feed," said Geoff.

"I like to play straight man," answered George.

"Because it's the only time anyone calls *you* straight." Janice hustled the kids out to the car. "Talk some sense to him, George."

"I already have. I think he's on the right track."

"I think he's a fool."

"See you tonight," said Geoff.

Maybe she would. Maybe she wouldn't.

It was more than an hour to her grandmother's house in Barnstable, where she left the kids. She'd be damned if she made that drive many more times just so he could go wandering in search of his *connections*. But for the time being, she'd be damned to pay for day care.

She drove too fast back 6A, but in Dennis she slowed down to read the marquee for the Cape Playhouse. Now Showing: *Ain't Misbehavin'*. Coming Next: *On Golden Pond* with Mary Muldowney and Henry Shay. Two war-horses in a war-horse. Maybe they'd get to see it.

Maybe. Her life was steady rhythm of maybes, hitting her between the eyes like waves hitting the beach. Maybe everything would be in place and they could break ground when the estate cleared probate. Maybe Geoff would see that their security and his profession were more important than his uncle's crazy legacy. Maybe he'd realize that if *he* didn't develop the land, someone else would. And if he didn't realize it, *maybe* she'd leave him.

She pushed that last miserable *maybe* out of her mind and drove all the way back to Eastham, to a little cottage colony near Campground Road, where Methodists had once gathered for revival meetings. This one had a fireplace, and *maybe* the owner would be interested in selling to a battered wife with a buck and a quarter to spend. Then *maybe* Geoff would realize how tough life on a broker's commission could be.

She hated these cold calls. Excuse me, but would you be interested in selling your house? Don't you think it's time you stepped up to something better than this? You look pretty old, and wouldn't you like to live in a nice garden apartment without all this upkeep? My husband's out to lunch and my kids are going to go hungry if you don't sell your house so I can get the commission.

She had to be realistic. Somebody had to.

The car in the driveway was a BMW, New York plates. Somebody upwardly mobile, or maybe just a renter slumming it in a little dump near the beach.

She had scouted half a dozen little dumps. Then she had remembered this old place. Her father's office had listed it in the early eighties and she hadn't been here since, but there was still something strangely familiar about the place. It wasn't the television antenna, or the addition on the back, and she'd never seen a house before that was painted sky blue all over. But she felt that she knew the house . . . from somewhere.

"Sell my house? I only *bought* it six months ago." He was about thirty, oiled and tanned, wearing one of those bathing suits that looked like a red nylon jockstrap.

"What would you take for it?" Janice was sitting in the living room, by the fireplace. There was even something familiar about *that*.

His name was Vinnie. He gave her coffee. He listened politely to her spiel. But he seemed almost indecent, sitting there with his balls moving up and down every time he breathed. She didn't look at the suit, but if she made eye contact, he gave her one of those stares straight out of a dating-bar training book.

Speak your piece and get the hell out. "There must be some price you'd take."

"Not for sale."

Now his friend came up from the beach. Good tan, another skimpy little nutpouch suit, enough chest hair to braid a rug, and a gold coke spoon on a chain around his neck.

"Hey, Charlie, the lady wants us to sell our house."

Our house. Were they gay? Both of them were wearing wedding bands, but that didn't mean anything.

Charlie gave her his own Romeo eyes. "Sell? Gedoudaheah. We just bought the place. Bargain city."

"Yeah. We'll tear down this shithole and put up somethin' good, with a roof deck so our wives can see the water."

She was glad to hear about wives. "They'll be disappointed with the zoning restrictions. You'll never get three stories here."

"Ehhh." Charlie brought thumb and forefinger together in the universal gesture: money talks.

Time to leave. Money talked everywhere, but on Cape Cod, it seldom spoke the pig latin of graft. These guys might be drug dealers or mafiosi. Of course, money was money. She forced herself to stay. Always exhaust all options. That was what her father had taught her when she was selling years ago.

"If your wives are interested in modern three-story fun houses, I could show you some beauties down in Truro. Maybe when they come up from the beach—"

"They ain't here." Charlie sat down next to her and lit a cigarette. "They're home in Queens."

"Yeah. We come alone, for a little fishin'."

"Wet our lines, like they say. Heh-heh." Charlie moved a bit so that his oiled leg bumped against her skirt. Now she had a cleaning bill.

"Got a sister blond like you? Maybe we could all go fishin'."

There was a maybe to turn the stomach. "Just a husband and two kids."

She got up and headed for the door. She had already given them her card, for which she was extremely sorry.

One of them made a comment about the pretty legs. Then Charlie jumped between her and the door and gave her one more of those looks, as though she didn't know what she was missing. She might have laughed if she hadn't been so frightened.

"Excuse me." She was wearing heels, and the two of them were barefoot. She decided to count three and bury a heel in Charlie's instep. Then she could take a good kick at Vinnie's little swimsuit and be gone. One . . . two . . .

Charlie executed a ridiculous little bow, which caused the coke spoon and other things to dangle. Then he pushed open the door. "If we change our mind, we'll call you."

"If *you* change *your* mind, you call us," said Vinnie.

She hit the pavement and screamed "Son of a bitch!" at the top of her lungs. She didn't need this. She'd gone along with Geoff when he wanted to leave Boston. But this was not what she had bargained for.

She was *not* going to subject herself to this again, no matter how sorry she felt for the battered wives of the world, no matter how desperately she wanted a sale. She had to bring Geoff to his senses, or two mortgages would.

iii.

Half and half, split right down the middle. Half for Geoff and his heirs, half for Emily and hers. That was what Rake's will decreed, though Geoff guessed the old man wasn't thrilled at leaving it to either of them.

Maybe he could get the house onto the National Register of Historic Places—Home of the Man Who Sank the *Somerset*. Or maybe he could design the whole development around Rake's house. *That* would bring him back from the dead.

Something Professor Digges said had drawn Geoff to the house: Why would a man from verdant Hertfordshire choose to live on this desolate arm of sand?

The Tom Hilyard painting, *Voyage from Hertfordshire: A Journey from the Past to Secure the Future,* hung in the shadows at the top of the stairs. It showed a grim-faced young shipmaster, hands clamped behind his back, riding the canted quarterdeck of a schooner. The template identified him as Sam Hilyard, and the feathered Indian at the helm as Charlie Kwennit.

He took the picture off the wall and carried it downstairs for a better look. As he held it to the light, something slipped from behind the backing on the frame and fell on the floor.

An envelope. Hidden. A list written in Rake's hand:

> *Carolyn Hallissey*
> *comeuppance in the book of history*
> *Hertfordshire voyage to secure the future*
> *Nance / Iron Axe / charcoal on the floorboards*
> *Tom Hilyard paints Pilgrims from life?*
> *"The book of history will set us free from*
>   *the evil that bricks us up."*
> *State senator scared shitless*
> *Mary Muldowney and the doorstop*
> Murder on the Mayflower *by Tom Hilyard*

A message from the grave? A gag?

Then there was a *pop*. Nothing else. He didn't even see the arrow come through the doorway and dig into the pile of newspaper against the wall.

Geoff felt his stomach drop, and it was such a good idea that his whole body followed it. He shoved the list into his pocket and shouted, "For chrissakes, Arnie! What are you doin'?"

"What are *you* doin'?" Arnie Burr lowered the bow.

"Reading old newspapers."

"I saw a strange car."

"A blue Chevy Cavalier? Body-rot, stickers for all the beaches? Next time ask questions before you shoot."

"Next time, let me know when you're plannin' to snoop."

"It's my house, too, Arnie. Fifty-fifty. And he left the Tom Hilyard to me, free and clear."

Arnie raised the bow and pointed the arrow at Geoff's forehead. "Could've parted your hair and your brains, too . . . right down the middle."

Now Emily came through the back door. "We don't need any Hilyards over the mantelpiece. We got deer heads, bear rugs, stuffed stripers—"

"What's he worried I'll find here, Emily?" Geoff grabbed a paper from the pile behind him and read the headline. "That Nixon's mined Haiphong Harbor, maybe?" He threw the newspaper onto the table, and so much dust rose that Arnie began to sneeze.

"Oh, Jesus, here we go." Emily grabbed the arrow so that he didn't shoot anyone in the process.

"Until—*achoo!*" Arnie's sneeze hit Emily in the ear.

"Gesundheit." Geoff stepped back from the mist of spit.

"Until I know what this guy is plannin'—*achoo!*"

Geoff ducked. "No decision until I do a little more digging."

Emily pulled a cigarette from her pocket, lit it, and sucked in three or four breaths to settle herself. "It's our dream to sell this place, Geoff. It's a bitch of a life."

"As bad as fishin' for a livin'." Arnie grunted.

"Yeah. With the money, we can visit our daughters in California all winter, live in a house right here all summer."

"Did you ever ride dirt bikes in the hills around Santa Barbara?" said Arnie. "I did it once. Never had so much fun in my life."

"Dirt bikes . . . yeah. Great, Arnie." Geoff began to back toward the door. He hated daydreams, especially when he could make them come true.

Emily hacked once or twice. "You can't stand in the way of this. You'll screw it up for everyone."

Slam. He was out the door with the list in his pocket and two more futures in his hands.

And he had the feeling that the list might determine the futures . . . of a lot of people. He memorized it and made two copies. One he gave over the phone to Ma Little and told her to give it to Jimmy.

The other he took to George's dune shack, but George wasn't home. Probably out wandering with his new summer friend, the one he said was named Dave. So Geoff left the list in an envelope with a note: "Think about this, but don't tell anyone."

iv.

Janice was back in Barnstable, in the 1700 house. Her grandmother lived on the second floor, and there were law offices on the first floor, as there had been for most of the eighteenth century.

Hiram Bigelow kept his main offices in Boston, but he'd been hanging a Bigelow, Holden, and Hoar shingle here all his life. He looked over his reading glasses at Janice. "Why do *you* want to know about community property?"

She watched the cars passing the little oval of grass on 6A, the old town green. "I just want to know."

"Have you talked with anyone about this?" Hiram was a year younger than Dickerson, but had developed a completely different persona. Where Dickerson was bombastic, Hiram was subtle, where Dickerson played his bulk, Hiram folded a slender frame into a seersucker suit and folded the suit into a leather chair. Where Dickerson was smart, Hiram preferred to be wise. "You really should talk with someone, Janice."

"I'm talking with *you*, Hiram."

"About the wrong thing. One of the problems of your generation is that you run at the first sign of trouble."

"I'd like to get Geoff's attention." She went to a window and looked out. "We're getting ready to fight the town Conservation Commission and then the Cape Cod Commission tooth and nail—"

"To build ourselves the security our land entitles us to."

"Right. But my husband is thinking about killing the development before we even start."

"I'm a firm believer in using what God gives us." He leaned back in his chair and made a little tent with his fingers. "Unfortunately he gave us consciences, and your husband's seems to be working overtime."

She watched the traffic on 6A. During the summer, it flowed like a stream, sometimes rushing fast, sometimes meandering, but always running, like questions she could not hold back. "What are my rights if . . . if something should happen?"

He laughed, as though the possibility was too much to consider. "You're joint tenants. Unless otherwise stipulated, whatever he inherits becomes community property . . . provided you don't leave him before the estate clears probate."

"What's his is mine, what's mine is his?"

"Your Pilgrim ancestors would have said that *you* were his. That was before we had divorce lawyers."

She wasn't sure what she'd do with that knowledge, but she was glad to know. Now there was something else. God gave us all consciences, and hers had not been treating her well. "Tell me, Hiram. Is a handwritten will legal?"

"Absolutely."

She clutched at her purse as though she thought Clara's will might come flying out. For a moment, the future of the whole project was in her hands as much as Geoff's.

"But in Massachusetts a will has to be witnessed by two people," Hiram added.

Good. Clara's will was invalid. But what would old Hannah Bigelow have said about a young woman who carried someone's last bequest in her purse and did nothing about it?

On her way upstairs, she stopped to look at Hannah, painted rather primitively in the 1790s by some local portraitist. Hannah was wearing a yellow dress, her hair was simple and severe, and her brown eyes stared like beacons across the centuries. The only resemblance Janice saw to herself was in the stiff spine. The old girl had backbone. . . .

She had long ago read Hannah's letters and wanted to read them again, just to remind herself of backbone—especially when dealing with Hilyard men.

Agnes Bigelow looked up from the pile of papers on her lap. "I went across to the Sturgis Library and got Hannah's letters. They keep them so well over there, and they're so nice. Not like the snoops from Old Comers."

Janice brushed her lips across the fuzz on her grandmother's cheek. Agnes was eighty-nine, with no more than a hunchback slowing her down. No sad smell of urine, no cranky old temper, no memory loss. That was why Janice was happy to leave her children in the old woman's care.

"Letters from Sam Hilyard to Hannah, from Eldredge Dickerson to Hannah, a few that Hannah wrote and never sent, or maybe copied and sent."

Janice hefted the pile. "A lost art, correspondence."

"They *are* art. You've read them before, but come back to them again and they'll give you new insights, like great books."

Janice picked up the first one; it came from Sam Hilyard.

June 18, 1784

Dear Hannah,

Word reaches me that you have wed. This saddens me, as I always hoped to sail your way, but the winds do blow contrary. I wish you and John Digby best wishes, and as a patriot, will welcome you back to the new nation whenever you choose to come.

CHAPTER 24

May 1793

The Story of Hannah and Sam

Sam Hilyard reread Hannah's answer nearly ten years later, when word arrived that John Digby had gone down off Hatteras and Hannah was coming home. He had saved the letter that long.

Dear Sam,
    Thank you for your kind thoughts. We cannot return, in that my husband's family embraced the Loyalist cause with great passion. I shall always miss Cape Cod, but Nova Scotia is my home now. May our ships sail always on friendly seas, each with its own special mate.

Sam hoped that by now she had changed her mind.
He mastered a big-bellied draft horse out of Boston called the *James Otis*. For crew, he counted on his brother Will, Charlie Kwennit, who had survived the Revolution, and Mr. Barmy Burt, who found the sea a greater inspiration than William Thayer's doctoring. For love, he counted on women in Boston, London, and Jamaica, but as he reached age thirty, he had come to realize that his only true legacy might be the children he left behind.
    It was thought that Hannah Bigelow, after a childless decade

with John Digby, might be barren. But Sam decided to write to her nevertheless.

Dear Hannah,

As I have been at sea these last six months, I could not express my sympathy personally, and I would not now interrupt your grieving. They say John Digby was a good man. To win you, he must have been. But as your heart heals, you must look to the future. It is the only direction our wind will take us. We must follow it or founder. Should you need anything that I can offer, I will stand at your service.

A week later, on the day he was due to ship for Jamaica with a cargo of rum, her answer arrived in Boston.

Dear Sam,

Many thanks for your kind thoughts. I am most happy to be back at Cape Cod, and I agree that we must take the future at full canvas. Be assured that when I have strength, I will raise my sail again. And we will again sail on the same seas. But it may be a long time before I think of sharing another quarterdeck, so don't stay in port for me.

ii.

From the last will and testament of Benjamin Bigelow: "And to my niece Hannah, I bequeath the whole of that certain property known as Jack's Island, including the surrounding marsh, all buildings thereon, and saltworks. It is my confidence that she will make good use of the land. In a world where power passes from father to son, a childless uncle is happy to make his bequest to a trusted niece. . . ."

Hannah told her driver to stop on the causeway so that she could admire her island.

"You'll have all the help that your father can give." Sitting beside her was Solomon, now sixty-two and completely gray, though still ramrod-straight and as querulous as an old gull.

"Thank you, Father," answered Hannah, "but I intend to conduct my affairs here on my own, so that you may learn confidence in me for the future."

Jack's Island was now a spring-green meadow from one creek to the other. But when the wind blew, few tall trees waved in the sky. Instead, the sails of the windmills spun above the saltworks.

The first settlers on the Cape had found that boiling a kettle of seawater would effectively render salt. In a place where wood was abundant, this was the cheapest route to profit. But the sea was endless and the woods were not, and in time, firewood for boiling the seawater grew more expensive than the salt.

Yet Cape Codders were ingenious people where a dollar could be made from the elements. They built vats, some a hundred feet long and ten feet wide, though no more than a foot deep, then fitted them with shutters that could be closed in rainy weather, and let the sun evaporate seawater into salt. Five thousand feet of saltworks now lined Jack's Creek and Nauseiput, and as the sun gained strength each May, spindly-legged windmills began pumping water into the vats.

"Fine saltmakin' weather." Jacob Bigelow, the youngest of Shearjashub's sons, welcomed them to the island. He had retired from the sea to run the saltworks, but everyone still called him Cap'n Jake.

"A fine saltmakin' *crew*," said Solomon.

Scrooby Doone and Leyden were out among the vats, opening the shutters so the morning sun could begin its work. When they saw Hannah, they came running.

"We heard the news, Miss Hannah, 'bout you inheritin'—"

"I'm Widow Digby now, Scrooby," she said gently.

"That means she husband's kicked the . . . passed the . . . he's dead." With the shovel that he always carried, Leyden whacked his brother in the seat of the pants. Then he took off his hat and bowed his head to Hannah.

"I'm very happy to be back, boys." She patted Leyden on his bald spot, and he gave her a toothless old grin.

"Scrooby and Leyden know almost as much about the windmills as I do," said Jacob.

Scrooby pulled off his hat and bowed to the ground. "And I know more than Leyden."

"You see," said Solomon, "your land is in good hands."

"I intend to learn how salt is made, Father, and how the windmills run."

"I can teach you that good enough," said Cap'n Jake, "but it's like learnin' how to sail. You gotta know how to make canvas and wind do your biddin'."

"She needs to learn only how to find herself another husband," said Solomon. "One who can give her children."

"I need also to learn what my father and brother do at Barnstable, so that I can do it as well." Hannah offered her arms to the Doone brothers. "Gentlemen, a tour of the saltworks, if you please."

Scrooby and Leyden looked at her arms as though they were sleeping snakes; then they looked at each other. So Hannah took one of Scrooby's arms and hooked it into her own.

Scrooby beamed at Hannah and scowled at his brother. "Take she other arm, damn fool. Ain't no one ever taught you how to treat a lady?"

As the Doone brothers led Hannah toward the vats and windmills that stood like giant herons on the sand, she announced, "It's a new era, Father."

"A new era for men of vision," muttered Solomon, "not for young widows who should be keeping house."

. . .
iii.

A new era, indeed. Those who lived through the time between the closing of the Barnstable Court and Washington's inauguration had seen Benjamin Bigelow's prophecies on independence fulfilled. Most of those not impoverished by blockade and rebellion were bled white by what followed. The British closed their ports to American shipping, and while a loose confederation of states, with little foreign credit, struggled to organize itself, the system of national currency remained in a shambles.

But on Cape Cod, those who held land could raise cattle or corn. Those who had hooks could fish. And even in bad times, there were shipmasters and speculators who could smell change in the wind before it blew over the horizon. By 1793, the bravery of the shipmasters and the money of the speculators were bringing prosperity. And it would soon be said that most Cape mariners knew the sea route to China better than the land route to Boston.

One of the most respected mariners was a small and precise Barnstable man named Eldredge Dickerson. He mastered the merchantman *Benjamin Bigelow,* owned by a family whose speculations had brought income in even the hardest days. Upon his return from a China run, he learned that the Widow Digby had moved to Jack's Island. With her father's permission, he courted her.

Upon return from an Indies run, Sam Hilyard learned that the Widow Digby was receiving suitors. With no one's permission, he courted her, bringing both flowers and a schooner laden with lumber.

Hannah was pleased by the flowers, curious about the schooner, and surprised by the appearance of a man she had often imagined since girlhood. Compared to Eldredge Dickerson's condensed and careful presence, Sam seemed brawny and a bit wild. He wore the loose-fitting clothes of a sailor, a straw hat instead of felt, and shoulder-long hair he had never powdered or tied in his life.

Sam had courted many beautiful women and some not so beautiful, but he had never before courted one fresh from the strawberry field. A sun hat shaded most of Hannah's face, the handle of a small trowel hung from a pocket in her apron, a film of perspiration beaded on her upper lip, and she looked as handsome to Sam as his first memories of her.

She smelled the irises and poppies, which had little scent, and out of politeness said they smelled beautiful. Then she invited him to the house for tea. They strolled along the path from the Nauseiput dock through the cornfield, where the scarecrows stood sentinel over the crows, toward the forlorn grove of trees that protected the house. Jack's Island now looked like a table in the midst of marshland and flat, something God had forgotten to carry away when he made the coastline.

"Your uncle gave you a great gift."

"A great responsibility as well. We have much to do here"— she held out her hands, tanned brown and callused—"though the sun may leave me looking like an old fisherman."

He bent down slightly to look under the brim of her hat. "Little chance of that, Widow Digby."

"You've grown more skilled in seventeen years, Sam."

For a moment, he thought he might kiss her, as he had done so clumsily that night in 1776. But it was true. He had grown more skilled in his dealings with women. After all, he had paid enough of them to learn. Still, for all his careful charting of this conversation, he ran himself straight onto the rocks of bluntness: "Did Eldredge ask for your hand?"

"I thought you came here to flatter me, Sam . . . then sell me a boatload of lumber."

"They say you live in a hundred-forty-year-old fallin'-down house. The lumber's a gift."

She had known that they would come when her mourning was over—the widowers, the bachelors, the seafarers who had come to realize that while they were at sea, all the women had married and their youth had fled. Who among them wouldn't take a chance with Hannah, widowed young as she was, childless, and blessed with a fine inheritance?

The Reverend Mr. Kite of Barnstable, a middle-aged widower with an odd eye and a penchant for quoting Scripture, had paid her an inordinate amount of attention. James Stubbs, a young fisherman, brought her halibut and cod after every voyage. And Eldredge Dickerson had already made his intentions known to her father.

Eldredge had the best chance. He was an honorable man, a churchgoer, and as a China trader he was gone for years at a time. That was to the good, because Hannah had plans for which a man would be nothing more than a nay-saying hindrance. But here was Sam Hilyard, looking as nervous and unpredictable as the boy who had enticed her so long ago.

She let him into her house, the first of her suitors she had so honored. "It was built by one of your ancestors. It's very old."

"Very old post and beam." He pulled out his knife and probed a corner post, working downward until the knife slipped easily into the wood. Scores of slimy white bugs slithered out and fell to the floor. "Very old post and beam, very new termites."

He said nothing of the wing chairs beside the fireplace, but he stuck his head up the flue and said it probably hadn't been pointed since it was built. He did not notice the red curtains on the windows, but told her how small seventeenth-century windows were and how much more efficient was the double-hung design. He did not notice his flowers in a vase on the great room table, but banged his head on the door frame leading to the sitting room.

She tucked her hands into the pockets of her apron. "You're too big, Sam."

"The house is too small. Let me build you another one."

"I'm happy here where I am."

Her resistance was something he had prepared for, but he had not foreseen the midday silence, the quiet intimacy made closer by the distant crump of the waves. So he sought another blunt question from the course he had charted before coming. "Why did you marry John Digby?"

"I loved him." She threw open the back door. Out beyond the barn, windmills turned in the breeze. Ocean and sky made their pact at the horizon.

"Did you ever think of me in Halifax?"

"I saw your ship. I saw the bloodstains. I cried . . . for us all."

He stood behind her. She had taken off her sun hat and shaken out her hair, and the smell of her intoxicated him. "The British took us right out there. They came out of these creeks in longboats."

"We had to grow up quickly." She stepped away and went toward the barn. It was said that Quakers had met there during the persecutions, and she was often drawn to it, as if she could summon her own strength by contemplating theirs, and at the moment, she needed her strength.

But Sam followed her. "Sell me this land and let me build you a new house."

She stopped at the barn door. "*Sell* you the land?"

"Sell me half the island. I'll pay whatever you wish and build you a house wherever you want . . . a barn as well."

"I like *this* barn." She went inside.

"Then it shall be yours."

"Build a house . . . buy my island . . ." She moved into the shadows as he pursued her from the sun, the young privateer stepping out of her girlhood memories. "I don't think you know what you want."

"I think I do." He stalked toward her. He put his hands on her shoulders. She raised her face to his—

And Leyden Doone stepped from the shadows and hit Sam Hilyard over the head with a shovel. "You got to be careful, Miss Hannah. You ain't seen what some fellers got between their legs."

iv.

Sam stored the lumber beneath a sailcloth and came often to check on its seasoning. By the following autumn, they had seen more of each other than most couples ever did before deciding on marriage, but she had decided only to hold off Eldredge Dickerson's proposal. When Sam was at sea, she mapped her calendar, so that she might imagine where he was each week. When Sam slipped into a prostitute in some port city, he imagined Hannah beneath him.

But Hannah would not allow him to build her a house or buy half the island, because those proposals were prelude to one of a more personal nature. She was not yet ready to commit herself to any man, and even if she loved Sam, she feared her father, whose disapproval of Sam was well known.

"Why do you hate him?" she once asked.

"He is not a God-fearing man."

Hannah could not know that Solomon had killed one Hilyard because of her ideas, betrayed another out of fear, and detested a third who coveted his daughter. Those were things a man kept to himself.

In the spring of 1794, Sam sailed for South Carolina with a cargo of rum and barrel staves, which he exchanged for flour and rice. From Charleston he wrote Hannah that if they did not begin building by fall, the fine lumber would rot. Then he headed for Spain.

Hannah understood his meaning and gave it much consideration. But her father had made a promise: if she continued to oversee Jack's Island skillfully and married a God-fearing man like Eldredge Dickerson, he would include her in the larger deliberations of Bigelow and Son.

It was during this time that she was most thankful for Leyden Doone and his shovel. She had never enjoyed her couplings with her husband. They were brief and to the point, and she had come to expect nothing more. Had she submitted to Sam that day in the barn, she might have found that not all men were so dry, and her passion might now have overwhelmed her good sense. But she kept her head . . . until the French Revolution threatened Sam's.

Before reaching the Spanish port of La Coruña, Sam's ship was waylaid by a French frigate and taken to the city of Brest. France was in turmoil, its people starving, and a cargo of flour and rice had no future but the French belly. While barrels and sacks came off the ship, Sam and the crew were brought before a citizens' tribunal, which promised to recompense them, in due time.

Sam knew what that meant. He sent his crew home and con-

veyed to the tribunal his determination to wait for payment until hell
froze over . . . or the French stopped drinking wine. Then he went
to Paris, where the American envoy wrung his hands and said there
was nothing he could do.

On Cape Cod, there was nothing that Hannah could do but
write letters:

> Dear Sam,
> No seafaring metaphors. No playful words. I love you.
> Know that. But you are a silly, stubborn man. You do not
> remain in France for the money, but for the principle. And
> principles get people killed. Before you choose to fight for
> them, make sure they are worth your head. I cried for you
> last night. I shall cry for both of us if you lose your head.

But there was no need to cry for Sam. He spent two months
holding out his hand in one revolutionary office after another, and
partaking, with some disappointment and at considerable expense,
in the carnal pleasures for which Paris had once been famous. He
also studied the French manner of slicing through their chains with
the guillotine and found it wanting.

Hundreds were ridden past his window to their death, but he
watched a beheading only once.

A married couple caught his attention, middle-aged and graying,
simple folk, from the look of their clothes, brave folk, from their
bearing. As the tumbril took them through the screaming streets,
something drew him after them. He could not guess at their
offense—nor, perhaps, could they—but they stood with hands
linked, eyes only on each other. In a world of madness, they had
found their bearings. When they reached the platform, they went up
together. They embraced without tears or a glance at the mob. Then
the wife lay beneath the blade, as though settling down for a nap.
After it fell, the husband did not look at the headless body twitching
in the basket but went quickly to join his wife in spirit.

Sam left Paris with government bills of exchange, payable in
London, and the vision of two people who knew their bearings even
in death. He was hailed by the merchants of Boston and welcomed
by the woman he hoped would help him to keep his bearings for the
rest of his life.

"The bonnet is beautiful, Sam."

"It ain't Paris fashion. There ain't much of that these days. It's a good Boston hat, the same yellow as the one you wore to the *Serenity* that day."

Yellow flattered her, bringing out the intense brown in her eyes. In egalitarian France, women still wore lip salve and astringent powders that scarred their skin. They plucked their brows to thin strands and piled their hair high on the top of their heads. Hannah was unadorned and all the handsomer for it, a new breed of woman, an American.

The clouds were blowing east, ragged purple remnants of an autumn storm, as Hannah and Sam went walking out behind her house. "I worried for you, Sam."

"That's what men and women are supposed to do."

"Worry?" A cloud threw a shadow across her face.

"Worry . . . help . . . keep each other on course. I can build you a house by Christmas."

"You're not a God-fearin' man, Sam."

"I fear God whenever I go to sea." The cloud passed.

"You're not a churchgoer." She went toward the barn, her haven of contemplation.

"I'll take a pew in the First Church."

"My father won't approve."

"He will once he sees what I pay for the land."

"Why must you have half the island?"

"Pride. If we each own half, we start as equals."

Sam stopped in the doorway and peered into the corners.

"Leyden is at the saltworks." She laughed.

"Good. I'll build the house to last, like this barn, with a foundation." He stamped across the floorboards. Then he knelt and rapped his knuckles against a plank. "Somethin' here."

With a pinch bar he pried up the board. Neatly mortised into the joists was a compartment large enough to hold an abandoned mouse nest and some sort of tool wound in several thicknesses of marsh hay.

The outer layer disintegrated. The second layer, wound in the opposite direction, was better preserved. A third layer, wrapped again as the first, smelled rancid and oily.

"An axe," said Hannah when the last strands fell away.

"A damn strange axe." Sam smelled the residue on his fingers. "Whale oil. Somebody covered it with whale oil to keep it."

"Look at the lettering on the shaft."

Sam studied the four symbols engraved into the metal. "I know what it says."

"What?"

"It's a message from the past. It says, 'With this axe, build Hannah a house." Then he kissed her.

v.

Six weeks later, Solomon returned from a London trip to learn that his daughter had accepted the proposal of the one suitor to whom he objected.

"We can't reverse the sale, but we can damn well stop the marriage," he told his son in the office of the Barnstable House.

"I tried." Elkanah was a copy of his father and sought to heighten the effect by adopting his father's sudden gestures, colorless wardrobe, and small potbelly. Like his father, he was slender of shoulder and chest, but the belly, which he hoped would lend stature, looked like nothing more than a pillow hung upon a coatrack. "Hannah said Sam Hilyard is the best shipmaster on Cape Cod, and we are far better served if he serves our family than someone else's."

It may have occurred to Solomon that this union represented a final victory over the Hilyards, but he could never allow Bigelow blood to be mingled with that of the invective-spewing Outcast of Billingsgate. "Hannah loses everything."

"What?"

"If she marries Sam Hilyard, she loses any claim to our future. If she takes Eldredge Dickerson, I give her half of everything upon my death."

"Half?" Elkanah nearly slipped from his chair.

"Not to your liking, but suitable to our future."

vi.

As the days grew shorter, Sam hurried to finish the house. He broke down Jack Hilyard's old saltbox, no mighty task, given the work of the termites; he saved what timbers were sound and burned the rest in a great conflagration of dry wood and crackling bugs.

Then he dug a foundation hole and lined it with ballast stones that rose two feet above the sand. This meant the termites would have a harder time reaching wood and beginning their work. The foundation was wide, but the house would hug the ground.

"A short hoist and a long peak" was the Cape Cod saying. A story-and-a-half house presented a low profile to the ceaseless wind, which the windowless roof deflected. And though the upper rooms were small and low, they were all the warmer for their size. On the first floor, three rooms surrounded the chimney—a parlor to contain good furniture and family mementos, a master's chamber, and a great room where the family cooked, ate, and spent most of its time.

As a family grew, the house could grow, with new wings to accommodate new arrivals. The most frugal or penurious might even begin with half a house and expand as fortune permitted, but Sam Hilyard was neither, and he built with the best materials, indulging in dentil molding along the fascia boards, a fanlight above the doorway, and elegant pine paneling around the fireplaces.

On a warm November afternoon, he was pegging pine planks in the great room. Salt making had ended for the season, so Scrooby Doone was helping Sam, while upstairs, Kwennit, Will, Barmy Burt, and Leyden Doone put down rough flooring.

The house echoed with the sound of hammering and chatter, and Sam laughed to imagine what flights of conversational fancy might be transporting Burt and Leyden. In the way that he attracted misfits, he had drawn the Doones into his circle. Scrooby, by far the more scrutable, seemed the happier for it. He was at the other end of the board, using a pinch bar to hold it in place. When Sam laughed, he laughed, though he could not have known why.

"Gettin' married makes a man happy, don't it?"

"Happier than a ship's cat findin' rats in the bilge."

"I'm glad. I was a-scared of you at first."

"So was your brother."

"Yeah, but . . . yeah, but he's stupid. I'd never hit you with a shovel."

A drop of perspiration rolled from the tip of Sam's nose and splattered onto the new board.

"Leyden believed all what he heard 'bout you, back in the Revolution. But I didn't. I knew that if I ever worked for you, you'd treat me good."

Sam did not notice the agitation creeping into Scrooby's voice.

His attention was on the peg in front of him, and his mind was on Hannah. He gave no more thought to Scrooby's chatter than to the crying of the gulls.

"So . . . so, since you're my boss now, I just want to say I'm sorry."

Sam's mallet drove the peg downward. "Mmm-hm? What for?"

"Tellin' cousin Solomon what you was doin' that night."

"What night?"

"September the fourth, 1778."

Sam stopped hammering and turned to the childlike old man at the other end of the floorboard.

"Solomon . . . he always said, 'If you ever hear anythin' 'bout the Hilyards, let me know.' So . . . when I heard about you smugglin' salt, so . . . I told him."

"And what did he do?"

"He sent me and Leyden with a letter to the captain with the brass buttons. He said you was bad guys and you'd be caught. But I . . . I don't think you're a bad guy now, Sam, and I just wanted you to know that."

Scrooby's words mixed once more with the cry of the gulls.

vii.

Hannah had gone to Nova Scotia to settle affairs with her late husband's family, and she had returned by way of Barnstable, so that she could visit her father. Then she headed for Jack's Island.

The twenty-mile ride from Barnstable to the north parish of Harwich was never pleasant. Roads built upon sand were unstable, no matter how often they were rolled or covered with crushed shells. Cape Cod horses wore large shoes to support them, and the carriages went on wide wheels, because there were places where the road was no better than the beach.

Still, Hannah was thankful for the long journey from her father's home, because she had much to consider after seeing him. It was near dusk when she reached the island. She found Sam sitting on the half-finished floor, a fire of wood scraps roaring on the hearth, a rum bottle at his side. "My father's given me a choice."

Sam kept his eyes on the fire. "Renounce him."

"He said if marry I you, I'll never have an interest in the business."

"Do you love me, Hannah?"

"Of course."

"Then prove it."

"We agreed that until our marriage, you could satisfy your lust elsewhere."

Sam grabbed her hand and pulled her down to his side. "My lust is not the issue . . . though you smell very good."

"You smell like rum."

"Rum clears my head."

"What clouds it?"

"Love."

"I don't understand."

Nor did Sam. He had counted on her to help him find his bearings, and she brought only more confusion. He threw his arms around her, as if she were a buoy.

"Sam—" She had come to find strength, and he asked her to be strong. His stubble scraped against her cheek. His arms surrounded her. His scent of rum and sweat, of tobacco and tar, comforted her in a way she could not define.

The effect of her body was no less upon him. The smoothness of her skin, the softness of her breasts, the sweet scent of vanilla, these conspired to draw him from his anger and point him north once more.

They remained like this for some time, and though their flesh knew the quickening that came to all lovers, they did not seek to satisfy it. The embrace was satisfaction in itself, taking them beyond desire, toward sustenance.

A chunk of wood tumbled from the firebox, spattering sparks across the floor. The wood was pushed back, the sparks extinguished. They found each other's arms once more. Their silence enfolded them, except for the small sigh when he kissed her . . . and the greater sigh when her bared breasts touched his chest.

Sam Hilyard had rutted his way through the ports of America, the Indies, and Europe, and when he glanced at the shadow rocking on the wall, he thought once more of Kwennit's term: the beast with two backs. Perhaps he and Hannah looked no more dignified than that, he with his ass in the air and his breeches at his ankles, she with her dress front unbuttoned and her skirts hiked up around her waist. But this was different. The spiritual pact they made in their embrace they sealed with the joining of their flesh.

It was a long time before they spoke, before the world once more invaded their small circle of warmth.

"Renounce him," whispered Sam.

"He's my father."

"He informed the British of my father's final voyage."

Hannah sat up and pulled her dress across her breasts. "Where did you hear this? Why have you not spoken of it before?"

"Scrooby told me yesterday, by way of tellin' me I've neither horns nor forked tail."

"You believe the words of a man-child?"

"That was your father's thinkin' when he sent two half-wits to the *Somerset*."

"You must let my father answer this charge."

Sam put his arm around her. "We own this island. I hold stock in the *Nathan Hale*. We have each other."

For Hannah, the glow of their love was fading like the warmth from a glass of wine. In its place was the heaviness that came when the wine wore away. "I cannot renounce my family, and if you believe this story—"

"I leap a wide river to reach you, Hannah. Let your father keep his property. We'll begin a life together."

Hannah stood, and as she collected herself, a reminder of their intimacy trickled onto her thigh. "I deserve part of what my father owns. And if I renounce him, there is no promise that your hatred for him will die."

"I'll kill my hatred"—Sam sipped his rum—"by takin' his daughter in exchange for my father."

"Is this how you see me? And what we just did, was it some kind of victory?"

"You misunderstand."

The trickle on her thigh grew colder. She turned away and pressed one of her petticoats between her legs. "I'll not be used as comeuppance for my father's failings."

He stood, hitched his breeches. "Renounce him."

"You cannot love me too well if you know me no better than that."

Sam drained the bottle and shattered it in the fireplace. The flames jumped angrily.

"Let my father answer this charge. I cannot live knowing you burn to kill him." Hannah pulled on her shawl. "I'll stay at Cap'n Jake's."

"I'll finish the floor, in honor of what we done on it."

That night Cap'n Jake brought Sam a note from Hannah:

Dear Sam

You must trust me, and I must trust my father, you for the sake of our love, I for the sake of my blood. I do not wish to separate myself from you, yet there are times when a man must be alone, hearing nothing but the sounds of his own heart and unspoken voice. And it is these, more than the happy din of a noisy household, that will make him understand how much he needs the gentle things, a loving woman's voice, the laughter of children. You and my father must speak, for we cannot marry under such conditions.

viii.

Solomon Bigelow came to Jack's Island on a miserable rainy morning a few days later, but not to speak to Sam Hilyard. He came to take the Doone brothers and their flapping mouths back to Barnstable. For help, should they prove uncooperative, he brought his Negro driver Gamaliel and Thornton Brace, Barnstable blacksmith.

Hannah had hoped for reconciliation, but Solomon had neither time nor interest for that.

"Where are those fools?" he demanded of his daughter without so much as a greeting.

"At the windmill, with Cap'n Jake, grinding corn."

Solomon turned back into the rain and ordered his driver to take him up the road to the mill.

Hannah called for him to wait, but he ignored her, so she threw on her shawl and went running to the new house, where Sam was pegging floorboards. She could not let her father leave the island without speaking to Sam, no matter the anger of either man.

While the pumping mills looked like delicate herons feeding on the marsh, the grinding mill near the causeway stood as solid and serene as the First Church itself, and nearly as revered. The arms turned in the relentless wind that Cape Codders had come to know as God's breath. The wooden gears squeaked in the cap. The gears turned the great stones on the middle level of the mill. And the corn filled the bins on the first floor.

Solomon and his blacksmith found the Doones and Cap'n Jake working at the millstones. He had to shout over the noise. "They've learned all they need to here. I need 'em in Barnstable."

"Ain't we . . . ain't we done good here?" said Scrooby.

"I don't want to go." Leyden gripped his shovel.

Brace grabbed him by the collar and he pulled away like a dog ducking a blow.

"I don't want to go, either," said Scrooby. "Cap'n Jake been good to us, and Aunt Sarah, she makes blueberry cobbler and—"

"Now, Scrooby," said Cap'n Jake, "if Solomon says he needs you up in Barnstable—"

"Maybe he needs you to betray another patriot." Sam Hilyard's voice boomed up the stairwell as he came pounding from the grain-bins to the grinding level. "Maybe someone's runnin' salt to Washington's army!"

"This is private property, Hilyard," said Solomon. "Get out."

"I asked him to come!" Hannah rushed up after Sam, tripping on her shawl as she came.

"He has no business here!" Solomon's voice sounded as harsh as the wooden gears. "Mr. Brace, throw him out."

The blacksmith had no neck, arms like most men's thighs, and a face like a barnacle-crusted hull. He suggested that Sam should move along. Sam ignored him.

Hannah put herself between the blacksmith and Sam. She shivered from fear and the cold rain that had soaked through her shawl and plastered her hair to her face in wet ringlets. All she wanted was time to reconcile her father and Sam, and herself to each of them.

All Sam wanted was the truth, because the truth would tear Solomon's daughter away from him forever. "Scrooby Doone says you betrayed my father."

"You believe them? They're idiots."

"Idiots?" cried Scrooby. "We ain't idiots."

"We is," said Leyden, "but I'm smarter."

"You ain't ever."

"Am so."

Cap'n Jake grabbed their collars and pulled them back against the wall. "Shut up. This here's serious stuff, more'n either of you understands."

"Idiots," repeated Solomon.

"The captain of the *Somerset* believed them," Sam cried over the roar of the mill wheel. "And you believed that if they said where they'd gone, no one would believe them. But I believe Scrooby."

Scrooby grinned and his Adam's apple wagged up and down. "I was on that British ship, just like I said, Sam."

"They're idiots."

"Scrooby, what did the captain look like?" asked Sam.

"A dark man, dark eyes, black brows . . . like a raccoon."

"And he had brass buttons," said Leyden. "Shiny buttons to see you face in. I liked the brass buttons."

"Enough of this," said Solomon.

"Yep. And Scrooby couldn't find the letter, 'cause he's stupid, but I had it in me hatband, just like Mr. Bigelow told me—"

"Quiet, both of you!" cried Solomon.

Hannah had heard her father described as an old gull, a sharp-eyed, grasping scavenger. Now, in his rain-soaked gray coat, with streaks of chalk running from his powdered hair down the sides of his face, he even *looked* like a gull.

His eyes met hers for an instant; then his head twitched away. "Brace, move my daughter aside, and give this impudent Hilyard rascal what he deserves."

Sam gave the blacksmith no more than a glance. "Move and you'll wear the mill wheel around your neck."

"Send him down the stairs, Brace. 'Tis time he had his comeuppance."

"My what?"

"Comeuppance! Your bloody grandmother's favorite word. Take your own, for swindlin' my daughter and screwin' her as well, I'd wager!"

"Father!"

"Comeuppance!"

That voice, screaming over the roar of the mill, became a voice, screaming over the roar of the wind, screaming of comeuppance, and for a moment, Sam saw a burning cat.

And in that moment, Thornton Brace struck. A hand sank into Sam's throat like a lobster claw. A fist crashed into his face, then again. And Sam's knees went weak. Now Brace smiled. He might bully a small town with his bulk, but he had never fought in a dockside tavern brawl. So he let go of Sam's throat and reached for Sam's collar, to throw him down the stairs.

And Sam butted him square in the breastbone.

Brace's eyes opened wide, and like a great bellows, he began to gasp. He got down one gulp of air, then another. Then Sam's foot drove his balls into his body, and Sam's fist drove his body down the stairs.

Solomon screamed for Gamaliel, who stood outside the mill near the carriage. But standing between Gamaliel and the door was Charlie Kwennit, harpoon handle in his hands. Charlie asked the slave why a red man and a black man should bother with white men's arguments, and the slave had no answer but to stand where he was in the pouring rain.

Solomon called again for his slave. Then the gull became a crab, scuttling sideways toward the stairs, never taking his eyes from Sam, who studied him now as the osprey studied the creatures on the tide flat, coldly, without passion.

Then Sam pulled his knife.

"Sam! Stop!" Hannah threw her arms around Sam, but he shoved her aside. Her shawl slipped from a shoulder, tangling her foot and causing her to stumble against the wheel casing. She felt the rumble grinding into the pit of her stomach and up her spine. She whispered the word "please," but above the roar, she knew he did not hear. The osprey consumed its prey to survive. Sam would consume the object of his hatred.

Then something above him caught his attention. Hannah's eyes followed his gaze into the cap of the mill, where the wind shaft turned the brake wheel, engaging the wallower gear to turn the spindle shaft that spun the stone. She did not know what he had seen in the works, but now he looked again at Hannah. His gaze had grown cold enough to make her shiver, yet she smiled, as if to calm him. And he reached toward her. So she offered her hand. And he ripped the shawl from her shoulder.

In a single motion, he flung the shawl upward, into the gears. Then he drove his knife into the end of it and grabbed Solomon. The old man kicked and screamed and swore his imprecations, but Sam lifted him into the air and neatly spliced the collar of his coat to the shawl.

It looked as if Solomon had been hanged, but instead of dropping toward the floor, he was rising toward an end far more gruesome than a simple snapped neck.

"Cut me down!" Solomon flailed his limbs like a newborn. "Hannah! Cap'n Jake! Leyden! Scrooby!"

"I can't help. I'm an idiot!" Scrooby brought a finger to the side of his head and stirred. "Ooohhh."

"Shut up!" said Leyden.

Sam stood by the brake and watched Solomon rising toward the gears. "Did you kill my grandmother and betray my father?"

Solomon mustered whatever he had in his terror-dry mouth and spit it into Sam's eye. Sam smashed a backhand across his face.

"Stop it!" screamed Hannah.

"Tell the truth, and them gears won't crush you."

Solomon craned his neck to see how close he was to the mill cap. Then he grabbed madly at the knife in his collar.

Hannah rushed for the brake, and Sam flung her back. "Stay away!" he commanded. "If you ever hope to have me, hear the truth right now."

"Stop this, or I never hope to want you!"

"Let me down!" screamed Solomon.

"This is killin', plain and simple," cried Cap'n Jake.

Yet the wooden gears squeaked, the shawl wound 'round them like yarn on a bobbin. And Solomon rose.

"Did you kill my grandmother? Did you tar and feather her and set fire to her cat?"

It may have been that Solomon saw the cat before him or heard the gears, grinding closer and closer, or realized the enormity of his guilt. But he screamed in a voice that sounded to Sam like that terrified black cat, screamed until there was no air left in his lungs, screamed until the roar of the mill could not be heard, and he passed out.

For a time, nothing moved, but for the limp body of Solomon Bigelow, rising in little jerks like a figure in a German clockwork. Then Hannah shivered. Sam took a step toward her.

And Leyden Doone stepped from the shadows and hit Sam Hilyard over the head with his shovel.

"What did you do that for?" Scrooby asked.

"I hate cats, too. I set fire to a few meself."

ix.

Three days later, Sam Hilyard accepted command of a merchantman called the *Parnassus*. He and his crew of friends, augmented by twenty more, sailed for China.

What hope was there that Hannah would have him, after the fury she had seen in him? How could they live as man and wife when their parents had been such enemies? He would always love her, but until her father was gone and her ambition for Sam equaled her ambition for her father's property, they could have no future. He set these thoughts down in a letter, which he put on a Boston-bound ship in Valparaíso.

While at anchor with the other foreign vessels at Whampoa, he received Hannah's answer. It came on a vessel captained by Eldredge Dickerson, who deferred Sam's invitation to visit until after Sam had read the letter.

There was good reason for this. Hannah had taken the surname Dickerson and was now with child. She said she forgave Sam, "but with your departure, I felt compelled to marry Eldredge. He is a good and honorable man, as you are, but untouched by the furies. Yours have caused the invaliding of my father and may one day bring you to greater grief. Learn to fear God, and someday will you find love."

Sam and Eldredge dined that night. With a brave smile, Sam toasted Eldredge's health, his bride, and his baby. Afterward, he stood at the stern of the *Parnassus* and stared at the alien landscape of China. On the distant hills, Chinese lords and coolies drank their tea. Along Whampoa Reach, the leaves of the poplars quivered in the moonlight breeze. He was far from home and would have to find his bearings on his own. . . .

He did not see Hannah again for thirteen years.

X.

By October 1807, three new towns had appeared on Cape Cod. Merchant shipping and fishing had brought prosperity, which brought larger populations and more contentiousness. So Eastham's south parish had become Orleans, Dennis had been born of Yarmouth, and the north parish of Harwich had broken away to become Brewster. Not that Sam Hilyard cared whether Jack's Island was in Harwich or Brewster. He visited Cape Cod at Christmas and Easter, if he happened to be in New England, but he was now a man of the world.

His crew called him Hard Sam Hilyard. Shipowners called him money in the bank. The Chinese who had seen him fight the Macao pirates called him Huoyan Jinqang, Determined Fury. And beneath his cutaway, he wore a white waistcoat of Chinese silk, on which two luxuriantly embroidered black dragons breathed fire.

With a few extra pounds around his bedragonned belly, he considered himself the finest, if least godly, figure of a man ever to stand before the First Church in Brewster. At the door of the church stood the finest figure of a girl he had ever seen. Her yellow dress and bonnet brought out her brown eyes in a way that caused Sam to stop and tip his hat.

She nodded, then saw the dragons on his waistcoat, which caused her expression to change from mere politeness to recognition, then caused her to call her mother.

Hannah Bigelow Dickerson stepped from the shade of the portico. "Why Sam, we hoped we'd see you here today."

Sam's brother Will, who had long since left the sea, was taking a wife, Mary Burr by name, the eighth daughter of a salt-caked old Brewster fisherman, and Sam was the best man. "When Will said he'd invited his neighbors, I thought he meant the Doones."

"He did." Hannah gestured to a pair of old men who were sitting in a back row. One of them held a shovel around which he had tied a ribbon.

Sam laughed at the Doones and swallowed back the consternation he felt at the sight of Hannah. But he recovered sufficiently to give her daughter Dorothy a courtly bow and European kiss upon the back of the hand, causing the girl to blush mightily.

"You grow even more skilled." Hannah laughed.

Yes, he thought, more skilled, but still alone when he returned to Boston after years at sea. "Your lovely daughter favors you in all save her black hair."

For a moment, Hannah seemed at a loss. Then she extended her hand for him to kiss. "New England ladies are seldom greeted so graciously."

He brought the hand to his lips and held it there, inhaling the vanilla scent he remembered from so long ago. "Your skin is very white. Eldredge has seen to it that the sun didn't leave you looking like an old fisherwoman."

She withdrew her hand. "I've seen to that myself, though our company always takes an interest in vessels mastered by my husband. In fact, he is at sea even now."

"The dragons," said Dorothy, "my father says they're called Determination and Fury."

"Determined Fury is my Chinese name. Huoyan Jinqang."

As if she could not help herself, the girl reached out and touched the orange silk circle floating above the dragons. "Is that the sun?"

"My Chinese mistress says the fireball is love. The dragons breathing flames, they are the lovers."

"Sam! My daughter is a lady."

"So I see. As much a lady as her mother."

Just then Hannah's brother Elkanah came up the steps. He had grown to resemble his father even more as he grayed, which caused Sam to dislike him even more. He was followed by two young men who resembled him enough to be his sons, though Elkanah did not bother to introduce them.

He gave Sam a limp handshake. "'Tis a great day for the Hilyards, marrying into a good family like the Burrs."

"'Tis a great day for the Burrs," answered Sam.

"I suppose, now that your Jack's Island caretaker marries, you'll look to sell that property." Elkanah smiled, something that Sam did not remember Solomon doing.

"Yes," offered Hannah, "my brother would like to buy it, just as he has bought my half of the island. My husband and I believe in ships, but Elkanah believes in land."

"Come, Sam," said Elkanah. "Unite the island once more under the Bigelow name. For a fair price."

"I have the deed right here." Sam extracted from his pocket an envelope, which he passed in front of Elkanah's nose. "My wedding gift to my brother, that he and Mary may fill the island with Hilyards. I can't think of better comeuppance for the Bigelows."

Elkanah's cloying smile faded. "You, sir, are a son of a bitch."

"And proud of it." Sam tipped his hat to Hannah and bowed to young Dorothy. "You must forgive your elders their foolishness. May your generation be not so burdened."

Dear Huoyan Jinqang,

I cannot say that it was a pleasure to see you again, for your old anger still burns. You brought comeuppance to my father and the Royal Navy. Let that be enough. You must by now have forgotten how sweet the air smells on warm June mornings, how pretty our Cape Cod daughters look in their Sunday pews. Let the past fade. Let us enjoy each other's table talk once more. Eldredge returns within a fortnight, and we would consider it an honor if you would sup with us.

Dearest Hannah,

Forgive me my ancient anger, but when I learned I could never have you, I saw no reason to curb it. As that philosopher, Captain Ourry of the *Somerset*, once said, hate keeps a man alive.

I thank you for invitation. I would gladly bank my rage to dine with you, your lovely daughter, and as honorable a man as Eldredge Dickerson. However, my new ship stands ready.

She is a Baltimore clipper with raked bow to cut the water and hermaphrodite rig for speed in the lightest wind. I've painted her hull black and given her a red dragon for a figurehead, as that is her name, *Dragon*. She is not the biggest China trader, at one hundred forty feet, but she'll be among the fastest and her tea the freshest.

I leave my brother on Jack's Island and am off. Will was never cut for the sea. He is a gentle man who can happily live the life of handlines and hoes that suits most Cape Codders. They till their corn patches when the sea is rough, they keep cattle because the marsh hay is free, and they hearken to windy ministers who promise something better beyond the bar.

I have other ambitions and will sail on, warmed by the sight of you and your beautiful daughter. For your sakes will I try to strike the word "comeuppance" from my brain.

xi.

But he could not. And a year later, with time on his hands, curiosity overcame him.

England and France were once more at each other's throats, this time attempting to garrotte each other with naval blockades. Napoleon had decreed the British Isles off limits to neutral shipping. The British had decreed all ports from the Elbe to Brest interdicted. So ships were forever liable to seizure by someone.

To protect American sailors and vessels, Thomas Jefferson declared an Embargo Act prohibiting all but coastwise trade. New Englanders likened this to an eagle playing at ostrich. Shipmasters hurried to clear before the navy closed their ports, and those caught at sea made for European cities rather than sail home to unload their cargoes and step down their masts.

Sam cleared for England. He felt no loyalty to the English, but his experiences during the Reign of Terror had left him suspicious of the French. And he had taken more than his ounce of flesh for what the Royal Navy had done to his father. Now he rather liked the English, especially the young women with whom he strolled arm in arm along the Thames. Delivering comeuppance, he decided, could clear the mind.

So, while waiting to reach agreement with an English trading house for a tea run, he dredged up a name from the past, a name given him by Dr. William Thayer, and sent a letter to Squire Bellamy of Hertfordshire. Much to his surprise, the squire invited him for a weekend.

The journey to Bellamy's home took the better part of a day, north out of the teeming, twisted streets of London, past the factories and foundries where this latest war would ultimately be won, and into the farmlands of Hertfordshire. On distant hilltops, sheep grazed and horses gamboled and hired men earned their pay. Across the fields, a dozen riders in red coats rode after their hounds. The sun was bright, the breeze fresh and fair. English life unfolded according to a master plan that ordered the world in neat concentric circles, radiating from the miseries of London to the serenity of Hertfordshire, and within these circles were smaller circles that organized the shires around seats of privilege and power like Moseby Hall.

These circles were made literal in the yew hedges that surrounded the house like a fortress. Moseby Hall looked to be over two centuries old, a grand structure of oak, stucco, and slate, and though Sam was not one to be impressed by such things, he concluded that if there was a God, he must truly be an Englishman.

He was assisted from the carriage by a liveried footman. At the door, a servant took his hat and cape. A butler in white wig led him into the library and announced, to the man at the fire, "Mr. Samuel Hilyard."

A gentleman, Sam concluded, as comfortable in London clubs as in the fields of Hertfordshire.

"Welcome, Mr. Hilyard." He extended his hand. "I've always hoped to meet my American cousin."

Sam felt the dragons jump across his waistcoat.

Squire John Bellamy was about Sam's age, but there the resemblance ended. He was taller and more slender, hair light brown and very short, except on top. His clothes were cut in the latest fashion, his pantaloons reaching his ankles, his waistcoat straight around the bottom, the collar of his cutaway fitted to his neck. His features were smoothed into a mask of complete calm, yet his eye betrayed the pleasure he took in shocking his guest.

"Cousin?" said Sam when he was able to speak.

Bellamy poured two sherries and raised his glass to the portrait above the fireplace. "My grandfather and your great-uncle, Lemuel Bellamy."

"Sam Bellamy's brother?"

The Englishman shook his head. "An adopted name. He was once known as Solemnity Hilyard."

Sam threw down the sherry and stepped closer to the portrait. The plate read, "Lemuel Bellamy, 1697–1775, by Sir Joshua Reynolds." A bewigged English gentleman, dressed in silk finery, reclined against a hunt board in some half-world, neither indoors nor out. On one side were bookshelves, on the other, bright sunlight, blowing clouds, waving palm fronds. Two beagles slept peacefully at his feet, and there was . . . serenity in his gaze, yes, and in the pursed lips, the sure sign of bad teeth and the only resemblance to Serenity Hilyard.

"A tormented man," said Bellamy.

"The teeth?"

"The life." And over a meal of pheasant and sweetbreads, the squire told the story.

Lemuel Bellamy, born Solemnity Hilyard, had appeared in the West Indies some time in the 1720s, in the company of his wife Samantha. To anyone who would listen, he announced he had come to build his fortune. Then he bought a small piece of land and began to grow sugarcane. He worked hard, and Samantha worked with him, but she was not made for the steamy climate and soon took to her hut.

In those first years, Lem built nothing but debt and one day went to a Kingston bookseller to ask what a ship's log would fetch, if the ship had brought the first Separatists to Massachusetts. Inquiries were made, and a widow of considerable means and not inconsiderable charm named Patience Moseby Moore expressed interest, as some in her family had been Separatist. She invited the Bellamys to tea, though Lemuel came alone. His wife, he said, was ill. In truth, she was drunk.

What went on between Lemuel and the widow, many guessed at. There was no doubt that they examined the log together. There was talk that they examined each other. And there was further talk that Lem Bellamy was buying rum every day at the local tavern to poison his wife. His motive could not be proved, but a year later Samantha died, nothing more than a skeleton in rum blossoms.

If Lemuel mourned the death of Samantha, he did it privately. After an acceptable time, he married Patience Moseby Moore and became lord of her plantation. Then he was able to secure credit to buy more acreage and more slaves. He bought only the best specimens and treated them with kindness, because even a little kindness would win the loyalty of such terrified creatures.

But early on, he learned that kindness was not enough. Such terrified creatures were also the strongest of the strong. When slave traders raided an African village, they took only the strongest young men and women. Only the strongest of *them* survived the trek from the interior to the coast. Only the strongest of *them* survived the five-week voyage in the fetid, shit-stunk tween-decks of the slave ship. Only the strongest and most wilfull of all lived long enough to reach the block. And for them, terror could turn easily to fury.

After one fine auction, Lem brought his new bucks back to the plantation and, according to his tradition, ordered that a pig be roasted to welcome them. While the meat turned on the spit, Lem went among them to hand out ragged clothes and deliver his message: God loved them, and their master was God's spokesman on earth.

In the midst of this sermonizing, one of Bellamy's new possessions flew at him. But Lem was ready. He had been watching this one because he was big and spirited, just the sort to cause trouble. Before the buck had moved three steps, Lem drew a pistol and shot him. Then he finished the sermon and left his slaves to their pig, though there were few appetites among them that night.

From that time forth, Lem conducted his welcomings as before, with one change. Soon after new slaves arrived, he would find one who had transgressed some rule, real or imaginary, and shoot him dead.

The other planters admired this, though they questioned the expense of killing a prime buck when a good flogging might do as much. Lem answered that one dead kept the rest docile, so that he could bring them to Christ while they brought riches to him.

He built a fortune on the backs of those dead Africans and, later, on the thousands who crossed the Atlantic in Bellamy ships and rendered two hundred percent profit on the block. Finally, after thirteen years, he crossed the Atlantic himself. Patience Moseby Moore Bellamy, mother of Lemuel's three sons, had inherited Moseby Hall, and the new squire grew quickly in the esteem of Hertfordshire. He helped the poor and paid a good wage to his hirelings. He attended the Church of England. He rode to hounds and was received at court.

No one questioned the black sweat he had used to build his sweet fortune. After all, London chartered many companies to deal in Negro flesh. And Lemuel Bellamy was a learned man. He had even taken to collecting ancient books for his library. What slave would not be the better for having known him?

Lem thought, on occasion, of his sister, but he had come so far from her world and betrayed it in so many ways that he never considered returning. As for the Bigelows, what would victory over a handful of backwater aristocrats be worth, considering all that he had since achieved? Revealing himself to any of them, he concluded, could only endanger his standing in Hertfordshire.

So he lived his long and prosperous life and at the end had his comeuppance. His wife died before him, then his first son, killed in the siege of Quebec, and his second son, lost on a voyage out to India. His third son, the ne'er-do-well who once enlisted the care of Dr. William Thayer, stood as his only heir. This prospect sent Lem to his deathbed.

In his final days, he had the bed put by the window. Though the night air was known to be unhealthful, he wanted to watch the stars turn out in a moonless sky, to feel their cold gaze and wonder once more. What could God care of the earth in the majesty of the universe? What did he care for the devotion of the colony of Massachusetts in the black enormity of the American continent? Had he cared that a minister chose love over holy loneliness? That he deserted one love for a richer one? In a universe so vast, what had the death of a few niggers mattered? And would the death of an unfrocked Cape Cod minister matter more?

"My grandfather asked astute questions."

"For which there may be no answers," said Sam.

"You are not a God-fearing man, then?"

"It's been said of me."

"Nor am I, I must admit. But my grandfather feared a great deal, which spoiled his enjoyment of all that his sins had gained for him."

They had returned to the library for cigars and brandy. Sam sank into a leather chair and inhaled the smooth tobacco. The food and drink, the newfound consanguinity, and the story of Solemnity Hilyard had nearly distracted him from why he had come. "You could not have been more than five or six when your grandfather died. Where would you learn of slaves and Separatist manuscripts?"

"A book." Bellamy took the cigar from his mouth and studied the tip. "An even burn shows good tobacco. Bellamy tobacco, grown on a Bellamy plantation."

"A fine smoke," said Sam, believing that he and not Bellamy was leading this conversation. "But this book, and the Separatist manuscript—"

"They are stored together." Bellamy went to a shelf and took down a metal box that sat among the red and brown leather backs of his books.

Sam looked at the dragons on his belly, to be sure that they were not jumping.

In the upper corner of the box was a foundry stamp: TW. Inside was a thin brown notebook on which the name Lemuel Bellamy had been written in several scripts, as though the writer were testing a signature and, perhaps, an identity. Bellamy took it out and flipped through the pages of tiny handwriting.

"This was my grandfather's diary. He wrote in the hope of moving his sins from his soul to the paper. He wanted his descendants to learn that riches are not the end in life. It's a hollow lesson, though he considered it valuable enough to store next to this." John Bellamy lifted the other book from the box.

When Sam held it in his hands, he felt no surge of energy. No grand thoughts filled his head. Yet this book might have changed lives . . . and might yet.

"My grandfather deemed this the most valuable book in his possession. I can't fathom why he would consider the ramblings of some ordinary sea captain, observing the activities of an ill-planned colony, to be more valuable than a Shakespeare Folio." Bellamy puffed his cigar and studied Sam. "Perhaps because it brought him to Patience Moseby."

Sam wiped his hands on his breeches and opened the book. " 'July 15, 1620. At berth in Thames. This day have been en . . . engaged by agents of the London Adventurers, Mr. Thomas Weston, prop., to bring a company of colonists to the northern reaches of Virginia.' " Sam looked at his cousin. "This is the beginning of America."

"Want it?"

"You'd give me this?"

"For a price." Bellamy stood. "There's a fine reading lamp in your chamber. Tell me in the morning."

xii.

Sam read the night through—of the sixty-six-day voyage, the arrival off Truro, the first encounter, the first winter—and he searched for comeuppance. Was it to be found in the intimations surrounding Dorothy Bradford's death? But such things would be meaningless today. Otherwise, the Bigelows came out quite well.

His own ancestor seemed the far greater troublemaker. In that respect, nothing had changed. The Bigelows stood for orthodoxy; the Hilyards were still casting about for . . . something.

Nevertheless, Sam wanted this log. He wanted it because of

what it represented and what it might be worth . . . and what it still might do to the Bigelows.

The next morning, on their way to the stables, John Bellamy repeated his question to Sam.

"What is the price?" Sam asked.

"A voyage."

"To where?"

"Africa might be nice." Bellamy said it as though it had come into his head while he was buttoning his red riding jacket. "Yes. Africa, for a small cargo, then on to our plantations in the West Indies."

Sam followed him into the stable, which was larger than most Cape Cod churches, and redolent of nothing worse than leather and horse liniment. The stablemen stopped their work and pulled politely at their forelocks.

"Mornin', squire," said the foreman, a semi-toothed brute called Runkle.

"Say hello to Sam Hilyard. He's about to guarantee the wages of all the men in this room."

Runkle executed a courtly bow that should have seemed ridiculous, if not for the sense of threat that accompanied it. Then he turned to the others and called three cheers for Sam Hilyard.

"Listen, John," Sam whispered, "I've agreed to noth—"

"Come, Sam, these men have children, families all."

"That has—"

"They've heard what service you will perform."

"Indeed we 'as, sir," said Runkle, scraping and bowing once more. "And we'll not forget you for it."

Before Sam could say more, Bellamy was mounting his horse and galloping off. Sam had no choice but to go bouncing after him on the fractious gray mare that Runkle seemed to have saddled just for the occasion.

Though the wind was willful and the sea had a mind of its own, there was never a horse yet that Sam Hilyard preferred to the deck of a ship. Riding was pure misery under the best of circumstances, for he never knew when to put his ass in the saddle and when to lift it out, and this bone-crushing gallop took them from one end of the estate to the other, through streams and over fences and at last to the highest hill in the shire.

Bellamy dismounted and looked down at the cloud of verdure and gray mist below. "Isn't it beautiful?"

Sam slid from the saddle and stood on legs that felt like pieces of twisted line. "This isn't how I do business."

"This is not business. I offer you a chronicle of your familial history, your national history. In return, you help me to preserve all of this. Do *not* call it business."

"You planned this all, didn't you?"

"Your fame precedes you."

"And Africa?" said Sam. "There can be only one purpose in an African journey."

"What you see below you did not come about by accident. It was built on the backs of the peasants it now supports. It is supported by Bellamy sugar and tobacco, which in turn are supported by Bellamy slaves."

Sam went back to his horse. "Won't do it."

"Why?"

"Principles."

"Principles?" The word and accompanying laughter rolled back to Sam from thirty years before.

"Principles." Sam lifted a foot to the stirrup.

"Your backers are New England merchants, are they not? Of Boston, Salem, Newport?"

"Of course."

"And they invest in other ships?"

"If they invest in my ship, they have profits to invest in other ships."

"Which profits many have invested in New England's own triangle trade—molasses to rum to slaves, I believe."

Sam tried, with some pain, to swing his other leg over the rear of the horse. "I am no slaver."

"You trade with China, and on your voyages, you often put in at Turkey. Turkish opium for Chinese tea. Enslavement for a nation."

"I'm a shipper." Sam settled onto the horse. "I deliver cargoes. It's for others to use them."

"On the one hand you beg principle. On the other you decree that there is no morality in what goes in the hold. Which do you believe, Sam?"

"You're a clever man, John Bellamy."

"I am a desperate man, Sam, as yourself."

"I am *not* desperate."

Bellamy grabbed the bridle of Sam's horse. "I am desperate because my father drank most of *his* father's fortune. I have sustained my family's holdings through the slave trade. Now the British lion grows scruples beneath its tail and outlaws the trade, as you Americans have. That makes the sailing more dangerous . . . and immeasurably more profitable."

Sam tried to pull the horse away, but the animal heeded its master.

"*You* are desperate, Sam, because if you go home, you can't ship until Jefferson lifts his embargo. London merchants know this, and they'll cut your share on any tea run you make."

"Where have you heard that?"

"You're a man without a flag, Sam. Such men are used." He put his hand on Sam's thigh and gripped it hard. "But flesh and blood pass over national boundaries. They cast aside worn principles. I offer you something of immense value in exchange for—"

"A piece of my soul?"

Bellamy relaxed his grip. "You said you were not a God-fearing man."

"I'm not."

"Then why speak of your soul?"

Sam reined the horse around and rode down the hill. But he did not go far, because Bellamy was right. He could not claim principle. He could not worry for a soul besmirched already by countless sins. He stopped and turned. "Why not sell the log instead of the slaves?"

"Because you want the log more than any London bookseller will. It is why you came here. The log will profit me only once. A good slave will breed for generations."

Sam had once dreamed of owning all of Jack's Island. With the log, he might yet. Comeuppance was good for the soul, likewise the profit that this book might bring. But he lived now for challenge, for the danger of the Barbary Coast or the Horn, for the intrigue of bargaining in Canton or Constantinople. Hard Sam Hilyard, they called him, Determined Fury, afraid of nothing. He had no wife or children that he knew of. His voyages would be his legacy, and what braver voyage could there be than to run the blockades of the African and American coasts?

Besides, men had been slaving since the beginning of time. Slavery was a pillar of the American economy, north *and* south. If there was a God, how could he have let slavery go on for so long, unless he approved?

Sam looked out on all that slavery had preserved. It was beautiful beyond words, and he made his choice. "I'll not sail without the book."

"You shall have it. But fail, and I shall send agents to retrieve it."

. . .
xiii.

What struck most was the stench. A week out of Africa, and his beautiful *Dragon* stunk the stink of death, of living death, of puke and shit and piss, of bodies that died during the night and released their contents and began to rot before dawn, a stink that could not be washed away by buckets of salt water or blown away if all hatches were thrown open or prayed away by all the souls in Christendom.

The *Dragon* carried four hundred naked Africans, chained three apiece, hands and feet, without regard to sex or age. Fifty of them were on deck now, exercising their limbs so that they would not shrivel, then partaking of horsebeans cooked to mush. Some ate; some refused any food or water whatever.

"It's all right, Cap," said Mr. Milt, an Africa hand who had been slaving on Bellamy ships for thirty years. "Them what don't eat, 'less they're prime, we lets 'em die. The prime ones we chains down and opens their mouths, and if they don't eat, they gets a burnin' coal to suck on."

Sam kept his eyes straight ahead. He did not look at Milt, because Milt had only one expression, the smile of a man who had just worked his way through a brothel. Sam could not reconcile this to the work Milt did, nor could he reconcile the beauty of the *Dragon* to the three slave decks that Milt had built into her. Yet, in the overhaul of the ship and the handling of the slaves, Sam had deferred to Morley Milt, because Milt, in his way, separated Sam from the horror, as if Milt were the supercargo and Sam merely the hired shipper.

And while the living ate, the dead rose. Each morning the crew passed a rope basket to the tween-decks, and the strongest of the blacks would load in those who had died in the night. Sons piled fathers, while mothers, with what tenderness they had left, piled their babies. Then the bodies would rise from below, but to no resurrection. Without so much as the doffing of a seaman's cap, the filth-covered black flesh was sent over the side.

Then came a sound that Sam could never ignore, the splashing and snapping frenzy of the sharks. They followed the ship day and night, as if they knew how well they would feed, and the *Dragon* left a wake of shark fins and blood all the way across the Atlantic.

"You'll get used to it, Cap," said Milt. "We be in the middle passage now, when most of the dyin' gets done. The first week out, they stays pretty strong. The last week out, only the strongest is left. It's these five weeks in between when we does the best service by weedin' out the weak ones."

Sam looked down into the boil of legs and arms and flashing jaws at the stern. Inexplicably, a face turned toward him. It was a little girl. Her eyes were open, and she seemed to look right at him, right through him. Then she was pulled into the blood.

A voice whispered in Sam's ear, "You'll get used to it, Cap."

It was Kwennit, and he was wearing a headband. In the twenty years he had been Sam Hilyard's mate, never once had he worn a piece of Indian clothing, beyond the whales'-tooth necklace Ned Hilyard had given him when he went off to join the Continental Army.

"Where did you find that?"

"I made it from the loincloth of a dead nigger."

Sam clamped his hands behind his back. "Stand your men ready for the starboard tack."

"All of this for a book, Sam? About the first white men in America? I seen the book in your cabin, Sam. I read what I could of it. They robbed Indian graves, but they called the Indians savages."

Sam glanced around the deck at Milt and his crew of slaving veterans. They were all watching him. And so was the cargo. Sam could not let this go on or he would lose all respect, and a captain who lost respect might just as well go over the side with the dead niggers.

"Stand down, Charlie," he said softly.

Kwennit did not move. His eyes were as piercing as the little black girl's.

"Stand down before we face mutiny."

"We're all dead men, Sam. All dead."

"Stand down, damn you."

Kwennit turned abruptly. "Mr. Burt, prepare for starboard tack."

"Starboard tack to Boston and back. When they go to face God, even white men are black."

"Tell him to quit 'is pomes," cried Milt. "They upset me men."

Burt's voice echoed down the deck. "I upset his men. I make 'em sad. But they steal frightened niggers, so it's too damn bad."

And the August sun beat down, and the *Dragon* beat to windward, and the weak ones died.

A fortnight into the voyage, Kwennit went to Sam's cabin again. This time, he read the journal of Solemnity Hilyard, which Squire Bellamy had not bothered to remove. It told of killing slaves simply to strike fear. The next day, Kwennit went shirtless on deck, his chest and arms covered with grease to deflect the sun.

"Kwennit takes off his shirt and puts on his paint, and maybe it's him who'll end up a saint," said Barmy Burt.

And August beat into September, and the sun beat down, and black flesh fed the sharks. Burt grew barmier each day and made up a new poem for every order. Mr. Milt continued to smile and finger his whip. Kwennit put on breechclout and feathers.

Sam Hilyard studied the trim of the sails and the run of the swell and tried not to think about his cargo. Each night, he wrote in his own log, which then he placed in the box with the foundry stamp. If something happened, he would save the box before anything.

He had gambled that once he evaded the British patrols on the African coast, he would face little difficulty in running into the West Indies. Most British ships were blockading Napoleon, while the tiny American Navy was overtaxed simply keeping American vessels bottled up in American ports.

He was right about the navies. But he had also gambled on the weather, and here his hand was not so steady. It was autumn, the time of the hurricanes that swirled off the Brazilian coast, beat northward until they slammed into the Indies, then spun on to havoc Florida and the Carolinas. He could not outrun the hurricanes.

The *Dragon* was no more than two days from the West Indies when the pressure began to fall in the glass.

"Kautantowit's mad." Charlie Kwennit had now painted his face black, as his ancestors did when they went into battle.

"Kautantowit?"

"He's mad about the niggers, and he been mad a long time. About Witawawmut and King Philip and Mashpee Indians who came home from the rebellion and found white overseers running their town. He's madder now than ever. If you don't throw over that book and cut loose the niggers, we're all dead men."

"Put on your pants," said Sam.

The following day, the wind faded entirely. The sea grew silent. The air became still. The sky went a strange yellow-gray. Even the creatures in the hold seemed to sense something terrible in the air, and their wailing, once as constant as the wind, ceased as completely.

"Mr. Kwennit, lower 'maphrodites and tops'ls."

"Lower?" cried Milt. "You should be wettin' 'em down and kedgin' out ahead. Anything to catch a wind."

"Tend to your cargo, Mr. Milt. I'll tend to the ship."

"Sails are in, Captain," cried Kwennit, who played the perfect mate, though he now looked like one of the slaves.

"We'll scud with spanker and jib."

"Shall I loose the niggers?"

"Loose the niggers?" screamed Milt.

"No!" answered Sam Hilyard.

And the rain began to fall. And the sea rolled into swells that grew into great black mountains. And the wind began to roar, loud and louder, until neither the renewed screaming of the slaves nor the praying of the crew could be heard above it.

Sam stood at the stern, the dragons on his waistcoat soaked to his skin, Barmy Burt lashed to the wheel beside him.

"The pumps!" Kwennit came sliding aft. "They can't keep up, Sam."

"Keep pumping!" screamed the captain.

"Loose the niggers!" cried Kwennit through cupped hands. "Throw over the book! Or we're all dead men!"

"Loose the niggers! Throw over the book! Or it's sure that in hell we all three will cook!" Burt began to laugh.

Sam had not heard the madman's cackle since the *Somerset*. It chilled him colder than the scream of the storm.

"I been chained in the cable tier, and so has you, and your old dad, Ned . . . but he knew what to do."

"What?" Sam turned on Burt with sudden fury. "What did he do?"

"He held to his principles, but you, you ain't got any."

"Loose the niggers!" screamed Kwennit again.

"Loose the niggers?" Milt was running down the deck, unfurling his whip as he came. "Loose the niggers?" He raised his whip, and the tip blew back like a piece of loose line. As he turned to see where it went, Kwennit drove his knife into Milt's belly and opened him all the way to the throat, spilling blood and intestines like stew onto the deck.

Then Kwennit cut Burt free from the wheel, which spun wildly with the running ship and swung the stern away from the wind. "Loose the niggers, Burt!"

"No! Not the niggers!" Sam grabbed for the wheel, and the spinning spokes nearly threw him over.

"Loose the niggers." Kwennit gave Burt the keys from Milt's belt. "I'll get the book."

"No!" screamed Sam. "Not the book."

Kwennit kicked open the companionway and went below while Barmy Burt went laughing toward the forward hatch. And Sam could follow neither of them, for if he let go of the wheel, his ship would swing broadside and be gone.

One of Milt's men came out of the forecastle and skulled Barmy Burt with a belaying pin. Burt fell to the deck, grabbed a halyard, and pulled himself up, only to be smashed again.

Sam found line to lash the wheel and lurched toward Burt. Then he thought of the book. Kwennit would throw it over the side, a sacrifice to the Indian God, but the wind would not stop, nor the waters part, and the book would be lost forever.

Through the sheeting black rain, Burt and the sailor suddenly seemed to Sam like mockingbirds fighting for a branch. But the book . . . the book was alive, for what it was worth, for what it meant, for what it had cost. So Sam left Burt fighting for his life and stumbled to his cabin.

The sailor hit Burt again and again with the pin. But Burt clutched his halyard and laughed like a madman. With each blow, the laugh grew louder, the eyes opened wider, and the sailor struck harder, as though shocked that this crazy old man could stand the beating. But Burt stood it until a black sea boiled up and carried the sailor over the side.

Then he let go of his line and unlocked the hatch. His last act was to drop the keys into the hold, freeing black men chained as he once had been. Then he disappeared in another wave of blackness.

From blackness into blackness men went. From the blackness of his cabin, Sam emerged to the living blackness of the storm. In his arm, he clutched the box. Its corner was covered with blood and hair, and his hands were covered with lampblack from Charlie Kwennit's face.

And now black men were rising from the belowdecks blackness to the blackness of the storm. They must have thought they had reached the bottom rung of hell, where torment was not steady and predictable, but an insatiable, roaring monster. The first few to emerge were washed overboard, chained and squealing like pigs.

Two of Milt's sailors tried to drive the others back with whips and pistols. But the blacks were swarming now, screaming their rage at the white faces and the black storm. They swept their chains down the deck and sent slavers over the side. They wound their chains around the chests of their tormentors and crushed them to death.

And now they were coming after Sam, like black ghosts, their chains clanking above the wind, their eyes flashing with the fury of God. He clutched the book tighter, as if it could protect him and his beloved *Dragon*.

But the *Dragon* was doomed. Her open hatches were filling. She was going over with the next sea, or one after that. The captain was supposed to be the last man to leave the ship. But these were not men. This was cargo. And the sailors cowering in the forecastle, Milt's men, they were not friends. Sam's friends were dead. Now only the book mattered.

He threw himself into the lifeboat, and as another sea washed over the deck, he deserted the *Dragon*, just as he had deserted everything else.

.

CHAPTER 25

July 14

Dead Letters and Greenheads

"This letter was written in 1809. It seems that Sam had disappeared," said Janice.

"She never stopped worrying about him," said Janice's grandmother.

" 'Dear Sam, I send this to your last London address, though I have no hope of its reaching you, as you have responded to none of my letters the last two years. If you still read missives from home, hear this: Everything has a cost, and yours grows higher by the day. Do your shipping profits cost you your country? Does your search for comeuppance cost you your happiness? I will continue to write, but only you can make your hard decisions. Hear the words of one who was an exile: come home to your country.'

"At the bottom, it says, 'Never Sent.' "

"Have these helped you?" asked Agnes.

"They've given me an idea." Janice looked at her watch. "Could I come back and read the rest tonight?"

"Take them, if you want."

"I'd rather leave them here . . . and the kids, too."

"Janice—"

That *tone*. Janice headed quickly for the door when she heard it. There were two reasons why her grandmother had aged so well:

she did not marry Rake Hilyard when she had the chance, and she brooked no nonsense. That tone said she smelled nonsense.

ii.

Geoff now had the list in his head, and Old Comers was the place to test it.

Carolyn Hallissey said she would talk if he joined her on a boat ride down to Chatham, to inspect the last topsail schooner on the East Coast. "If we buy it and anchor it in our pond, maybe Old Comers can nail down the *Whydah* collection."

Why not? Her name was on the list, she knew something, he liked her. But he hadn't expected that they would go alone, or that she would be wearing nothing more than a wraparound skirt over a two-piece bathing suit.

She guided her shallow-draft Novie across the salt pond, through the little channel called the Portanimicut River, and into the calm expanse of Pleasant Bay. The water was warm and shallow here, dotted with islands and limned with salt marshes that looked, in the bright sun, like the land's living aura.

"The Monomoyick Indians lived here," said Carolyn. "And they lived very well on the oysters and scallops. Have you ever seen an Indian shell midden?"

"A few small ones."

She glanced at her watch. "We have time, and I know a good one nearby. Want to see it?"

Of course. Anything to gain a little more of her trust.

She took a channel behind a deserted island and ran the boat up to a beach on the extreme northeast shore. It was so quiet he could hear the Atlantic, wearing itself against the other side of the barrier beach, half a mile away.

"We'll have to wade in."

Geoff threw over the anchor and took off his shoes.

Carolyn undid the skirt. Geoff tried not to do a double take. And of course, she was very cool. She said she did this for all her friends. She put on a black baseball cap, smoothed some sunscreen onto her arms, and stepped into the water.

He reminded himself of a few things as he followed: if he thought

Rake was killed because of the log, he should not trust her. It was just as likely that he was killed because of Jack's Island. But the log and the island were linked. And she wanted the log as much as he did. None of this, however, kept him from admiring the high-cut thighs of that bathing suit.

A thirty-foot embankment, covered with trees and brush, rose from the beach. Until you got close, you couldn't tell that part of the embankment was composed entirely of shells.

It looked as if someone had backed a truck to the edge and dumped shells from every restaurant on the Cape—clams, quahaugs, scallops, oysters—then planted a few trees in the middle of the mess to cover it up. But *this* dump had been open before the Pilgrims sailed.

"The Indians would have had their village up above." She poked into the midden with a stick. "They probably lived there for generations, growing corn, hunting deer, harvesting shellfish."

What revels this hillside had seen, he thought. What feasts of corn and scallops, what peaceful days beneath a canopy of blue. What a setup—the boat, the solitude, the shell midden, the bathing suit. Stay cynical or you could get into trouble.

But he liked her. He could not deny that, and she seemed to be working toward the same end as he was, even here. She said the shell midden could give him a sense of perspective about his work. And in a way that was all he was looking for. Architects dreamed grand dreams, but whole cultures came and went without leaving anything more than a pile of shells.

What happened next might have been planned. But it took a small and random series of events to set it in motion.

Somebody, someplace in the bay, had thrown a beer bottle over the side of a boat. The bottle was carried by the tide to this beach. A little boy looking for arrowheads broke the bottle in the thoughtless way that little boys do such things. The glass worked itself into the sand. Carolyn stepped on it, and it sliced into her foot.

Time to be cool. He put an arm under her shoulders and helped her to the boat. She sat on a bow seat. He perched on the gunwale, her foot on his thigh.

Seawater. Best thing for infection. A clean bucket of seawater over the foot, towel it dry, two butterfly bandages to hold it together. "And next time, wear your shoes." Very *cool*.

"You have gentle hands."

Here the cool began to melt. He could not resist sliding his fingers up to the little gold chain around her ankle.

He was new to this—whatever *this* was—and he couldn't tell from the look on her face if she was encouraging him or just counting style points. But she was in no hurry to move her foot.

Setup. This is a setup. She wants something.

But the flesh was weaker than he thought. He brushed his thumb across the pads of her toes. Her expression did not change, so he did it again. The toes were soft, the nails painted a subtle pink.

An outboard puttered in a distant channel, two terns squawked over the barrier beach, the tide lapped against the side of the hull . . . and the whole bay, for a moment, seemed to pivot around his thumb and the tips of her toes.

He traced a delicate line along her instep to her ankle. Still her expression did not change. Was she waiting for him to go further? Subtracting points? He let his touch travel the soft curve halfway to her knee. There he stopped.

If this was a game, she had to start playing. After a moment she slid her foot along his thigh, to the cuff of his tennis shorts.

Setup. This is a . . . the little voice in the back of his head faded like a Boston television signal. He leaned forward to kiss her.

And the first greenhead found them. This is a fly that breeds in the salt marshes. It is born with an enormous green head, a taste for salty flesh, and a sting like a hot needle. Geoff felt a small tickle at his ankle, a little pain, then a shock. But these flies would have had to be carrying knives to interrupt—

Slap! Carolyn nailed one on her neck.

He pressed his lips to hers, and another little green-skulled bastard landed on his ankle. It bit just as her lips parted, and it bit . . . and bit, and the sting traveled from his ankle right up his backbone. But he kept kissing until—*slap*—she whacked at another one on the side of her neck and hit him right in the jaw, which jolted his brain back into working order.

He sank into a sitting position on the deck. "If this is a setup, next time bring some Raid."

"What?"

When he was at ease within his tennis shorts, he jumped up and started the engine. "You want as much from me as I do from you." He turned the boat back toward the Portanimicut River and the museum. "We're playing a game."

"I'm a divorced woman who hasn't been kissed in months."

"I'm a sucker for nice legs." He threw her her skirt. "And soft toes." He picked up his sweat socks and threw her those, too.

The skirt she put on. The sweat socks she tossed over the side.

"Thank God for the greenheads," he said.

"I agree." She got very businesslike again, as though covering hurt feelings.

And she was good enough at it that he felt bad. Maybe he had been too harsh with her. Maybe she really *did* like him and couldn't help herself. But remember, you're married.

She limped over and took back the wheel. "You said you had some questions."

"What do you know about a doctor from Hertfordshire?"

Her arm stiffened on the throttle and the boat jerked forward. "Who?"

"His name was Thayer, ship's doctor of the *Somerset*."

"*He* came from Hertfordshire?"

She was covering up. He could tell by the way she stared ahead with that neutral look on her face, the one she used when she turned on the tape recorder and waited for him to talk or when he touched her toes and she waited for him to touch her thigh. Go ahead, say a little more, do a little more before I reveal anything. A game.

Trade a little knowledge for a little more? "The transcript of your interview with my uncle mentions a painting called *Voyage from Hertfordshire*."

She puttered back into the pond and headed for her dock. "He showed me all his Hilyards, the Pilgrim paintings, the House on Billingsgate studies. Are you saying there's a connection?"

"Coincidence, connection . . . who knows?" He thought of another item on the list. "Considering that Tom Hilyard usually painted the Pilgrims, why would he paint something like *Voyage from Hertfordshire*?"

"Who knows? Why did he start painting the Billingsgate house? For the last years of his life, all he painted was the Billingsgate house, from every angle. He started off as a Howard Pyle rip-off, and turned into the forerunner of Edward Hopper? Why?"

Like a sphinx, he thought, a smart, beautiful sphinx. "You *started* all this with your questions, you know. Now my uncle's dead."

At that, she stopped the boat, right in the middle of Portanimicut Pond. "You were ready to climb into my bathing suit ten minutes ago. Now you're saying *what*?"

"I'm trying to find the log. So are you. As for your bathing suit, that was a setup."

She slammed the throttle forward. The boat lurched. And Geoff toppled over the side. "Swim to your car," she shouted, "and don't come around with any more questions."

iii.

When he got home to Truro, he was still wet, soaked through with a miserable mixture of pond scum, guilt, and confusion that got worse when he found a letter taped to the door.

Dear Geoff,

It was true a hundred and seventy years ago, and it's true today: there are no easy answers. Everything has a cost, and yours is getting higher by the day. Does your concern for a slash-covered island cost your professional future? My family's future? Does your treasure hunt cost your family? I've tried to help you, but you are a silly, stubborn man. Only you can make your hard decisions. So make them. Read your broadsides, see your imaginary stalkers, watch the fog turn silver and float away. But remember that winter is coming.

I don't like to do this. But there are times when a man has to be alone, hearing nothing but the sounds of his own heart and unspoken voice. And it is these isolated sounds, more than the happy din of a noisy household, that will make him understand how much he needs the gentle things, a loving woman's voice or the laughter of children.

I'll call day after tomorrow.

She didn't talk like this. But it was her handwriting. Had the guys who followed him in the boat been here? Kidnapped Janice and the kids? But why this and not some kind of threat? Or had she, by some enormous coincidence, seen him in that boat with Carolyn Hallissey? Impossible.

He picked up the phone and called her father's house.

Dickerson answered. The usual growl sounded soft and distant. "Hiya, Geoff. That bluefish was terrific. Had it—"

"Where's Janice?"

"She says she doesn't want to see you for a few days."

"Where is she?"

"I can't tell you."

"Tell me, or you'll never get my land."

"I don't know."

Geoff hung up and called their Boston home. No answer. That didn't mean they weren't there. It was eight o'clock. He could reach Boston in two hours and stop this before it did some kind of damage to the kids.

Sixty-five miles an hour all the way to Beacon Street. There was a light on. He let himself in. But the door wasn't chained from the inside. The timer had turned on the light. The refrigerator was empty. He took a leak and turned right around again.

iv.

It was midnight when he pulled up at Ma Little's tiny house on Wakeby Pond. Maybe Janice was sitting at the kitchen table, complaining to Ma and Samantha about men.

He left his car on the road and walked up the dark driveway. He guessed he looked suspicious, and somebody agreed, somebody who knew exactly where to hit the back of his neck to knock him out.

The ammonia capsule woke him up like a cigarette burning his nose hairs. He heard the good-natured laugh of Ma Little, echoing in her own kitchen.

"You shouldn't be sneakin' up on somebody's house like that, Geoff. Massy and the boys are a little jumpy."

"What are they doin'? Strippin' cars?"

"I only ever stole one car." Massy, who wore a blue bandanna around his head, took the ammonia capsule and gave it a couple of snorts. "Pretty good."

Ma slapped it out of his hand. "Somebody been snoopin' around. We was at dinner. The boys down at the pond seen him."

"Yeah," said Massy. "He was dressed like some kind of jogger, man. Let himself in the house. Almost got his ass shot off."

"I don't jog." Geoff rubbed his neck. "Is Janice here?"

"She left you?" asked Samantha.

"She says it's time for me to make up my mind."

"Her or the island?" Jimmy was wearing pajamas and a monogrammed robe, a very upper-crust Indian, his finger jammed into a copy of *Presumed Innocent.* "She knows how to reduce things to the simplest terms."

"And Bigelows know how to hit below the belt." Ma laughed. "You want us to go and occupy their real estate office till they give you your wife back? Or maybe we could occupy Jack's Island when the Conservation Commission goes there. We haven't done anything like that in years."

"Like, a demonstration?" said Massy.

Jimmy said, "Stop worryin' about demonstrations and get a job."

"Fuck you, big shot." Massy grabbed a beer from the refrigerator and stomped outside.

Ma filled the teakettle. "Sometimes I wonder how I got such a smart son with one husband and such a . . . normal one with the other."

"That's not fair, Ma," said Samantha.

Ma looked at Geoff. He realized he had stumbled into a family squabble. Ma was mad about something. "They're leavin' on Friday, goin' up to her family's house in Pride's Crossing. More comfortable in a fancy house on the North Shore than here at Ma's."

"That's not true," said Samantha.

But it was. It was a small kitchen in a small house beginning to feel smaller. The table was covered with a red-check vinyl cloth, the same one Geoff remembered from their college days. The linoleum showed wood through all the holes. A bungee cord held the refrigerator door shut. Rustic verging on poor. Jimmy had more refined tastes now. But Ma looked as if she could have gone into the woods, built herself a *wetu,* and raised a few more Wampanoag *pinses* or Harvard lawyers without a bit of help.

She put a cup of tea in front of Geoff. "Find your wife and bring her around for some smoked bluefish. The size of my house never mattered to *her.*" Ma gave a squint at her daughter-in-law. "Janice, she's good people."

Samantha pulled her robe around herself and went huffing off to the bedroom where she and Jimmy slept with their two kids. Ma and Jimmy were left glaring at each other—the old woman who hunted squirrels in the woods, just because her ancestors had done it, and the young man who was her greatest pride and damnedest disappointment.

Geoff had enough problems without sitting in the middle of this, so he drained his tea. "Janice might be good people, but she's not doing anything good for me right now."

"She's just trying to make you see the light," said Jimmy. "Your first responsibility is to your family."

Ma laughed at that, and Geoff headed for the door.

"Don't forget," called Ma. "Us Indians, we know all the enviramentalist troublemakers around here. They trot us out whenever they need to get a picture in the paper. I can get a hundred of 'em at Jack's Island day after tomorrow. Raise holy hell."

"Rake might have liked that."

"It's not worth it, Geoff," said Jimmy.

"Mother Earth gotta be worth somethin'," said Ma.

V.

Geoff worried all the way to Barnstable. It was one o'clock now. He parked on 6A and walked through the opening in the fence of Agnes Dickerson Bigelow's house. The night breeze had kicked up from the southwest. Hiram Bigelow's shingle was making such an annoying squeak it was a wonder anyone could sleep.

From the window above the shingle, Janice watched him go around to the back. He was looking for the Voyager, but he wouldn't find it unless he went to the neighbors' garage. He slumped out of the barn and gave the house another long look. And she heard Hannah's words to Sam in France: "You are a silly, stubborn man. You do not remain in France for the money, but for the principle. And principles get people killed. . . . Make sure they are worth your head." Janice glanced over her shoulder at the portrait of Hannah that hung on the landing.

Geoff was too sleepy to drive to Truro, so he made Jack's Island his refuge for the night. At the causeway, he stopped. How beautiful the marsh was, almost iridescent in the moonlight, just as it must have looked to men a century ago.

CHAPTER 26

July 1814

Huoyan Jinqang

Wisps of fog scudded past the moon like rags of raw silk. It was a full moon, what the Indians called the corn moon.

Though the man traveled most of the time by night, he had not been here in many years and was thankful for the light to guide him. At the end of the causeway, the road forked, but a path still wound through the cornfield to the house in the middle of the island. The house was not lighted, and the man hoped it was not deserted.

From the elevation of the moon he guessed the hour to be about midnight. He traveled late, but time no longer mattered, nor distance, nor the way he looked to the world. His shadow on the moon-yellowed ground was the only image he had of himself. It did not show the sunken eyes, the whitening beard, the layer of filth that clung to him like moss to a tree. It showed only his shape, a fishhook hunched over the box he held to his chest.

When he was close enough to see the dentil molding on the house, he nearly turned away. It had taken him many years to bring himself this far, yet the blackness still beckoned. It would be easy to retreat into it, as he had done so often before. He even took a step backward.

Then, from somewhere in the house, a baby cried, new life

come to brighten the blackness, and he pounded at the door. But no lights came on.

A mourning dove mourned in a scrub pine near the barn. A windmill was spinning and squeaking down by the saltworks. On the bay, a ship's bell rang out the hour. He pounded again. And he felt the gun press against his neck.

"Be gone. You and your friend both."

"I brung no friend."

"I told you last year and the year before that, my brother's dead. He ain't comin' back."

"I *am* your brother."

"Sam?"

The man turned slowly, so he would not be shot. Then he opened his ragged coat. Beneath it was a filthy vest on which two dragons spit fire across his belly.

That night Sam Hilyard saw his infant nephew Isaac asleep in a shaft of moonlight. In five years of wandering, he had seen nothing as peaceful, nothing so touched by the hand of God, nothing, anywhere, that spoke so certainly for the goodness of life.

Over cups of steaming tea, he talked. Will and Mary sat a good distance from him, perhaps because he smelled stronger than sun-baked mackerel, and most certainly because they felt they were in the presence of an apparition.

Sam Hilyard had last been seen by honest men when the *Dragon* cleared Southampton five years before. Of his own volition, he had then descended into hell.

He had prayed that the boat carrying him from his ship would become his coffin. But the swirling wind drove him into the eye of the storm, and by the time the blue sky had passed, his boat was run up on a deserted beach somewhere in the Leewards. He stayed there for many months, living on bananas and fish, before deciding to make for a larger island.

His travels took him to Jamaica, where he saw a bookseller and learned the value of his treasure. But unlike Solemnity Hilyard, he reaped no riches from the book, no earthly reward to compensate for his eternal damnation. In truth, he could not even bring himself to sell it.

He signed on with a coasting schooner, and when the work became familiar enough that his mind could once more dwell on the *Dragon,* he disappeared. He turned up in the French city of New Orleans and worked a Mississippi cargo barge, from which he disappeared six months later. In the village of Pittsburgh, he killed a man who tried to steal the box. And he disappeared again. Then from Baltimore, then Philadelphia did he disappear.

By now another war was begun with Great Britain. New England seafarers won glory for the fledgling navy, but New England politicians spoke of secession. In a newspaper, Sam saw a drawing of the king, sitting on a throne of blockaded goods, his arms outstretched to the four dithering gentlemen who represented the four seafaring states of New England.

Sam could not conceive of such an attitude among Cape Codders. But it burned there brighter than anywhere, because this new war had destroyed the commerce so painstakingly built since the Revolution. In a New York tavern, he met a Cape Codder and learned that once more, ships rotted in Cape Cod harbors while British men-of-war blockaded the coast.

"I heard things were bad, so I come back to help," he said in the scratched-over whisper of one who seldom spoke.

"You're nothin' but another mouth to feed," said Mary. "We got all we can do to keep the kids in cornmeal and clams."

"Now, now," said Will, "he's my brother. Without him, we wouldn't even own this island."

"Can he work?"

Sam looked at Mary's salted-cured face and bony body, on which nursing breasts seemed as misplaced as teats on a tree. "I can work. And I brung this." Sam slid the box across the table.

"The book?" Mary's eyes narrowed to angry slits.

"You know of it?"

Will's face matched his wife's, line for line. "Two men come lookin' for you every summer—"

"And they always ask 'bout the book. They always says they want the book back."

"Englishmen, they are. With this war, they must sneak down through Halifax."

Mary touched the box. "What's in it?"

"Comeuppance," said Sam, "for the Bigelows."

Will and Mary both sat back, as though hearing at last the blasphemy they expected from this creature.

"You won't find many who think that's a good idea," said Will. "Bigelow and Dickerson ships have kept Cape Cod goin' all durin' this war."

"Privateers," said Mary. "Without the prize money, folks in Brewster could never have paid the British."

"*Paid* 'em?" said Sam. "For what?"

"The saltworks. The British commanders said they'd destroy the saltworks of any town that didn't pay ransom. Eastham paid fifteen hundred dollars. It cost Brewster four thousand, on account of more board feet."

"We *fought* the British," muttered Sam.

"Maybe *you* had less to lose." Will wrapped his hands around his teacup. They were big, muscular hands, nicked with tiny nail cuts and splinters, the hands of a man who kept his eyes close to the job in front of him. "Countin' the Bigelow works, which we been runnin' since the Doones died, and what I built, we have sixty-one hundred feet right here on Jack's Island."

"Hilyards workin' for Bigelows. Times do change."

"Don't you come steppin' out of the past and start to criticizin' us for gettin' along in a hard world." Mary looked at Sam with a cold eye. "The Bigelows pay us good for what we do. Better than we could do by turnin' against 'em."

Sam looked at the flames on the hearth. He had once made love to a Bigelow woman before that fire. He could not fault his brother for doing business with Bigelows now. So he drew the book back and wrapped it in his ancient vest.

ii.

Word soon spread that a bearded stranger now lived in the hay crib of Will Hilyard's barn. He was seen many times that summer, lost in the work of Jack's Island. When the weeds grew up, he hoed the corn rows. When thunderclouds rose, he rushed out and closed the roofs on the salt vats. And when the tide ran out, he built a weir on the flats, so that the Hilyards would not risk British capture and impressment to catch fish.

Will told the townspeople that he had hired a new man. Mary said they had taken on another mouth to feed, but God would provide. And God did, though he did not see fit to free Sam from his guilt.

Sam told no one the nature of the *Dragon's* cargo or the bargain he had made. He had wandered thousands of miles, but his sins haunted him still, and only forty miles of the easternmost peninsula in America remained to him. Somewhere between here and Provincetown, he would have to find his peace.

But there was no peace on Cape Cod.

This latest war found only four of fourteen towns in support of the American government. On the Upper Cape, Barnstable and Sandwich could afford to defy British ships because they were protected by barrier beaches and salt marshes. Falmouth supported the government but was open to the deep water of Nantucket Sound, so her ships were seized, her buildings cannonaded, and her local militia tested by British landing parties.

On the Lower Cape, only the town of Orleans remained loyal to the United States. Wellfleet had gone so far as to instruct the Committee of Safety to negotiate with the British and "at all times to keep in as much friendship with the enemy as possible, making the Constitution and laws of the United States . . . their guide as far as they can with safety to the particularly exposed position of the town to the enemy."

Sam did not admire this attitude, but Cape Codders had learned to compromise with what surrounded them, and the Royal Navy remained a force of nature. So Cape Codders remained rebels, standing for independence, even if it was only their own.

With such political confusion a mirror of his own turmoil, Sam sought to lose himself in simple labor. His brother seemed a happy man for all the angles to his face and sharp edges to his wife. Perhaps the making of salt and the catching of fish could bring happiness to any man, though Sam thought the making of children also played a part.

And one child helped Sam. Will's daughter Ruthie, for reasons that Sam could not fathom, made herself his closest companion. She followed him everywhere, helped him with his work, sat with him in the evenings, and asked him to help her in her Bible study.

"I'm not much for the Bible," he answered, though kindly.

"We all must learn to fear God."

"Deep wisdom for an eight-year-old."

"My mother told me. She said it was something you should learn, too."

And he was learning, but not in the way that the churchgoing

Mary Burr Hilyard would recognize. God did not dwell beneath the steeple of the First Church, but on the flats that Sam and Ruthie rode over each day.

Sam had found few sights like the Brewster flats. There were many more impressive—the Whampoa Reach and the Bosporus—but nowhere had he felt so soothed. At dawn, a man looked out upon sand, six miles of sand from Quivett Creek to Rock Harbor, sand stretching two miles into the bay. By afternoon, the sand was covered complete in a deep blanket of blue. Then the sea ran out, revealing the flats to the silvering moon. More water weighing more than anything ever made by man, moving as effortlessly as the wind. He could live forever within such rhythms and come to feel part of the turning of the spheres, as natural as the tide in his failings and ambitions.

And if his ambition was to do no more than see his weir full of fish, the tide would satisfy him. Weir fishing lacked a certain nobility, to be sure, and luck played an even greater role than in most fishing pursuits, but it was also without the dangers of handlining, netting, or blockade-running. And most of all, it was simple.

A long stretch of net, suspended from twelve-foot poles, ran straight out from the beach. If the fish swam into it, they instinctively followed it toward deeper water, which led them into a wide circle of net and poles. The poles were usually no more than the trunks of sapling trees chopped down and stripped, and the net hung upon them like curtains in an unfinished room.

Upon entering this chamber, the fish would swim about until they found the opening to deeper water. Following their instinct, they would take this to the smallest part of the net, where most would remain in milling confusion and panic, until the tide ran out.

Then the net minder put on oilskins and boots waterproofed with tallow and collected the tools that he would need: a pitchfork or thin-tined manure fork to harvest the fish, a shovel to pound fresh mud into holes where the tide had loosened poles, and heavy twine, splicing awl, and sailmaker's needle to mend any net that needed attention. To these, Sam added the axe he had recently rediscovered in the barn, as it was the perfect tool to cut thrashing sand sharks out of the netting.

Then he and little Ruthie climbed onto their horsecart and went out to see what nature had provided.

Sometimes nature provided nothing. Sometimes the netting churned with bluefish, mackerel, or the king of fishes, the striped bass. Sam wondered that the First Comers had not named this place Cape Striper. No fish was more delicious or plentiful, and this day he and Ruthie harvested them with a pitchfork.

He tried not to imagine the panic of the fish as the tide receded and they swirled to escape. Hundreds of stripers lay flank to belly, like bodies stuffed belowdecks. Their gill rakes stretched out, grasping for the last drops of oxygen. Their magnificent black stripes faded in the sun. But their eyes remained like dull coins, neither accusing nor comprehending. And that was the mercy of nature.

"I hate it when they die, Uncle."

"The bass ate the squid and we eat the bass," Sam said to his niece. "One creature serves the next."

"A bit like slavery, eh, guv?"

The voice caused the hair to rise on the back of Sam's neck. If he sought to lose himself in his work, he had done it too well and had not noticed two strangers crossing the flats.

He grabbed Ruthie and put her behind him. His body and the flimsy wall of netting were their only protection. He pointed the pitchfork at the bigger man, a semi-toothed brute who smiled and bowed to the metal tines. "We're a bit late this year, what with the bloody war and all."

"What do you want?"

"Why . . . the book. What else would bring a good Englishman into this backward country every summer?"

Sam did not remember this man but sensed that he should. "I don't know what you're talkin' about."

The man's brow sloped as he laughed. "I'm Runkle, foreman of Moseby 'all, 'ere on a bit of a . . . 'oliday."

The other one cackled. He was smaller than Runkle, but no less scrofulous in filthy clothes and eye patch. From the top of his left boot protruded the haft of a knife, and in the pocket of his coat was the outline of a pistol.

"Squire Bellamy wants his book back, and 'e promised me 'arf of whatever it fetches, if I get it."

"What made him so certain that I survived?"

"The Jamaican bookseller you went to. *Your* uncle brought the book to 'is uncle eighty years ago."

And Sam was reminded of an old saying, that coincidence was God's way of preserving his anonymity. God did not want Sam to have this book. But Sam would have it, if only to control its destiny.

He gave Ruthie a reassuring little wink. She was staring at him, wide-eyed yet unable to comprehend the threat. For an instant, her face became the face of the little African girl, staring up at him from the swarming sharks.

"Step out of the weir, now, folks, and we'll go get what we come for, what's rightful our employer's."

"We'll be stayin' here."

"Squint," said Runkle, and the little one pulled the pistol from his pocket.

Sam laughed, his teeth showing white through his beard. "You tryin' to scare me with that little thing? This nor'west wind's liable to blow the ball back in your face."

"Put down the pitchfork and step out the net."

"All we need's to wait. Someone'll see us soon enough."

Runkle looked up and down the coast. "No 'ouses in sight, but for your brother's. And no one to 'ome just now."

Runkle was right about that. The family had sailed to Barnstable for provisions. If Sam called for help, his cries would be lost in the wind that boomed across the bay and blew little froths across the tide pools.

Runkle pulled out his knife and cut into a net string. "Maybe we'll take the little girl's thumb for a souvenir, if we can't get what we come for."

Ruthie clutched tighter to her uncle's leg.

"Stay away." Sam jabbed the pitchfork in the air.

Runkle cut another string, as methodically as a surgeon trimming a wound. "She's awful pretty. That thumb'll look grand on the tack room wall."

"Hurt her and get nothin'."

"I'm gettin' nothin' as it is. So I'll take a bit of somethin'." Runkle cut the net halfway to the ground.

Sam felt the little girl's arm twined around his leg. The cold wind gusted against his neck. And he studied his predicament calmly as he could.

There was Runkle to his left, Squint to his right, and the little horsecart backed up to the opening in the net between them. In the boot of the cart, he noticed his tools, among them the shovel he had brought to reset the loosened poles on the right side of the net. If one pole came down, he had told Ruthie, half the net could come down with it.

Now he prayed that it would be so. He said his Chinese name in his head, like the "amen" to his prayer: Huoyan Jinqang.

He swung the pitchfork away from Runkle and drove it, with all his strength, into the loose pole. The swiftness of his motion paralyzed the two thugs for just a moment, which was long enough. The pole came out of the mud and began to fall. Another came with it, then another, and down came a ten-foot section of netting onto Squint, whose pistol went off with an impotent little pop.

From the other side, Runkle slashed with his knife and lunged into the fortress of string. Sam, better-footed among the fish, skittered toward his cart, so Runkle turned on Ruthie, who turned to run.

Runkle's left hand grabbed her collar, his right hand swept the knife to her throat . . . and his left hand came off—clean off. His fingers were still hooked into the fabric, but his forearm was now pumping blood like bilge.

As Ruthie stumbled away, the hand fell into the dead fish. As Runkle reached out instinctively to save it, the axe struck him in the back of the neck and took off his head.

Squint screamed and flailed madly, but Sam Hilyard hacked him in half as though he were no more than a sand shark caught in the net.

Then he felt his own blood trickling into his mouth and running onto his beard. The impotent little pop of Squint's pistol had not been so impotent after all.

iii.

There were as yet no newspapers to affirm the facts and suspicions of daily life on Cape Cod. The disappearance of two drifters was nowhere officially noted, and given the present "ruinous and unhappy war," neither was it spoken of at the inns or taverns. Many years later, a dragger would pull from the sea a beheaded, dishanded skeleton, and another severed completely in half, but by then the players in the drama would be dead, save for Ruth Hilyard, who had buried the event in the depths of her mind, even as it happened.

For their news, Cape Codders relied on town criers, broadsides, and those time-honored methods of discourse, gossip and rumor. Good ministers warned against the last of these, but gossip and rumor, if nurtured long enough, sometimes grew into legend.

About a month later, a story was told of a Barnstable woman making boat trips down the bay. She was well known, the daughter of First Comers, married to a China trader turned privateer. She had traveled the world on her husband's ships and now oversaw the family investments while her husband raided British commerce. But for most of the autumn of 1814, she devoted herself to nursing a man on the dunes of Billingsgate Island.

Most people believed the man to be Sam Hilyard, since he had begun in the employ of Will Hilyard and had later taken up residence in the Billingsgate house that Ned Hilyard had built almost sixty years before. It was also rumored that the woman had once been in love with the man.

When his identity was finally revealed, heads nodded and tongues wagged, and there was talk in some parishes that Eldredge Dickerson had been cuckolded by a Hilyard. When the war ended and the fortunes of the Dickersons and Bigelows began to grow, a few of the more resentful farmers and fishermen took comfort in this. But the truth was somewhat different.

When she heard rumors of Sam's return, Hannah Bigelow Dickerson went to Jack's Island to see for herself if he was alive and if he could take the helm of a privateer. She considered *huoyan jinqang* as a fine quality in wartime as her husband's calm calculation.

But she learned from Mary and Will that he had gone to Billingsgate under rather shadowed circumstances. . . . His enemies had come back. . . . There had been a shooting. . . . Little Ruthie had been endangered. . . . Sam had left for the good of the family, in spite of his wound. . . .

"Wound?"

"He'll survive," said Will, studying his hands and cracking his knuckles. "He's tough and we'll pray a prayer for him."

"He's gone from here," said Mary harshly. "That's what matters. He's gone, and that damn book with him."

That damn book. Now Hannah had another reason to see Sam, though she did not believe what she saw.

He lay on a mold-rotted mattress in the dark of a September morning. Blood was caked in his beard, in his ear, on his pillow, and on the grotesquely swollen right side of his face. His eyes were staring at the ceiling as though it might hold the answer to some question of infinity.

"Sam?"

His eyes turned to her, sad, old man's eyes. When he recognized her, he closed them and shook his head.

"Sam?"

Painfully he managed a rasp, "Go away."

She touched his forehead. "No fever."

"Go away."

"Sam, you could die."

He closed his eyes and put his head back, as though that would be all right.

The pistol ball had struck him in the upper lip, passed through his sinuses, and come to rest near the hinge of his jaw, causing every movement of his mouth to feel like a knife stab. But the bleeding had stopped, and a clean crust had begun to grow over the surface of the wound.

"No infection," she said, touching around the edges.

"Go away. Let me die. If Ruthie don't see me again, she won't remember. . . . Let me die."

She looked around the little cottage, at the sand-filled corners and rodent droppings and the cold ashes on the grate. She built him a fire, then took to the broom.

Hannah was a woman of some standing on Cape Cod, and there were others to do physical labor for her now. But she could still work. Many Cape Codders considered it a matter of honor to work hard, others took it as a sign of virtue, and even among the rich, there were few who were fat.

Hannah swept the place clean and brought in water. She washed his bloody pillowcase and dirty clothes. She brewed tea. She ordered her servant to buy a piece of haddock at one of the other shanties on the island. From this she made a thin fish soup, which she forced him to swallow.

When she was done, he was sitting up in a shaft of sunlight. She felt enormously satisfied at the difference she had made in his little world, but he did not smile.

"Next time I'll trim your beard," she said cheerfully.

"Let me die, Hannah. That's why I came here."

She sat on the edge of the bed and looked into his eyes, searching for some reflection of the man she had once loved.

It could be said of some men that they were God-fearing, and that would tell everything . . . or stern or loving or ambitious. But Hard Sam Hilyard had never been one to label. He had been a man of enormous appetite—for everything. Her own Eldredge, at fifty-six, was no less a man than he had been twenty-five years before, steady and calm through success and tribulation. But the bright-burning passion of Sam Hilyard, which had caused her to love him and then to hate him, now seemed to have guttered at last.

"What happened, Sam?"

"I lost my bearings."

She gripped his hand in both of hers. "I'll help you to find them again."

He shook his head. "I hoped to give you comeuppance. For stickin' by your father, for marryin' Eldredge. Instead, I destroyed myself."

"Comeuppance?" she whispered. "The book of history? The book mentioned in Serenity's broadsides? Is it real?"

"The log of the *Mayflower*. The story of our ancestors. I ran slaves to get it. I killed Kwennit to keep it—"

At this, Hannah let go of his hand.

"I never meant to. We struggled, the ship lurched . . ." Every word was as great an agony to speak as to recall. "I ran. When I stopped runnin', God sent for the book, but I would not give it up even with a little girl at my side. I defied God, right there on the flats."

"Sit back, Sam. If you become agitated, you may start to bleed again."

"Whether I do or not, you have no worry from the book."

"You've destroyed it, then?"

"'Twill never be seen again."

"Miz Hannah," her servant came to the door. "British barge up Pamet way, workin' south. We'd best leave now."

Hannah touched his face. "You still have friends, Sam."

"My friends are all dead."

She did not return to Billingsgate Island for a week, as the British patrols coasted close to intimidate blockade-runners between Orleans and Sandwich. They would not detain an empty vessel for long, especially one carrying women, but the wise wife of a privateer could not endanger herself recklessly.

Though it was a bright, chilly day, she saw no smoke curling from the chimney, and the ragged curtains were pulled tight. She hiked up her skirts and ran to the house. His body lay, as it had that first day, in darkness and squalor. She gasped at the smell. She whispered his name. She cursed herself for coming too late.

Then she drew closer and saw that he was breathing. His eyes were open, still staring at the ceiling.

"Go away," he whispered. "I'm dying."

"And damn near killed me with fright in the bargain." She took a pitcher of water from the bedside and threw it in his face. "Get up!"

His eyes widened with shock, and he gave her a furious glare. "Can't you let a man die in peace?"

"You'll not die around me, nor kill me with the stench of a shitted bed." She pulled back the blankets. "Get up."

"I can't walk."

"You *won't* walk."

A doctor had told her that if the wound had not killed him by now, he would survive, though he might spend the rest of his life in misery.

"You try me, woman. I been in bed a week . . . dyin'."

She grabbed the broom and whacked his legs. "Get up!"

He rolled away and she whacked him again, across his skinny rump. "Get up. Get out of your own shit. Take your fate like a man!"

He buried his head in his hands and tried to curl into a ball. "No!"

"Yes!" Hannah was a woman who could not stand waste. And this, regardless of its history or its future, was a life wasting away. "I thank God for that day in the mill, when I saw what kind of man you are."

And she struck him again with the broom.

"Stop! My face. My teeth. They pain like knives. Stop!"

"I thank God that I never came to love you more." She hit him one more resounding thwack that knocked him over the edge of the bed and onto the floor. "I thank God."

For a time, there was silence from the space between the wall and the bed.

"Sam?" she leaned over his body and wondered if she had given him his wish.

Then he looked up, but his eyes seemed to be focused on a sound. "What do I hear?"

It was the sound that had pointed him north after the sinking of the *Somerset,* the sound that had drawn him, almost against his will, to his brother's house the night he returned to Cape Cod.

"What do I hear?"

"That's . . . your granddaughter," she whispered.

"Granddaughter?"

"Yours . . . and mine."

He raised himself to the window and peered out. Hannah's daughter was crossing the dunes with a six-month-old child in her arms.

"Your daughter brings *her* daughter to visit an old friend of her mother's. Reveal this truth to anyone, especially to them, I'll give you reason to wish you had died this week."

"My daughter and granddaughter," he whispered, staring into the bright September afternoon.

Hannah watched his shock turn to joy, then consternation. He jumped up, straightened his clothes, pulled the covers up, and wrinkled his nostrils at the stench.

"I cannot meet them like this," he said.

"No. You're right." Though she remained outwardly calm, her inner turmoil overwhelmed her. To save Sam from drowning, Hannah had sailed into the sea of her own past. She had endangered not only herself but her family as well. She decided that throwing him a rope was enough. He would have to climb it himself.

"Clean yourself and perhaps I will bring them next time." Then she hiked up her skirt and hurried out.

When she returned the following week, Sam was bathed and his beard neatly trimmed. The cottage was straightened. Tea brewed upon the hearth. But Hannah brought only a doctor from Barnstable. He gave Sam a dose of laudanum, then extracted four teeth, the roots of which had been shattered by the pistol ball.

She left him in misery, though she promised that when she returned, she would bring his daughter and grandchild at last.

By the following week, the swelling had gone down. Sam was mending net when she approached, and she felt a rush of pity at the sight of him, his face filling with anticipation, then collapsing with disappointment because she was alone once more. And this time, she did not promise that they would come. Instead, she made him promise never to try to see them.

"Let them be the ideal of your life. Remember that they exist because of you. But don't endanger their happiness to find your own."

iv.

The knowledge that he had fathered a daughter did not save Sam Hilyard from his demons. They still danced on the Billingsgate dunes and whistled in the corners of his brain. But the vision of the child, the purity of her cry echoing across the sand, had saved him from death.

There was a reason to endure, after all, if only to make amends.

He spent the autumn gaining strength. He rebuilt an old fishing boat, which he named the *Nancy*, after his granddaughter. When the British were not about, he dug quahaugs, cut them into pieces, and baited them onto a long line of hooks. Sometimes he caught cod, sometimes bass, and often nothing. But in this, he joked to himself, he was like one of the Apostles.

The fishermen no longer deserted Billingsgate as winter approached. Near the southern tip of the island there were now a dozen year-round families. A schoolhouse was planned, and there was even talk of building a lighthouse when the war ended.

But farther north, where Sam lived, the population grew sparse and the wind shaped the world. And Sam came to study all that he had taken for granted as a boy. He remembered his father making a lesson of the ospreys that nested in the old whale tower. The tower was gone, and there were no tall trees left on the Cape, so the ospreys were gone as well. But Sam found truth in the tides and the migration of the shorebirds and the browning of the dune grass that would green again in spring.

Neither wars fought with British frigates nor petty hatreds fired by ancient feuds could interrupt the orderly pattern of the natural world. Birth, death, survival, family—these were what mattered.

Each night Sam stood near the spot where his grandmother had died and gazed west toward Barnstable, home of his daughter and granddaughter and the woman he still loved. And the wind rattled the dune grass. So fragile, he thought, and yet without it, the island would blow away like a man without friends, a man without a family.

He yearned to see them. More than once he planned to go to

Barnstable as a fisherman selling his catch, simply to gaze upon them again. But the time never seemed right.

Instead, he stayed on Billingsgate and watched the war play out. The British attacked Rock Harbor and burned whatever lay at anchor. Cape Cod sailors ran the blockade in whaleboats. But Cape Cod selectmen dined on British ships, and British officers paid gold guineas for goods in friendly towns. Principles, Sam decided, were a thing of the past.

Then he found his grandmother's principles rolled into the barrel of the blunderbuss he had once hidden in the wall. And he remembered his father facing Captain Ourry on the deck of the *Somerset*. And he decided there was a principle to hold him as well.

Hannah had revealed her deepest secret to save him. It would be the noble thing to honor her wishes, to keep no more dreams of his children. They were his only in their conception, after all. He would hold to a principle and deprive himself of the greatest joy he might know. There could be no worse punishment, yet nothing more cleansing.

When word arrived that the Treaty of Ghent had been signed and the foolish war was over, Sam sent a letter to England. He did not know if he could ever exorcise his demons, but he had begun.

Squire Bellamy,

The log of the *Mayflower* is gone, as are the black children who fed sharks to pay for it and the white men you sent to find it. If you send more men to the island spoken of in the book, they will not find me. If they do find me, they will meet the strange-lettered axe spoken of in the book, as did their predecessors. You have no recourse. You are as guilty as I. My mind may brew a storm, but I will keep my world tranquil.

Yr. Obedient Srvt.
Sam Hilyard

CHAPTER 27

July 15

Board Meetings and Floorboards

Sam's letter to Bellamy won Carolyn Hallissey her job.

Now, with the snap of a manicured finger, she could convene the board of trustees—three real estate developers, two bankers, a selectman, a lawyer, a minister, and a retired teacher—for a breakfast meeting to discuss the purchase of a topsail schooner.

Once, the trustees had all been related, tweedy old Bostonians who summered on the Cape and kept their fists tightly clenched. But as times and endowments changed, so did the board. More than one seat was now held by a major contributor, like John M. Nance, who sprawled in a wing chair in Carolyn's office after the meeting.

"Hilyard and his faggot Hollywood friend went metal-detecting on Billingsgate the other day."

She laughed. "It's not there. And don't be so critical of our gay friends, John."

Her secretary David brought coffee, served it, and left.

"You mean, like him?"

"David is very efficient. He's doing a lot of good work for us. At night he goes home to Provincetown."

"Another faggot." Nance stirred his coffee. "Too bad that old Rake bastard got killed. He was the best hope to know the truth."

"Sam Hilyard said the log was gone in 1815. Maybe we should believe him."

"William Bradford's diary was gone, but somebody found *that*. Dumb luck led you to Sam Hilyard's letter. Rake thought the log was gone until you got him thinking about it." Nance took a rose from the vase on her desk and slipped it into the lapel of his white suit. The rose matched his tie. "I don't think Rake knew what was in that log. We can only speculate. But finding it could make or break the most satisfying deal of my life. I want it found."

It had not been dumb luck that drew Carolyn Hallissey to Hertfordshire a year earlier, but intelligence, planning, ambition, *then* dumb luck.

As curator of Cape Cod paintings for Old Comers Plantation, she had tapped the deep pockets of contributor Nance to bid against the Boston Museum of Fine Arts for works by Sandwich Impressionist Dodge McKnight, against the Heritage Plantation for the seascapes of Frank Vining Smith and C. D. Cahoon, against *anybody* for the work of Provincetown modernists like Robert Motherwell and Ross Moffett. And she had thrilled the art world when she found, in the attic of an old Truro house, a study of shadow and light called *Tom's Hill, Winter*, an undiscovered Edward Hopper.

But Old Comers needed a signature collection, and for that, she had chosen the eclectic and relatively inexpensive work of Tom Hilyard.

She had followed the movement of his paintings via mailing lists, call lists, and trade publications. When a British newsletter reported that the contents of the Bellamy estate in Hertfordshire were being auctioned, she recalled a Cape Cod legend that Black Bellamy was an ancestor of the Hilyards. And one of the missing Hilyard paintings was called *Voyage from Hertfordshire*. Coincidence or . . . connection?

She went to her board connection, which had been forged during job interviews, over drinks and dinner, on business trips to New York and Boston, and in a dozen hotel rooms. She had no guilt over her relationship with John M. Nance. She had been dealt enough bad luck that she took whatever good came her way, including a free trip to England.

The Bellamys, like the empire, had long passed their peak when the buyers descended on Moseby Hall. But there was little for Carolyn Hallissey to bid on. The magnificent Joshua Reynolds portrait of

Lemuel Bellamy was going to the Royal Gallery, and there were no Tom Hilyards hidden in the corners. Her voyage to Hertfordshire did not uncover the *Voyage from Hertfordshire*.

But here was where dumb luck played its role. On the day before the auction she was perusing the collection from the Bellamy library. The most valuable volumes had been sold already. All that remained was a set of common editions of Swift, Smollett, Defoe, Dickens, and Sterne.

She found Sam Hilyard's letter in a copy of *Robinson Crusoe*. Neither the letter nor the book, it seemed, had been read since 1815. She bought the set for $1,000. She knew the story of the axe, Nance's ancestors, and Jack's Island. Now a letter linked them all to a volume that any museum in the world would kill for. John M. Nance was very much interested.

A month later, she was appointed director of Old Comers Plantation, and the oral history project began. She talked first with Rake Hilyard, who told her that *Voyage to Hertfordshire* had been in his house for years.

ii.

Geoff had not slept well. In the middle of the night he had felt the ghosts ambling through the old house, Sam Hilyard and Hannah, Rake, and all the rest. Once, the wind banged the barn door open and he was certain he saw the ghost of Jack Hilyard skitter through the moonlight.

It had been the kind of night to bring out the black dogs, as he called them, thoughts of mortality that could make you question whatever you were doing at the time and that usually fetched a little religion right behind them. His had been Catholicism, learned from a mother who kept her faith though she married a lackadaisical Protestant and brought this lackadaisical half-Catholic into the world.

If he started asking hard questions, he knew he'd be up all night and useless when he went after the answers in the morning. So he contemplated the effortless majesty of whales gliding through the bay and finally slipped back to sleep.

Around eight o'clock he decided to walk down to his brother-in-law's house. Maybe Janice was there.

The bobwhites whistled in the woods along the road. The shade was cool and dense. The underbrush grew so thick around pitch pine and oak that you couldn't see more than a few feet into the woods. It was dark and primeval, seemingly indestructible, though not much more than a generation old and as fragile as . . . well, his marriage.

The road came into a meadow about a hundred yards from the L-shaped Greek Revival house the Bigelows had built in 1850. Geoff was wearing jeans so that he could slip into the brush and case the place, like some rip-off artist with a screwdriver in his pocket. But he didn't see the Now Voyager or hear his kids.

He picked a few blueberries from a bush by the road. They were fat and juicy and tasted of pine. Pick some for your cereal, grab a few blackberries. Enjoy life. But first, find your family and straighten out this mess.

Then, a stretch Cadillac about the size of a coal barge came down the west side road and pulled into Doug Bigelow's driveway. Was he so confident that he now had a chauffeur?

But it wasn't a chauffeur. It was much worse—John M. Nance, Strip-the-Plants Nance, Public Enemy Number One on the environmentalists' hit list, also on the lists of the several conservation commissions, the EPA, a few horned husbands . . . and Rake Hilyard.

Doug seemed to treat Nance like the long-lost uncle who also happened to hold the mortgage on the house. They shook hands, and Doug invited him in. But Nance wanted to go for a walk, so they went for a walk—right down the road toward Rake's house.

Geoff didn't think he'd look too good if they saw him spying from the brambles. He'd look even worse if he popped out of the woods like some tourist hunting for the beach. So he hunkered down and hoped he hadn't grown allergic to poison ivy in his old age.

". . . doesn't know what's good for him," Nance was saying.

"He seems very interested in this *Mayflower* log."

"You'd better hope he doesn't find it. If he does, he won't be a struggling architect with two mortgages, two car payments—"

"And a few pretensions."

Pretensions? Geoff almost jumped up right then. He had *principles,* not pretensions, but they were right about the rest.

"He'll have a lot of dough," Nance was saying, "and very little incentive to make the sale."

"My sister has become his incentive."

Geoff raised his head and peered past three shiny leaves. They looked like mafia dons in conference while their bodyguard idled along in the car behind them.

"She's left him," said Doug.

Nance laughed. He had never met Geoff Hilyard or his wife or kids, and he *laughed*, the bastard.

"If he can't find the log, what will he do next?"

"Protect the bones," shouted Geoff from the brush.

Nance dropped into a crouch, as though somebody was about to shoot him. "Who said that?"

Nance's driver sprang from the car, gun in hand.

"Morning, gentlemen." Geoff decided to march straight out of the brush. Act as if he owned it, because he did.

"What the hell are you doing?" demanded Doug.

Geoff ignored him and went up to Nance. "I'm thinking of an archaeological survey, to protect the bones."

Nance looked at Doug. "The brother-in-law?"

Geoff kept talking. "Did you know the best collections of Indian artifacts on Cape Cod belong to backhoe operators?"

"You're going off the edge, Geoff," said Doug.

"How many backhoes do you have, Nance?"

"None. I'm a venture capitalist."

"And my island is your latest venture?"

"*Our* island," said Doug.

Geoff slipped the rose from Nance's lapel and inhaled its aroma. Let him know he wasn't frightened by bodyguards and rich men in white suits. "I didn't think the Bigelows and Cousin Blue could develop this island by themselves, Dougie . . . but Strip-the-Plants Nance?"

Nance looked at Geoff as though he were a job seeker, not the obstacle to the job. "Only idiots call me that, people who don't know any better, like your uncle."

"Let's see . . . there's the Mount Hope Mall, built on a wetland in Rhode Island, and that monstrosity in Sandwich, right on top of the watershed—"

"All legal."

Geoff studied the sleek features and the perfect tan. Sometimes the ones at the top didn't show a trace of the struggle to get there. He decided to throw something out and see how it played. "Nance, Iron Axe, and charcoal on the floorboards."

That was the strangest entry on Rake's list, but Nance just looked at him, as though he made no sense at all. "*This* is the guy the project hinges on?"

Geoff looked around him. " 'Whose woods these are . . .' are mine. That makes me the guy."

Nance stalked to the car and opened the door. "You need an architect, Douglas. If this guy isn't interested, find someone who is. And if this guy won't sell, we'll build around him."

Geoff watched the Cadillac disappear around the bend. "Does your father know about him?"

"We need deep pockets on this one, Geoff."

"I thought your father and that guy had a grudge—"

"I'm running things now. Besides, grudges are wasteful, as wasteful as pinning your future on a myth."

"Pin it on a principle. Know the truth before you act rashly. Then you won't be acting rashly. If you talk to Janice, tell her that."

. . .
iii.

Doug talked to her in the sitting room of the Bigelow 1700 house. She was wearing a red bathing suit under a wraparound skirt. She had not slept well, but she looked composed and serene.

"It might be a good tactic to stay away from him a bit longer," said Doug.

"You may have played the breakup of your first marriage like a game, Doug, but that's because you're a man."

"Low blow."

"I think a little differently." She tucked her feet under her, though the ancient Victorian settee was not quite made for the posture. "Geoff and I, we've started seeing the world differently. I don't know how or why, but it's happened."

"He said he was doing this because of principles." Douglas laughed.

That word again. Janice looked at the letters on the table. Hannah had lectured Sam about foolish principles. Yet she had done a few foolish—and principled—things herself when she got older.

"Let him stew a while longer," said Doug. "If not for me, for Dad."

"For Dad. For the future . . . I want to look to the future, and Geoff keeps looking to the past."

Doug got up. "I'm going over to the island. We're doing wetlands prelims on Clara's land. Emily and Arnie are hot to trot."

That she did not need to hear. She sat there for a long time, looking at her purse, wondering why she didn't just get rid of that damn will. It didn't carry any legal weight, and it felt as heavy as a soapstone sink in her purse. But she couldn't do it.

iv.

On summer nights, up and down 6A, candles flickered in the windows of the inns where Yankee sea captains once lived, and where chefs now put raspberries on chicken, cooked duck in orange sauce, and did things to mussels that no self-respecting Cape Codder would do to a barnacle.

At the Bell-in-Hand you could still get a fisherman's platter—deep-fried seafood with a side of slaw for $9.95. Add to this a salad in a little wooden dish, dressing from a bottle, a big highball in one of those heavy glasses, and serve it on a paper place mat featuring a Cape Cod map. Not that the locals cared about maps. The Bell-in-Hand didn't even have windows.

There was, however, a jukebox filled with fifties rock, and somebody was spending his week's pay on Buddy Holly songs.

Geoff preferred to eat at the inns, but they were one more sign of what he called the creeping chichi of Cape Cod. They had been catering to tourists for nearly a century down here, but it had only been in the last twenty years that Off-Capers had rubbed away the character of the place, that sense of stiff-spined, chowder-eating independence that had made Rake Hilyard such a hard case right up to the night of his death.

"If I were you, I'd be looking for my wife. Not the log," said George. "I *do* have a sense of priorities. Once I found her, I'd take out that list and look for the log."

Maybe so, thought Geoff. But a bad night's sleep, the day's revelation, and three beers had left him pretty depressed. Not even "Peggy Sue" could cheer him up. That was why he had called on his friends to do the job. George was chowing on the fried clam plate, and Jimmy was on the way. "Let Janice look for me."

"She won't want to if you hang around that museum director," said George.

"The museum director is in it for herself. I wouldn't trust her any more than those guys over there."

Four big guys, in work shirts, jeans, and mortar-stained boots, were at the bar watching the ball game on television. Geoff would not have noticed them, but sitting in the middle of them was the Humpster, working a beer and a shot.

And they didn't notice Geoff until the door opened. Guys at a bar always checked out a new arrival, because it might be a pretty girl or a troublemaker or an Indian named Jimmy Little, wearing jeans, T-shirt, and a new Red Sox baseball cap. They watched Jimmy go over to Geoff's table, and someone whispered something in the Humpster's ear.

Jimmy pulled out a chair and straddled it backwards.

Geoff gave him the once-over. "I thought you wore a blue blazer after five o'clock."

And Jimmy said one word: "Nance."

Geoff nodded.

"This changes things. If Nance is in it, I might occupy that island myself."

"Was Nance one of the plaintiffs in the '77 land suit?" asked George.

"He's the guy. Dirty fighter. Tried to make the Indians look like a bunch of lazy reds, screwin' the good white developers just to get their land. All we were trying to do was save it." Jimmy raised his hand and called for a beer.

Geoff had always liked Jimmy because he was so cool, a perfect foil for George. But there was no cool tonight. The name of Nance had touched something in the old alligator brain or, more likely, in the ancient anger that most Indians carried around whether they knew it or not. "Do I smell vengeance in the wind?"

"A little vengeance is good for the soul," said Jimmy. "It gets us in touch with our roots."

"Unh, I signed on for a treasure hunt," said George. "Is this thing going to get ugly?"

"If Nance is involved, it already is ugly. But he papers over the ugliness with money." Jimmy ordered a beer. "When the Wampanoags brought the land suit, I was the young crusader, ready to get something back for all that the tribe had given up. But we weren't quite as high-powered as the other guys."

"Money won the fight," said George.

"It always does. And the idealistic young lawyer went off to Wall Street to get some money of his own."

"And Ma's still mad," said Geoff.

"More disappointed than mad." Jimmy snatched a fried clam from George's plate. "She doesn't think they care too much about Mother Earth down on Wall Street."

"Mother Earth . . ." Geoff sipped his beer. "I've always liked the way Ma talks. She's known all along what this is really about."

"She says Mother Earth is the spiritual center of everything. Indian mysticism. Simplistic, but it works." Jimmy took another clam from George's plate. "Respect Mother Earth."

"And order your own clams," said George.

Geoff drained his beer. "I guess that's what I've really been trying to do here."

"Order your own clams?" George played his role as the one who kept things light.

"Respect Mother Earth," answered Geoff. "But I've let a good commission slide, my uncle's gotten killed, my wife's walked out . . ."

"Mother Earth as bitch goddess." George looked at Jimmy. "So how is Nance's money helping the Bigelows to scar Mother Earth's face?"

"Blue Bayou" was playing now. A couple of people were singing it at a nearby table. The noise level was rising as the supper crowd came in.

Jimmy drained his beer and ordered another round. "As far as I can tell, Nance must have saved Bigelow Development from Chapter Eleven. He probably figures that the 1904 subdivision will let the Bigelows slam dunk every agency in the county, from the Cape Cod Commission on down. Any that stand in their way get hauled into court, because Nance has deep pockets. Once they get all the permits, that land will be worth a fortune."

"I'd love to see the written agreement between Nance and Bigelow," said Geoff.

"I'll go to the county registry and check the mortgage listings tomorrow," said Jimmy.

"And if you find something, where does that leave Geoff?" George fished through the bread basket for a hard roll.

"Right where he is. He can do the deal they offered and live like a king, sit back and watch the Bigelows develop from his designs in conjunction with Nance, who does quality work, the bastard."

"Especially to old men on Suicide Six."

George stuffed a breadstick into Geoff's mouth. "Don't say that too loud. The walls may have ears. They certainly have some ugly fixtures." George smiled up at the Humpster, who had pushed his way through the tables and smoke and now stood over them, all belly and beer breath.

"Blue Bayou" ended and "True Love Ways" began.

The Humpster gave that choke-a-dog grin and leaned over them. "Rub-a-dub-dub, three men in a tub, a faggot, a Mo-nig, a fool."

An old man at the next table looked up, then slid his plate of fried clams to the other side of his table. His wife twitched around to see what was going on.

"What did you call me?" said Jimmy.

"This is a family place. Let's step outside and me and the boys'll tell you there. We'll tell you all about how tough it is when there's no work because of faggots, Mo-nigs, and fools."

"Mo-nig" could light Jimmy's fuse faster than "Nance." They were outnumbered, but Geoff knew that wouldn't stop Jimmy now. "Easy," whispered Geoff.

Jimmy slipped off his chair and looked the Humpster in the eye, even though he was a head shorter.

Geoff slid to the edge of the booth and prepared to spring. He noticed George slip his knife and fork into his hands and eye the roll of truck-stop kidney fat peeking out over the back of the Humpster's belt. This wasn't going to be pretty.

But this was a family place, the town hangout, and before anything else happened, the flannel shirt of Bill Rains appeared between the Humpster and Jimmy. He smiled at both of them. There was tartar sauce in his beard. "It is not a good day to die, Jim. And, Clarence, over in the corner is off-duty Brewster police officer Bob Shine, straightest arrow between here and the Mashpee Indian Museum. If he decides to administer field sobriety tests in the parking lot, you could lose your license for a year, under Massachusetts law. You couldn't even drive a bulldozer."

The Humpster's big eyes roved around the room until he saw the cop, then he glugged the rest of his beer, almost in defiance. "Bulldozers. Yeah. We can't live without them, can we? Bulldozers comin' real soon to Jack's Island. *Brrrrrmmmmm.*" He splattered his lips together and made the sound of an engine.

The old man at the next table put his napkin over his plate like an umbrella.

"Watch out for my bulldozer." Using his beer bottle as a gear shift, the Humpster turned himself around and *brrrrrmmmm*ed all the way back to the bar, where his three pals were laughing their asses off.

When the spit-mist had cleared, the old man took the napkin from his plate and looked up at Bill Rains. "Blue Bigelow says it all the time. His kid's a stupid son of a bitch."

"Yeah," said Rains. "Too bad he's so big."

"We may cut him down to size." Geoff threw a twenty on the table. "Him and John M. Nance."

"Nance?" said Rains.

"So even the Conservation Commission doesn't know?"

"Strip-the-Plants is in on this?" said Rains.

"Go finish your clams, Bill, before they get cold," said Jimmy.

"And count on seeing us at Jack's Island the day after tomorrow," said Geoff.

"And, unh"—George put the knife and fork back on the table—"thanks. I don't know what I was going to do with these."

Buddy Holly sang "It's So Easy."

In the parking lot, Jimmy turned to his friends. "Okay, Rake may have known he was up against Nance along with the Bigelows. So he needed big medicine. So what happened three hundred and seventy years ago that matters today?"

"Whatever it was got him killed"—Geoff pulled the list from his pocket—"just when he was figuring it out."

Jimmy studied the list and scratched his head.

George begged off. "I've done my share for the night, guys. And there's a young man up in Provincetown who thinks 'Legal Eagles' is the best show on television."

"Be careful," said Jimmy.

"Don't worry, James. These days I no longer rely on the kindness of strangers."

"That's not what I mean. Don't trust *anyone* if Nance is around."

"Better yet, stick around." Geoff waved the list at him. "We could find the log if we put our heads together."

George laughed. "Heads. Yeah. One in particular that I'm thinking about."

The Humpster and his pals were coming out now. It was time to leave before any more trouble started.

George jumped into his Bronco and headed for P-town.

Jimmy drove Geoff back to Jack's Island. And as the car crossed the causeway, Geoff felt the eloquence in a few extra glasses of beer. "I guess an Indian lawyer has to be the most careful guy on the block, but you know better than anybody what this island was, what all of the Cape was."

"What?"

"Freedom. Thoreau said a man could stand here and put all of America behind him."

"He said that about the outer beach, not Brewster. This town was built by hidebound Yankee shipmasters who would have laid Georgie's backbone bare just because of who he was."

"But the island, Jimmy . . . before the shipmasters, it meant freedom, for Indians, for Quakers."

The headlights bumped along the road, skittered over the front of Rake Hilyard's house, and lanced into the back.

Jimmy said, "No place meant freedom for Indians— Hey!"

In the glare of the headlights, a man raced out the door of Rake's barn.

"Who's that?" said Jimmy.

Geoff was already out of the car, running down the shaft of headlights into the woods behind the barn. "Hey!" he called, and he ran without thinking. The darkness closed in quickly around him. He stopped and tried to listen. All he could hear was Jimmy's thrumming engine and the slop of the waves.

Then a thought cleared his brain and dropped him onto the path. He'd had an arrow shot at him. Somebody had killed Rake. Somebody could be taking aim at his white shirt right now. He waited for a time as his eyes adjusted. Then he rose to a crouch and saw a big black spot expand, right in front of him . . . but not in front of him, *inside* him. The blood and beer rushed so fast to his brain that he almost passed out.

He waited for the spot to fade. Then he heard footfalls behind him, pounding down the path from the house. Jimmy? He almost said the name. He saw a flash of nylon, a logo, a puma—then a knee struck him. His nose cracked and stars burst around it. He landed on his ass and grabbed the leg. Like steel cable. But Geoff held tight, and the man thudded onto the path, kicking cold sand into Geoff's face.

Geoff leaped at him and an elbow caught him right in the sternum. This took both his wind and his enthusiasm and the man scrambled off. A moment later Geoff heard an outboard pull away. From the sound, it was heading toward Rock Harbor. He cursed and kicked the sand. But what would he have done if the guy had had a knife?

Jimmy was at the barn door, looking very angry. "Son of a bitch blind-sided me. I haven't been blind-sided in years."

He pointed to the trapdoor in the middle of the floor. "It looks like they went through the whole house, then came out here."

Geoff aimed Rake's work light into the hole.

"What's down there?"

"Don't know." Geoff took a rusty old gaff from the wall, led with the tip, and lowered himself.

The ground crunched under his feet—mostly charcoal and shells. And the top sheet from a package of Polaroid film lay there. Somebody had taken a picture, somebody careless.

He tried to stand and banged his head on the floorboards. Charcoal . . . floorboards.

He pointed the light above him and saw strange marks, like letters, scratched into the wood. Beside them was a drawing that looked like a drinking cup. And words, very faint, almost gone: "God Bless the good Bigelows, God damn the bad and God bless our baby."

"My sentiments exactly," said Jimmy.

" 'Nance, Iron Axe, and charcoal on the floorboards.' That's it, whatever it means."

Jimmy dropped into the hole beside him. "That cup looks like the Big Dipper—the Drinkin' Gourd. That's what runaway slaves called it. Follow the lip of the Drinking Gourd to the North Star and you'll be free."

CHAPTER 28

October 1850

Follow the Drinkin' Gourd

September 18 had been a black day. Of that Nancy Drake Rains had no doubt. President Fillmore had signed the Fugitive Slave Law, thus violating a higher law that no politician could compromise.

Nancy Drake Rains: Cape Cod aristocracy of the first salt. Her husband's memorial stone stood on a plot in the Dennis cemetery, though his body lay at the bottom of a distant sea. Her father descended from James Drake, who in 1660 had bought up a thousand acres of Monomoyick land in what was to become Chatham, for a small boat and a greatcoat. Her maternal grandfather, as far as she knew, had been the famous Eldredge Dickerson. And her grandmother's name, Hannah Bigelow Dickerson, echoed back to the *Mayflower* itself.

There could be no finer pedigree for a young widow of thirty-six with two growing sons, none finer in a young nation searching for a sense of its own past, a nation that had come to define 1620 as the moment of its spiritual conception. The First Comers had always been revered in the Old Colony, but as the nineteenth century unfolded, they had grown in stature across America.

Nancy remembered the bicentenary of the Pilgrim landing and Daniel Webster, then a young man of mighty voice, proclaiming,

"Who would wish that his country's existence had otherwise begun? . . . Who would wish for other . . . ornaments of her genealogy, than to be able to say, that her first existence was with intelligence; her first breath the inspirations of liberty; her first principle the truth of divine religion?"

On that day, Webster turned a bedraggled band of religious rebels and fortune seekers into the ancestors of the American ideal, and he made Plymouth Rock the touchstone of American myth. That was good, thought Nancy later, because a nation built upon a lie needed its myths to remember its ideals.

After Webster had praised the Pilgrims, he unleashed his fury upon slavery. "I hear the sound of the hammer, I see the smoke of the furnace where the manacles and fetters are forged for human limbs. I see the visages of those, who by stealth and at midnight, labor in this work of hell, foul and dark."

Not all of America had heard the hammer or seen the smoke, however, because the wind of commerce blew a hurricane that sometimes carried conscience before it. Despite the ports into which commerce had blown her vessels and the prosperity they had brought back, the Cape where Nancy grew up had remained a close-bred place. On occasion, a pair like the Doone brothers blossomed forth. But in the main, the twining of the old names had produced a forest of families, hard-headed and Protestant to the core, whose roots held the land in place where the trees were gone. And in such earth, conscience sometimes thrived.

Many Cape shipmasters, among them Nancy's late husband, had risked lives and livelihoods to smuggle living cargo from the slave states to ports on the south side of the Cape. No manifest mentioned this cargo, because it was always hidden in steerage until a vessel was well out to sea. And no customs officer taxed it because, in Massachusetts, no price could be put upon human life.

Of course, not all Cape Codders believed that slavery was their concern, any more than their use of herring for fertilizer should be the concern of the Georgia planter. Many of the churches of the Cape—indeed, of the nation—refused to condemn a practice that brought Negroes to Christ, no matter the fashion. Some even considered the theft of a Negro a greater crime than his enslavement.

But until the Compromise of 1850, slaves were free when they reached ports like Hyannis or Harwich. They could take themselves to Mashpee and mingle with the Indians there. Or they could cross to a bay-shore town like Barnstable and continue their journey aboard a north-coasting schooner.

But, to avert civil war, Daniel Webster had acceded to Henry Clay's compromise. California would join the Union as a free state, the territories of New Mexico and Utah would decide the issue on their own, and the Fugitive Slave Law would be enacted, so that any runaway in any state could be apprehended and remanded.

In Boston, three thousand Whig merchants signed pledges of support for the compromise. At the same time, abolitionists created a Committee of Vigilance to watch the docks for southern slave catchers. The pivotal moment had come for men and women of conscience, among whose number Nancy counted herself and her grandmother, founder of the Barnstable Anti-Slavery Society.

"Your Dennis Methodists have been a disappointment." Hannah Bigelow Dickerson sat by the window in her upstairs sitting room. She was now eighty-seven and had outlived her daughter and any affectation but a stiff spine. She wore a simple brown dress, a yellow shawl, and a net on her white hair. People were still struck, however, by the stern brown eyes and the brows which had remained dark, even into old age.

Nancy had her grandmother's eyes but hair as black as mussel shell and skin translucent white, untouched by the sun that leathered most Cape wives. She did not deny that she had been more pampered than most, but now that she had taken up the task of her late husband, she would not falter.

She fluffed a pillow and leaned back on the new settee. "The congregation denied a slave permission to speak from the pulpit, so one parishioner marched in and tore his pew right out of the floor."

Hannah laughed. "I hear that *you've* decided to leave as well and become a Come-Outer."

"A Come-Outer of the new style."

"No fence-walking and singsong for you, I hope." Hannah looked into the road, where Nancy's two sons played at kick-the-can. "It wouldn't do them any good."

"A Come-Outer of conscience."

The first Come-Outers had followed the call of evangelists who urged them to come out of their hidebound churches and express their faith in every aspect of their lives. The result seemed more affliction than religion. When the spirit was upon them, Come-

Outers spoke in strange voices, walked fences, swung from trees, and sang their talk, like characters from Gilbert and Sullivan.

When others came out of their churches because they disagreed over slavery, they were called Come-Outers as well. In the eyes of the orthodox, the abolitionist Come-Outer and the religious lunatic merely pulled at different oars in the same boat.

"Whatever we call ourselves," said Hannah, "we must move runaways to Canada quickly. The new law may prove toothless. But given our notoriety, Massachusetts may be crawling with federal marshals and southern agents already."

"We'll treat them the way we treated the British when you were a girl."

" 'We hold these truths to be self-evident, that all men are created equal.' " Hannah stared out her window, lost in memory. Then she noticed a man striding up the road. "My word, an answer to our prayers."

Captain Jonathan Walker was about fifty, an altogether unremarkable specimen in frock coat and stovepipe hat. But like others who looked unremarkable on land, this man and his stovepipe stood out like boldness itself on the stern of a Boston ship.

In 1844, he had attempted to smuggle seven runaways aboard his ship. For his efforts, he spent eleven months in the jungle dampness of a Florida prison and had the letters "SS," slave stealer, branded into his palm. A pariah in the South, he needed only raise his right hand to become a hero in the North. John Greenleaf Whittier even wrote "The Branded Hand," making Walker one of the few Cape Codders ever to appear in a poem longer than five lines, without the word "Nantucket" in the rhyme scheme.

He sat on the straight-backed chair beside Hannah's knitting frame and balanced his hat on his knees.

"To what do we owe the honor of your visit," asked Hannah over the hat.

"Ladies, I've circled the world three times, and the trip from Harwich to the Barnstable Courthouse is the thirstiest journey I know."

"Tea is all we can offer." Hannah poured a cup.

"A fine drink." He balanced the cup on top of the hat, as though it were a table that traveled with him wherever he went. "But after I do my business, I always take somethin' stronger at Crocker's Tavern, which this afternoon put me in the presence of Mr. Heman Bigelow."

"My great-nephew," said Hannah, "one of my brother Elkanah's grandchildren."

"A lawyer, is he?"

"A banker and businessman."

"He *talked* like a lawyer, puffin' and opinionatin' that it was 'bout time all this slave runnin' was put stop to. So one of the locals—didn't catch his name—said he heard that Heman's own *relatives* was runnin' slaves."

"Our fame spreads."

"And may sink you, if Heman keeps talkin'. He said if he thought there was slaves in his aunt Hannah's house, he'd send the sheriff to arrest 'em and think nothin' about it."

At that, there was a thump loud enough to startle Captain Walker's stovepipe right off his knee. Then something rolled across the attic floor above them.

The captain looked up at the ceiling. "It sounds like somebody's been pressing his ear to a glass on the floor, listenin' to everythin' we say."

"Not a glass," said Hannah. "A jelly jar."

She led them into a closet and, with a broom handle, rapped twice on the ceiling, which then rose. But there was neither sound nor movement in the little space above.

"Jacob," said Hannah gently, "come down, Jacob . . . You and Dorothea both."

After a moment a ladder was lowered, and the pink soles of a black man's feet appeared in a shaft of light. The black man did not descend tentatively. Once he had decided to come, he dropped like a big cat, fixed Nancy and Captain Walker with a furious glare, and puffed his chest in threat.

Then the reason for his ferocity appeared. A young woman hung down her feet, a young woman with child, nearing her time. In fact, she was too far along to back down the ladder properly, so she descended as if on a narrow staircase, an African princess in a blue gingham dress, her hand placed for support upon the shoulder of her devoted retainer.

She had coffee-colored skin and hazel eyes that showed a mother's fear, not for herself but for her unborn child. It was a fear that every woman who had carried a child understood, just as Jacob's protectiveness was known to every father.

They had lived on a Virginia plantation owned by a gambling drunkard. Jacob, the plantation carpenter, and Dorothea, a seamstress, had paid no mind to their master's ways until he began to sell off what he called prime breeders to pay his gambling debts. One night, as they lay together, feeling the baby kick in her belly and fearing a sale that might tear them apart, they resolved to go to a place where they would be treated like human beings rather than breeders.

Making the trek to Norfolk, hiding in the cellar of a sympathetic Quaker, being smuggled onto the Yankee ship at midnight—their safe passage through these they had seen as evidence of God's guiding hand. When the Yankee schooner leaned into the wind, they thought their ordeal had ended. But somewhere between Chesapeake Bay and Cape Cod, old white men had made a new law, and the northward journey stretched now even farther, like a trip the wrong way down a captain's glass.

"We ain't a-goin' back, Miz Hannah," said Jacob. "If this feller comin' to—"

Walker held up his hand, causing Jacob to fall silent. The Negro could not read, but he had seen the symbol branded into other white men, and he knew its meaning.

"We'd best get them on their way to Canada right now," said Hannah, "what with the tavern talk."

"Canada's a fair distance," said Walker. "Why not Boston instead? There's men on the Boston Vigilance Committee who can handle a schooner."

"We cannot be certain what's happening in Boston or how intent the federal forces have become."

"I wouldn't move them to Thatcher's house or Howe's," offered Nancy. "Those houses are watched, and there's some Cape Codders who'd gladly turn in a runaway for five dollars."

Hannah went to the window, looked out on the plot where once the liberty pole had stood. "Indeed."

"I know fishermen who'll make the run to Nova Scotia"— Walker rubbed his palm and studied the Negroes—"but it might take a day to track 'em down."

"I fear we may not have days," said Hannah calmly, "in that Heman Bigelow is coming up the walk this very moment, with Sheriff Whittaker in tow."

Jacob grabbed his wife. "We ain't a-goin' back."

"Just go back to the attic," answered Hannah.

ii.

At the front door, Heman Bigelow doffed his beaver hat. He always said that prosperous men wore prosperous hats, and at the bottom of this dispute was the matter of prosperity. Like most who supported the Compromise, he believed that anything was better for the country, and for trade, than civil war. And no part of the country slept more soundly upon the bed of trade than Cape Cod.

"What a surprise," said Hannah upon his arrival, with little enough emotion that he could not tell what *kind* of surprise. Then she led Heman and the sheriff into the downstairs sitting room, where Nancy awaited. Captain Walker, however, had wisely hidden himself in the pantry.

Heman was thirty-two, in height and hard edges most surely a Bigelow. But somewhere along the line, his maternal ancestry— Snows and Linnels of old Cape stock—had bestowed upon him a pair of bespectacled eyes and a bald pate that seemed to shine with irony itself, in that he resembled no one so much as Abolitionist William Lloyd Garrison.

While his brothers went to sea or to Boston, Heman had chosen to remain on Cape Cod and plow the fields of local investment. Fisheries, saltworks, cranberry farms, tanneries, the Sandwich glass-works, boatyards, and above all, the merchant marine had brought prosperity to Barnstable County. The first cracks in the prosperous facade had begun to show when saltworks met competition from the western mines. But prosperous men in prosperous hats would find ways to keep prosperity flowing, provided there was no war.

Nancy considered Heman an ass who wore his status as pomp-ously as his hat. But through the whole of his visit, she felt as if *she* were about to have the baby, rather than the poor colored woman trembling in the attic.

"Sheriff Whittaker and I been talkin' about the Underground Railroad. He's heard that some members of our family are engaged in it, and"—Heman smiled as though he were about to grant a loan—"I just want to assure him of the otherwise."

"Then assure him." Hannah smiled sweetly.

Nancy looked straight at the sheriff. "I pity you, Emulous Whittaker. This Fugitive Slave Law may make you busier than a one-armed mackerel jigger."

"A jigger for niggers." Emulous Whittaker laughed, a disagreeable sound from a scrawny little body.

"You are also a plain-speakin' man," said Hannah dryly.

"On the lookout, upholdin' the Constitution."

" 'We hold these truths to be self-evident . . .' " said Hannah.

Heman laughed, "Very good . . . a quote from the Preamble, is it not?"

"A pleasure to meet learned folks," said the sheriff.

"Remember, ladies, tell your abolitionist friends that running an underground railroad is now a crime, even in the state of Massachusetts." Heman put on his hat.

After they left, Hannah went to her desk, took out pen and paper, and scrawled a note. "We're going to smuggle these people out right under Heman's prosperous nose."

"On a Bigelow boat?" Captain Walker now appeared from the pantry.

"No. Young Heman, by virtue of inheritance, owns half of Jack's Island. There are Hilyards on the other half."

"Hilyards?" Nancy laughed. "My husband never had a good thing to say about a Hilyard in his life, especially that drunkard Isaac."

"If you want to run the railroad, you're about to meet Hilyards in the flesh." Hannah sealed the envelope and shoved it into her granddaughter's hand. "Get goin'."

"When?"

"Now, dear, now."

Nancy had not expected this moment to arrive so quickly. She had hoped that she would have time to consider her tactics, choose her cohorts, select a wardrobe.

"Hannah, are you sayin' that crazy old Come-Outer Will Hilyard's a *conductor*?" asked Walker, still rooted to his spot in the middle of the rug. "Or any of his durn-fool spawn?"

"No, but Sam Hilyard has a fine sloop."

"Sam? He's even crazier than his brother . . . and older."

"He is exactly my age." Hannah raised her chin haughtily, then turned her gaze to Nancy. "Will can take you to Sam. Give Sam the letter, and he'll run you north."

iii.

Just after dark, Captain Walker's carriage left Hannah's barn and pointed east on the County Road. As it happened, Emulous Whittaker and Heman Bigelow were just then coming out of Crocker's, and Whittaker gave a wave. Walker's driver, a retired seaman named Quintal, nodded politely, and the man seated in the carriage gave a wave of his own.

"They recognized your carriage." Nancy hunkered down in the shadows beside Captain Walker.

"Nonsense," he whispered. "There are dozens of carriages on Cape Cod. And this is not the only one that's closed up and battened down against the weather."

"Then your hand . . . they saw your hand in the window."

"Don't act the nervous nellie. It won't help if we *are* stopped."

As the carriage took the turns before the courthouse, she watched Emulous and Heman walking into the road. Were they merely crossing, or stopping to inspect the depth of the wheel tracks? Then the carriage rolled down the hill and out of their view, and Captain Walker was jostled against Nancy.

He laughed now, as though he was enjoying himself. "This slave runnin' makes folks awful close awful fast, don't it, Miz Rains?"

"If I didn't know you were an honorable man, Captain, I'd warn you that I carry a long hatpin."

"You've nothin' to fear from me. But Jacob must be gettin' a nice view, along about now."

Their legs were immodestly raised and their feet pressed against the front of the carriage. A blanket was draped over the legs, and the two frightened Negroes hid beneath.

"I can't see nothin'," came the muffled voice from beneath.

"Good," said Nancy.

The carriage ground through the village and started up the hill at the east end. If Emulous and Heman decided to follow, this was where they would catch up, and if they saw the way the horses labored to pull such a small load, suspicion would rise. Then Nancy and the captain would have to lie about their purpose for being alone together on a Tuesday night. If they did it well, they would endure gossip, if they did it poorly, arrest.

Up they went, slow and slower, the steady snap of the driver's whip popping in the night air, up past the Custom House, slower and slower, until at last Nancy could look out at the lighthouse on Sandy Neck.

"Hallelujah," she whispered.

Then they heard horses coming up the hill. The captain raised his hand in a calming gesture. The hoofbeats came closer . . . faster . . . and went past with a rumble and a greeting to the driver.

"See now," whispered Walker, "most storms blow themselves out before they ever do a bit of damage."

And Nancy felt a bit better. It could not be said, however, that she felt brave or at all confident. She would have given anything that night to have been in her own house, reading her Jane Austen.

But on they went, through the desolate stretches of Yarmouth and Dennis. To the south, on the treeless hills of the mid-Cape, the sails of the windmills turned in the moonlight, grinding the autumn grain, and their creaking echoed eerily across the land. To the north, beyond the meadows and marshes, the lighthouse beams pierced the blackness of the bay.

From time to time, however, the desolation gave way to groves of new-planted pitch pine. Nancy had read that the Pilgrims found Cape Cod covered with trees and their descendants had stripped it bare in a few generations. She could not believe this, could not imagine it, for in the moonlight, the stunted trees looked like lost children wandering the sand, as homeless as the Negroes hidden beneath her legs.

Along toward midnight, the carriage rocked into Brewster, where, it was said, there were more shipmasters than anywhere else in America. And most had built fine homes for land-bound quarterdecks.

"Here's where you see what seafarin' has brought these last thirty-five years," said Walker. "These fancy places tell you why most Cape Codders want no war over slavery."

"All lumber," she muttered.

"Eh?"

"I rode the stagecoach last year. A miserable rainy day it was, and I said how inviting these houses looked. The man next to me laughed."

"Bad manners, I'd say."

"He was an Off-Caper, more plain-speaking than impolite." Nancy watched the houses go by in stately procession. The windows in a few were illuminated, and here and there a lantern hung on pillar or fence post, awaiting a seafarer who might return that night or that month . . . or never. "He said these houses were nothing but lumber."

"Sounds like a charlatan. What was his name?"

"Thoreau."

"What's his claim?"

"He's a philosopher, makin' a book about Cape Cod."

Walker laughed. "Easy life, ridin' stagecoaches and scribblin' words about the sights."

"Easier'n slavery." Jacob now came up for air.

Nancy rubbed her legs, which had begun to cramp in this strange position. "He said all men made themselves slaves to riches, and slavery was just one of many abominable institutions. I asked him what he would do to lead a worthwhile life. This was just after my husband's death, you must realize, and I welcomed the words of a philosopher."

"Did he tell you to run slaves?" asked Dorothea.

"He said to simplify. That was all . . . to simplify." On this night, as she broke the law for the first time in her life, the words echoed in her mind.

"Seems like we're *complicatin'* things," said Walker.

"Only to simplify something greater."

iv.

Will and Mary Hilyard still lived in their house on Jack's Island with their daughter Ruth. Their son Ephraim lived with his family in a little place on the east side of the island. Isaac, whose infant cry had drawn Sam Hilyard through the night in 1814, lived with his parents when he was not fishing the Grand Banks.

The Hilyards were simple people. They grew corn, fished, and when the tide ran out, dug clams on the flats. Their days were a succession of large labors, their nights a litany of small tasks. They celebrated the Fourth of July and Christmas and voted in every election. They helped out when a friend's barn burned or a friend's baby was born, and they counted among their dead a son, drowned during the Great Gale of 1841.

That they were not good Congregationalists did not cause them to be ostracized. The uncompromising faith of the First Comers was still strong. But in a place where God was made manifest twice a day by the tides, where all faced common hardships, tolerance had become necessity rather than virtue.

Mary Burr Hilyard, her daughter, Ruth, and her son, Ephraim, were good Methodists. Isaac subscribed to no faith, but visited many churches in search of Jesus and attractive widows. Will went to Cape Cod's famous Methodist camp meetings each summer, because he loved the spectacle of good folk stirred by a preacher and seized by the spirit, and he rejoiced to hear a congregation chanting out the devil and singing in the Lord.

But for him, even *this* faith was too tame.

As Nancy Rains and her two charges scurried toward the Hilyard house, having left Captain Walker and his carriage at the edge of the causeway, they heard singing from somewhere in the cornfield.

"No farmer I ever knew sung to his corn," said Jacob.

"That's the tune to 'Old Dan Tucker,' " said Dorothea.

An old man's voice, high and thin, wavered up from the dried stalks: "Holy good God, make my corn grow. Holy good God, make my debts low. Holy good God, let me know thee, from here to kingdom come."

"Hallelujah," grunted Jacob.

"He's the man we want." Nancy called his name.

The voice fell silent, and the white hair dropped below the corn plants.

Nancy hiked up her skirts and went into the field. "Will! Will Hilyard!"

"Who are you?" he cried in an even higher voice. "An angel or"—the voice dropped to a deep rumble and the head popped up in a new place—"a devil?"

"I'm Nancy Rains."

The head appeared again, in another place, and he said, in a normal voice, "You're a Come-Outer, ain't you?"

"Of a sort."

The cornstalks rustled, and the head rose a few feet away. "And you brung others?"

"Friends . . . in need," she said.

Will thought about this, scratched his head, stared at the moon, as though it held some answer. Then he sang out, "A friend in need, he's a friend indeed, and Come-Outers is better friends than most."

"If he the best we got," muttered Jacob, "I for a-goin' on my own."

"It's his religion," explained Nancy.

"What is he? One of them Jews?"

"Hell no!" cried Will, surprising them with the power of his hearing. "I'm a good Christian with a different way."

"And we're two black Baptists who still believe," said Dorothea, "no matter what Christian slave owners done."

"Do you believe in slaveholdin'?" asked Jacob.

And Will exulted, "We are all Come-Outers of the spirit, we are all white men in our souls."

"I think he tryin' to be nice, but I ain't white, inside or out."

Meanwhile, Captain Walker's carriage was making its way from the causeway back to the County Road, and the lights of another carriage were bouncing toward the island.

As the carriages approached each other, Walker heard Heman's mother, Achseh, squawking away. She had taken up residence with her oldest and slowest son, Abraham, in a new house on the west side of Jack's Island. Before good sense had set him on another tack, Walker had courted her, widower to widow, and knew her to be one of the busiest bodies on Cape Cod.

"Who on earth are they, out so late at night? And what in tarnation are you doin'?" she shouted when Abraham turned their carriage onto the shoulder to let the other pass.

"We're out late, Ma," said Abraham.

"We been a-visitin'. What can *they* be doin' on our island?"

"'Tain't *all* ours."

"The Hilyards, they'd never have a guest ridin' a fine carriage like that, not them iggorant swamp Yankees."

"Ma, that ain't . . . Why, good evenin', Mr. Quintal."

Walker had hoped to escape recognition.

"Quintal?" Achseh's sagging old udder of a face peered out. "And Cap'n Walker?"

"Good evenin', Achseh." Walker doffed his hat.

"So, you come skulkin' 'round in the middle of the night, thinkin' to get my affection back?"

"Nice to see you again."

"Nice? Nice, is it? You old slave stealer, you can just go and . . . and smell my feet!"

At about this time, Will Hilyard was rapping on the door of his house. When he was in a prayerful mood, he did this by climbing a small ladder, scuttling across the roof, and banging on the door from above with a bull rake that left tooth marks in the wood. If nothing else, his strange faith had kept the old man quick and spry.

A lantern appeared, the door opened, and a woman peered out. "Pa! Come d-d-d-down!"

"Daughter Ruth, stop your stammerin' and say hello to fellow Come-Outers, found in the cornfield."

Ruth Hilyard glanced into the shadows, as though expecting to see nothing. Then she looked again. Her eyes opened wide at the sight of the Negroes, her hand came to her breast, and she fainted dead away, right there in the hallway.

Jacob looked at Dorothea, "Mebbe we was better off in that attic . . . or in the South."

Will was down the ladder now, fanning his daughter with his floppy hat and singing "Old Dan Tucker" to wake her.

"Quiet!" shrieked Mary from her room. "Quiet that damn song and let a good Methodist get some sleep."

"That woman got no tolerance," Will said. "Get out the way, Old Dan Tucker. Get out the way . . ."

A man stumbled down the stairs, wearing nothing more than a red union suit. "Pa, we'll be puttin' blinders on you when that full moon pops out, 'less you start actin'—"

At the sight of Isaac Hilyard, Nancy stiffened her spine. Her husband had once taken him as mate and vowed never to do it again, for he was a crude and dangerous man.

"Good evening, Mr. Hilyard." Nancy stepped over Ruth and smiled a proper smile. "I thought you might be at sea."

Isaac furrowed his brow, as if trying to recall where he had seen this woman. His black hair and heavy beard were well matched to his presence, and he seemed not the least embarrassed to be seen in his underwear. "You thought wrong."

"She and her friends are Come-Outers," offered Will.

"I see two runaways and a slave stealer." Isaac went into the great room and emerged a moment later, in a pair of greasy trousers that looked as though they could stand alone. "Who told you to come here?"

"Mrs. Hannah Bigelow Dickerson," said Nancy.

"Got no use for Bigelows." Isaac helped his sister up.

Ruth brushed herself off and, with stammering cordiality, invited her late-night visitors into the parlor. At the mantel, she lit the two lanterns.

Nancy might now have given Ruth a bit more attention but for the wreath above the fireplace, which Ruth delicately straightened, as though hoping her visitors might notice. It was made of hair. Not just any hair, it would seem, but the hair of the Hilyard family, a vine of beautifully woven browns, auburns, blonds, and whites, decorated with hair flowers. A lost art, thought Nancy, well worth losing.

Isaac opened a panel near the fireplace and took out a bottle. "No use for Bigelows, none for runaway darkies, neither."

"Coloreds." Jacob put his arm around Dorothea. "And we ain't stayin' where we ain't wanted."

"That's never stopped me." Isaac took a long swallow from the bottle.

Nancy turned to Will. "You're the one we came to see, one Come-Outer to another."

Will pulled himself up straight and raised his chin. "Fire away to old Will Hilyard. He'll do what he can."

"We need you to take us to Billingsgate, to your brother, Sam."

Will's face dropped. "Him and me don't have much truck. He thinks I'm an old fool. I think he's an old hermit."

"You're both right," said Isaac.

"I was told he has a boat that can take my friends to Canada," said Nancy.

Isaac laughed, loud and liquor-stunk. "The *Nancy?* That old thing'll roll your eyes out, then drown you."

"That's a risk we must take." Nancy spoke firmly, feigning a confidence she knew she would need in truth, were she to accomplish her task with no better help than these Hilyards for help.

"Smart people risk their necks for nobody," answered Isaac.

And Ruth asked Nancy, "Why . . . why would you risk your n-n-neck?"

Nancy looked closely at her for the first time. Her features suggested that she was not more than forty-five, but her gray hair and palsied hands made her seem far older.

"I risk my neck," said Nancy, "for principle."

"Principle?" Isaac took another drink. "The only principle Bigelows know earns interest compounded quarterly."

"What's this talk? Principle?" Mary Burr Hilyard, pickled in salt and dried in the wind, shuffled down the stairs. "Whose principle? And whose niggers?"

"*Coloreds*," said Jacob.

"If none of you are willin', I'll look elsewhere," said Nancy.

Ruth took Nancy's hand. "I c-c-c-can sail. I'll take you to Billingsg-g-g-gate."

"You row a skiff up and down the bay, collectin' hair from all your friends for another damn hair wreath, and you decide you're a sailor?" said Isaac.

Ruth ignored her brother and kept her eyes on Nancy. "I . . . I admire a person with pr-principles."

"I won't allow it," said Isaac.

"You won't, eh?" Mary smacked her toothless gums a few times to wake herself up. "Who died and made you king?"

"*I* think we should do it," said Will.

"You don't run things, either," said Mary.

"Petticoat democracy . . . I'm livin' in a petticoat democracy." Will began to hum "Old Dan Tucker," which he did whenever he lost the courage to sing it.

"I won't allow it," said Mary. "'S against the law."

Meanwhile, at Achseh Bigelow's house, the old woman's mind was spinning faster than her tongue.

"Can you imagine the nerve of that Walker, comin' to our island? *Our* island? I bet they was peekin' in the windows lookin' for us."

"I bet not." Abraham yawned over a glass of buttermilk.

"Then what, tell me, what was they doin' here? Visitin' the Hilyards? And why would that slave-stealin', lawbreakin' abolitionist son of— Why would he be visitin' the Hilyards? Unless he was breakin' a law . . . stealin' a slave. Yes . . . stealin' a slave!"

Up the stairs she scurried to the spyglass she kept trained on the Hilyard house. And just as she had expected, a light was burning there. The Hilyards were up at an ungodly hour, and up to no good in the bargain. She was so excited that her hair fell out of its bun.

She said that Heman and the county sheriff should know about this right away, and she insisted that Abraham ride to Barnstable. He offered to ride to the constable's in Brewster, but that was not good enough. By Achseh's lights, the constable was an abolitionist, while *she* was a good Daniel Webster Whig.

Didn't the Grand Old Man of Massachusetts come to Cape Cod

every summer? He stayed in Mashpee and fished for trout. In Chatham he cast his feathered drail into the surf after bluefish. How could Webster support a law inimical to Cape Cod? And by simple logic, how could anyone opposing his law have Cape Cod interests at heart?

Now, from the little attic window, she saw Hilyard's front door opening. A long, rectangular beam of light cut into the blackness, and for a fleeting instant, she saw a man in a stovepipe hat enter the house.

In the Hilyard parlor, Captain Walker caught his breath. "Where are they?"

"Hid when we heard you comin'," said Nancy.

"Good. Achseh saw me. Move out as soon as the tide can take you, or you may get a visit from the sheriff."

"If we're caught," said Isaac, "the fine is a thousand dollars for each slave."

Will asked the captain, "Can't *you* take them to Billingsgate?"

"Too many people smell me in the wind. I don't mind playin' the bluff, but—"

The sound of hoofbeats thumped past. Isaac peered out and announced that Abraham Bigelow was going down the road.

Mary pulled her shawl around her shoulders. "Ridin' off to warn the law, at a thousand dollars a slave."

Will went over to a corner and stood on a chair. "Good Lord, let us to know what to do."

"Shut up," said Mary.

Ruth wrung her hands. "'Tis t-t-time to get dressed."

Walker acted as if he saw none of this. He pulled his watch from his vest and turned to Isaac. "You got a good wind out the west—thank God for that—and an outgoin' tide, I cal'late, in an hour and a half."

"I'm goin' back to bed."

Walker took a step toward him. "I heard it said that you're a bad man when the goin's good and a worse one when it's bad."

"Here, now." Mary pushed herself between Isaac and the captain, like any mother shielding a wastrel son from the truth. "You'll speak with Christian charity in this house."

"Why should he s-s-s-speak with Christian ch-charity," said Ruth, "in a house where there ain't any?"

And Will began to sing "Old Dan Tucker."

While this was going on, Jacob and Dorothea were hiding in the root cellar of the barn behind the house. It was cold and damp and the floor had a strange, burned smell that, once it struck, stayed in the nostrils.

Dorothea put her head back against the stones and closed her eyes. The journey from another attic to another cellar to the hold of yet another ship had been more arduous than ever she had imagined. And her fear for her unborn child magnified her pain. "I hope they know what they doin'."

"I know one thing. The slave catchers ain't takin' us without no fight. We through with 'yassuh' and 'nosuh.' "

"What you doin'?"

"Lookin' for stuff." He was on the other side of the little hole, holding a lantern up between the floor joists. Whatever he was looking for, he found a tool hidden atop two spreaders. Its head was wrapped in oily rags. He tore the covering off and held up an axe with a blade the width of a man's hand, sharp and shining. "Here's somethin' for a colored man to fight with."

She scrambled over to him. "Kill a white man, you won't never live to see your . . . to see the baby."

"But havin' a weapon, *that* make you a man." He slid down beside her.

"*This* make you a man." She took his hand and put it on her belly.

"I know." His hand lingered a moment; then his arm encircled her waist. With his other hand, he held up the axe. "It's still a fine-lookin' tool, honey, what with that writin' and all. What do it say?"

"The Quaker ladies, they didn't teach me no letters like that," said Dorothea. "I don't know what it say, and I don't care, neither."

Jacob laughed a bit, to calm her. "Mebbe it's Ibo for God bless the good Bigelows and God damn the bad."

"Or God bless our baby." With a piece of ancient charcoal, she wrote the four strange letters on the floor joist above her. After them she wrote, "God bless the good Bigelows, God damn the bad, and God bless our baby." Then she drew the Drinkin' Gourd so that other slaves would know who had been here.

V.

It was said on Cape Cod that three things were most likely to kill you—the sea, childbearing, and old age. If a man quit the sea before it got 'round to taking him, if a woman lasted till her monthlies were finished, they would usually reach three score and ten with their sails blown full.

Sam Hilyard was eighty-seven, as tough as smoked mackerel, with a beard that fanned from a black mustache to a fringe of white that looked like melting snow around the top of his collar. Some had taken to calling him Methuselah, for they saw in the length of his life a sign of God's reward to a good man. Sam saw it differently.

In the gray dawn, when the mist hung heavy on the sand and the bay and sky were the color of bilge, when he sat in the shadows and wondered what his days might have been like had he lived them out with Hannah Bigelow, Sam knew that God had given him longevity to curse him, so that he might meditate upon his fury a bit longer, hear the screaming of the slaves once more, and in his madness kill Kwennit again—all to own a book that proved nothing.

He was cooking corn mush in the dawn light when he heard voices on the dune.

He threw a dash of cinnamon into the pot, in case some island children were coming to visit. Then he heard a high, thin voice singing "Old Dan Tucker."

He threw open the door and shouted, "I told you I got no interest in *real* religion. Don't come down here singin' your damn fool songs and doin' your Jesus jumpin'."

Will grinned. "Me and the girls sailed down alone."

"Hello, Uncle Sam." Ruth smoothed her hair and straightened her blouse.

Sam touched the scar that still showed beneath his mustache. He felt a familiar twinge of pain from the pistol ball in his jaw. Then his gaze fell upon the other woman.

He had seen her only a few times in thirty-six years. The last had been at the service for her mother, who died in India, while "keeping house" aboard her husband's ship. Sam had taken Nancy's hand that day and held it longer than any mere stranger should have. She must have wondered why one who had barely known her mother would struggle so to hold back his tears. She could not have known that he had been crying for himself.

But he had held to his principle. He had protected the honor of Hannah Bigelow Dickerson.

Now his granddaughter stepped boldly forward and introduced herself. "Mr. Hilyard, we need your help."

"There's nothin' I can do for you, young lady."

She shoved an envelope into his hands. "It comes from my grandmother."

Dear Sam,

The day is here. Your life has been comeuppance for your sins. Now comes your chance for redemption. Do not misuse it.

Your oldest friend,
Hannah

P.S. Eldredge has gone to his reward, and you and I face ours. Perhaps the time for truth is here. Help the girl and tell her what you will. Hunker in your cottage, and forever hold your peace.

Sam read the letter twice, holding it close because he did not want the others to read it, though not too close because his eyes were not good. He turned it over to see if anything was written on the back, perhaps a second note, suggesting that it was all a joke. Then he said, "What could an old man do for you?"

"It's what you can do for *them*." Nancy pointed toward the catboat run up on the beach between two rotting blackfish carcasses.

A week earlier, a herd of blackfish, known also as pilot whales or puffin' pigs, had come into Blackfish Bay, sending the men of Billinsgate rushing for their boats. A blackfish rendered a barrel of oil worth twenty dollars, and before anyone from Wellfleet or Eastham had the chance, the Billingsgaters got their boats around the herd and drove them right onto the beach. There they slaughtered them, skinned them, and took their heads for the melons of oil.

It was bloody business, not something Sam Hilyard relished. As the blackfish died, they gave out strange, childlike cries, and their sad smiles made them seem almost human. And for weeks after, the carcasses would lie there, rotting in the sun, filling the sky with the stench of death, like black Africans washed up from their ocean graves.

At first, Sam did not see the faces peering over the bow, as they were all but covered with sailcloth to ward off the stench, and he was not looking for black skin. He saw *that* every night as he drifted to sleep, but he had not seen a living Negro in many years. Now two of them were rising from the sea, alive amidst the dead whales.

"There's a new law against what we're doin'," Will said proudly, as though defiance of his wife had taken him across the bar to a brave new sea.

"I know," said Sam. "There ain't much place to hide 'em on an island with no trees."

"We don't want for you to hide them," said Nancy.

"I can't put 'em to work cleanin' up the carcasses from the slaughter or—" Sam saw a little sharpie coming by the lighthouse and running north along the shore. This was no good. He went down to the catboat, pulled away the sailcloth, and looked into the eyes of Jacob the slave.

"You the one sailin' us to Canada?" asked Jacob.

"'Tain't been discussed."

"Why, mister, you as old as Methuselah."

Sam saw the weapon in the Negro's hand. "I thought I hid that axe good and proper."

"*We* was hid good and proper, too."

Sam tucked the sailcloth down tight. "Stay hid, and keep the axe the same way."

Will scurried over the dune. "That's Isaac comin' up."

The sun had just risen above the Eastham tableland, so that long red rays struck the sail and the man at the tiller. "By gar, you're right," Sam said. "Haven't seen him in years. Haven't missed him, neither."

The sharpie, a little flat-bottom boat of the sort that most Cape Codders learned to sail in their childhood, bumped neatly to rest a few feet from the catboat. Before he dropped the sail, Isaac was shouting, "When are you people gonna drag off your whales after you flense 'em?"

"Breathe deep the stench," said Will, "and think on the fate of the godless man."

"Shut up, Pa."

"What happened?" Nancy rushed over the dune, followed by Ruth.

Isaac ignored them and took a long swallow from a rum bottle.

"Still a good thirst, I see," said Sam.

"It burns out the stink of a place like this."

"Then why sail here to breathe it?"

"Because no Bigelow comes to my house and tells me I'm hidin' niggers, then calls me a liar when I say I ain't, even if I am."

"*Coloreds* is what we is." Jacob rose from under the sailcloth.

Isaac took another drink. "*Slaves* is what you'll *be*, if'n we don't get goin'."

"Did Abraham b-b-b-bring the constable?" Ruth was fanning the air in front of her face to hold back the stink.

"He rode all the way to Barnstable. Must've killed his horse. Brung back Heman and that green-toothed snake Emulous Whittaker. They said if Cap'n Walker been visitin' us, we must be runnin' slaves, and there was a law 'gainst all that now. I said I didn't know nothin' 'bout no slaves, and even less 'bout some law."

Will pinched his nostrils against the stink, causing his voice to sound even higher. "What did your mother say?"

"She told 'em they could go screw horseshoe crabs."

Sam laughed. "If I didn't know that domineerin' old witch, she wouldn't be hard to like."

"Heman guessed we moved the slaves off, to someplace like Billin'sgate."

"We ain't a-goin' back," said Dorothea.

"Last I saw of Heman and the sheriff, they were thumpin' out of Jack's Creek in that old sow of a schooner, the *Hannah*." Now Isaac held his nose. "I cal'late every seam's opened since last time they caulked her."

"Will she sink?" asked Nancy.

"Who cares? So long's the seams on the *Nancy* are pounded tight."

"She's a drum, sonny," Sam said indignantly. "I could sail her to Jamaica tonight."

"Can you sail her to Nova Scotia?" asked Nancy.

Sam knew the dangers, but if this was his last trip, he would not complain. "I wouldn't be much of a man if I refused these brave *colored* folks, would I?"

"No one'll think less of you if you give me the helm and stay behind," said Isaac. "Me and the widow can do fine."

Sam slipped the rum bottle from Isaac, took a drink, and threw the rest into the water. "*I'd* think less of me. Come as mate."

"Sail comin' 'round the point!" cried Will.

"That old sow's faster'n I thought," said Isaac.

Ruth fanned the air. "I'm frightened. I thought I wouldn't be, but I'm . . . I'm . . . f-f-f-f—"

"We're all frightened," said Nancy.

"*We* ready to go goin'," said Jacob.

"Then let's go," answered Sam.

The *Nancy* was thirty feet, with a shallow draft and a broad beam, which meant she rolled but always righted herself. In his younger days, Sam had sailed her alone. Now he took a crew of two, Isaac and Nancy. "A misfit and a mother who should be home with her kids."

"What about me and Ruthie?" asked Will.

Ruth continued to fan herself. Her grand moment of defiance had come and gone in the parlor of her parents' home. Now her courage faded completely. "Oh, I don't know. I don't . . ."

"We need you two to distract 'em," said Sam. "Take the catboat and sail for Wellfleet. If they catch up to you, just tell 'em— Tell 'em you're . . . I don't know."

Ruthie suddenly brightened. The hand stopped waving. "I'll tell 'em we're out c-c-collectin' hair for a wreath."

"You do that, sister," Isaac said gently.

"Hair for a hair wreath," muttered Sam. She had been ruined by that damn book, too, and he wished he could do something to make amends. But when he went to embrace her, she pulled away, as she did from all physical contact.

Will's voice rose. "Hair for a hair wreath, prayer for a song. Get thee behind me, Satan."

Sam held up a finger, and Will stopped singing. "Decoy, Will. Haul 'em off. That's what we need you to do. 'Sides"—Sam smiled now, the first sign of warmth he had shown his brother—"you start to singin' 'Old Dan Tucker' in the Gulf of Maine, I'm liable to take and cut your pecker off with the axe that nig—that *colored* found in your barn."

Ruthie pulled out her shears and asked Jacob and Dorothea for a few locks of that curly, curly hair.

It took the *Hannah* twenty minutes to weather Billingsgate Point against an east wind. By the time she came around to north'ard, she had tacked halfway to the Eastham coast, while Sam had provisioned, slipped his cables, and raised sail.

"We try to run past 'em, we could hang up on Billin'sgate point," warned Isaac.

"We ain't goin' out to south'ard," answered Sam.

"The Slew?" Isaac clapped his hands and gave out a hoot. "If you're game, me too."

Blackfish Bay, which people now called Wellfleet Harbor, was like a long seine of sand with the cod end at the north. Once you started north there was no escape, except for the hole between Jeremy Point and Billingsgate Island known as the Slew.

The passageway was no more than thirty feet wide, maybe fifty long, a shallow and shifting little channel where even the best fishermen might take the tide going out and ground on a new bar coming back. Bluefish and striped bass loved to feed in the rips around it, but captains cursed it.

Sam was taking it under the best conditions, an easterly wind and a tide just ebbing. He stationed Isaac in the bow to watch for green water, warned the others to stand by the sails and listen for the first rush of sand against the hull. Then he threw over the helm.

He knew the *Hannah* could never follow him through, but she might be fast enough to catch him before he made it, so he pointed for the rip and prayed for some luck.

Suddenly the sand rose on the port side. Isaac shouted. Sam spun the wheel. He felt the current clutch at the hull like a living creature. For a moment, the little sloop was broadside to the tide, and no more than ten feet from plugging up the Slew like a cork. But the ebb was steady and so was Sam's hand, and he lifted the *Nancy* out of the current at the last instant.

Now she would have to wear around and come at it once more, and by then the *Hannah* might be upon them.

Sam bellowed at Isaac, "Sharpen your eyes, you bloody squint. Sing out afore the sand kisses the keel!"

"Just point 'er east and keep 'er east, old man."

"*Hannah's* comin' fast!" cried Nancy.

Jacob turned the axe twice in his hand. "I ain't a-goin' back. My baby be born a free man."

Suddenly, with a great luffing of her sails, the *Hannah* swung away from them, and into the wind!

"What's she doin'?" asked Jacob.

And Sam let out a wild old laugh.

The *Hannah* was turning after the catboat now bucking its way across Wellfleet Harbor. The faint sound of "Old Dan Tucker," sung by a father and his stuttering daughter, could be heard on the wind.

"Get out the way, all you sand shoals!" cried Isaac.

And old Methuselah, Hard Sam Hilyard, Huoyan Jinqang, steered the *Nancy* into Cape Cod Bay.

The clean air struck first. The stench of dead whales was gone. Sam Hilyard breathed deep and told his black passengers to breathe free.

vi.

By evening, they were cruising north, just off Portsmouth, New Hampshire. The wind had backed into the southwest, promising warm blue days and starry nights. The sea rolled in long, gentle swells, and the *Nancy* became as a cradle in a bower, rocking its two black children to their rest in the forecastle.

In his berth at the stern, Sam Hilyard could have slept through a storm. As it was, he slept more peacefully than he had in thirty-five years.

The little sloop was silent but for the hiss of the waves along the hull. Isaac stood the helm. Nancy Drake Rains hunkered against the bulkhead, keeping her distance from him and keeping her thoughts to herself.

It was good that this had happened so quickly, she thought. Courage came more easily when there was little time for reflection and a staunch grandmother giving the orders. Even with the *Hannah* pounding after them and her knees shaking uncontrollably, Nancy had not questioned the rightness of what she had done. Her sons, eating their supper that night in Hannah's dining room, would be proud. Her husband would have been.

She had acted upon a simple truth, and it had clarified her life. There would be time for Jane Austen later. She felt the coolness of the night and the comforting scratch of a woolen pea coat against her neck, and she knew that she would be able to help other runaways, even if it meant acting in concert with a man such as Isaac Hilyard.

Isaac looked at her, then at the stars. "Niggers call it the Drinkin' Gourd."

"*Nigger* is a crude word, Mr. Hilyard."

"The Drinkin' Gourd . . . we call it the Big Dipper. Find it and follow it to the North Star."

"Go north and be free." Nancy pulled the pea coat more tightly around her neck.

"There's no place free, 'cept in here." He tapped his skull.

"Do you stay free in here"—she tapped her skull—"with rum?"

"Rum, women, and never fear death. Fear death, the sea smells it and comes to take you. Beyond that, you brook the bad tongue of no man and stick your neck out for none."

"You stuck your neck out for Jacob and Dorothea. You may be more principled than you let on."

"Heman made me mad." Isaac adjusted the heading a bit, with nothing more than a small, skillful movement of his thumbs. "I did it to make Heman mad."

"I suppose we could call *that* a principle."

Isaac grunted. "There's many a principled man on the sea. But the sea takes principled men just like it takes the rest of us."

Scores of running lights dotted the sea around them; scores of vessels carried the commerce of New England on the endless black highway of night. A great going and coming of lights, a north and south passage of lumber and fish, cotton and rum, tanning arsenic and hemp, gingham and steel gears, a silent waltz of lights, a dance to the richness of America. Some of the lights coasted close, but most remained no more than distant stars, and no more interested than the stars in the cargo of this little sloop.

Yet none of them, thought Nancy, carried the future as surely as they did, and it cried out an hour later, in the voice of Dorothea, daughter of slaves who would be mother to a free man.

Nancy thought the first muffled noise was merely a sleep sound, the dreaming whimper of one whose mind still lived under the lash. Then she heard it again and hurried into the forecastle.

"Miz Nancy? Is that you Miz Nancy? I'm a-scared."

Nancy took her hand, said the appropriate words, and asked the appropriate questions. Then Jacob rolled from the deepest slumber he had known in months.

Nancy heard the whistling of his axe a moment before it struck. She ducked, and it sliced off the top of her bun.

Axe in hand yet still asleep, Jacob jumped up to protect his wife, struck his head on the bulkhead and collapsed.

The night passed quickly, especially for Jacob.

The ocean, lead gray in the hour before dawn, came pink with life. The sun appeared on a horizon as sharp and cloudless as honesty itself. The sea rose and fell with the rhythm of the ages. And the birth pains drew closer together.

Nancy stayed with Dorothea, held her hand, mopped her brow, and timed the pains. When they came, she put the leather strap between Dorothea's teeth and told her what a beautiful day was rising to greet her baby.

Dorothea said, strangely, that she prayed the night would be as kind.

On deck, Jacob studied the lettering on the axe, balanced it in his hands, polished it with his sleeve, spun it on the deck and watched it fall, polished it again.

"You're like to wear that thing out," said Sam.

"I so jumpy, I nearly kill Miz Nancy with it."

Isaac laughed. "Don't worry 'bout that. Ruthie'll use the hair you cut off to make a wreath, a freedom wreath."

From the forecastle came another scream.

"Easy, lad." Sam pressed a hand on Jacob's shoulder.

"Yes, yes," said Isaac, "nothin' for us men to do but keep the *Nancy* on course."

"Mebbe they is." Jacob looked Sam in the eye. "If'n you a real sea cap'n, I mean."

"I got you through the Slew, didn't I?"

Jacob slipped the axe into the length of rope that held up his pants, planted both feet on deck, and announced, "We wants to be married."

"I don't think Sam's that kind of cap'n," said Isaac.

"I damn right well am. If this boy—"

"Man!" said Jacob.

"If this man wants me to hitch him, then I'm proud to be asked."

From the sea bag in his cabin, Sam took the ancient silk vest, which he had put away thirty-five years ago. He smoothed it over his bony chest and patted each determined, furious, passionate dragon in turn. Then he took the Bible and led the men to the forecastle. He was now closer to forgiveness than ever he had been.

First, he read: " 'If I speak with the tongues of men and of angels, but have not love, I am become a soundin' brass or a clangin' cymbal. And if I have the gift of prophecy and know all mysteries and have all knowledge; and if I have all faith, so as to remove mountains, but have not love, I am nothin'.'"

After another pain had passed, he told Jacob to kneel and take Dorothea's hand. He promised to speak quickly, as the pains were not more than three minutes apart. He had never performed a marriage ceremony and had seldom heard one, in that his glowering presence was rarely welcomed at Cape Cod weddings. But he smoothed his vest and administered as fine an oath as any of them had ever heard.

He asked Jacob and Dorothea if they loved each other. They said yes. He asked if they loved each other enough to live through the good days and the gales, the doldrums and the freshening breezes. They said yes.

Then he asked, "Does each of you promise to help the other find the Drinkin' Gourd when he's thirsty or lost?"

And they said yes, as though they understood exactly what he meant.

"All right, then, by the power vested in me by the sea god Neptune, the real god Christ, and the dragons on this here vest, I now say you're man and wife."

Dorothea let out the loudest scream yet.

But there was one more matter. A couple needed a last name. Jacob and Dorothea had tried Hilyard, Rains, and Bigelow, and decided those names were already worn proudly by others. So they said they were going to take a first name as their last name: Nancy.

"Boats get named for people." Isaac laughed. "Not the other way 'round."

"They're takin' the name of a lady, not a boat," said Sam. "Seems to me a man ought to be able to call himself whatever he wants so long as there's honor in it, and there's honor in Miz Nancy, for all she's done."

Nancy was touched and yet a touch embarrassed. "My mother always had a little name for me, and it might sound better. She called me Nance."

Jacob and Dorothea tried on the name and declared it the best they had heard. Then Dorothea screamed again, and Nancy ordered the men outside. "This is a female time. Just stand by and wait."

A half hour later, the forecastle door swung open, Nancy cried out that it was a boy with all his fingers and toes, and the forecastle door slammed shut.

"A free citizen of the open sea," exulted Sam Hilyard, pulling a bottle of brandy from a sea chest. "To the father."

Jacob drank, and looked into the eyes of each of them, as though he understood the significance of a simple fact—if a man drank with you, he took you as an equal. He swallowed, then passed the brandy to Isaac, who honored him further by not wiping the neck of the bottle before drinking.

In the cabin, Nancy took the child and bathed it in warm water. Her hands were shaking and she felt giddy from the excitement. But she willed herself to be calm, a force of confident experience.

"You can't let a man see a baby all covered with cheese and afterbirth. He'd never understand."

"Is he beautiful?"

"The most beautiful baby that ever was." She wrapped the child up tight in several layers of blanket and gave him to his mother.

"He sure cryin' a lot."

"He wants your breast, dear. Give him your breast."

"Can I see his eyes?"

"Give him your breast first," Nancy urged gently, and she guided the tiny face toward the nipple. "Let his mouth find it, and he'll do the rest."

Dorothea made a soft, almost passionate sound. "It feel strange . . . nice."

"It's supposed to," said Nancy. "It's what God wanted."

Dorothea watched for a time, her face a mask of calm. Then the little sloop struck a wave and rolled, first to starboard, then to port. When she righted herself, the look of calm had left Dorothea's face. She seemed again filled with the fright that a good birth was meant to relieve.

"What's wrong?" asked Nancy.

"His eyes. What color his eyes?"

"Why, they've been mostly closed, but brown, I imagine. That's if they have any color at all."

Dorothea looked down at the tiny coffee-colored face. "I gots to know." She pushed him from her breast, ignoring his hungry squawk, and pulled back one of his eyelids.

On the deck, Jacob nervously plucked the brandy bottle from Isaac and took another long drink. "I gots to see him."

Sam had heard about niggers and drink, and he wanted nothing to spoil this day. So he took the axe from Jacob's belt and held it up as though it were the sword of an Arthurian knight. "Jake, where you're goin', there'll be tall trees, whales to flense, and maybe—if you're as good a carpenter as your wife says—things to build. Receive this from me as the first tool in a new life."

Jacob studied it as if for the first time. "'Tain't as good as a hammer or a saw, but it's somethin', and no white man never give me nothin' afore."

Soon Nancy let him in to see the child, and if anything could equal the expansiveness of the sea around them, it was the pride of a new father about to see his son.

Nancy closed the door and came to the helm.

"Samuel Isaac Nance," said Sam. "It's a grand day."

"I smell brandy," said Nancy. "I'd appreciate a taste."

Isaac took a sip for himself and handed the bottle to Nancy. "There somethin' wrong?"

The forecastle door smashed open and Jacob lurched out, as if trying to escape. He came toward them, then turned and hurried forward, shaking his head, looking at the sky in an attitude of unendurable pain.

Finally he cried out one word: "Blue."

"What?" said Sam.

"They blue."

"What's blue?"

"His eyes is *blue*. He ain't my baby."

"All babies' eyes are blue when they're born," said Nancy.

"He *ain't* my baby."

vii.

The *Nancy* put in at Annapolis Royal, which was still known, on some charts, as Port Royal.

The organization that would later assist runaways in Canada was still in its infancy, but Nancy Drake Rains knew the identities of sympathetic families, and she left the Nances with a Presbyterian couple named Frederick and Alice Campbell, whose home was within the shadow of the old French fortress.

The Campbells promised that the Negroes would be treated well.

Since each of them knew a trade, there would be work for them, and an enclave of other runaways to join. But sometime during the night, Jacob took his axe and slipped away.

Dorothea was inconsolable. Alice Campbell urged her to think of the child, but Dorothea's milk stopped flowing. The old woman, who had never had a child of her own, fed little Sam milk from a bottle and wondered at the blue of this Negro baby's eyes.

But there was no wonder in it. Dorothea had been one of her master's most desirable possessions, light-skinned and fine featured, a house slave unbowed by heavy work. And beyond that, she had intelligence. She knew that a master would not sell a slave who made him happy. So, when her master came to her, she made him happy, in hope that she and Jacob could remain together. . . .

Unlike his ancestor, Jack, Sam Hilyard left Port Royal with a sense of ineffable sadness. There was no redemption in life, no forgiveness. The joy they felt at Samuel Isaac's birth had faded in Jacob's despair.

"So old Jacob's gone off on his own to follow the Drinkin' Gourd." Isaac stood the helm on a bright southbound day.

"Maybe he'll come back." Nancy touched the blisters she had earned hauling tarred line, a small physical pain to distract from her heartsickness. "I hope he comes back."

"He might." Isaac laughed. "Where's a nigger gonna find another high-yeller woman in Nova Scotia, anyway?"

"You're a crude man."

"A plain-speaker."

"He'll come back because he loves her," said Sam. "He'll see that she done it because she loved him."

"For a lonely man, you speak well of love," said Nancy.

"It's the loneliness makes you appreciate it."

Sam had done what Hannah asked. Now he was free to do as he wished. He had much to tell Nancy, a legacy to give her, whether she wanted it or not. He had traveled to this moment over many years. But still he hesitated, because nobody ever reached the North Star. They simply beat on, sloops thumping over the waves.

"Did you love someone once?" Nancy asked him.

"More than one . . . more than once." Sam smoothed his hands over the ancient vest and went into his cabin.

"I love women," announced Isaac. "All kinds."

"I think you love something else, Mr. Hilyard. 'Lust' is the most polite word for it."

"The world could do with a little more lust. It might take everyone's mind off all this do-goodin'."

Nancy found herself amused by Isaac's honesty, her first amusement since the blue-eyed birth. "You do good rather well, for a man who professes so little interest in it. Perhaps I shall ask you to do more good, on another voyage."

"*Perhaps* I'll do it . . . if the fish ain't bitin'."

viii.

Sam plotted his course as though dropping a plumb line from Nova Scotia onto the sand at Provincetown, and he guided his little sloop straight and steady for two days of clear weather. But on the second afternoon, high, thin clouds came striping across the blue.

The mackerel sky, Sam knew, swam in the current of a changing wind. And by the following morning, the mackerel had become a raging serpent of a northeaster.

On Cape Cod, tight-lipped women watched the wind rip sheets of rain across the dunes and prayed for their men at sea. Hard-eyed masters went down to the harbors to secure their vessels against the tide. And sharp-eyed scavengers walked the back shore, watching for salvage thrown up by the storm.

In the Hilyard house, there was quiet. After a prayer, which Mary led and Will did not sing, the family went about its rainy-day business as though none of their number were in mortal danger. They had lost one son to the sea. They knew that worry would not save the other from the fate that God had designed. Best to keep busy.

In her house at Barnstable, Hannah watched the rain wear at the window while her great-grandsons played checkers by the fire. From their nervous talk, she knew that double jumps were not what concerned them. They had lost a father to the sea, but they lacked the stoicism of a fisherman's family. They were too young for that, and Hannah was too old to lie to them.

The wind that shook the Cape Cod houses and thrashed the stands of pitch pine blew like a breeze compared to the living gale that consumed the sea. In the center of the storm, there was neither time nor place . . . only sensation.

The head throbbed from the roar, the skin stung from needle pricks of rain, the stomach churned with each sickening rise and precipitous drop and vomitous roll of the sea. Liquid cold seeped through every crevice between oilskin and flesh, filling the boots and soaking the body and dulling the brain to distraction. And where there was only sensation, thought retreated to the barriers of instinct.

For six hours, instinct held the *Nancy* before a wind that pounded her ever southward, allowing her no more control than a bottle cast over the side. But a mariner who had not merely *lived* fourscore and seven, but spent most of it at sea, was the kind who might pilot that bottle.

Sam lashed himself to the helm and watched the compass. Isaac and Nancy tied lifelines to the mast and watched for the beams of light that meant safety or disaster. If, in that time, Sam thought to reveal his truth to his granddaughter, he did not act upon it. There was too much else to do.

An hour after dark, as best they could tell, the *Nancy* came down on the tip of the Cape.

Isaac saw the Race Point light flash off the starboard bow.

"How far?" shouted Sam.

"A mile sou'west."

"Sou'west?" Sam turned to Nancy, "Look for Highland! And pray you see it afore you hear breakers!"

"Can you hear breakers over this wind?"

"Hear 'em or hit 'em."

"Long Point just showed for a bit," Isaac hollered.

"Port or starboard?"

"Starboard."

"Damn." Sam Hilyard's instincts had failed him.

Race Point to port and Long Point right after—that had been his plan, to come at the bay with room to spare, swing around Long Point, and into the lee of the Provincetown shore. But the lights told him he was northeast of the Cape, coming down on the back shore before a following wind.

"I see it!" cried Nancy.

The rock-steady beam of Highland Light appeared through the storm three miles to the south. That meant the *Nancy* was straight on the Peaked Hill Bar.

Then, like a pair of evil spirits greeting each other somewhere beyond the bow, the roar of the wind met the thundering surf.

Nancy remembered the rest as a dreamer recalls small pieces of a sleeping story.

When the sloop struck, the shock threw her to the deck and a sea as black as the grave poured over her. Then a loop of rope was passed around her waist.

At the helm, Sam was shouting about principles and honor . . . and comeuppance.

He raves, she thought. His words rushed like water bursting an ancient dam.

The mast was down, the sail blown off, the sloop breaking apart in the surf, and yet Sam's voice screamed above it. "You've saved me again, Nancy, just as—"

A crashing sea lifted Nancy over the side, and she grabbed madly for a line to pull herself aboard. Then she felt the pressure around her waist, holding her against the tons of cascading water, holding her in this world when the ocean would take her to the next.

As the wave receded, Isaac dragged on the line that tethered her to him, lifting her back to the canted deck.

". . . I let slaves die, little children and all, just to own a damnable book, just to get comeuppance on the Bigelows."

Isaac reached Sam and cut one of the lines that lashed him to the helm.

"I sinned against God, against principle, all for the log of the *Mayflower*."

Isaac tried to cut the other lashing, but Sam shouted, "Leave me. Let me go down with my ship. Save yourself and find the book, in—"

The sea struck again, and this time the sloop split open like a rotten melon.

Sam screamed, "Save her! Save my granddaughter."

Then there was blackness, cold, a tumbling, turning ride through the surf, wet sand in her eyes . . . and Isaac's hands pressing into her breasts, pressing hard, a rough lover, pressing the water out of her, and now his mouth on hers, wide open, breathing life, as intimate as . . . two people huddled together in a Humane Society hut, beneath heavy dry blankets, their wet clothes stripped off and hung before the fire, their arms around each other for simple animal warmth.

ix.

"He lashed me to himself, though I could have pulled him under."

Nancy and Hannah were sitting once more in the upstairs parlor. Outside the window a locust tree shed its yellow leaves.

"He saved my life."

"And for *that* you wish to marry him?" asked Hannah.

"He asked to marry *me*."

"He asked?"

Nancy nervously tucked her hair behind her ears. It was now cut very short, as she no longer needed a bun. "Well, actually, he said it was time he settled down with a well-padded woman, someone who could keep his mind occupied as well as his . . . instincts."

"He's a crude man."

"He's a plain-speaking man, and a brave one."

"He's a mackerel fisherman, Nancy. You come from shipmasters."

"And when have you ever seen a Cape Cod mackerel fisherman step aside for a shipmaster?"

Hannah well understood the attraction that Nancy might have for a plain-speaking Hilyard. "Have you said yes?"

"Not yet." Nancy folded her hands and stared at her grandmother. Her face, but for a bruise beneath her left eye, was composed beyond any imagining of impulsiveness.

In the foyer, the grandfather clock chimed three times. Hannah's teacup rattled against its saucer. A horse clopped by on the road.

"Do you love him?"

"I may."

"Perhaps you should spend more time with him." Hannah cast her eyes toward the ceiling, which had just creaked. "You might ask him to transport my current houseguests to Nova Scotia. See if he is still brave."

"He's already agreed. And we both agree that you shouldn't hide any more runaways, at least until Heman and Sheriff Emulous have gotten over their resentment."

"On that, I agree with both of you. On other things, I have my reservations." Hannah furrowed her brow.

Nancy did the same. "Such as?"

"Did Sam reveal anything before he died?"

"He spoke of a book—the log of the *Mayflower*."

This caused Hannah's brows to rise. "He mentioned it?"

"He said he killed slaves to get it, for comeuppance. He tried to tell us where it was, but—"

"It still exists." Hannah shook her head and fixed her eyes on the pattern of colors in the Oriental carpet—blue, gold, much red. "He told me he had destroyed it."

"Why should you worry about it?"

"'Tis poison. It poisoned his grandmother. It poisoned my father. It poisoned him."

Nancy knelt by her grandmother's side. "You sent us to Sam so that he could salve his conscience by saving those slaves, didn't you?"

"I sent you to the best seaman I knew." Hannah pulled her shawl around her shoulders. "It happened to be Sam."

"You once loved him?"

"I loved what he was before he became obsessed with comeuppance. We're not meant to look to the past each morning and fill ourselves with resentment and dreams of revenge. We should look to the past for examples, then get on with our lives."

"You loved a Hilyard. Why can't that be my example?"

"Because Isaac is your *cousin*, girl."

Nancy sat back as though she had been struck. She thought she had heard Sam say the word "granddaughter," but she had not believed it.

"I may be old now, but I had my passions, even before I married your grandfather."

"But, Grandmother—"

"I'm too old for apologies."

"You need make none." After a time to digest this news, Nancy laughed and threw her arms around her grandmother's neck. "From what I saw of Sam Hilyard, I'm proud to have his blood in my veins."

"That's the problem, dear. There's an old Cape saying and not a very gentle one: As the cousins get closer together, the eyes get farther apart. Do you remember the Doone brothers?"

"Their parents were *first* cousins. Isaac and I are—"

"Your children may yet turn out idiots."

"Or geniuses."

"Whatever they are, don't let them waste their gifts in search of a book. Think of the future, always the future. It was the past in that book that ruined your grandfather . . . that kept you from ever knowing him and him from ever knowing you."

And that was a tragedy for both of them, thought Nancy.

X.

On a June afternoon seven years later, Nancy Drake Rains Hilyard packed the book into a satchel that also contained several sticks of smoked herring, some bread, a dozen stalks of asparagus, fresh strawberries, and a jug of water.

She and her son Tom, the only child she had had by Isaac, took the stagecoach from East Dennis to Pond Village in Truro. From there, it was a hard walk down a sandy path to the back shore. The drisk—Cape Cod for a miserable combination of drizzle, mist, and rain—had settled onto land and sea, making the hearth more attractive than the heath. But as this was Nancy's first anniversary without Isaac, she thought to make some gesture to his memory.

They had married, after several Canada runs during which Isaac had proven as resourceful as any Cape shipmaster.

To be sure, the Fugitive Slave Law had seldom been exercised in Massachusetts after Boston abolitionists rescued a slave named Shadrach from federal custody. In the decade that the law was in force, only seven slaves would be remanded, six from Boston and one from Hyannis. Yet any man or woman who worked on the Underground Railroad risked freedom and fortune with every slave.

Isaac did dangerous things with a smile and principled things without a hint of self-importance. If he had a passion, beyond Nancy and an occasional drink, it was for fine-lined vessels. He built one, a fast mackerel schooner. And from Captain Rains's house above the Shiverick shipyard, he watched many more take shape.

Clippers, they were called, and they came down the ways with steeply raked bows and hulls like the flanks of fine racehorses—*Hippogriffe, Belle of the West, Wild Hunter*—ships to break hearts and break records, whether hauling around the Horn in a hundred days or speeding tea from China in a few days more.

And every one was mastered and mated by men of East Dennis. When Captain Joshua Sears took command of the *Wild Hunter*, he offered Isaac a position as third mate. The railroad, said Isaac, would have to run without him.

Nancy, her two older sons, and little Thomas journeyed to Boston to bid him farewell. The older boys, nearing their twenties, went reluctantly, as they had nothing but resentment for the man who had replaced their father. Little Tom went even more unwillingly, because he feared that a year's voyage would mean forever.

The *Wild Hunter* had left the Shiverick shipyard without masts, a fledgling towed north by a steam tug. In Boston, riggers transformed her into an eagle. As each sail puffed open, she seemed to gather the light around her, to rise higher on the water, to dwarf all the schooners and squat smoking steamboats plying the harbor. When she entered Nantasket Roads and made for the open sea, she seemed truly to be flying. And that was how Nancy always remembered her husband.

Dearest Nancy,

As wife of a ship's officer and widow of a shipmaster, you know that letters from men other than your husband do not bring good news. So it is with this missive, which I compose as *Wild Hunter* sails in ballast for Calcutta.

Isaac is dead. No more painful words can be written or read. I know you will weep, as you have wept before, but know that it is the way of the sea. And after your bereavement, you will wish to know the circumstances of his death, so herewith I offer them.

We were cruising off the Formosa Strait, where Chinese pirates are known to prowl in lateen-rigged boats called proas. They arm themselves mostly with lances, axes, and dastardly things called stinkpots. These contain a foul herb, which they light and hurl onto the deck, so that the crew inhale the smoke and fall to retching and blindness.

As we passed Quemoy, out they came, scores of proas, each manned by forty or fifty screaming chink devils. They had been waiting for some unsuspecting Yank, but they did not reckon on the speed of *Wild Hunter* or the courage of men like your husband.

I bore straight into them at fifteen knots while Isaac meanwhile meted out the muskets, which soon were meting out lead. Then he took command of our two four-pounders and directed the fire with such accuracy that they dismasted five proas and created thriving confusion amongst the cut-throat fleet. But they kept coming—Lord there are so many heathen chinks—and enough drew close that soon the stinkpots came over.

I'll blame the foul-smelling herb for the fact that several of our seamen fell to their knees and began to pray like women at a Methodist camp meeting. Prayer is fine in its place. But the Lord wants action in hard straits, and Isaac got those prayerful cowards to tossing the stinkpots right back at the chinks.

But it was our bad luck that some of the chinks had themselves guns, big blunderbusses that spread bird shot like sand grains in a windstorm. It was our worse luck that three of our men were struck, among them your Isaac.

He lingered three days. On the last he was calm and even made a joke or two. He said that if he met Sam Hilyard when he got to where he was goin', he'd see that the old b——told him exactly where the book was hidden, then he'd find a way to tell you. Knowing nothing about this, I simply nodded and said some soothing words, but his last remarks may have meaning for you.

He died with your name and little Tom's on his lips.

Thy ways, O Lord, are past finding out.

Captain Joshua Sears

Nancy now carried this letter as a bookmark, so that whenever she read the Pilgrim story, she would think of the husband who inherited his courage from the First Comers.

She and little Tom walked north several miles. The sand cliffs rose like a wall on the left, the gray Atlantic rolled eternally to the right, and the deserted majesty of the beach beckoned her through the fog, as if through time. In one sweep of the eye, she saw near past and close future, and yet the generations before her and the generations to come were lost in sea mist and fog.

Isaac and Hannah and Sam had now faded behind her. The sons she had made with John Rains raced ahead. Only little Tom remained at her side, his breeches rolled up to his knees, his childish laughter flung against the roar of the surf. He chased the waves when they receded and ran frantically up the beach when they rolled in again, and she tried to fix this moment in her memory, for she knew that all too soon he would be lost in the mists as well.

At last they came to a hollow in the bluff, where a small hut materialized. Above the door was a sign.

"What do it say?" asked Tom.

" 'For Cases of Distress Only.' "

"What's distress?"

"Trouble. Your father and I were in trouble the night we found this hut. We kept each other warm till mornin'. That's what these houses are for. They shelter shipwrecked sailors who make it out of the surf."

"Are we in trouble now?"

She tousled his hair. "More sadness than trouble."

It was chillier in the little hut than outside, and there was about it the leaf-mold smell of an old animal nest. The gray light coming through the door revealed a fireplace, firewood, benches, a tin case with matches and candles, and filling most of the room, a lifeboat for the brave soul who, once saved from the storm, might brave it again to save his mates. . . . Just as she remembered it.

They built a fire and ate their lunch. Then she told him of their first trip to help the slaves, emphasizing the bravery of his father, not the sad ending. Afterward, as the surf breathed like a sated beast upon the beach, little Tom slept.

Nancy took out her book. She picked up at the place where she had been reading of the First Encounter: "Thus it pleased God to vanquish their enemies and give them deliverance, and by his special providence so to dispose that not any one of them were hurt or hit. . . ."

There was a knock and Nancy looked up with a start. A man stood in the doorway, a traveler, dressed in rough clothes, with a pack on his back, a walking staff in his hand, and tallow-covered shoes on his feet. He had a prominent nose and dark eyes that might have seemed threatening but for his benign smile and familiar presence. "I saw smoke from the chimney and thought there might have been a shipwreck. Would you need help?"

Nancy shook her head and instinctively put herself between the man and her son.

"May I come in?"

She closed her book and set it aside. "If you are in distress, the Massachusetts Humane Society welcomes you."

"It's cold for June. *That's* distressing."

"Cape Cod can be cold in any month."

"But a warm hearth . . . the heart of charity. It'll warm for a time, but inevitably grows cold." He dropped his pack and rubbed his hands together over the flames. "What would a woman and her son be doing here on such a gloomy day?"

"I revisit a place with happy memories."

He looked around. "We are fortunate not to meet in one of your sadder places."

"And you?"

"A deserted beach is more beautiful to me than the finest houses in Cambridgeport or Brewster."

From his talk she knew him now. "You travel alone this time. You have simplified your existence even further." And she described their first meeting in a coach.

"I have scribbled a bit on that journey," said Henry David Thoreau. "You may have seen it in *Putnam's.*"

"Beyond the *Liberator* and the Yarmouth *Register*, my reading is limited."

"The *Liberator*? You hold with the abolitionists?"

" 'We hold these truths to be self-evident . . .' A simple vision that the abolitionists put to practice. You once told a new widow to simplify, and she became an abolitionist."

"Even simple things become complicated in the modern world." He noticed the book she had set on the bench. "What do you read today?"

"The newspapers call it the log of the *Mayflower.*"

Thoreau opened the book. " *'Of Plymouth Plantation, 1620–1647*, by William Bradford." And with a reverence that the well-made volume inspired in the well-made man, he turned the leaves and here and there read a phrase to himself. "This publication has caused quite a sensation."

Bradford's manuscript had disappeared from the New England Library when the British left Boston in 1776. Some blamed British soldiers for the theft; others blamed Thomas Hutchinson, the last civilian royal governor. Then, in 1855, the original appeared in the library of the Bishop of London, and while controversy over its ownership simmered, the published version was recognized as one of the seminal volumes in American history.

Nancy had decided that this must be the book her grandfather had spoken of. She knew it was not an actual log, as the newspapers had proclaimed. But could there be a companion, with a history as unusual? She thought not. Somewhere in time, the Bradford journal had become part of a family myth that now must fade.

" 'So they left that goodly and pleasant city which had been their resting place near twelve years.' " Thoreau looked up. "There is no such thing as a goodly and pleasant city." Then he continued to read. " 'But they knew they were pilgrims, and . . . lifted up their eyes to the heavens, their dearest country, and quieted their spirits.' "

"Mr. Bradford was a fine writer."

"Indeed he was," said Thoreau, handing her back the book. "But the sentiment is not to my taste."

"They were brave people, sir."

"They thought they brought God to the wilderness when all the while, God was here waiting for them if only they cared to look." Thoreau went to the door and gazed out at the ocean. "Be thankful your Cape is as yet unknown to the fashionable world. You still have the chance to find something greater here. But the time must come when this coast will be a place of resort."

Nancy laughed. "That I cannot believe."

"Mother?" Little Tom rolled out of his sleep. "I was dreaming of a bird, a bobolink."

Thoreau cocked his head. "I believe I hear a bird, and a bobolink it is, back up in the hollow."

The boy sat up and rubbed his eyes. "What makes he sing so sweet, Mother? Do he eat flowers?"

Thoreau laughed. "A fine observation."

The fog thinned for a moment, and the sun knifed down, turning the beach to gold, the sea to delft blue.

"I must be off." Thoreau shouldered his pack. "Remember, Mrs. Hilyard: drink deep of this place before it's gone. You may stand on this beach and put slavery and compromise, cotton gins and railroads, peddlers and politicians, indeed, you may stand here and put all of America behind you."

They watched Thoreau through the doorway for a time. Then little Tom looked over his shoulder. "All I sees behind me is a wall."

CHAPTER 29

July 16

Polaroids

The Philosopher and the Beach was one of Tom Hilyard's earliest works.

It hung in Agnes's upstairs sitting room, between the windows. Janice liked the flatness of it, the child's eyes through which were seen sky, sea, and golden sand in three horizontal bands, a man in blue and brown sauntering along, content with the world and whatever deep thoughts were in his head. And there was a bird flying behind him. It looked like a bobolink.

"I found that painting in a barn in 1949. I bought it for fifty dollars. Worth a bit more today." Agnes poured coffee and offered Janice a doughnut. "It's supposed to be Thoreau."

"Without a care." Which was not how Janice felt. She unfolded the last of Hannah's letters. She had read them all now, absorbed them, seen the world through Hannah's eyes, lectured her husband with Hannah's words. But, buried in a box that no one had opened in decades, she had found a letter that said maybe it was time for her to come back to the present. "The artist's mother was bothered by the same thing that's been bothering *me* lately."

Agnes sat in her rocker, hummed a bit, as she sometimes did, and pressed the remote button to start the TV. "It's about time you told me what's really going on between you and Geoff."

Janice began to read: " 'Dear Nancy, The news reaches me—' "

"It sounds as if they were worlds apart," said Agnes, "and yet Hannah was here and Nancy was in your father's house down in Dennis."

" '—of your husband's tragic death at the hands of Chinese pirates. The Lord's ways are past finding out. He was a good man, no matter what. You showed great good sense to marry him over my objections. We shall all miss his courage and laconic humor.' "

"Cape Cod virtues for certain."

" 'But I am concerned about his last words, as told by Captain Sears, for I fear that they have been on your mind. That damn book—' " Janice looked at her grandmother for some reaction, but Agnes's eyes were on the television set. " 'That damn book must be forgotten.' Now, here's the crossed-out part. 'Whatever Sam did with the book, he left no key to its whereabouts. Let us not search for it, either in this world or in the next. It will only bring sadness.' "

"I wonder what she meant by 'this world or the next.' "

"I wonder about 'that damn book.' " Janice had her qualms about the will she carried in her purse. If she also buried the information in this letter, she wouldn't sleep at night. "Could the book have been the *Mayflower* log?"

Zap. Agnes killed the TV picture with the remote. "The *Mayflower* log? Is that at the root of this thing between you and Geoff?"

"You know about it?"

Agnes laughed as though she'd just heard a gentle little joke. "Let me straighten you both out. . . ."

ii.

Janice called the Truro house, but there was no answer. She let the phone ring, hoping Geoff was in the studio with his phone unplugged.

After four rings, Keith's little voice came on. "Hello. This is the Hilyard residence in Truro. We can't come to the phone now, but—ssh, I'm not done."

"It's my turn." That was Sarah, whispering angrily.

"No! Give it back. Ma-ah!"

Now Janice's own voice came on the line, calm and composed. "As you can hear, things are about normal at the Hilyard house. We can't come to the phone right now, so leave your name and number and the time that you called—"

Sarah jumped in. "Andwe'llgetbacktoyouassoonaswecan."

"Dork," whispered Keith.

Beep. "Geoff, this is Janice. I said I'd call this morning, in case you forgot. We have to talk. I'm at my grandmother's house. And erase that tape."

What had they been thinking of when they let *that* go out over the phone lines?

Then she called Rake's house. No answer. She called Ma Little's. The same.

So she left the kids with her grandmother and drove to her father's office in Dennis. It would have been logical for Geoff to show up there, but Geoff was being far from logical. Still, she went in. When she needed logic or a pep talk on how important this development was to the future of company and family, there was always her brother.

He was sitting on his desk, playing with a golf ball. Dickerson and Blue Bigelow studied an overlay map of the wetlands on Jack's Island.

"Don't start dividing it up yet." Janice kissed her father and tugged at his beard.

"We're not, thanks to your dimwit husband," said Blue.

"With a son like the Humpster, I guess you're an expert in dimwits." Defending Geoff did not feel unusual, but she didn't want to do too much of it. "Have you seen *my* dimwit?"

"Why? Did your toilet overflow again? I'll send the Humpster to pump it. He's good at pumpin'. Good at perk tests, too." Blue gestured to an arcane mistake on the map. "But he still don't know how to mark off wetland, the stupid son of a bitch."

"Don't talk about your son like that." Dickerson patted his pockets until he found his medicine bottle. He counted out four pills. "Trust him. Build him up, even when he makes mistakes. Then, when you come back from sick leave and find him doin' a lot of things he doesn't want to tell you about, you won't worry that he's done anything stupid."

Blue stuck his little finger into his ear and pulled out a wad of wax. He inspected it for a moment, then consigned it to the leg of his trousers.

Janice saw this nervous little twitch, and she knew that her father did as well. People had once called Dickerson "The Lobster" for the invisible antenna that let him pick up the vibrations in any negotiation. He couldn't miss something right in front of him.

Doug grabbed his putter and began to twirl it, which was one of his nervous twitches. "Jan, tell Geoff that when the Conservation Commission leaves, we'll be bringing in a backhoe to do preliminary perk tests for the septic system. *Without* the Board of Health looking over our shoulder."

"That quick?" asked Janice.

"We want to know what to expect before they come in. We may also clear out a space to park some heavy equipment." Doug began to tap golf balls into a cup. "Like Dad always says, when everyone's runnin' away, jump in."

"Words to live by." Janice sensed the tension, almost another dimension, like time.

"Yeah, jump right in, right over the edge." Dickerson went to the water cooler and swallowed down a fistful of pills. Then he looked at Janice. "I've been back in my office for over two weeks, and every time I start to talk about financing, Doug says he's made *arrangements*, and I shouldn't worry. Do you know anything?"

Before she could answer, Doug jumped in. "When you took sick, Dad, I said, leave the money to me. You're the idea man now. I'll fight the town and the banks and the Cape Cod Commission. *You* come up with the concepts."

"They're kickin' the old man upstairs, Jan," said Dickerson.

"We worry about you, Dad," she said. "Doug's tried to protect you."

"I worry, too." He looked at his son. "But I'm done with it. Tomorrow the attorney power expires. Before the Conservation Commission visits that island, I want some answers. And if you think the answers will kill me, I'll take a nitro first." He grabbed his fishing rod and headed for the door. "Now I'm going out to work the pond lilies."

Blue rubbed his hand across his face, as though searching for another orifice to clean. Janice hoped he'd stay away from his nose.

Doug tapped three balls toward the little cup in the middle of the floor.

And Janice said, "Douglas, who's behind you?"

"Just find your husband and straighten him out. It doesn't matter who holds the note."

"Is it the one who came at us a few years ago? Nance?"

Doug missed a two-footer.

John M. Nance. For an instant, she wondered if she could make Clara's will stand up. "This'll kill Dad."

Doug stood up from the ball. "Janice, work with me on this. When everything is in place, Dad will love the deal. Convince yourself, then go find Geoff and convince him."

She decided not to fight her brother. What was done was done. Her first priority was her husband. She was going to exercise her gloating rights. Then she would straighten things out. "Any idea where Geoff might be?"

"Try Old Comers." Doug hit another one. "I hear he's been talking a lot with the director about this log foolishness. They say she's, uh, pretty smart."

Pretty smart. Pretty? Smart? Pretty and smart? A dangerous combination.

"How much talking can he do with a museum director?" she asked.

"Enough . . . I guess. Walking out on him hasn't worked. I think you better go back to him, work on him from within."

Doug was telling her more than he was saying. She heard it in his voice, in that halting advance toward and retreat from honesty that was so familiar.

"I told you before, Doug, I'm not playing a game—"

Just then the phone rang.

"I'm not here," said Doug.

"Me neither," said Blue.

Maybe it was Geoff, so Janice answered.

"Hello, Jan!" That *voice.* "Phyllis Baxter here. Any luck on a rotten little rathole house?"

"A few possibilities."

"Any addresses? My client would like to do some drive-bys. I guess she has some time to kill."

Janice fished in her purse for her notebook and gave Phyllis the addresses of three houses, including the place in Eastham. She recommended staying away from that one, but couldn't have cared less.

What she did care about was the will, also written in the notebook. She glanced at it and almost showed it to her brother. Then she shoved it back.

She drove to Old Comers. Geoff's car was not in the lot, which was a bigger relief than she was prepared to admit. Pretty and smart. She should never have left.

. . .
iii.

John M. Nance sat in the lounge at the Indian Valley Country Club in Mashpee. The bartender was polishing glasses. The shades were drawn to keep out the morning glare. But Nance wore his sunglasses. "A young lady out on the first tee awaits my charms. This better be good."

John Lambeth opened a manila envelope containing a photo enlargement. "I took this. Nearly got caught."

Nance peered over his sunglasses. "Caught?"

"Charcoal on the floorboards, just as you suspected." Lambeth held a magnifying glass over the picture. "Things have faded, but you can still see the four marks, just like the ones on your axe."

"So the family story is true. Maybe Carolyn knows what else this means." Nance thought a minute. "And Hilyard's friends? Did you sow a little confusion among them?"

"One of my people followed them to the Bell-in-Hand last night, then paid a visit to Provincetown."

"Good. Anything to keep them guessing. We don't want any of them to know who's coming at them or from what angle."

Now Lambeth slipped another folder from the envelope. "The material on Bill Rains, the conservation commissioner. Credit history, academic records, whatever else we could come up with. Why?" Lambeth slipped a stick of gum into his mouth.

"We're in a fight." Nance slipped a black golf glove onto his left hand, a nice contrast to his white sweater and white slacks. "What do you think of my course and all the condos?"

"Real nice." Lambeth folded his arms. He wore a black polo shirt and tan slacks, and his machine-made Nautilus muscles seemed to move by hydraulics.

"We had to fight to build it. Back in 1977, the Indians decided they wanted all the open land in the town, whether they owned it or not. And *they* were the ones who'd sold most of it to begin with."

"Even this?"

Nance gestured to the first fairway, a five-hundred-yard dogleg around a marsh. "Beautiful, isn't it?"

"Yeah, but not if you have a slice."

"Fifteen years ago, it was nothing but scrub pine around an old cranberry bog that some half-breed had been nursing for years. He made more money selling that land to me than he'd made in his whole life from cranberry sauce."

"No harm in that."

"Now it's beautiful, and people enjoy it. The hand of man making the most of nature, no matter what the tree huggers say. It's a good thing. And it's legal. There's nothing more fundamental to this country than property rights. We fought to remind the courts of that in 1977, and we're fighting today."

"That still doesn't explain what you want with Rains, or why I sent someone down to P-town last night."

"It's part of the fight." Nance finished his iced tea and stood. "And there are a lot of ways to win. How old are you, Lambeth?"

"Thirty-two."

"Young to have your own detective agency, and with nothing more than a Harvard degree, not the best qualified. You should be paying me for the privilege of learning from a master. When it's over, I won't be surprised if you turn down your fee." The clatter of his spikes on the floor made him sound like some kind of badly lubricated machine, but he was very smooth.

iv.

Janice drove to Truro. Forty minutes through thickening Route 6 traffic, and found no one at their house. Her last shot was George, sitcom writer in the dunes.

It was near noon. The parking lot at the National Seashore was filling fast. To drive into the dunes, you needed four-wheel drive, which she didn't have, and enough backup gear to launch the space shuttle. So she parked in the broiling sun and walked.

She loved the bleakness of the dunes, the mountains of sand and heat, the little brows of dune grass trying to hold them in place, the forests of bleached tree trunks rising like ghosts from the sand that smothered them. But she wanted none of it in the July heat.

Instead, she took to the beach, walking barefoot beside the cooling surf. There were bathers, sand castle architects, surfers enjoying the minor leagues of their sport, surf casters enjoying the major leagues of theirs, vacationers living for two weeks in their fifty-week Cape Cod fantasy.

Everyone had Cape Cod fantasies. Sometimes Janice needed to come to the National Seashore, away from the increasingly suburban Upper Cape, to remember that this was a place of dreams for everyone, from the first Englishmen to those two teenagers wrapped in a beach towel, hiding behind a dune, going at it like, well, two teenagers.

What was her fantasy? Not a question she usually asked. Maybe it was the heat that brought it on. Or the intense clarity of a place colored only in gradations of blue and brown. Or the hunt for a husband whose fantasy had colored everything else.

Up in the dunes, the sand was so hot it burned her insteps. By the time she reached George's shack, the little tar-paper roof and sun-silvered shingles looked like an oasis.

She heard music—the sunny-day jazz of Pat Metheny. She followed it around to the deck and stopped.

A young man was giving George a back rub. He had one of those haircuts that took everything off the sides and left the curls on top, and another indecent little jockstrap bathing suit.

"Hello, George."

"Janice, honey." George rolled over and turned off the boom box. He didn't seem at all embarrassed. But why should he? This was George, and at least he was wearing bathing trunks. "Meet my friend David."

David gave her a little wave and sat back with a kind of disinterested look, like a mechanic interrupted in the middle of an oil change.

George sent him down to the pump to get some cold water and invited Janice into his shack. After the intense sunlight, the little place seemed air conditioned.

But when her eyes adjusted, Janice saw that George's shack had been trashed. The table was broken, the bookshelf had been torn from the wall, and somebody had spray-painted "Faggots, Mo-nigs, and fools" on the door.

Then Georgie took off his sunglasses. His eyes looked like two plums. Same color, almost the same shape. "Won't be needing any eyeliner for a while." He pulled down his bathing trunks so she could see one buttock. "Fork marks."

"Who did this?"

"They came in on four-wheel drive. Three of them. I think your cousin Clarence sent them. But he wasn't here."

"That pig. We should press charges." She tried to touch his face, but he pulled away.

"No proof." He looked out into the bright sunlight, as though he didn't want to talk about this. "Do you like my friend David? He's a fan. He loves 'Legal Eagles,' and he's an amateur historian. It was good to have him last night, after they left."

"Do you have any ice?" She looked around for the refrigerator. But the dune shacks had no power. "Oh, shit, Georgie, you have to be more careful."

"Helluva life, isn't it? On top of all we go through, now we got Mother Nature shoutin', Hey, faggot, be careful—disease."

"I'm not Mother Nature."

"More like Mother Courage, wandering the Cape with your children."

"I'm not her, either. I'm just looking for Geoff, and you should be looking for some ice."

"*Geoff* is looking for Geoff, even as we speak."

"Where?"

"Someplace with his list." George looked around at the mess. "There's something to this log-and-island business, Janice."

"Maybe to the island business, but forget about the log."

David appeared with a bucket of water. "It's good and cool." He dipped a cloth into the bucket and pressed it against George's eyes.

George didn't even flinch. He told Janice that when she found Geoff, she should warn him to watch out for the Humpster.

v.

Hammer drills. That was all Geoff could think of when he woke up. Hammer drills running inside his head.

The night before, he and Jimmy had killed a six-pack while they ruminated over the charcoal markings they had found in the barn cellar. And should they call the police about the break-in? But what would the police do? Dust for prints and keep them awake. So they killed another six-pack, which nearly killed Geoff by morning.

The only painkiller he could find in Rake's medicine cabinet was a tin of crumbling Bayer aspirin. He took three and drove to the junkyard near Allen Harbor in Harwich.

Men with saws and drills and sparkling acetylene torches were working over the carcasses of dead cars, like morticians. It was a surrealistic place to match the surrealistic experience of having a construction crew working on your skull. And only a surrealist would have put a junkyard on a promontory overlooking one of the prettiest yacht-filled harbors on the Cape.

The two guys dismantling the Corvette by the gate showed him the '68 Olds Cutlass parked among a half-dozen other relics of Suicide 6.

He didn't dwell on the business end of the accident. One of the baloney-skin tires was blown—that could have done it. The hood was pleated like a piece of drapery. The windshield was an exploded star of glass. They said the old man was dead as soon as he struck. Geoff hoped so.

It was the rear that interested him, and just as the police had said, there was no sign of dent or scratch. The old chrome bumper was smooth and shiny.

But there was something the police had missed, assuming they had bothered to look: a little piece of fabric, caught on the corner of one of those long 1968 brake lights, blue nylon with a little anchor woven into it, about an inch square, ripped off of something. A skirt, maybe?

Right. A girl in a blue skirt pushed Rake off the road at fifty miles an hour. He put the fabric in his pocket.

Little men ran their hammer drills against the backs of Geoff's eyes all the way home to Truro. When he saw Carolyn Hallissey waiting for him on the deck, it felt as if they had broken through.

Geoff had expected Janice, looking . . . contrite, pissed off . . . something.

This was not good.

He tried to be cool to her. "How's your foot?"

"Better. I'm sorry about the other day."

"Sorry about what?" He rubbed his forehead.

"I got a little mad about your speculations."

She was acting . . . friendly? Seductive? What? "You came here to tell me that?"

"I came on a little too strong. It's just that when it comes to history, we're on the same wavelength."

"Let's forget about it." He noticed the Polaroid 600 on her lap. "What's the camera for?"

"I have a few ideas . . . about Tom Hilyard. I was hoping you'd show me your House on Billingsgate painting."

He went into the house and got a can of Coke. He held it to his forehead to soothe the throbbing, then used it to wash down the last three aspirin. It was Tom Hilyard she had come to see, not him. But he was still operating under the assumption that whatever she knew could help him. Even if she had sent someone to Rake's cellar the night before.

So he took her down to the barn. In his office he pulled the shades across the skylights. Only then did he dare take off his sunglasses.

"This is nice." Carolyn's eyes were drawn to the sketches on the drafting table; then she saw the painting on the wall above it.

"Before you tell me your Tom Hilyard theory, what does 'Nance, Iron Axe, charcoal on the floorboards' mean to you?"

"That someone's dealing in non sequiturs."

Good timing, he thought. And with even better timing, Janice pulled into the driveway. She got out of the car and gave a once-over to the Datsun 240Z parked beside Geoff's Chevy, which sent the jackhammers into overdrive. Geoff told Carolyn to sit down and act natural.

Carolyn dropped onto the sofa and crossed her legs primly. "Will this do?"

"It'll have to." He pulled his stool as far from Carolyn as he could get.

And Janice pounded up the stairs. "I've been looking for you all morning. Where the—"

Geoff widened his stupid grin—very guilty—and introduced the young woman from Old Comers Plantation.

Janice seemed to step back, as though the name "Old Comers" had hit her in the solar plexus.

And Carolyn seemed to twitch nervously. Was this what happened when an offended wife met the offender? Did they give off some kind of scent?

"Pretty." Janice looked her up and down. "Smart, too?"

Carolyn wound her fingers around the camera strap.

"C'mon, Janice. What kind of question is that? How do you think she got to be the director of Old Comers?"

"I could guess."

"Hey, if I'm in the way here, let me just take another picture and I'll take off." Carolyn went back to the painting on the wall.

"No need." Janice pivoted for the stairs.

Geoff pressed his thumbs against his temples to keep the jackhammers from lifting off the top of his head.

Janice stopped on the top step. "I've called after you everywhere. I've driven the whole damn Cape. But I guess talking with Miss Pretty Smart—or is it Mrs.?"

"Ms.," answered Carolyn.

"—is more important than taking my call."

"Janice—"

Carolyn raised the camera. "I'll be done in a second."

"When you are, chew on this: Georgie had the shit beaten out of him last night. And that log you're so interested in . . . sometime around the turn of the century, it burned up in a fire."

"What?" cried Geoff.

The Polaroid flash went off and blinded Geoff Hilyard.

CHAPTER 30

January 1885

Pilgrims' Progress

Tom Hilyard's artwork was considered a joke by his mates at the High Head Lifesaving station, yet he sketched every night.

"Hold still while I get the mustache," he said.

"I'm like to get a stiff neck settin' here," said Jeff Parker, "and what good'm I with a stiff neck?"

"Better than you are with a stiff somethin' else, or so your wife says." Brawny Kimball sat by the wood stove, dealing out solitaire and insults.

Steam from the teakettle fogged the windows, not that the surfmen could have seen out; blowing sand had long ago pitted a permanent fog into the glass. Not that they *wanted* to see out; on nights like this, when the wind made the station rattle like a loose shroud, they most relished the quiet of the hearth, because on nights like this it was most likely to be shattered.

It had been calculated that if all the wrecks on the back shore were raised and laid end to end, a man could walk the forty-five miles from Race Point to Chatham without getting his feet wet. Cape Cod reached into the most important sea-lane in America, and like a toll collector, demanded a ship a month for the hundreds that passed safely. The U.S. Lifesaving Service, organized in 1871 to replace the Humane Society, helped those made to pay.

"Patrol should be in anytime," said Parker.

"Good reason to finish the mustache." Tom Hilyard sketched with the tip and shaded with the side of the pencil, all the while keeping his tongue wedged firmly in the corner of his mouth.

He had a hard little face, pinched and withered by the wind, but the calm eyes of a man who had seen the worst nature could do and still saw her beauty.

"Never met a surfman liked to draw before." Jeff Parker was new to the station.

"Been drawin' since I was a kid. Thirty-three now."

"What do you draw?" Parker pushed his tobacco plug from his right cheek to his left.

"People, things, but Cape Cod, mostly. . . . Put the chaw back in your right cheek."

"Can I spit first?"

"Yes, yes, I guess."

Parker hit the spittoon dead square in the middle. Surfman Smith stopped tootling his harmonica long enough to say they should sign Parker up for the Sunday spittin' contests. Then Ellis and Doane came in, looking like two salt snowmen, oilskins covered with sleet and rime ice.

"Patrol's back!" barked Captain Pervis. "Next shift!"

Tom finished the mustache and got into his gear. "How far can you see?"

"Forty yards, maybe, through the sleet," said Ellis.

"We got much of a beam showin' out there?" Smith asked about the Highland lighthouse.

"Showin' half a mile, no more," answered Doane. "Kind of night a schooner makes ice in the riggin' every time she hits a wave. Good luck."

"You have to go out, but you don't have to come back," said Tom. Somebody, in every one of the thirteen stations between Provincetown and Chatham, repeated the surfman's psalm of duty before every shift. Between every two stations, at every hour of the day and night, ten months of the year, there was a surfman walking the beach, watching.

Tom did not mind the solitude of the work or the communal life at the station. In childhood he had grown used to both.

His mother had been lost at sea while running slaves to Nova Scotia in 1859, leaving Tom in the custody of his two half brothers, who considered him no more than a product of their mother's bad judgment. They invested his money, along with their own, in Shiverick clipper ships. Then they sent Tom to a miserable Boston boarding school where a boy was taught a trade rather than the classics.

Tom learned sums, sentence diagrams, and sailmaking. Physically small, he learned to defend himself like a badger. Naturally withdrawn, he learned to find companionship in his own creations. And he came also to sense that he was different in other ways.

When he was thirteen, he lied about his age and joined the Thirty-third Massachusetts as a drummer boy. He was as brave as any in his troop, but when the men guffawed at bawdy jokes, he merely smiled. When they spoke lecherously of the corseted figures on playing cards, he said nothing. And when he drew the human figure, he never drew women.

He was different. So was a rangy Roxbury lad named Jack, whose hands were rough, whose face was gentle, and who, at age sixteen, knew much about the world. Tom believed that what they did in the midnight shadows was wrong, but still they did it, two motherless boys embracing in the bloody spring of 1864. Then came the day at Cold Harbor. One instant Jack was there, pounding retreat beside him, and the next he was gone, beheaded by a Confederate cannonball. Blood splattered in Tom's eyes, and Jack's body fell, hands twitching drumsticks, neck pumping blood, a grotesque sign of God's anger at his sin.

Such a deep scar made it hard for Tom to see the familial irony of the war: his mother had done her part to bring war about, and war had brought about the demise of the Shivericks, the clipper ships, the American Merchant Marine, and the fortune that her first husband had accumulated. When it was over, one of Tom's half brothers lay at the bottom of the Atlantic, sent there by a Confederate raider, the other had sold Heman Bigelow the Sesuit house and gone west. And Cape Cod itself was slipping into an economic backwater where it would stagnate for fifty years.

Tom went home to Jack's Island. His uncle Ephraim taught him how to work handline and hoe and keep his belly full in bad times. His stuttering aunt Ruth taught him that if bad memories arose, whether from a bloodbath in a Cape Cod fish weir or on the drummers' line at Cold Harbor, you *made* something. Ruthie made hair wreaths and tea. Tom drew pictures and joined the Life Saving Service.

Now he glanced up at the lighthouse, as he did every night. He gauged the wind at a steady thirty knots out of the northeast, shooting sand and sleet like needles against his face. He bowed his head and pointed himself into the roaring black solitude.

On clear, calm nights, there was a majesty to earth and sky that made him feel a small part of some grand design. But on dirty nights like this, the sleeted cold blew through the holes in his wool muffler and under the brim of his sou'wester, his ears ached, his chin went numb, the blowing sand scoured his skin. And no matter how much wool he wore under his oilskins, his toes and fingertips soon felt like pieces of lead.

So he sought a steady pace, his lantern swinging rhythmically before him, his eyes turning like beacons every twenty seconds to the sea, and he tried to think about pleasant things like a sketch pad or—

Suddenly a flare showed through the sleet. A hundred yards offshore, the sea was bursting over a medium-size schooner and her sails slatted like cannon fire in the wind.

The first time he heard cannon fire, he had shit his pants. But in the Life Saving Service, he had learned to conquer his fear by following the drill. He lit a red Coston flare and drove it into the sand. Then he hurried back to the station.

"All turn out!" shouted Captain Pervis at the word.

The doors of the boat room slammed open, and out clomped a big old mare pulling the surfboat on a wide-wheeled cart. Directly behind her pounded five surfmen in the traces of the gun cart. They weren't big men, but there was an almost simian strength in the slant of their gait and the slope of their shoulders, and it took them less than ten minutes to get back to the flare.

The beach around it was littered with cut lumber, barrels, spars, rigging, and the broken body of an old Negro with an axe in his belt.

"Dead," shouted Pervis above the roar of the surf. "Let's save his mates." He ordered Tom to stay ashore and prepare the Lyle gun. Then he called for the surfboat.

Cape Cod surfmen were, by instinct and training, the best small boatmen in the world. They had drilled the launch hundreds of times, performed it under these conditions dozens more. With a few quick commands, Captain Pervis directed the boat up over one wave, into the trough of the next, and turned for the ship.

But for all their skill, surfmen needed luck, and halfway to the ship, Pervis's luck deserted him. He rode the side of a ten-foot comber, up and up, straight up until the boat seemed to be standing on its stern. Then, like a ballerina on a music box, the boat did a little pirouette and came down broadside in the trough.

Tom could not see what was happening. But over the roar of wind and surf, he heard the almost human shrieks of splitting wood. The schooner was breaking up. Her crew would be taking to the masts. If they weren't rescued, they would freeze in the rigging, then drop one by one into the sea, or remain until morning, like icicles hanging from a leaky downspout.

But where was the surfboat?

There. In the surf itself, spat from a wave like a bone from the mouth of a great woolly dog.

Tom's stomach turned. He reminded himself of his training. He could rig the breeches buoy himself if he had to.

But training and cork life belts helped surfmen to survive in the surf, and Captain Pervis soon came cursing out of the waves, followed by Ellis and Baker, then Kimball, all save Parker. And there was no time to hunt for him, because the death shrieks of the schooner were growing louder. Without waiting for orders, Tom fired the gun.

Its rocket flared through the storm like a shooting star, trailing line that snagged perfectly in the schooner's rigging. Attached was a hawser, whip block, and tally board, which read: "Fix to lower mast, well up. If masts are gone, then to best place you can find. Cast off rocket line. See that rope in block runs free and show signal to shore."

Meanwhile, the surfmen raised a V-shaped frame to create a pulley between ship and shore. Despite frigid water and ice that froze in their mustaches, they worked well, for they had trained well. When the signal flare showed above the ship, they hung the breeches buoy on the line and, one by one, hauled the survivors over the furious sea.

Two were black men, which was unusual. The third looked to be brava, a Cape Verde islander, descended from Portagee criminals and African slaves. He was the mate and, though shivering uncontrollably, was able to tell them that captain and cook had gone over the side. Then he saw the body of the Negro on the horse cart. He went over to it, tenderly touched the face.

Tom threw a blanket around his shoulders. "The cook?"

"Yep," said the man, "and part owner of the *Dorothea N.*, named for his late wife. This was Mr. Jacob Nance."

"Make a report when we get back to the station," said Pervis. "Let's move afore we all freeze."

The man slipped the axe from Jake Nance's belt. "He cut loose the deck load. We thought we might float free if we wasn't carryin' so much. But when we pushed the lumber off, he went with it."

"Should save the axe for the next of kin," said Pervis.

"I *am* the next of kin. Name's Samuel Isaac Nance."

Tom looked at the black body on the horse cart. Then he held up his lantern and looked into the blue eyes before him.

Mighty strange, he thought. But his puzzlement was forgotten when pain, pure and excruciating, exploded before his eyes. The wagon had gone over his foot, a common enough occurrence and harmless in the sand. But beneath the sand was a rock, rolled there by the waves, buried there by tide, the perfect anvil on which to shatter Tom Hilyard's instep.

He spent two months in the hospital and suffered through three operations. To speed the time, he drew. Sometimes the drawing distracted him from his pain. Sometimes he drew with pain popping sweat beads all over his face. But he never stopped drawing, because he sensed that now he would *have* to draw.

When the doctors were finished with him, his left foot was no more than a few twisted shards of bone to be dragged painfully along wherever he went. He could never trudge miles of beach or help his mates in the surf again, and so he was dropped from the service. That was the way of things. His salary of sixty-five dollars a month —plus twenty cents a day for food—was gone. But there was an old saying—most often used when things went irretrievably wrong—that where God closed a door, he opened a window. The wreck of the *Dorothea N.* had closed the door on his foot but opened a window onto his new career.

Soon after, there appeared in *Frank Leslie's Illustrated Newspaper* a story called "Bravery at Cape Cod," featuring engravings made from "genuine eyewitness drawings of seashore tragedy, done by one of the staunch rescuers himself." Tom had sent many drawings to the pictorial weeklies before, but they had always been rejected.

"This story," the editors wrote him, "shows the terrible price lifesavers may pay when they seek to outwit Neptune. Yet they pay it with bravery and resourcefulness, the stuff of nobility. Besides, this is the first time anyone has sketched a surfman an hour before his death. The public will lap it up."

A drawing of Jeff Parker appeared at the top of the page. He looked calm and relaxed, not a trace of foreshadowing on his face. His sou'wester was pushed back jauntily on his head, his chaw bulged in his right cheek, and every hair of his mustache stood out. The caption read "Bravery in Repose."

Beneath it were drawings of the surfboat riding a wave, the breeches buoy, and most touching of all, the body of a white-haired Negro on a horse cart, and his son removing the axe from his belt. The caption read, "A Father's Final Gift." The engravers had given the son more Negroid features than Tom had. Their vision of Samuel Isaac Nance had huge lips, rolling eyes, torn trousers, and looked more like a character from Uncle Remus than a brave seaman.

The relationship between Tom's parents and the dead cook Jacob Nance never came to light. The New York writer interviewed the lifesavers, but the survivors had shipped back to Nova Scotia—except for Samuel Isaac Nance himself.

Had anyone bothered to ask, he could have told the story of his parents' flight in 1850, though he knew nothing of his father's brief desertion. A reporter might then have asked if the Hilyards who saved his parents were related to the one who saved *him*, and the story would have become the sensation of 1885. But no one asked and Samuel Isaac Nance did not read *Frank Leslie's Illustrated*.

When the story appeared, Nance was aboard a Provincetown Grand Banker. He had chosen not to return to Nova Scotia and the backers who believed the *Dorothea N.* was insured. He had also fallen for the daughter of a Portuguese fishing captain and hoped that, with his light skin and blue eyes, he might pass for something he was not.

For his part, Tom Hilyard remembered the tale of his mother's first slave run, but he had never been told of its sad conclusion or the name the slaves had taken. Besides, a new career awaited him, and he began to draw everything he saw for the illustrated weeklies.

But the weeklies didn't need everything he saw. They had photographers who could take their new lightweight Eastman cameras anywhere, make their pictures, then pass them on to staff engravers who rendered photographic truth in line. So Tom took his savings, his broken foot, his palette of oils, and moved to the old house on Billingsgate . . . and he painted.

He filled hundreds of canvases. In winter he took the train to Boston to see the works of the masters and the wonders of the French school called Impressionism. In summer he went to Provincetown to meet the men of the Boston Paint and Clay Club. He called himself an American Impressionist and painted some more, but no one noticed.

"Progress passes me by," he told his aunt Ruth on a Thanksgiving visit two years later. "*I* see with paint and pencil. The world prefers chemicals and photographic plates."

"Pr-pr-progress cannot be st-st-stopped, Tom." Her hands worked steadily at the squash on the cutting board. A black stove sat in the hearth and the stovepipe ran up the flue. Heat and good smells steamed the windows.

Ruth was now eighty-one, and her eyes seemed to gaze toward ever more distant horizons. Of course, to Tom, she had aged little since his return from the war. She had been as lined and gray at fifty-eight, as concerned with the neatness of the house, as obsessed with the long strands of hair she was always shaping, the braids of the children she never had.

"Can't be stopped," repeated Tom sadly.

"So you d-d-d-do things to move ahead. Find yourself a good w-w-w-woman and switch to engraving."

Tom scratched out the sketch he had made of her. She always mentioned women when they talked. She could not understand that some men had no desire for them and denied whatever other desires they might have. But she meant well, and she was the only one who had ever loved him. He began to sketch her again.

"Y-y-you don't want to grow old alone. I was lucky. I always had Ephraim and his family over on Nauseiput Creek. 'Course, his sons have notions of their own."

Some Cape Cod brothers were as close as clams in a flat. Others were like high tide and low.

Ephraim's older son, Zachary Hilyard, took after his late father, a big, slow, calculating kind of man who counted himself blessed at having Jack's Island to live on and a fine wife to bear him children. He tilled the soil and worked the weirs, wore a fringe of whiskers around his face and held up his trousers with honest red braces.

His younger brother, Elwood, taller and pencil-thin, had chosen to shape his beard and his passions to the future. He wore a neat Vandyke and a gray four-button suit, favored silk cravats, and always wore a monocle when he visited Boston's mansions.

Of course, at Boston's mansions, he always went to the back door, because this fine figure of a man was a peddler. He sold the latest buttonhooks and cheese graters and carried an ample supply of basics like sewing thread and gas mantles, too. On Cape Cod, his visit had been the highlight of a woman's week. In Boston, sales were tougher, but tougher sales made tougher salesmen, and he said that with a new century gallivanting toward them, those who could *sell*, not those who could cut the eyes from scallops, would thrive.

He always came to Thanksgiving with a bottle of French wine from S. S. Pierce on Tremont Street . . . and an idea. It took him most of the meal to get around to his latest idea. Long after they had all given thanks and wondered about their ancestors, Tom mentioned *progress*. Elwood jumped right in.

"It's a good thing, progress. If you've seen the world, like I have, you agree. And I don't say that to be a braggadoccio." Along with his Edwardian wardrobe, Elwood favored inflated words and foreign phrases.

"I like the progress from one season to the next," said Zachary. "It suited the ancestors we honor today. It'll suit our children."

Elwood turned to Ruthie, perhaps in the knowledge that the aged were the best allies of youthful enthusiasm. "What would you say, Auntie, to a hotel on Nauseiput Creek?"

"A-a-a-"

"Hotel?" shouted Zachary. "On my island?"

"*Our* island." Elwood blew on his Indian pudding. "Yours, mine, and Aunt Ruthie's."

"And the Bigelows', too," added Tom.

"A ho-ho-ho-"

"They live on the other side. It's none of their business."

"They can damn quick *make* it their business." Zachary pushed his son's fingers away from the Indian pudding.

Tom slipped out the sketch pad and began to draw the face of Elwood P. Hilyard. He liked the way the enthusiasm brightened Elwood's eyes. Enthusiasm was something most Cape Codders kept to a minimum. Elwood fairly dripped with it. He had been to the city.

Tom asked, "Why a hotel?"

"Why not? They've built them in Hyannis, in Dennis. Lorenzo Dow Baker put up a veritable Tajma Hall in Wellfleet."

"Where do you plan to build this?" asked Tom.

"Where Pa's house is now."

Zachary grew very still. "That's *my* house."

"It's the best spot, Zach, and you'll have a market for what you grow and catch. And your little ones will get to know quality people."

"Hote-hote-hote-hote*l*?" shouted Ruth.

"Yes, Ruth."

"I like it."

She liked it enough to change her will. When she passed away in 1890, she bequeathed the Hilyard property on Billingsgate to her nephew Tom so that he could paint in solitude, her Jack's Island property to Elwood, her hair wreaths and $229.97 in savings to Zachary.

"This bequest may disappoint Zachary," the will stated, "as he shall own only one-fourth of the Hilyard parcel. But if he will transfer to Elwood his one-fourth and allow the hotel to be built upon it, he shall receive *all* of my personal property and Elwood's bequest. I believe this life is nothing unless we make things to leave behind. This agreement needs only the assent of Zachary to become binding." With some reluctance, Zachary assented.

"Hotel? On Jack's Island?" Heman Bigelow's voice echoed off the oak tellers' windows of his bank. Shipmasters' widows and frugal scallop fishermen stopped in the middle of their transactions.

Elwood P. Hilyard put his monocle into his eye and lowered his voice. "That's not the tonality I was hoping to hear from the president of the First Comers Cooperative."

"I moved to Jack's Island for peace and quiet . . . and good gunnin'. Not many places where a man can roll out of bed and into the duck blind."

"This could be a fine place to put Cape Cod money."

"I've done more than anyone to keep Cape Cod money workin' since the Civil War, sonny. I need no lectures on how to use what these fine people have put in my trust"—he pointed an arthritic old finger at the faces of his customers beyond the gate—"and I didn't move to Jack's Island to see a hotel scare off all the ducks!"

Elwood looked at the carriages and carts clopping past the Harwich town green. It was a bright day in March 1891. The sun poured down through the bare trees, as though scrubbing the world clean for spring. He took off his monocle, polished it, and looked hard at Heman Bigelow's spectacles. "You lent Levi Snow a substantiated sum to build his inn last summer, right here in Harwichport."

"The word is *substantial,* you fool. He's a man of substance. You're nothin' more than a peddler, with pretensions. And what's wrong with your left eye? Why don't you wear spectacles like every-body else?"

Elwood stood and tugged on the points of his vest. "There *are* other lenders."

"But *no* other neighbors. You try to build a hotel on that island, you'll have to get 'round *me*. Good afternoon." Heman swiveled his big oak chair and looked at the painting behind him, an enormous print of Boughton's *Pilgrims Going to Church*. Copies hung in all the offices of First Comers Cooperative, to remind the customers of just *who* was granting them their loans.

Elwood tried not to look at the faces of the other customers, but before he reached the door, he heard the voice of Widow Sears: "Say, we need one of them newfangled can openers. You sellin' 'em these days?"

A few hours later Heman's son Charles rose from his chair. "A hotel! On Jack's Island?"

Heman had taken the afternoon train to Barnstable and gone straight to the 1700 house, Hannah's runaway stop. There his son Charles now kept a law office. "Every generation, they come up with somethin' to bother us. I'm too old to have strangers sneakin' around my duck blind. Ignorant swamp Yankees!"

"At least they're Cape Codders. Maybe they'll listen to reason."

The next day Charles Bigelow, Esq., rode the train to Wellfleet, a journey of almost forty miles that took not much more than an hour. Progress was a magnificent thing.

Yet the miseries of travel on Cape Cod—rolling packet runs and spine-pounding coach rides—had protected it before the coming of the trains. Charles recalled that, in his boyhood, there were almost no strangers in Barnstable. Contentious people, to be certain, but the faces you saw at town meeting, at church, at the wharf, had been there from the beginning. American faces they were, English faces, the stock that had founded a nation.

Now there were bravas arriving on the whalers and fishing boats. Negroes had been intermarrying with Indians in Mashpee since before the Underground Railroad. Portagees were taking over the Province-town fishing fleet. And the papist Irish, who bred like rabbits and voted with one mind, were slowly moving into Barnstable County. The train that rocked Bigelow through the pine groves, across the winter-burned bogs, and over the open wastes of Eastham now brought strangers from every point of the compass. A hotel would only bring more. Perhaps an artist might object to a hotel on his ancestral island.

"Nope," said Tom Hilyard. "Did at the beginning, but that was before I thought about it."

Bigelow sat in the ancient cottage at Billingsgate, in a shaft of sunlight from one of the south windows. Unlike his father, he had a full head of hair and features that were large and expansive rather than hard and precise, a Saint Bernard to his father's terrier. His widening paunch and gold watch fob looked distinctly out of place among Tom Hilyard's stick furnishings.

"Rembrandt and the Dutch preferred the north light. Cool, indirect. I like Cape light. It reflects off beach and the sea, seems to come from everywhere." Tom mixed gold and brown and spread the oil across the canvas. "This is Thoreau."

"He wouldn't have liked another hotel."

"He came here when there were forty thousand people. Now there's less than thirty. What with the end of shippin' and salt makin' and such, the Cape's shrivelin' up. Young folks are movin' off." Tom limped back and forth before the canvas. A little blue, a little more gold. A little bird flying over Thoreau. "A hotel would bring folks in."

"Cooks and maids and porters. Off-Cape immigrants, taking work from our own." Bigelow came over to the canvas and pretended to study Tom's technique. "I've bought some of your paintings. They're excellent."

Tom had grown hard doing a job where "well done" meant a life saved and seldom less. But there had been few compliments for his painting. "What have you collected?"

"*Sunset at Nauseiput, Jack's Island Clam Diggers*—"

"I'd been studyin' Millet before *Clam Diggers*."

"It shows," said Bigelow, though he hadn't the foggiest idea who Millet was. "Jack's Island clam diggers. That's how the banks think of the Hilyards, Tom, rightly or wrongly. Not many banks lendin' money to clam diggers. Tell your cousin that. Tell him, so he doesn't waste his time."

And Tom did. Nevertheless, Elwood wasted his time until every Cape Cod bank had proven the Bigelows prophetic. Then he went back to peddling and dreaming. Zachary fished, raked clams, impregnated his wife. And out on Billingsgate, Tom painted Cape landscapes and scenes of Cape life. He sold them to friends and businesses. He sold them in shavings shops, beside whittled windmills and hand-carved weathervanes that visitors bought to remind them of Cape Cod. He sold them wherever he could.

But soon his friends had all the art they could hang, and summer visitors were as fickle as April winds. It was not too many years before Tom could no longer support himself with his painting. So Zachary—steady, stolid Zachary—came each week with fish. Elwood, wandering Massachusetts in his four-button suits, butterfly collars, and peddler's pack, could send only letters about his hotel, his turreted, gabled, flag-festooned dream.

Finally, on a June day in 1896, Tom came to the bottom rung of artists' hell. He ran out of paint. He still had canvas, paper, and when all else failed, scavenged cedar shingles to paint upon. But he had no paint.

And he had to paint. If he did not, he would come to meditate on his loneliness, on the pain in his foot, on the impulses he had denied since the day at Cold Harbor, on his inability to create anything to remain after him. Every morning, when he looked at the play of light upon the water, he wanted to give permanence to the ineffable beauty of it. But if he had no paint . . .

Or was it inspiration that he lacked? Weren't sea and sky inspiration enough? Could it be that he lacked talent?

They said the Indians had made paint from berries, from animal blood, from bark and squid ink and seaweed. . . . Tom ground pigments with mortar and pestle and created watercolors to keep painting. He painted the tide flats with a seaweed paint because tide flats were a muddy green. He painted an ocean with blueberry-based paint and created a blueberry-colored ocean.

He prayed for a stranding, so that he could make paint from whale oil. But no whales came. So he tried to make new paint from old paint and simply made a mess. He took a piece of red cloth and soaked the color out of it, then he painted with the pink water, which faded on the paper.

One gentle June evening, he sat in the little cottage, soaked his foot in hot water, and read a newspaper he had found blowing along the beach, dated May 5, 1896:

> Barnstable attorney Charles Bigelow, a Republican, has announced his intention to run for the State Senate. He

says it is time to return to the values of hard work, honesty, and good Protestant faith that founded this country.

Said Bigelow: "I believe that my Pilgrim ancestors would agree, if they could come to the Cape today, that she is changing. It will be the job of the next state senator to see that the change is for the better in the birthplace of America.

Tom cursed. If he'd had something to drink, he would have drunk. He and his beloved Jack had fought a war to prove that all men were created equal. Now men like Charles Bigelow waved the flag of nativism, when in simple truth, they hated outsiders. And hadn't they all been outsiders once? Tom dried his foot on the old newspaper, then threw it into the kettle of water and wondered if he could make paint from newsprint.

Then he put his head back and studied the evening light filling his room. The light was his friend, and the light of the summer sunset seemed as certainly alive as the terns darting across the tide flats. And on June evenings, the red light reached deeper into the room than at any other time of the year, so that its rays met the red of the fireplace bricks, creating a color that Tom Hilyard yearned to paint. And perhaps it was a color he could turn *into* paint.

He got out a hammer and chisel. He placed the chisel on the corner of the fireplace and made a single, gentle tap. To his surprise, the whole brick popped free, as though the mortar had been weakened . . . or perhaps replaced.

Behind it should have been another course of brick, but instead, there was a piece of metal. He tapped it with his hammer. It sounded hollow. He tapped a few more bricks, and the mortar around them crumbled like sand. He pulled them out, so that the shaft of red sunlight now illuminated a box in a little space inside the chimney.

At first, Tom was merely curious. An iron box? With the initials TW in the corner? A strange house this was, with surprises everywhere.

He recalled the broken-off barrel of the blunderbuss that he had found behind a wall. It had contained a dozen ranting broadsides, antiques of Revolution and a long-lived family feud. He had dried them in the sun, read them, and painted a woman in tar and feathers.

What surprise might this box contain? He peeled away the wax seal and pried off the top with a knife. He pulled out a thin brown notebook on which was written the name Lemuel Bellamy in different scripts. Beneath was a thicker book, like a ledger. "Log of the *Dragon*. Southampton, June 21, 1808. Have taken a large load of lumber, which will show on manifest. Have also taken aboard Morley Milt and his crew of 'Africa hands.' Milt will use the lumber to build three new decks into the *Dragon* while we make for Africa. This is not a proud day, but my grandmother yearned for the book of history, and now it is mine."

The book of history. Tom knew of it from the broadsides. He took a third book out of the box. This one was bound in brown vellum and very old, much older than the others. The paper was heavy, tight-fibered, a pleasure to touch, especially for a man who knew the quality of such things.

Only after he had familiarized himself with its feel, shaken its hand, in a way, did he read the first entry: "*July 15, 1620. At Berth in Thames. This day have been engaged by agents of the London Adventurers. . . .*"

The book of history. The perspiration from Tom's fingertips soaked into the paper. He wiped his hands on his shirt and read on through the names of history—Brewster, Bradford, Standish—and the two families from which he descended.

The red of sunset seemed to linger far longer than usual. The wondrous Cape light lit Tom Hilyard toward his future. He read in the gloaming and into the night. He read through the first entries, the descriptions of winter, to the final words: "I agree to give over the log to Thomas Weston. I consider that I have no choice and little strength for dispute."

And sometime during the night, Tom knew he had found his inspiration. When the sun poked through the front windows, its rays struck the broken spot in the chimney, as though its setting and rising formed latitude and longitude of America's conception.

He could not guess at the value of the book. It would easily be worth as much as the famous Bradford manuscript. But he would not sell it. Instead, he would draw it, every scene.

He did a sketch and sent a letter to *Frank Leslie's*. "I have tried, these last few years, to be a Cape Cod Impressionist, capturing light that vibrates with life. But I now see that there is no better vibration than that of humanity, without which the Cape light would have no meaning. In that I descend, on both sides, from those who gave birth to American history, I propose to give light to them. Herewith, a pencil sketch called *First Light*. It shows my ancestor, Christopher Hilyard, in the crow's nest of the *Mayflower*, sighting Cape Cod after two months at sea."

Tom labored longer on the letter than on the sketch to convey the proper tone of calm confidence at a time when he feared he might starve. And it worked. Leslie ordered half a dozen more.

In short order, Tom delivered the *Mayflower* riding the waves; the Pilgrims shoring up the main beam; something called *Saints and Strangers, Psalms and Slop Buckets*, which was not used; *Reading the Compact*; *The First Encounter*; and *The Gravediggers*.

After his sketches had filled his belly, he bought oils and brushes and went back to working in a medium that would last. Paintings were his alone, not part of an assembly line. But he painted only from the book—of Pilgrims, Indians, men and women bravely facing the wilderness.

On December 21, celebrated among Pilgrim descendants as Forefathers' Day—the day the *Mayflower* reached Plymouth—*Frank Leslie's* Pilgrim edition was published. By then, Tom had completed two dozen Pilgrim paintings. He sold all of them through a Boston dealer, and most were engraved by license in Leslie's studio or reproduced in garishly tinted mass editions. One, *Reading the Compact*, was bought by Charles Bigelow, new state senator, for his Beacon Hill office. Tom charged him top price.

The critics considered his depictions energetic but crude. The public found them irresistible. They showed the Pilgrims as human beings with human foibles, and that was something that Pilgrim art had not done before. But Tom never forgot sentiment, handmaiden to popular success, and always cast the eyes of *someone* piously toward heaven.

By spring he felt he could go beyond the Pilgrim tale. But he went with caution. He took out the box once more and read the stories of Lemuel Bellamy and Sam Hilyard. These were tales not of human greatness but of depravity. Even the worst of the Pilgrims redeemed themselves through courage. Lemuel Bellamy had known no redemption in life and deserved none after death. Sam Hilyard had died bravely, but no death could make amend for the lives lost on the *Dragon*.

One spring morning, Tom was painting Sam Hilyard and his Indian mate on the deck of the *Dragon*. He had decided not to paint the box under Sam's arm and was debating whether to show Africans being dumped over the side, when Elwood P. Hilyard appeared at the door.

That day, the cousins walked the shore barefoot, with their trousers rolled to their knees. The daffodils in the window boxes had shot up several inches since sunrise. The Billingsgate shore had fallen back five feet since fall.

Whatever currents had created the island from the sand were now taking it away. Year by year, it grew smaller. Season by season, more houses were taken off. This was not unusual on Cape Cod. It was simply part of the bargain Cape Codders made with the place they lived. They pulled houses back from bluffs and floated them off eroding islands as readily as peddlers moved carts on Boston street corners.

The cousins came to a set of greased ways running from a little cottage to the water, as though the cottage were a boat about to be launched. "When labor's cheap and wood's expensive," said Tom, "moving houses makes good sense."

"You'll have to move soon. I could guarantee you a room in your own hotel, if you cared to help."

"I'm an old hermit." Tom picked up a wad of grease on his finger. A year earlier, he would have stolen it to make paint. His fortunes had turned quickly, but he cared little for fortune itself. "They say you're marrying a Brewster widow. How old?"

"Forty-six, like me."

"Too old to bear children, then."

"Some men proctorate children. I'd build something, if I had help."

After giving up any dreams of love, Tom had dreamed only of inspiration and a public to appreciate his art. His dream had come true. How could he resist the cry of another dreamer? He agreed to cosign loans and paint a picture to flatter an investor.

The investor was Lorenzo Dow Baker, a square-hulled old Wellfleet Methodist who first imported bananas to America, founded United Fruit, and built the Chequesset Inn, the grand wave of gray wood and gables rising on Wellfleet Harbor.

At Baker's office, Elwood put in his monocle and presented a proposal—a hotel on Jack's Island to handle the guests that the Chequesset could not accommodate. Tom presented a painting called *First House*, of Stephen Hopkins finishing the thatch on his roof.

And even Baker could fall to flattery when Tom Hilyard compared him to his Pilgrim ancestors.

He agreed to give them a loan, but first he would have his attorneys ask "a few friendly questions" about the Hilyards. His local attorneys were Bigelow, Holden, and Hoar, and his friendly questions received decidedly unfriendly answers. The convergence of the Hilyards and the Bigelows at the worst possible moment now seemed to have become a Cape Cod tradition.

A few days later, Tom arrived at Jack's Island with hotel sketches in hand. The sun was bright, but Elwood was in his cottage, the shades drawn, a half-empty gin bottle on the table in front of him. He wore only his union suit and a pair of fishy trousers. As for his Vandyke, it was disappearing into the fringe of beard like a lawn giving up to the weeds. "Damnable Bigelows" was all he said.

Tom learned the story from Zachary.

"What will you do?" Tom asked.

"What I always done. Got mouths to feed." Zachary picked his teeth with a match.

"Don't this make you mad? The Bigelows doin' it to us again?" Tom asked.

"But what do we have to fight with?"

Tom slipped the match from Zachary's teeth. "The book of history will set us free from the evil that bricks us up."

The lamps burned bright on Billingsgate that night and for many nights after. Tom Hilyard had an ancient story to use in an ancient fight . . . and a gathering of ancients in which to use it.

Before dawn on May 26, 1897, he put on his best suit, rolled a sketch into a tube, and tied it with string. As the first streaks of red came into the sky, he sailed his sharpie across to Wellfleet. He hurried to the depot, moving briskly in the morning chill, and caught the 4:15 local, which carried iced fish and mail from Provincetown, stopped in Eastham to take on milk, then rattled on through every town until Boston.

Once he was settled, he opened the newspaper: "Mayflower Log Returned." That was the name that the Consistory Court of London had given to William Bradford's journal.

At ten o'clock today, a Joint Convention of the Great and General Court will be held at the State House to receive

Captain William Bradford's *Mayflower* Log from Thomas F. Bayard, former Ambassador to the Court of St. James's, who has personally conveyed the book from England.

His Honor Governor Roger Wolcott will preside. In attendance will be the Honorable George F. Hoar, senator from Massachusetts, along with members of the American Antiquarian Society, the Pilgrim Society, and the New England Society of New York.

"A marvelous day for all Americans," enthused State Senator Charles Bigelow, Republican of Barnstable. "There may be nothing like this book in human annals since the story of Bethlehem. It tells of the birth of America, and it belongs in Massachusetts, America's birthplace." Senator Bigelow, descendant of Pilgrim Ezra Bigelow, will address the assembly.

Tom Hilyard reached the State House around seven. The corridors were deserted. His limping footsteps echoed and scraped ahead of him until met in the distance by janitors' voices and the scraping of mop buckets across marble.

At Bigelow's office, he tried the door. It swung open, revealing *Reading the Compact*, which was hanging between the windows. The draperies were a rich blue and gold, the spittoons shining brass.

"Mrs. Pierce? You're early, Mrs. Pierce," came a familiar voice from the inner office.

Tom had not expected it to go so easily. He was tempted to put the tube on the desk and leave. But he had learned in lifesaving how to summon his courage when it would not come forth on its own. And he had come here to save a life—Elwood's. He stepped into the inner office.

Bigelow's chair was turned toward the window. A morning coat hung on the rack, and a pair of gray striped trousers stretched from Bigelow's chair to the windowsill, where two polished boots crossed at the ankles. "Mrs. Pierce?"

"Not Mrs. Pierce. Tom Hilyard."

Bigelow spun in his chair, and several sheets of paper fluttered from his lap. He had grown heavier. His face was full, his belly fuller, and he now had a most opulent gray mustache. A tracery of red veins showed on his cheeks and nose. Nothing extreme, of course, just a delicate little coloration that looked healthy, though it was not.

"Tom Hilyard?" Bigelow spread a smile over his shock. "Why, I didn't know you were invited."

"I wasn't."

"You should have been, considering what your art has done for the Pilgrim tale."

"I'm planning to do more." Tom kicked the door shut.

The color drained from Bigelow's face. This pleased Tom, who knew his own face was as gray as his trousers.

"Well, I can't think of anything I'd rather see than more of your paintings." Bigelow got up slowly and went toward the door. "Have you seen the place of honor that I've given to *Reading the Compact?*"

Tom did not try to stop him. In his younger days, it would not have bothered him that Bigelow was nearly twice his size, but he had not come with a physical threat.

Bigelow practically jumped into the outer office. "Yes, Tom, come out and see it. Mrs. Pierce?" Bigelow stuck his head out the door and called up and down the marble corridor. "Mrs. Pierce? Pierce . . . ierce . . . ce!"

"Nobody here yet," said Tom, "except for one of today's honored guests . . . and someone come to honor him."

Bigelow pulled his head back into the office. "Honor?"

"With a new painting." Tom handed the tube to Bigelow. "This is just the study."

Charles looked at the tube as though it might explode, took it, then tore it open. "What is this?"

"The master of the *Mayflower* in his cabin, looking out at the wife of the man who brings us together today."

"Captain Bradford, you mean?"

"That's what the newspapers call him. But he was no captain, and his book's no log. I know that for a fact."

"What are you saying?"

Tom pointed to the sketch like a patient instructor. "That's Dorothy Bradford, who drowned the night of December 10, 1620. Her husband's book doesn't mention it. Was it an accident? A suicide? I think someone killed her. I've painted him in."

Bigelow's eyes searched the rough-penciled shadows and turned again to Tom Hilyard.

"Master Jones seemed to think it was a killing—"

"You haven't come here to honor me or my family."

"I honor your hypocrisy." Tom felt a touch of pride at phrasing himself so well before such a well-spoken man.

"Get out and take this with you." Bigelow tried to shove the sketch back into Tom's hands.

Tom imagined an angry wave building before his surfboat. "The ancestor on whose name your father built First Comers Cooperative, the one you praise in all your speeches, is the man in the shadows of my painting, and he's about to *push* Dorothy Bradford."

"What?" Bigelow closed the outer door. "Where did you hear this?"

Tom jerked his thumb at the painting behind him. "Same place I learned about the reading of the Compact."

"Where?" demanded Bigelow. "*Where*, damn you?"

The wave rolled toward him, threatened to overturn him, but Tom kept calmly to his oars. "I read it in a book as genuine as the one we're making such a fuss over today."

"This is *invention*." Bigelow straightened his waistcoat. "You've invented this to . . . to blackmail a member of the Great and General Court of Massachusetts. Well, I won't stand for it."

Blackmail. Tom had not considered it such, but blackmail was what he was about, and like a raging surf, once embarked upon, it was as dangerous to back away from as to face. "What will the members of the Great and General Court think, or the voters who put you there, if they learn that a man who's bragged on the purity of his ancestry, who claims descent from the first white Americans, descends from the first white murderer?"

"Why . . . this is absurd."

Tom threw the sketch on the desk. "The painting is finished. Dark, shadowy, splashes of yellow lanternlight . . . and the template names all the players. I even gave the first murderer in America *your* face."

Charles Bigelow began to sputter. He was, quite simply, speechless.

If Tom had so demanded, Bigelow would have given up his opposition to the hotel right then, but Tom had no experience in these negotiating games, and so he started to leave. "There are a lot of people in this country who cry 'America for Americans.' You've gotten votes doing it, and you'll do it again when you run for Washington. Maybe I'll save the painting until then."

"The nativist plank is as honorable as any in the platform of the Republican party."

"My mother was a Republican. She believed that all men were created equal." Tom limped into the hall and headed for the stairway. "We all came as outsiders from somewhere else."

Bigelow went after him. Their footsteps echoed and scraped along the marble. "I refuse to let a hotel be built on Jack's Island. Do you understand that?"

Tom listened only to the echoes coming back and bouncing away again, until he put his hand on the brass rail of the stairway and took the first step. Then he stopped, as he had planned. "There is a way to keep this story private."

"You have no story. You've made this up."

"See what people say when the painting is exhibited." Tom decided to go and leave Bigelow standing there, his great day spoiled before it began.

"Wait!" Bigelow grabbed Tom's elbow, but Tom pushed him away.

The staircase had been built with extra-deep treads and shallow risers to create a magisterial slope . . . and very unfamiliar footing.

Tom led with his bad foot and missed the step. His ankle turned. The poorly knit bones snapped. He grappled with Bigelow for a handhold, but it seemed as if Bigelow was helping him to fall.

He cried out as he tumbled. He heard the echo of his own cry. Then he heard a thump, like a melon striking a sidewalk—the back of his head hitting the nosing of a step. Then . . . nothing, for months. . . .

. . . Golden shafts of afternoon light came through the windows of the Billingsgate house. They settled, as always, upon the side of the brick chimney. It was summer 1898.

Tom studied the shaft of light, for he loved the light. It was hard and simple and told the truth.

But now the light began to move. Not slowly, as light should move on a summer afternoon, but like a lighthouse beam passing through one window and then the next. His own shadow fled across the wall, reached the corner, bent strangely, and disappeared.

He raised his hands to his temples to try to stop the spinning in his head. He looked out the window to take his eyes off things that seemed to be spinning with him. He saw, as always, the familiar sand of Billingsgate, the fringe of dune grass, the blue sky. But then the window moved away from the sand and he saw . . . water? *Water.* Wellfleet Harbor, swinging into view.

His ears were pierced by a shattering whistle. The window swung farther, and he saw the little steam lighter. Its cable snapped taut. His house began to move.

Now a face came toward him. It was Elwood who had brought him here, to sit in his favorite room for a final time. Elwood was saying something about floating the house off the island before the sea took it. Tom watched the light, still moving. . . .

At Campground Landing in Eastham, a farmer with an ox team slipped the raft onto rollers and dragged the house away. The Hilyards had no use for it. Zachary and his family lived in the solid house Sam Hilyard had built; Elwood and his wife had taken Tom to live with them in the family quarters of the new Hilyard House Hotel.

Only Tom cared, but he could tell no one. He had spent six months in a coma. And he had not spoken since, nor did he seem to understand what had happened. But when Elwood put him in front of a canvas and slipped a paintbrush into his hand, the first thing he painted was the house. And it was all that he had painted since—from the inside, from the outside, in daylight, by starlight, under clouds, in the sun. *House on Billingsgate,* Number 1, Number 10, Number 15 . . .

Tom Hilyard was left in a fog that no one would ever penetrate. And two days after his accident, a dory fisherman named Samuel Isaac Nance disappeared into a Grand Banks fog from which he would never emerge.

There had been a strange symmetry in these lives. Nance had been born on the voyage that brought Tom's parents together. They were forced to begin a new life on the same night and the same beach. They were lost to their families in the same week.

And the next generation—Sam Nance's son Perez, Tom Hilyard's nephew Johnny—would continue the tradition. They would glance at each other on a brilliant August afternoon in the year 1911, but both would be focused on Charles Bigelow and his political ambitions.

ii.

A photoflash burst and damn near blinded Johnny Hilyard, but people across America wanted to see a Pilgrim descendant, a Cape Cod lad with rosy cheeks, straw hat, new red braces holding up his pants, and a gen-u-ine Cape Cod clam rake in his hands, so Johnny stood still for the picture.

But the music. Good Lord, he'd never heard anything so loud in his life—Marine Band blasting "Stars and Stripes Forever" right in his ear, louder than the Pamet foghorn.

This was the greatest day that had been seen at Cape Cod since the signing of the Mayflower Compact, that's what Johnny's uncle Elwood had said: the dedication of the Pilgrim Monument. And here was Johnny, right in the middle of it, holding the hand of his uncle Tom, who held a canvas-covered painting and smiled, as though he knew exactly what was going on.

On the speakers' platform beside Tom stood the Dickersons— husband in buckled plug hat and breeches, wife in white cap and apron—playing the Pilgrim couple with their Pilgrim daughters. Dorothy, nineteen, held the key to Provincetown. Little Agnes, ten, twitched about as though the only thing she was holding was a full bladder.

From the platform at the base of the monument, Johnny looked out across a sea of straw boaters and summer bonnets, celluloid collars, starched blouses and bustles, a human sea held back by a double line of sailors, from the monument all the way to the wharf. And out in the harbor lay seven warships of the Great White Fleet, symbol of the nation that Johnny's ancestors had founded right here in Provincetown.

A good Protestant nation, his uncle Elwood called it, but in this crowd, not all faces were Yankee faces. The Mashpee Wampanoags in the receiving line were easy to pick out. Uncle Elwood had also taught him to know the florid Irish, the dusky Portagees, the bravas . . .

Brava. No compliment, but Perez Nance would rather be called brava than nigger, and better nigger than half-breed.

Nance was standing down by the wharf, near the line of roadsters at the President's gangplank, waiting.

When the first dignitaries emerged from the grand saloon on

the presidential yacht, the Navy Band began to blare "Washington Post," and the brass nearly blew Perez's straw boater off his head.

He had dressed in his best for this occasion. He had carefully bleached his only pair of white ducks. He had bought a new-style rounded collar and pinned it to his only fancy shirt, the one with the red stripes. To that he had added a blue silk necktie. And he had given his black handlebar an extra coating of wax. Before the day was out, Perez Nance, age twenty-three, would be famous.

Would the reporters call him brava or Portagee? Nance would have said Portagee. That was what his mother's father had been, married to a woman whose parents had been brava. Portuguese blood for certain. On the other side, his grandfather had been a slave owner, his grandmother a light-skinned slave, probably part white herself.

With each generation, the Nances had grown whiter, and when Perez fell in love with Dorothy Dickerson, daughter of one of the oldest Provincetown families, he had imagined that his children would be the whitest of all, Pilgrim Portagees in the place where America began.

But the man now standing on the fantail of the President's yacht had seen to it that Dorothy Dickerson would never be Perez's wife: Charles Bigelow, Republican state senator, cousin of the Dickersons.

Bigelow had come to Provincetown when he heard what he called an ugly rumor: Dickerson was allowing a brava to court his daughter. This was unacceptable, he said, in a family that descended from the Pilgrims. It was also unacceptable that a politician who had run regularly on the nativist plank should be related, however distantly, to a brava. Dickerson had been looking for just such an excuse to prohibit his daughter from seeing Perez Nance. And Dorothy being an obedient girl . . .

Perez put his hand into his pocket and wrapped it around the grip of the .22 pistol. Since the assassination of McKinley, the Secret Service protected their Presidents like jealous husbands, but no one would be worried about a state politician. If Perez could breach the double line of sailors, he might be able to rush the yacht . . .

The yacht was called *Mayflower*, appropriately, thought Charles Bigelow. It had carried Teddy Roosevelt, and now, settling lower into the water, it carried all three hundred and twelve pounds of William Howard Taft. Before the day was out, Bigelow would appear in a photograph with the monumental Taft in the foreground, the

Pilgrim Monument in the background, and guarantee himself another ten thousand votes in the senatorial primary.

"A big fat puffin' pig, if you ask me." Heman Bigelow had been invited aboard as the oldest living descendant of the First Comers, and would say whatever he damn well pleased.

Fortunately for Charles, the President and the rest of his entourage were still inside the yacht's grand saloon. The Bigelows were leading the way because they were assigned to the first of the roadsters lined up on the wharf below.

"You have to show some respect, Pa," Charles chided as he led his father toward the gangplank. "He's the *President*."

Heman Bigelow's ninety-three-year-old head wobbled along under the weight of a prosperous top hat. "Fat is *fat*. Belly like that could capsize a Cape dory."

"Men of girth are respected men," Charles slapped the belly beneath his blue jacket.

"Eh? Men of birth?" Heman aimed his brass ear trumpet at his son.

"And who's had better birth than the Bigelows?" Charles said.

"Bigelows havin' a birth? Who?"

As Charles and his father came to the top of the gangplank, a great cheer rose from the crowd on the dock. Charles Bigelow's belly filled with pride. He had fought for these people. He had stood against the Irish Democratic horde of Massachusetts, and he took the applause as a vote of approval in the political sunshine.

He raised his chin and gave the crowd a wave. Then the yacht listed slightly. He realized they were cheering for the President, who was emerging from the grand saloon, behind Charles and his father. Pride turned to bile in Bigelow's stomach. He brought his outstretched hand to rest, like some kind of tethered bird, atop his head, and he smoothed his hair. Then he hurried his father down to their roadster.

Most people were watching the President descend the gangplank, and a few were betting on whether it would hold him, but as Bigelow settled into the open car, he noticed a man in a straw boater and a big black mustache—very familiar—looking straight at him.

"Damn Eye-talian pile of rocks."

Charles turned to his father. "What?"

The old man was looking at the tower that now loomed over the town. "Design an Eye-talian tower, bring in a bunch of Irishmen to build it, make all the Congregationalists turn over in their graves."

The old man was right. The monument to the Pilgrims had been modeled, for some unfathomable reason, after the Mangia tower at Siena, Italy. All that Charles Bigelow could think of was a Roman pope standing at the top, arms outstretched, spewing a Latin blessing on the Pilgrim land.

All that Johnny Hilyard could think of as he waited on the speakers' platform was the majesty of it, rising two hundred fifty-two feet above the town, the tallest thing between London and New York.

"Hey, Johnny." Mr. Dickerson leaned down so that the bogus buckle on his Pilgrim hat glinted in Johnny's eye. "What's the paintin' your uncle's brought for the President?"

"*First Light*, it's called. Ain't that the one, Uncle Tom?" Johnny called him "uncle," though he was a second cousin. Johnny's grandfather, Ephraim and Tom's father, Isaac, had been brothers.

Jesse Dickerson peered at Tom Hilyard as though he were inanimate. Most people believed that, in all save his art, he was. "Do you think he'd mind if we took a gander at it, a little sneak of a peek?"

So Johnny gently lifted the canvas that covered it, and Tom grabbed the painting away like a starving man snatching food.

"Tom"—Johnny's stomach went cold—"this ain't the right one."

"What?" asked Dickerson. "What's wrong?"

"Why's he so mad?" Little Agnes was frightened by the strange, sudden anger in the old man beside her.

"The wrong paintin'," said Johnny.

Tom shook his head.

"Can't give that to the President."

Then the cheers rolled up the hill. The brass of the Navy Band rose to do battle with the Marine Band at the monument. The parade was coming. The President would soon be here . . . and with him Charles Bigelow.

In his roadster, Bigelow thought about his introduction, which would be neither too long nor too windy. Afterward, they would remember him for his brevity as much as his eloquence.

In the crowd behind the procession, Perez Nance surged along, his hand wrapped around the gun.

On the speakers' platform, Johnny Hilyard tried to grab the painting, but Tom shook his head and held tight. A line of spittle dripped from the corner of his mouth.

Then Johnny saw Uncle Elwood's white linen suit, pushing through the crowd. He was carrying a large square package that had to be *First Light*.

So Johnny let go of his uncle's arm, stroked his hand, said whatever soothing words he could think of. It was now a race between the procession and Elwood P. Hilyard.

The two bands drew close enough that they could play "Stars and Stripes Forever," like two streams becoming a single river. At the sight of the President, Mr. Dickerson straightened his hat and shouldered his old blunderbuss. Mrs. Dickerson's hands began to flutter around her daughters.

Good Lord, what a walrus the President was, thought Johnny, right down to the drooping gray mustache. But he was no jolly fat man. He took to the job of greeting the public like a lawyer might take to cleaning fish. And whoever had laid out that dark suit in the heat must have been trying to torture him. As he lumbered up to the platform, his face went from a peaked white to a kind of whale-meat red that was truly frightening.

Charles Bigelow stepped up to the lectern, smoothed his mustache, patted his brow, and announced, "Ladies and gentlemen, 'The Star-Spangled Banner.' "

Ten thousand hats were removed as one, and twenty thousand people turned to the flag. Johnny scanned the crowd for his uncle's white Vandyke. Once, twice, and even on the third pass, his eyes fell on the face of a man near the speakers' platform, a dark man with a black handlebar mustache.

The face was not unusual in a town that was half Portuguese, but the man was not looking at the flag. His eyes were fixed on someone on the platform. And Dorothy Dickerson's eyes were fixed on him. She looked as distressed as a fisherman's wife watching a storm roll over the bay. She might even have shaken her head and moved her lips, as if to say something to him.

But Johnny didn't have time to think about Dorothy or the Portagee, because the anthem was ending, the hats were going on again, and Bigelow was declaiming to the President and the crowd, "It is our honor to descend from the people who founded America at this place in 1620, and our privilege to honor *them* with the tower that Americans of Pilgrim descent from across the continent have built. . . ."

And so on and so on and so on. Johnny's father Zachary said Bigelow was one of the biggest windbags on Cape Cod. Uncle Elwood always added, "But he's *our* windbag."

"And now let me introduce our Pilgrim family, the Dickersons of Provincetown, to bestow upon you, Mr. President, the key to Cape Cod."

Johnny didn't watch the Dickersons. His knees were beginning to shake. Elwood seemed to have filled with water and sunk into the sea of people. And when Johnny and Tom were introduced to the President and to the audience, Johnny wanted to drive his rake into the planking and anchor himself right where he was.

"Go ahead," whispered Agnes. "Just don't get too close. His belly's so big, you can't see his face."

"Thanks, Aggie."

"And he *smells*."

Johnny glanced once more into the audience. No white suit, no Vandyke . . . only the eyes of that Portagee.

"Come along, John," urged Bigelow, "can't hold up the ceremony."

All right, then, thought Johnny. Let Bigelow face the damn painting, right here, in front of the Pilgrim Monument, the President, and twenty thousand people. He took his uncle by the elbow and led him forward.

And Bigelow introduced them: "A little Cape Cod clam digger and the finest artist we know."

The boy raised a finger in front of his uncle's nose, a sign for the old man to wait. Then he took a deep breath and looked over the big hillside of the President's belly, rolling up to the turkey-stuffed double chin.

"Mister-President-this-is-a-Cape-Cod-clam-rake-the-gift-of-the-people-of-Brewster-We-hope-you-like-it."

Taft leaned forward and took the short-handled rake, then made a few remarks about digging clams on the Chesapeake. "I thank you, young Mr. —" It seemed the President had forgotten Johnny's name, so he invented one. "Young Mr. Clamrake."

That was why he was President, thought Johnny. He could always think of *something* to say. "Johnny, sir, Johnny Hilyard is the name."

"Johnny *Clamrake* Hilyard," corrected the President, and everyone on the platform laughed politely.

"Now then"—Charles Bigelow thrust his mustache into Johnny's line of vision—"bring your uncle Tom forward."

Johnny could see the white suit at the platform steps. Elwood was talking to one of the Secret Service men, and Johnny thought about stalling. Perhaps he could give the President a demonstration with the clam rake.

But the mute—and some said incoherent—Tom Hilyard seemed to understand what Bigelow had said. He stepped forward and held out the painting.

Johnny looked at the beaming faces of the President, the governor, old Heman with the hearing trumpet in his ear, Charles Bigelow with his political ambitions stitched like his watch fob across his vest, and he thought, I've done what I could. He pulled the cover away.

"*Murder on the Mayflower*," Johnny mumbled, so softly as to be unheard. And he saw what he had expected—benign puzzlement on the President's face, curiosity from the dignitaries surrounding him, and a red, sputtering rage flooding from Bigelow's chin to his hairline.

"Mr. President"—Bigelow pulled a handkerchief from his pocket and mopped his brow—"there's been a mistake."

"Steak?" shouted Heman Bigelow, who could see about as well as he could hear. "The Pilgrims didn't have steak."

"Quiet, Pa."

Heman looked at the President. "Steak dinners on the *Mayflower*. Who ever heard of such a thing? Take him away."

"Johnny," said Charles Bigelow, "perhaps you should show your uncle back to his place."

Tom shook his whole body and tried to shove the painting into Taft's hands. Secret Service men were moving. Johnny was grabbing his uncle by the arms. Bigelow was saying something about Tom's violent rages, and Elwood's white linen suit was squeezing through the crowd on the platform.

But the confusion lasted only a moment, like a little williwaw of sand blowing up on the beach. Then there was a *pop*. The sound of a firecracker. Or a gunshot.

People in the crowd ducked. Secret Service men put their hands on their guns and pressed themselves around the President. Memories of William McKinley's death were still fresh. But not even a puff of smoke rose from the crowd.

That was because the smoke was contained in a pocket.

The little explosion, whatever it was, punctuated the scene. Tom Hilyard's emotion faded, and he was led back to his seat. The President accepted *First Light* from Elwood while Charles Bigelow shoved *Murder on the Mayflower* into the hands of Dorothy Dickerson. Then the band began to play.

Perez Nance kept his hand around the gun in his pocket until the President came to the lectern. Then he limped away, leaving a trail of blood from the twenty-two caliber hole he had shot in his foot.

. . .

iii.

That afternoon Charles Bigelow hosted a clambake for members of the Pilgrim Association at the Hilyard House Hotel. He conveyed them from Provincetown on a chartered white steam yacht that came gaily in on the high tide. The band oom-pahed at the dock, pennants fluttered atop every turret, and red, white, and blue bunting danced in the breeze.

Elwood Hilyard could not have been prouder than Bigelow was of his investment in the great white edifice that rambled along the shore like the *Rosa rugosa* along the fence in front of it. The hotel had been a fine idea after all.

Bigelow was disappointed that neither the President, the governor, nor Senator Lodge had accepted his invitation. A nod from a Republican stalwart would have been most welcome as the 1912 campaign approached. Nevertheless, it was a day to celebrate his heritage with others of like blood, and some of them would open their pocketbooks when he set his sights on Washington.

So he played the gracious host on the veranda, in the tent on the lawn, and down at the beach, where lobsters, clams, and corn were steaming in a pit of seaweed and hot stones. He had lost his wife the year before, but thanked God for his three sons, the best ambassadors a man could want, and he was especially pleased that his youngest, Theodore, was escorting a beautiful Pilgrim and distant cousin, Dorothy Dickerson. He and his fine family would make everyone forget the strange little scene on the speakers' platform that morning.

Beer flowed in the tent, barrels of raw oysters rolled, and the band went to the gazebo to play "In the Good Old Summertime" and "Let Me Call You Sweetheart."

No one complained that the original Pilgrims had frowned on any music but psalms. And when an old Congregationalist lady complained about the kegs, Charles reminded her that the Pilgrims had put in at Provincetown because they were running low on beer. Then he poured her a sarsaparilla.

While the party went on, Johnny Hilyard was charged with keeping Tom in his room, and he did a good job of it for an hour or so.

But the longer he sat there, with Tom rocking silently and scowling out the window, the louder grew the voice in Johnny's head. It wasn't fair. Outside, there was music. People were laughing. Kids played ring-a-lievio. It . . . wasn't . . . fair. And across the lawn, the Japanese lanterns that he had helped to string glowed like fireflies. After all he had been through that day, it wasn't *fair*.

He pulled out a canvas and set it up on the easel. Then he opened Tom's paint box and squeezed tubes of red, orange, yellow, green, blue, and violet onto the palette. At the sight of the paints, Tom stopped rocking and began to fish in his pockets. Something in his fractured mind always told him he had a paintbrush in his pocket.

Johnny slipped a brush into his hand. "That ought to keep you busy."

About an hour later, a game of hide-and-seek was rambling across the lawn, through buildings and tents, under the feet of the grown-ups, and off into the darkening woods. Johnny's sister Clara was "it," counting to a hundred by tens with her face pressed against a pillar on the veranda.

Johnny scampered through the refreshment tent and snatched the last piece of blueberry pie. Before any of the grown-ups could make him put it back, he wrapped it in his red handkerchief and went outside.

But where, in all this excitement, could he hide with his pie? *Down there*, behind the gazebo. The band had taken a rest and the gazebo was deserted. Slip in between the shrubbery and the knee wall and no one would ever see him.

After he was settled, he tried to decide what was most delicious—that purloined piece of pie, the knowledge that his sister would never find him here, or the view of Dorothy Dickerson, down on the beach, spoonin' with Teddy Bigelow.

The pie, he decided. He raised it to his lips, let the bittersweet aroma bring the juices to his mouth, and a girl's voice whispered from the other side of the rhododendron, "I was here first."

Aggie Dickerson's Pilgrim dress was torn and grass-stained, and a smudge of dirt sat right at the tip of her nose. "I was here *first*, Johnny Hilyard."

"Call me Clam—uh, call me *Rake*. That's what the President called me. And so what if you was here first?"

"This spot's mine. You can stay if you give me a taste of your pie."

Johnny— Rake, gave this some thought, then took the bite he had been planning. He closed his eyes and smacked his lips as though someone had put the rapture of the Lord right on his tongue.

"Hah-hah, very funny," said Aggie. "Gimme a bite or I'll scream your name. Then Clara, she'll find you and you'll be it."

That would be no good. In the dark, he would never find all the kids. As he reluctantly offered her the pie, he heard a funny toot, almost a yelp, as though somebody had stepped on a dog's paw. It was followed by a whistle.

Johnny peered over the knee wall into the gazebo. What he saw caused him to drop like a rock. Tom Hilyard was methodically wiping off the mouthpieces and testing each untended instrument, while Uncle Elwood and Charles Bigelow hurried down the path.

"I thought you told that nephew of yours to watch him." Bigelow was shouting in a furious whisper.

Toot . . . tootle-toot-toot. Clarinet.

"He could have destroyed my career," Bigelow went on. "How could you let him out of the house with that painting?"

"He's gettin' devious."

Johnny heard the screen door open, then shut, which meant Elwood and Bigelow were in the gazebo now, and Johnny was in trouble.

"The painting should have been destroyed years ago," said Bigelow.

"It should have been, but . . . but my brother said we should hide it, in case you ever turned against us."

"Turned against you? After the participation of First Comers

Cooperative in building your hotel? After we agreed to subdivide the island in 1904 so you could build cottages all over it if the hotel was a success? We had an *agreement*, Elwood."

"I'm sorry."

"I honor my agreements. *Ours* made you a prosperous man, and it should have protected *my* reputation."

Plink. Plink-plinkle-plunk. What was that? The triangle? The ⟨ylophone?

"Put that down," said Elwood.

Johnny peered over the wall again. Charles was in shirtsleeves, but Elwood, for all the tension in his voice, still looked as fresh as the morning paper.

"C'mon, Tom," said Elwood.

Tom shook his head and picked up the trombone.

Bigelow snatched it out of his hands. "Get back to the hotel and out of sight before you remind the guests of that painting."

"Almost no one saw it," said Elwood, "and *First Light* made a peace de grace."

"But what happens when the reporters ask about it? We can't very well destroy it."

"No one saw the nameplate," said Elwood. "We can make a new one. Name someone else as the murderer."

Tom shook his head.

Charles wiped his red silk handkerchief across his forehead. "Blame it on someone who died that first winter?"

"Someone without any offsprouts. That way none of your"— he gestured to the veranda of the hotel—"bonofactors will be offended."

Tom shaped his angriest face and tried to plant his feet, as if to say he would not be moved. But the ruined left foot collapsed and he fell to the floor.

Johnny wanted to help him, but Johnny was in trouble enough already. If they caught him eavesdropping on a grown-up conversation, his father would warm his hide.

But Elwood and Bigelow were treating Tom like an enfeebled animal. They just stood over him, watching him struggle to get to his feet. This wasn't right.

Finally Elwood crouched down next to him. "We'll help you, Tom. Just come back to the house, like a good fellow."

"If Tom could find this painting, wherever you and your brother hid it," said Bigelow, "he may be able to produce the book he spoke of, the one he called 'as authentic as Bradford's log.' "

This was the first time that Johnny "Rake" Hilyard had ever heard mention of the book, and it meant nothing to him.

"You wouldn't do that, would you, Tom?" asked Elwood.

Tom continued to struggle.

"How much do you think gets through to that devious mind?" asked Bigelow.

"Who knows? What can doctors know about the brain? They could see his fractured skull and six-month coma, but not whatever happened inside—stroke, cerevral hemorrhage. Can't talk, can't communicate, keeps painting one little sliver of his past, like it's the only shaft of light that still gets through to him."

"And he still hates me," said Bigelow, "in spite of all I've done."

"We're grateful," said Elwood.

"And trusting." Bigelow was seized by fury. He dropped to his knees and grabbed Tom by the shoulders. "You said Bradford's log was not the log. Is there another one? The log of the Mayflower? The book of history?"

Tom just looked at him.

"Tell me!" Bigelow shook Tom like a shark shaking a piece of meat.

Johnny jumped up, but he had no courage and dropped down again. These were grown-ups. They were supposed to know how to act. He looked at little Aggie. She scraped her top teeth across her lower lip and looked back as though Johnny would know what to do.

"Where is the book!" demanded Bigelow.

Elwood crouched beside him and whispered, as if to remind Bigelow that voices carried far through the night. "There is no book. We went through his old house from top to bottom before we moved it. There was nothing hidden but the old . . . the old broadswords."

"Broadsides. They spoke of the book more than a hundred years ago." Bigelow released Tom, stood, straightened himself. "I think it still exists."

"Is my trumpet down there?"

Another voice. Johnny peered over the knee wall and saw old Heman tottering down the path.

"My trumpet! My hearin' horn."

Charles Bigelow whispered to Elwood, "Did Tom ever go back to the old house?"

"Zachary took him when he went out there fishin' or clammin'. Tom liked Billingsgate. He liked to go there."

"And I'll bet the devious old snake brought that book back with him. If we find it, we should burn it."

"Burn what?" demanded Heman.

"I thought you were deaf," said his son.

"What? Where's my horn, my hearin' horn?"

Charles picked up a trumpet and gave it to his father.

While Heman pressed the valves and held the horn to his ear, Charles whispered to Elwood, "If we find it, we burn it. If we don't, maybe we should burn the hotel to make sure it's gone."

"Burn the hotel?" said Heman. "Good idea. Hotels bring strangers, and we got strangers wanderin' all over the island tonight, scarin' the ducks."

"It's not duck season, Pa."

"You don't want the ducks thinkin' that."

"Ducks don't think, Pa."

"But they *see*, and they'll be glad to see that hotel burn."

"Just a figure of speech, Pa." Charles put his arm around his father and led him back up the path. "Let's go find your trumpet, so you can hear when the band starts up. And no more talk of burnin'."

Elwood helped Tom to his feet, brushed off his trousers, and said a few calming words, but Tom would not go. Elwood tugged gently, because he was a gentle man, but Tom would not move. Then Elwood understood. He picked up the slide trombone, the one instrument Tom had not tested.

Honk. Hoooonk! And Tom left with his cousin.

Johnny looked at Aggie, and Aggie looked at the pie. "Can I have my bite now?"

Johnny handed her the whole piece.

Then they heard, from somewhere on the beach, a slap.

"Uh-oh," whispered Clara. "Teddy's gettin' fresh."

Their attention was turned from the frightening world of grown-up affairs to the more interesting, though confusing, world of older kids kissing in the shadows.

It seemed that Teddy Bigelow had taken his spoonin' too far, and Aggie's big sister had taken exception.

Dorothy jumped up and started down the beach, but Teddy caught up to her, said something, and kissed her. This time she kissed him back.

Then they disappeared arm in arm into the night. A moment later, another man came down out of the woods. Johnny could not tell who he was. He seemed to be following Dorothy and Teddy, perhaps spying on them, but his limp made it hard for him to keep up.

iv.

On a windy night a month later, long after all the summer guests had left the Hilyard House, Rake was awakened by the sound of a shotgun blast.

Then he heard the most terrifying cry of all. *"Fire!"*

By the time he and his family rushed through the woods, the flames were dancing in the windows of the hotel and licking at the eaves.

Elwood and the remaining hotel staff were fighting with bucket brigades and hand-pump hoses. But the Hilyard House, a honeycomb of long, drafty hallways and high ceilings, was going up like a drift-wood pile on the beach.

Johnny heard his father say, "We might just as well spit on it, but let's see if we can help."

Then, from the room off the kitchen, there came the sound of an explosion.

"That'll be Tom's linseed oil goin' off," said Zachary, and he called to his brother, "Where's Tom?"

"We got him out," shouted Elwood, "he's in the gazebo."

But Tom was not in the gazebo. He was nowhere to be found until the fire was out and the Hilyard House was a smoking pile of ashes. What there was of him lay in his room, with his exploded paints and ruined canvases.

No one ever knew why he went back, though Charles Bigelow suspected that it was the book that drew him.

As for the fire, there was no doubt that it was set, and most people thought that crazy Tom himself had done it. A can of linseed oil was found near the veranda where the fire was thought to have started, along with the footprints of a man who limped, a man with a hole in his shoe. Tom limped. Tom had holes in his shoes.

But who had fired the shotgun to awaken those who might have died by this act of arson? The shell casings found at the edge of the beach were Remington twelve-gauge bird shot. Charles Bigelow knew that this was the ammunition his father used. But his father was found the following morning, in his house on the west side of the island, in his bed, in his nightshirt, with his shoes on his feet, sleeping soundly. So soundly in fact that he would never awaken.

Charles Bigelow removed his father's shoes, dumped out the sand, and put his finger through the hole in the sole.

CHAPTER 31

July 16

Mechanical Monsters

"Whenever I go to Provincetown," said Agnes, "which isn't too much, what with all those queer folk—"

"*Gays*," Geoff said.

"Strange word . . . Well, whenever I go there, I always smell b.o., and it's not the *gays*. It's Taft. Huge man in a dark suit, sweatin' to beat the band. And whenever I taste blueberry pie, I always think of that hotel, glitterin' like a jewel."

Geoff had forgotten his hangover, but confusion kept his head pounding. "Who set the fire? Did they find out?"

She shook her head. "Wooden hotels were like wooden ships, very susceptible to flame."

"Did you wonder about Charles Bigelow, after what you heard in the gazebo? Would he have burned the hotel to burn the log?"

"Of course not. That's a plug-ugly lie." Agnes sat back for a moment and started to hum. She always kept a little tune going in her head, if only to hold off the silence.

"Did anybody investigate Tom's fall at the State House?"

"What was there to investigate? He went to Boston to see Charles about a painting and fell down the stairs. He cracked his skull and had some kind of cerebral hemorrhage. The brain surgeons weren't too good then. Neither were the lawyers, because he didn't get much of a settlement."

"But the fire? Rake must have told his father what Charles said."

"The idea that Charles Bigelow would torch the Hilyard House was beyond anyone. He'd financed it after Tom's accident. And he made his father sign the subdivision plan when Elwood wanted to build a cottage colony all around it."

"The 1904 subdivision was a Hilyard's idea?"

"It was *Elwood's* idea. He had some big dreams. But after the fire, he lost interest. He took the insurance money and built himself the house they use now for the sailing camp. He said it was time to *respire* like a gentleman. A fool, that Elwood. Silver-plated fool. Zachary preferred work, like a man. I could never see how the same soil that nurtured your grandfather grew Elwood."

Geoff couldn't see how the soil that nurtured Aggie had grown her son Dickerson or her grandson Douglas, and her granddaughter Janice was beginning to bother him, too, but he didn't say so. Even if he had, Agnes might not have noticed, because her mind was now traveling down the highways to the two-lanes to the crushed-shell roads of her youth.

"They'd gotten around to building a canal in Sandwich, after three hundred years of talking about it, and a lot of Cape schooners were hauling granite for the breakwaters. Your grandma was pregnant with your father." Agnes laughed. "Pregnant at forty-five. Some woman. So Zach, he decided to get in on the hauling, make some diaper-pin money. Last anyone saw of Zach's old schooner, Zach, or his three eldest sons, they were off Cape Ann, wobblin' along with a deck load of rocks halfway to the mast."

"The sea has taken a lot of Hilyards."

"Bigelows, too. My sister and Teddy Bigelow took their honeymoon trip to England and came home on the *Titanic*. My sister came home a widow."

Though she rambled, every path led to another, which led to another, which led ultimately to the log.

It was Agnes's sister Dorothy who had been handed *Murder on the Mayflower* in 1911, who later married one of the Coles of Orleans and had three daughters, two of whom never married, one of whom moved to California and had four children, none of whom cared more for the Orleans home they inherited than to auction it and its contents, among which was a painting found in the attic, which hinted at the identity of the first murderer in America, which could not be proved without the log, which had inspired Tom Hilyard, who had died in the hotel fire, which satisfied Rake for eighty years that the log was gone, until the arrival of the woman named Carolyn Hallissey, who paid sixteen thousand dollars for the painting and somehow inspired Rake to start looking for the log once more. *Whew.*

"Did you and Rake ever talk about the log after that night in the gazebo?"

"A few times. I remember a Sunday morning, July of 1918 it was. I was visitin' my sister in Orleans, mostly so I could be close to Jack's Island. You know, Rake was just about the handsomest boy on the Lower Cape. Black hair, blue eyes to make you melt, and—gals weren't supposed to notice these things—he was spun like steel cable." She stared off again . . . *hum, hum.*

Geoff waited silently. Downstairs, the grandfather clock in the foyer chimed twice.

"Rake picked me up in Elwood's carriage. He brought me a bouquet, simple old snapdragons and a few strands of marsh grass. Most romantic thing a seventeen-year-old girl could ask for . . ." She looked out the window at the cars whizzing past on 6A, then continued down this sandy old path.

"We rode through the Barleyneck dairy field to Nauset Beach. It was deserted, of course. Everyone was at church, praying for an end to the Great War. The only thing out on the water was an old tug pulling a string of coal barges.

"We went a ways toward the inlet, just to be sure no one would spy on us. Then he pulled off his shirt and sat on a big piece of driftwood to take off his shoes. I just stood there, feelin' my dress blowin' against my bare legs and fidgetin' with my bouquet. I didn't want to admit it, but I was a little scared."

"That was kind of scandalous then."

"An unchaperoned boy and girl strippin' down on a deserted beach—we thought we were the first rebellious generation but—"

"Every generation thinks that, Aggie."

"—I was a good Methodist and a very reluctant rebel. I didn't know *what* I'd do if he decided to kiss me."

Geoff was back there with her, in the heart of her youth. He could almost feel the hot sand burning his toes, hear the roll of the surf.

"I was still afraid to let him see my bathing bloomers. Compared to today, they were a suit of armor, but I thought if I made a joke, he might laugh and forget whatever was on his mind. The driftwood log he was sittin' on gave me an idea. 'Jump up,' I said. 'I think you're sittin' on the log of the *Mayflower.*'"

"And you know what? He didn't laugh at all. He just said, '*This* isn't the log, Aggie. I'll guarantee you that.'

"'It was just a joke,' I said. 'The log burned in the Hilyard House fire.'

"He allowed as how it had. Then he said, 'The book of history will set us free from the evil that bricks us up.'"

Geoff was right. Her ramblings *did* lead back to the point, and the past led back to the present, and to the list that he carried in his pocket. "Why did he say that?"

"That's what his father told *him* when he asked about the log. I'm not sure he knew what it meant, and it puzzled me. Then we heard the first explosion."

"Explosion?"

"German U-boat. U-156, firing her deck gun. You could barely see it, about a mile offshore, long and flat, with a little tower that looked like nothing more than an oil barrel floating upright on the water. One shot hit in front of the tug, one hit the bluff right above us—blew out a great big chunk. Rake threw me down and threw himself on top of me, and I remember thinkin' how brave he was, and how happy I was to have his body on top of me but his mind on something else."

"Anybody hurt?"

"The crew got off the tug. Then the German commenced to sinkin' her and all the three barges. By now, everybody in Orleans was comin' out to watch, and it must've made the German nervous, because it took him about a hundred shots, which we thought was *some* funny, until he sent a few more at the bluff. Somebody said he was firin' at the cottages that showed the American flag, but . . ."

She stared out the window, hummed a bit, then said suddenly, "More than anything else, you know what I remember? How puny that gun sounded. Like the sky couldn't be bothered with the noise and just swallowed it up. Then we heard the putt-putt of an airplane engine."

"Navy fliers?"

"Un-huh, but the feller with the key to the bomb locker at the Chatham Naval Air Station was off playin' baseball. So the plane flew over and dropped a *monkey wrench* at the submarine. And that was that for the only German attack ever on American soil."

Geoff laughed. "The world sure has changed."

"Rake thought it changed right then. He said we weren't safe on our own beaches anymore, and it was time he did something about it. Hitched up for two years, which is a very long time in the life of a young girl. While he was gone, I fell in love with a man ten years older . . . and a Bigelow to boot." *Hum, hum,* tuneless, thoughtless, a sound track for the past.

"Rake felt betrayed, of course. We'd written letters, thought we were in love . . . but he got over it. People get over things. I thought the truth about the log would help you and Janice get over your problems, but an hour ago here she came, snatched up the kids, and away she went."

After an hour with Agnes, Geoff was ready to believe that everything was related—Rake's hunt for the log, Geoff's hunt for what Rake knew, Rake's anger at Agnes, Geoff's at Janice. A wheel, coming around again and again.

"Where did she go?"

"She didn't say."

Geoff picked at the thread coming loose on the arm of the sofa. "Why didn't you say anything about the log burning up before?"

"I'm old, Geoffrey. Nobody *asked* me."

ii.

Geoff wanted to believe Agnes, to free himself of the past that threatened to brick *him* up. But who had ransacked Rake's house and prowled in his barn? Who were those guys on the boat? Was the Humpster really stupid enough to beat up George? And for what, beyond a little fag-bashing? And, as always, there was the list. Why was Carolyn Hallissey's name at the top?

If Agnes's story was true, Janice's skepticism had triumphed. But Carolyn Hallissey might have some skepticism of her own—for Agnes's story.

It was five-thirty when he arrived at Carolyn's little Cape near Arey's Pond. From somewhere in the house he heard the sound of an afternoon game show. Two hamburger patties were frying on the range, two plates already arranged with sliced buns, ketchup, pickles, chips. . . .

He was surprised at how homey, and homely, she looked, barefoot, in jeans and baggy T-shirt.

And for the first time since they'd met, Carolyn did not seem happy to see him. Nor did she offer any skepticism. "If it's gone, it's gone. End of story. Go back to your wife and tell her I'm sorry for spoiling your reunion this morning."

"One word from Agnes Bigelow and you quit? Why haven't you interviewed her before this?"

"She's on the calendar. But I'm less interested in interviews than I am in art—pictures." She pointed to a picture on the wall. "My little boy did that."

It was a crudely drawn stick figure with long hair and the words "My Mother."

"How old is he?" asked Geoff.

"Eleven."

It looked like the work of a five-year-old. Another setup? he wondered.

But Carolyn called to Robby, who came shuffling in from the living room.

He seemed small for his age, a little round-shouldered, maybe, and he carried his head at a strange, crooked angle. As he approached, Geoff first saw the sandy hair, the friendly smile, then the unaccountably old face and sad eyes of Down's syndrome.

Carolyn introduced Geoff as Mr. Hilyard, and the boy took Geoff's hand with a practiced politeness that was all the more touching for the pride he took in it.

"Nice to meet you, Robby."

"Nice to meet you, Mr. Hilyard. Do you . . . do you like to fish?"

"I love to." Geoff told the boy about his fishing boat and promised to take him out someday.

After the boy had gone back to the television, Carolyn pulled out a chair. "Get the surprise off your feet."

"Nice boy," said Geoff.

"You're a nice guy. When I meet a man, I always gauge him on how he'll do with Robby. I pegged you for a good one. But you're taken. End of another story."

They talked a bit about the boy and his drawings, and that led naturally back to Tom Hilyard's paintings.

"He had the log, he painted from it, he lost it." She took two beers from the refrigerator. Then she jumped to the stove and flipped the hamburgers before they burned. Not nearly as cool in the kitchen as in the office.

He went to the counter to open the beers for her. That was when he noticed the black wig and sunglasses. Strange. And something stranger lay beneath them: a set of proofs for an Old Comers promotional brochure, with head shots of the directors, including John M. Nance.

Geoff took a moment, took a sip of beer, swallowed his anger at his own ignorance. Then he softly said Nance's name. "You told me you didn't know anything about him."

Carolyn took a tomato out of the refrigerator. "I told you I didn't know anything about his entry on the *list*."

"I never mentioned a list."

She put the tomato on the cutting board and sliced into it, as though it were a prop. "Your friends, Geoff . . . choose them more carefully. One of them talks a lot."

"And one of them was beaten up last night, by your boss's Bigelow friends. Did they do that to get information?"

"I don't know a thing about that. But I sent people into Rake Hilyard's barn last night, because I knew about the list and could deduce a bit more, thanks to one of your friends. Now it's over, so it doesn't matter which friend. I see no reason why Agnes Bigelow would tell you anything but the truth."

Another setup, after all? He stood there, hating the smell of hamburger fat in a kitchen. "You've been lying to me since I laid eyes on you, Carolyn. Why should I believe you now?"

"Listen"—she slammed the knife on the cutting board and sent tomato seeds splattering—"I have two loyalties: to that boy in there and to the job that lets me give him the best life I can. Nance gave me the job. Guess the rest of the syllogism."

Life was full of surprises. A lot of them were bad. Some were sad. More than anything, he wanted to see his kids.

iii.

As he drove over the causeway, he imagined the lives Jack's Island had lived. Those lives had been full of surprises, too, a lot of them bad. And some sad.

He saw it as Jack Hilyard must have seen it, covered with tall hardwoods, dense and primeval. Then it was treeless, with corn growing and windmills pumping water into salt vats. Then the great white hotel rose on Nauseiput Creek. Then the red cedars began to fill in the meadows, making way for the pitch pine forest that now was giving way to oak and that might someday become beech and maple again.

He drove by the house that Elwood had built on the hotel foundation. Nothing else remained of the Hilyard House. Nature covered her scars, if given time. But bulldozers gouged deep.

And damned if he didn't hear one when he got out of the car in front of Rake's house. Then he saw the Voyager. A bad surprise, then a good one. From somewhere, his kids came scampering and falling over each other, covering him with kisses and questions. Where had he been? Why wasn't he staying in Truro? When was he going to make up his mind so they could all be back together again? What had she been telling them?

She had her arms folded across her chest, which meant she was ready for a fight, but her words were the neutral color of sand. "I thought you'd stay here tonight, to be ready for the Conservation Commission walk tomorrow."

A snappy answer would have been good, but that bulldozer . . .

Janice told the kids to go down and play with Jimmy and Jason.

"Jimmy's kids?" Geoff asked. "Are Jimmy and Samantha here, too? Is this, like, a party?" More like a wake, he was thinking, and from the way she was standing in the doorway, she could be the guest of honor.

"I asked them to come. To help us."

Crack! The sound of a tree snapping at the trunk. "What's that bulldozer doing?"

"Geoff, do I have to worry about this Carolyn Hallissey?"

"You have to worry about *us* . . . and that bulldozer." If she wanted to make him feel squeezed, she couldn't have done a better job. The bulldozer, the kids, the questions—bring it all to a point right now, right in the open.

Somewhere off on the west side of the island, another tree trunk split, then snapped. The crown sweeping through the surrounding branches sounded like the wind.

"Forget the bulldozer," said Janice, still frozen in the doorway. "The log burned. My family's in trouble. We're in trouble—"

"Because you ran away."

"*You* ran away."

"And your family's in trouble, Janice, because your brother's on the hook to John M. Nance."

She didn't move, didn't even seem shocked, which surprised him. "I heard. Jimmy went to the registry. There's a mortgage on file, between Bigelow and Iron Axe."

"Yeah"—Jimmy came out of the house and distributed beers to Geoff and Janice—"but I couldn't get any further than the catalog, because in the summer they close at four o'clock on Mondays around here. Librarian called me a typical Indian. Day late and a dollar short."

"Nobody's called him a *typical* Indian in a long time," Samantha followed her husband. "I'm not sure I like it."

Jimmy took a swallow of beer. "Ma laughed like hell when I told her."

"Did she laugh about Nance? Strip-the-Plants, stomp the foe, run him off the road." Geoff pulled from his pocket the piece of fabric, blue with a little white anchor woven into it. "I found this on the bumper of Rake's car."

Just then George's Bronco came banging down the road and into the driveway. He had his new friend with him, and he didn't look too bad for all that had happened to him. He even got out of the car with a little spring in his step, though his friend stayed inside.

Geoff went over to him and lifted his sunglasses and he looked a lot worse. "Hiya, George."

George tried to smile, but it looked as if it hurt too much. "It got uglier, Geoff."

"The Humpster?" asked Geoff.

George just shrugged.

Now Samantha came over to him and pinned a purple paper heart to his shirt. "The kids made this."

"Cute," said George.

"Are you sure the Humpster did this to you?" asked Janice.

"They wrote his favorite line on the front door."

In the woods, the bulldozer growled, shifted gears.

"Now he's cuttin' new scars in Mother Earth," said Jimmy.

"What would Ma Little do about that?" asked Geoff.

"As long as they're a hundred feet from the wetlands," answered Jimmy, "not a thing. Legally, that is."

Geoff picked up a garden spade leaning against a fence post. "Ma would kick a little ass. And old Rake would say, 'Fuck 'em, let's fight about it.' You guys with me?"

George fitted the glasses back on his nose gingerly. "Hey, guys, I'm a lover, not a fighter."

"So bring your friend along." Geoff looked into the car, at George's friend. "What about— David? The secretary?"

The young man from Provincetown who served coffee and fetched files for Carolyn Hallissey. He gave Geoff a little wave with his fingertips and then looked straight through the windshield.

"Secretary?" George looked in at David from the other side of the car. "Of what?"

"Old Comers Plantation. He's been passing everything you know to Carolyn Hallissey, Georgie."

George looked at David, and David just shrugged. No big deal. Nice knowin' ya. See ya around. He got out of the car and started down the road.

And for a moment, the others stood there listening to the growling of the Humpster's bulldozer in the woods, while George hid whatever he was feeling behind his sunglasses.

Finally George shouted, "Thanks for bein' there last night, David. And thanks for nothin'." Then he smoothed the little purple heart on his chest. "Helluva life, isn't it, kids?"

The thunderous echo of an empty scoop striking a boulder made them all jump. Geoff grabbed his shovel and said the Humpster should pay for what he had done to Georgie.

"This is stupid," said Janice.

Jimmy patted her arm. "I'm still a lawyer. I still know how to talk. We'll let the Humpster know he shouldn't do what he's doing. We're not that stupid."

Geoff was already halfway down the road. Jimmy gave his wife a little kiss and went hurrying after him.

George said, "I can't be a lover, so I guess I'll be a fighter."

And Janice went in to call her brother.

A chain saw was baying after the bulldozer. And as Geoff approached the edge of the woods near Doug's house, he smelled diesel exhaust.

The baloney roll hanging over the Humpster's belt jiggled. At first he didn't see them. Running a rig like this was demanding work, and the Humpster was no amateur. Give him that much. He drove the yellow monster the way most men drove a car.

The trees fell, and the rocks rolled, and the scanty topsoil came scraping up like sunburned skin under a fingernail. And three other guys went about the business of cleaning up after him, one with a chain saw, two with shovels.

"Hey, fat ass," shouted Geoff.

"What the fuck do *you* want?" screamed the Humpster.

"What are you doin'?" demanded Geoff.

"I'm fuckin' a snake. What does it look like?"

The guy with the chain saw gunned his little monster into the air, just for show. The others raised their shovels.

"You need Conservation Commission approval to cut these trees," said Jimmy.

The Humpster pointed across the road, to a red stake about thirty feet from Doug's driveway. "There's the hundred-foot wetlands marker. Beyond it, we can do anything we want outside of buildin' a house. So fuck off, Hiawatha."

Jimmy took a few steps. "I'll have the C.C. here in twenty minutes. Cutting these trees threatens the watershed."

"In twenty minutes, they'll all be down. One acre."

"Then you'll be fined," said Jimmy.

The Humpster gave them the finger and leaned on the throttle. The earthmover scraped into another clump of trees. The earth beneath it was a strange yellow color. Then he backed up, crunching and grinding over broken branches and rocks, straight at Geoff Hilyard, without even looking.

Geoff raised his shovel. Jimmy stood at his shoulder.

Fat jiggled, wood chips flew, and somebody finally saw that the Humpster wasn't going to stop. George grabbed Jimmy, Jimmy grabbed Geoff, and the three of them went sprawling sideways into the sand as the treads crawled past, like a Japanese tank in a war movie.

"You guys remember *Back to Bataan?*" George picked up a rock. "If this was a hand grenade—"

Now the guy with the chain saw decided to get into it, but he didn't get far. Geoff swung his shovel like a baseball bat and caught the saw right under the blade. It flew up, spun backwards, and nearly cut the guy's nose off. He jumped back so fast that he tripped on one of the fallen trees, and before he was on his feet, Jimmy had the saw in his hands, holding it like a spear to keep the others off.

"Better odds today, fatso," shouted George.

"What are you talkin' about?" The Humpster threw the shift into neutral so he could trade a few more insults.

" 'Faggots, Mo-nigs, and fools'?" said George.

"You said it, not me." The Humpster was probably an inveterate liar, but he was no actor. Geoff could see that he was puzzled by George's remark. Then the Humpster revved his engine like a challenge.

And Geoff smashed his shovel against the blade of the bulldozer. It was like taking a hammer to a battleship, but he didn't care. After a week and a half of frustration, it was better than sex. If these were the odds, he'd take them.

And now Blue Bigelow and Douglas came skidding down the road in Blue's Lincoln Continental. Blue leaped out, shouting, "What's goin' on here?"

"Clearin' the woods." The Humpster backed halfway to the road for some running room, then he shifted again.

However stupid it might have been, Geoff kept himself in the way. And his friends decided to act as stupid.

The Humpster gunned the engine. The little cap on the exhaust tube popped open. The fat jiggled. The Humpster looked like some kind of heavy-haul Buddha in a John Deere temple. The sand and rolling rocks in front of the blade built like a wave.

"Stand your ground," said Geoff.

"That's what they told us when the white men fired their guns," said Jimmy. *Brmmmm.* He fired the saw.

"Scissors cut paper, bulldozer breaks chain saw"—George seized a rock and wound up like Roger Clemens—"and rock breaks Humpster." But George had no control. The Humpster just laughed at a wild pitch.

Closer and higher the wave came. Blue shouted something at his son. Closer, higher, louder . . .

Geoff stopped thinking. Thought retreated behind the barrier of instinct. He knew he would know just when to jump, or whether to jump at all.

Closer, higher, louder . . .

Blue Bigelow moved fast for a big man. By the time he leaped onto the bulldozer and grabbed the brake, the blade was so close that Geoff could see no more than two heads above it.

"Talk about scared straight," whispered George.

Blue's first words were "Stupid son of a bitch."

"Fuck you, Dad. You said to clear an acre before the perk tests."

"*Before* the tests," Doug explained gently, "*after* the C.C. walks the ground."

"Stupid son of a bitch," repeated Blue.

"It's quittin' time, Hump." Geoff laughed. Someone who had done something this stupid and survived *had* to laugh.

"Fuck you, too." The Humpster's big face was turning a medium-rare shade of red. The sweat patch widened on his belly.

"Excuse me, guys." In the confusion, no one had seen a rental Chevy come down the road. The driver called, "Isn't Rake Hilyard's house this way?"

"Who's asking?" Geoff stepped out of the mess the Humpster had made, just because he was a stupid son of a bitch.

"My name's Mary Muldowney." The famous old actress.

Geoff had wondered about her since he found the list.

"Rake asked me to come and visit when I got here."

"I'm his nephew."

"He asked me to bring a painting he gave me years ago." On the seat of the Chevy was *House on Billingsgate*, Number 17.

CHAPTER 32

August 1928

Summer Stock

Rake Hilyard swore off love the day Aggie Dickerson sent him a Dear John that would have lifted the stripes off a bass.

"I am writing to tell you that next month I marry Ethan Bigelow." A potbellied lumber salesman ten years her senior, and Agnes turned over Rake Hilyard for him. What man wouldn't swear off love after that?

Spark with the local girls, sure. Take a New York divorcée out on the boat and promise to visit her come January. Go to Boston and pay for it when you couldn't clear your pipes any other way. But no more falling in love.

He had seen this Mary Muldowney gal only once, and he hadn't even talked to her. When she appeared in her maid's uniform, dusting and fluttering about the stage, her beauty reached through the darkness and grabbed him right by the belt. This one was for him—at least for the summer.

The play was called *The Barker*, and it was the second time Rake had seen it. Most fishermen didn't see a play in a lifetime. Who could be bothered when the tide turned at three in the morning and you lost the best fishing of the day if you missed it? But Rake could be lured if someone gave him tickets to the Cape Playhouse.

And tickets came regularly from a Boston gentleman named Mr.

Flip. Though they did not know his real name, the Hilyards did business with Flip. They conducted this business on moonless nights, because the business was liquor, and liquor was illegal.

No one knew when the first man fermented a grape. It was probably soon after he met the first woman. Possibly before. But after the Great War, some people decided that a country without drink would be a better place. So they passed the Eighteenth Amendment and called it a Noble Experiment.

Rake called it the work of busybodies and fools. By 1928, few disagreed, and most would say that America wasn't even as *good* a place as it had been before Prohibition.

People who wanted to take a drink now and then flouted the law from the boweries to the Harvard reunions, and they pumped a flood of illegal cash into the aquifer of America's economy. The Noble Experiment made a lot of people criminals, made a lot of criminals rich, and put a high premium on dark stretches of beach.

Flip had visited several of Brewster's seacoast mansions, searching for a place that was secluded and above suspicion, where no coast guardsman or hijacker would ever think to look for liquor. He found Jack's Island and the shingle-style Victorian owned by Elwood P. Hilyard, who still wore a monocle and called himself a respired businessman.

In their only meeting, Flip presented himself as a man of cultivation who spent more time discussing theater than bootlegging. Afterward, business was conducted by telephone, but whenever a load came in at Jack's Island, two theater tickets accompanied the landing fee of a dollar a case.

The old Cape Cod, the one that had dozed in the sun the morning that Rake took Agnes to the beach, that Cape was gone. Postwar prosperity had seen to that. Summer people poured onto the Cape in their Model A Fords and poured cash into theaters, hotels, guest houses, and roadside stands where farmers sold butter-sugar corn, beach plum jelly, and bootleg. They paid fools' prices for whatever Cape wives dug from their attics and called "anteeks." And they bought land.

But not only did they buy. They speculated. The year-round population was still less than it had been in 1850, but ambitious people were buying up woodlots and waterfronts, building cottage colonies and subdivisions, while people whose speculations succeeded were building mansions on the Gold Coast of Nantucket Sound.

The sandy roads were now oiled, the oiled roads were now tarred. In Dennis, an old Quaker meetinghouse became the Cape Playhouse, while new houses of worship gave play to Catholicism. And the last of Provincetown's Grand Bankers had been chased from the sea by the same submarine that shelled Nauset Beach.

Some had seen the voyage of U-156 as comic opera. But to Rake, it had meant that the old ways were ending. The tourist dollar would gain sway in a place where men had always taken their living from the elements. He would not complain, however, if the new ways brought gals like Mary Muldowney to that meetinghouse in Dennis.

She looked at the flowers in his hand and laughed. "Take a hike, Stage Door."

"Stage Door?"

"Stage Door Johnny."

"How'd you know my name was John?"

"It's the lingo, Johnny. Now go on. I got a fella." She took a drink from the silver flask on the table in front of her, tilting her head all the way back to get out the last drops.

The other girls did not seem bothered that a man was in the dressing room. Rake guessed theater folk were a little different that way. One was tightening her brassiere to flatten her breasts. Another was curling her hair with a hot iron. Another was slipping a flask into her garter. But they all had an eye on Rake, because a young fisherman was something they seldom saw beyond the footlights.

"I thought you were just fine tonight," he said.

"Everybody's a critic." She turned to the mirror and applied the lower half of a red bee sting to her lips.

"I'm a fisherman," he said.

"That gives us exactly zero in common."

He put the flowers in front of her and studied her like a man inspecting the hull of a new boat—twenty or twenty-one, marcelled black hair, eyes the color of a summer sky, lower lip as red as a berry in his father's old bog, and a full, round figure that put the boy-chested flappers to shame. But he'd be damned if he'd say any of that now, the way she was treating him.

"Friends don't call me Johnny. Call me Rake, Rake Hilyard. Ask at Jack's Island . . . if you ever want any fish."

The other girls snickered, and Mary's face broke into a grin that looked pretty stupid with one bee-stung lip.

"*Sell* 'em to you or, considerin' what I saw on the stage tonight, give you a job cleanin' 'em."

"Say, you dirty— Why, Hank!" Someone had appeared behind Rake, and Mary became Miss Demure, 1928. "Hank, you're early. I'd be ready now, but this Stage Door Johnny—"

"The name's John," Rake said fiercely as he turned. "You can call me . . . Mr. Hilyard."

Rake recognized him from the play. He was a bit taller than Rake, with black hair, a gentle face, and a soft, drawling manner of speech. "Nice to meet you, Mr. Hilyard. Hope you liked the play."

A little warmth softened Rake considerably. "It was fine. Liked it fine. Thanks."

"I'll call ya if I need any fish," said Mary.

When he got to his car, Rake took the program and looked up the name. Hank . . . Henry Fonda. Another actor. Bet Hank couldn't bait a tub of line. Bet he didn't know when the stripers came to Dennis Hole. Bet he wouldn't be man enough to do what Rake was plannin' that night. But Hank had the girl . . . for now.

Rake put the car in gear and headed out to collect the boys.

ii.

An engine . . . distant voices . . . The panic snapped Aggie Dickerson Bigelow straight off the pillow. Her first thought was that someone had broken into the boathouse. She elbowed Ethan. His breathing stuttered, then settled back into the rhythm of the waves.

So she found her slippers with her toes and scuffled to the window. The boat could be stolen only at high tide, which meant it was now somewhere between one-thirty and three-thirty.

Then she heard the engine again. A truck . . . two trucks. One of them shifted, and the grinding of the gears struck her at the base of the skull. She had heard rumors about her old beau Rake Hilyard. . . .

She scurried past the room where her little boys slept, to the room where her father-in-law lay in a codeine stupor. She peered out the front window but could see nothing through the pitch pines in the middle of the island.

So she climbed the narrow stairs to the attic. There an old captain's glass sat on a tripod by a window. With shaking hand, she swept the glass back and forth until she found the raised shadow of the causeway in the middle of the marsh. And then she saw them, the big, square outlines of two trucks straining into the woods, all lights out. She bolted for her bedroom.

"Rumrunners! Ethan, wake up. Rumrunners!"

He rolled over like a lazy wave flopping onto the beach. The middle button on his pajamas had come undone, revealing a slice of luminous white skin. She poked it with her fingernails.

"Huh? Rum . . ."

"We have to call the Coast Guard."

"Why? Who? Coast Guard? Is someone in trouble?"

"No! Rumrunners! Right here on Jack's Island!"

Ethan sat up. "Get the keys to the gun case."

"They're rumrunners, not ducks! They'll shoot back. Call the Coast Guard." She was shouting and whispering at the same time, so as not to wake the children or Grampa Charlie.

But Grampa Charlie was awake and wandering the hallways in search of more codeine. "Who's callin' the Coast Guard?"

Aggie was startled by the voice, still strong and certain, coming from the withered old silhouette. Charles Bigelow's daunting bulk was gone. His belly sagged beneath the tie on his robe, and the fringe of white hair around his head looked like the disheveled halo he was trying on for size.

"I think the Hilyards are running rum," she said.

"Scotch, more likely." He flipped on the light in their room.

"You *know*?" Ethan squinted like a bat caught in the beam of a lantern.

"Scotch, if we're lucky." He smoothed his hand over his upper lip, but even the mustache was gone, shaved by some orderly in the hospital where his death sentence had been pronounced. "Maybe a few bottles of beer."

"Grampa, that's illegal."

"You like a glass of wine, don't you, girl? Where do you think I get that? Out of a seed catalog? Elwood brings it after every run."

"You stocked your cellar before the law passed."

"That was *eight years ago*. Get back to bed." He flipped off the light and went shuffling toward the bathroom. A moment later a medicine bottle shattered and the old man cursed.

"Go on," said Ethan. "I'll take care of him."

She climbed under the covers and, with her conscience churning her stomach, listened: another truck, several passenger cars, then a muffled boat engine. She got out of bed again and went to the window that looked out at the bay. No running lights showed, but the phosphorescence of the wake glittered eerily, like a snake in the darkness.

iii.

Perez "Iron Axe" Nance puttered past the Coast Guard cutter at the end of Town Wharf in Provincetown.

"Catch anybody this week?" he shouted to the Lieutenant at the stern.

"Gonna catch *you* this week."

"Whatchew wanta with us?" called Perez's cousin, Manny Souza. "They gots prohibition on halibuts, now?"

"Don't be ridin' 'em." Perez laughed. "No good gettin' the Coast Guard mad."

"Eh, they mad awready," said Manny out of the corner of his mouth, "'cause they got no chance to catch the Iron Axe."

Perez guided his boat through the harbor and around Wood End. In his boyhood, he had stood on that barren sandspit and watched the Grand Bankers, with their clipper-trim hulls and cloud-like spreads of canvas, sweeping majestically toward the fishing grounds. But beam trawlers and draggers had replaced the beauties of the past. Independent men now put to sea in thirty-foot gasoliners like the *Pilgrim Portagee*.

A little gasoliner for a big man. That's what they said about the *Portagee*, because after the boat, everything about Perez Nance was big—big voice, big belly, big arms, big black mustache, a highliner who always filled his hold.

He had long ago forgotten Dorothy Dickerson, though not her father's insult. He had enlisted in the Great War, in spite of a slight limp and, when he came home, had fallen in love with an East End Yankee girl named Helen Tinker.

And it was the same old story. Her father objected, because the Tinkers descended from the *Mayflower* and Perez came from the West End. But instead of pocketing a pistol, Perez put on his Purple Heart from Belleau Wood and went courting. And the medal worked its magic.

He and Miss Tinker were married at the Catholic church in

1920. Though out of the ordinary, this was not the first Provincetown wedding of Protestant and Portuguese. The old order accorded a grudging respect to the newcomers, because the Portuguese had proved themselves where it mattered most in a seafaring town—at sea.

Few knew that Perez's grandmother had passed from slavery to freedom, that he had passed from the dark brava to light-skinned Portagee, or that he dreamed of seeing his son pass into any port of American life he chose. Perez named his boat the *Pilgrim Portagee*, for the mingling of the stocks, and those who didn't like it could go to hell.

That included the Ku Klux Klan, who burned a cross in front of the church a few months after his marriage. In a last flurry of nativism, Klansmen went about the Cape, frightening Catholics and foreigners both, but by 1928, most night riders rode rum. There was more money in bottles than in bed sheets.

Once past Race Point, the *Pilgrim Portagee* turned east. The gray and white town sank behind the dunes, which soon faded into the haze. After about twenty minutes, an old schooner appeared, snoozing at its anchor like a dog leashed to a stake. Off to the south a rotten five-master rolled on the swell. And to the north, an old bucket of bolts rusted away.

This was Rum Row, the beggars' blockade that stretched along the American coast from Maine to Florida. The challenge for this navy, however, was not to keep things *out*, but get them *in*. Only ships of American registry could be seized outside the three-mile limit. So rum-ship captains registered in Britain, set their anchors ten miles offshore, and left the landing to men who could handle small boats in coastal waters—men like Perez Nance.

He guided the *Pilgrim Portagee* around the stern of a three-master named *The Dalmatian*, and tethered her to the seaward side, out of sight of patrolling cutters.

As soon as the *Portagee* was tied up, the loading began. She could carry three hundred cases, worth a hundred dollars apiece to the syndicate that owned the *Dalmatian* and the delivery trucks, five dollars apiece to the man who got the booze from one to the other. The liquor was packed in straw-filled burlap sacks—still called cases—and fitted into every corner. The work went quickly, because as soon as there was liquor on board the *Portagee*, she was hot.

Perez unsnapped the leather sheath that covered the axehead

and went aboard. He and the men of the *Dalmatian* worked for the same syndicate, but when he went aboard without a weapon, he felt as if he had gone without his pants. These were not sailors to trust in heavy seas—or with your back turned. In such company, an old battle-axe demanded respect.

"Hey, Iron Axe," said one of them, "Sbardi come all the way out from Boston to see you. You in trouble?"

Perez swallowed the fear that rose with the linguiça he'd had for lunch. "Just load the booze."

Sbardi and his three bodyguards sat in the captain's cabin, playing poker. When Perez knocked, three hands went for shoulder holsters.

"Easy, boys." Sbardi flicked his stubby fingers and Sammy the Snake made room for Perez.

Sammy had slicked-back hair and sleepy eyes, and always wore a life jacket because he was afraid of the water. Beneath the life jacket, he always wore a shoulder holster. Perez didn't like Sammy or any of the others. The dark, disinterested faces said that any of them would chop him up with his own axe, stuff him into a burlap liquor case, and send him back to P-town without twitching a nose hair, and there were plenty of those in sight.

Of course, most of Sbardi's hair was in his ears. His olive-colored skin was as smooth as an eggshell. And the way he hitched his pants up over his potbelly, he even *looked* like an egg. He waved his black Parodi cigar like a wand, and a glass of Haig & Haig appeared before Perez.

"Nice boat you got tied up at the stern." Perez sipped the scotch and felt it burn through the linguiça.

"*The Gray Lady*. Ran it out from Boston in two hours. Forty foot, twin Fiats. Make most Coast Guard scows look like rowboats."

"You . . . you on a pleasure cruise?"

"Uh-uh." Sbardi blew a stream of smoke. "We got a problem with one of the other syndicates. Bunch of fuckin' Irish bums. They got Southie, Quincy . . . halfway down to Plymouth, they got. But they greedy."

"No good to be greedy. Plenty to go around."

"Yeah, well, these fuckin' Irish bums, we gotta teach 'em a lesson. I want you find out who's runnin' for a guy goes by the name Flip."

Nance could think of several. But he scratched at his chin as though he'd never heard the name.

"You tell us who's runnin', where they land, when . . . we get some boys go visit 'em."

Nance was as tough as anyone, but he steered clear of things beyond the beach. He knew only that along the dark roads between Cape Cod and Boston, men like Sbardi's thugs were at their best. "This . . . this ain't my line of work. I'd do you a lot more good outsmartin' the Coast Guard."

"And you'd make a lot more money with a bigger boat. More money to pass on to that little bambino." Sbardi laughed like an old man buying his grandchildren gelato from a pushcart. "He a good boy?"

"Good boy. Big and strong."

Sbardi puffed thoughtfully on his cigar. "Save what you make from this work. Save it, put it away, set him up in business. None of this . . . dirt."

Nance swallowed a bit more scotch. "For the boy, I do some dangerous things, but no gunplay, no head-knockin'."

"Eh"—Sbardi shrugged—"you play with fire, maybe you get burned. But maybe I give you the *Gray Lady*. Carry six hundred cases, so fast she outrun Coast Guard *bullets*, never mind the boats. Make you three thousand bucks every fuckin' trip. You help, she's yours."

iv.

Rake went to the Cape Playhouse a week later. The play was called *Mr. Pim Passes By*. Henry Fonda had passed *it* by and was now in some other summer theater someplace in Connecticut.

Good riddance, thought Rake. With luck, that would be the last he'd see of Fonda. The backstage talk this week was of a young actress with big eyes and a bad temper named Bette Davis. Rake thought Mary was a lot better, but he hadn't come with compliments.

"Hiya, fisherman," said one of the girls in the dressing room. "Got any haliddock?"

"How 'bout some chow-dah?" called another.

Rake ignored them. He went to the corner where Mary was

slicking off her stage makeup with cold cream. "You and *Hank* want to go fishing?"

"Get lost," she said, without looking up.

He put the bouquet under her nose.

"Is that supposed to be funny?" She glanced at the dandelions and lousewort and other weeds, festooned with cattails and marsh grass.

"Thought this might be more to your taste than the first one." He set it on the table. "Don't need a vase."

"You got that right, fisherman." She picked the bouquet up to throw it into the trash, but the heft of it made her curious. It had its own vase, wrapped in woven marshgrass.

She peeled back the dandelions and sliced a long red fingernail into the weaving. Beneath was the corner of an orange label with juniper berries—Gordon's gin. "Where would a fisherman get—"

But the fisherman was gone.

She gently unscrewed the top, passed her nose over the lip, and smelled merry old England, uncut and unadulterated. She had learned to tell the good stuff from the rotgut. She had also learned to ignore the insult when a gentleman brought gin instead of candy. Candy she could buy at the general store.

A few days later, Mary hitchhiked to Jack's Island. It seemed that she had gotten herself fired. She had bobbled a line, causing Bette Davis to miss a cue. Afterward, Davis had accused her of being drunk on stage, which was a lie. Mary drank no more than the other girls, and never before the show. But the producers sided with the rising star, who was not Mary.

At the causeway, she put down her suitcase and sat on it. She rubbed her knuckles, where she'd smacked Davis, but her pride felt worse than her knuckles. And her feet felt worse than her pride. She slipped off her shoes and rubbed the soles of her feet. She should have known that on Cape Cod you needed something more than heels. And a wide-brimmed hat would have helped, too, instead of a cloche that you'd wear to some West Eighties speakeasy.

But it was all for the best. She was on her way to Provincetown. Dennis was nothing but a backwater of summer families and tooth-sucking old Yankees looking to make a buck from the Off-Capers. She'd heard that Provincetown was like Greenwich Village gone to summer school. There were artists at easels in the dunes, writers in the cafés, speakeasies right in the town, and the Provincetown Players, the first company to produce the plays of Eugene O'Neill.

But Mary was broke. To get to P-town, she needed another ride, and she *was* a little thirsty . . . and come to think of it, that fisherman did look a bit like Hank Fonda.

It was a sparkling afternoon, the kind she wrote about in letters to her New York girlfriends when she wanted to make them envious: "There's a hot sun but a cool breeze. A clean stillness hangs over the marshes and meadows, letting you hear sounds you never hear in New York—the chatter of a mockingbird when you pass her nest, the slamming of a screen door down the road, the faraway cries of kids at the beach. . . ." Her friends wouldn't envy her now.

The west side of the island was covered with stunted pitch pines, the only kind of forest on Cape Cod. In the middle of the island, the trees thinned to meadows dotted with cedars, as though somebody had painted them in, thinking they'd look nice against the blue of the bay. And over on the east side, seedy lawns and hedges grew up around a big house.

She took the west fork. The sandy shoulders of the road were kind to her feet, and the scrawny trees threw more shade than she'd expected. Not bad walking at all. And there was a sweetness in the air, of pine and berries. Soon she came to a boathouse at the edge of the creek.

It was low tide. Nothing more than a trickle of water ran through the creek and onto the tideflats, like a river fading into an alkali sink in some cowboy serial. Two little boys were scrambling around a motorboat in the mud.

"Hey, you kids got names?"

"I'm Dickerson," said the big one, who looked to be about eight. He had a layer of fat around his belly and an aggressive little scowl. The other one studied her with a sweetly quizzical expression that made him look a bit like an inbred, of which she had seen more than one in these parts.

"This here's Hiram," offered Dickerson. "He's five. Who're you?"

"Name's Mary. Are you Hilyards?" And was this fisherman stepping out on his wife and two kids?

"Nah. We're Bigelows. The Hilyards live down the road."

"Next house?"

"The one after. Next one's my grampa's. He was a senator."

"A Washington senator?"

"Nah, just a state senator. Now he got a cancer."

"Oh, uh, sorry." She wasn't much for small talk with little boys, especially about cancer. She left them to hot-wire the boat and hurried on. Soon she passed a decrepit old windmill, all over-grown with brambles and vines, and she had the feeling she was walking back in time. Then she came to a big house, built in a style she'd read about somewhere. French Provincial? Greek some-thing-or-other? She couldn't quite remember. The name on the shingle read Charles Bigelow, Lawyer. She turned east and followed the road.

She found Rake in the barn behind his old Cape house. He was caulking a catboat.

"Hiya, Stage Door." She dropped her suitcase.

He gave her no more than a glance, as though he had been expecting her all along. "What happened to your shoes?"

She wiggled her toes. They were coated all over with dust, which made her red nails look as cheap as rhinestones. She daintily lowered her ass to the edge of the suitcase, brushed off her feet, put on her shoes. And if she just happened to show more leg than this fisherman might have seen in his whole life, where was the harm?

However, if he was impressed by the whiteness of her thighs, he had a peculiar way of showing it. He fit his caulking iron into a joint and pounded some oakum. "Looks like somebody come to see Stage Door 'cause she got kicked out the front door."

"*Back* door's more like it. That Davis dame said I was drunk on stage. So I smacked her."

"By gar, you're a feisty one." He put down his caulking tools and opened a trapdoor in the floor. "That deserves a beer."

"But, gee-golly-gosh, it's Prohibition." She widened her eyes and gave her voice a little Betty Boop squeak. "Ain't beer illegal?"

He laughed and pulled a burlap bag from below.

She heard the tinkling music of beer bottles tapping against one another, and soon she was licking the foam from her lips. The beer had a fresh, nutty taste, as cool as the earth it came from. "Guess you must've wanted to smack me, the way I treated you."

"Yes, yes, I guess. And maybe you wanted to smack me for giving you a bouquet of weeds."

"I liked the vase." She sipped and let the coolness of the beer fizz on her gums. In this light, he really did look like Hank Fonda. "So . . . you a rumrunner?"

"'Fore Prohibition, nobody much cared 'bout booze. These days, win more friends with a bottle of gin than a halibut steak, and don't know *who* to trust. If someone ain't watchin' to find your hidin' place, they're out to weasel on you." He crouched in front of her and looked her in the eye. "Helluva way to live, but don't trust anyone, girlie-girl. Now, what're you after?"

Indignation. She summoned it from her bag of expressions. "What makes you think I'm after anything?"

"Can tell when the mackerel are gettin' ready to rise. Ought to be able to tell when someone's after somethin'."

She took another swallow of the beer. She could stomp out and keep hitchhiking. Or swallow her pride. Or settle for something in between. She poured the last of her beer onto the floor. Refuse to swallow the beer, *then* swallow the pride. "All I want's a ride to P-town. I'm broke and I don't know anybody else. If you can't be civil, I'll get up there—"

"*Down* there."

"*Up* there! It's *north.* Don't you people know geography?"

"Rake?" A dark-haired young woman appeared in the doorway.

The wife, thought Mary. He *was* stepping out, the bastard. She got ready to spit in his eye and skidoo.

But the woman was Rake's sister Clara and she didn't give Mary a second look. "Elwood wants to see you. Flip called about tonight."

"Where's Billy?"

"Gone clammin'."

Rake told her to go get him, told Mary to sit tight because she might get her ride to Provincetown, then started toward the big house. But Clara didn't move.

"What's wrong?" Rake took Clara by the arm and kicked the barn door shut, leaving Mary inside.

What did he think she was going to do? Eavesdrop? She lifted another beer out of the burlap sack and tiptoed to the open window.

They were arguing—something about a shipment that night and Rake needing his little brother to help. But his sister didn't want their little brother getting arrested.

"Ain't been arrested yet," Rake said. "Want him waitin' tables at Harvard, feelin' poor 'cause he comes from a hardworkin' family? There ain't no quicker way to make money than what we been doin'."

"We could always ask Elwood about the sailin' camp."

Rake just laughed and held up his hand. "Five dollars a case, two hundred and fifty cases. *That's* money. But I can't do it by myself."

"Get somebody else," said Clara.

"Can't *trust* somebody else."

"Trust me," Mary said through the window, "for three hundred and a ride to P-town."

And so began the rumrunning partnership of Rake Hilyard and Mary Muldowney.

Clara gave her a pair of men's trousers and some flat-heeled shoes. Rake gave her a baseball cap and asked her if she had any strength in those skinny arms.

"I grew up in Hell's Kitchen, me and four brothers in two rooms. I'm stronger'n most *guys*."

And she was. The sailors on the rum ship laughed when they saw her, but they weren't laughing when Rake's boat rumbled away. "As strong as a stevedore and tits that bounce," muttered one awe-struck sailor.

Mary liked the money. Three hundred dollars cash was more than she had ever made in a single night. And the run went so well that she couldn't imagine quitting. A week later, they were still working. The most Rake would admit was that he had found a partner, but that was enough.

One night they were held up an extra hour at the landing and missed the tide on the way back to Jack's Island. Rake's boat, the *Paintin' Tom*, had a bit over two hours on either side of high tide to cross the Brewster flats. So Rake came in as close as he could and threw out the anchor.

Then they walked, barefoot and cuffs rolled up, through the receding water.

In some places, the bottom was firm and sandy, but in others, Mary sank to her ankles in mud that sounded like a fart when she pulled a foot free—and didn't smell much better. And there were night creatures scuttling about in the wash—crabs, brine shrimp, panicked minnows splattering before their feet.

It was the sort of midnight stroll a girl could have bitched about, but Mary kept her mouth shut. The money was too good, and she wanted to impress this fisherman, whether she would have admitted it or not. Anything he could take, she could take—until a crab bit her toe, and her scream echoed across the flats.

"Kick him off. Kick him," said Rake. "Don't scream or you'll have every busybody in Brewster down here."

"The little shit's drawin' blood!" She danced about on one leg in the moonlight until the crab flew off and she fell against Rake. He smelled of gasoline and boat exhaust.

"You been doin' good. Don't spoil it." In his whisper he sounded more like a lover than a mentor. "These flats are a tough test."

"Huh?" She felt his arms closing around her waist.

"Gettin' to like havin' you around. So you better know what the mud feels like 'tween your toes, what crabs feel like when they bite. They're a part of this life."

"This life?" She laughed nervously. "I'm kind of independent Rake. Matter of fact, I'm about as independent as a . . . a Cape Cod fisherman."

When he kissed her, she told herself to pull away, to say she wasn't interested, but she was. Even if "this life" wasn't for her.

V.

Aggie Dickerson Bigelow looked out at her father-in-law, who sat on the lawn in his bathrobe. While his sons stalked back and forth before him, Charles methodically cleaned his shotgun, as though preparing to use it on himself . . . or them.

Unseemly, that's what it was. Downright unseemly for them to be treating him so. He had risen high in his life, all the way to the Massachusetts State House, and now they were fighting over his leavings before he was even gone.

Clarence wanted him to sign a permission so that they could exercise the subdivision plan that he and Elwood had agreed upon in 1904: a cottage colony from marsh to beach to creek. Agnes's husband, Ethan, wanted a more stately development, something they could propose to Rake as well.

"Elwood will go for anything, especially if we call it Elwood Manor. But Rake, he likes his privacy."

"I've decided I like this island just like it is," said Charles. "In a few months, you can do whatever you want."

"But, Pa"—Ethan sat his heavy ass down on the chair next to his father—"your name on a plan will mean a lot to the Hilyards. They respect you."

Charles went on cleaning, oiling, polishing, checking the sight. His sons talked at him for a time, then turned their attention to each other, and the argument grew hotter. Many cottages or a few houses? Several small gambles or a few big ones? Summer hordes or people of quality? And finally—*boom!*

Aggie went running out the door, half expecting to see someone dead on the lawn. A gray puff of smoke was blowing off toward the beach. The two sons were standing like trophy animals, stuffed and mounted. The subdivision blueprint for Pilgrim's Rest at Jack's Island was fluttering on the little table between them. And Charles stood over it, gun in hand. "I am still the master of this place, and I will agree to nothing that chews it up while I'm alive."

Now his grandsons came running over the dune, drawn by the sound of the gun.

"Grampa!" shouted Dickerson. "What are you shootin' at?"

"Buzzards, boy, comin' to feast on your birthright." Charles looked at his sons, then bored his eyes into Aggie. "I've seen a lot of changes on this Cape. I brought some of 'em about myself. It might be good to leave this island *un*changed, make it a gift to the future."

"Ethan and Clarence are *plannin'* for the future," said Aggie, "for Dickerson and Hiram and Clarence's boys, too."

Just then the blueprint flew off the table and went tumbling across the lawn. Little Dickerson chased after it and stopped it before it blew into the creek.

vi.

One hot night in August, Mary put on her cloche hat and heels, Rake donned a starched shirt and straw boater, they bundled their old clothes below, and they took the *Paintin' Tom* to Provincetown.

In a little café they had bouillabaisse, floating with fish, mussels, lobster, and linguiça. They soaked up the broth with thick, crusty Portuguese bread and wished they had some wine. They bought tickets for the Provincetown Players, then strolled along the streets.

There were artists, actors, someone who looked like John Dos Passos, more sophisticated-looking people than Mary had seen in months. And from every other door came the jazzy wail of a sax or a clarinet. She relished the long, lonely rum runs with Rake, but Provincetown throbbed with the kind of life that a New York girl loved.

She told Rake she wanted to meet someone famous, so he introduced her to Perez Nance, who was sitting on a bench in front of Town Hall, watching the world go by.

"The best rumrunner in Provincetown," said Rake.

"Shhh. My little one don't know that." Perez pointed to the baby carriage beside him. "But your lady friend, I hear she's a better rumrunner than most men."

Rake put an arm around her. "Better to look at, too."

Mary liked the compliment, but this was a cosmopolitan place, and a girl of her talents should have been on the arm of someone fancier than a fisherman, talking to someone who didn't smell so much of garlic and sweat. The thought shamed her as soon as she thought it. But she slipped out of Rake's grasp and pretended to be interested in Nance's baby.

"John M. Nance," Perez said proudly. "M. for Manuel. Someday he'll go to Harvard, like Rake's brother. Be whatever he wants. Lawyer, doctor, fisherman—"

"Rumrunner?" said Rake.

Perez laughed. He and Rake were part of a brotherhood. They stayed out of one another's way, helped if someone was in trouble, and passed words to the wise when they might be sufficient. They were fishermen before anything else, and they lived by the rules of the sea, not the syndicates.

Perez asked, "You goin' out tonight?"

"Never come to P-town without goin' on to Rum Row."

"Watch yourself. It's gettin' dangerous."

"Too dangerous for Iron Axe?"

Perez tapped his knuckles against Rake's chest. "Too dangerous for you, too, my friend."

"How dangerous?" Mary's interest in the baby faded. She didn't mind tempting the Coast Guard and risking a few months in jail. But this sounded serious.

Rake looked into the Portagee's eyes and laughed. That made

her feel better. Rake was daring, but no fool. And when he told Mary not to worry, she stopped worrying. She couldn't think of another man who could do that to her.

At 2:00 A.M. the trucks were waiting for *Paintin' Tom* at Ballston Beach in Truro. This was the back shore, with sandbars and surf that made for the most dangerous landing of all. On a rough night, Rake would have refused, but heat and humidity were like a weight smoothing out the surf, so he ran right onto the beach, as bold as a gull.

The lead trucker, a burly Irishman named Malloy, had been needling Rake since he first saw Mary. But tonight he stood on the dark beach and applauded as the tide gently lifted the *Paintin' Tom* off. "Mary, that's one helluva rumrunner you got. Only man I ever met could land liquor on the back shore. A helluva catch, darlin'."

"And you're a helluva truck driver," she called.

Rake went fast along the shore and didn't muffle the engine, because all they carried now was three bottles of scotch. "'Nother great night. 'Nother twelve hundred and fifty dollars, cash money." He handed her the roll. "Count out three—make it four hundred."

She threw her arms around his neck and gave him another kiss. "Like the man says, one helluva rumrunner."

"And one helluva catch."

She took her arms away. "But, Rake—"

"But, but, but. You like me well enough out here, when we're on the boat, in rumrunner's rags, but when we go to P-town, you twitch every time I touch you."

"Rake—"

"Well, honey, watch this." He sped up the beach until they were about a mile south of Race Point Light. Then he ran the boat onto the sand. There were half a dozen shacks along the rim of the dune, others scattered through the great desert beyond, and kerosene lamps lit the darkness in spite of the hour. "Writers, mostly, thinkin' great thoughts."

He grabbed two bottles of scotch, took her by the hand, and without a word, went toward a big cottage.

"Rake, that's a Coast Guard station."

"*Was.*" He marched her right up to the door. "Gene! Gene! It's Rake Hilyard."

An intensely thin man with a black mustache appeared at the screen door. "Rake Hilyard?"

"Brung some Haig and Haig. Gen-u-ine pinch bottle."

"I haven't seen you since last summer."

"Been workin' for a syndicate." Rake shoved the bottles into the man's hand. "But was thinkin', when I come by and seen your light, what a good customer Eugene O'Neill always was, back when I was independent."

Mary made a funny noise and stiffened like a bluefish left in the sun.

"Can't stay, Gene, but wanted you to meet Mary Muldowney. Fine actress."

O'Neill studied her with his dark, sad eyes.

And she overcame her shock enough to mumble, "I . . . I like your work, very much, Mr. O'Neill. I think it's very . . . uh, entertaining."

"She's good, Gene. Take it from me."

O'Neill was already retreating behind the screen. They said he was shy, and a visit in the middle of the night could not have made him more gregarious. "Get in touch with me in New York this fall," he said to Mary. "Mention Rake's name, we'll see what you can do."

They were halfway back to the boat before Mary could say anything else. "You look awful smug, Rake Hilyard."

" 'I like your work, Mr. O'Neill. I think it's very *entertaining.*' His plays'd depress Will Rogers."

"He's the greatest dramatist in America."

"Who introduced him to you? *Hank*, or a fisherman?"

"A fisherman." She agreed, but she didn't like to surrender without a fight. So she stopped and unbuttoned her blouse. "But *Hank* went skinny-dippin'."

"Skinny-dippin'?"

"What's wrong?" She let the shirt drop in the sand, then unbuttoned her baggy borrowed trousers. "You afraid?"

"Well, uh, the water's cold."

"The night's hot." She unhooked her brassiere.

He kicked off his shoes.

"That's a start." She slipped off the brassiere and stood frankly before him, her exquisite breasts round and white, tipped with delicate buds of flesh.

"Should be ready if the undertow gets you." The words caught in his throat. "It's dangerous."

"Don't you like a little danger?" And as if it were the most natural thing in the world, she slipped her hands into her bloomers and pushed them down. "I'm goin' swimmin'."

He watched the white body glisten in the black water. He felt the warm southwest wind on his face. Was she enticing him or showing him that a fisherman and a New York actress could never be well matched, even on a beach at night? Or was it both? There was only one way to find out. So he stripped and waded in.

He chased her through the waves. She swam away. He caught her, and she laughed and swam away again. And then again. And then she rode a wave to the shore, where he caught her again and threw his arms around her.

He kissed the salt from her neck and her nipples. She touched the hard muscles lining his flanks and the hardness thriving in the cool water. They sank to their knees and the foam came up around their legs. They lay back on the sand slope. The sea surged over them, and in the swirl they lost their bearings.

He rolled over her and she over him, and they were the wave and the sand, and their rhythm was the rhythm of the waves, and the waves drew them back, fast and faster, back, past Adam and Eve, back, to the first moment, the first coupling at the edge of the sea.

There was an old blanket on the boat. They wrapped themselves together afterward and sat on the dry sand. Their bodies were naked and cool in the scratchy wool.

"Now, who's done more for you? Hank Fonda or me?"

"Rake, you're the best man I ever met."

"Then stay." He twined his fingers into her wet curls and pulled her face to him.

"I have to go to New York."

"O'Neill goes to New York and comes back. You can, too."

"Maybe I will."

"I'll go with you. We can have that world of yours, all flash and pretend, then come here and have this."

The sea rushed up, foaming around their bodies. She felt him growing against her. She gave a lascivious little laugh and slipped herself onto him. "Nothin' like a man."

"Nothin' like a man . . . to grow old with," he whispered.

The softness of his voice above the rush and retreat of the waves was more seductive than anything she had ever known.

Then he shouted, "Oh, Jesus!" and pushed her off. The tide

was lifting the boat, and Rake went running, bare-assed as birth, after the *Paintin' Tom*.

vii.

"Boat comin' . . . comin' fast," said Manny.

"Let him come." Perez kept hauling the trawl from the starboard bucket.

"You got anything?" asked Manny.

"Haddock. Gimme a hand."

"Bait and haul. Bait and haul." Manny took the tail. "Break your balls doin' this."

"This the way *men* used to fish, the way my father fished, before draggers . . . and rumrunners."

"So why we no more runnin'?"

"I told you. We're done with it. Too dangerous."

"Eh, maybe so"—Manny watched the boat—"but it no done with us."

It was the *Gray Lady*, pounding so fast across the waves that she seemed to be riding on top of them.

Nance loosened the axe in his belt. "Keep doin' what you're doin'."

Sammy the Snake, strapped tight in his life jacket, was holding up a gaff.

"Maybe he want to tie up," said Manny.

"Don't throw him no rope," answered Nance.

The *Gray Lady* made a circle around the *Pilgrim Portagee*, and the smaller boat began to rock drunkenly as the wake rolled in, whacked against itself, and rolled back out again. Perez and Manny bumped into each other, and Manny fell on the pitching deck.

A half a dozen faces were at the stern of the *Gray Lady*, laughing at Perez and Manny like kids at the Keystone Kops. Then Sammy fished the gaff into the water and caught the Portagee's trawl. A switchblade sprang to life in his hand and slashed the line.

"Dat sonamabeetch!" cried Manny.

Perez felt the line go slack in his hand. "Twenty bucks' worth of fish!" he shouted over the thrumming of the Fiat engines. "*Full trawl.*"

Sbardi appeared from the wheelhouse. "You been duckin' your job, Nancie. I don't like when somebody ducks a job."

The *Gray Lady* drifted closer, and Sammy hooked his gaff into the transom of the *Portagee*. Then he and half a dozen others stepped aboard. One of them was dressed in a white suit and wore a pasted-on white Vandyke. He looked about the foolishest thing Perez had ever seen.

"Your new crew," said Sbardi from the stern of the *Gray Lady*. "We gonna give you a chance to show you still our buddy."

"I don't want no crew, I don't want to be your buddy, and I don't want your boat."

"You ain't *gettin'* the fuckin' boat, Nancie. That offer been withdrawn. You made me do my own spyin'. But you do what the boys say, you get back in my good graces."

"I'm done runnin' rum. Too dangerous."

"Too dangerous if you don't," said Sammy the Snake.

Sbardi stuck a Parodi into his mouth, and one of the others lit it for him. "We busted a few Irish legs, found out what you could've told us three weeks ago. We know where Flip's trucks are goin' tonight."

viii.

It was September. The summer people had left. Rake's brother Billy had gone to Harvard. Rake's sister had married an Orleans fisherman named Eri Hartwig and gone to live with him. Jack's Island had grown quiet. The days grew short.

Mary often thought she should have left him that night at the beach, gathered up her clothes and simply walked off into the dunes, but she could not. Rake hoped, after that night at the beach, that she might stay, but he asked for something only once.

So they took what the summer gave them of blue seas and warm days, of decks piled high with liquor and pockets stuffed full of cash. And they hoped that the cool winds would not come.

"How much you figure you got now?" he asked.

"Close to five thousand. More'n I've ever had in my life." She leaned back and looked up at the sky. "I do love it here, Rake. When you're on the water, under the stars, you feel that you're somethin' special."

"You *are* somethin' special." He pulled a package from under the wheel. It was flat, crudely wrapped in newspapers, with a red bow in one corner. "Was plannin' to give you this when we got in. But—"

"It feels like a picture."

He lifted the blanket that covered the V-berth hatch. "Go in and open it."

"But the light?"

"Ports are blacked out. Keep the blanket down."

A rumrunner loaded to the gunwales was not a swift beast. Without speed or claws, it relied on darkness, quiet, and stealth, like any creature of the night. The *Paintin' Tom* always went blacked out, the engine muffled by a U-shaped length of pipe that funneled the exhaust into the wake. But they could never be too careful.

While the *Paintin' Tom* slid through the bay, Mike Malloy drove his truck across the causeway. Tonight they were landing on Jack's Island, and never once had there been trouble there. But Mike was always cautious, even with an empty truck. When he saw the body lying face down in the road, he almost drove around it.

"Hey," said his partner, Eddie. "That's Elwood."

"Never stop on the causeway."

"C'mon. Who else you know wears a white suit and has a white Vandyke beard?"

So Malloy stopped the truck a few feet from the body and pulled a thirty-eight revolver from under the seat. Then he waved a white handkerchief out the window to tell the boys in the second truck to keep their eyes sharp.

Eddie took the shotgun and got out. He nudged the white jacket with the muzzle; then he knelt. That was a mistake. Elwood turned out to be someone with very black hair, a pasted-on Vandyke, and a .45 automatic.

Ten minutes later Malloy looked at Eddie. "Bebber mop ob de cobway."

"Ahhh?"

Malloy looked at the driver of the second truck and made the sounds again. What he was saying, through a knotted gag, was "Never stop on the causeway."

"Bebber min bat. Bis maht ink," said the other driver. Never mind that. This marsh stinks.

"'N a bide bill isin." And the tide's still risin'.

"Baby it ust ese ancupps." Maybe it'll rust these handcuffs.

Maybe . . . but it would take more time than Malloy and his friends had, or Sbardi's men needed. . . .

Aggie Dickerson Bigelow never slept well on the island, especially when Ethan was off in Boston on business. She heard everything, even the clunk of an oar against the side of a boat.

A little while ago, that clunk had brought her straight out of bed, and she had seen a fishing boat going up the creek, with men on either side using oars as poles. At the boathouse, six men had gotten off, including, of all people, Elwood Hilyard.

Now she rocked in the chair by the window, hummed a nervous little tune, fidgeted with the braid that hung over her shoulder, and watched the boat glide back to the mouth of the creek.

She didn't care how good the the beer tasted on a hot afternoon. The Hilyards were now using the Bigelow side of the island, where *her* children slept. She had to do something. So she went into her father-in-law's room.

"Wake up, Grampa. Wake up."

It was nearly time for his painkiller, and he was easily roused. He smelled old, not simply sick, but used up, like a pile of autumn leaves turned over in March.

"Elwood and five other men snuck up the creek a while ago. They're running rum on *our* property now."

Out on the *Pilgrim Portagee*, Sammy the Snake was listening for the sound of an engine.

Perez had already heard two trucks, but Sammy hadn't budged, and Perez wasn't helping him with any of this. He considered gangsters bad luck on a boat. He considered this island worse luck. Here his old nemesis lay dying. Here he had seen things that had broken his youthful heart.

"Hey, Sammy," Manny was saying, "where you get dat name, 'Sammy the Snake'?"

"Shhh. Tryin' to hear the boat."

"Sammy the Snake. You don't look like no snake."

"Shut up, you stupid Portagee."

Manny looked at Perez. "Eh, a sure thing, with dat life jacket on, dey no call him Sammy the *Water* Snake."

Perez whispered for Manny to be quiet.

When Manny was frightened, he talked. And right now his mouth was going faster than when the *Portagee* lost an engine on

Handkerchief Shoals and drifted halfway to Georges Banks before they got it started.

Perez was frightened, too. For himself and for the Hilyards. But he had made a deal with Sbardi. He had done what he could to warn Rake off. There was no escaping.

Suddenly something splashed in the black water a few feet from the bow . . . something big.

"What was that?" said Sammy the Snake.

Meanwhile, in the V-berth of the *Paintin' Tom*, Mary Muldowney was holding the painting to a kerosene lamp. "It's beautiful," she said through the blanket. "A real study."

It was called *House on Billingsgate*, Number 17—the inside of a cottage, south-facing windows on either side of a fireplace, windows angled into the east and west walls, silky curtains waving in the breeze. A shaft of light slanted through the east window and struck the fireplace. Beyond the south windows were three bright strips of color—gold for the sand, blue for the sky, and bluer for the sea.

"It's like you can see forever out those windows."

"Look at the paintin' he painted in over the fireplace," Rake yelled from above.

"It's a copy of the painting itself, with an even smaller copy inside the copy."

"In the first copy, the light's comin' through the west window, but it hits the same spot as the light comin' through the *east* window. In the copy of the copy, the light's comin' from the east again." Rake's voice, muffled by the blanket and the rumble of the engine, sounded distant and disembodied, as though their drifting apart had begun.

She blew out the lantern and went on deck. "I love it."

"Used to think there was hidden meanin' in it, all tied up with bricks and the book of history."

"What kind of meaning?"

"Don't know. Don't care. Did when I was a kid and thought there might be some money in it, or some trouble for the Bigelows. But the Bigelows let us land the booze, and the booze brings more money than I know what to do with."

"The painting still says something."

"It says on Cape Cod, you can see forever. Even in your own house, you can feel the turnin' of the earth."

"Oh, Rake"—she threw her arms around his neck—"giving me this doesn't make this any easier."

"Do what your gut tells you." He took his hands off the wheel and held her. "But if you look long enough at that paintin', you'll come back."

The wheel of the *Paintin' Tom* turned by itself and pointed the boat back toward Provincetown. Then they heard something splash . . . something big.

In the big house on Jack's Island, the phone rang. Elwood was on the veranda, listening to the splashes in the creek. Charles Bigelow was calling to find out where he was.

"I'm right here, waitin' for a . . . for a deliverance."

"Aggie says she saw you sneakin' around our creek."

"She didn't see me, but maybe she heard something, 'cause I heard a sound down at our creek."

"What did you hear?"

"A whale."

On the *Pilgrim Portagee*, Sammy the Snake was shivering with fright. "Another splash! Over there!"

"Eh, just some sea monster," said Perez calmly.

"Sea monster?" Even in the dark, Perez could see Sammy turn a funny green.

"What's the matter?" asked Perez. "No sea monsters in Boston?"

"Never mind dat," said Manny. "Whatsa matter he no tell us where he get his nickname? I teenk maybe it mean he got a big dick or somethin'."

"Shut up, you fuckin' Portagee, or I'll pull out somethin' more than my dick." Sammy slapped at the holster under the life jacket.

"How 'bout we call him One-Eye, for short?" said Manny.

Now Perez let him talk, because the talk was making Sammy more nervous, and if he was nervous enough, he might not hear the sound of Rake's boat, and this whole ambush would go to hell. "One-Eye for short? Short for what?"

"Sammy the One-Eyed Trouser Snake." Manny laughed.

Suddenly something burst from the water just ahead of the *Pilgrim Portagee*, something slick and black.

"Holy Jesus!" cried Sammy, and he came scrambling back from the bow. "Another fuckin' sea monster!"

Then something broke the surface near the stern.

"Mother of God!" Perez blessed himself. "They're everywhere!"

Sammy crouched below the gunwale and fumbled his pistol from his holster.

"Careful with that," said Perez. "You might shoot yourself in the foot or somethin'."

"And no be shootin' into no water," said Manny. "Dem sea monsters, dey get mad."

"Nobody told me there was fuckin' sea monsters."

"Live and learn," said Perez.

"I *hate* fuckin' sea monsters." Sammy raised his head just as a great black back burst from the water and blew its spout into his face. He screamed and his gun went off.

On the *Paintin' Tom*, Rake thought he had heard a shot. He cut the engine and listened.

"I can't hear anything but the whales," said Mary, who was all but hanging over the side to touch them. "My God, it's beautiful."

As far as she could see, from one side of Jack's Island to the other, black-backed waves were rolling through the sea, misting spouts were rising in the night, and the water glowed with the phosphorescence of the squid that were drawing them on.

"Heard a shot," said Rake. "Start tyin'."

"You're too jumpy. There was no shot."

"On calm nights like this, sounds travel across water like pine needles blowin' across a frozen pond. Tie."

"You're the boss." She hauled out a length of line and began to lash cases together so that they'd all sink at once.

A whale spouted just a few feet away. Mary shrieked, then threw her head back and laughed like a little girl on a roller coaster, laughed for the sheer joy of the moment.

At Jack's Island, Elwood was greeting the men in the trucks. The one in white got his attention first. "Nice suit. Looks, uh, familial."

He started to back away. There was a pistol under the porch. If he sensed danger, he was supposed to fire it into the air. But they collared him before he reached it.

"Where's Malloy?" he asked.

"Bog-hoppin'," said the one in the suit, "like a good mick."

"I . . . I must warn you, gentlemen—"

"Yeah, yeah. What's that splashin'?"

"Whales. They've come into the creek after squid."

"Whales in a tide creek?" asked the hulk twirling brass knuckles on his little finger. "No fuckin' way."

"*Pilot* whales. Puffin' pigs." Elwood put his monocle into his eye and looked at the hijackers as though they were illiterate, not a bad bet. "In the Latin, it's grampas."

"Gram*pas*?" laughed the hulk. "They got any gram*mas*?"

On the other side of the island, Aggie Dickerson Bigelow was now dragging her sleepy little boys along the path that led from the house over the dune to the beach. She should never have brought them out. With rumrunners all over the island and that strange boat in the creek, she should have been hiding in the root cellar, but her father-in-law had taken a shotgun and a box of shells and gone stumbling out the door before she could stop him.

For a moment she had weighed his life against that of her children. If he died, it would be a loss of only a few months, but she couldn't think that way, and she couldn't leave the little boys alone in the house.

"Grampa," she cried, "if you shoot at that boat, they'll shoot back."

"Elwood said he saw whales. They're comin' in." He had not moved this quickly in months.

"You're not gonna kill 'em?"

"Hell, no! Gonna *save* 'em."

"I want to go back to bed!" cried little Dickerson.

The cold sand found its way into Aggie's slippers and ground at her feet. The little boys dragged at her arms. And in the meager light of a quarter-moon, she tripped over a piece of driftwood. Dickerson fell on top of her. Little Hiram landed in the knife-sharp dune grass and began to wail.

On the *Pilgrim Portagee*, Sammy the Snake heard the sound, like an animal cry, coming from the island. "What's that?"

"Maybe a land monster!" said Perez.

"Holy shit, they got them, too?"

Then a shotgun blasted into the sky.

"Christ!" cried Manny. "Dem land monsters got guns!"

In the next muzzle flash, Perez saw the old man he had once stalked, like a ghost stalking the night itself. He had once wished the man dead; now the man was dying. There was bad luck in this. He blessed himself and revved his engine. "We gotta get away from these monsters, Sammy."

Aggie left the boys at the top of the dune and ran to her father-in-law. "What are you doin'?"

"Scarin' the whales. Savin' 'em."

"Come home. Save yourself." The waves rolled in around her feet, and a dozen slimy squid came slithering at her ankles. She jumped back just as he fired again.

Suddenly a huge old bull pounded his flukes in shallow water ten feet away. Charles's next shot sent up an enormous splash just in front of the whale. "Swim. Don't come here or you'll die."

"Grampa!" It was Dickerson. "Stop shootin'. Stop it!"

"I'm warnin' 'em off, son." The gun thundered again. "Swim! Swim for every bit of life you can!"

Aggie grabbed him by the arm, but he pulled away with more strength than he had shown in months.

"I'm dyin', girl. My life's over. And my sons want to chew up my island, and I'm not even gone yet. That's my punishment for the bad I've done." He fired again, and her ears began to ring. "This is a little good. I'll save somethin' before I'm gone, even if it's a bloody whale."

"Grampa," said Dickerson. "Stop."

The old man fired again and screamed at the whales, at the spiritlike spouts, at the blackness itself. "Go away!"

And little Dickerson began to cry.

Though Charles Bigelow could no more keep the whales away than he could stop the cancer, his firing accomplished several things.

Rake was warned off the island. He dumped his load, found a quiet spot, threw out the anchor, and made love to Mary in the V-berth.

Sammy the Snake was so frightened by the sea monsters that he didn't even notice when Perez put his hand on the throttle and started for Provincetown.

With a crazy man firing on the beach, the hijackers knew there would be no work for them that night, so they watched the "grampas" churning up the water until the search beam of a Coast Guard cutter pierced the night.

At four in the morning Perez Nance sat in his kitchen and dialed Sbardi's Boston number.

Sbardi picked up the phone on the first ring.

"Uh, Sammy the Snake, he's afraid of sea monsters."

"What fuckin' sea monsters?"

"The same ones that brought out every old fool on Jack's Island. Turned the beach into a shootin' gallery, warned off the whiskey, too." Perez slipped his axe out of his belt. "I done what you asked, Sbardi. We square, now?"

There was a long pause on the other end of the line. "You still want to run rum?"

"No rough stuff."

"I'm a religious man, Nancie. I make nine first Fridays every year. If God sends a sea monster when I pull a fuckin' scam, I guess he tellin' me to keep the rough stuff on my own turf."

"I guess maybe he is." Perez turned the axe over in his hands and wondered how often God had sent sea monsters to change men's minds.

Rake and Mary came in a half an hour before sunrise. The tide was dropping fast, and the gulls were settling onto the hummocks of sand that rose in advance of the flats. The gulls made Mary laugh. They reminded her of New Yorkers collecting at a bus stop.

Then, through the rising mist, she saw the whales. From one side of Jack's Island to the other, the black bodies covered the sand and splashed in the shallows.

They screamed like scared children. They snorted and gasped like dying old men.

And Mary Muldowney cried.

"This life has good things," said Rake gently, "and things like this."

"What will you do with them?"

"Cut out the melons, then haul 'em off 'fore they start to stink."

"Melons?"

"Sacks of oil in the heads. Fetch fifty bucks a gallon. Purest oil there is."

"That's all? Can't you save them somehow?"

Rake shook his head.

"They were so beautiful . . . just a few hours ago."

"Nothing stays beautiful forever, honey."

She jumped off and went splashing among the dying whales. A big bull studied her sadly and made a strange sound, as if it were trying to speak. But when she touched its slick black skin, it pounded its flukes and nearly knocked her over.

"The way of things," Rake called. "Can't change it."

"Mornin', kids!" Elwood came down to the dock and threw Rake a rope.

"What happened?"

"All kinds of conflications. Where's the liquor?"

"Lowered it into Ellis's weir."

"Well, even if we lose a few bottles, we'll make it up in whale oil." He was holding two knives. "Best get to initiallin' right away."

"Initialling?" cried Mary. "Initialling what?"

"Cut your initials into the whales, or somebody might come along and take the melons," explained Rake. "Could use some help."

"No thanks. I need some sleep."

"Take eight hours. See you this afternoon."

"All right. See ya." She hesitated to say more. They both knew, but she could not say good-bye. "See ya this afternoon. We'll go out and bring up that load."

She went to her room in Elwood's house, washed, packed, and put on her New York clothes.

By nine o'clock, the smell of dead whale was lifting into the breeze, and she could see Rake, far down the beach, working with his knife in the head of a beast. His arm was covered to the elbow in blood. He did not see her, and she did not call to him.

She wore no makeup now and, when she arrived in New York, people would call her a natural beauty. Her feet no longer hurt, and she'd built such strength that her suitcase felt like a purse. That was good because she would carry it for many years. And she clutched the painting under her arm, because she knew she would look at it every day of her life. But she was crying as she left the island.

Mike Malloy saw her on the causeway and called to her. "Bary! Bary! Own ere. In e barsh." Mary! Mary! Down here. In the marsh.

She didn't hear. She just went as quickly as she could, across the causeway and into the canopy of scrub pine.

"Bary! Bary! Ome bat. Ate ove oo!" Mary! Mary! Come back. Rake loves you.

ix.

Rake read books that winter. He had never been much of a reader, but he found that reading took him out of himself on lonely, dark nights.

He read the Cape Cod novels of Joseph C. Lincoln and the poetry of Conrad Aiken, who lived back in the Brewster punkhorn. He read a novel by Ernest Hemingway, *The Sun Also Rises.* But the book he liked most did not take him into other worlds. It opened his eyes to the place where he lived, and in the process drove him deeper into himself.

It was called *The Outermost House, A Year of Life on the Great Beach of Cape Cod,* by Henry Beston. The author had moved into a tiny cottage on a dune in Eastham and from there had watched the drama of earth, ocean, and sky unfold.

Beston spoke to Rake more eloquently than any minister, playwright, or woman ever had. All the things that Rake had taken for granted became, in Beston's eyes, the wonders of life, the mighty works of the natural world.

Like Beston, Rake had seen how the turning of the earth remade the beach in each season. But he had drunk the vintage of Cape Cod as a peasant drank in the wine cave, swallowing without tasting the subtlety. Beston had made him a connoisseur.

Here, in the endless change and renewal, there was a completeness that man could never achieve. The sea pounded Cape Cod, drove it back, broke its beaches, and yet Cape Cod greened each spring and came to vintage each fall. Cape Cod endured. It was a good lesson in that first year after Mary left.

But whenever Rake looked from Nauset toward the sea, he imagined U-156, something new and ugly and far more dangerous than anything man had brought before. And he knew there would come a time when this fragile place, to endure, would need the help of friends.

x.

Thirteen years later he met the man who would come to agree with him.

Repeal had long since killed the booze boom and sent Rake

Hilyard back to fishing. Depression had killed the real estate boom and sent Charles Bigelow's sons back to remodeling old houses. German U-boats were once more cruising off the Cape, and Americans were once more off to war.

Rake was forty-two, a reserve officer, a bachelor, experienced in handling small boats—prime fodder for the most dangerous service in the navy. He turned up, in the terrible summer of 1942, at the PT boat school in Melville, Rhode Island.

"You seem pretty old for this business, Pops," said the guy who sat beside him on the first day of gunnery class. "What brings you into it?"

Rake hated to be called Pops. "I'm a fisherman. Used to be a rumrunner."

"My father dabbled in booze a bit, too." The young guy was as skinny as a fishing pole. If not for his Adam's apple and flashing teeth, he would have had no shape at all. "Where you from?"

"Cape Cod."

The young guy offered his hand. "One Cape Codder to another. My family has a place in Hyannis Port."

Rake looked at the face and the shock of chestnut-colored hair, "Another one of those two-toilet Irish from Dorchester who come down for the month of August and think they're Cape Codders?"

The young guy smiled. "If I'm not mistaken, my house has seven toilets."

From that uncertain beginning, they became friends. They drank together, exchanged notes on women and PT boats, and shipped at the same time. Rake was given PT 104. His young friend went out in PT 109.

When the war was over and his friend ran for Congress, Rake wrote him a note. "From an old Cape Cod Yankee to a seven-toilet Irishman. Watch your back, your front, and your midships. The politician can be as unpredictable as the Jap destroyer. If you win, I have an idea you might like to hear: a Cape Cod National Park."

CHAPTER 33

July 16

House on Billingsgate

"It didn't work out so badly for us after all," said Mary. "Rake got to be friends with Jack Kennedy. I got to sleep with Darryl F. Zanuck."

"You *shtumpfed* Zanuck?" asked George. "How was he?"

Jimmy hit George with his hat.

Mary sipped her scotch. "Slam-bam-and-no-thank-you, ma'am."

They were gathered under the oak tree behind Rake's house. The painting had been hung on a nail in the tree, and Geoff had not taken his eyes off it.

"I'm damn sorry about Rake," Mary said. "We got together whenever I came through in stock. We'd sit in the barn there, get out of the sun, have a beer . . . like old times."

"Did he say why he wanted to see the painting after all these years?" asked Jimmy Little.

She pointed to the lacquered log holding open the back door. "Something to do with that silly doorstop I gave him."

" 'Mary Muldowney and the doorstop,' " said Geoff.

She coughed out one of those famous scotch-soaked laughs of hers. "It was a joke. I was here the summer the *Mayflower* replica came from England. 'Fifty-seven, I think it was. Terrible weather, but Provincetown was mobbed—fluttering pennants, hot-dog vendors, kids dressed like Pilgrims."

Geoff remembered. He'd been one of them. So had a little girl named Janice Bigelow. It was where they first saw each other, Geoff holding the hand of his Irish Catholic mother and feeling ridiculous in a plug hat, Janice marching with her father as though born to the costume.

"When that little ship sailed in, I said, 'It's like God ordered up a November day in June so we could know what it felt like.'

"Rake said, 'It was freezing that day. And overcast.'

"I asked him how he knew.

" 'I looked it up,' he said, 'in the log of the *Mayflower*.' "

"When?" asked Geoff.

"When what?"

"When did he look it up? Before or after 1911?"

She swirled the cubes around in her glass. "It was a joke. He never looked up anything. So I gave him the doorstop. One joke log deserved another."

"*Joke* logs," said Janice from the kitchen window, "I like that."

"You would . . . as funny as joke bulldozers." Geoff went back to the painting. "But why did he want to see this?"

"And why did Tom Hilyard's broken brain allow him to paint nothing but this house after his accident?" George Flynn studied the canvas. "From the outside, from the inside, and in this case, the inside inside the inside."

"It's like M. C. Esher meets Edward Hopper," said Samantha.

Geoff stared at the painting, at the painting within the painting, at the square of light that fell, three times, on the same corner of fireplace bricks. " 'The book of history will set us free from the evil that bricks us up.' "

"What?" Mary looked up from her scotch.

"That's what my grandfather, Zachary Hilyard, told Rake when he asked about the log. It was on his list."

Mary furrowed her brow, a neat trick in a face full of California sun-dried folds. "The night Rake gave me this painting, he said something like that. But it's been . . ."

George looked at Geoff. "Could it be that the book of history was *bricked up*, not burned in a hotel fire, and once it's set free it sets us free?"

"That's a reach," said Jimmy. After the fight with the Humpster's bulldozer, he seemed to be regaining his lawyerly reserve.

"Maybe," said Geoff, "but thanks to Georgie's friend, Carolyn Hallissey and Nance know all the things we know." He apologized for that as soon as he said it. But it was true.

George made no apologies. "We all need someone to get us through the night."

Mary Muldowney sipped her drink. "Ain't it the truth."

"Let's face it, guys"—George fixed his eyes on the painting—"an Indian married to a blond white woman, or a Hilyard married to a Bigelow, or a Hilyard who may descend from Serenity Hilyard and Black Bellamy . . . any one of you knows there are some things you can't fight."

They also knew that George was explaining, not apologizing. He had stopped apologizing a long time ago.

"It's okay," said Geoff. "We've all made some mistakes."

"And we'll make some more," said Jimmy.

"Ain't it the truth," Mary said again.

George laughed a bit nervously and touched the picture frame. "At least I never got to tell the bad guys about this painting."

"Which you'd better take a Polaroid of," said Mary, "because I have to get to makeup."

The crash sounded like a gunshot. Janice was standing in the doorway, the tea tray shattered at her feet. "That house . . . I've been in that house."

ii.

"She said they'd painted it blue all over." Geoff glanced at a Polaroid of one of Rake's paintings, a full frame—*House on Billingsgate, Number 12*, propped up on the dash. Then he glanced out at the house. "Sky blue, but that's *it*."

"What . . . a . . . dump." George did his best Bette Davis from the backseat.

"Go slow," said Jimmy, who rode shotgun, "but not too slow. We don't want these guys to notice."

The door of the cottage was opening. The owners were stepping, or slinking, out for the night. Silk shirts open to their navels showed off more cheap gold than the Home Shopping Network. Very tight black trousers displayed the other cheap stuff.

"Dressed to kill," said George.

"No joke," answered Jimmy. "Charlie Testaverde, known also as Charlie Balls, and Vinnie McGinnis, the Irish Eye."

The two men got into a BMW and drove away. Geoff drove down to a little lot rimmed with dune grass at the end of the road. They had to park on the shoulder because the lot was full. There was no better show than sunset over the tideflats. After dinner on warm nights everybody came out to chase Frisbees, comb for shells, and watch their children grow up as the sun went down.

"So who are they?" Geoff turned off the ignition, but no one got out. Three strangers strolling through a neighborhood of summer cottages might look a little suspicious.

"Wise guys," said Jimmy. "If you're on the New York Bar, you know about them. Bad dudes. I heard that Vinnie keeps a fifty-foot Chris-Craft at East Wind up in Chatham. Twin diesels, twenty-foot bridge, loran, radar, the works. The kind of thing you could take to Florida, which he does, about once a month. The other one, Testaverde, runs around in a slick speedboat, visits Panamanian freighters at sea."

"Drug runners?"

"Not much call for *rum*runners anymore."

"So what are they doing on the bay?" asked George.

"Maybe their wives like Eastham . . . bay beaches are safer for kids or something."

Geoff craned his neck. From where they were parked, he could see through the corner lot to the ancient house. According to Janice, the two men had bought the corner lot and were planning to put up a modern house with a view across the bay.

Geoff got out of the car. "I'm going to have a closer look."

"We'll stay here," said Jimmy. "One fool snoopin' around after supper's enough. And remember the difference between a closer look and a b-and-e."

"I don't need any more legal-voice-of-reason stuff, thanks. It's time for a little action." Then he looked at George. "And if *you* come along, we'll probably read about it in the Brewster *Oracle*."

"Low blow," said George.

Geoff stuck his hands into his pockets and began to whistle. Up ahead, a group of kids were playing stickball in the street. A dog was barking.

A modest summer neighborhood, the kind that sprang up in the early fifties, when ten-thousand-square-foot lots could be had for a few grand, and every GI could put up a one-story shell for a song. Now the houses were worth a quarter-million, minimum.

Even at dusk the neighborhood rang with the sounds of *improvement*. Hammers hammering, saws sawing, paint compressors compressing. . . . One-stories becoming two-stories, Capes sprouting additions. . . . and a bulldozer sleeping behind the House on Billingsgate, like a lion beside the carcass of a gazelle.

This house didn't have much time, so neither did Geoff. He went right up to the door and knocked. No answer. Not surprising. What wife would let her husband go off looking like some cheap Romeo while she stayed home in this dump?

He peered into the front window for a closer look. Time for the b-and-e part. He gave the neighborhood another glance. The stickballers weren't paying any attention. An old man was fumbling with a kinked hose and sprinkler next door. Across the street, behind a wall of wild blueberries, two carpenters worked late on an addition.

He opened the screen. He tried the door. . . .

No wonder it wasn't locked. There was nothing inside but a few chairs, a boom box, and a pile of pizza cartons and beer bottles in the middle of the floor. Even the refrigerator and stove were gone. Stripped for demolition.

Geoff took out the Polaroid of Mary Muldowney's painting and stood in the middle of the room, where Tom Hilyard might have sat with his easel. He held up the picture and looked at the fireplace.

This was it.

Windows flanked the fireplace, though they no longer looked to infinity, just into the scrub pine. No curtains fluttered in the breeze. But Geoff saw Serenity lettering broadsides at her son's table, Sam wishing to die, Tom wondering at the beauty and harshness of his world. Then a shaft of sunlight fell through the window and brought the brick to life.

Geoff touched where the sunlight touched. Was the log of the *Mayflower* really here? Beneath these bricks? Or burned to a wisp of ash in the Hilyard House fire?

Only one way to find out. But where was he going to get a hammer in a house that didn't even have a refrigerator?

And another problem presented itself. How was he going to get out of the cottage, now that a car was pulling up outside? A red Toyota, stopping in the road.

He dropped down beneath the window and scrambled for the back door—the next Frank Lloyd Wright scuttling around like one of the cockroaches in the pizza box on the floor.

The driver had long black hair, sunglasses, a white raincoat. She aimed a camera and took three quick snapshots. Then she looked around to see if anyone was watching her.

"As suspicious as we are." From the car at the bottom of the road, Jimmy watched her go toward the house, then he got out and went striding up the road like he owned the place. "Can I help you?" he called, and while he kept her busy, Geoff made his escape.

"She's the one Janice told us about," said Geoff on the way back to Brewster. "Strange lady . . . very twitchy . . . sunglasses at dusk, looks like a battered wife. . . ."

"Wearing a black wig," said George.

"Black wig?" Geoff glanced into the rearview. "How can you tell?"

"In my line"—George straightened his Panama hat—"you're smart to know what's a wig and what isn't."

Geoff wasn't quite as much of an expert, but he could tell a black wig when it lay on a counter in Carolyn Hallissey's house.

iii.

"They moved houses all over the Cape in the nineteenth century," said Jimmy.

They were back at Rake's house again, sipping beers and cooking franks on the grill. Jimmy and Geoff were pumped full of excitement, like little kids who had found a new cave to explore. Janice and Samantha were very tense. And George was in the kitchen talking on the telephone in a funny voice.

"It was the land that mattered in the old deeds, not the houses," Jimmy went on. "When some of these places were moved, especially little dumps like the house on Billingsgate, they just disappeared. There was no electricity to disconnect, no water, so no permits to leave a paper trail. There might be legends, but nothing concrete."

"So if you're hunting for a needle in a haystack, and you have a haystack as big as the bay shore, what can you do?" Geoff put half a dozen rolls on the grill to toast.

"You hire a real estate agent." Janice took a sip of beer. She wanted to get very drunk. "Let *her* find the house."

"Congratulations." Geoff smacked her on the ass, which she did not like at all. "The lady in the black wig used both of us."

"She didn't wear the wig around you. Did she wear anything else?"

"Her ambition."

Janice turned the hot dogs. They were burned on one side. She was burned on both. She had done everything to make Geoff face the real world, and she had led him straight to the source of his fantasy. Well, she was nothing if not stubborn. "Agnes says the log burned in a hotel fire in 1911. I still believe her."

"There's only one way to find out," said Geoff. "And we have to do it tonight, before the house is bulldozed away."

"You have children, Geoff. These men are dangerous."

"We stood up to the Humpster."

"And he would have killed you if I hadn't called in the cavalry. And if you think Nance killed Rake, you really *are* crazy." She took four franks off the grill and called the kids. The screen door banged open, and Samantha came out with a tray of beers and soft drinks. The smell of franks on Rake's old grill mingled with citronella smoke that was supposed to keep the mosquitoes away but didn't. The voices of the kids carried over the wash of the waves. A mustard bottle sneezed. God, this felt familiar.

In some irrational corner of her mind, Janice had hoped that if they all got together around the grill, they could solve this problem, just as they'd solved all the world's problems every summer of their lives.

Geoff put a frank into a bun, loaded it with mustard, and spread it with onions. "That log's worth millions. And it may contain information that would stop the development. Financial freedom for my family, freedom for this island. How can I do anything but follow it to the end?"

Janice turned to Jimmy, who used to be the cool one. "Are you in on this?"

"I counsel against breaking and entering."

Still cool, she thought gratefully.

"The book's a cultural treasure," said Geoff.

"It belongs to the owners of that house."

Geoff jumped up. "They're *drug dealers.*"

"Their *house* is a treasure, too," said Jimmy. "We can tell the judge it's a historic landmark. Get a restraining order. Go from there."

"That could take days," said Geoff. "And a restraining order won't stop Nance."

"Nance." Jimmy sat up straighter and looked at his wife. "We can't forget he's in the middle of this."

Now, George came out of the house. A walking bad influence. "I called East Wind marina, pretended I was an old friend, asked for Charlie Balls and the Irish Eye. They took off an hour ago."

Geoff looked at his friends. "Nance could have people watching the causeway. We'd better take Rake's whaler."

"I won't be here when you get back," said Janice. "You're all three endangering yourselves like fools."

The guys looked at one another. It was near eight o'clock. The sun was setting. The night would soon belong to the mosquitoes.

"Are we fools?" said Geoff.

"The expression," said Jimmy, "is faggots, Mo-nigs, and fools."

"Not very nice," said Geoff.

iv.

"You want a trowel and mortar?" Emily's voice echoed down the stairs of the big house.

Geoff stood in the foyer. "Arnie does the masonry here, doesn't he?"

"Yeah. Come on up."

The house was quiet. No more noise than a few campers flipping through the magazine rack in the library.

Geoff followed the metallic stink of cigarette smoke to Emily. "I have a little work to do on Rake's fireplace."

She took a puff and pushed the smoke out the corner of her mouth. "Arnie's in the parlor watching TV."

She led him down the hallway. The place felt strange without Clara's presence. The floors were new-waxed and squeaked against his heels. The usual cloud of urine didn't waft out when he passed Clara's room. In fact, something made him stop.

A new mattress and box spring, all shining blue and white rayon, sat like an altar on the bedstead.

"Arnie got rid of the old one last week. Makes the place smell a lot better . . . the way she wet the bed at the end." Emily began to cough.

"Didn't you buy out a whole mattress factory once?"

"We sure did." *Hack-hack.* Emily could keep a conversation going through the worst coughing fit. "Back in the days when we bought everything by the truckload for the camp." *Hack.*

"I slept on one when I was a kid."

She held the back of her hand to her mouth and coughed and laughed at the same time, while the smoke from the cigarette made her squinty-eyed.

Arnie Burr and his friends were watching the Red Sox. His friends were a marlin over the fireplace, a glass-eyed deer head, and a raccoon stuffed like a Halloween cat—back arched, fangs bared, tail standing straight up—on an end table.

"Trowel and mortar. Hammer and cold chisel?" Arnie didn't take his eyes off the game. "What the hell for?"

Geoff said, "Got a little job to do."

Arnie squinted over the tops of his bifocals. "What is it that can't wait till tomorrow?"

"A . . . a hobby."

Arnie buckled his pants and tied his shoes. "It's all in the shed. I'll show you."

"I'll find it on my own."

"No, I'll come."

Geoff no more wanted Arnie Burr along than he wanted the damn raccoon. He plucked it off the table and shoved it into Arnie's hands. "Stay here. You don't want your friend to get lonely."

He patted the raccoon, which gave off a farting little cloud of dust.

"Ah-ah-ah—"

"Here we go," muttered Emily.

Arnie threw his head back and splattered a sneeze all over the raccoon.

He was still sneezing when Rake Hilyard's Boston Whaler left the boathouse five minutes later. Aboard were three men, a fifty-pound bag of mortar, and some masonry tools.

V.

How much booze could his father have run in this boat? Whenever he eased the throttle and the powerful inboards began to hum, John M. Nance imagined his father, right beside him, watching for the lights of a Coast Guard boat.

He often wished that old Perez had lived long enough to see what his son had attained. But Perez had died in 1961, when his son was considered no more than a bottom fisher.

Nance ran his cigarette boat up the back shore, from Chatham to Provincetown, in less than two hours. Even a man called Strip-the-Plants could feel the majesty of the dusk-red dunes, the calm beauty of the sea at sunset, a little tug of nostalgia when he tied up at the Provincetown Wharf where his father had once unloaded fish.

P-town was a strange, two-faced kind of place, he thought. And it had been that way even in his youth, a hardworking town where a lot of people seemed to be playing all the time.

The fishing fleet still tied up here, a row of rusty, smelly old trawlers handled by salt-of-the-earth Portagees and Pilgrim descendants, men who still made their living doing the most dangerous work there was, who still sent their kids to the schools Nance had gone to, who still lived in the houses where their fathers had lived.

But a block from the wharf was that other world, of galleries and restaurants, of chitchat about pesto and Post-Modernism, of gay bars and drag shows, of mobs of tourists swarming on a Sunday afternoon, of midwestern couples looking disoriented and disappointed because they had come to the place where American self-government was born and found that on a Saturday night, they were the only straight people on the street.

Cramped, claustrophobic P-town, surrounded by the eternity of the ocean. A lot of people thought that the contrasts made it a great place. Nance thought the summer frenzy of the streets and the dead silence of the dunes and ocean made it feel as much like the end of things as the beginning. The town with two faces was no longer for Nance, perhaps because he had been called two-faced too often himself.

And what he was doing right now was among the most two-faced things in his career. But it was all for a good cause.

He pulled a wad of bills from his pocket—a hundred wrapped

around a fist's worth of singles—and gave it to Lambeth. "This Bill Rains is the toughest guy on the Conservation Commission. Let's soften him up."

"Did you read my report?" Lambeth glanced at the money as though it had teeth. "Every contractor I talked to said Rains is Mr. Honesty. The only thing worse than trying to bribe a guy like that is threatening him first."

"So threaten him, then offer him the cash."

"I don't get it."

"You don't have to. Let him think you're an unemployed construction worker. Tell him a lot of people will be very unhappy if the town Conservation Commission tries to make it tough for the Bigelows on their own island."

"That will only turn him against you."

"Just do what I tell you." Nance watched Lambeth go down the dock to the *Stellwagen Star*, one of the whale watch vessels disgorging passengers after a sunset cruise. It was a few minutes before he saw Lambeth emerge on the upper deck and approach the pilothouse. Then Rains stepped out.

They talked briefly. Lambeth reached into his pocket and pulled out the bills. Then something happened very quickly. From a distance, Nance couldn't quite tell, but for all his muscle, Lambeth ended up in Provincetown Harbor, and the money went fluttering after him.

Good thing they were mostly singles, thought Nance.

Then the tourists began to jump in. None of them worried much about Lambeth, but one was heard to say, "Two more dives and I can pay for all my photo processing."

John M. Nance wondered if his father would approve of all he had gone through to work his revenge.

CHAPTER 34

May 1957

The Pilgrim Portagee

The postwar expansion, they called it. Men were working, women were having babies. In jukeboxes, Patti Page sang about old Cape Cod. And the mid-Cape Highway moved toward Orleans.

When people could drive from the canal to the elbow in an hour, the windswept land beyond would turn to gold. And John Nance planned to have plenty of it. Motels, cottage colonies, restaurants, miniature golf—and the tourists to pay for it.

In spring, Nance did his prospecting. The sun, when it managed to burn through, was high and bright and reached into places it would never go when the trees leafed out. He could stomp through the tender underbrush to get the lay of the land, see what to buy, and know where to build.

As he walked on this early May morning, he came upon two surveyors. They wore green uniforms, spoke with hard-edged accents that dug into every r like barbed hooks, and their shoulder patches read "U.S. Department of Interior, NPS."

He met them on a wild knoll of bear oak on Bound Brook Island, a piece of mainland surrounded by small streams. There was land for sale there, and Nance meant to buy it, though it might put him in debt. He approached the surveyors warily. "Hi, fellas."

"Good morning, sir," said the older one.

"What are you guys doin'?"

"Surveying, sir."

Nance looked at the USGS marker in the ground. "I didn't think that grew from a seed. Surveying *what?*"

"Bound Brook Island."

"What's NPS mean?"

"National Park Service," said the older one. "Interior's considering Cape Cod for a National Seashore. We're doing the preliminary studies."

The Cape Cod *Times* had carried the story in the fall. Ever since, the coffee shops and fishermen's bars had burned with the argument. Would the federal government save the Cape—or destroy it? Until now Nance had not worried. Now he wanted to mount a horse and go riding like Paul Revere. "The Feds are coming, the Feds are coming."

ii.

But the Pilgrims came first. The *Mayflower II*, a gift from the people of England, had sailed for America in April. In mid-June, she arrived off Cape Cod.

It was the nicest time of year, but on the day she approached Provincetown, the clouds lowered and the mist came in on a nasty northeast wind. Still, ten thousand people lined the beaches and wharfs to watch the ship arrive.

"Looks like they've come back to start the whole bloody mess all over again," said Perez Nance when he saw Rake Hilyard on Commercial Street.

"Everyone wants to see history." Rake was still rod-thin but nearly all gray. Perez's hair remained the color of coal, but arthritis had crippled his joints and set him ashore, where he had grown as fat as a monkfish.

Time had been gentler to the woman on Rake's arm. She hennaed her hair to keep down the gray, and her skin had a deep-tan wrinkle, but there was a regality about her that she could not hide with sunglasses or ugly orange kerchief. Rake introduced her as an old rum-running pal. Mary Muldowney enjoyed her privacy, because now that she played a regular character on one of the Warner Brothers' television westerns, she was recognized all the time.

"Rum-runnin'," said Perez. "Great days, Rake. Big money days."

"Depression got mine."

Perez clapped Rake on the shoulder. "Best place to keep your money in them days was in the mattress. That's what I did. Had enough when it was over to send the boy to college, set him up in business, too."

"How's he doin'?"

"Good. Wish I could do as good when I was twenty-nine. But he don't like this National Park talk at all."

"Better get used to it."

A welcoming party had gathered at the wharf. It included politicians, customs officials, Indians wearing feathered headdresses, and, of course, members of the Pilgrim Association, including Dickerson Bigelow, who had been elected to carry a copy of the Mayflower Compact to the ship, and John M. Nance, who had learned at Harvard that a Pilgrim heritage could go a long way toward gaining a little acceptance.

But the *Mayflower* was out at Race Point, having one hell of a time with wind and ebbing tide. So the welcoming committee was still ashore.

"Hey, Johnny," Perez called to his son, "you remember Rake?"

John Nance wore the costume of a seventeenth-century sailor —high stockings, loose trousers, leather jerkin, red stocking cap— in which he seemed quite comfortable. He gave them a disinterested smile that Rake didn't like right off.

"You know, Johnny," Perez went on in a loud voice, "Rake been tellin' me how he thinks this National Park—"

"Seashore."

"—is some good idea to protect Cape Cod."

Now Rake felt a much colder gaze from John Nance.

"And," Perez continued, "he thinks it's gonna happen, no matter what we say."

"We'll have plenty to say!" boomed Dickerson Bigelow. He wore a black cape, buckled shoes, a buckled plug hat, and for once, his fringed beard did not look plain silly. He said hello all around and ushered forth his daughter, Janice, a cute little blonde wearing Pilgrim apron, cap, and hand-sewn cape. "She's coming out with me to the ship."

Rake crouched down and shook her hand. "My nephew's one of the little boys who are going out."

"Is his name Geoffrey?" asked Janice.

"Yeah."

"Well, when he saw the boats rockin' up and down, he turned kinda green. Don't think he's goin'."

"Hope he's not some kind of sissy," said Dickerson.

Rake stood. He didn't like Dickerson. He especially didn't like Dickerson's big mouth.

"You better watch out." Perez laughed. "No sissies in Rake's family."

"But some damn strange notions," answered Dickerson. The wind blew up under his cape and made him look like he might lift into the air. "The way he's goin' around talkin' about this National Park—"

"Seashore," corrected Rake.

"Say, why are you callin' it a good idea?" asked Dickerson.

"It is."

Dickerson threw an arm around John Nance, who did not look pleased. "Here's two Pilgrims who think it's a *terrible* idea. As past president of the Cape Cod Association of Planning Boards, I can tell you it's not going to happen."

"That's good," said Perez, "'cause Johnny, he's so worried, he's thinkin' of selling what land he has and gettin' off the Cape altogether."

"Guileless"—a good word for Perez Nance, thought Rake. "Stupid" was another one. Or maybe his brain had gotten old faster than the rest of him. Because he was standing there, spilling his son's secrets, and Dickerson Bigelow was drinking in every drop.

"Yep," Perez went on, raising his voice over the booming wind, "just last week Johnny said he'd rather pull out now than deal with the gover'ment. Take a little profit just to be clear of any land he owns in the park areas."

"Uh, Dad—"

Perez looked at Mary. "'Less you want my son to lose what he worked for since he left Harvard, you tell your friend Rake here to talk to that Senator Kennedy in Washington."

"Kennedy's stayin' out of this," answered Rake. "Doesn't want to make Dicker Bigelow mad."

"A wise position," said Dickerson.

The bell chimed in the steeple of the First Church. Then the bells in the rest of the town joined. Then the foghorn lowed into the wind.

"Here she comes!" Dickerson puffed up and bellowed, "Everyone to the boats!"

But Nance gave Rake a last nasty look. "Your name shows up every time I read about this federal land grab. Don't forget that the first people who came here in rags like I'm wearin' didn't want the king or the pope telling them what to do. Neither do the people who live here now."

That was a truth that Rake Hilyard had never disputed.

When the boats were away and Dickerson's voice was fading into the wind, Mary said, "It sounds as if you've made yourself a few enemies lately."

"National Seashore's the best thing could happen to the Cape. Save it from beady-eyed profiteers like Nance and big-arsed thieves like Bigelow."

She shivered. She was wearing a light sweater, which should have been enough for June, but not today. "It feels like November, as if the good Lord sent us the same kind of weather the Pilgrims had when the first *Mayflower* arrived."

"Let's see"—Rake scratched his throat—"on that day, it was twenty-nine degrees and overcast."

"How do you know?"

"Looked it up"—he gave her a little half-smile—"in the log of the *Mayflower*."

"The what?"

"Just a joke"—he pointed out to sea—"like that."

The *Mayflower II* was rounding Wood End at last, but not on her own. After sailing from England to Bermuda and up the American coast to Cape Cod, an epic journey that no high-pooped caravel had made in three centuries, the *Mayflower II* simply could not weather Race Point.

So this wooden symbol of man's questing spirit arrived under tow, courtesy of a Coast Guard cutter called the *Yankton*.

Even the church bells sounded disappointed.

. . .
iii.

A year later, the *Mayflower II* had gone to her permanent berth in Plymouth, while across the bay, in the towns of the Lower Cape, the fight was getting ugly.

Two Off-Cape congressmen, O'Neill and Boland, had filed a bill to authorize land-takings in six towns—Chatham, Orleans, Eastham, Wellfleet, Truro, and Provincetown—for the establishment of the Cape Cod National Seashore. Cape Cod's own Congressman Nicholson was squirming like a speared eel.

A week after the filing, Rake got a call from Washington. He knew the voice immediately. "I—ah—I hear that Tip O'Neill was booed out of a hearing in Eastham the other night."

"Booed ain't the word," Rake said. "Damn near shit on him, Jack . . . and on Boland, too."

"HR 12449 doesn't seem to be going over."

"The Truro folks even hung O'Neill in effigy."

Kennedy chuckled. "Like Tip says, all politics is local."

"That's why *you* should bring the bill, Jack. You're a Cape Codder . . . kind of."

"Thanks for the honor, Rake. But that's why I'm *not* filing. The only support's come from the Great and General Court of Massachusetts and the—ah—Garden Clubs of America. I haven't heard from a Cape businessman yet who likes the idea of the government taking land out of circulation."

"How do you feel about it, Jack?"

A hand muffled the receiver. Someone was saying something to Kennedy—perhaps that he had spent enough time on such an insignificant matter. Well, this was *not* insignificant. The skinny kid who had sat beside him at gunnery class was going to hear what Rake had to say.

Kennedy came back on the line. "Ah, thanks for the update Rake. I'm being called to a vote now."

"Jack, are you with us?"

"I have to go."

"Jack . . . Senator, wait." He felt that he was sticking his arm through the phone line and hooking a finger into Kennedy's lapel. "Plenty here in favor of a National Seashore, Jack—a lot of selectmen, people in the streets—but even the supporters are scared of the fed'ral gover'ment. Everyone else is just plain scared. People who own houses are scared they won't be able to stay in them, never mind pass them on to their kids."

"Mmm-hmm."

"People who own land are scared they won't be able to build on it or get a fair price."

"Uh-huh."

"The towns are scared that if the Feds take land, they won't have the property taxes to operate."

"Uh-huh."

"You have to make people stop bein' scared, Jack."

"Ah—right, Rake, good. Keep up the good work and keep me posted."

Rake's throat was as dry as sand. He'd talked more since this seashore fight started than he had in his whole life, and for all his talk, he couldn't even get Kennedy to come down on one side or the other.

iv.

By the following spring, the opposing forces had marked their positions like dogs pissing on the same beach.

Those in favor of the taking of 28,465 acres of land said they were protecting nature, the past, the future, the Great Beach, apple pie, the flag, and motherhood. Those who opposed federal intrusion said they were protecting property rights, property values, home rule, homeowners, independence, the Fourth of July, Thanksgiving, Christmas, and, of course, motherhood.

But in May, a senator from Oregon filed a no-more-Mr.-Nice-Guy bill, to let the Department of Interior acquire a hundred thousand acres of land in three unspecified places, without public hearing or local approval. As bad as taxation without representation.

Even Rake Hilyard had a hard time swallowing it.

John M. Nance read the bill and decided the end was near. The Feds were coming, and eminent domain would follow—wholesale takings of private property with wholesale prices paid. For almost two years, he had been fighting, but now it looked like time to retreat.

In Dennis, Dickerson Bigelow agreed that this was a bitter thing, but Dickerson never retreated. His first question was always "How can I profit?"

If he bought wisely and took advantage of the fear and greed that drove any deal, he couldn't lose. If the seashore proposal failed, he would own enormous tracts of land, purchased at bargain prices. If it succeeded, he would control commercial property along the main roads and profit from that.

In the newspapers, officials were warning of "business interests outside of your communities who know what this development is going to mean. . . . They are among you, acquiring land in anticipation of the establishment of the Area. They know that there will be a large influx of people and that land values will rise. . . . Hold your lands within your communities; don't let outside speculators come in and take over."

Much better, thought Dickerson, for an Old Comer to do the speculating, a member of a local planning board, a Cape Cod businessman whose family had owned property in the target area since . . . well, since Jeremiah Hilyard sold his Eastham farm to Ezekiel Bigelow in 1717.

"What's this, Pa?" Douglas had a baseball glove on one hand, a ball in the other.

"A battle plan, son." Dickerson stood over his desk. "A map of every piece of property and every property owner on the Lower Cape."

"What are you going to do?" Doug tossed the ball into the glove.

"I'm looking for the weak links—people who might sell because they're overextended or undercapitalized or just plain scared."

"Oh." *Smack, smack.* The ball hit the glove a few more times. "I thought you said this National Seashore was a bad idea." *Smack, smack.*

"It is, but like I've told you, when everyone's runnin' away, think about jumpin' in."

"Right." *Smack, smack.* "And when the goin' gets tough, the tough get goin'."

Dickerson was proud of his son's curiosity. Douglas was twelve now and as bright a boy as a man could want. He liked the usual things that boys liked—baseball, bubble gum, Steve Reeves movies, his uncle Blue's bulldozer—but he also liked real estate. Maybe he liked it because any boy was interested in what his father did. But maybe he had a future, to go with his family's illustrious Cape Cod past.

Dickerson's target was John M. Nance. He knew nothing of his family's history with the Nance family. He knew only that Nance's father had loudly played one of his son's aces on a Provincetown wharf two years before, and a man who *wanted* to sell could be schooled into thinking he *had* to sell.

On a bright June day, Dickerson had lunch with Nance at the Orleans Inn, overlooking Town Cove. Dickerson ordered chowder, Nance the fried clam plate.

For all his barrel-chested bulk, Dickerson ate carefully, in small spoonfuls, and never let a dribble sit on his beard for more than a moment. Nance covered everything with ketchup and ate with both hands.

Nance wore a crew cut, the button-down collar, his Harvard tie, and tweed. He never became ruffled, never got mad, and carried himself with the air of a summer tourist, smug and condescending to the locals. But at heart, thought Dickerson, he was just a Cape Cod boy who ate as though he was afraid someone might snatch the plate away.

Which gave Dickerson his approach pattern: snatch at nothing until you gain his trust . . . then take it all.

So they talked about the seashore.

A land grab, Nance called it.

Absolutely, agreed Dickerson. *Sip the chowder.*

Terrible for the economy, too.

And don't believe that stuff about boom times outside the park. The Feds'll find a way to control commercial development from here to P-town. *Dab your napkin at your lips after a lie like that.*

You own land north of Nauset Harbor. What will you do?

Put down the spoon and sit back. Seem resigned. I have to. It's the Bigelow heritage. I'd like to bail out and leave entirely, but I'll hold on and think about buying more land, so I can influence policy, however it goes.

Nance's eyes lit up, as though he had found a sucker washed up on the wrack line. So you want to stay when a lot of people want to sell?

After three centuries here, I have no choice.

I guess not.

He wants out. He hasn't bought anything since the *Mayflower* came back and America claimed her for its own. Now America is going to claim Cape Cod, too. Let the frightened Mr. Nance believe it. *Pick up the check.* "It's good to know that you're on my side in this, John."

"Oh, yes."

"Like Ben Franklin once said, if we don't hang together, we will surely hang separately."

And now take two paths. Rouse opposition to the National Seashore, but learn what you can about the government's payment plans. Buy cheap and sell at . . . a small profit.

v.

That summer brought Mary Muldowney to the Falmouth Playhouse in a stock production of *Oklahoma!*, and Mary drew Rake to Falmouth, as pretty a town as there was, with white churches, fine old Victorian homes built for rich vacationers before the turn of the century, warm-water beaches at the foot of every street, an atmosphere that seemed more settled and established than the windswept Lower Cape.

In Falmouth, the National Seashore entered the conversation only after people had talked about Ted Williams's batting average, the doings at the Falmouth Zoo—a row of Victorians rented by fraternities who moved in lock, stock, and beer barrel on Memorial Day and stayed until September—and the star at the Falmouth Playhouse.

"As Mae West says, 'Is that a gun in your pocket or are you just glad to see me?' "

Rake knew a lot of women. Most of them just wanted to talk. But Mary, when she kissed you, she pressed herself against you and made you feel young again.

And she always brought a present. Like last summer, that funny lacquered log. Well, this summer, he had a present for her—cocktails at the home of the senator who had come within a whisker of the Democratic nomination for vice president in 1956.

They took Route 28 from Falmouth to Hyannis Port. This was the main road along the south coast, in some places running for miles through scrub pine forests, but in others a strip of plastic and neon junk shops, just the kind of thing that the National Seashore would stop.

Kennedy came ambling across the lawns between his father's house and his own. It was the lawns that impressed Rake most when he visited the Gold Coast. In Brewster and beyond, the sandy soil and salt air did not make for the best fertilizer. Here they could truck in the fertilizer, truck in the loam, truck in the air if they had to. They had already trucked in the money.

There were few Cape-made fortunes in Cotuit, Osterville, Wianno, Centerville, or Hyannis Port—not that there were many anywhere else. The men who summered here brought their money from Wall Street or oil fields or manufacturing in the heartland and settled on the Cape's south coast, where the waters were warmed by the Gulf Stream rather than chilled by the Labrador Current, where the majesty of great white houses gazing out at the yachts replaced the drama of the Great Beach and the Atlantic.

They had drinks on the veranda. Rake took a beer. Kennedy suggested that Mary have a daiquiri, his own favorite drink. "I only suggest it to special people."

As smooth as ever, thought Rake. Part of his charm was that he could say something flattering and slightly silly at the same time, and a woman would hear whatever she wanted.

"Nice of you to ask us down here," Rake said.

"A lot of people are going to take credit for this National Seashore"—Kennedy sipped his drink—"but as far as I'm concerned, it was your idea first, back in '46."

"The idea don't matter a damn 'less we get somethin' that makes people happy."

"You can't always make people happy. The trick is to make them less mad." Then he talked about the bill he planned to file in September, a joint effort with Republican Senator Saltonstall. "This one will settle a lot of stomachs."

The bill would allow people to retain their houses and three acres of land to sell or bequeath. The towns would be protected against tax losses. And there would be a local Advisory Commission with influence in park policy. The plan was going to be made to work, one way or the other.

"Guess you were listenin' after all," said Rake.

Kennedy looked out at the Sound, sparkling and blue in the afternoon sun. "The story of this Cape is the story of America, Rake. I want my kids to be able to read it, too."

Afterward Mary told Rake she was more impressed than she had been the night she met Eugene O'Neill.

So Rake suggested they go skinny-dipping.

vi.

A good commander kept spies in every camp. Dickerson Bigelow had learned that as an OSS functionary in 1945.

One of his Cape Cod spies was Arnie Burr, whose family had intermarried with the Hilyards once and was about to do it again.

Arnie had gotten himself engaged to Rake's niece, Emily Hartwig. It was known that Rake loved Emily like the daughter he never had. She was no beauty. Her nose took care of that. And she had reached twenty-seven without a single marriage proposal. But Rake had urged her not to accept Arnie Burr.

This surprised no one. "More selfish than a he-lobster in matin' season" was the way one old fisherman described Arnie Burr.

Arnie was an independent who followed the seasons. He took Pleasant Bay scallops in the winter, set trawls on the back shore in spring, and chartered from summer through the big bass runs of fall.

"*Jig*, damn you, *jig* the line," Arnie growled at vacationers who were paying him for the privilege of fishing. And he cursed them when they lost fish, because he said a charter captain built a reputation on how many fish he boated, nothing more. And in summer there were new customers every two weeks.

Off-season, it was different. He couldn't keep a trawling partner when he trawled or a shucker when he scalloped. Married scallopers usually relied on their wives to clean their catch while they went after more. Bachelors came home to barrels of cold shells, knuckle-slicer knives, and slimy little squares of scallop flesh. Or they hired women at four cents a cleaned quart.

Emily Hartwig was one of the best shuckers in Brewster, and one winter, when Rake put off scalloping, she took on Arnie Burr's catch.

She might have heard about his temper and his reputation as a "soaker" who put scallops in fresh water and cornmeal to make them swell. But she must have found some good in Arnie, too, because pretty soon they were cleaning scallops together. She didn't mind when he sneezed on the shells; he didn't care if she left a trail of ash in the bucket. Amid scallops, sneezes, and cigarette ashes, they fell in love.

But if love softened Arnie, Rake hardened him right up again. And he was willing to give out information to Rake's enemies for nothing.

"Hello there, Arnie." Dickerson came down to the wharf in

Sesuit Harbor. Where the Shivericks had built their clippers, day boaters and charter captains now held sway.

Arnie was scrubbing fish blood from the deck.

"Any luck?"

"Hit a school of bluefish. Chopped 'em up real good. Sent the landlubbers home happy."

That was enough small talk. "Any news?"

Arnie sprayed the hose onto the deck. "Rake had a invitation to Hyannis Port yesterday. When he came back, he told Clara that the good guys were going to win."

For Dickerson, this was reason enough to look Rake in the eye. He drove to Jack's Island. He parked at his mother's house, took off his shoes, and headed out onto the flats.

It didn't take him long to reach the clam digger picking along near the tide line. "Hello, young feller."

Rake scooped up a big quahaug with his rake and dropped it into the bucket. "Be careful, Dicker. The tide's turnin'."

Dickerson pressed his feet into the mud and watched it ooze through his toes. "You mean the Feds are floodin' us?"

"Can't stop the tide."

"You can't stop the tide of people who want to come here. Everybody wants to see this"—he swept his arm at the land and sea around him—"but take twenty-eight thousand acres out of circulation, and that tide may swamp *you*, Rake. It may even swamp Jack's Island."

"That'll be the day." Rake pressed his foot into the sand and turned up a big rock.

"People have to live somewhere. Builders build because there's buyers. The federal government can't stop that, not Eisenhower, not the National Park Service, not even Kennedy of Hyannis Port."

Rake dug into the sand again and turned up a few squirming seaworms.

"Of course, Kennedy hasn't done you much good, has he?" said Dickerson.

"Come September."

"Come September, what?"

"Introducin' a bill to make everyone happy."

This was what Dickerson had feared all along. At least he had come to the right place to hear about it. He looked out at the terns working the waterline. "That can't be done, Rake Hilyard."

"Sure can. Come September."

Dickerson pumped reticent Rake for every detail Kennedy had given him. And Rake was no different from any other man. He had won a victory and he would gloat.

When he had learned what he wanted, Dickerson gloated back. "What'll happen when the world finds out that Cape Cod's most famous rumrunner is giving old man Kennedy's kid advice on this bill?"

"No threats, Dicker."

"Half the country thinks that mick bastard's fortune came from booze, and here you are, helpin' his son to steal some of the most beautiful real estate in America. A thief to a thief."

"Old man Kennedy and rum-runnin'—that story's nothin' but chum. And it *don't* draw fish."

"It could hurt the seashore plan *and* those presidential fantasies everybody talks about." Dickerson was toying now, a dangerous thing to do with Rake Hilyard. But if an idle threat could make him quit the fight, fine. It would serve him right for the trouble he'd caused. "So long, Rake."

"Don't try to use rum-runnin' against me, you son of a bitch," Rake's voice came rolling across the flats, "because there's people who think the Bigelows burned a hotel to destroy one of the most valuable books in history. I can spread *that* around."

Dickerson stopped in his footprints and turned. He knew nothing about this. And Rake just looked small and ridiculous, his pants rolled up to his knees. "You're standin' on the flats, Rake, but you're off the deep end. See ya."

Dickerson no longer cared about the seashore fight. Kennedy had made the end inevitable. His job was to use his new information to improve his position before Kennedy introduced his bill. But he still had to keep up appearances. And he always appeared to Rake Hilyard as a son of a bitch.

vii.

"Back to you, David, in Washington."

"Thank you, Chet. President Kennedy today signed into law the Cape Cod National Seashore Bill, which puts much of the outer arm of Cape Cod under federal protection. . . ."

John M. Nance sat in his Boston apartment, watched the Huntley-Brinkley Report for August 8, 1961, and seethed. He had seethed many times over the land he had sold, at distressed prices, to Dickerson Bigelow. They had played poker, and Nance had lost.

But until now, he had never known if he had been outsmarted, outguessed, or beaten by an insider who knew that the government would allow landowners to keep as much land as they did.

Now, as Kennedy signed the bill and handed out souvenir pens, Nance saw a face he remembered among the grinning congressional leaders. He almost didn't recognize him in necktie and ill-fitting shirt. It was his father's old friend and his new enemy, Rake Hilyard.

Nance had vowed that he would make Dickerson Bigelow pay. His accomplice Hilyard would pay as well. Someday.

But first, there were other matters: the blonde he was meeting for supper, the new idea he had been discussing with a few investors—something called a shopping mall. And then there was his long-range project: developing the town of Mashpee. What money he had made from his Lower Cape lands he had invested in the old Indian town, where the federal government had had no interest, where nobody had much money, where they had nothing but some of the prettiest ponds and pine woods around.

He was not finished yet with Cape Cod.

CHAPTER 35

July 16

The Lost Log of the *Mayflower*

"Nance could have people there right now." Geoff leaned on the throttle of Rake Hilyard's Boston Whaler and pointed toward Eastham. "I wish I borrowed Arnie Burr's bow and arrow."

Taking the boat had been the right idea. And with the tide rising, they would have plenty of time to get in and get out. In fifteen minutes, they were anchored innocently among several moorings on the Eastham flats.

Geoff filled a bucket with mortar mixture, threw the tools in after it, and they slipped into the knee-deep water like three commandos.

George said they couldn't be far from where the Pilgrims anchored their shallop before the First Encounter.

"And started all the trouble," added Jimmy.

Geoff said, "Forget the history lesson. Let's just get across the beach . . ." and up through the parking lot, across the yards, around the great sleeping bulldozer, to the back door of the Billingsgate house.

"Nobody home," whispered Jimmy.

"Lights out," said George.

Geoff looked into the street. Nobody out front. Then he opened the screen door, which squeaked like a tire on wet pavement. All three froze, waited, heard nothing, went inside.

Geoff scuttled through the kitchen. At the living room door he paused, listened, heard a gentle brushing sound.

"What's that?" asked George.

"Roaches."

"Roaches . . . I can't stand roaches."

Geoff went straight to the chimney. He fitted the chisel against the smooth mortar, raised the hammer. No thoughts about what might be in there . . . how it might change his life . . . how it already had. Just *clink, clink.* The mortar flew into little pebbles.

"One more hit," said Jimmy.

Clink! The brick came loose. Geoff told Jimmy, "Shine the flashlight. There should be a second course of brick behind this. If there isn't—"

The shaft of light struck something dark, metallic.

"There isn't," gasped George.

"Hit the brick above," said Jimmy.

No thoughts. No connections. Just *do it.* The mortar flew and three bricks came out.

The beam of light played over the outline of a box, fitted like two bricks into the chimney.

It was there, right in front of him. But don't think about it now. Don't think about the ways it's changed your life. Not now. Just one more sharp whack. Two bricks fell. He scratched his knuckles on the jagged edges of mortar. He slipped his hands around the corners of the box.

"Iron." That was all he could say when he finally held it in his hands. "Iron, sealed over with wax. You were right, George. The metal detector would have found it."

George grabbed the flashlight and played it over the box until he found the stamp. "T.W."

"Thomas Winslow?" asked Jimmy.

"*Edward* Winslow was the name," said George. "But Thomas . . . T.W., T.W., uh . . . iron box . . . T.W., ironmonger . . . Thomas . . . Thomas Weston!"

"Who?" said Geoff.

"Never mind. This has to be it! The Holy Grail."

"Okay, okay." Geoff tried to focus on the task at hand. If there was energy emanating from that box, he couldn't let himself feel it, not until they were safe. "We all know what to do."

He grabbed the hammer and chipped the old mortar from the bricks. George took a whisk broom from his pocket and swept the chips from the floor. Jimmy went into the kitchen and mixed the new mortar with water.

It was quick and clean. Geoff mortared the seven bricks back into the fireplace, smeared a little dirt into the joints, and hoped it would suffice until the house came down. Considering how the rest of the place looked, it was a good bet that no one would notice the patch.

And the headlights that lanced through the windows as Geoff finished were a good bet for trouble. The guys didn't wait. They were out the back door and halfway to the beach before the car engine turned off.

They did not see the flashlight beam come on inside the cottage, hear the sneakers squeak across the bare wooden floor, or see Carolyn Hallissey's hand touch the wet mortar.

But as they waded back through the rising tide, they heard a sneeze.

The water was now up to their armpits, but warm and cloying, like bathwater. Geoff held the box high over his head and peered into the darkness. He could make out the shadow of a big cabin cruiser about a hundred yards away. And someone sneezed again.

"Sounds like a fish with a cold," said George.

"Or a fisher*man*," said Geoff.

"Fisherman or fish, hurry up," said Jimmy, "before somethin' swims by and bites off our nuts."

When Geoff started the engine, a beam of light came to life on the cabin cruiser and began to sweep across the water like a snake slithering along a path.

"Hit it!" Jimmy cried.

Geoff leaned on the throttle and the engine jolted. George nearly fell over the stern. Jimmy gripped the box, stumbled, and braced a leg against the transom.

The powerful Merc lifted the boat like a hydrofoil, so that only the three keels were touching the water, and they took off across the waves.

But the beam of light took off right after them.

"Big boat!" Jimmy cried over the roar of the engine.

"Can we outrun 'em?" shouted George.

"We'll try," said Geoff.

But before long the beam of light began to grow like the bulge in a feeding snake. And it was feeding on *them*.

"Restricted Zone!" shouted Jimmy. "We're in it!"

"Restricted? From what?" cried George.

Geoff saw the black shadow of the *Longstreet* ahead. The canted bow looked as if it was sinking into the mud, the stern was crumbling, and the midships was gone—bombed, rusted, vaporized—from the deck plates to the waterline.

Why not? The Whaler drew so little and they were going so fast they just . . . might . . . make it. "We're goin' through."

"Through what?" shouted Jimmy.

"The boat. No time to be timid," answered Geoff. "Georgie, get in the bow!"

"The what?"

"The bow! Even out the keels and keep low."

George slipped onto one of the bow seats. Geoff aimed at the middle of the shadow. "Hold *on!*"

"Holy shit!" George covered his head with his hands.

"This is craaazy!" shouted Jimmy.

The roar of the engine doubled, trebled, deafened, echoed madly off the rusted mountain around them. The wind rushing past was focused, blowing straight down the metal canyon in the middle of the wreck. The searchlight beam was broken by enormous shadows on either side of them.

From somewhere in his youth or beyond, Geoff heard the words of the old psalm, "Yea, though I walk through the Valley of the Shadow of Death . . ."

And they were out.

"All riiight!" George filled with bravery.

But the light was out right after them, still chasing . . . and getting closer.

"They followed us through!" Jimmy shouted.

"Let's go again!" Geoff threw the helm to starboard. The Whaler spun so sharply that the water slopped in over the gunwales on the inside of the turn.

And the beam of light came straight at them.

"Who *are* those fuckin' guys?" shouted Jimmy.

"Who knows?" cried Geoff.

"How many you figure aboard?" George asked.

"At least two! One to drive, one to use that light."

They sped around the stern of the *Longstreet*, bumping hard over the waves from their own turning wake.

But the light kept coming.

"What we do know," shouted George, "is that one of them has an allergy!"

Allergy? thought Geoff. A sneeze? He finished the circle and aimed into the midships hole again.

A sneeze . . . a new mattress to replace Clara's old one . . . a piece of blue and white fabric caught in the bumper of a ruined car, familiar fabric with little white anchors . . . from an old mattress, a mattress tied to a bumper, to protect it . . . while it ran Rake Hilyard off the road. . . .

Arnie Burr!

"That son of a bitch!" Geoff turned his head to check the light. It was chasing them into the break once more.

The Whaler sped through and broke out into open ocean.

Geoff shouted, "This time, we keep goin'."

But this time, the light didn't follow them.

Because Arnie Burr sneezed. His hand slipped from the wheel and he struck something in the water, one of the rusted ribs of the old ship, something sharp enough to poke a hole in the hull of Arnie's boat.

Then there was a dull *thunk*. The shock of the collision set off the small charge in an ancient target bomb, which set off the charge in a misfired rocket, which set off the gasoline leaking from Arnie's boat, which blew into the sky.

ii.

Emily's cigarette flared in the darkness. She was standing on the dock at the sailing camp, waiting.

And Geoff could tell, just from her shadow, that she knew.

He jumped out of the Whaler. "We went back, but—"

She flipped her cigarette into the water.

The sound of the explosion had brought kids and counselors out of the camp barracks, but Emily had ordered them all back to bed. Competent Emily, keeping order.

"He chased us through the target ship," said Jimmy.

"Crazy." George's voice was shaking.

Emily pulled out another cigarette and lit it with a Bic lighter. "Damn fool."

Geoff showed her the fabric, told her where it came from.

She studied it in the glow from the lighter. "Ma always said he was a selfish bastard."

"Who was on the boat with him?"

"Clarence Bigelow . . . Arnie liked the Humpster. They thought the same about this island. Tonight the Humpster said that he was going to settle this thing a lot faster than his father could. Just to show Blue who was the real stupid son of a bitch."

"He'd been called that once too often," said Geoff.

"Every boy has to prove something, even the Humpster." Emily took a long drag. "He came here the night Rake died . . . with a bicycle in the back of his truck. I could never figure that one out."

But Geoff could. A bike to make an old man swerve.

Far out on the bay, lights were flashing now. A Coast Guard cutter was probing the *Longstreet*.

Emily hacked against the back of her hand. "As far as I know, Arnie went chasin' bluefish around the target ship. If he killed Rake, I'd rather not have it known."

It was a deal worth taking, as long as Rake's killers had been punished. Geoff wanted nothing to tie him to the house from Billingsgate . . . or to its owners.

Competent. That was Emily. She walked to the edge of the dock and watched the Coast Guard searchlight sweeping the water.

iii.

The barrels of a shotgun pressed against the side of Geoff's head.

"Hello, Massy," said Jimmy through the open window on the passenger side.

"I thought Ma's place was the *safe* house," George said.

"It *is*," said Jimmy, "because Massy and his friends are in the woods with guns. Nance's thugs won't get near us."

Massy told the three of them to get out. "You guys go on inside. We'll hide the car."

Then one of Massy's pals got behind the wheel and went pounding off into the woods with two wheels off the ground, then three, and sometimes four.

"Hey, watch the springs," shouted Geoff.

"And the *trees*," said Jimmy.

Samantha and Ma Little were were having tea at the kitchen table. The kids were bedded down.

"Nice surprise," said Ma, "havin' you all here tonight. Now, are we on for a little hell-raisin' tomorrow or not?"

"Let's see what's in the box first," said Jimmy.

"Where's Janice?" asked Geoff.

"Wouldn't come. Went to her grandmother's instead," said Samantha. "She said she wasn't going to play a little boys' game with a—here I quote—'very stubborn little boy.' I almost went with her."

"But you stuck by your man." Ma gave Samantha a pat on the back, which she hadn't done too often, and told Geoff she had sent a couple of Massy's pals to Agnes's house, so that Nance wouldn't get close.

That made Geoff feel a bit better. He opened the plastic bag he'd been carrying and pulled out the box. There was no ceremony. He was too exhausted, too shocked at the explosion of Arnie's boat, too disappointed that his wife was not here.

His shorts had dried out after his wade through the water, but the salt on his skin made his ass sting and itch like a case of poison ivy. The hunt for this box had led him to the truth about Rake's death. Its contents would vindicate him, and Janice didn't even care. He wanted a shower. But that could wait.

It was time for the box. Geoff touched it. He felt the cold, smooth surface. He ran his fingers over the initials in the upper right corner. He was almost afraid to open it. They all were. Except Ma.

"Well, goddamn. I ain't sittin' here all night. I need my sleep." And she attacked the wax seal with a table knife.

Then Jimmy grabbed a pair of pliers and bent off the little clasp. Then Geoff pushed at the lid, but it was rusted on.

George handed him a hammer. "Let's see if Samuel Eliot Morison was right about the wrapping paper."

"And whether we're millionaires," said Jimmy.

Geoff tapped the corners of the lid, lifting it a little, then a little more, and the excitement began to fill him, driving away his exhaustion, his disappointment, and his doubts over what he had done.

Be careful. Hurry up. The box is fragile. Don't be afraid of it.

Don't hit too hard. C'mon, *hit* the damn thing. They were all talking at once. *One more tap.* The top popped off and clanged onto the table.

Before them lay a thin brown notebook on which was written the name Lemuel Bellamy in several different scripts.

"That's no log," whispered Jimmy.

Geoff lifted the notebook out and gave it to George.

Beneath it was a thicker book, like a ledger.

"That *is.*" Geoff grabbed a dish towel from the refrigerator door and wiped his hands.

"But is it the right one?" asked George.

Without lifting it from the box, Geoff flipped it open and read, "Log of the *Dragon.* Southampton, June 21, 1814."

"There's another one beneath it." Ma Little gently lifted the log of the *Dragon* from the box and revealed a third book.

It was bound in brown vellum and very old, much older than the others. The cover crackled with dryness when Geoff turned it back, but the binding was still solid after—he read the first entry: "*July 15, 1620*"—three hundred seventy years. The electricity traveled from his fingertips straight up his spine and jumped across every synapse in his head.

" 'At Berth in Thames. This day have been engaged by agents of the London Adventurers . . .'

George whispered, "The book of history—"

"—will set us free from the evil that bricks us up." Geoff leafed through the parchment pages, through the names of history—Brewster, Bradford, Standish—and the names of the families from which he and his wife and their children descended.

Then he put the book on the table, as though its energy was too much, or maybe it was the vision that passed before him—of himself, with his wife and family at his side, on the deck of the *Mayflower,* with the pristine continent spread before them.

Then the refrigerator kicked on and Ma clapped her hands together. "This deserves a toast."

After the clinking of beer cans, Geoff began to read. And he read for an hour, soft and steady, stumbling a bit on the illegible words and strange seventeenth-century spellings, but hypnotized by the tale.

" 'Upon the buckling of the main beam, a sailor cried that we should turn back, causing several of the passengers to voice their fright. Bradford chided his people and told them to put faith in God. I told the sailor it was no place of his to make such remarks and ordered him to the deck.' "

"Decisive. I like it," said Jimmy.

"This is a time machine," whispered George.

" 'The elders then fetched an iron screw jack, brung to raise their houses, and supported the beam. This will hold, said I. Bradford added that God would see to it. Their faith is a thing to see. It calms their fears as if it could calm the storm. Yet the storm does blow and I must put my faith in my ship, cracked beam and all.' "

"An existentialist," said George.

"Just a man, trying to get by," said Geoff.

Ma Little yawned, and her false uppers dropped onto her tongue. "Let's get 'em to America, guys. I'm sleepy."

Geoff flipped to the entry for November 9, 1620, the landfall. " 'Before this joyful moment, there came promise of conflict, when the Stranger Jack Hilyard emptied a slop bucket during morning prayer—' "

"Sounds like something a Hilyard would do." George laughed.

" '—which incurred the wrath of Ezra Bigelow, who berated him for such a blaspheming act. The high-minded Bigelow takes it to himself to chide everyone when the spirit is upon him.' " Geoff glanced at his friends. "It's genetic."

"Keep reading," said Jimmy.

" 'Thus giving proof to one truth—no matter where men are, there be contention.' "

At that, Ma began to cackle.

"What's so funny?"

"The Hilyards and the Bigelows are *still* contendin'," she said, "and still contendin' over where to put the shit."

"Not on Jack's Island," said Geoff, "no matter how good their septic system is."

They read on through the scenes that had inspired Tom Hilyard's paintings. *Reading the Compact, Finding the Corn,* and *Firebrand at First Encounter* all came to life.

Jimmy looked at Ma. "We sure missed our chance at the First Encounter."

"We missed a lot of chances." Ma got up to make coffee. "Even missed our chance for a good night's sleep."

Geoff didn't hear the birdsong beginning or the gentle snoring of Samantha, who had put her head down on the table, or the ineffable sadness in Jimmy's voice. He had been drawn completely into the tale, which now told of "terrible news awaiting William Bradford."

" 'Terrible news,' " George whispered. *"Murder on the Mayflower?"*

And there it was, in a few words—the suspicion that had paralyzed the Bigelows from the time of Ezra to . . . when?

Geoff read of Bradford's resolve at learning of his wife's death, of Master Jones's suspicion. " 'I called the elders together in the great cabin, for a master can shut his eyes to nothing aboard his ship.' "

"Who?" George came around the table to read over Geoff's shoulder. "Who does he suspect?"

"Ezra Bigelow," whispered Geoff. "My wife's Pilgrim ancestor."

"You make it sound as if *she* did it," said Jimmy.

There were more birds singing now, though the sky was barely streaked with light. Ma got up and started banging the coffee pot around.

Geoff kept reading and paraphrasing and reading. "On the night of her death, Jones says he heard voices. 'Sharp voices, they were, 'twixt Ezra and Dorothy, as though they had come to some terrible pass.' "

Then Bradford uttered his verdict: "suicide." But was it? Elder Brewster said no. As if to comfort Bradford, protect Dorothy's soul, or defend one of their own, he pronounced the death an accident.

And Christopher Jones didn't believe it. Geoff felt the suspicion in every line. Jones thought Ezra Bigelow had killed Dorothy Bradford. "Guys, I think this book solves the first murder mystery in America."

"The first *white* murder mystery," corrected Jimmy.

"And what a whitewash," added George. "Right on the *Mayflower.*"

Geoff read the last lines. " 'Every man, innocent or not, will be needed. As for me, I've done my honor in this.' "

" 'Innocent or not,' " repeated George. "They *knew* Ezra did it, but they needed bodies. They couldn't string up one of the elders. Think of what it would have done to morale."

"But why would he kill her?" Jimmy was skeptical.

"He'd gotten her pregnant. . . . She had something on him. . . . Who knows?" George had the imagination to come up with reasons all morning.

But this couldn't be it, thought Geoff. There might have been a time when the identity of Dorothy Bradford's murderer would have mattered—to a WASP politician in an America overrun by immigrants, to Loyalists claiming the high ground before the Revolution. And it would rewrite a few history books. But could it stop the development of Jack's Island? Geoff didn't think so.

Outside, the sky was now brightening quickly.

Geoff's ass still itched from the dried salt, and the smell of coffee reminded him that he was exhausted. He had that speed-freak up-all-night buzz in his head, and the edges of everything were beginning to vibrate. It was like being back in college, during finals, with his buddies buzzing beside him.

He wondered if he should keep reading or go to sleep. After all, if Rake had pinned his hopes on this scandal, he was about eighty years too late. And what else could there be, other than the money that the book itself would be worth?

But how could he put this book down now?

iv.

It was six-thirty when the phone rang at Carolyn Hallissey's bedside.

"It's Nance." He told her that Arnie Burr's boat had blown up, the guys had cleared off Jack's Island. "You have any ideas?"

"Unh . . ." She yawned and pretended she had been pulled out of a deep slumber, but she had been awake most of the night.

Nance prodded her a little. "Burr's wife told the Coast Guard he was fishing around the target ship."

"Then maybe he was."

"I think he was chasing the log."

"He wouldn't have had to go out in a boat to do that."

"Why?"

"If the book still exists, I think it's somewhere on that island."

"Why?"

She flipped open a folder that lay on the other pillow. It contained photostats of the works of Tom Hilyard—old engravings from pictorial weeklies, paintings, lithographs. It fell open to one of the early paintings, *Barn with Stone Cellar.* "Just a hunch."

"Why didn't you call about this?" Nance's voice sounded like cement hardening.

"It's a new hunch." Carolyn heard her son get up and go into the bathroom. He was happier than he had ever been. The quickest way to jeopardize his happiness would be to cross Nance. She had to give him *something,* and the barn was the oldest thing on the island. It would seem logical for the log to have been found there. "Try the cellar of the barn, where your ancestors hid."

V.

"Don't start sloppin' food around, Ma," said Jimmy. "You spill maple syrup on these books and—"

Ma waved a knife at Thomas Weston's box. "That thing protected 'em for near four hundred years. It can protect 'em through breakfast."

Jimmy's son Jason, dark and black-haired, came scuffling into the kitchen.

Then Massy Ritter came in for coffee. "I smell pancakes."

"You sure do." Ma Little laughed, and her leathered hands began to fly back and forth above the skillet.

"We're thirsty, too," said Massy. "How about a few beers?"

Ma raised the spatula like a tomahawk.

Geoff decided to get out of the line of fire and took the log into the living room. He scratched at his salted ass and dropped onto the sofa with the maple trim. He had forgotten that the log was worth a few million dollars. The money was almost secondary. It was, quite simply, a helluva story.

George took the vinyl recliner with the cracked arms and flipped through the Lemuel Bellamy notebook. "Guaranteed best-seller."

Jimmy agreed, but he said he couldn't stand the salt on his skin any longer and went off to the shower.

Geoff was reading now of the death of Kate Hilyard, of the gravediggers, of Jack Hilyard standing on a hilltop, cursing the God he did not believe in, just like a modern man: " 'When the first shovel was drove into the sand to bury his wife, Jack Hilyard cried out as though the shovel had struck his own belly.' "

Just the way Geoff had felt when he found Janice's note pinned to the door.

He read a bit more, then paraphrased for George. "Get this. Jack runs off, goes to a place where the whales strand, so Jones and Simeon Bigelow go after him in the shallop, sailing five hours south southeast, across *tideflats*."

George sat up straight. "The only tideflats south southeast of Plymouth are the Brewster flats."

"This means Jack Hilyard went to that island in the first winter."

"That isn't mentioned in Bradford."

"The log says Bradford was sick when it happened. He never wrote about it." Geoff felt the kind of excitement that gripped him when he had been fighting a design idea for days and suddenly it came clear before him, just as he was planning to give up and go to bed. That jolt of energy could keep him going all night. Or all day.

He dug his toes into the braided rug. "Jones and Simeon Bigelow find Jack Hilyard and his kid in a clearing—listen to this—'around a square of stones, perhaps half a rod on each side, around what once had been a hole in the ground. Jack says he'll use it as root cellar for the house he will build over it.' Now, get this: 'The stones were all of the same size, like ballast stones, and went down deep, as if builded for a foundation. I found this most puzzling, as it looked like the work of civilized man.' "

"Foundation?" Jimmy came into the room, toweling off after his shower. "Who in the hell would've built a foundation on Jack's Island?"

"No Indian," said George.

"Maybe the friends of that corpse they found buried in Corn Hill," said Geoff.

"Keep reading," said George.

Geoff gave him a look. "Okay. Jack finds an axe on this island—an iron axe 'engraved with a strange kind of writing, here shown.' " He studied the blocklike letters, which looked somehow. familiar.

Geoff read verbatim now. " 'Simeon thought it came from an Indian grave and should be put back, but Jack said he found it in the mud when digging for clams. Simeon disbelieved this, for what metal can survive in seawater?' "

"It would have rusted after a few months," said George. "It must have been French fishermen."

"But the French have the same alphabet we have."

George shrugged and pointed to the letters. "There's P, Q, O, J . . . Wait a minute." He studied the letters, then picked up Bellamy's notebook, flipped a few pages, and found it—in the tiny, tortured script of Lemuel Bellamy, the same letters and a dozen more.

"Bellamy was a Cape Cod preacher before he went off to become an English lord," George explained. "One night he went 'to fetch from Jack's Island a stepping-stone for the church. I found it buried in sand at the back of the barn.' "

"Ra. 's barn," said Geoff.

George kept reading. " 'The stepping-stone must have been the front of an ancient dwelling that looked from this place to the sea. Who built it, I cannot tell, for' "—here George slowed his pace—" 'the doorstep was covered with markings that looked like letters, the scratchings of some language now forgotten. As I rode home beneath a black and starry sky, those letters spoke to me of the void. The God we pray to is no more personal than the stars, no more knowable than the letters on that stone.' Another existentialist."

"Another man," said Geoff. "Keep reading."

" 'I had reached nearly to my parish in the west of Sandwich when I was overwhelmed by this truth. In an unknowable universe, I chose to know a woman. I chose what I thought was love. Yet now, at the end of my life, those letters remain in my mind's eye, cold and unblinking. I set them down so that someone may someday decipher their meaning:

And the connections came quickly. The strange letters on axe and stepping-stone were the same. An *iron* axe, one of them said. *The* Iron Axe? one of them asked. And a *lettered* stepping-stone? Why did those letters look so familiar?

And then Geoff knew. "Because they're the letters on the Bourne Stone. The Bourne Stone was found on Jack's Island."

"The Bourne Stone"—Jimmy raised his voice—"which some say came from Scandinavia."

"Where the Vikings lived," said George.

"And made their iron axes," added Geoff.

"A legend for everything," shouted Ma from the kitchen.

CHAPTER 36

July 17

Answers and Questions

Geoff felt much better after a hot shower. He borrowed a pair of Jimmy's jeans and a tight green T-shirt that read, "I played Fireball, Wampanoag Powwow, July 4, 1986."

The Conservation Commission would be at Jack's Island by eight o'clock. And he would be there to meet them, with a welcoming committee of the frightened, the nervous, the greedy, and maybe, the enlightened.

First he called Carolyn Hallissey. "I have the log."

"I never thought you'd find it in the cellar of Rake's barn."

And he broke the basic rule of negotiating. He spoke before he thought. "I didn't."

"We wouldn't want Charlie Balls and the Irish Eye to know that."

And he heard the familiar echo in her voice: always negotiating. Just like his wife. "What do you want?"

"Give Old Comers first option. A preemptive bid."

"This could bring millions at auction." That was better, he thought.

"If a pair of drug runners find out what you stole from their chimney, you'll never spend a nickel without looking over your shoulder," she said.

He couldn't argue with that one. "And if I accept?"

"Get three appraisals and take the median. You get the money. Six million, minimum."

Too good to be true, which meant it probably was. "What's the catch?"

"No catch. You get money; I get prestige and a bonus. If I'd found it myself, my contract wouldn't give me much more."

"Why should I trust you?"

"One word: Robby. I'm doing this for my little boy. He likes this place. It's good for him. We want to stay."

So Geoff took the deal. He didn't have much choice, and he believed he could trust her. But there was one thing more: "Nance's axe. The one in his company logo. Is there writing on it?"

And, as if to show her good faith, she told the whole story. She even quoted Sam Hilyard's 1814 letter word for word.

And for Geoff, the connections grew stronger. The strange-lettered axe still existed, and it belonged to Nance. "Can you bring the axe to Rake Hilyard's barn?"

"I'll try. But Nance might come with it."

"The more the merrier."

Next call: his wife. He should have called her first, but this morning business came first, and so far the business had been better than he could have expected.

He said, "Grandma Agnes was wrong."

"Geoffrey? Thank God. They're talking about a boat explosion on the radio."

A couple of nasty answers spun through his head, but they never got out. The relief in her voice was too real. He was still furious with her, but it wasn't going to last forever. He told her to be at Rake's barn that morning. "And bring your father."

"He's in trouble, Geoff. Douglas really blew it."

Now he got annoyed. Underneath the plea, she was negotiating again. Always negotiating.

But he was making no more deals. "The truth may clear up the trouble, and answer a few of the questions."

"Including ours?"

"Maybe."

ii.

Geoff sent George, Ma Little, and the log straight to Jack's Island, along with an armed guard of Massy Ritter and three of his friends.

Then he and Jimmy made a stop at the Brewster General Store, where the tourists and the locals mingled over newspapers and coffee and chitchat about the weather. The store had been the heart of the town since 1858. Now, there were a few too many souvenirs for sale and not enough staples, and the place felt more like a museum of Americana than a real store, but the doughnuts were always fresh, which guaranteed that Conservation Commissioner Bill Rains would be sitting on a bench out front every morning.

"The Commission postponed the visit to Jack's Island," said Rains when he saw them. "I don't think Blue Bigelow will be in any condition to go over the wetland surveys that his son and Arnie Burr did last week."

"We'd still like you to come down," said Geoff.

"What for?" Rains bit into a big sugar cruller that left little flakes of white in his beard and mustache.

"Isn't the Conservation Commission in charge of archaeological remains?"

"Yeah." Rains put the doughnut on a piece of wax paper and opened his Boston *Globe* to the sports page.

"Well, we think we've found something that might be Viking."

"Oh, Christ, not that again." He threw down the paper. "There's never been a shred of hard evidence—"

"You know more local history than anyone," said Geoff. "And you've heard all the Viking myths."

"So I've read all the sagas, a lot of imprecise oral tradition that somebody set down in the fourteenth century. So what?"

Geoff sat next to him. "And you've also been on archaeological digs."

"But none of them were Viking." Rains took another bite and talked with his mouth full. "When people read the sagas about the Wonder Strands of Vinland, they want to think its the Great Beach of Cape Cod, with the wild grapevines in the woods. They hear about the Norse wall in Provincetown—"

"What's that?" Jimmy Little carefully peeled the plastic top from a coffee cup and took a few slurps.

"In the nineteenth century an excavator hit a wall in the sand, thirty feet under the original ground level. Supposedly it's made of ballast stones."

"Why hasn't anybody dug it up?" asked Geoff.

"Because all these theories have holes you could sail through in a longboat. They're bullshit. But fun bullshit."

Geoff understood the skepticism. It was the right attitude. But when Rains got going on something that interested him, you couldn't shut him up.

"Take Frederick Pohl." Rains licked the sugar from his mustache. "An English teacher from Brooklyn. In 1948 he used the sagas to plot Leif Ericson's voyage from Greenland to Vinland. He said Ericson must have hit Nantucket, turned north to the Cape, and sailed right up the Bass River to Follins Pond. He even found rocks in Follins Pond, with mooring holes like the ones in the fjords of Norway. Ergo, the Vikings had been in Dennis. *Ta-dah*, big article in the *Saturday Evening Post*, then a book. Of course, those holes can be found all over North America. And so can fake rune stones—you know, rocks with Viking inscriptions. There's even a town in *Oklahoma* that claims they have a runestone. Give me a *break*."

"Would you give *me* a break if I told you I'd found a Norse ruin that could keep Nance off Jack's Island?"

Rains ate the rest of his cruller in one gulp. Five minutes later they turned off 6A and drove toward the causeway. Rains was still talking.

"This is like comedy, don't forget. You buy the premise, you buy the bit. Your premise is that Vinland the Good was Cape Cod. So you buy what people have been selling for a hundred years: Leif Ericson's brother Thorwald stopped at the tip of the Cape to repair his keel and raised a monument of timbers, naming the place—what else?—Kiarlness. Keel Cape. And the base of the monument was that Norse wall that nobody gives a shit about."

Jimmy laughed. "Maybe he stopped off in Napi's for bouillabaisse."

"C'mon, Jim. One smartass is enough," said Geoff.

"Yeah, or Ciro's for pasta," added Rains. "Then he sailed west. This would have taken him to Boston or even up the coast to Maine. But some benighted souls have argued that he ended up in Yarmouth."

"Which isn't too far from Brewster."

"Have it your way. Thorwald's bunch wanted to set up light housekeeping someplace near good water, wood, game, shellfish—someplace with a decent anchorage, of course."

"That would rule out the flats," said Jimmy.

"The channels through the flats were probably deeper then. Don't forget, Billingsgate was still an island. The sand hadn't been spread around."

"We're experts on Billingsgate," said Geoff.

"Now, the Indians—the Vikings called them Skraelings—they were friendly at first, probably traded a bit, until they found out the Vikings were planning to settle. And there goes the neighborhood. The Indians attacked. Thorwald got sent to Valhalla. The Vikings got sent home."

Up ahead, Jack's Island now appeared. The tops of the trees looked sharp and shadowed in the fresh morning light. A delicate gray mist rose from the marsh. And a blue heron poked along the edge of a little stream.

In the middle of the causeway, Geoff put on the brake.

"What are you stopping for?" asked Jimmy.

"So we can remember why we've gone through all this."

Rains leaned over the front seat and peered through the windshield. This morning he was wearing a blue flannel shirt. "They call me a tree-hugger because I want to protect sights, and sites, like this. We've lost so many. People just don't understand how valuable this is, just as it is."

"Just as it is," repeated Geoff. Then he pulled a postcard from his pocket and offered it to Rains. "I assume you've seen this."

"The Bourne Stone? That old hoax?"

"If I could tie the Bourne Stone to John Nance's iron axe and a root cellar on Jack's Island, what would you say?"

"I'd say what the archaeologists say: if no hard evidence has been found, don't assume it doesn't exist."

iii.

When they got to Rake's house, they found George, sitting at the dining room table, holding a shotgun over the box and shaking like a frightened dog.

The barricades of newspapers around the room had been pushed in front of the windows so that no one could see in. And two of Massy's friends guarded the doors.

George said, "We went out to the barn and heard noises."

There was the pop of a pistol, answered by the blast of a shotgun, and Jimmy and Geoff went rushing out the back door.

"Son of a bitch!" Massy Ritter was shouting at the barn floor. "Son of a bitch shot me in the foot!"

"He just took off the toe of your sneaker!" Ma Little was standing at the open door of the barn, holding a pump-action shotgun at her side.

Pop!

"Shoot again!" cried Ma.

Boom! Massy's shotgun sent another blast into the open trapdoor.

The gunshots sounded like firecrackers going off or trucks backfiring. From a distance, at the sailing camp, that's what they *would* sound like.

As Geoff and Jimmy scrambled toward the barn, Ma whirled and leveled her Remington at them.

"Easy, Ma!" cried Jimmy. "We're not ducks."

"There's two guys diggin' around down there. Told 'em to come out but they— Who's this?" Now Ma pointed the gun at the big black limousine rolling into the yard.

Carolyn Hallissey climbed out first, hands up. "Sorry, Geoff. I forgot to warn you." And she moved toward the barn.

"Hey!" said Ma. "Don't go in there. There's two guys in the cellar, with guns."

Geoff followed Carolyn into the barn. It smelled of gunsmoke and chewing gum.

"Did you bring the axe?" Geoff asked.

"Nance, too." Then she called into the hole. "Guys, you can come up now."

"Nance said to tear this cellar apart until we found it," came a voice from below.

"It's *been* found. Come out."

"Tell them to put up their shotguns," said the voice.

"Tell them to throw out their pistols," said Massy.

"Tell him to go and fuck himself."

"Tell them to send up the guns or we'll lock them down there and call the cops," said Geoff.

"Lambeth." John M. Nance appeared in the doorway of the

barn. He was wearing a blue blazer with red tie, white shirt, white ducks. New York Yacht Club–cool, about as far from his ancestry as he could get.

Ma, just as cool, placed her shotgun against Nance's neck. "We was plannin' a big demonstration, but I thought maybe just a few shotguns, blow off a few heads."

As if it were no more than an annoying branch he had brushed against, Nance pushed the gun away from his neck. "Excuse me."

"Been excusin' you since '77," answered Ma. "Just watch your step around here."

A hand appeared in the hole and a .22 came skittering across the floor.

"And the other one," said Carolyn calmly.

After the second gun came her bodyguard, followed by the face that Geoff had seen at the auction, at the town meeting, on the stern of the boat—John Lambeth in his running suit. The new-look detective.

"Never sail away from a bluefish blitz," Geoff told him. "It makes people suspicious."

Lambeth ignored him and went over to Nance. "My contract is fulfilled."

"Not so fast," said Geoff. "Trespassing, breaking and entering, and somebody beat up a friend of mine, tried to make it look like gay-bashing."

Nance turned toward his car. "The Conservation Commission is due at Douglas Bigelow's house."

"It's been canceled, but Bill Rains is inside—reading the log," said Geoff.

"It's here?"

"I've won, Nance." Geoff shoved his hands into his back pockets and leaned against the doorjamb. Doing business in jeans and T-shirt while his opposition wore suit and tie—one of Geoff's Cape Cod dreams fulfilled. "Now you have to talk to me."

iv.

Janice drove the Voyager onto the island and pulled up at her brother's house. She felt as if she had come on an outing with her father, her two kids, and her grandmother in the back.

The kids piled out and went scampering toward the dunes. Dickerson went into the house muttering about an old bladder that made him so twitchy he couldn't sit in a car for a few minutes without needing to take a leak. Janice and Agnes went up onto the veranda and watched the kids.

Sarah's long coltish legs sprayed sand down the path while Keith shouted, tripped, stumbled, and fell into the dune grass. They were squabbling, as always. But there was life in it, thought Janice, something pure and elemental in the morning sun . . . her kids.

"Not a parent yet who ever looked at two kids on a beach but didn't think of her own, no matter how old she'd gotten." Agnes stood at the railing.

Dickerson reappeared, zipping his fly. "Doug just got off the phone. The CC isn't coming, considerin' what happened last night."

Doug came out now, dressed all in black and his hair fresh-slicked. "Let's get down to Rake's house and see what Geoff has cooked up this time."

But Agnes kept talking, as though wherever her mind was going was a lot more important than wherever Doug wanted the rest of them to go. "You know, I never look at that path through the dunes, but I don't think of the night Grampa Charlie tried to chase off the whales."

"Maybe we can get to this later." Douglas looked at his watch. "And maybe you could stay here and watch the kids, Grandma? My wife's gone shopping."

"What a surprise," said Janice.

"We ought to get this over with," said Doug.

"Wait a minute, son," said Dickerson. "Listen to your grandma."

"Grampa Charlie was old then," Agnes went on, "older than you, Dicker. He fired his shotgun and made you boys cry."

"I remember." Dickerson leaned against the house. He looked big enough to hold it up all by himself, though it was holding him. "Sometimes, I wonder what I was so scared of, the shotgun or the darkness."

The children appeared on the crest of the dune again, then dropped from sight in a whirl of arms and legs.

"It takes just that long," said Agnes, "and they're grown up and gone. Sometimes for good. I guess old Blue regrets all the names he called his son now."

"We struggle to screw each other, win and lose, destroy and build," added Dickerson, "and all the while, we don't see how fast time's goin' by. Then it's over, just like that."

It seemed to Janice that her father could sense defeat. His lobster antennae were working. So she laughed and slapped him on the shoulder. "Don't go getting philosophical on us, Dad. We're going to need you."

"No, you won't. You're the generation who gets to make the mistakes now."

"We're just trying to survive." Doug stepped off the veranda and headed for the van.

"Whatever mistakes you've made, son, I'm behind you." Dickerson turned to his daughter. "But maybe it's the ones who ask the questions who survive the best."

"Maybe." Janice told her grandmother to watch the kids.

"I'll watch them run on the beach. There's no happier sight."

V.

It was growing into a hot day, but the rocks in the root cellar were as cool as night. Geoff Hilyard and Bill Rains were bumping around down there while the shells crunched under their feet. The strange markings and the words "God bless the good Bigelows, God damn the bad, and God bless our baby" were barely visible on the floorboards of the barn above them. The yellow work light threw wild dancing shadows. And the eyes peered down.

"Well?" said Geoff.

Bill Rains measured several of the rocks with a small tape. "Uniform size, to stack neatly."

"What's he saying?" called George.

"It looks good." Geoff glanced up and saw Nance, Carolyn, George, still clutching the metal box to his chest, and Jimmy Little and Massy Ritter holding shotguns.

Ma was sitting under a tree outside the barn, having a smoke with Emily Burr. A fresh-made widow had taken her daily walk to soothe her grief and found a two-time widow to comfort her.

"Looks good." Nance shook his head. "That's too bad."

"Or good," said George.

Then Janice's face appeared, then Dickerson's and Douglas's. A drop of somebody's perspiration hit Geoff on the cheek. He thought it came from Dickerson, but it was Douglas who was sweating, and shooting nervous glances at Nance.

Geoff boosted himself up and sat so that his legs were swinging in the hole, like a kid perched on the edge of a pier. He didn't even bother to say hello. "According to the log of the *Mayflower*, which some of you said did not exist, this root cellar was here when Jack Hilyard arrived in 1620."

Then he extended his hand to Nance, who offered his axe, as though surrendering to whatever fate the island held. Geoff was glad that the only shotguns in sight were on his side, because he didn't trust Nance, no matter how docile he seemed.

"The log also says that Jack Hilyard found this axe in the marsh mud near the mouth of Nauseiput Creek." Geoff delivered every word as though squeezing off a bullet at Janice.

He had the right, she supposed. He had gotten what he went after.

"Metal, wood, and leather doesn't last in the acidic New England soil," he went on. "But in a bog in England, the remains of a whole society were found."

"They called them the Bog People," offered George, who now perched on the edge of a sawhorse.

Rains popped up from the hole. "The artifacts of the Bog People survived because they were buried in anaerobic marsh mud. No oxidation." Then he dropped back like a bearded animal protecting its burrow.

Geoff admired the axe. "Bill thinks that if something of great weight buried this axe—"

"What? A steamroller?" demanded Dickerson.

"Who knows? *Something*, and sank it into the mud at just the right moment, it might have survived since, say, the time of the Vikings."

Janice shook her head. This was too much for anyone to believe, but then, so was the story of the log.

Rains popped up again. "Those are ballast stones. Somebody used them to build that cellar. That's all I can say. But this"—he wiped his hands on the front of his shirt, then took the axe reverently by the handle—"this is the key. If these letters are the same as those on the Bourne Stone, which apparently came from this foundation, I'm going to recommend that the whole island be surveyed for Viking artifacts."

Janice watched the color drain from her brother's face.

"You can't do that," said Douglas, "except within a hundred feet of wetlands."

"Don't tell me the law." Rains lifted himself out of the hole and stood toe to toe with Douglas. He might have been an amateur archaeologist and ecologist, but it was the strength of some small towns that amateurs ran for the commissions, learned the laws, took them seriously, and gave a damn.

"We can't stop you from developing," Rains continued, "much as we'd like to. You've got your rights. But we'll find out what's here before you start."

"A survey might take nine or ten months," mused Nance, looking up at the ceiling.

Why did this make him so happy? Geoff wondered.

Rains mopped his brow. "The chances of finding anything can't be very good. When we're done, we'll probably all laugh that we ever thought it was Viking. But we have to look."

"Hey," said George, "maybe we'll be able to open a theme park."

"Welcome to Viking World," said Nance.

Carolyn Hallissey laughed. "No competition with Old Comers, please."

Janice wanted to smack her, lay her right out in her denim skirt and cowboy shirt and fancy silver jewelry.

Then Nance asked for his axe back. His demeanor seemed to be changing. He was doing what he did naturally—taking over.

"If you should need it, call." He looked into the hole. "Amazing, isn't it? My own great-grandmother was down there. 'God bless the good Bigelows, God damn the bad, and God bless our baby.' "

"God damn you," growled Doug.

"Easy, Doug." Nance looked at Geoff again. "Does Miss Hallissey get the log now, or must we come back for it?"

He couldn't have done a better job of shocking everyone, if he had dropped a cherry bomb into the root cellar.

George clutched so hard at the box, he almost fell off the sawhorse. Jimmy and Massy both raised their guns and pointed them at Nance.

He slipped a hand into his jacket pocket, hooked the thumb over the outside, and struck a pose. "You boys are too damn jumpy."

"Besides, we have details to iron out," Carolyn explained.

"We can't just sell the log to them," said George.

Geoff kept his eyes on his wife. He knew her suspicions were spinning so fast inside her head they were making her dizzy. "Carolyn and I made a deal. We'll stick by it."

"I'll bet you drove a hard bargain," said Janice.

Nance reached across the hole and offered Geoff his hand.

Geoff looked at it as though it might have fangs. But he was still winning. So he shook it.

"A pleasure doing business with you." Nance's capped teeth seemed to grow in the middle of his tan. "And it will be a pleasure to be your neighbor."

Geoff felt the fangs sink in and hold. With Nance still clamped to his hand, Geoff looked at Douglas. "You put up your half of the island as collateral, didn't you?"

Douglas stepped back into the shadows.

"Well, what else would the Bigelows have that I would want?" Nance released his grip.

"The company," grunted Dickerson, eyes on the floor.

Nance was getting downright cheerful. He slapped Dickerson on the back. "It takes a son of a bitch to know how one thinks. That's right. The *company*."

"My son gave you a second mortgage on all our properties, didn't he?" Dickerson rolled his eyes toward Douglas, who sank to the floor and drew his knees up against his chest.

"I was the only investor ready to save another overextended real estate company from Chapter Eleven." Nance walked over and stood beside Douglas. "So Doug did what he had to. But if the Jack's Island subdivision isn't approved, he has nothing here but raw land. Without permits, it isn't worth anywhere near enough to liquidate my loan."

"Written on a one-year note, I assume?" asked Jimmy.

"I can't afford to have six million tied up for longer than that. Debt service costs money."

"Why do you think I've been pushin' so hard?" Doug's voice sounded distant and disembodied, coming from the dark corner.

"Doug believed that the 1904 plot plan guaranteed success," Nance said. "I didn't. So he secured my loan with the rest of the company—appraised at twenty million dollars' worth of assets, mostly in unsold real estate, my favorite medium of exchange. It's worth less today. But the wheel will turn, like it did in the eighties. And I can wait."

"You wanted this development to fail all along," said Janice softly.

"Smart girl." Nance slipped the rose from his lapel and offered it to her. "Maybe you should have gotten power of attorney, instead of Douglas."

"Now I know who tried to bribe me," said Bill Rains. "Just to turn me against this project."

"And who spray-painted George's shack so I'd turn against the Bigelows completely." Geoff felt as if he was about to be dropped into the hole. For eternity. He looked at Rains and tried to backpedal. "You know, this Viking stuff could be exaggerated. Maybe there's no need to survey the whole island."

"Once this news breaks in the paper," said Nance, "you'll have no choice. I'll see to it personally." He took Carolyn by the arm and led her toward the limousine. "You've got eight months to meet the note, and you've got nothing else to mortgage, Dickerson. You're done."

Janice whirled so angrily on Geoff she nearly fell into the hole. "You and your questions. If you hadn't pushed for this, and done your pushing with Ralph Lauren's sister, here—"

"Congratulations, Geoff," said Nance.

Dickerson brought his hand to his chest, as if to hold down the pain. He turned and staggered out into the yard.

"Dicker?" Emily rose from her lawn chair. "Are you all right?"

"Dad, do you want me to call the doctor?" Janice came after him.

"Screw the doctors." He lumbered across the yard like an old bull whale looking for a place to die. He stopped and leaned on the lawn table, knocking Emily's cigarettes to the ground. Then his eyes fell upon Ma Little's pump-action Remington.

She picked it up and slapped it into his hand. "Shoot him, Dicker. None of us'll tell."

"Dad, be careful with that thing." Douglas came out of the barn.

Dickerson pointed the gun at the sky, as if to chase away the darkness. But the blue must have been too bleak, because after a moment, he lowered it.

And Nance moved calmly across the clearing, sidestepping Dickerson and offering his condolences to Emily.

Like he owned the whole place already, thought Geoff.

"I'll call on you when your mourning is over, Mrs. Burr," said Nance. "And we can discuss the sale of the camp."

Emily sucked on her cigarette and blew the smoke in his face.

Nicely done, thought Geoff.

But Nance didn't miss a beat. He turned to Dickerson one last time. "Payback, Pilgrim, thirty years later. I learned the American way from a real American. The Pilgrim Portagee learned from the original Pilgrim himself. Now I'm the original American. I come from the Pilgrims, from the bastard of a slave owner and his slave mistress, from a Portagee fisherman—old blood, mixed blood, immigrant blood—and now, I want my piece of the future." He jabbed his finger into Dickerson's big, broad chest. "Deal with it."

Dickerson just stood there, the shotgun at his side.

And Nance turned his gaze to Geoff once more. "Keep your piece of the island pristine. Once all this foolishness is over, we'll need some green space between the condo units."

"Condos!" cried Rains. "You'll never get condos in here. We won't let you."

"I have very deep pockets, and I'm very patient," said Nance. "Just ask Dickerson."

Geoff had never seen anyone gloat so well. But the winner had the right. The doors of the limousine slammed shut, and Nance rode off with Carolyn Hallissey. A cloud of car dust flattened out in the air above the clearing.

And Geoff noticed a strange thing—the sweet, damp smell of pine needles, as thick as the shock.

He looked at Janice, but she looked away.

Her concern now was for her father. She put an arm around him and twined her fingers into his beard, which no longer gave him the look of a seafarer but of an anachronism. When she gave the whiskers one of her traditional little tugs, he didn't make a sound. And she could think of nothing comforting to say.

It was left for Ma Little to voice the first opinion. "That Nance was a son of a bitch fifteen years ago, and he's a son of a bitch today."

Then Emily said, "I have a mind not to sell at all."

"What?" said Janice.

"Arnie thought that I should, but . . ."

And for the first time all morning, Janice felt as if she could do something. If she could, she always *did* something, even if it was the wrong thing. When she couldn't turn her husband away from a fantasy, she took the kids and left. And now she pulled out something that had been burning a hole in her purse since it went in there.

She handed it to Emily and told her that this might change her mind.

"Your mother wrote that," said Janice.

Emily's eyes scanned the will, through cigarette smoke and rising tears. "Christ, she hated us that much?"

"She loved the island that much," said Janice. "Maybe you should think about this."

"Maybe I should."

Geoff was reading, too, over Emily's shoulder, shocked by what he saw. "A handwritten will and you kept it hidden?"

"It would never have stood up in court," said Jimmy. "It isn't legal."

"Think of the *spirit* of the thing." Geoff was furious with her.

"Like the spirit of your deal with Carolyn," snapped Janice.

The distrust was growing between them, right there in the sand. In ground so well fertilized, it could not wither.

"If you hadn't gone chasing after that log—"

"If you had stayed by me—"

"Stop it!" Douglas grabbed the shotgun and fired it into the air. "I'm to blame. I wanted to push us ahead, and I put us in the crapper."

"We all have to gamble sometime. Just too bad you lost the whole pot," said Dickerson, "to Nance."

Geoff turned away from the Dickersons' defeat, Douglas's guilt, his new anger at his wife, and the betrayal on the faces of his friends. He took the path behind the barn and went toward the beach. He thought if he moved, he would not feel so paralyzed.

Within a few strides, the pine woods surrounded him. A bobwhite whistled off in the thicket. The wash of the waves on the shore was almost musical. He felt the peace of the island all around him.

And down there on the beach, his kids were running and playing. The future belonged to them, he thought, and they to it. But John M. Nance would soon take a piece of their future by taking the peace of this island. All because their father had found the log. The irony almost made him laugh out loud.

And in the quiet of the pines behind Rake's barn, Geoff realized what he had to do. There was only one way to stop John M. Nance. He turned and hurried back up the path. "Hey, Douglas, how big is the note, again?"

"What?"

"The note? How big?"

"Why, six million."

Geoff looked at Janice. "Watch." Then he turned to George and slipped the metal box from his arms. "You'll like the poetic justice in this one, Georgie." He looked at Jimmy. "You and Ma will like the sentiment." And he held the box in front of Douglas.

Douglas looked at it as though it might explode.

"Leverage, Doug, in here." Geoff kept his eyes on his brother-in-law, though he felt Janice moving closer to him. "Nance's money buys the log from me. You agree to leave your side of the island open, unless and until we agree on development. Then you liquidate Nance's note with Nance's money."

"That simple?" said Douglas.

"Simple and beautiful." Dickerson let out the kind of gusty laugh that no one had heard since the glorious Fourth, when he wanted everyone to believe he was back in control. Now he grabbed the shotgun from Douglas and fired it into the sky.

"Grampa! Grampa!" Keith and Sarah came running up the path from the beach. "What are you doing?"

"Savin' a little bit of this island, kids, and sealin' a deal."

Janice went over to her husband, so that he was the only one who could hear her. "Geoffrey, sometimes you surprise me."

That didn't sound very good, she thought, and the anger in Geoff's answer even surprised him.

"If what I just did surprised you," he said, "we have a long way to go."

"Maybe so, but thanks."

"As somebody once said, 'The book of history will set us free from the evil that bricks us up.' "

CHAPTER 37

Autumn

Connections

Geoff saved the Bigelow company, but it seemed that Geoff and Janice could not save their marriage. Too much damage had been done.

Janice went back to Boston with the kids.

Geoff stayed on Cape Cod and saw them on weekends.

Apart, they tried to understand what had happened to them together. Disagreement bred misunderstanding which became distrust and bred anger. It had begun long before the Fourth of July traffic jam.

And they were as stubborn as snapping turtles. *You* wouldn't stand beside me when I reached for the unreachable. *You* wouldn't accept a realist's vision of a real world. *You* wouldn't tell me the truth when Clara tried to save her part of the island with the will. *You* wouldn't quit even if it cost you your marriage.

But sometimes the stubbornness faded. Janice knew that he had not been chasing a foolish dream but trying to make things right in a world spinning out of control. Geoff knew that without her pragmatism to balance his dreams, the center would not hold.

The log was hailed, within a few days of its discovery, as the historical, if not literary, equal of William Bradford's *Of Plymouth Plantation*.

It and the accompanying manuscripts were sold to Old Comers for seven and a half million dollars, which liquidated the note and left a profit for Geoff, Jimmy, and George. Geoff stayed to watch the archaeologists peel away layer upon layer of the palimpsest that was Jack's Island. Jimmy went back to New York, though he contributed his profits to the Indian museum and considered opening a practice in Mashpee. George gave up on sitcoms and took a place in Provincetown to edit and annotate the log for publication.

"It will sell forever," John M. Nance said in *People* magazine, "because it's a story of people surviving—some through faith, some through love, and some through pure cussedness."

He got that part right. And some of those people had joined together to defeat him. He didn't mention that.

But of everything that the *Mayflower* log contained, it was the love that drew the most attention. Especially love that led to scandal.

"Murder on the *Mayflower!*" shouted the *People* headline, over a photo of the Tom Hilyard painting. "Dorothy Bradford: Separatist Floozy?" asked the *National Enquirer*. Serious journals also explored the possibility: "A New Suspect in America's First Murder Mystery?"

In her Boston condo, Janice read the stories and laughed. Who could know the truth of what had happened? Christopher Jones merely speculated on what had gone on, had seen it in shadow from the chartkeeper's cabin.

The papers were right to say that history had been made on the deck of the *Mayflower*. The history of the world could be written in those passages about Ezra Bigelow and Dorothy Bradford, because no part of history was untouched by the mystery of a woman and a man reaching out to each other in the dark.

Though the truth was unknowable, Janice became obsessed by the story. She read all that she could. She attended lectures. And on a chill November Saturday she went to the *Mayflower II*, so that she could stand in the place where the captain had stood and look toward the rail where her ancestor and Dorothy Bradford had talked.

Part of the experience when you visited the Pilgrim village or went aboard the *Mayflower II* at Plimoth Plantation, was that you met interpreters who dressed, spoke, and thought like the Pilgrims.

Talking to them could be exasperating, but if you made the effort, the effect was magical. They could very quickly make you forget the school kids swarming about the ship, the traffic, and the Frostee-Freeze Ice Cream and Souvenir Shop directly across the road.

It was late when she got there. And a calm November cold was settling down with dusk.

She let the children explore the tween-deck while she climbed to the poop deck and stood in front of the chartkeeper's cabin. She took a deep breath and looked forward, to the spot where, according to the Tom Hilyard painting, it had happened.

"Good evenin' to thee, dear lady."

He was big and bearded, a robust-looking man in a black wool suit with red ribbon points and a sea cape of heavy wool lined with rabbit skin. He had about him the proprietary air of the ship's master. "Where be thee from, good lady?"

"Boston."

He frowned a bit. "Thou be a long way, marm."

"Just an hour," she said, forgetting the little game.

He laughed. "Thou jest, marm. It took us sixty-six days from Plymouth. There be no wind drive you much faster from Boston."

She smiled. "Uh, Boston, *Massachusetts*, I mean."

"Massachusetts? I know not this place." Then he smiled, as if they should not let such things stand in the way of their friendship. "Now, then, be there anything I can tell thee 'bout my vessel?"

"I'm curious about the things I read in your log."

"Log? My sea journal? How couldst thou know of my log?"

"It's in all papers."

"Papers? I know not of such things, good lady. And me log, as you call it, me log be in me cabin, where I always keep it."

Now she made a conscious effort to force her mind backward, to see him not as an actor but as the master of the ship. She had done this before, with the children, and it always helped the experience. "Could you tell me, sir, a little about the death of . . . of my friend Dorothy Bradford?"

"Friend? What be thy name?"

"Bigelow."

In the surprised little rise of the eyebrows, he came out of character for just a moment. But he dropped back quickly. "Be thou related to Ezra?"

"At some distance."

He warmed now to his part. He spoke delicately, as though not wishing to offend her, but took her forward to the place on the deck where Tom Hilyard said it had happened.

"Why did he do it?" Janice asked.

"Who can tell for certain if he did? And if he did, who can tell why?"

"I'm glad to hear you say that."

She looked out along the coast, at the lights of cars and houses, and the red flashes beyond the next hill, on the towers of the Pilgrim nuclear plant. And she closed her eyes. People talked about genetic memory, about things that nature had imprinted on us to help us survive, like fight, flight . . . and love.

But Janice sometimes thought there might be more to it than that. Maybe, if a person concentrated, in the right place, at the right moment, she could think herself back along her own genes, back through the memories of her parents and their parents before them. Back . . . back . . .

The lights of the nuclear plant stopped flashing. The cars disappeared. The night grew darker. And in her mind's eye, she became Ezra Bigelow. . . .

"Good Master Ezra, thou dost trouble me," said Dorothy.

"I must speak with thee," he whispered.

Dorothy Bradford pulled her heavy wool cape around her shoulders. "'Tis cold, good master. Miserable cold."

"Aye, too miserable for words, good lady." He leaned against her, and she pulled away. "Fear not, Dorothy. I seek only the touch of shoulders through our cloaks."

"'Tis unseemly, Master Ezra, 'specially with my husband out there, wanderin' the wilderness."

"'Tis merely a touch." He raised his voice slightly and looked about. The forward watch was nowhere to be seen. At the stern, the lights of the great cabin were out, the elders asleep. In the chartkeeper's cabin above, the taper burned. The master wrote.

Ezra turned back to Dorothy. "I have admired thee for many years, dear lady."

"Thou mustn't."

"I know how bitter this must be for thee, left to contemplate the wilderness while thy husband wanders this spit of sand. But think thee on his misery, helpin' shoulder the burdens of our community."

"Methinks too much on misery, Master Ezra. I see no future but death."

"Nor do I."

"Then why hast thou brought us here?"

Ezra looked out into the blackness and touched the wood of the rail, as if to feel something real, something solid. "God wills it. Men must do what God wills, else they are not men."

"Men must quest for God," she said bitterly, "whilst women are left to wash the bloody linens."

"'Tis the way of the world." He leaned against her once more.

She pulled away and turned to him, her eyes wide, her face a strange wax color in the starlight. "We have known each other for many years. I have long admired thee for thy constancy and felicitous preachments."

At this, he felt a small leap of joy in his heart, but she was the wife of a friend, and he had placed himself already in temptation enough.

"Thou must promise me," she went on, "that thou wilt speak nothing of the words I now say."

"So I do promise."

She took a deep breath and said, "God wills nothing. He hath forsaken us."

"Yes." It was as if he could not keep the word from rushing out of him.

Her eyes widened in shock. "Thou sayest such things also?"

It was blasphemous agreement to a blasphemous premise. Ezra felt a cowl of sin droop down over his face. He shook his head, as if to shake it off. But he could not drive from his eyes the image that had haunted him for days, nor could he keep from speaking of it.

"I would have gone with thy husband this time, but I could not. When I looked into the canvas sack on Corn Hill and saw the grim eyes of the corpse, I felt something wither in my heart. Then I did see the boy-corpse and *lost* heart. I saw us all dead afore our time, deserted by God." The steam from his mouth disappeared into the blackness, like his spirit rising into nothingness. "I read my Bible to drive the eyes of the corpse away. I remember that even Our Lord knew this terror in the Garden."

"Then he died." She looked out, along the arm of sand that for weeks had lain bleak before them. "They have been gone many days. I fear they may not come back."

"'Tis my fear as well."

"Without William, I shall be alone . . . completely."

He was overwhelmed by the need to touch her. He took her shoulders and drew her toward him. "Good lady, I *am* alone. I sailed without woman, without love. God guides my hand, but if I have not a woman to hold to my breast, I cannot know God's heart."

She looked at him, neither inviting more intimacy nor rejecting it, and in that moment he came as close to adultery as ever he would come. He wet his lips, as if to press them to hers. He brought his face so close to hers that he could feel the warmth of her breath. But the Lord had not forsaken him. The Lord gave him strength. He stopped and whispered, "If thy husband does not come back, I shall offer thee my love."

She looked at him with eyes that seemed as lifeless as two wooden pegs. "Where God has forsaken us, no love is sufficient."

"Do not *say* that!" he cried, then lowered his voice. "Do not say that. We must always believe the other. We must hope that love will come one day." He looked into her eyes for some sign of acceptance, of understanding, and he saw none. He released his grip on her shoulders. He could do nothing against this misery, though he would try. "The Lord is my shepherd. I . . . I . . . I will leave thee to thy thoughts. My nightly reading beckons."

He went to the great cabin and rummaged in the dark for his Bible. Then he heard something splash into the water, and a terrible thought froze his heart. He ran on deck and saw that her shadow was no longer there. He ran forward, but she was gone. . . .

And no one would ever know the truth of what passed between that man and woman. Not Janice Bigelow for all her effort, not the historians, not Christopher Jones himself.

And it developed, as the months wore on, that no one would know the truth about the Vikings and Jack's Island.

Geoff had been watching the dig. He had even learned how to plot a grid and excavate a small area himself. They had found many artifacts, from Rake Hilyard to Jack, from broken Carling bottles to clay pipestems. There were stone arrowheads and Indian jewelry buried in the shell midden. But the artifact they all dreamed of—a Norse coin that the midden might have protected—was not there.

The axe, which should have proved everything, caused only controversy. It did not take long before the world divided once more into anti-Vikings and pro-Vikings.

Yes, the axe looked Norse. Yes, it had the same strange markings found on the Bourne Stone. And yes, the log said this axe had been found in the marsh mud. But how could such an axe have survived a millennium? And what could have buried it?

What about the Bog People? the pro-Vikings cried.

The conditions were different, the anti-Vikings answered.

What about the letters on the axe? the pro-Vikings cried.

As meaningless as the letters on the Bourne Stone, the anti-Vikings answered. The axe was left by fishermen, they insisted, who had come the winter before the Pilgrims and had chosen to live on Jack's Island.

Do you have evidence? the pro-Vikings demanded.

Do you? the anti-Vikings responded.

In the seemly tradition of scientific discourse, New England towns that had always claimed Viking visitations aligned with the pro-Vikings and sold bumper stickers. Those who had laughed at Viking theories for decades laughed all the louder and said that Leif Ericson and his brother Thorwald had come no farther south than Nova Scotia.

One of the ballast stones was subjected to lithic thin sectioning and compared with similar kinds of rock from Scandinavia and Europe. The tests were inconclusive but suggested that the stones might have come as easily from France as from a Norse country, from French fishermen wintering over, with nothing to do but dig a foundation. But what about the axe? And the writing?

In the long run. Nothing was answered. Nothing more was found.

But Geoff read the sagas and studied the sea each day. It was always there, like a tangible god, giving the land mood and identity, giving the people a sense of limitless possibilities . . . or overwhelming odds.

And he imagined a Viking *knorr*, riding the godlike sea into the bay. Would there have been women aboard? he wondered. Why would men, exploring a new and unknown world, have constructed a dwelling with a root cellar and a doorstep, unless they were planning to bring their women? What men settled without women? Without women, what future was there?

On the cold Wednesday morning before Thanksgiving, he went to the back of Rake's barn and stood at the place where the doorstep had been. The archaeologists were gone. It was quiet. He closed his eyes and tried to see what the world might have looked like to someone perched on that doorstep. He had read somewhere about Einstein's theory of time, that it was like a river, and if one could somehow swim backward, if he could go back a few decades . . .

Geoff saw himself walking arm in arm along the beach with the Cape Cod girl he had met in Pilgrim garb. . . .

He went back half a century or more and saw Rake Hilyard and Mary Muldowney walking up the path. . . . A century and a half, and he saw Sam Hilyard kiss Hannah. . . . Three centuries and he saw a young man and an Indian girl, their loins locked, rocking back and forth in the shallow water. They were Christopher Hilyard and Amapoo. And now his mind was spinning back across the centuries, back a thousand years, to the mind of Gudrid, the first white woman on the Narrow Land. . . .

"Thorwald, the Skraeling comes from the strand."

Thorwald sat under a tree and, with a hammer and sharp chisel, tapped letters into the shaft of his second-best axe. "I have not finished my gift for him."

"It is not a gift that he comes for. He comes in great excitement. He waves to the sky and the gulls swarm."

"Gulls." Thorwald looked up. "What sign are gulls?"

"I know not." She twined her fingers into the single long braid of yellow hair that fell across her shoulder. She was not afraid. She had heard good stories of this Skraeling and his brothers. If he came with excitement, it would be for a good reason.

Her husband had explored this place the summer before. He had seen the Wonder Stand, had stopped at the place now called Kiarlness to repair his *knorr* and had found this island the finest place of all.

The creek was deep and would give good protection to the *knorr*. There were fish, game, timber, and a wide marsh where they could feed their cows. Everywhere grew the wild grapes that gave this land the name Vinland the Good. And the Skraelings had shown themselves to be gentle and kind and much taken with the ways of the Norsemen. They had traded much for the cloth and metal that Thorwald had brought, and even more for the white drink that came out of his cows.

So Thorwald had built here a house of timbers. Because he knew that he could fill his *knorr* with wood and pelt skins to take back to Greenland, he had used his ballast stones to build a root cellar beneath his house, big and wide, for the land was plentiful and they would have much to store there. Then he had taken the largest stone he carried, squared it with a chisel, and dug it into the sand before the door of his house, so that Gudrid would have proper welcome in Vinland the Good.

It was a handsome house, much finer than the dirt-walled caves where his brethren lived in Greenland, and when he sailed away, he had left it in the care of a Skraeling he much trusted.

On the doorstep of the house, the vigilant Skraeling had drawn his name:

$$\textrm{P} \, \textrm{Q} \, \Diamond \, \textrm{J}$$

Wompash, and the warning, "*Wetu* of white Gods who go on an island of wood. They will come back. Enter not."

Now Gudrid stood on the doorstep of her house, in the autumn sunshine, in a place she loved already. Here were trees, as in her Norse country, and here women would wish to settle.

Thorwald handed her the axe. "Put this in your skirts. Let the Skraeling not see it. We must give it to him with some ceremony."

"You are a silly man, to treat a Skraeling like a prince." She took the axe and slipped it beneath her jacket. "But I do love you for it."

"Treat the Skraeling like a prince, and he will treat you like a god. But we should not let him see gods kissing."

She grabbed his hand and pressed it against her swelling belly. "What else gods do cannot be hidden."

Wompash reached the clearing. He wore only a breechclout and feathers, and the sweat ran in rivers off his face. Now it was clear that his excitement was mingled with fright. He pointed to the sea and said several words.

Thorwald had learned some of their language, they a little of his, and with gestures as well, they talked. Wompash told them that something was coming that they must fear: "*Pootaop*."

"*Pootaop*? Whale?"

The Skraeling nodded many times.

"Whales!" Thorwald bellowed the word like a great laugh and began to sing the song he sang in Greenland when he told them of this land: "Let us return thither with our countrymen to rejoice while strong heroes live on the Wonder Strand, and there boil whales, which is a wonder to the land."

Gudrid laughed to hear this godlike sound, this man-sound.

The Skraeling nodded, then shook his head, and said many words that her husband could not understand.

"They're *whales*. And no Norseman yet has been afraid of whales. Gudrid, ring the bell and bring the brethren."

At the pounding of the bell, the other men came running from their labors in the woods. And the Skraeling went rushing off.

"Where does he go?" asked Gudrid.

"To bring his brethren, that they may see how the white gods slaughter whales." He threw his arm around her. "You are a fine big-boned woman. You'll bear many children."

Nothing could have filled her with more pride.

"And tonight you feed whale meat to the baby in your belly."

Now Gudrid saw a whale burst from the water down on the beach and drive itself forward. The cloud of gulls had come closer and skied high over the clearing.

Thorwald called for his axe. Bjarni, his friend, said that he had taken it, for he had broken the handle of his own.

"No matter." Thorwald took the axe on which he had engraved the marks of Wompash. "I will use this one a final time."

And, bellowing, the men ran down to the beach.

Gudrid and three other women stayed behind. While the others prepared a pit for the trying fire, Gudrid went into the house to sharpen the knives she would use to take meat from the whales.

The sharpening stone made a scraping sound. The cries and shouts of the men echoed up from the beach. The gulls cried overhead. The baby kicked. All was right.

Then Wompash appeared in the door. He motioned for her to come out. She would have obeyed, but then she heard one of the other women scream.

She shook her head and stepped back.

He came toward her. The fear on his face was reborn in fury. Behind him, she saw many Skraelings running through the clearing. One of the other women staggered toward the door and collapsed, blood spreading across her back.

But Gudrid would not scream. She would fight for her little baby.

As the Skraeling lunged for the knife in her right hand, she swept another knife from the table with her left and drove it into his back. He let out a bellow and grabbed for the haft, exposing his belly to the other knife. With it, she gutted him, right there in her house.

Then she ran to the door and saw a sight too frightening to behold. The Skraelings were everywhere in the woods, and all the women in the clearing were dead. She wanted to fight. Her blood was up and her man was threatened. But were she to venture out, she would be dead in a moment, and her baby never born.

So she fell back to her root cellar, and there she spent an eternity praying to the new Christian God she had been told of, all the while with one hand around her belly and the other around her knife.

And some of her prayers were answered. She was saved. But when the men came back for her, Thorwald was not among them.

It was Bjarni who opened the trapdoor and looked into the little cellar. "Gudrid, thank the gods."

"Thank the God Christ," she said. "Where is Thorwald?"

Bjarni did not answer but grabbed her by the elbow. "We must flee."

"Thorwald?"

"On the beach. You will see him on the beach." He dragged her past the body of Wompash. "Look straight ahead. Do not see the other women."

"Why has this happened?"

"The Skraeling Wompash, he was afraid. Perhaps their whales are gods. Perhaps their whales are gifts from their gods. Perhaps their whales are sacred to them. I know not. But they will be back."

"And Thorwald?"

"He will meet the gods in Valhalla this day."

And Gudrid cried out from the bottom of her soul.

Bjarni tried to keep her from seeing her man. He was afraid, she knew, of how she would keen, but she could not leave Thorwald on the beach. She found him, face down in the marsh mud, an arrow through his throat.

She knelt by his side and began to rock back and forth and sing her saddest song. Then she felt Bjarni's hands under her arms. He was urging her to leave, for the Skraelings would be back.

"No! We must bury him."

"No time. The tide will turn and we may ground."

"He was your leader. I am his wife. I will not allow him to rot here. He will go into the earth, like a Christian. He will be rooted to the place he loved." And her resolve was so great that it conquered his fear.

They buried Thorwald on the little hillside, not far from the house, and erected a Christian cross over his head. The grave was shallow, for they did not have the time or bravery to dig a six-foot hole. If the Skraelings did not dig him up, the wolves most surely would. But he had been buried and prayed over, and now Gudrid could grieve in peace. She thought to stay there and grieve forever, beside the grave of her mate. But she would go, if only to protect what she carried in her belly, which was the future.

As they ran back down the beach, she stopped by the old bull whale. Her husband's blood stained the mud around him. His axe was buried beneath the beast.

"Hurry," said Bjarni. "No more time."

The old bull made a great sigh, like a death rattle.

"You said that whales were Skraeling gods."

"I know not."

She picked up a rock that lay in the sand and went toward the whale. "If they are, I smite their god."

The old bull saw the rock raised above its head . . .

. . . and felt cool water pour down.

Then a television helicopter came clattering low over the beach, capturing the scene for the six o'clock news.

But not even that noise was enough to rouse the whale that Geoff Hilyard had been tending half the day.

"Geoff, I'm sorry, we're going to have to destroy that one," said the team veterinarian.

"No," said Geoff. "This is one of the youngest. You can't do it!"

The whales had come in on a northeaster.

Three hundred pilot whales, one of the biggest herds to beach since the nineteenth century, covered the flats and the marshes all around Jack's Island. So did police, newspeople, scientists from the New England Aquarium, and volunteers from the Center for Coastal Studies in Provincetown.

The volunteers put on survival suits and went into the water to try to help the scientists save the whales. Geoff and three others—a teacher, a lawyer, and the town clerk—had stood for hours in frigid water and blowing wind, wetting down the whale, and trying to turn him back. But each time they pointed him toward the sea, he came back to land.

Now the tide was ebbing, and this whale faced the same fate as the rest. Death by injection. A few would be turned back, only to beach farther down Cape, a few would be taken to the New England Aquarium, a few would find their bearings once more.

And that, in a way, was what Geoff was trying to do in the bitter water.

"We'll give you another ten minutes with him, but he's getting weak." The hood of the vet's dry suit had squashed his face so that he looked like some sort of tube creature. "Their weight crushes them."

"Let us push him off once more! You have to." Through the long, icy morning, Geoff had formed a bond with this beast. He had touched something elemental in the flesh. The whale looked up at him with a knowing eye and an upturned mouth that seemed almost human in its sad smile. By lunchtime Geoff thought he could understand the clicks and whistles and sad cries. By afternoon he knew he would cry if this one died.

And he knew it was crazy. The damn whale was bent on destroying itself for reasons that only the sea understood, but if he could try once more . . .

The vet threw his hands in the air. "I've got plenty more to do. If you can save him, good luck."

"Okay," Geoff said to the others. "The tide's starting to run fast. Let's douse him with water a few more times, let him know we love him, then try to persuade him to change his mind. Where's the bucket?" He reached behind him, and someone put the bucket into his hand.

"Thanks."

"You're welcome," said Janice.

He turned.

"I thought I'd find you here. Can I help?"

"Sure. I don't know how much chance there is, but—"

"Winter's here, and I need a little of that silver summer fog."

He liked that. It said a lot that only they would understand. "Where are the kids?"

"At my father's."

She took the bucket and poured the water onto the whale. The creature thrashed and almost lifted its body out of the water.

"Whoa!" shouted one of the others.

"He hasn't done that in a couple of hours."

"It's either the death throes or new life," said Geoff.

A bitter cold wind had come up, and a depressing gray drizzle was coming down, but for the next half hour, they worked to turn the whale toward the sea.

At one point, the creature swung its tail and knocked Janice right on her rear. She wasn't dressed for the water, but she did not quit, even as the cold turned her seams and stitches to ice. She would not quit, because this time, it seemed that they might succeed. And they did.

The whale turned back toward the ocean. It went out and swam in a wide circle, half in and half out of the water, as though it were dizzy, or trying to shake something out of its ears. Then, for a time, it swam parallel to the beach, and they ran along, shouting and waving their arms to keep it off. It was *their* whale now, and they couldn't let it come back.

Then suddenly the whale righted itself and turned north, away from the beach, away from the volunteers, away from Jack's Island.

While the others cheered, Geoff whispered to Janice, "We'd better get you out of those wet clothes."

The marine biologists were using Rake's house as a base of operations. When Geoff and Janice went inside, one of the biologists was on the telephone, giving an interview to an all-news radio station.

"No one knows why they do it," he was saying. "Some scientists blame it on parasites in the whales' inner ears, others on the turbulence in shallow waters during a storm. And recently we have found a magnetic anomaly in the earth beneath the elbow of the Cape, which may cause the whales' navigational system to malfunction. Whether it is one of these factors or a combination of several, we just don't know. It's a mystery."

"Like a lot of things," said Janice.

"But we'll solve it," said the scientist.

"We'll try," whispered Geoff.

They went through the living room, past the fireplace where Sam Hilyard had made love to Hannah so long ago, to the room where the crazy old Come-Outer Will Hilyard had coupled with iron-spined Mary Burr. And while Janice shivered, Geoff stripped off her clothes and his suit and they got into the bed where Rake Hilyard had made love to Mary Muldowney.

And they warmed each other. It did not take long, yet it said more than all the words between them since they crossed that bridge on the Fourth of July.

And when they were done, they wrapped themselves in a blanket and went to the window. The beach beyond the pine grove was littered with dead and dying whales, but out in the water, there were seven swimming north, and one of them was theirs. They knew.

They stood in the window, their arms around each other, the blanket around their shoulders, and they watched the whales until they disappeared into the gray mist. Then they got back into bed and made love again.

And the whales swam north, past the point that might once have been called Kiarlness, the sandspit that sheltered the *Mayflower* for six miserable weeks, north from the bay that brimmed with life, north along coastlines of rock, past rivers and inlets, north to the seas where the ice never melted, to the place where the glaciers shimmered, the great white mountains of ice, the shaping hands of God.

Printed in the United States
69180LVS00003B